BOOK OF WORSHIP
FOR
UNITED STATES FORCES

BOOK OF WORSHIP
FOR
UNITED STATES FORCES

A collection of Hymns and Worship Resources
for Military Personnel
of the United States of America

PUBLISHED UNDER THE SUPERVISION OF
THE ARMED FORCES CHAPLAINS BOARD

The Armed Forces Chaplains Board is indebted to all those who have granted permission to use hymns, tunes, or other worship materials under their control. Diligent efforts have been made to see that all copyrighted works are used by permission of the owners. Acknowledgment of such permission is given in the index of acknowledgments and sources, or below the hymns, as appropriate. If, through oversight, any copyrighted material has been used without permission, proper acknowledgment will be given in future printings. Reproduction of copyrighted material appearing in this hymnal is not authorized without permission of the copyright owners.

Library of Congress Catalog Card No. 73-600319

PRINTED 1974
BY
U.S. GOVERNMENT PRINTING OFFICE
WASHINGTON, D.C. 20402

Preface

Through the ages the people of God have related to their Creator through the medium of worship and song. Books of Worship record some of man's noblest expressions in his continuing search for understanding and meaning. Their pages flow in endless streams of song and Scripture, prayer and praise. They speak of the believer's faith in the daily renewal of life and love between creature and Creator.

The BOOK OF WORSHIP FOR UNITED STATES FORCES follows in this tradition. It is a repository of selected worship resources reflecting both traditional and contemporary communities from among the respective faith groups. Many dedicated chaplains and civilian consultants worked under the direction of the Armed Forces Chaplains Board to produce this volume. It is a unique interfaith publication. Hymns and worship resources have been carefully selected to provide for the spiritual needs of many diverse groups of worshipers within the military community. It was especially designed in language and style to appeal to young adults.

By tradition, lay leadership has been integral to the worship experience of military congregations. Therefore, this BOOK OF WORSHIP was arranged to include a wide variety of hymns, responses, and liturgical resources to assist the layman both in worship and in its direction.

Extensive indexes, instrumental chord symbols, varieties of hymn tune moods and styles, plus the use of both traditional and modern idioms, have been included to encourage creativity and flexibility in worship.

Appreciation is expressed to all who have contributed so generously of time and talent in the creation of this contemporary interfaith hymnal. Although space precludes listing their names, may they always be mindful of the many who will be blessed through their labor of love. Therefore, we joyfully offer the BOOK OF WORSHIP FOR UNITED STATES FORCES to the praise of Almighty God.

THE ARMED FORCES CHAPLAINS BOARD

Contents

The Hymns

O Mighty God, When I Behold the Wonder

1

Carl Gustaf Boberg, 1859-1940
Tr. by E. Gustav Johnson, 1893–

O store Gud 11. 10. 11. 10. 10. 8.
Swedish folk melody

1. O might-y God, when I be-hold the won-der Of na-ture's
2. When I be-hold the heav-ens in their vast-ness, Where gold-en
3. When I be-hold his Son to earth de-scend-ing, To help and
4. When, crushed by guilt of sin, be-fore him kneel-ing I plead for
5. When fi-nal-ly the mists of time have van-ished, And I in

beau-ty, wrought by words of thine, And how thou lead-est all from realms up
ships in az-ure is-sue forth, Where sun and moon keep watch up-on the
heal and teach dis-tressed man-kind; When e-vil flees and death in fear is
mer-cy and for grace and peace, I feel his balm and, all my bruis-es
truth my faith con-firmed shall see, Up-on the shores where earth-ly ills are

yon-der, Sus-tain-ing earth-ly life in love be-nign,
fast-ness Of chang-ing sea-sons and of time on earth,
bend-ing Be-fore the glo-ry of the Lord di-vine,
heal-ing, He saves my soul and sets my heart at ease,
ban-ished, I en-ter, Lord, to dwell in peace with thee,

1-4. With rap-ture
5. With rap-ture

filled, my soul thy name would laud, O might-y God! O might-y God!
filled, my soul thy name shall laud, Thanks be to thee, O might-y God!

With rap-ture filled, my soul thy name would laud, O might-y God! O might-y God!
With rap-ture filled, my soul thy name shall laud, Thanks be to thee, O might-y God!

2   Holy, Holy, Holy! Lord God Almighty!

Reginald Heber, 1783–1826

Nicaea 11. 12. 12. 10.
John B. Dykes, 1823–1876

1. Ho - ly, Ho - ly, Ho - ly! Lord God al - might - y!
2. Ho - ly, Ho - ly, Ho - ly! All the saints a - dore thee,
3. Ho - ly, Ho - ly, Ho - ly! Though the dark - ness hide thee,
4. Ho - ly, Ho - ly, Ho - ly! Lord God al - might - y!

Ear - ly in the morn - ing our song shall rise to thee;
Cast - ing down their gold - en crowns a - round the glass - y sea;
Though the eye of sin - ful man thy glo - ry may not see,
All thy works shall praise thy name, in earth and sky and sea;

Ho - ly, Ho - ly, Ho - ly! mer - ci - ful and might - y!
Cher - u - bim and ser - a - phim fall - ing down be - fore thee,
On - ly thou art ho - ly; there - is none be - side thee
Ho - ly, Ho - ly, Ho - ly! mer - ci - ful and might - y!

God in three Per - sons, bless - ed Trin - i - ty!
Who wert, and art, and ev - er - more shalt be.
Per - fect in power, in love, and pu - ri - ty.
God in three Per - sons, bless - ed Trin i - ty! A - men.

O Worship the King All-glorious Above

3

Lyons 10. 10. 11. 11.
J. Michael Haydn, 1737–1806
Arr. by William Gardiner, 1770–1853

Robert Grant, 1779–1838, cento, alt.

1. O wor-ship the King all-glo-rious a-bove,
2. O tell of his might, O sing of his grace,
3. The earth with its store of won-ders un-told,
4. Your boun-ti-ful care, what tongue can re-cite?
5. Frail chil-dren of dust, and fee-ble as frail,

O grate-ful-ly sing his power and his love;
Whose robe is the light, whose can-o-py space.
Al-might-y, your power has found-ed of old,
It breathes in the air, it shines in the light;
In you do we trust, nor find you to fail;

Our shield and de-fend-er, the An-cient of Days,
His char-iots of wrath the deep thun-der-clouds form,
Has stab-lished it firm by a change-less de-cree,
It streams from the hills, it de-scends to the plain,
Your mer-cies how ten-der, how firm to the end,

Pa-vil-ioned in splen-dor, and gird-ed with praise.
And dark is his path on the wings of the storm.
And round it has cast, like a man-tle, the sea.
And sweet-ly dis-tills in the dew and the rain.
Our mak-er, de-fend-er, re-deem-er, and friend! A-men.

4

Joyful, Joyful, We Adore Thee

Hymn to Joy 8. 7. 8. 7. D.
Ludwig van Beethoven, 1770–1827
Arr. by Edward Hodges, 1796–1867
Descant by Donald D. Kettring, 1907–

Henry van Dyke, 1852–1933, alt.

1. Joy - ful, joy - ful, we a - dore thee, God of glo - ry, Lord of love;
2. All thy works with joy sur - round thee, Earth and heaven re - flect thy rays,
3. Thou art giv - ing and for - giv - ing, Ev - er bless - ing, ev - er blest,
4. Mor - tals, join the hap - py cho - rus Which the morn - ing stars be - gan;

Hearts un - fold like flowers be - fore thee, O - pening to the sun a - bove.
Stars and an - gels sing a - round thee, Cen - ter of un - bro - ken praise.
Well-spring of the joy of liv - ing, O - cean depth of hap - py rest!
Fa - ther love is reign - ing o'er us, Broth - er love binds man to man.

Al - le - lu - ia! Al - le - lu - ia!

Melt the clouds of sin and sad - ness, Drive the dark of doubt a - way;
Field and for - est, vale and moun - tain, Flow - ery mead - ow, flash - ing sea,
Thou our Fa - ther, Christ our Broth - er, All who live in love are thine;
Ev - er sing - ing, march we on - ward, Vic - tors in the midst of strife,

Joyful, Joyful, We Adore Thee (cont.)

Al - le - lu - ia! In the tri-umph song of life. A-men.

Giv - er of im - mor-tal glad-ness, Fill us with the light of day.
Chant-ing bird and flow-ing foun-tain, Call us to re - joice in thee.
Teach us how to love each oth - er, Lift us to the joy di - vine.
Joy - ful mu - sic leads us Sun-ward In the tri-umph song of life. A-men.

O God, Our Help in Ages Past
5

St. Anne C. M.
Ascribed to William Croft, 1678-1727
Descant by Donald D. Kettring, 1907-

Isaac Watts, 1674-1748, cento, alt.

Descant

3. A thou-sand in your sight   Are like an eve-
5. Our help in ag - es past,   Our hope for years

1. O God, our help in ag - es past, Our hope for years to come,
2. Be - fore the hills in or - der stood, Or earth re - ceived her frame,
3. A thou - sand ag - es in your sight Are like an eve - ning gone,
4. Time, like an ev - er - roll - ing stream, Bears all its sons a - way;
5. O God, our help in ag - es past, Our hope for years to come,

ning gone,   Be - fore the ris - ing sun.
to come,   And our e - ter - nal home. A-men.

Our shel - ter from the storm - y blast, And our e - ter - nal home:
From ev - er - last - ing you are God, To end - less years the same.
Short as the watch that ends the night Be - fore the ris - ing sun.
They fly for - got - ten, as a dream Dies at the o - pening day.
Re - main our guard while life shall last, And our e - ter - nal home. A-men.

Descant copyright 1956 by W. L. Jenkins; from *Familiar Hymns with Descants*. Used by permission.

6

Praise Him! Praise Him!

Joyful Song 12. 10. 12. 10. 11. 10. with Refrain

Fanny J. Crosby, 1823–1915

Chester G. Allen, 1838–1878

1. Praise him! praise him! Je - sus, our bless - ed re - deem - er!
2. Praise him! praise him! Je - sus, our bless - ed re - deem - er!
3. Praise him! praise him! Je - sus, our bless - ed re - deem - er!

Sing, O earth—his won - der - ful love pro - claim! Hail him! hail him!
For our sins he suf - fered, and bled, and died; He our rock, our
Heav-enly por - tals loud with ho - san - nas ring! Je - sus, Sav - ior,

Refrain: Praise him! praise him!

high - est arch - an - gels in glo - ry; Strength and hon - or
hope of e - ter - nal sal - va - tion, Hail him! hail him!
reign - eth for - ev - er and ev - er; Crown him! crown him!

tell of his ex - cel - lent great - ness, Praise him! praise him!

give to his ho - ly name! *Fine* Like a shep - herd Je - sus will guard his
Je - sus, the Cru - ci - fied. Sound his prais - es! Je - sus who bore our
Proph-et, and Priest, and King! Christ is com - ing! o - ver the world vic -

ev - er in joy - ful song!

chil - dren; In his arms he car - ries them all day long. *D.S.*
sor - rows, Love un - bound - ed, won - der - ful, deep and strong.
to - rious; Power and glo - ry un - to the Lord be - long.

16

7

You Servants of God, Your Master Proclaim

Hanover 10. 10. 11. 11.
William Croft, 1678–1727
Descant by Donald D. Kettring, 1907–

Charles Wesley, 1707–1788, cento, alt.

1. You serv-ants of God, your Mas-ter pro-claim, And pub-lish a-
2. God rules up on high, al-might-y to save; And still he is
3. "Sal-va-tion to God, who sits on the throne," Let all cry a-
4. Then let us a-dore, and give him his right, All glo-ry and

broad his won-der-ful name; The name all-vic-to-rious of
nigh— his pres-ence we have; The great con-gre-ga-tion his
loud, and hon-or the Son; The prais-es of Je-sus the
power, all wis-dom and might, All hon-or and bless-ing, with

Je-sus ex-tol; His king-dom is glo-rious, he rules o-ver all.
tri-umph shall sing, As-crib-ing sal-va-tion to Je-sus our King.
an-gels pro-claim, Fall down on their fac-es, and wor-ship the Lamb.
an-gels a-bove, And thanks nev-er ceas-ing and in-fi-nite love. A-men.

8

To God Be the Glory

Fanny J. Crosby, 1823–1915

To God Be the Glory 11. 11. 11. 11. with Refrain
William H. Doane, 1832–1915

1. To God be the glo - ry: great things he hath done; So loved he the world that he gave us his Son, Who yield - ed his life an a - tone-ment for sin And o - pened the life-gate that all may go in.

2. O per - fect re - demp - tion, the pur-chase of blood! To ev - ery be - liev - er the prom-ise of God; The vil - est of - fend - er who tru - ly be - lieves, That mo - ment from Je - sus a par - don re - ceives.

3. Great things he hath taught us, great things he hath done, And great our re - joic - ing through Je - sus the Son; But pur - er and high - er and great - er will be Our won - der, our trans-port, when Je - sus we see.

Refrain

Praise the Lord, praise the Lord, Let the earth hear his voice! Praise the Lord, praise the Lord, Let the peo - ple re - joice! O come to the Fa - ther through

To God Be the Glory (cont.)

Je - sus the Son, And give him the glo - ry: great things he hath done.

Sing and Rejoice

9

Sing and Rejoice Irregular
William B. Bradbury 1816–1868

William B. Bradbury, 1816–1868
(Canon for 4 equal voices)

Voice 1
1. Sing and re-joice; Sing and re-joice; Let all things liv-ing now sing and re-
2. Ho-san - na! Ho-san - na! And on earth peace to all men of good

Voice 2
Sing and re-joice; Sing and re-joice; Let all things
Ho-san - na! Ho-san - na! And on earth

Voice 3
Sing and re-joice; Sing and re-
Ho-san - na! Ho-san -

Voice 4
Sing and re-
Ho-san -

Voice 1
joice.
will!

Voice 2
liv-ing now sing and re - joice.
peace to all men of good will!

Voice 3
joice; Let all things liv-ing now sing and re - joice.
na! And on earth peace to all men of good will!

Voice 4
joice; Sing and re - joice; Let all things liv-ing now sing and re - joice.
na! Ho-san - na! And on earth peace to all men of good will!

Words and music from the *Little Book of Carols*, published by Co-operative Recreation Service, Inc., Delaware, Ohio. Used by permission.

10   Halay, Halayluia

Paul Quinlan, 1938–

Halay 7. 8. 7. 8. with Refrain
Paul Quinlan, 1938–

Refrain

Ha - lay, ha - lay - lu - ia, ha - lay - lu - ia!

Ha - lay - lu - ia, ha - lay, ha - lay - lu - ia!

1. When to God I send a plea, Has - ten,
2. How long, hard - ened heart, how long, How long,
3. He is God; his praise we sing: Lord of
4. Ev - ery day we'll do the right; Think of

God; won't you set me free? Lis - ten to me;
heart, will you do the wrong? If you go to
all, God of ev - ery - thing. He is Lord; he
God in the still of night. Of - fer - ing we'll

hear my call; Help me, Lord; don't you let me fall.
God this day, He will help put you on the way.
hears our call; God will come and I will not fall.
make in trust, Sac - ri - fice of a life that's just.

Words and music used by permission of Paul Quinlan.

5. Come to us, Lord; come and bless;
   Be with us; that is happiness.
   Light our lives with a Father's grace;
   Lord above, show a Father's face.

6. Joy to men through bread and wine,
   God above in a holy sign,
   God of peace who knows no strife,
   You bring joy into every life.

7. Night will come when day is done;
   I'll have peace in a victory won.
   Joy will come when the sky grows gray;
   I have known yet another day.

Come, My Brothers, Praise the Lord 11

Michael, Row Irregular with Refrain
American Negro melody
Source unknown
Arr. by David Hugh Jones, 1900–

1. Come, my broth - ers, praise the Lord, Al - le - lu - ia!
2. For the Lord is a might - y God, Al - le - lu - ia!
3. Let us come be - fore the Lord, Al - le - lu - ia!
4. Joy - ous songs our voic - es raise, Al - le - lu - ia! To
5. Praise the Fa - ther, praise the Son, Al - le - lu - ia!

Praise the Lord, for he is God, Al - le - lu - ia!
He is King and Lord su - preme, Al - le - lu - ia!
He is ours and we are his, Al - le - lu - ia!
God a - bove we of - fer praise, Al - le - lu - ia!
And let's praise the Spir - it one, Al - le - lu - ia!

12 Blessed Assurance, Jesus Is Mine

Fanny J. Crosby, 1823-1915

Assurance 9. 10. 9. 9. with Refrain
Phoebe P. Knapp, 1839-1908

1. Bless-ed as-sur-ance, Je-sus is mine! O what a fore-taste of glo-ry di-
2. Per-fect sub-mis-sion, per-fect de-light, Vi-sions of rap-ture now burst on my
3. Per-fect sub-mis-sion, all is at rest, I in my Sav-ior am hap-py and

vine! Heir of sal-va-tion, pur-chase of God, Born of his
sight; An-gels de-scend-ing, bring from a-bove Ech-oes of
blest, Watch-ing and wait-ing, look-ing a-bove, Filled with his

Spir-it, washed in his blood.
mer-cy, whis-pers of love.
good-ness, lost in his love.

Refrain
This is my sto-ry, this is my

song, Prais-ing my Sav-ior all the day long; This is my

sto-ry, this is my song, Prais-ing my Sav-ior all the day long. A-men.

Blessing and Honor and Glory and Power

O quanta qualia 10. 10. 10. 10.

Horatius Bonar, 1808-1889, cento, alt.

La Feillée, 'Méthode du plain-chant,' 1808

1. Bless - ing and hon - or and glo - ry and power,
2. Ech - oes the heaven of the heavens with his name;
3. Ev - er as - cend - ing the song and the joy;
4. Give we the glo - ry and praise to the Lamb;

Wis - dom and rich - es and strength ev - er - more
Ech - oes the earth with his glo - ry and fame;
Ev - er de - scend - ing the love from on high;
Take we the robe and the harp and the palm;

Give un - to Him who our bat - tle has won;
O - cean and moun - tain, stream, for - est, and flower
Bless - ing and hon - or and glo - ry and praise—
Sing we the song of the Lamb who was slain,

His are the king - dom, the crown, and the throne.
Ech - o his prais - es and tell of his power.
This is the theme of the hymns that we raise.
Dy - ing in weak - ness, but ris - ing to reign. A-men.

14   O Day of Rest and Gladness

Mendebras 7. 6. 7. 6. D.
Anonymous German melody
Christopher Wordsworth, 1807–1885, cento, alt.   *Arr. by Lowell Mason, 1792–1872*

1. O day of rest and glad-ness, O day of joy and light,
2. On you, at the Cre - a - tion, The light first had its birth;
3. New grac - es ev - er gain - ing From this our day of rest,

O balm of care and sad-ness, Most beau - ti - ful, most bright,
On you, for our sal - va - tion, Christ rose from depths of earth;
We reach the rest re - main-ing To spir - its of the blest.

On you the high and low - ly, Through ag - es joined in tune,
On you our Lord, vic - to - rious, The Spir - it sent from heaven;
To Ho - ly Ghost be prais - es, To Fa - ther, and to Son;

Sing ho - ly, ho - ly, ho - ly, To the great God tri - une.
And thus on you, most glo - rious, A tri - ple light was given.
The church her voice up - rais - es To you, blest Three in One. A-men.

Safely Through Another Week

Sabbath 7. 7. 7. 7. D.
John Newton, 1725–1807, cento, alt.
Lowell Mason, 1792–1872

1. Safe - ly through an - oth - er week God has brought us on our way;
2. While we pray for par - doning grace, Through the dear Re - deem - er's name,
3. Here we come thy name to praise; Let us feel thy pres - ence near;
4. May thy gos - pel's joy - ful sound Con - quer sin - ners, com - fort saints;

Let us now a bless - ing seek, Wait - ing in his courts to - day:
Show thy rec - on - cil - ed face, Take a - way our sin and shame;
May thy glo - ry meet our eyes, While we in thy house ap - pear:
Make the fruits of grace a - bound, Bring re - lief for all com - plaints:

Day of all the week the best, Em - blem of e - ter - nal rest;
From our world - ly cares set free, May we rest this day in thee;
Here af - ford us, Lord, a taste Of our ev - er - last - ing feast;
Thus may all our Sab - baths prove, Till we join the church a - bove;

Day of all the week the best, Em - blem of e - ter - nal rest.
From our world - ly cares set free, May we rest this day in thee.
Here af - ford us, Lord, a taste Of our ev - er - last - ing feast.
Thus may all our Sab - baths prove, Till we join the church a - bove. A - men.

I Sing the Mighty Power of God

Ellacombe C. M. D.

Isaac Watts, 1674–1748, cento, alt.   *'Gesangbuch der h. w. kath. Hofkapelle,' Württemberg, 1784*

1. I sing the might-y power of God, That made the moun-tains rise,
2. I sing the good-ness of the Lord, That filled the earth with food;
3. There's not a plant or flower be-low But makes thy glo-ries known;

That spread the flow-ing seas a-broad And built the loft-y skies.
He formed the crea-tures with his word And then pro-nounced them good.
And clouds a-rise and tem-pests blow By or-der from thy throne,

I sing the wis-dom that or-dained The sun to rule the day;
Lord, how thy won-ders are dis-played, Wher-e'er I turn my eye:
While all that bor-rows life from thee Is ev-er in thy care,

The moon shines full at his com-mand, And all the stars o-bey.
If I sur-vey the ground I tread Or gaze up-on the sky!
And ev-ery-where that man can be, Thou, God, art pres-ent there. A-men.

Come, Thou Almighty King

Italian Hymn 6. 6. 4. 6. 6. 6. 4.
Felice de Giardini, 1716–1796

Anonymous, c. 1757, cento, alt.

1. Come, thou al - might - y King, Help us thy name to sing, Help us to praise: Fa - ther, all - glo - ri - ous, O'er all vic - to - ri - ous, Come, and reign o - ver us, An - cient of Days.

2. Come, thou in - car - nate Word, Gird on thy might - y sword, Our prayer at - tend: Come, and thy peo - ple bless, And give thy word suc - cess; Spir - it of ho - li - ness, On us de - scend.

3. Come, Ho - ly Com - fort - er, Thy sa - cred wit - ness bear In this glad hour: Thou who al - might - y art, Now rule in ev - ery heart, And ne'er from us de - part, Spir - it of power.

4. To thee, great One in Three, The high - est prais - es be, Hence ev - er - more! Thy sov - ereign maj - es - ty May we in glo - ry see, And to e - ter - ni - ty Love and a - dore. A - men.

18   Praise to the Lord, the Almighty

Joachim Neander, 1650–1680, cento
Tr. by Catherine Winkworth, 1827–1878, alt.

Lobe den Herren 14. 14. 4. 7. 8.
'Erneuertes Gesangbuch,' Stralsund, 1665
Arr. in 'Praxis Pietatis Melica,' 1668

1. Praise to the Lord, the Al - might - y, the King of cre - a - tion!
2. Praise to the Lord, who o'er all things so won-drous - ly reign - eth,
3. Praise to the Lord! O let all that is in me a - dore him!

O my soul, praise him, for he is thy health and sal - va - tion!
Shel - ters thee un - der his wings, yea, so gent - ly sus - tain - eth!
All that hath life and breath, come now with prais - es be - fore him!

All ye who hear, Now to his tem - ple draw near;
Hast thou not seen How thy de - sires e'er have been
Let the A - men Sound from his peo - ple a - gain:

Join me in glad ad - o - ra - tion!
Grant - ed in what he or - dain - eth?
Glad - ly for aye we a - dore him. A - men.

My Lord, What a Morning

What a Morning 6. 8. 7. 7. with Refrain
American Negro melody
Arr. by David Hugh Jones, 1900–

Spiritual

Refrain

My Lord, what a morn-ing, My Lord, what a morn-ing,
My Lord, what a morn-ing, When the stars be-gin to fall.

Solo

1. You'll hear the trum-pet sound, To wake the na-tions un-der-ground,
2. You'll hear the sin-ner mourn, To wake the na-tions un-der-ground,
3. You'll hear the Chris-tian shout, To wake the na-tions un-der-ground,

Chorus

Look-ing to my God's right hand, When the stars be-gin to fall.

20   From All That Dwell Below the Skies

Lasst uns erfreuen L.M. with Alleluias
Cologne, 'Geistliche Kirchengesänge,' 1623
Arr. and harm. by Ralph Vaughan Williams,
1872–1958

Sts. 1,3, Isaac Watts, 1674–1748
St. 2, Robert Spence, 'Pocket Hymn Book,' 1780

Unison

1. From all that dwell be - low the skies   Let   the Cre - a - tor's praise a -
2. In ev - ery land be - gin the song,   To   ev - ery land the strains be -
3. E - ter - nal are thy mer - cies, Lord;   E - ter - nal truth at - tends thy

Harmony   *Unison*

rise: Al - le - lu - ia!   Al - le - lu - ia! Let   the Re - deem - er's
long: Al - le - lu - ia!   Al - le - lu - ia! In   cheer - ful sound all
word: Al - le - lu - ia!   Al - le - lu - ia! Thy   praise shall sound from

Harmony

name be sung Through ev - ery land, in ev - ery tongue. Al - le - lu - ia!
voic - es raise And fill the world with joy - ful praise. Al - le - lu - ia!
shore to shore, Till suns shall rise and set no more. Al - le - lu - ia!

Unison   *Harmony*

Al - le - lu - ia! Al - le - lu - ia! Al - le - lu - ia! Al - le - lu - ia!
Al - le - lu - ia! Al - le - lu - ia! Al - le - lu - ia! Al - le - lu - ia!
Al - le - lu - ia! Al - le - lu - ia! Al - le - lu - ia! Al - le - lu - ia! A - men.

Arrangement and harmonization from *The English Hymnal.* Used by permission of Oxford University Press.

Come, Thou Fount of Every Blessing

Nettleton 8. 7. 8. 7. D.
American folk melody
Wyeth's 'Repository of Sacred Music,' 1813

Robert Robinson, 1735-1790, cento

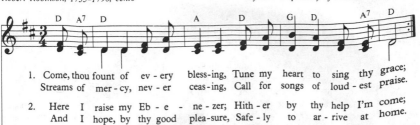

1. Come, thou fount of ev - ery bless-ing, Tune my heart to sing thy grace;
   Streams of mer - cy, nev - er ceas-ing, Call for songs of loud - est praise.

2. Here I raise my Eb - e - ne - zer; Hith - er by thy help I'm come;
   And I hope, by thy good plea-sure, Safe - ly to ar - rive at home.

3. O to grace how great a debt - or Dai - ly I'm con-strained to be!
   Let that grace now, like a fet - ter, Bind my wan-dering heart to thee.

Teach me some me - lo - dious son - net, Sung by flam - ing tongues a - bove;
Je - sus sought me when a stran - ger, Wan-dering from the fold of God;
Prone to wan - der, Lord, I feel it; Prone to leave the God I love;

Praise the mount; I'm fixed up - on it, Mount of God's un-chang-ing love!
He, to res - cue me from dan-ger, In - ter-posed with pre-cious blood.
Here's my heart; O take and seal it, Seal it from thy courts a - bove. A - men.

22　　Jesus Shall Reign Where'er the Sun

Isaac Watts, 1674-1748, cento

Duke Street L. M.
John Hatton, ?-1793

1. Je - sus shall reign wher - e'er the sun Doth his suc - ces - sive jour - neys run; His king-dom stretch from shore to shore Till moons shall wax and wane no more.
2. For him shall end - less prayer be made, And prais - es throng to crown his head; His name like sweet per - fume shall rise With ev - ery morn - ing sac - ri - fice.
3. Peo - ple and realms of ev - ery tongue Dwell on his love with sweet - est song, And in - fant voic - es shall pro - claim Their ear - ly bless - ings on his name.
4. Bless - ings a - bound wher - e'er he reigns; The pris - oner leaps to lose his chains, The wea - ry find e - ter - nal rest, And all the sons of want are blest.
5. Let ev - ery crea - ture rise and bring Pe - cu - liar hon - ors to our King; An - gels de - scend with songs a - gain, And earth re - peat the loud A - men. A - men.

God Himself Is with Us

23

Gerhard Tersteegen, 1697–1769, cento
Tr. by Frederick W. Foster, 1760–1835
and John Miller, 1756–1790, alt.

Arnsberg 6. 6. 8. 6. 6. 8. 3. 3. 6. 6.
Joachim Neander, 1650–1680

1. God him-self is with us: Let us now a-dore him, And with awe appear be-fore him. God is in his tem-ple— All with-in keep
si - lence, Pros-trate lie with deep-est rev - erence. Him a-lone God we own,
Him, our God and Sav - ior; Praise his name for - ev - - er.

2. God him-self is with us: Hear the harps re - sound-ing! See the crowds the
throne sur - round-ing! "Ho - ly, ho - ly, ho - ly"—Hear the hymn as-
cend - ing, An-gels, saints, their voic-es blend-ing! Bow thine ear To us here:
Hear, O Christ, the prais - es That thy church now rais - es.

3. O thou fount of bless - ing, Pu - ri - fy my spir - it; Trust-ing on - ly
in thy mer - it, Like the ho - ly an - gels Who be-hold thy
glo - ry, May I cease-less-ly a - dore thee, And in all, Great and small,
Seek to do most near - ly What thou lov - est dear - ly. A - men.

Great Day! Great Day

Spiritual

Great Day Irregular with Refrain
American Negro melody

Great day! Great day, the righ-teous march-ing. Great day! God's going to build up

Zi - on's walls, Zi-on's walls!

1. Char - iot rode on the moun-tain top,
2. This is the day of ju - bi - lee,
3. We want no cow - ards in our band,
4. Going to take my breast-plate, sword, and shield,

God's going to build up Zi - on's walls!
My God spoke and the
The Lord has set his
We call for val - iant -
And march out bold - ly

char - iot did stop, God's going to build up Zi - on's walls!
peo - ple free, God's going to build up Zi - on's walls!
heart - ed men, God's going to build up Zi - on's walls!
in the field, God's going to build up Zi - on's walls!

Holy God, We Praise Your Name

Anonymous German tr. of Te Deum, cento
Tr. by Clarence Walworth, 1820-1900, alt.

Grosser Gott 7. 8. 7. 8. 7. 7.
'Katholisches Gesangbuch,' 1774, Vienna

1. Ho - ly God, we praise your name; Lord of all, we
2. Hear the glad ce - les - tial hymn An - gel choirs a -
3. Lo! the a - pos - tles' holy train Joins your sa - cred
4. Ho - ly Fa - ther, ho - ly Son, Ho - ly Spir - it:

bow be - fore you; All on earth your scep - ter claim,
bove are rais - ing; Cher - u - bim and ser - a - phim,
name to hal - low; Proph - ets swell the glad re - frain,
three we name you; Though in es - sence on - ly one,

All in heaven a - bove a - dore you. In - fi - nite your
In un - ceas - ing cho - rus prais - ing, Fill the heavens with
And the white - robed mar - tyrs fol - low, And from morn to
Un - di - vid - ed God we claim you, And, a - dor - ing,

vast do - main, Ev - er - last - ing is your reign.
sweet ac - cord: Ho - ly, ho - ly, ho - ly Lord.
set of sun Through the church the song goes on.
bend the knee While we own the mys - ter - y. A - men.

26   Come, Let Us Join Our Cheerful Songs

Isaac Watts, 1674–1748, cento

Gräfenberg C. M.
Johann Crüger, 1598–1662

1. Come, let us join our cheer-ful songs With an-gels round the throne. Ten thou-sand thou-sand are their tongues, But all their joys are one.
2. "Wor-thy the Lamb that died," they cry, "To be ex-alt-ed thus!" "Wor-thy the Lamb," our lips re-ply, "For he was slain for us!"
3. Je-sus is wor-thy to re-ceive Hon-or and power di-vine; And bless-ings, more than we can give, Be, Lord, for-ev-er thine.
4. The whole cre-a-tion join in one To bless the sa-cred name Of him who sits up-on the throne, And to a-dore the Lamb. A-men.

Jesus, the Very Thought of Thee   27

Ascribed to Bernard of Clairvaux, c. 1091–1153, cento
Tr. by Edward Caswall, 1814–1878, alt.

St. Agnes C. M.
John B. Dykes, 1823–1876

1. Je-sus, the ver-y thought of thee With sweet-ness fills my breast;
2. No voice can sing, no heart can frame, Nor can the mem-ory find
3. O hope of ev-ery con-trite heart, O joy of all the meek,
4. But what to those who find? Ah, this Nor tongue nor pen can show;
5. Je-sus, our on-ly joy be thou, As thou our prize wilt be;

Jesus, the Very Thought of Thee (cont.)

But sweet-er far thy face to see, And in thy pres - ence rest.
A sweet-er sound than thy blest name, O Sav - ior of man-kind.
To those who fall, how kind thou art! How good to those who seek!
The love of Je - sus, what it is None but his loved ones know.
Je - sus, be thou our glo - ry now, And through e - ter - ni - ty. A - men.

28 O Come and Sing to God, the Lord

St. Peter C. M.

The Psalter, 1912, alt.

Alexander R. Reinagle, 1799–1877

1. O come and sing to God, the Lord, To
2. Be - fore his pres - ence let us come With
3. O come and, bow - ing down to him, Our

him our voic - es raise; Let us in our most
praise and thank - ful voice; Let us sing joy - ful
wor - ship let us bring; O let us praise the

joy - ful songs The Lord, our Sav - ior, praise.
psalms to him, With grate - ful hearts re - joice.
gra - cious Lord, Our Mak - er and our King.

29 Priestly People, Kingly People

Lucien Deiss, 1921–
Unison

Priestly People Irregular with Refrain
Lucien Deiss, 1921–

Refrain

Priest - ly peo - ple, King - ly peo - ple, Ho - ly peo - ple,
God's cho - sen peo - ple, Sing praise to the Lord.

The stanzas address Christ with the various messianic
and royal titles which Scripture gives him.

1. We sing to you, O Christ, be - lov - ed Son of the Fa - ther.
2. We sing to you, O Son, born of Mar - y the Vir - gin.
3. We sing to you, O bright - ness of splen - dor and glo - ry.
4. We sing to you, O light bring - ing men out of dark - ness.

We give you praise, O Wis-dom ev - er - last - ing, and Word of God.
We give you praise, Our Broth-er, born to heal us, our sav - ing Lord.
We give you praise, O Morn-ing Star, an -nounc-ing the com-ing day.
We give you praise, O guid -ing Light, who shows us the way to heaven.

5. We sing to you, Messiah foretold by the prophets.
   We give you praise, O Son of David and Son of Abraham.

6. We sing to you, Messiah, the hope of the people.
   We give you praise, O Christ, our Lord and King, humble, meek of heart.

7. We sing to you, The Way to the Father in heaven.
   We give you praise, The Way of truth, and Way of all grace and light.

8. We sing to you, O Priest of the new dispensation.
   We give you praise, Our Peace, sealed by the blood of the Sacrifice.

9. We sing to you, O Lamb, put to death for the sinner.
   We give you praise, O Victim, immolated for all mankind.

10. We sing to you, The Tabernacle made by the Father.
    We give you praise, The Cornerstone and Savior of Israel.

11. We sing to you, The Shepherd who leads to the kingdom.
    We give you praise, Who gathers all your sheep in the one true fold.

12. We sing to you, O Fount, overflowing with mercy.
    We give you praise, Who gives us living waters to quench our thirst.

13. We sing to you, True Vine, planted by God our Father.
    We give you praise, O blessed Vine, whose branches bear fruit in love.

14. We sing to you, O Manna, which God gives his people.
    We give you praise, O living Bread, which comes down to us from heaven.

15. We sing to you, The Image of Father eternal.
    We give you praise, O King of justice, Lord, and the King of peace.

16. We sing to you, The Firstborn of all God's creation.
    We give you praise, Salvation of your saints sleeping in the Lord.

17. We sing to you, O Lord, whom the Father exalted.
    We give you praise, In glory you are coming to judge all men.

30   Let All the World in Every Corner Sing

All the World 10. 4. 6. 6. 6. 6. 10. 4.

George Herbert, 1593-1632

Robert Guy McCutchan, 1877-1958

1. Let all the world in ev-ery cor-ner sing: My God and King!
2. Let all the world in ev-ery cor-ner sing: My God and King!

The heavens are not too high, His praise may thith-er fly; The
The church with psalms must shout, No door can keep them out; But,

earth is not too low, His prais-es there may grow. Let
more than all, the heart Must bear the long-est part. Let

all the world in ev-ery cor-ner sing: My God and King!
all the world in ev-ery cor-ner sing: My God and King! A-men.

O Saving Victim, Open Wide

Thomas Aquinas, 1227–1274, cento
Tr. by Edward Caswall, 1814–1878, alt.

O Salutaris Hostia L. M.
Abbé Duguet, ?–c. 1767

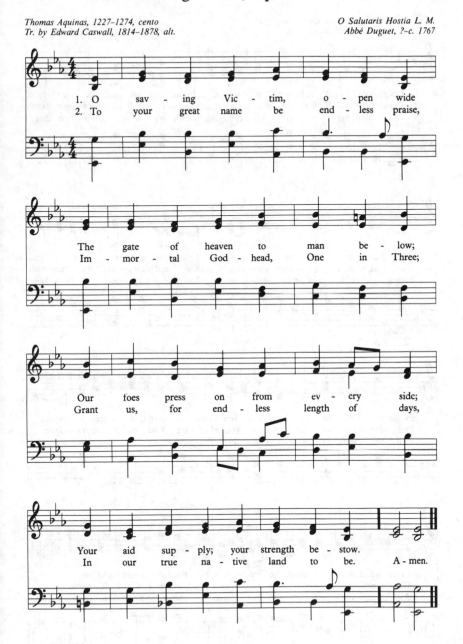

1. O sav - ing Vic - tim, o - pen wide
2. To your great name be end - less praise,

The gate of heaven to man be - low;
Im - mor - tal God - head, One in Three;

Our foes press on from ev - ery side;
Grant us, for end - less length of days,

Your aid sup - ply; your strength be - stow. A - men.
In our true na - tive land to be.

Praise the Lord! Ye Heavens, Adore Him

Sts. 1, 2, 'Foundling Hospital Collection,' 1796
St. 3, Edward Osler, 1798–1863

Hyfrydol 8. 7. 8. 7. D.
Rowland Hugh Prichard, 1811–1887

1. Praise the Lord! ye heavens, a - dore him; Praise him, an - gels, in the height;
2. Praise the Lord! for he is glo - rious; Nev - er shall his prom - ise fail;
3. Wor - ship, hon - or, glo - ry, bless - ing, Lord, we of - fer un - to thee;

Sun and moon, re - joice be - fore him; Praise him, all ye stars of light.
God hath made his saints vic - to - rious; Sin and death shall not pre - vail.
Young and old, thy praise ex - press - ing, In glad hom - age bend the knee.

Praise the Lord! for he hath spo - ken; Worlds his might - y voice o - beyed;
Praise the God of our sal - va - tion! Hosts on high, his power pro - claim;
All the saints in heaven a - dore thee, We would bow be - fore thy throne;

Laws which nev - er shall be bro - ken For their guid-ance hath he made.
Heaven, and earth, and all cre - a - tion, Laud and mag - ni - fy his name.
As thine an - gels serve be - fore thee, So on earth thy will be done. A-men.

Sing Hallelujah, Praise the Lord!

Bechler 8. 6. 8. 6. 8. 8. 8. 6.
John C. Bechler, 1784–1857

John Swertner, 1746–1813

1. Sing hal - le - lu - jah, praise the Lord! Sing with a cheer - ful voice;
2. There we to all e - ter - ni - ty Shall join the an - gel - ic lays

Ex - alt our God with one ac - cord, And in his name re - joice.
And sing in per - fect har - mo - ny To God our Sav - ior's praise;

Ne'er cease to sing, thou ran-somed host, Praise Fa - ther, Son, and Ho - ly Ghost,
He hath re-deemed us by his blood, And made us kings and priests to God;

Un - til in realms of end - less light Your prais - es shall u - nite.
For us, for us, the Lamb was slain! Praise ye the Lord! A - men.

Words and music used by permission of the Moravian Church in America.

34   Sing, My Tongue, the Savior's Glory

Thomas Aquinas, 1227–1274
Tr. by Edward Caswall, 1814–1878

St. Thomas 8. 7. 8. 7. 8. 7.
John Francis Wade, c. 1711–1786, alt.

1. Sing, my tongue, the Sav - ior's glo - ry, Of his flesh the
2. Of a pure and spot - less vir - gin Born for us, his
3. On the night of that Last Sup - per, Seat - ed with his
4. Christ, the Word-made - Flesh, by speak - ing, Earth - ly bread to

mys - tery sing, Of the blood, all price ex - ceed - ing,
love to show, He, as man, with man con - vers - ing,
cho - sen band, He, the pas - chal vic - tim eat - ing,
flesh he turns; Wine be - comes his blood so pre - cious—

Shed by our im - mor - tal King, Des - tined, for the
Stayed, the seeds of truth to sow; Then he closed in
First ful - fills the law's com - mand; Then as food to
Un - con - ceived in hu - man terms! Hearts sin - cere per -

world's re - demp - tion, From a no - ble womb to spring.
won - drous fash - ion This his life on earth be - low.
all his breth - ren Gives him - self with his own hand.
ceive this mar - vel; Faith its les - son quick - ly learns. A - men.

Stanzas 5 and 6 are sung when the procession arrives at the Altar of Repose.

5. Down in adoration falling,
   This great Sacrament we hail;
  Over ancient forms of worship
   Newer rites of grace prevail;
  Faith tells us that Christ is present
   When our human senses fail.

6. To the everlasting Father,
   And the Son who made us free,
  And the Spirit, God proceeding
   From them each eternally,
  Be salvation, honor, blessing,
   Might, and endless majesty.

36   What Wondrous Love Is This

Wondrous Love 12. 9. 12. 9.
'Southern Harmony,' 1835

American folk hymn

Harm. by Carlton R. Young, 1926–

1. What wondrous love is this, O my soul, O my soul, What wondrous love is this, O my soul! What wondrous love is this that caused the Lord of bliss To bear the dreadful curse for my soul, for my soul, To bear the dreadful curse for my soul.

2. What wondrous love is this, O my soul, O my soul, What wondrous love is this, O my soul! What wondrous love is this that caused the Lord of life To lay aside his crown for my soul, for my soul, To lay aside his crown for my soul.

3. And when from death I'm free, I'll sing on, I'll sing on, And when from death I'm free, I'll sing on. And when from death I'm free, I'll sing and joyful be, And through eternity I'll sing on, I'll sing on, And through eternity, I'll sing on. A-men.

Sing Praise to God, Who Reigns Above 37

Johann Jakob Schütz, 1640-1690, cento
Tr. by Frances Elizabeth Cox, 1812-1897, alt.

Praise (Af Himlens) 8. 7. 8. 7. 8. 8. 7.
Swedish traditional melody
Arr. by Leland B. Sateren, 1913-

1. Sing praise to God, who reigns a-bove, The God of all cre-
a - tion, The God of power, the God of love, The God of
our sal - va - tion. With heal-ing balm my soul he fills, And ev-ery
faith-less mur - mur stills: To God all praise and glo - ry!

2. The an - gel host, O King of kings, Thy praise for-ev-er
tell - ing, In earth and sky all liv-ing things Be-neath thy
shad-ow dwell - ing, A - dore the wis-dom which could span, And powerwhich
formed cre - a - tion's plan: To God all praise and glo - ry!

3. What God's al - might - y power hath made His gra-cious mer-cy
keep - eth; By morn-ing glow or eve-ning shade His watch-ful
eye ne'er sleep - eth: With - in the king-dom of his might Lo, all is
just, and all is right: To God all praise and glo - ry!

4. Then all my glad-some way a - long I sing a-loud thy
prais - es, That men may hear the grate-ful song My voice un-
wea - ried rais - es: Be joy - ful in the Lord, my heart: Both soul and
bod - y, bear your part: To God all praise and glo - ry! A-men.

38 Sing to the Lord of Harvest

Wie lieblich ist 7. 6. 7. 6. D.
Johann Steurlein, 1546–1613
Harm. by Jan O. Bender, 1909–

John S. B. Monsell, 1811–1875

1. Sing to the Lord of har - vest, Sing songs of love and praise; With
joy - ful hearts and voic - es Your al - le - lu - ias raise. By
him the roll - ing sea - sons In fruit - ful or - der move; Sing
to the Lord of har - vest A joy - ous song of love.

2. By him the clouds drop fat - ness, The des - erts bloom and spring, The
hills leap up in glad - ness, The val - leys laugh and sing. He
fill - eth with his full - ness All things with large in - crease, He
crowns the year with good - ness, With plen - ty and with peace.

3. Bring to his sa - cred al - tar The gifts his good - ness gave, The
gold - en sheaves of har - vest, The souls he died to save. Your
hearts lay down be - fore him When at his feet you fall, And
with your lives a - dore him, Who gave his life for all.

Songs of Thankfulness and Praise

Salzburg 7. 7. 7. 7. D.
Jakob Hintze, 1622–1702, alt.
Christopher Wordsworth, 1807–1885, cento, alt.   *Harm. by Johann Sebastian Bach, 1685–1750*

1. Songs of thank-ful-ness and praise, Je-sus, Lord, to you we raise,
2. Man-i-fest at Jor-dan's stream, Proph-et, Priest, and King su-preme;
3. Man-i-fest in mak-ing whole Pal-sied limbs and faint-ing soul;
4. Grant us grace to see you, Lord, Mir-rored in your ho-ly word;

Man-i-fest-ed by the star To the sag-es from a-far;
And at Ca-na, wed-ding guest, In your God-head man-i-fest;
Man-i-fest in val-iant fight, Quell-ing all the dev-il's might;
May we im-i-tate your way, And be pure, as pure we may,

Branch of roy-al Da-vid's stem In your birth at Beth-le-hem;
Man-i-fest in power di-vine, Chang-ing wa-ter in-to wine;
Man-i-fest in gra-cious will, Ev-er bring-ing good from ill;
That we like to you may be At your great e-piph-a-ny;

An-thems be to you ad-dressed, God in man made man-i-fest.
An-thems be to you ad-dressed, God in man made man-i-fest.
An-thems be to you ad-dressed, God in man made man-i-fest.
Let us praise you, ev-er blest, God in man made man-i-fest.

40   All the Earth Proclaim the Lord

Lucien Deiss, 1921–

Proclaim the Lord 9. 10. with Refrain
Lucien Deiss, 1921–

All the earth pro - claim the Lord, Sing your praise to God.

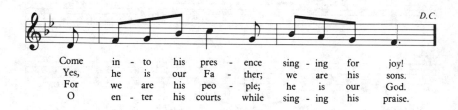

1. Serve you the Lord, heart filled with glad - ness.
2. Know that the Lord is our cre - a - tor.
3. We are the sheep of his green pas - ture,
4. En - ter his gates bring - ing thanks - giv - ing,

Come in - to his pres - ence sing - ing for joy!
Yes, he is our Fa - ther; we are his sons.
For we are his peo - ple; he is our God.
O en - ter his courts while sing - ing his praise.

5. Our Lord is good, his love enduring,
   His word is abiding now with all men.

6. Honor and praise be to the Father,
   The Son, and the Spirit, world without end.

Praise the Lord, Who Reigns Above

Amsterdam 7. 6. 7. 6. 7. 7. 7. 6.
J. A. Freylinghausen, 'Geistreiches
Gesangbuch,' Halle, 1704
Adapted by John Wesley, 1703-1791

Charles Wesley, 1707-1788, cento, alt.

1. Praise the Lord, who reigns a - bove, And keeps his court be - low;
2. Cel - e - brate th'e - ter - nal God With harp and psal - ter - y,
3. Him, in whom they move and live, Let ev - ery crea - ture sing,

Praise the ho - ly God of love, And all his great - ness show;
Tim - brels soft and cym - bals loud In his high praise a - gree;
Glo - ry to their Mak - er give, And hom - age to their King.

Praise him for his no - ble deeds, Praise him for his match - less power;
Praise him ev - ery tune - ful string; All the reach of heav - enly art,
Hallow - ed be his name be - neath, As in heaven on earth a - dored;

Him from whom all good pro - ceeds Let earth and heaven a - dore.
All the powers of mu - sic bring, The mu - sic of the heart.
Praise the Lord in ev - ery breath, Let all things praise the Lord. A - men.

42   Alleluia! Praise God in His Holy Dwelling

Psalm 150 8. 7. 8. 9. with Refrain

Omer Westendorf, 1916–

Jan Vermulst, 1925–

People

Al - le - lu - ia, al - le - lu - ia, al - le - lu - ia!

Choir (Stanzas)

1. Praise God in his ho - ly dwell - ing;
2. Praise him with the blast of trum - pet;
3. Praise him with re - sound - ing cym - bals;
4. Praise God the al - might - y Fa - ther;

Praise him on his might - y throne;
Praise him now with lyre and harps;
With cym - bals that crash, give praise;
Praise Christ, his be - lov - ed Son;

Alleluia! Praise God in His Holy Dwelling (cont.)

Praise him for his won - der - ful deeds;
Praise him with the tim - brel and dance;
O let ev - ery - thing that has breath,
Give praise to the Spir - it of love;

Praise him for his sov - ereign maj - es - ty.
Praise him with the sound of string and reed.
Let all liv - ing crea - tures praise the Lord.
For - ev - er the tri - une God be praised.

People

Al - le - lu - ia! al - le - lu - ia!

Stanzas 1, 2, 3 al - le - lu - ia! *Stanza 4* lu - ia!

43   Hail! Redeemer, King Divine!

Patrick Brennan, 1877–1952, alt.

St. George's Windsor 7. 7. 7. 7. D.
George J. Elvey, 1816–1893

1. Hail! Re - deem - er, King di - vine! Priest and Lamb, the throne is thine,
2. Christ, thou King of truth and might, Be to us e - ter - nal light,

King whose reign shall nev - er cease, Prince of ev - er - last - ing peace.
Till in peace each na - tion rings With thy prais - es, King of kings.

Refrain

An - gels, saints, and na - tions sing: "Praised be Je - sus Christ, our King;

Lord of life, earth, sky, and sea, King of love on Cal - va - ry."

We Praise You, O God, Our Redeemer

44

Julia Bulkley Cady Cory, 1882-1963, alt.

Kremser 12. 11. 12. 11.
Dutch traditional melody

1. We praise you, O God, our Re - deem - er, Cre - a - tor,
2. We wor - ship you, God of our fa - thers, we bless you;
3. With voic - es u - nit - ed our prais - es we of - fer,

In grate - ful de - vo - tion our trib - ute we bring.
Through life's storm and tem - pest our guide you have been.
And glad - ly our song of true wor - ship we raise;

We lay it be - fore you, we kneel and a - dore you,
When per - ils o'er - take us, es - cape you will make us,
Our sins now con - fess - ing, we pray for your bless - ing,

We bless your ho - ly name, glad prais - es we sing.
And with your help, O Lord, life's bat - tles we win.
To you, our great Re - deem - er, ev - er be praise. A - men.

45 Praise, My Soul, the King of Heaven

Henry Francis Lyte, 1793–1847, cento, alt.

Lauda anima 8. 7. 8. 7. 8. 7.
John Goss, 1800–1880

1. Praise, my soul, the King of heav - en; To his feet your
2. Praise him for his grace and fa - vor To our fa - thers
3. Fa - ther - like he tends and spares us; Well our fee - ble
4. An - gels, help us to a - dore him; You be - hold him

trib - ute bring; Ran - somed, healed, re - stored, for - giv - en,
in dis - tress; Praise him still the same as ev - er,
frame he knows; In his hands he gent - ly bears us,
face to face; Sun and moon, bow down be - fore him,

Ev - er - more his prais - es sing: Al - le - lu - ia!
Slow to chide, and swift to bless: Al - le - lu - ia!
Res - cues us from all our foes. Al - le - lu - ia!
Dwell - ers all in time and space. Al - le - lu - ia!

Al - le - lu - ia! Praise the ev - er - last - ing King.
Al - le - lu - ia! Glo - rious in his faith - ful - ness.
Al - le - lu - ia! Wide - ly yet his mer - cy flows.
Al - le - lu - ia! Praise with us the God of grace. A - men.

The God of Abraham Praise

46

Daniel ben-Judah Dayyan, 14th century
Tr. by Max Landsberg, 1845-1928,
and Newton Mann, 1836-1926, alt.

Leoni 6. 6. 8. 4. D.
Hebrew traditional melody
Arr. by Meier Leon, 1751-1797

1. The God of A-braham praise, All praise his bless-ed name,
2. His spir-it flows so free, High surg-ing where it will:
3. He has e-ter-nal life Im-plant-ed in the soul;

Who was, and is, and is to be, Ev-er the same!
In proph-et's word he spoke of old—He's speak-ing still.
His love shall be our strength and stay, While ag-es roll.

The one e-ter-nal God, Ere aught that now ap-pears;
Es-tab-lished is his law, And change-less it shall stand,
Praise to the liv-ing God! All praise his bless-ed name,

The First, the Last: be-yond all thought His time-less years!
Deep writ up-on the hu-man heart, On sea, or land.
Who was, and is, and is to be, Ev-er the same! A-men.

Praise the Lord, His Glories Show

Llanfair 7. 7. 7. 7. with Alleluias
Robert Williams, 1781–1821
Harm. by David Evans, 1874–1948
Descant by Donald D. Kettring, 1907–

Henry Francis Lyte, 1793–1847, cento, alt.

Descant

3. Praise the Lord, his mer-cies trace, Al - - le - lu - ia!

1. Praise the Lord, his glo - ries show, Al - - le - lu - ia!
2. Earth to heaven, and heaven to earth, Al - - le - lu - ia!
3. Praise the Lord, his mer-cies trace, Al - - le - lu - ia!

Praise his prov - i - dence and grace, Al - - le - lu - ia!

Saints with - in his courts be - low, Al - - le - lu - ia!
Tell his won - ders, sing his worth, Al - - le - lu - ia!
Praise his prov - i - dence and grace, Al - - le - lu - ia!

All that he for man has done, Al - - le - lu - ia!

An - gels round his throne a - bove, Al - - le - lu - ia!
Age to age and shore to shore, Al - - le - lu - ia!
All that he for man has done, Al - - le - lu - ia!

All he sends us through his Son. Al - - le - lu - ia! A-men.

All that see and share his love. Al - - le - lu - ia!
Praise him, praise him ev - er - more! Al - - le - lu - ia!
All he sends us through his Son. Al - - le - lu - ia! A-men.

O for a Thousand Tongues to Sing 48

Azmon C. M.
Carl G. Gläser, 1784-1829
Arr. by Lowell Mason, 1792-1872

Charles Wesley, 1707-1788, cento, alt.

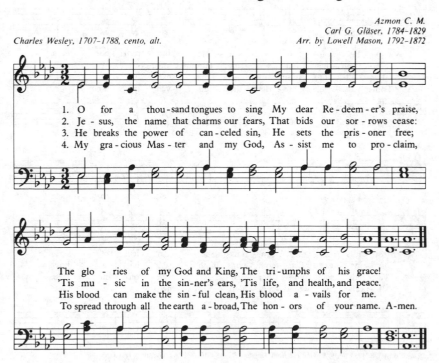

1. O for a thou-sand tongues to sing My dear Re-deem-er's praise,
2. Je - sus, the name that charms our fears, That bids our sor - rows cease:
3. He breaks the power of can-celed sin, He sets the pris-oner free;
4. My gra-cious Mas-ter and my God, As-sist me to pro-claim,

The glo - ries of my God and King, The tri-umphs of his grace!
'Tis mu - sic in the sin-ner's ears, 'Tis life, and health, and peace.
His blood can make the sin-ful clean, His blood a - vails for me.
To spread through all the earth a-broad, The hon-ors of your name. A-men.

49 Immortal, Invisible, God Only Wise

St. Denio 11. 11. 11. 11.
Welsh traditional melody

Walter Chalmers Smith, 1824–1908, cento, alt.

Descant by Donald D. Kettring, 1907–

4. Great Fa - ther of glo - ry, pure Fa - ther of light,

1. Im - mor - tal, in - vis - i - ble, God on - ly wise,
2. Un - rest - ing, un - hast - ing, and si - lent as light,
3. To all, life thou giv - est— to both great and small;
4. Great Fa - ther of glo - ry, pure Fa - ther of light,

Thine an - gels a - dore thee, all veil - ing their sight;

In light in - ac - ces - si - ble hid from our eyes,
Nor want - ing, nor wast - ing, thou rul - est in might;
In all life thou liv - est, the true life of all;
Thine an - gels a - dore thee, all veil - ing their sight;

O help us to see

Most bless - ed, most glo - rious, the An - cient of Days,
Thy jus - tice like moun - tains high soar - ing a - bove,
We blos - som and flour - ish as leaves on the tree,
All praise we would ren - der; O help us to see

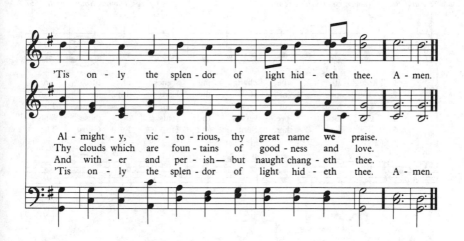

'Tis on - ly the splen - dor of light hid - eth thee. A - men.

Al - might - y, vic - to - rious, thy great name we praise.
Thy clouds which are foun - tains of good - ness and love.
And with - er and per - ish— but naught chang - eth thee.
'Tis on - ly the splen - dor of light hid - eth thee. A - men.

Praise to God, Immortal Praise   50

Pleyel's Hymn 7. 7. 7. 7.

Anna L. Barbauld, 1743–1825, cento

Ignace Joseph Pleyel, 1757–1831

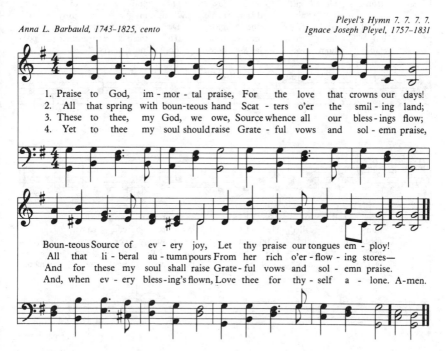

1. Praise to God, im - mor - tal praise, For the love that crowns our days!
2. All that spring with boun-teous hand Scat - ters o'er the smil - ing land;
3. These to thee, my God, we owe, Source whence all our bless-ings flow;
4. Yet to thee my soul should raise Grate - ful vows and sol - emn praise,

Boun-teous Source of ev - ery joy, Let thy praise our tongues em - ploy!
All that li - beral au - tumn pours From her rich o'er - flow - ing stores—
And for these my soul shall raise Grate - ful vows and sol - emn praise.
And, when ev - ery bless-ing's flown, Love thee for thy - self a - lone. A-men.

51 Through All the Changing Scenes of Life

Tate and Brady, 'New Version,' 1696, cento

Wiltshire C. M.
George Thomas Smart, 1776–1867

1. Through all the chang - ing scenes of life, In
2. O mag - ni - fy the Lord with me, With
3. The hosts of God en - camp a - round The
4. For God pre - serves the souls of those Who
5. To Fa - ther, Son, and Ho - ly Ghost, The

trou - ble and in joy, The prais - es of my
me ex - alt his name; When in dis - tress to
dwell - ings of the just; De - liv - erance he af -
on his truth de - pend; To them and their pos -
God whom we a - dore, Be glo - ry, as it

God shall still My heart and tongue em - ploy.
him I called, He to my res - cue came.
fords to all Who on his suc - cor trust.
ter - i - ty His bless - ing shall de - scend.
was, is now, And shall be ev - er - more. A - men.

We Gather Together

52

Dutch traditional hymn, 16th century
Tr. by Theodore Baker, 1851–1934, alt.

Kremser 12. 11. 12. 11.
Dutch traditional melody

1. We gath - er to - geth - er to ask the Lord's bless - ing; He chas - tens and
   has - tens his will to make known; The wick - ed op - press - ing now cease from dis -
   tress - ing. Sing prais - es to his name! He for - gets not his own.

2. Be - side us to guide us, our God with us join - ing, Or - dain - ing, main -
   tain - ing his king-dom di - vine; So from the be - gin - ning the fight we were
   win - ning; Thou, Lord, wast at our side; all glo - ry be thine.

3. We all do ex - tol thee, thou lead - er tri - um - phant, And pray that thou
   still our de - fend - er wilt be. Let thy con-gre - ga - tion es - cape trib - u -
   la - tion. Thy name be ev - er praised! O Lord, make us free! A - men.

We Praise Thee, O God

53

Julia Bulkley Cady Cory, 1882–1963

Kremser 12.11. 12. 11.
Dutch traditional melody

1. We praise thee, O God, our Redeemer, Creator;
   In grateful devotion our tribute we bring.
   We lay it before thee, we kneel and adore thee,
   We bless thy holy name, glad praises we sing.

2. We worship thee, God of our fathers, we bless thee;
   Through life's storm and tempest our guide hast thou been.
   When perils o'ertake us, thou wilt not forsake us,
   And with thy help, O Lord, life's battles we win.

3. With voices united our praises we offer,
   And gladly our songs of true worship we raise.
   Our sins now confessing, we pray for thy blessing;
   To thee, our great Redeemer, forever be praise. Amen.

54   Praise the Lord in Our Worship

Kent E. Schneider, 1945–

Laudate omnes Irregular with Refrain
Kent E. Schneider, 1945–

1. Praise the Lord in our wor - ship.
2. We have come from all o - ver to
3. Christ calls us in - to liv - ing to
4. Live your faith! Ev - ery - bod - y don't

Praise his ho - ly name. Sing a song
wor - ship at this time. With new sounds and
join his faith - ful band. Let your heart and
leave it in the pew. At work or play in

for the hope that in our lives he'll reign.
new in - volve - ment with God we re - a - lign.
mind be o - pened. Know he's close at hand.
slum or sub - urb, Make it part of you.

Refrain

Praise the Lord, ev - ery - bod - y!

Let Us with a Gladsome Mind 55

Monkland 7. 7. 7. 7.
J. A. Freylinghausen, 'Geistreiches
Gesangbuch,' Halle, 1704
Adapted in 'Hymn\Tunes of the United
Brethren,' Manchester, 1824
Arr. by John B. Wilkes, 1785–1869

John Milton, 1608–1674, cento, alt.

1. Let us with a glad - some mind Praise the Lord, for he is kind:
2. Let us sound his name a - broad, For of gods he is the God:
3. He, with all - com - mand - ing might, Filled the new-made world with light:
4. All things liv - ing he will feed; His full hand sup - plies their need:
5. Let us then with glad - some mind Praise the Lord, for he is kind:

For his mer - cies shall en - dure, Ev - er faith - ful, ev - er sure. A - men.

56 Lift Up Your Heads, Ye Mighty Gates

George Weissel, 1590–1635, cento
Tr. by Catherine Winkworth, 1827–1878

Macht hoch die Tür 8. 8. 8. 8. 8. 8. 6. 6.
J. A. Freylinghausen, 1670–1739

1. Lift up your heads, ye might - y gates; Be - hold the King of
2. The Lord is just, a help - er tried, With mer - cy ev - er
3. O blest the land, the cit - y blest, Where Christ the Rul - er
4. Re - deem - er, come! I o - pen wide My heart to thee: here,

glo - ry waits! The King of kings is draw - ing near,
at his side; His king - ly crown is ho - li - ness,
is con - fessed! O hap - py hearts and hap - py homes
Lord, a - bide! Let me thy in - ner pres - ence feel:

The Sav - ior of the world is here. Life and sal - va - tion
His scep - ter, pit - y in dis - tress. The end of all our
To whom this King of tri - umph comes! The cloud - less Sun of
Thy grace and love in me re - veal. Thy Ho - ly Spir - it

he doth bring; Where - fore re - joice and glad - ly sing:
woe he brings; Where - fore the earth is glad and sings:
joy he is, Who bring - eth pure de - light and bliss:
guide us on, Un - til our glo - rious goal is won:

Lift Up Your Heads, Ye Mighty Gates (cont.)

We praise thee, Fa - ther, now; Cre - a - tor, wise art thou.
We praise thee, Sav - ior, now; Might-y in deed art thou.
O Com-fort-er di - vine, What bound-less grace is thine.
E - ter - nal praise and fame We of - fer to thy name. A- men.

All People That on Earth Now Dwell   57

William Kethe, ?–1593, cento
Alt. by Benjamin Caulfield, 1890–

Old Hundredth L. M.
Louis Bourgeois, c. 1510–1561

1. All peo-ple that on earth now dwell, Sing to the Lord with cheer - ful voice;
2. Know that the Lord is God in - deed; With-out our aid God fash-ioned man;
3. O en - ter then his gates with praise, Ap-proach un - to his courts with joy;
4. To all, the Lord our God is good; His mer - cy is for - ev - er sure;

Serve him with joy, his bless-ings tell; Come all be - fore him and re - joice.
We are his peo-ple; we have fed From pas-tures where fresh wa-ters ran.
Laud, bless, and thank his name al-ways, For praise is seem - ly to em - ploy.
His truth at all times firm-ly stood, And shall from age to age en - dure. A- men.

Yo Ri-bohn O-lahm V'-ol-mah-yo

Yoh Ribon Olam Irregular with Refrain
Hebrew traditional melody

1. Yo ri-bohn o-lahm v'-ol-mah-yo
ahnt hoo mahl-ko me-lech mahl-chah-yo. O-
vahd g'-voor-taych v'-sim-chah-yo, shah-
peer ko-do-moch l'-hah-ch'-vah-yo.

2. Sh'vo-cheen ah-sah-dayr tzahf-ro v'-rahm-sho,
loch e-lo-ho di-v'ro chol nahf-sho. Ee-
reen kah-dee-sheen oo-v'nay e-no-sho chay-
vahs bo-ro v'oh-fay sh'-mah-yo.

3. Rav-r'-veen ov-doch v'-sah-kee-feen, mo-
chaych ro-mah-yo zo-kayf k'-fee-feen.
Loo y'-chay g'-var sh'-neen ahl-feen
lo y'ay g'-voor-taych b'-chosh-bo-na-yo.

Refrain

Yo ri-bohn o-lahm v'-ol-mah-yo
ahnt hoo mahl-ko me-lech mahl-c'hah-yo.

Rock of Ages, Let Our Song

Hebrew hymn by "Mordecai," 14th century
German tr. by Leopold Stein, 1810–1882
Tr. by Marcus Jastrow, 1829–1903, and
Gustav Gottheil, 1827–1903

Maoz Tsur 7. 6. 7. 6. 6. 6. 3. 3. 6.
German Ashkenazic melody

1. Rock of Ag - es, let our song   Praise thy sav - ing pow - er;
2. Kin-dling new the ho - ly lamps,   Priests, ap-proved in suf - fering,
3. Chil-dren of the mar - tyr race,   Wheth - er free or fet - tered,

Thou, a - midst the rag - ing foes,   Wast our shel-tering tow - er.
Pu - ri - fied the na - tion's shrine,   Brought to God their of - fering.
Wake the ech - oes of the songs   Where ye may be scat - tered.

Fu - rious they as - sailed   us,   But thine arm a - vailed   us,
And his courts sur - round - ing   Hear, in joy a - bound - ing,
Yours the mes - sage cheer - ing   That the time is near - ing

And thy word Broke their sword When our own strength failed us.
Hap - py throngs, Sing - ing songs With a might - y sound - ing.
Which will see All men free, Ty - rants dis - ap - pear - ing.

Yis-m'choo, Yis-m'choo

Yismechu Irregular
Hebrew traditional melody

Yis - m' - choo, Yis - m' - choo v' - mah - l'choo - s'cho

shoh - m'ray shah - bos v' - koh - r'ay oh - neg.

Ahm m' - kah - d'shay m'kah-d'shay sh' - vee - ee, koo - lom

yis - b' - oo v' - yis - ah - n' - goo mi - too - ve - - cho,

v' - yis - ah - n'goo v' - yis - ah - n'goo mi - too - ve - cho.

Oo - vah- sh'vee-ee ro - tzee-so boh v' - ki - dahsh - toh,

chem - dahs yo - meem oh - soh ko - ro - so zay - cher

l'mah - ah - say v' - ray - shees, chem - dahs yo - meem oh - soh

ko - ro - so zay - cher l' - mah - ah - say v' - ray - shees.

Yig-dahl E-loh-heem Chahi 61

Leoni 10. 10. 10. 10.
Hebrew traditional melody
Adapted by Meier Leon, 1751–1797
Harm. by Abraham Wolf Binder, 1895–1966

Daniel ben-Judah Dayyan, 14th century

1. Yig-dahl e-loh-heem chahi, v'-yish-tah-bahch, nim-tzo v'-ayn ays el-m'tzee-oo-soh. E-chod v'-ayn yo-cheed k'-yi-choo-doh ne-e-lom v'-gam ayn sohf l'-ahch-doo-so.

2. Ayn loh d'-moos hah-goof v'-ay-noh-goof, loh nah-ah-rohch ay-lov k'-doo-sho-soh. Kad-mohn l'-chol do-vor a-sher niv-ro, ree-shohn v'-ayn ray-shees l'-ray-shee-soh.

3. Hi-noh Ah-don oh-lom l'-chol noh-tzor, yoh-reh g'-doo-lo-soh oo-ma-l'choo-soh. She-fah n'-voo-o-soh n'-so-noh el ah-'n'-shay s'-goo-lo-soh v'-sif-ahr-toh.

4. Loh kom b'-yis-ro-ayl, k'-mohshe ohd no-vee u-mah-beet es t'-moo-no-soh; Toh-rahs e-mes no-sahn l'-ah-moh ayl, ahl yahd n'-vee-oh ne-e-mahn bay-soh.

5. Loh yahchahleef hoayl v'loh yohmeer dosoh, l'ohlomeem l'zoolosoh;
Tzohfe v'yohdayah s'soraynoo, mahbeet l'sohf dovor b'kahdmosoh.

6. Gohmayl l'eesh chesed k'mifoloh, nohsayn l'rosho rah k'rishosoh.
Yishlahch l'kaytz yomeen m'sheechaynoo, lifdos m'chahkay kaytz y'shooosoh.

7. Mayseem y'chahye ayl, b'rohv chahsdoh borooch ahday ahd shaym t'hilosoh.
Mayseem y'chahye ayl, b'rohv chahsdoh borooch ahday ahd shaym t'hilosoh.

From the *Union Hymnal,* copyright by the Central Conference of American Rabbis. Used by permission.

71

62   Sho-lohm Ah-lay-chem

Shalom Aleychem 8. 8. 8. 6.
Israel Goldfarb, 1879–1967
Harm. by Abraham Wolf Binder, 1895–1966

1. Sho - lohm ah - lay - chem mahl - ah - chay hah - sho - rays, mahl-ah-chay el - - yohn; mi - me-lech mahl-chay hah- m'lo-cheem, hah - ko - dohsh bo - rooch hoo. 2. Boh-ah-chem l' sho-lohm
4. Tzay - s'chem l' sho - lohm mahl - ah - chay hah - sho - lohm, mahl-ah-chay el - - yohn; mi - me-lech mahl-chay hah- m'lo-cheem, hah - ko - dohsh bo - rooch hoo. 3. choo - nee l' sho-lohm

mahl-ah-chay hah-sho-lohm, mahl-ah-chay el - yohn, mi - me-lech
mahl-ah-chay hah-sho-lohm, mahl-ah-chay el - yohn, mi - me-lech

D.C. al Fine

1. *2.*

mahl-chay hah-m'lo - cheem, hah-ko-dohsh bo-rooch hoo. 3. Bo-r'
mahl-chay hah-m'lo - cheem, hah-ko-dohsh bo-rooch hoo.

Ahl Hah-ni-seem V'-ahl Hah-poor-kon 63

Al Hanisiym Irregular
Hebrew traditional melody

Ahl hah - ni - seem v' - ahl hah - poor - kon v'-

ahl hah-g' - voo - - rohs v'ahl hah - t'shoo - ohs,

v'ahl hah - mil - cho-mohs she - o - 'see - so lah - ah - voh-say-noo

bah - yo - meem ho - haym bah - - z'mahn hah - ze.

73

64   Hah-l'loo-yo Ahv-day Ah-doh-noi

Haleluya Avdey Adonai Irregular
Hebrew traditional folk tune
Harm. by Harry Coopersmith, 1902–

1. Hah - l' - loo - yo, hah - l' - loo - yo, hah - l'- loo ahv - day Ah - doh - noi. Hah - l' - loo - yo, hah - l' - loo - yo, hah - l' - loo es shaym Ah - doh - noi.
2. Hah - l' - loo - yo, hah - l' - loo - yo, y'hee shaym Ah - doh - noi m' - voh - roch. Hah - l' - loo - yo, hah - l' - loo - yo, may - ah - to v' - ahd oh - lom.
3. Hah - l' - loo - yo, hah - l' - loo - yo, m' - kee - mee may - o - for dol. Hah - l' - loo - yo, hah - l' - loo - yo, may - ahsh - pohs yo - reem ev - yohn.

Ah-dohn Oh-lom A-sher Mo-lahch

Adon Olam Irregular
Elieser Gerovitsch, 1844–1913

1. Ah - dohn   oh - lom   a -   sher   mo -   lahch,   b'-
2. V' - ah - chah - ray   ki - ch' - lohs   hah - kohl,   l'-
3. V' - hoo   e - chod   v' -   ayn   shay - nee   l'-
4. V' - hoo   ay - lee   v' -   chay   goh - ah - lee,   v'-
5. B' - yo -   doh   ahf - keed   roo - chee,   b'-

te - rem   kol   y' - tzir   niv - ro.   Le - ays   nah - ah - so   v'-
vah -   doh   yim - loch   noh - ro.   V' - hoo   ho - yo   v'-
hahm - sheel   loh   l' - hach   bee - ro.   B' - lee   ray - shees   b'-
tzur   chev - lee   b' - ays   tzo - ro.   V' - hoo   ni - see   oo-
ays   ee - shan   v' - o - ee - ro.   V' - im   roo - chee   g'-

chef - tzoh   kol,   a - zahy   me - lech   sh' - moh   nik - ro.
hoo   hoh - ve,   v' - hoo   yih - ye   b' - sif - o - ro.
lee   sach - lees   v' - loh   ho - ohz   v' - hah - mis - ro.
mo - nohs   lee,   m' - nos   koh - see   b' - yom   ek - ro.
vi - yo - see,   Ah - doh - noi   lee   v' - loh   ee - ro.

76

Eyn Keloheynu Irregular
Julius Freudenthal, 1805–1874

1. Ayn kay - loh - hay - noo, ayn kah - doh - nay - noo, ayn
3. Noh - de lay - loh - hay - noo, noh - de lah - doh - nay - noo, noh - de

k' - mahl - kay - noo, ayn k'moh - shee - ay - noo. 2. Mee chay - loh - hay - noo,
l' - mahl - kay - noo, noh - de l'moh - shee - ay - noo. 4. Bo - rooch e - loh - hay - noo,

mee - chah - doh - nay - noo, mee ch' - mahl - kay - noo, mee ch'moh-shee-
bo - rooch ah - doh - nay - noo, bo - rooch mahl - kay - noo, bo - rooch moh - shee-

ay - noo. 5. Ah - to hoo e - loh - hay - noo; ah - to hoo ah - doh - nay -

noo, ah - to hoo mahl - kay - noo, ah - to hoo moh - shee - ay - noo.

From the *Union Hymnal*, copyright by the Central Conference of American Rabbis. Used by permission.

Ay-lee-yo-hoo Hah-no-vee

Eliyohu Hanoviy Irregular
Traditional Ashkenazic folk tune
Harm. by Harry Coopersmith, 1902–

Ay - lee - yo - hoo hah - no - vee, Ay - lee - yo - hoo hah - tish - bee, Ay - lee - yo - hoo, Ay - lee - yo - hoo, Ay - lee - yo - hoo hah -

gi - lo - dee! Bim - hay - ro v' - yo - may - noo,

yo - voh ay - lay - noo, im m' - shee - ahch

ben Do - veed, im m' - shee - ahch ben Do - veed.

79

68   Come, O Sabbath Day, and Bring

Sabbath Hymn 7. 7. 9. 7. 3. 3.

Gustav Gottheil, 1827–1903   *Abraham Wolf Binder, 1895–1966*

1. Come, O Sab-bath Day, and bring Peace and heal-ing on thy wing; And to ev-ery trou-bled breast Speak of the di-vine be-hest: Thou shalt rest, Thou shalt rest!

2. Earth-ly long-ings bid re-tire, Quench the pas-sions' hurt-ful fire; To the way-ward, sin-op-pressed, Bring thou thy di-vine be-hest: Thou shalt rest, Thou shalt rest!

3. Wipe from ev-ery cheek the tear, Ban-ish care and si-lence fear; All things work-ing for the best, Teach us the di-vine be-hest: Thou shalt rest, Thou shalt rest!

God of Might, God of Right

69

Hebrew traditional hymn, 17th century
Tr. by Gustav Gottheil, 1827–1903, et al.

Addir Hu 6. 6. 6. 6. 6. 6.
Hebrew traditional melody, 17th century

1. God of might, God of right, Thee we give all glo - ry;
2. Now as erst, when thou first Madest the proc - la - ma - tion,
3. Be with all who in thrall To their task are driv - en;

Thine all praise in these days As in ag - es hoar - y,
Warn - ing loud ev - ery proud, Ev - ery ty - rant na - tion,
In thy power speed the hour When their chains are riv - en;

When we hear, year by year, Free-dom's won-drous sto - ry.
We thy fame still pro - claim, Bend in ad - o - ra - tion.
Earth a - round will re - sound Glee - ful hymns to heav - en.

81

70

In the Peace of Christ We Sing

Peace of Christ Irregular with Refrain

Lucien Deiss, 1921–

Lucien Deiss, 1921–

Unison

Refrain

In the peace of Christ we sing our thanks to God.

1. We give you thanks, O Lord. You have giv-en us Your
2. We give you thanks, O Lord. You have giv-en us Your
3. We give you thanks, O Lord. You have giv-en us A

Repeat Refrain

sa-cred word to light our path to heav—en.
bread that is our pledge of e-ter-nal life.
song to praise your name through-out all the earth.

Words and music © World Library Publications, Inc. Used by permission.

71

God of Earth and Planets

Whitehills 6. 5. 6. 5.

William Watkins Reid, 1890–

Cyr de Brant, 1896–

1. God of earth and plan - ets Rang - ing out - er space,
2. God of worlds and at - oms, Each a mas - ter - piece,
3. God of flower and o - cean, Fra-grance, beauty, and power,
4. God of home and fam - ily, God our par - ents know,
5. God who sent us Je - sus— Mas - ter, Friend, and Guide—

Copyright 1965 by The Hymn Society of America; from *Twelve Children's Hymns.* Used by permission.

82

We in si - lent won - der Glimpse thy might and grace.
Deep-est probes of sci - ence Awe and faith in - crease.
Of thy love and beau - ty Share we ev - ery hour.
In thy love and knowl - edge We would live and grow.
We would call thee Fa - ther, In thy care a - bide.

God of Concrete, God of Steel 72

Arfon 7. 7. 7. 7. 7. 7.

Richard G. Jones, 1926–
Welsh traditional melody

1. God of con - crete, God of steel, God of pis - ton and of wheel,
2. Lord of ca - ble, Lord of rail, Lord of free - way and of mail,
3. Lord of sci - ence, Lord of art, God of map and graph and chart,
4. God, whose glo - ry fills the earth, Gave the u - ni - verse its birth,

God of py - lon, God of steam, God of gird - er and of beam,
Lord of rock - et, Lord of flight, Lord of soar - ing sat - el - lite,
Lord of phys - ics and re - search, Word of Bi - ble, faith of church,
Loosed the Christ with Eas - ter's might, Saves the world from e - vil's blight,

God of at - om, God of mine— All the world of power is thine.
Lord of light - ning's flash - ing line— All the world of speed is thine.
God of se - quence and de - sign— All the world of truth is thine.
Claims man - kind by grace di - vine— All the world of love is thine.

73 Lord, Dismiss Us with Your Blessing

Sts. 1, 2, ascribed to John Fawcett, 1740–1817, alt.
St. 3, Godfrey Thring, 1823–1903, alt.

Sicilian Mariners 8. 7. 8. 7. 8. 7.
Sicilian traditional melody

1. Lord, dis-miss us with your bless-ing; Fill our hearts with
2. Thanks we give and ad-o-ra-tion For your gos-pel's
3. So that when your love shall call us, Sav-ior, from the

joy and peace; Let us each, your love pos-sess-ing,
joy-ful sound; May the fruits of your sal-va-tion
world a-way, Let no fear of death ap-pall us,

Tri-umph in re-deem-ing grace: O re-fresh us,
In our hearts and lives a-bound: Ev-er faith-ful,
Glad your sum-mons to o-bey: May we ev-er,

O re-fresh us, Trav-el-ing through this wil-der-ness.
Ev-er faith-ful To the truth may we be found;
May we ev-er Reign with you in end-less day. A-men.

Come, Ye Thankful People, Come 74

St. George's Windsor 7. 7. 7. 7. D.

Henry Alford, 1810–1871

George J. Elvey, 1816–1893

1. Come, ye thank-ful peo-ple, come, Raise the song of har-vest home;
2. All the world is God's own field, Fruit un-to his praise to yield;
3. For the Lord our God shall come, And shall take his har-vest home,
4. E-ven so, Lord, quick-ly come, Bring thy fi-nal har-vest home;

All is safe-ly gath-ered in Ere the win-ter storms be-gin;
Wheat and tares to-geth-er sown, Un-to joy or sor-row grown;
From his field shall in that day All of-fens-es purge a-way,
Gath-er thou thy peo-ple in, Free from sor-row, free from sin,

God, our mak-er, doth pro-vide For our wants to be sup-plied;
First the blade, and then the ear, Then the full corn shall ap-pear;
Give his an-gels charge at last In the fire the tares to cast,
There, for-ev-er pu-ri-fied, In thy pres-ence to a-bide;

Come to God's own tem-ple, come, Raise the song of har-vest home.
Lord of har-vest, grant that we Whole-some grain and pure may be.
But the fruit-ful ears to store In his gar-ner ev-er-more.
Come, with all thine an-gels, come, Raise the glo-rious har-vest home. A-men.

85

75   Now Thank We All Our God

Martin Rinkart, 1586–1649
Tr. by Catherine Winkworth, 1827–1878, alt.

Nun danket 6. 7. 6. 7. 6. 6. 6. 6.
Johann Crüger, 1598–1662

1. Now thank we all our God With heart and hands and voic - es,
2. O may this boun - teous God Through all our life be near us,
3. All praise and thanks to God The Fa - ther now be giv - en,

Who won-drous things has done, In whom his world re - joic - es;
With ev - er - joy - ful hearts And bless - ed peace to cheer us,
The Son, and him who reigns With them in high - est heav - en,

Who, from our moth - ers' arms, Has blessed us on our way
And keep us in his grace, And guide us when per - plexed,
The one e - ter - nal God, Whom earth and heaven a - dore;

With count-less gifts of love, And still is ours to - day.
And free us from all ills In this world and the next.
For thus it was, is now, And shall be ev - er - more. A-men.

This Is My Father's World

Terra beata S. M. D.
Franklin L. Sheppard, 1852–1930
Harm. for 'The Hymnbook,' 1955

Maltbie D. Babcock, 1858–1901, cento, alt.

1. This is my Fa-ther's world, And to my lis-tening ears All
2. This is my Fa-ther's world: The birds their car-ols raise, The
3. This is my Fa-ther's world: Oh, let me ne'er for-get That

na - ture sings, and round me rings The mu - sic of the spheres.
morn-ing light, the lil - y white, De - clare their mak-er's praise.
though the wrong seems oft so strong, God is the rul - er yet.

This is my Fa-ther's world: I rest me in the thought Of
This is my Fa-ther's world: He shines in all that's fair; In the
This is my Fa-ther's world: The bat-tle is not done; Je-

rocks and trees, of skies and seas; His hand the won-ders wrought.
rus-tling grass I hear him pass, He speaks to me ev-ery-where.
sus, who died, shall be sat - is - fied, And earth and heaven be one. A-men.

77 Wonderful and Great Are Your Works

Wonderful and Great Irregular with Alleluias
Lucien Deiss, 1921–

Lucien Deiss, 1921–
Unison

Al - le - lu - ia! Al - le - lu - ia!

1. Won-der-ful and great are your works, O Lord God Al-might-y.

2. Just and true are your ways, O King of all na - tions.

3. Who shall not re-vere you, O Lord! Who shall not give glo-ry to your name! You a - lone are ho-ly. 4. All na-tions shall come to

Words and music © World Library Publications, Inc. Used by permission.

Wonderful and Great Are Your Works (cont.)

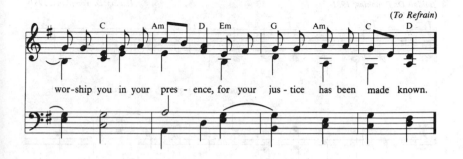

wor-ship you in your pres - ence, for your jus - tice has been made known.

(To Refrain)

Heaven and Earth, and Sea and Air 78

Lübeck 7. 7. 7. 7.

Joachim Neander, 1650–1680, cento
Tr. composite, 1868

J. A. Freylinghausen, 'Geistreiches
Gesangbuch,' Halle, 1704

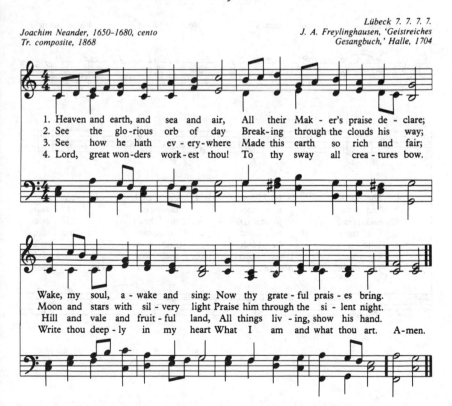

1. Heaven and earth, and sea and air, All their Mak - er's praise de - clare;
2. See the glo-rious orb of day Break-ing through the clouds his way;
3. See how he hath ev - ery-where Made this earth so rich and fair;
4. Lord, great won-ders work-est thou! To thy sway all crea - tures bow.

Wake, my soul, a - wake and sing: Now thy grate-ful prais - es bring.
Moon and stars with sil - very light Praise him through the si - lent night.
Hill and vale and fruit-ful land, All things liv - ing, show his hand.
Write thou deep-ly in my heart What I am and what thou art. A-men.

Music from *The Oxford American Hymnal,* Oxford University Press, Inc. Used by courtesy of Mrs. Carl Pfatteicher.

79 Let All Creation His Glory Proclaim

Let All Creation Irregular with Refrain
Haldan D. Tompkins, 1931–

Haldan D. Tompkins, 1931–

Unison
Refrain

Let all cre - a - tion his glo - ry pro - claim; with

praise and thanks we bless his name!

1. The earth is filled with the fruit of your works,
2. And wine to cheer the heart of man,
3. And bread to strength - en the heart of man,
4. The trees of the Lord ob - tain their fill,
5. There - in the birds their nests do build,
6. Up - on his moun - tains the wild goat dwells,
7. The moon you've made to sea - sons de - fine,

D.C.

that you may bring forth food, O Lord;
and oil to make his face to shine;
to feed your sons in ev - ery land;
the ce - dars of Leb - a - non on his hills;
the stork in his fir trees finds his home;
and there the rab - bit a ref - uge makes;
your sun o - beys and sets at your word;*

*(To Conclusion)

Conclusion

All glo - ry be to the Fa - ther and
As was, is now, and ev - er shall

Son, and Ho - ly Spir - it, with them One;
be, in ev - ery age, e - ter - nal - ly.

Glory Be to God on High

Gwalchmai 7. 4. 7. 4. D.

Theodore C. Williams, 1855–1915

Joseph David Jones, 1827–1870

1. Glo - ry be to God on high,
   Let the whole cre - a - tion cry.
   Peace and bless - ing he has given;
   Earth re - peat the songs of heaven.

2. Crea - tures of the field and flood, Al - le - lu - ia!
   Earth and sea cry, "God is good." Al - le - lu - ia!
   Toil - ing pil - grims raise the song, Al - le - lu - ia!
   Saints in light the strain pro - long. Al - le - lu - ia!

3. Stars that have no voice to sing
   Give their glo - ry to our King.
   Si - lent powers and an - gels' song
   All un - to our God be - long.

A - men.

The Heavens Declare Thy Glory, Lord

Isaac Watts, 1674-1748

Hebron L. M.
Lowell Mason, 1792-1872

1. The heavens declare thy glory, Lord; In
2. The roll - ing sun, the chang - ing light, And
3. Sun, moon, and stars con - vey thy praise Round
4. Nor shall thy spread - ing gos - pel rest Till

ev - ery star thy wis - dom shines; But when our eyes be -
nights and days, thy power con - fess; But the blest vol - ume
the whole earth and nev - er stand; So when thy truth be -
through the world thy truth has run, Till Christ has all the

hold thy Word, We read thy name in fair - er lines.
thou hast writ Re - veals thy jus - tice and thy grace.
gan its race, It touched and glanced on ev - ery land.
na - tions blest That see the light or feel the sun. A - men.

5. Great Sun of righteousness, arise!
    Bless the dark world with heavenly light.
    Thy gospel makes the simple wise;
    Thy laws are pure, thy judgments right.

6. Thy noblest wonders here we view
    In souls renewed and sins forgiven.
    Lord, cleanse my sins, my soul renew,
    And make thy Word my guide to heaven.

82 God of the Earth, the Sky, the Sea

Pater omnium L. M. with Refrain
Samuel Longfellow, 1819–1892, cento
Henry J. E. Holmes, 1839–1905

1. God of the earth, the sky, the sea! Mak-er of all a-
2. Thy love is in the sun-shine's glow, Thy life is in the
3. We feel thy calm at eve-ning's hour, Thy gran-deur in the
4. But high-er far, and far more clear, Thee in man's spir-it

bove, be-low! Cre-a-tion lives and moves in thee,
quick-ening air; When light-nings flash and storm-winds blow,
march of night; And, when thy morn-ing breaks in power,
we be-hold; Thine im-age and thy-self are there—

Refrain

Thy pres-ent life through all doth flow.
There is thy power; thy law is there. We give thee thanks, thy
We hear thy word, "Let there be light."
Th'in-dwell-ing God, pro-claimed of old.

name we sing, Al-might-y Fa - ther, heav-enly King. A-men.

94

Great Ruler Over Time and Space

83

Melita 8. 8. 8. 8. 8. 8.
John B. Dykes, 1823-1876

Mildred C. Luckhardt, 1898-

1. Great Rul - er o - ver time and space, Who hold - est gal - ax -
2. O Source of power for wheels and wings, O Key to un - dis -
3. In all the tur - bu - lence to - day, With - in our hearts or

ies in place, Thou Mak - er of the mas - ter plan,
cov - ered things, Thy chil - dren search the skies to trace
far a - way, Where - e'er we be — land, sea, or sky —

Great Source of ev - ery hope of man, Crea - a - tor of vast
The un - solved mys - ter - ies of space. Kind Fa - ther of each
Help us to know that thou art nigh. In fu - ture years, on

worlds un - known— Be thou our guide, and thou a - lone.
air - borne man, Keep us har - mo - nious with thy plan.
paths un - trod, We would walk close to thee, our God. A - men.

84 The Spacious Firmament on High

Creation L. M. D.
Franz Joseph Haydn, 1732-1809
Adapted by Isaac B. Woodbury, 1819-1858

Joseph Addison, 1672-1719

1. The spa - cious fir - ma - ment on high, With all the
2. Soon as the eve - ning shades pre - vail, The moon takes
3. What though, in sol - emn si - lence, all Move round the

blue e - the - real sky, And span-gled heavens, a shin - ing frame,
up the won - drous tale, And night-ly, to the lis - tening earth,
dark ter - res - trial ball? What though no re - al voice nor sound

Their great O - rig - i - nal pro - claim. The un-wea-ried sun, from
Re - peats the sto - ry of her birth; Whilst all the stars that
A - midst their ra - diant orbs be found? In rea-son's ear they

day to day, Does his Cre - a - tor's power dis - play, And pub - lish-
round her burn, And all the plan - ets in their turn, Con-firm the
all re-joice, And ut - ter forth a glo - rious voice, For - ev - er

es to ev - ery land The work of an al-might-y hand.
ti - dings as they roll, And spread the truth from pole to pole.
sing - ing, as they shine, "The hand that made us is di-vine." A-men.

All Beautiful the March of Days

Forest Green C. M. D.
English traditional melody
Collected, adapted, and arr. by
Ralph Vaughan Williams, 1872-1958

Frances Whitmarsh Wile, 1878-1939, cento, alt.

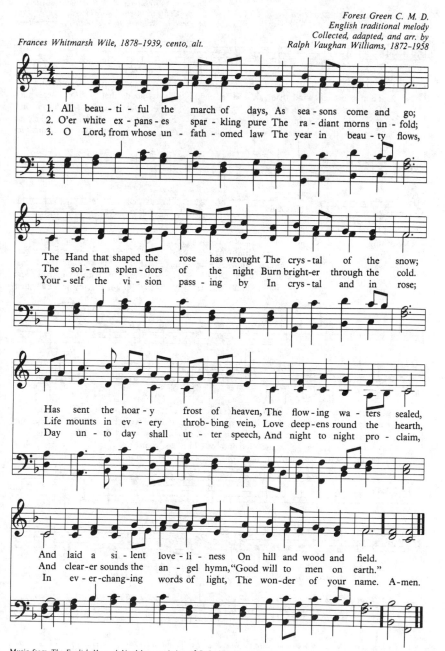

1. All beau-ti-ful the march of days, As sea-sons come and go;
2. O'er white ex-pans-es spar-kling pure The ra-diant morns un-fold;
3. O Lord, from whose un-fath-omed law The year in beau-ty flows,

The Hand that shaped the rose has wrought The crys-tal of the snow;
The sol-emn splen-dors of the night Burn bright-er through the cold.
Your-self the vi-sion pass-ing by In crys-tal and in rose;

Has sent the hoar-y frost of heaven, The flow-ing wa-ters sealed,
Life mounts in ev-ery throb-bing vein, Love deep-ens round the hearth,
Day un-to day shall ut-ter speech, And night to night pro-claim,

And laid a si-lent love-li-ness On hill and wood and field.
And clear-er sounds the an-gel hymn, "Good will to men on earth."
In ev-er-chang-ing words of light, The won-der of your name. A-men.

Music from *The English Hymnal.* Used by permission of Oxford University Press.

86 All Creatures of Our God and King

Francis of Assisi, 1182–1226, cento
Tr. by William H. Draper, 1855–1933

Lasst uns erfreuen 8. 8. 8. 8. 8. 6. with Alleluias
Cologne, 'Geistliche Kirchengesänge,' 1623
Arr. and harm. by Ralph Vaughan Williams, 1872–1958

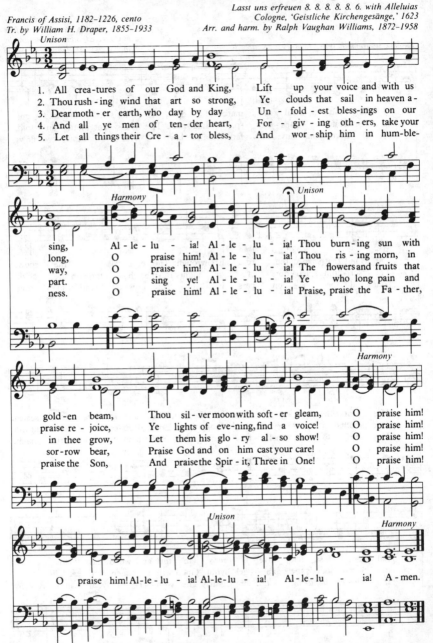

1. All crea-tures of our God and King, Lift up your voice and with us sing, Al-le-lu - ia! Al-le-lu - ia! Thou burn-ing sun with gold-en beam, Thou sil-ver moon with soft-er gleam, O praise him!
2. Thou rush-ing wind that art so strong, Ye clouds that sail in heaven a-long, O praise him! Al-le-lu - ia! Thou ris-ing morn, in praise re-joice, Ye lights of eve-ning, find a voice! O praise him!
3. Dear moth-er earth, who day by day Un-fold-est bless-ings on our way, O praise him! Al-le-lu - ia! The flowers and fruits that in thee grow, Let them his glo-ry al-so show! O praise him!
4. And all ye men of ten-der heart, For-giv-ing oth-ers, take your part. O sing ye! Al-le-lu - ia! Ye who long pain and sor-row bear, Praise God and on him cast your care! O praise him!
5. Let all things their Cre-a-tor bless, And wor-ship him in hum-ble-ness. O praise him! Al-le-lu - ia! Praise, praise the Fa-ther, praise the Son, And praise the Spir-it, Three in One! O praise him!

O praise him! Al-le-lu - ia! Al-le-lu - ia! Al-le-lu - ia! A - men.

Declare, O Heavens, the Lord of Space

Lasst uns erfreuen L. M. with Alleluias
Cologne, 'Geistliche Kirchengesänge,' 1623

Robert Lansing Edwards, 1915–
Arr. and harm. by Ralph Vaughan Williams, 1872–1958

Unison

1. De - clare, O heavens, the Lord of space; Re - ply, broad lands in ev - ery place;
2. Launch forth, O man, and bold - ly rise. Be - yond our plan - et pierce the skies;
3. Yet see this world with prob - lems filled; Earth longs for life the Mas - ter willed;
4. O Lord, whose power all space ex - tols, Draw near our lives, en - large our souls;

Tell his splen - dor! Al - le - lu - ia! New realms we find he first hath
Bound-less ven - ture! Al - le - lu - ia! No soar - ing flight can e'er out -
Light its dark - ness! Al - le - lu - ia! Reach out all bro - ken lives to
Dwell with - in us! Al - le - lu - ia! Stir deeds of grace to serve thy

made; All be - ing is his power dis - played. Al - le - lu - ia! Al - le -
run Truth God has shown us in his Son. Al - le - lu - ia! Al - le -
mend; In Christ win peace no war will end. Al - le - lu - ia! Al - le -
plan; Wake joy the morn - ing stars be - gan. Al - le - lu - ia! Al - le -

lu - ia! Al - le - lu - ia! Al - le - lu - ia! Al - le - lu - ia! A - men.

For the Beauty of the Earth

Dix 7. 7. 7. 7. 7. 7.
Conrad Kocher, 1786–1872
Arr. by William H. Monk, 1823–1889
Descant by Donald D. Kettring, 1907–

Folliott S. Pierpoint, 1835–1917, cento

1. For the beau - ty of the earth, For the beau - ty of the skies,
2. For the won - der of each hour Of the day and of the night,
3. For the joy of ear and eye, For the heart and mind's de - light,
4. For the joy of hu - man love, Broth - er, sis - ter, par - ent, child,
5. For thy church that ev - er - more Lift - eth ho - ly hands a - bove,

For the love which from our birth O - ver and a - round us lies,
Hill and vale, and tree and flower, Sun and moon, and stars of light,
For the mys - tic har - mo - ny Link - ing sense to sound and sight,
Friends on earth, and friends a - bove, For all gen - tle thoughts and mild,
Of - fering up on ev - ery shore Her pure sac - ri - fice of love,

Refrain

Lord of all, to thee we raise This our hymn of grate - ful praise. A - men.

Many and Great, O God, Are Thy Things 89

American Indian (Dakota) hymn, cento
Para. by Philip Frazier, 1892–1964

Lacquiparle Irregular
American Indian melody
Harm. by Stephen R. Riggs, 1812–1883

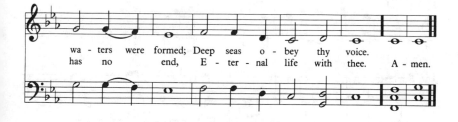

1. Man - y and great, O God, are thy things, Mak - er of
2. Grant un - to us com - mu - nion with thee, Thou star - a -

earth and sky. Thy hands have set the heav - ens with stars;
bid - ing one. Come un - to us and dwell with us;

Thy fin - gers spread the moun - tains and plains. Lo, at thy word the
With thee are found the gifts of life. Bless us with life that

wa - ters were formed; Deep seas o - bey thy voice.
has no end, E - ter - nal life with thee. A - men.

90   O Jesus, Crowned with All Renown

Kingsfold C. M. D.

Edward White Benson, 1829–1896,
cento, alt.

Melody coll. by Lucy Broadwood, 1858–1929
Harm. and arr. by Ralph Vaughan Williams, 1872–1958

1. O Je-sus, crowned with all re-nown, Since thou the earth hast trod,
2. Lord, in their change, let frost and heat And winds and dews be given;
3. That we may feed the poor a-right, And, gath-ering round thy throne,

Thou reign-est, and by thee come down Hence-forth the gifts of God.
All fos-tering power, all in-fluence sweet, Breathe from the boun-teous heaven.
Here, in the ho-ly an-gels' sight, Re - pay thee of thine own:

Thine is the health and thine the wealth That in our halls a - bound,
At - tem - per fair with gen - tle air The sun - shine and the rain,
That we may praise thee all our days, And with the Fa - ther's name,

And thine the beau-ty and the joy With which the years are crowned.
That kind - ly earth with time - ly birth May yield her fruits a - gain:
And with the Ho - ly Spir - it's gifts, The Sav-ior's love pro - claim. A-men.

Another Year Is Dawning

Frances Ridley Havergal, 1836–1879

Aurelia 7. 6. 7. 6. D.
Samuel S. Wesley, 1810–1876

1. An - oth - er year is dawn - ing, Dear Fa - ther, let it be
2. An - oth - er year of mer - cies, Of faith - ful - ness and grace,
3. An - oth - er year of serv - ice, Of wit - ness for thy love,

In work - ing or in wait - ing An - oth - er year with thee;
An - oth - er year of glad - ness In the shin - ing of thy face,
An - oth - er year of train - ing For ho - lier work a - bove.

An - oth - er year of prog - ress, An - oth - er year of praise,
An - oth - er year of lean - ing Up - on thy lov - ing breast,
An - oth - er year is dawn - ing, Dear Fa - ther, let it be

An - oth - er year of prov - ing Thy pres - ence all the days;
An - oth - er year of trust - ing, Of qui - et, hap - py rest;
On earth, or else in heav - en, An - oth - er year for thee. A - men.

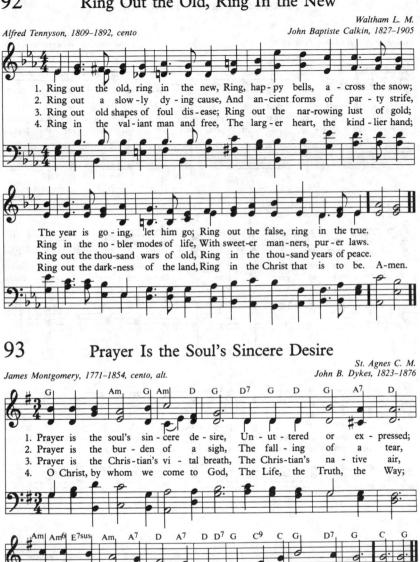

92   Ring Out the Old, Ring In the New

Waltham L. M.

Alfred Tennyson, 1809–1892, cento

John Baptiste Calkin, 1827–1905

1. Ring out the old, ring in the new, Ring, hap-py bells, a-cross the snow;
2. Ring out a slow-ly dy-ing cause, And an-cient forms of par-ty strife,
3. Ring out old shapes of foul dis-ease; Ring out the nar-rowing lust of gold;
4. Ring in the val-iant man and free, The larg-er heart, the kind-lier hand;

The year is go-ing, let him go; Ring out the false, ring in the true.
Ring in the no-bler modes of life, With sweet-er man-ners, pur-er laws.
Ring out the thou-sand wars of old, Ring in the thou-sand years of peace.
Ring out the dark-ness of the land, Ring in the Christ that is to be. A-men.

93   Prayer Is the Soul's Sincere Desire

St. Agnes C. M.

James Montgomery, 1771–1854, cento, alt.

John B. Dykes, 1823–1876

1. Prayer is the soul's sin-cere de-sire, Un-ut-tered or ex-pressed;
2. Prayer is the bur-den of a sigh, The fall-ing of a tear,
3. Prayer is the Chris-tian's vi-tal breath, The Chris-tian's na-tive air,
4. O Christ, by whom we come to God, The Life, the Truth, the Way;

The mo-tion of a hid-den fire That trem-bles in the breast.
The up-ward glanc-ing of an eye, When none but God is near.
His watch-word at the gates of death; He en-ters heaven with prayer.
The path of prayer you, Lord, have trod: Now, teach us how to pray! A-men.

104

William W. Walford, 1772–1850, cento

Sweet Hour L. M. D.
William B. Bradbury, 1816–1868

1. Sweet hour of prayer, sweet hour of prayer, That calls me from a world of care,
2. Sweet hour of prayer, sweet hour of prayer, Thy wings shall my pe - ti - tion bear

And bids me at my Fa - ther's throne Make all my wants and wish - es known!
To him, whose truth and faith - ful - ness En - gage the wait - ing soul to bless.

In sea - sons of dis - tress and grief, My soul has of - ten found re - lief,
And since he bids me seek his face, Be - lieve his word and trust his grace,

And oft es - caped the tempt - er's snare, By thy re - turn, sweet hour of prayer.
I'll cast on him my ev - ery care, And wait for thee, sweet hour of prayer. A - men.

He's Got the Whole World in His Hands

In His Hands Irregular
American Negro melody
Arr. by David Hugh Jones, 1900-

Spiritual

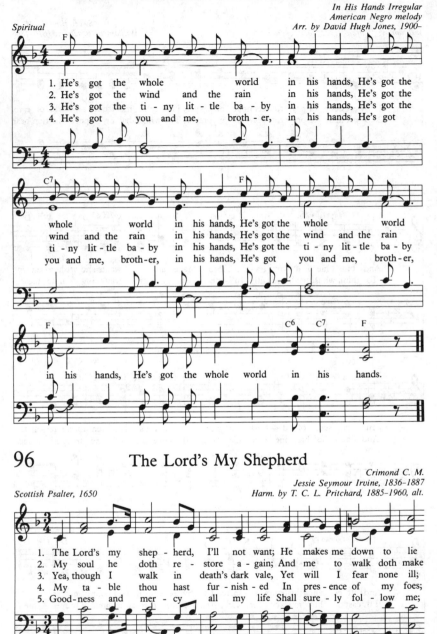

1. He's got the whole world in his hands, He's got the whole world in his hands, He's got the whole world in his hands, He's got the whole world in his hands.
2. He's got the wind and the rain in his hands, He's got the wind and the rain in his hands, He's got the wind and the rain in his hands,
3. He's got the ti-ny lit-tle ba-by in his hands, He's got the ti-ny lit-tle ba-by in his hands, He's got the ti-ny lit-tle ba-by
4. He's got you and me, broth-er, in his hands, He's got you and me, broth-er, in his hands, He's got you and me, broth-er,

in his hands, He's got the whole world in his hands.

The Lord's My Shepherd

Crimond C. M.
Jessie Seymour Irvine, 1836–1887
Harm. by T. C. L. Pritchard, 1885–1960, alt.

Scottish Psalter, 1650

1. The Lord's my shep-herd, I'll not want; He makes me down to lie
2. My soul he doth re-store a-gain; And me to walk doth make
3. Yea, though I walk in death's dark vale, Yet will I fear none ill;
4. My ta-ble thou hast fur-nish-ed In pres-ence of my foes;
5. Good-ness and mer-cy all my life Shall sure-ly fol-low me;

Music from *The Scottish Psalter.* Used by permission of Oxford University Press.

The Lord's My Shepherd (cont.)

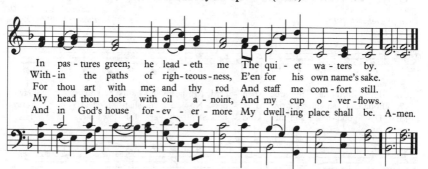

In pas - tures green; he lead - eth me The qui - et wa - ters by.
With - in the paths of righ - teous - ness, E'en for his own name's sake.
For thou art with me; and thy rod And staff me com - fort still.
My head thou dost with oil a - noint, And my cup o - ver - flows.
And in God's house for - ev - er - more My dwell - ing place shall be. A - men.

Unto the Hills Around Do I Lift Up 97

John D. S. Campbell, 1845–1914

Sandon 10. 4. 10. 4. 10. 10.
Charles H. Purday, 1799–1885

1. Un - to the hills a - round do I lift up My long - ing eyes;
2. He will not suf - fer that thy foot be moved: Safe shalt thou be.
3. Je - ho - vah is him - self thy keep - er true, Thy change - less shade;
4. From ev - ery e - vil shall he keep thy soul, From ev - ery sin;

O whence for me shall my sal - va - tion come, From whence a - rise? From God, the
No care - less slum - ber shall his eye - lids close, Who keep - eth thee. Be - hold, he
Je - ho - vah thy de - fense on thy right hand Him - self hath made. And thee no
Je - ho - vah shall pre - serve thy go - ing out, Thy com - ing in. A - bove thee

Lord, doth come my cer - tain aid, From God, the Lord, who heaven and earth hath made.
sleep - eth not, he slum - bereth ne'er, Who keep - eth Is - rael in his ho - ly care.
sun by day shall ev - er smite; No moon shall harm thee in the si - lent night.
watch - ing, he whom we a - dore Shall keep thee hence - forth, yea, for - ev - er - more.

98   The Lord Is My True Shepherd, My Needs

Psalm 23 7. 6. 7. 6. D.

Omer Westendorf, 1916–

Russell Woollen, 1923–

Unison

1. The Lord is my true shep - herd, My needs and wants he knows; He
2. Though I should walk in dark - ness, No e - vil shall I fear; Your
3. His good - ness and his kind - ness Shall ev - er fol - low me; His

feeds me in green pas - tures And there gives me re - pose. He
rod and staff give com - fort, For you are ev - er near. You
house shall be my dwell - ing For all e - ter - ni - ty. *Give
The

leads me to cool wa - ters, Where he re - fresh - es me; A -
spread a sump-tuous ban - quet In sight of all my foes; With
praise to God the Fa - ther, To Christ, his on - ly Son, And
Lord is my true shep - herd, My needs and wants he knows; He

long safe paths he guides me; True to his name is he.
oil you do a - noint me: My cup now o - ver - flows.
to the Ho - ly Spir - it, True God in es - sence One.
feeds me in green pas - tures And there gives me re - pose.

Words and music © World Library Publications, Inc. Used by permission.
* Alternate wording for end of Stanza 3 is given in italics.

108

What a Fellowship, What a Joy Divine 99

Leaning on Jesus 10. 9. 10. 9. with Refrain
Elisha A. Hoffman, 1839–1929
Anthony J. Showalter, 1858–1924

1. What a fel-low-ship, what a joy di-vine, Lean-ing on the
2. O how sweet to walk in this pil-grim way, Lean-ing on the
3. What have I to dread, what have I to fear, Lean-ing on the

Ev-er-last-ing Arms! What a bless-ed-ness, what a peace is mine,
Ev-er-last-ing Arms! O how bright the path grows from day to day,
Ev-er-last-ing Arms! I have peace com-plete with my Lord so near,

Refrain
Lean-ing on the Ev-er-last-ing Arms! Lean - ing,
Lean-ing on Je-sus,

lean - - ing, Safe and se-cure from all a-larms; Lean - - ing,
Lean-ing on Je-sus, Lean-ing on Je-sus,

lean - - ing, Lean-ing on the Ev-er-last-ing Arms.
Lean-ing on Je-sus,

100 Trust the Eternal When the Shadows Gather

William P. McKenzie, 1861–1942

Willingham 11. 10. 11. 10.
Franz Abt, 1819–1885, adapted

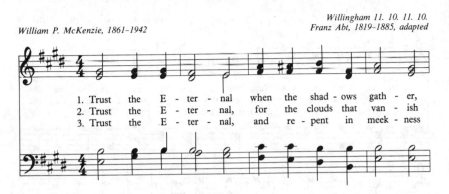

1. Trust the E - ter - nal when the shad - ows gath - er,
2. Trust the E - ter - nal, for the clouds that van - ish
3. Trust the E - ter - nal, and re - pent in meek - ness

When joys of day - light seem so like a dream;
No more can move the moun-tains from their base
Of that heart's pride which frowns and will not yield;

God the un-chang - ing pit - ies like a fa - ther;
Than sin's il - lu - sive wreaths of mist can ban - ish
Then to thy child - heart shall come strength in weak - ness,

From the *Christian Science Hymnal.*

110

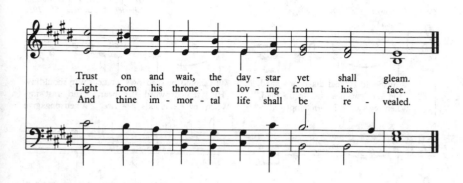

Trust on and wait, the day - star yet shall gleam.
Light from his throne or lov - ing from his face.
And thine im - mor - tal life shall be re - vealed.

I to the Hills Will Lift My Eyes 101

'The Psalter,' 1912, cento, alt.

Dundee (French) C. M.
Scottish Psalter, 1615

1. I to the hills will lift my eyes; O whence shall come my aid?
2. He will not let your foot be moved, Your guard - ian nev - er sleeps;
3. Your faith - ful keep - er is the Lord, Your shel - ter and your shade;
4. From e - vil he will keep you safe, For you he will pro - vide;

My help is from the Lord a - lone, Who heaven and earth has made.
With watch - ful and un - slum - bering care His own he safe - ly keeps.
'Neath sun or moon, by day or night, You shall not be a - fraid.
Your go - ing out, Your com - ing in, For - ev - er he will guide. A - men.

102   Why Should I Feel Discouraged

His Eye Is on the Sparrow
7. 6. 7. 6. 7. 6. 7. 7. 7. 7. *with Refrain*

Civilla D. Martin, 1868–1948   *Charles H. Gabriel, 1856–1932*

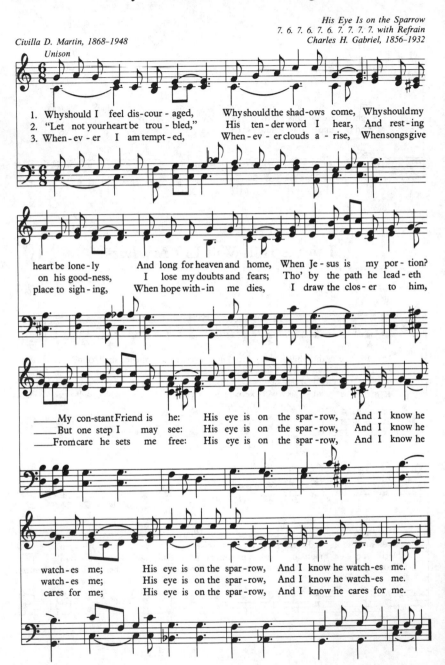

1. Why should I feel dis-cour-aged, Why should the shad-ows come, Why should my heart be lone-ly And long for heaven and home, When Je-sus is my por-tion? ___My con-stant Friend is he: His eye is on the spar-row, And I know he watch-es me; His eye is on the spar-row, And I know he watch-es me.

2. "Let not your heart be trou-bled," His ten-der word I hear, And rest-ing on his good-ness, I lose my doubts and fears; Tho' by the path he lead-eth ___But one step I may see: His eye is on the spar-row, And I know he watch-es me; His eye is on the spar-row, And I know he watch-es me.

3. When-ev-er I am tempt-ed, When-ev-er clouds a-rise, When songs give place to sigh-ing, When hope with-in me dies, I draw the clos-er to him, ___From care he sets me free: His eye is on the spar-row, And I know he cares for me; His eye is on the spar-row, And I know he cares for me.

Refrain *Harmony*

I sing be-cause I'm hap-py (I'm hap-py), I sing be-cause I'm free (I'm free),

For his eye is on the spar-row, And I know he watch-es me.

God Is Our Refuge and Our Strength 103

Winchester Old C. M.
Christopher Tye, c. 1500–1572
Alt. from 'Este's Psalter,' 1592

'The Psalter,' 1912

1. God is our ref-uge and our strength, Our ev-er-pres-ent aid,
2. Though hills a-midst the seas be cast, Though foam-ing wa-ters roar,
3. A riv-er flows whose streams make glad The cit-y of our God,
4. Since God is in the midst of her, Un-moved her walls shall stand,

And, there-fore, though the earth re-move, We will not be a-fraid;
Al-though the might-y bil-lows shake The moun-tains on the shore.
The ho-ly place where-in the Lord Most High has his a-bode;
For God will be her ear-ly help, When trou-ble is at hand. A-men.

104   There's a Peace in My Heart

Constantly Abiding Irregular with Refrain
Anne S. Murphy, ?–1942
Anne S. Murphy, ?–1942

1. There's a peace in my heart that the world nev-er gave, A peace it can
2. All the world seemed to sing of a Sav-ior and King, When peace sweet-ly
3. This trea-sure I have in a tem-ple of clay, While here on his

not take a-way; Tho' the tri-als of life may sur-round like a cloud,
came to my heart; Trou-bles all fled a-way and my night turned to day,
foot-stool I roam: But he's com-ing to take me some glo-ri-ous day,

I've a peace that has come there to stay!
Bless-ed Je-sus, how glo-rious thou art!
O-ver there to my heav-en-ly home!

Refrain

Con - - stant-ly a-
Con-stant-ly a-bid - ing,

bid - - - ing, Je - - sus is mine;
con-stant-ly a-bid-ing, Je-sus is mine, yes, Je-sus is mine;

Con - - - stant-ly a-bid - - - ing, rap - - ture di-
Con-stant-ly a-bid - ing, con-stant-ly a-bid-ing, rap-ture di-vine, O

Children of the Heavenly Father 105

Sandell L. M.

Caroline V. Sandell Berg, 1832–1903, cento
Tr. by Ernst William Olson, 1870–1958

Swedish folk song
Descant by L. David Miller, 1919–

1. Chil-dren of the heav-enly Fa-ther Safe-ly in his bos-om gath-er;
2. God his own doth tend and nour-ish, In his ho-ly courts they flour-ish.
3. Nei-ther life nor death shall ev-er From the Lord his chil-dren sev-er;
4. Though he giv-eth or he tak-eth, God his chil-dren ne'er for-sak-eth,

Nest-ling bird nor star in heav-en Such a ref-uge e'er was giv-en.
From all e-vil things he spares them, In his might-y arms he bears them.
Un-to them his grace he show-eth, And their sor-rows all he know-eth.
His the lov-ing pur-pose sole-ly To pre-serve them pure and ho-ly.

Words and music from the *Lutheran Service Book and Hymnal*; used by permission of the Commission on the Liturgy and Hymnal. Descant copyright 1962 by Muhlenberg Press; used by permission of Fortress Press.

What a Friend We Have in Jesus

Joseph Scriven, 1820–1886

Converse 8. 7. 8. 7. D.
Charles Crozat Converse, 1832–1918

1. What a friend we have in Je-sus, All our sins and griefs to bear!
2. Have we tri-als and temp-ta-tions? Is there trou-ble an-y-where?
3. Are we weak and heav-y-lad-en, Cum-bered with a load of care?

What a priv-i-lege to car-ry Ev-ery-thing to God in prayer!
We should nev-er be dis-cour-aged: Take it to the Lord in prayer!
Pre-cious Sav-ior, still our ref-uge— Take it to the Lord in prayer!

O what peace we of-ten for-feit, O what need-less pain we bear,
Can we find a friend so faith-ful, Who will all our sor-rows share?
Do your friends de-spise, for-sake you? Take it to the Lord in prayer!

All be-cause we do not car-ry Ev-ery-thing to God in prayer!
Je-sus knows our ev-ery weak-ness— Take it to the Lord in prayer!
In his arms he'll take and shield you, You will find a sol-ace there. A-men.

When Peace like a River

Horatio G. Spafford, 1828–1888, alt.

It Is Well 11. 8. 11. 9. with Refrain
Philip P. Bliss, 1838–1876

1. When peace like a riv-er at-tends all my way, When
2. Tho' Sa-tan should buf-fet, tho' tri-als should come, Let
3. My sin— O the bliss of this glo-ri-ous thought— My
4. And, Lord, haste the day when our faith shall be sight, The

sor-rows like sea bil-lows roll, What-ev-er my lot, you have
this blest as-sur-ance con-trol, That Christ has re-gard-ed my
sin— not in part but the whole— Is nailed to his cross, and I
clouds be rolled back as a scroll, The trump-et shall sound, and the

taught me to say: "It is well, it is well with my soul."
help-less es-tate, And has shed his own blood for my soul.
bear it no more; Praise the Lord, praise the Lord, O my soul!
Lord shall de-scend— "E-ven so"— it is well with my soul.

Refrain

It is well with my soul, it is well, it is well with my soul.
It is well with my soul,

Lord God of Hosts, Whose Mighty Hand

Lest We Forget 8. 8. 8. 8. 8. 8. 8.

John Oxenham, 1852–1941, cento, alt.

George F. Blanchard, 1868–?

1. Lord God of hosts, whose might-y hand Do - min - ion holds on sea and land,
2. For those who weak and bro-ken lie In wea - ri - ness and ag - o - ny,
3. For those to whom the call shall come, We pray your ten - der wel-come home;
4. For those who min - is - ter and heal, And spend them-selves, their skill, their zeal,

In peace and war your will we see Shap-ing the larg - er lib - er - ty;
Great Heal - er, to their beds of pain Come, touch and make them whole a - gain.
The toil, the bit - ter - ness, all past, We trust them to your love at last.
Re - new their hearts with Christ-like faith, And guard them from dis - ease and death:

Na-tions may rise and na - tions fall, Your change-less pur-pose rules them all.
O hear a peo-ple's prayers, and bless Your serv - ants in their hour of stress!
O hear a peo-ple's prayers for all Who, no - bly striv-ing, no - bly fall!
And in your own good time, Lord, send Your peace on earth till time shall end. A-men.

Words from *"All's Well!"* by John Oxenham. Used by permission.

Peace, Perfect Peace

Pax tecum 10. 10.
George Thomas Caldbeck, 1852–1912
Harm. by Charles J. Vincent, 1852–1934

Edward H. Bickersteth, 1825–1906, cento

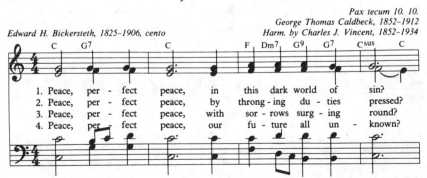

1. Peace, per - fect peace, in this dark world of sin?
2. Peace, per - fect peace, by throng - ing du - ties pressed?
3. Peace, per - fect peace, with sor - rows surg - ing round?
4. Peace, per - fect peace, our fu - ture all un - known?

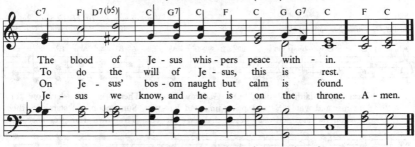

The blood of Je - sus whis - pers peace with - in.
To do the will of Je - sus, this is rest.
On Je - sus' bos - om naught but calm is found.
Je - sus we know, and he is on the throne. A - men.

5. Peace, perfect peace, death shadowing us and ours?
Jesus has vanquished death and all its powers.

6. It is enough: earth's struggles soon shall cease
And Jesus call us to heaven's perfect peace.

Take Time to Be Holy 110

Longstaff 6. 5. 6. 5. D.

William D. Longstaff, 1822–1894, alt.   *George C. Stebbins, 1846–1945*

1. Take time to be ho - ly, Speak oft with your Lord; A - bide in him
2. Take time to be ho - ly, The world rush - es on; Much time spend in
3. Take time to be ho - ly, Let him be your guide, And run not be-
4. Take time to be ho - ly, Be calm in your soul; Each thought and each

al - ways, And feed on his Word. Make friends of God's chil - dren; Help those who are
se - cret With Je - sus a - lone; By look - ing to Je - sus, Like him you shall
fore him, What - ev - er be - tide; In joy or in sor - row, Still fol - low your
mo - tive Be - neath his con - trol; Thus led by his Spir - it To foun - tains of

weak; For - get - ting in noth - ing His bless - ing to seek.
be; Your friends in your con - duct His like - ness shall see.
Lord, And, look - ing to Je - sus, Still trust in his Word.
love, You soon shall be fit - ted For serv - ice a - bove. A-men.

119

111   "Great Is Thy Faithfulness"

Faithfulness 11. 10. 11. 10. with Refrain

Thomas O. Chisholm, 1866–1960

William M. Runyan, 1870–1957

1. "Great is thy faith-ful-ness," O God my Fa-ther, There is no shad-ow of
2. Sum-mer and win-ter, and spring-time and har-vest, Sun, moon, and stars in their
3. Par-don for sin and a peace that en-dur-eth, Thy own dear pres-ence to

turn-ing with thee; Thou chang-est not, thy com-pas-sions, they fail not;
cours-es a-bove, Join with all na-ture in man-i-fold wit-ness
cheer and to guide; Strength for to-day and bright hope for to-mor-row,

Refrain

As thou hast been thou for-ev-er wilt be.
To thy great faith-ful-ness, mer-cy, and love. "Great is thy faith-ful-ness!
Bless-ings all mine, with ten thou-sand be-side!

Great is thy faith-ful-ness!" Morn-ing by morn-ing new mer-cies I see; All I have

need-ed thy hand hath pro-vid-ed—"Great is thy faith-ful-ness," Lord, un-to me!

When We Walk with the Lord

Trust and Obey 6. 6. 9. 6. 6. 9. with Refrain

John H. Sammis, 1846–1919, cento

Daniel B. Towner, 1850–1919

1. When we walk with the Lord In the light of his word What a glo - ry he
2. Not a shad - ow can rise, Not a cloud in the skies, But his smile quick - ly
3. But we nev - er can prove The de - lights of his love Un - til all on the
4. Then in fel - low - ship sweet We will sit at his feet, Or we'll walk by his

sheds on our way! While we do his good will, He a - bides with us still,
drives it a - way; Not a doubt nor a fear, Not a sigh nor a tear,
al - tar we lay; For the fa - vor he shows And the joy he be - stows
side in the way; What he says we will do, Where he sends we will go—

And with all who will trust and o - bey.
Can a - bide while we trust and o - bey.
Are for those who will trust and o - bey.
Nev - er fear, on - ly trust and o - bey.

Refrain

Trust and o - bey, for there's

no oth - er way To be hap - py in Je - sus, But to trust and o - bey. A - men.

113   All the Way My Savior Leads Me

Fanny J. Crosby, 1823–1915

All the Way 8. 7. 8. 7. D.
Robert Lowry, 1826–1899

1. All the way my Sav - ior leads me; What have I to ask be - side?
2. All the way my Sav - ior leads me, Cheers each wind - ing path I tread,
3. All the way my Sav - ior leads me; O the full - ness of his love!

Can I doubt his ten - der mer - cy, Who through life has been my guide?
Gives me grace for ev - ery tri - al, Feeds me with the liv - ing bread.
Per - fect rest to me is prom - ised In my Fa - ther's house a - bove.

Heav - en - ly peace, di - vin - est com - fort, Here by faith in him to dwell!
Though my wea - ry steps may fal - ter, And my soul a - thirst may be,
When my spir - it, clothed im - mor - tal, Wings its flight to realms of day,

For I know, what - e'er be - fall me, Je - sus do - eth all things well;
Gush - ing from the Rock be - fore me Lo! a spring of joy I see;
This my song through end - less ag - es: Je - sus led me all the way;

For I know, what - e'er be - fall me, Je - sus do - eth all things well.
Gush - ing from the Rock be - fore me Lo! a spring of joy I see.
This my song through end - less ag - es: Je - sus led me all the way. A - men.

A Mighty Fortress Is Our God

114

Martin Luther, 1483–1546
Tr. by Frederick H. Hedge, 1805–1890

Ein' feste Burg 8. 7. 8. 7. 6. 6. 6. 6. 7.
Martin Luther, 1483–1546

1. A might-y for-tress is our God, A bul-wark nev-er fail - ing;
2. Did we in our own strength con-fide, Our striv-ing would be los - ing,
3. And though this world, with dev - ils filled, Should threat-en to un-do us,
4. That word a - bove all earth - ly powers, No thanks to them, a - bid - eth;

Our help-er he a - mid the flood Of mor-tal ills pre-vail - ing:
Were not the right man on our side, The man of God's own choos - ing:
We will not fear, for God hath willed His truth to tri-umph through us:
The Spir - it and the gifts are ours Through him who with us sid - eth:

For still our an - cient foe Doth seek to work us woe; His craft and power are
Dost ask who that may be? Christ Je - sus, it is he; Lord Sab - a - oth his
The prince of dark - ness grim, We trem-ble not for him; His rage we can en-
Let goods and kin - dred go, This mor - tal life al - so; The bod - y they may

great, And, armed with cru - el hate, On earth is not his e - qual.
name, From age to age the same, And he must win the bat - tle.
dure, For lo! his doom is sure; One lit - tle word shall fell him.
kill: God's truth a - bid-eth still; His king - dom is for - ev - er. A-men.

Glorious Things of You Are Spoken

Austrian Hymn 8. 7. 8. 7. D.

John Newton, 1725-1807, cento, alt.

Franz Joseph Haydn, 1732-1809

1. Glo - rious things of you are spo - ken, Zi - on, cit - y of our God;
2. See, the streams of liv - ing wa - ters, Spring-ing from e - ter - nal Love,
3. Round each hab - i - ta - tion hov - ering, See the cloud and fire ap - pear

He whose word can - not be bro - ken Formed you for his own a - bode:
Well sup - ply your sons and daugh-ters, And all fear of want re - move:
For a glo - ry and a cov - ering, Show - ing that the Lord is near:

On the Rock of Ag - es found - ed, What can shake your sure re - pose?
Who can faint, while such a riv - er Ev - er flows their thirst to as - suage—
Thus de - riv - ing from their ban - ner Light by night and shade by day,

With sal - va-tion's walls sur-round-ed, You may smile at all your foes.
Grace, which, like the Lord the Giv - er, Nev - er fails from age to age?
Safe they feed up - on the man - na Which he gives them when they pray. A-men.

Jesus, Savior, Pilot Me

116

Pilot 7. 7. 7. 7. 7. 7.

Edward Hopper, 1818–1888, cento

John E. Gould, 1822–1875

1. Je - sus, Sav - ior, pi - lot me O - ver life's tem-
2. As a moth - er stills her child, Thou canst hush the
3. When at last I near the shore, And the fear - ful

pes - tuous sea; Un - known waves be - fore me roll,
o - cean wild; Bois - terous waves o - bey thy will
break - ers roar 'Twixt me and the peace - ful rest,

Hid - ing rock and treach-erous shoal; Chart and com - pass
When thou sayest to them, "Be still!" Won - drous Sov - ereign
Then, while lean - ing on thy breast, May I hear thee

come from thee: Je - sus, Sav - ior, pi - lot me.
of the sea, Je - sus, Sav - ior, pi - lot me.
say to me, "Fear not, I will pi - lot thee." A - men.

117

God of Our Life

Hugh T. Kerr, 1871-1950

Sandon 10. 4. 10. 4. 10. 10.
Charles H. Purday, 1799-1885

1. God of our life, through all the cir - cling years, We trust in thee;
2. God of the past, our times are in thy hand; With us a - bide.
3. God of the com - ing years, through paths un - known We fol - low thee;

In all the past, through all our hopes and fears, Thy hand we see.
Lead us by faith to hope's true Prom - ised Land; Be thou our guide.
When we are strong, Lord, leave us not a - lone; Our ref - uge be.

With each new day, when morn - ing lifts the veil,
With thee to bless, the dark - ness shines as light,
Be thou for us in life our dai - ly bread,

We own thy mer - cies, Lord, which nev - er fail.
And faith's fair vi - sion chang - es in - to sight.
Our heart's true home when all our years have sped. A - men.

Words from *The Church School Hymnal for Youth,* copyright 1928; renewed 1956 by Board of Christian Education of the Presbyterian Church in the U.S.A. Used by permission.

If Thou but Suffer God to Guide Thee 118

Georg Neumark, 1621–1681, cento
Tr. by Catherine Winkworth, 1827–1878, alt.

Neumark 9. 8. 9. 8. 8. 8.
Georg Neumark, 1621–1681

1. If thou but suf - fer God to guide thee, And hope in
him through all thy ways, He'll give thee strength, what - e'er be - tide thee,
And bear thee through the e - vil days; Who trusts in God's un -
chang - ing love Builds on the rock that naught can move.

2. On - ly be still, and wait his lei - sure In cheer - ful
hope, with heart con - tent To take what - e'er thy Fa - ther's plea - sure
And all - de - serv - ing love have sent; Nor doubt our in - most
wants are known To him who chose us for his own.

3. Sing, pray, and keep his ways un - swerv - ing; So do thine
own part faith - ful - ly, And trust his word, though un - de - serv - ing;
Thou yet shalt find it true for thee; God nev - er yet for -
sook at need The soul that trust - ed him in - deed. A - men.

119   Lead, Kindly Light

Lux benigna 10. 4. 10. 4. 10. 10.

John Henry Newman, 1801–1890

John B. Dykes, 1823–1876

1. Lead, kind-ly Light, a-mid th'en-cir-cling gloom, Lead thou me on;
2. I was not ev-er thus, nor prayed that thou Shouldst lead me on;
3. So long thy power hath blest me, sure it still Will lead me on

The night is dark, and I am far from home; Lead thou me on!
I loved to choose and see my path, but now Lead thou me on.
O'er moor and fen, o'er crag and tor-rent, till The night is gone;

Keep thou my feet; I do not ask to see
I loved the gar-ish day, and, spite of fears,
And with the morn those an-gel fac-es smile

The dis-tant scene: one step e-nough for me.
Pride ruled my will: re-mem-ber not past years.
Which I have loved long since, and lost a-while. A-men.

Whate'er My God Ordains Is Right

Samuel Rodigast, 1649-1708, cento
Tr. by Catherine Winkworth, 1827-1878

Was Gott tut 8. 7. 8. 7. 4. 4. 8. 8.
Severus Gastorius, 17th century

1. What-e'er my God or-dains is right; Ho-ly his will a-bid-eth.
2. What-e'er my God or-dains is right; He nev-er will de-ceive me;
3. What-e'er my God or-dains is right; Though now this cup in drink-ing
4. What-e'er my God or-dains is right; Here shall my stand be tak-en;

I will be still, what-e'er he doth, And fol-low where he guid-eth.
He leads me by the prop-er path; I know he will not leave me,
May bit-ter seem to my faint heart, I take it all un-shrink-ing;
Though sor-row, need, or death be mine, Yet am I not for-sak-en;

He is my God; Though dark my road, He holds me that I
And take con-tent What he hath sent; His hand can turn my
Tears pass a-way With dawn of day; Sweet com-fort yet shall
My Fa-ther's care Is round me there; He holds me that I

shall not fall: Where-fore to him I leave it all.
griefs a-way, And pa-tient-ly I wait his day.
fill my heart, And pain and sor-row shall de-part.
shall not fall, And so to him I leave it all. A-men.

121 Father Almighty, Bless Us with Your Blessing

Loammi J. Ware, 19th century, cento, alt.

Flemming 11. 11. 11. 5.
Friedrich F. Flemming, 1777–1813

1. Fa - ther Al - might - y, bless us with your bless - ing; An - swer in
   love your chil - dren's sup - pli - ca - tion; Hear now our prayer, the
   spo - ken and un - spo - ken; Hear us, our Fa - ther.

2. Shep - herd of souls, you bring all those who seek you To pas - tures
   green be - side the peace - ful wa - ters; Ten - der - est guide, in
   ways of cheer - ful du - ty Lead us, good Shep - herd.

3. Fa - ther of mer - cy, from your watch and keep - ing No place can
   part, nor hour of time re - move us; Give us your good, and
   save us from our e - vil, In - fi - nite Spir - it. A - men.

122 God Moves in a Mysterious Way

William Cowper, 1731–1800, cento, alt.

Dundee (French) C. M.
Scottish Psalter, 1615

1. God moves in a mys - te - rious way His won - ders to per - form;
2. Deep in un - fath - om - a - ble mines Of nev - er - fail - ing skill
3. O fear - ful saints, fresh cour - age take; The clouds you so much dread
4. Blind un - be - lief is sure to err, And scan his work in vain;

130

He plants his foot-steps in the sea And rides up-on the storm.
He trea-sures up his bright de-signs And works his sov-ereign will.
Are big with mer-cy, and shall break In bless-ings on your head.
God is his own in-ter-pret-er And he will make it plain. A-men.

Rock of Ages, Cleft for Me   123

Toplady 7. 7. 7. 7. 7. 7.

Augustus Montague Toplady, 1740–1778   *Thomas Hastings, 1784–1872*

1. Rock of Ag - es, cleft for me, Let me hide my - self in thee;
2. Not the la - bors of my hands Can ful - fill thy law's de-mands;
3. Noth - ing in my hand I bring, Sim - ply to thy cross I cling;
4. While I draw this fleet - ing breath, When my eye - lids close in death,

Let the wa - ter and the blood From thy wound - ed side which flowed
Could my zeal no res - pite know, Could my tears for - ev - er flow,
Na - ked, come to thee for dress, Help - less, look to thee for grace;
When I soar to worlds un - known, See thee on thy judg - ment throne,

Be of sin the dou - ble cure; Cleanse me from its guilt and power.
All for sin could not a - tone; Thou must save, and thou a - lone.
Foul, I to the foun - tain fly: Wash me, Sav - ior, or I die.
Rock of Ag - es, cleft for me, Let me hide my - self in thee. A-men.

124 Redeemer of Israel

Joseph Swain, 1761–1796, cento
Recast by William W. Phelps, 1792–1872

Beloved 6. 5. 8. 5. 6. 8.
Freeman Lewis, 1780–1859

1. Re - deem - er of Is - rael, Our on - ly de - light, On
2. We know he is com - ing To gath - er his sheep And
3. How long we have wan - dered As stran - gers in sin, And
4. As chil - dren of Zi - on, Good ti - dings for us. The

whom for a bless - ing we call, Our shad - ow by day,
lead them to Zi - on in love; For why in the val -
cried in the des - ert for thee! Our foes have re - joiced
to - kens al - read - y ap - pear. Fear not, and be just,

And our pil - lar by night, Our King, our de - liv - er - er, our all!
ley Of death should they weep Or in the lone wil - der - ness rove?
When our sor - rows they've seen, But Is - rael will short - ly be free.
For the king - dom is ours. The hour of re - demp - tion is near.

125 Father, Lead Me Day by Day

Posen 7. 7. 7. 7.
John Page Hopps, 1834–1911, cento, alt.
George C. Strattner, 1650–1705

Eb Ebmaj7 Eb6 Eb Ab6 Bb7 Eb Bb7 Eb Bb Cm7 F7 Bb

1. Fa - ther, lead me day by day, Ev - er in your ho - ly way;
2. When in dan - ger, make me brave, Make me know that you can save;
3. When I'm tempt - ed to do wrong, Make me stead - fast, wise, and strong;
4. May I do the good I know, Serv - ing glad - ly here be - low;

132

Father, Lead Me Day by Day (cont.)

Teach me to be pure and true; Show me what I ought to do.
Keep me safe by your own side; Let me in your love a - bide.
And when all a - lone I stand, Shield me with your might - y hand.
Then at last go home to you, There for - e'er to dwell with you. A-men.

Holy Spirit, Lord of Light   126

Anonymous, 12th century
Tr. by Edward Caswall, 1814–1878

Veni Sancte Spiritus 7. 7. 7. 7. 7. 7.
Ascribed to Samuel Webbe, Sr., 1740–1816

1. Ho - ly Spir - it, Lord of light, From the clear ce - les - tial height,
2. Thou, of all con - sol - ers best, Thou, the soul's de - light - ful guest,
3. Light im - mor - tal, Light di - vine, Vis - it thou these hearts of thine,
4. Heal our wounds, our strength re - new; On our dry - ness pour thy dew;
5. Thou, on us who ev - er - more Thee con - fess and thee a - dore,

Thy pure beam - ing ra - diance give. Come, thou Fa - ther of the poor,
Dost re - fresh - ing peace be - stow. Thou in toil art com - fort sweet,
And our in - most be - ing fill. If thou take thy grace a - way,
Wash the stains of guilt a - way. Bend the stub - born heart and will;
With thy sev - en - fold gifts de - scend. Give us com - fort when we die;

Come with trea - sures which en - dure; Come, thou Light of all that live.
Pleas - ant cool - ness in the heat, Sol - ace in the midst of woe.
Noth - ing pure in man will stay; All his good is turned to ill.
Melt the fro - zen, warm the chill; Guide the steps that go a - stray.
Give us life with thee on high; Give us joys that nev - er end. A - men.

127 Brood O'er Us with Thy Sheltering Wing

Love 8. 6. 8. 6. 8. 8.

Mary Baker Eddy, 1821–1910

Walter E. Young, 1878–1945

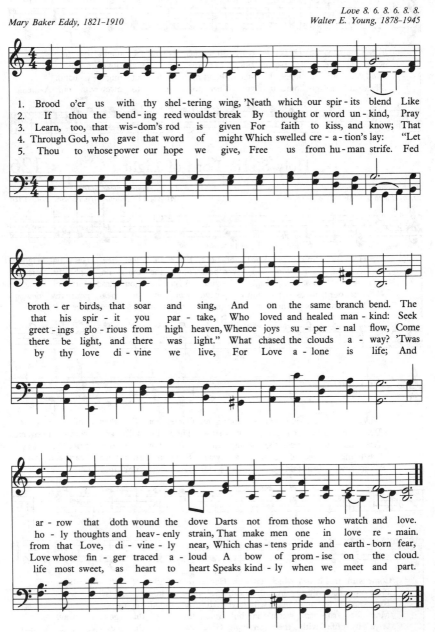

1. Brood o'er us with thy shel-tering wing, 'Neath which our spir-its blend Like
2. If thou the bend-ing reed wouldst break By thought or word un-kind, Pray
3. Learn, too, that wis-dom's rod is given For faith to kiss, and know; That
4. Through God, who gave that word of might Which swelled cre-a-tion's lay: "Let
5. Thou to whose power our hope we give, Free us from hu-man strife. Fed

broth-er birds, that soar and sing, And on the same branch bend. The
that his spir-it you par-take, Who loved and healed man-kind: Seek
greet-ings glo-rious from high heaven, Whence joys su-per-nal flow, Come
there be light, and there was light." What chased the clouds a-way? 'Twas
by thy love di-vine we live, For Love a-lone is life; And

ar-row that doth wound the dove Darts not from those who watch and love.
ho-ly thoughts and heav-enly strain, That make men one in love re-main.
from that Love, di-vine-ly near, Which chas-tens pride and earth-born fear,
Love whose fin-ger traced a-loud A bow of prom-ise on the cloud.
life most sweet, as heart to heart Speaks kind-ly when we meet and part.

Shepherd, Show Me How to Go

Guidance 7. 5. 7. 5. D.

Mary Baker Eddy, 1821–1910

Lyman Brackett, 1870–1937

1. Shep - herd, show me how to go O'er the hill - side steep,
2. Thou wilt bind the stub - born will, Wound the cal - lous breast,
3. So, when day grows dark and cold, Tear or tri - umph harms,

How to gath - er, how to sow— How to feed thy sheep;
Make self - right - teous - ness be still, Break earth's stu - pid rest.
Lead thy lamb - kins to the fold, Take them in thine arms;

I will lis - ten for thy voice, Lest my foot - steps stray;
Stran - gers on a bar - ren shore, La - boring long and lone,
Feed the hun - gry, heal the heart, Till the morn - ing's beam;

I will fol - low and re - joice All the rug - ged way.
We would en - ter by the door, And thou know'st thine own;
White as wool, ere they de - part, Shep - herd, wash them clean.

129 Lonely Voices Crying All Around Me

Lonely Voices 10. 9. 10. 9. 7. 9.
Billie Hanks, Jr., 1944–
Arr. by David Hugh Jones, 1900–

Billie Hanks, Jr., 1944–   , alt.

1. Lone-ly voic-es cry-ing all a-round me, Lone-ly voic-es
2. Lone-ly fac-es look-ing for the sun-rise, Just to find an-
3. Lone-ly eyes, I see them all a-round me, Bur-dened by the
4. A-bun-dant life He came to tru-ly give man; But so few His

sound-ing like a child. Lone-ly voic-es come from bus-y
oth-er bus-y day. Lone-ly fac-es, va-cant stares, sur-
wor-ries of the day. Men at lei-sure, but they're so un-
gift of grace re-ceive. Lone-ly peo-ple live in ev-ery

peo-ple; To dis-turb, to stop a lit-tle while.
round me, Men a-fraid, but too a-shamed to pray.
hap-py, Tired of fool-ish roles they try to play.
cit-y, Men who face a dark and lone-ly grave.

— Lone-ly voic-es fill my dreams;
— Lone-ly fac-es do I see;
— Lone-ly peo-ple do I see;
— Lone-ly fac-es do I see;

136

Lone - ly voic - es on my mem - o - ry.
Lone - ly fac - es on my mem - o - ry.
Lone - ly peo - ple on my mem - o - ry.
Lone - ly voic - es call - ing out to me.

Jesus Loves Me! This I Know 130

Renar 7. 7. 7. 7. with Refrain

Anna B. Warner, 1820–1915

William B. Bradbury, 1816–1868

1. Je - sus loves me! this I know, For the Bi - ble tells me so;
2. Je - sus loves me! he who died, Heav - en's gate to o - pen wide;
3. Je - sus loves me! loves me still, Though I'm ver - y weak and ill;
4. Je - sus loves me! he will stay Close be - side me all the way;

Lit - tle ones to him be - long; They are weak, but he is strong.
He will wash a - way my sin, Let his lit - tle child come in.
From his shin - ing throne on high, Comes to watch me where I lie.
If I love him, when I die He will take me home on high.

Refrain

Yes, Je - sus loves me, Yes, Je - sus loves me, Yes, Je - sus loves me—The Bi - ble tells me so.

131   My Soul Is Longing for Your Peace

Lucien Deiss, 1921–

My Soul Is Longing 9. 10. with Refrain
Lucien Deiss, 1921–

My soul is long-ing for your peace, near to you, my God!

1. Lord, you know that my heart is not proud,
2. Loft-y thoughts have nev-er filled my mind,
3. In your peace I have main-tained my soul,
4. As a child rests on his moth-er's knee,

And my eyes are not lift-ed from the earth.
Far be-yond my sight all am-bi-tious deeds.
I have kept my heart in your qui-et peace.
So I place my soul in your lov-ing care.

5. Israel, put all your hope in God,
   Place your trust in him, now and evermore.

6. Glory, praise be to the Father,
   Son, and Spirit, now and evermore.

Encamped Along the Hills of Light

Victory 8. 6. 8. 6. D. with Refrain

John H. Yates, 1837–1900
Ira D. Sankey, 1840–1908

1. En-camped a - long the hills of light, Ye Chris-tian sol-diers, rise, And
2. His ban-ner o - ver us is love, Our sword the Word of God; We
3. On ev - ery hand the foe we find Drawn up in dread ar - ray; Let
4. To him that o - ver-comes the foe, White rai - ment shall be given; Be-

press the bat-tle ere the night Shall veil the glow-ing skies. A-gainst the foe in
tread the road the saints a - bove With shouts of tri-umph trod. By faith they, like a
tents of ease be left be-hind, And on-ward to the fray; Sal - va-tion's hel-met
fore the an-gels he shall know His name con-fessed in heaven. Then on - ward from the

vales be - low Let all our strength be hurled; Faith is the vic-to-ry, we
whirl-wind's breath, Swept on o'er ev - ery field; The faith by which they con-quered
on each head, With truth all girt a - bout, The earth shall trem-ble 'neath our
hills of light, Our hearts with love a - flame, We'll van-quish all the hosts of

know, That o - ver-comes the world.
death Is still our shin - ing shield.
tread, And ech - o with our shout.   Faith is the vic - to - ry! Faith is the
night, In Je-sus' con-quering name.

vic - to - ry! O glo - ri - ous vic - to - ry That o - ver-comes the world.

139

133 O Love That Wilt Not Let Me Go

George Matheson, 1842–1906

St. Margaret 8. 8. 8. 8. 8. 6.
Albert L. Peace, 1844–1912

1. O Love that wilt not let me go, I rest my wea - ry
2. O Light that fol - lowest all my way, I yield my flick - ering
3. O Joy that seek - est me through pain, I can - not close my
4. O Cross that lift - est up my head, I dare not ask to

soul in thee; I give thee back the life I owe,
torch to thee; My heart re - stores its bor - rowed ray,
heart to thee; I trace the rain - bow through the rain,
fly from thee; I lay in dust life's glo - ry dead,

That in thine o - cean depths its flow May rich - er, full - er be.
That in thy sun - shine's blaze its day May bright - er, fair - er be.
And feel the prom - ise is not vain That morn shall tear - less be.
And from the ground there blos - soms red Life that shall end - less be. A-men.

134 Immortal Love, Forever Full

John Greenleaf Whittier, 1807–1892, cento

Serenity C. M.
William V. Wallace, 1814–1865

1. Im - mor - tal Love, for - ev - er full, For - ev - er flow - ing free,
2. We may not climb the heav - enly steeps To bring the Lord Christ down;
3. But warm, sweet, ten - der, e - ven yet A pres - ent help is he;
4. O Lord and Mas - ter of us all, What - e'er our name or sign,

For - ev - er shared, for - ev - er whole, A nev - er - ebb - ing sea!
In vain we search the low - est deeps, For him no depths can drown.
And faith has still its Ol - i - vet, And love its Gal - i - lee.
We own thy sway, we hear thy call, We test our lives by thine. A - men.

My Faith Looks Up to Thee 135

Olivet 6. 6. 4. 6. 6. 6. 4.

Ray Palmer, 1808–1887

Lowell Mason, 1792–1872

1. My faith looks up to thee, Thou Lamb of Cal - va - ry,
2. May thy rich grace im - part Strength to my faint - ing heart,
3. While life's dark maze I tread, And griefs a - round me spread,
4. When ends life's tran - sient dream, When death's cold, sul - len stream

Sav - ior di - vine: Now hear me while I pray, Take all my
My zeal in - spire; As thou hast died for me, O may my
Be thou my guide; Bid dark - ness turn to day, Wipe sor - row's
Shall o'er me roll, Blest Sav - ior, then, in love, Fear and dis -

guilt a - way, O let me from this day Be whol - ly thine!
love to thee Pure, warm, and change - less be, A liv - ing fire!
tears a - way, Nor let me ev - er stray From thee a - side.
trust re - move; O bear me safe a - bove, A ran - somed soul! A - men.

136 He Leadeth Me: O Blessed Thought!

Joseph H. Gilmore, 1834–1918

He Leadeth Me L. M. with Refrain
William B. Bradbury, 1816–1868

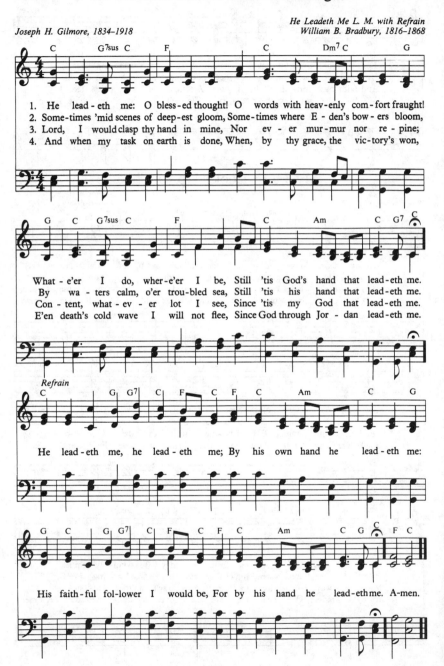

1. He lead-eth me: O bless-ed thought! O words with heav-enly com-fort fraught!
2. Some-times 'mid scenes of deep-est gloom, Some-times where E - den's bow-ers bloom,
3. Lord, I would clasp thy hand in mine, Nor ev - er mur-mur nor re - pine;
4. And when my task on earth is done, When, by thy grace, the vic-tory's won,

What - e'er I do, wher-e'er I be, Still 'tis God's hand that lead-eth me.
By wa - ters calm, o'er trou-bled sea, Still 'tis his hand that lead-eth me.
Con - tent, what - ev - er lot I see, Since 'tis my God that lead-eth me.
E'en death's cold wave I will not flee, Since God through Jor - dan lead-eth me.

Refrain

He lead-eth me, he lead - eth me; By his own hand he lead-eth me:

His faith-ful fol-lower I would be, For by his hand he lead-eth me. A-men.

My Jesus, I Love Thee

William R. Featherstone, 1842–1878

Gordon 11. 11. 11. 11.
Adoniram J. Gordon, 1836–1895

1. My Je - sus, I love thee, I know thou art mine,
2. I love thee, be - cause thou hast first lov - ed me,
3. I will love thee in life, I will love thee in death,
4. In man - sions of glo - ry and end - less de - light,

For thee all the fol - lies of sin I re - sign;
And pur - chased my par - don on Cal - va - ry's tree;
And praise thee as long as thou lend - est me breath;
I'll ev - er a - dore thee in heav - en so bright;

My gra - cious Re - deem - er, my Sav - ior art thou;
I love thee for wear - ing the thorns on thy brow;
And say when the death - dew lies cold on my brow,
I'll sing with the glit - ter - ing crown on my brow,

If ev - er I loved thee, my Je - sus, 'tis now. A-men.

138 Standing on the Promises of Christ My King

R. Kelso Carter, 1849–1928, cento

Promises 11. 11. 11. 9. with Refrain
R. Kelso Carter, 1849–1928

1. Stand-ing on the prom-is-es of Christ my King, Thro' e-ter-nal ag-es let his prais-es ring; Glo-ry in the high-est, I will shout and sing,
2. Stand-ing on the prom-is-es that can-not fail, When the howl-ing storms of doubt and fear as-sail, By the liv-ing word of God I shall pre-vail,
3. Stand-ing on the prom-is-es of Christ the Lord, Bound to him e-ter-nal-ly by love's strong cord, O-ver-com-ing dai-ly with the Spir-it's sword,
4. Stand-ing on the prom-is-es I can-not fall, Lis-ten-ing ev-ery mo-ment to the Spir-it's call, Rest-ing in my Sav-ior, as my All in All,

Refrain

Stand-ing on the prom-is-es of God. Stand - - ing, stand - - ing,
Stand-ing on the prom-is-es, stand-ing on the prom-is-es,

Stand-ing on the prom-is-es of God my Sav - ior; Stand - - ing,
Stand-ing on the prom-is-es,

stand - - ing, I'm stand-ing on the prom-is-es of God. A-men.
stand-ing on the prom-is-es,

144

Steal Away to Jesus!

Spiritual

Steal Away Irregular
American Negro melody

Steal a - way, steal a - way, steal a - way to Je - sus!

Steal a - way, steal a - way home, I ain't got long to stay here.

Tacet

1. My Lord, he calls me, He calls me by the thun - der; The
2. Green trees are bend - ing, Poor sin - ners stand a - trem - bling; The
3. My Lord, he calls me, He calls me by the light - ning; The

trum - pet sounds with - in my soul: I ain't got long to stay here.

140 "There Shall Be Showers of Blessing"

Daniel W. Whittle, 1840-1901

Showers of Blessing 8. 7. 8. 7. with Refrain
James McGranahan, 1840-1907

1. "There shall be show-ers of bless-ing": This is the prom-ise of love;
2. "There shall be show-ers of bless-ing"— Pre-cious re-viv-ing a-gain;
3. "There shall be show-ers of bless-ing": Send them up-on us, O Lord;
4. "There shall be show-ers of bless-ing": O that to-day they might fall,

There shall be sea-sons re-fresh-ing, Sent from the Sav-ior a-bove.
O-ver the hills and the val-leys,Sound of a-bun-dance of rain.
Grant to us now a re-fresh-ing,Come, and now hon-or your Word.
Now as to God we're con-fess-ing, Now as on Je-sus we call!

Refrain

Show - - ers of bless-ing, Show-ers of bless-ing we need:
Show - ers, show-ers of bless-ing,

Mer-cy-drops round us are fall-ing, But for the show-ers we plead. A-men.

146

God Be with You Till We Meet Again
141

Deus vobiscum 9. 8. 8. 9. with Refrain

Jeremiah E. Rankin, 1828–1904

William G. Tomer, 1833–1897

1. God be with you till we meet a-gain, By his coun-sels guide, up-hold you,
2. God be with you till we meet a-gain, 'Neath his wings pro-tect-ing hide you,
3. God be with you till we meet a-gain, When life's per-ils thick con-found you,
4. God be with you till we meet a-gain, Keep love's ban-ner float-ing o'er you,

With his sheep se-cure-ly fold you, God be with you till we meet a-gain.
Dai-ly man-na still pro-vide you, God be with you till we meet a-gain.
Put his arms un-fail-ing round you, God be with you till we meet a-gain.
Smite death's threaten-ing wave be-fore you, God be with you till we meet a-gain.

Refrain

Till we meet, till we meet, Till we meet at Je-sus' feet;

Till we meet, till we meet, till we meet, Till we meet,

Till we meet, till we meet, God be with you till we meet a-gain. A-men.

Till we meet, till we meet, till we meet,

142   When I'm Feeling Lonely

Orange Square Melody 6. 5. 6. 4. D.

Richard K. Avery, 1934–
and Donald S. Marsh, 1923–

Richard K. Avery, 1934–
and Donald S. Marsh, 1923–

1. When I'm feel-ing lone-ly, When I need a friend, When I need to know this Is-n't the
2. There are lots of times, Lord, When I want to pray, But I don't know how to. What should I
3. I've heard peo-ple say, Lord, How you cared so much That you sent us Je-sus, To keep in
4. I've got lots of ques-tions I want an-swers for; Though I've asked a cou-ple, I've plen-ty
5. I be-lieve you care, Lord, And watch o-ver me, E-ven though I won-der Where you can

When I'm Feeling Lonely (cont.)

end; When I'm need-ing some-one Just to see
say? Do you real-ly lis-ten To each per-
touch. So we'll fol-low him, Lord, Hop-ing that
more. If my prayers are an-swered, If my dreams
be. I have learned to trust in Ev-ery-thing

me through All my trou-bled times, Lord,
son's prayer? If I find the words, Lord,
it's true; And through him we all can
come true, Lord, are you the rea - son?
you do. Since you sent us Je - sus,

1. 2. 3. 4.

Can it be you?
Will you be there?
Keep close to you.
Can it be you?
I come to you.

149

143   Hush, Little Baby, Don't You Cry

All My Trials Irregular with Refrain
Bahamas traditional melody
Harm. by David Hugh Jones, 1900–

Bahamas spiritual

1. Hush, lit - tle ba - by, don't you cry, You know your Ma - ma was born to die;
2. I've got a lit - tle book with pag - es three, And ev - ery page spells lib - er - ty;
3. If liv - ing was a thing that mon - ey could buy, You know the rich would live but the poor would die;
4. There grows a tree in par - a - dise, And the pil - grims call it the Tree of Life;

All my tri - als, Lord, soon be o - ver.

Refrain Too late, my broth - ers, Too late, but nev - er mind;

When Israel Was in Egypt's Land

Let My People Go 8. 5. 8. 5. with Refrain
American Negro melody

Spiritual

1. When Is - rael was in E - gypt's land,
2. Thus says the Lord, bold Mo - ses said, Let my peo - ple go,
3. No more in bond - age shall they toil,

Op - pressed so hard they could not stand,
If not I'll smite your first - born dead, Let my peo - ple go.
Let them come out with E - gypt's spoil,

Refrain

Go down, Mo - ses, 'Way down in E - gypt's land,

Tell old Phar - aoh To let my peo - ple go.

Words and music altered from *American Negro Songs and Spirituals*, by John W. Work III, copyright 1940 by John W. Work III. Used by permission.

145
This Day God Made

This Day 4. 6. 4. 6. with Refrain
American Negro melody
Adapted from 'Slave Songs in the
United States,' 1867
Harm. by Angelo A. della Picca, 1923–

Omer Westendorf, 1916–

1. This day God made A great and glo-rious day, Re-
2. This day shines forth In God's e-ter-nal plan, This
3. This day has dawned A day of des-ti-ny, This

Refrain

joice in him As joy-ful-ly we pray.
day we see God's good-ness shown to man. Al - le - lu-
day will live for all e-ter-ni-ty.

ia, al - le - lu - ia, al - le - lu - ia, al - le - lu - ia.

When Morning Gilds the Skies

Laudes Domini 6. 6. 6. 6. 6. 6.

Anonymous German hymn, c. 1800, cento
Tr. by Edward Caswall, 1814–1878, alt.

Joseph Barnby, 1838–1896
Descant by L. David Miller, 1919–

1. When morn-ing gilds the skies, My heart a-wak-ing cries,
2. The night be-comes as day When from the heart we say,
3. You na-tions of man-kind, In this your con-cord find,
4. Be this, while life is mine, My can-ti-cle di-vine,

May Je-sus Christ be praised: A-like at work and prayer
May Je-sus Christ be praised: The powers of dark-ness fear
May Je-sus Christ be praised: Let all the earth a-round
May Je-sus Christ be praised: Be this th'e-ter-nal song,

To Je-sus I re-pair; May Je-sus Christ be praised!
When this sweet chant they hear, May Je-sus Christ be praised!
Ring joy-ous with the sound, May Je-sus Christ be praised!
Through all the ag-es long, May Je-sus Christ be praised! A-men.

Descant copyright 1962 by Muhlenberg Press. Used by permission of Fortress Press.

147 See the Morning Sun Ascending

Unser Herrscher 8. 7. 8. 7. 8. 7.
Joachim Neander, 1650–1680
Descant by Geoffrey Shaw, 1879–1943
Charles Parkin, 1894–

Ah _____ Ah _____

1. See the morn-ing sun as - cend-ing, Ra - diant in the east-ern sky;
2. So may we, in low - ly sta - tion, Join the cho - ris - ters a - bove;
3. For his lov - ing - kind - ness ev - er Shed up - on our earth - ly way;
4. "Wis-dom, hon - or, power, and bless-ing!" With the an-gel - ic host we cry;

Ah _____ Ah _____

Hear the an - gel voic - es blend - ing In their praise to God on high!
Sing - ing with the whole cre - a - tion, Prais-ing God for his great love.
For his mer - cy, ceas - ing nev - er, For his bless-ing day by day.
Round thy throne, thy name con - fess - ing, Lord, we would to thee draw nigh.

Ah _____ Ah _____ Ah _____ A - men.

Al - le-lu - ia! Al - le - lu - ia! Glo - ry be to God on high!
Al - le-lu - ia! Al - le - lu - ia! Glo - ry be to God a - bove!
Al - le-lu - ia! Al - le - lu - ia! Glo - ry be to God al - way!
Al - le-lu - ia! Al - le - lu - ia! Glo - ry be to God on high! A - men.

Sun of My Soul, O Savior Dear 148

Hursley L. M.

John Keble, 1792–1866, cento, alt.

'Katholisches Gesangbuch,' Vienna, 1774

1. Sun of my soul, O Sav - ior dear, It is not night if you are near;
2. A - bide with me from morn till eve, For with - out you I can - not live;
3. Watch by the sick; en - rich the poor With bless - ings from your bound - less store;
4. Come near and bless us when we wake, Ere through the world our way we take,

O may no earth - born cloud a - rise To hide you from your serv - ant's eyes.
A - bide with me when night is nigh, For with - out you I dare not die.
Be ev - ery mourn - er's sleep to - night, Like in - fants' slum - bers, pure and light.
Till in the o - cean of your love We lose our - selves in heaven a - bove. A - men.

Savior, Breathe an Evening Blessing 149

Evening Prayer 8. 7. 8. 7.

James Edmeston, 1791–1867

George C. Stebbins, 1846–1945

1. Sav - ior, breathe an eve - ning bless - ing Ere re - pose our spir - its seal;
2. Though de - struc - tion walk a - round us, Though the ar - row past us fly,
3. Though the night be dark and drear - y, Dark - ness can - not hide from thee;
4. Should swift death this night o'er - take us, And our couch be - come our tomb,

Sin and want we come con - fess - ing: Thou canst save, and thou canst heal.
An - gel guards from thee sur - round us: We are safe if thou art nigh.
Thou art he who, nev - er wea - ry, Watch - est where thy peo - ple be.
May the morn in heaven a - wake us, Clad in light and death - less bloom. A - men.

155

150 God, Who Made the Earth and Heaven

St. 1, Reginald Heber, 1783–1826, alt.
St. 2, Frederick Lucian Hosmer, 1840–1929, alt.

Ar hyd y nos 8. 4. 8. 4. 8. 8. 8. 4.
Welsh traditional melody
Harm. by Luther Orlando Emerson, 1820–1915

1. God, who made the earth and heav - en, Dark - ness and light,
2. When the con - stant sun re - turn - ing Un - seals our eyes,

Who the day for toil have giv - en, For rest the night,
May we, born a - new like morn - ing, To la - bor rise;

May your an - gel guards de - fend us, Slum - ber sweet your mer - cy send us;
Gird us for the task that calls us, Let not ease and self en - thrall us,

Ho - ly dreams and hopes at - tend us, This live - long night.
Strong through you what - e'er be - fall us, O God most wise! A - men.

Day Is Dying in the West

151

Chautauqua 7. 7. 7. 7. 4. with Refrain

Mary A. Lathbury, 1841–1913, cento
William F. Sherwin, 1826–1888

1. Day is dy - ing in the west; Heaven is touch - ing
2. Lord of life, be - neath the dome Of the u - ni -
3. When for - ev - er from our sight Pass the stars, the

earth with rest: Wait and wor - ship while the night
verse, thy home, Gath - er us who seek thy face
day, the night, Lord of an - gels, on our eyes

Sets her eve - ning lamps a - light Through all the sky.
To the fold of thy em - brace, For thou art nigh.
Let e - ter - nal morn - ing rise, And shad - ows end.

Refrain

Ho - ly, ho - ly, ho - ly Lord God of hosts! Heaven and earth are full of thee!

Heaven and earth are prais - ing thee, O Lord Most High! A - men.

152 The Shadows of the Evening Hours

Adelaide Anne Procter, 1825–1864, alt.

St. Leonard C. M. D.
Henry Hiles, 1826–1904

1. The shad-ows of the eve-ning hours Fall from the dark-ening sky;
2. The sor-rows of your serv-ants, Lord, O do not now de-spise,
3. Let peace, O Lord, your peace, O God, Up - on our souls de-scend;

Up - on the fra-grance of the flowers The dews of eve-ning lie;
But let the in-cense of our prayers Be - fore your mer-cy rise.
From mid-night fears and per - ils, now Our trem-bling hearts de-fend.

Be - fore your throne, O Lord of heaven, We kneel at close of day;
The bright-ness of the com-ing night Up - on the dark-ness rolls;
Give us a res-pite from our toil; Calm and sub-due our woes.

Look on your chil-dren from on high, And hear us while we pray..
With hopes of fu-ture glo-ry, chase The shad-ows from our souls.
Through the long day we la-bor, Lord, O give us now re-pose. A-men.

153 Abide with Me: Fast Falls the Eventide

Henry Francis Lyte, 1793–1847, cento

Eventide 10. 10. 10. 10.
William H. Monk, 1823–1889

1. A - bide with me: fast falls the e - ven-tide; The dark-ness deep-ens;
2. Swift to its close ebbs out life's lit-tle day; Earth's joys grow dim, its
3. I need thy pres-ence ev - ery pass-ing hour. What but thy grace can
4. I fear no foe, with thee at hand to bless; Ills have no weight, and
5. Hold thou thy cross be - fore my clos-ing eyes; Shine through the gloom, and

Lord, with me a - bide. When oth - er help - ers fail and com-forts flee,
glo - ries pass a - way; Change and de - cay in all a-round I see.
foil the tempt-er's power? Who, like thy - self, my guide and stay can be?
tears no bit - ter - ness. Where is death's sting? Where, grave, thy vic - to - ry?
point me to the skies; Heaven's morn-ing breaks, and earth's vain shad-ows flee:

Help of the help - less, O a - bide with me.
O thou who chang - est not, a - bide with me.
Through cloud and sun - shine, O a - bide with me.
I tri - umph still, if thou a - bide with me.
In life, in death, O Lord, a - bide with me. A-men.

O Splendor of God's Glory Bright 154

Puer nobis nascitur L. M.
'Piae Cantiones,' 1582

Ambrose of Milan, 340-397, cento
Tr. composite, alt.

Adapt. by Michael Praetorius, 1571-1621
Harm. for 'Songs of Praise,' 1925

1. O Splen-dor of God's glo - ry bright, From light e - ter - nal bring-ing light;
2. Con-firm our will to do the right, And keep our hearts from en - vy's blight;
3. O joy-ful be the pass-ing day With thoughts as clear as morn-ing's ray,
4. Dawn's glo - ry gilds the earth and skies; O now, our per - fect Morn, a - rise;

O Light of life, light's liv - ing Spring, True Day, all days il - lu - min - ing:
Let faith her ea - ger fires re - new, And hate the false, and love the true.
With faith like noon-tide shin-ing bright, Our souls un-shad-owed by the night.
The Fa-ther's help his chil-dren claim, And sing the Fa-ther's glo-rious name. A-men.

Father, We Praise Thee

Christe sanctorum 11. 11. 11. 5.

Gregory I, 540–604
Tr. by Percy Dearmer, 1867–1936

LaFeillée, 'Méthode du plain-chant,' 1808
Harm. by Ralph Vaughan Williams, 1872–1958

1. Fa - ther, we praise thee, now the night is o - ver; Ac - tive and
2. Mon - arch of all things, fit us for thy man - sions; Ban - ish our
3. All - ho - ly Fa - ther, Son, and e - qual Spir - it, Trin - i - ty

watch - ful, stand we all be - fore thee; Sing - ing, we of - fer
weak - ness, health and whole - ness send - ing; Bring us to heav - en,
bless - ed, send us thy sal - va - tion; Thine is the glo - ry,

prayer and med - i - ta - tion: Thus we a - dore thee.
where thy saints u - nit - ed Joy with - out end - ing.
gleam - ing and re - sound - ing Through all cre - a - tion. A - men.

Music from *The English Hymnal.* Used by permission of Oxford University Press.

156   Father, We Thank You for the Night

Onslow L. M.
Daniel Batchellor, 1845–1934

Ascribed to Rebecca J. Weston, 19th century, alt.
Harm. by Austin C. Lovelace, 1919–

Unison

1. Fa - ther, we thank you for the night, And for the pleas - ant morn - ing light,
2. Help us to do the things we should, To be to oth - ers kind and good,

For rest and food and lov - ing care, And all that makes the day so fair.
In all we do in work or play, To grow more lov - ing ev - ery day.

Music copyright 1955 by John Ribble; from *The Hymnbook.* Used by permission.

Savior, Again to Thy Dear Name We Raise 157

Ellers 10. 10. 10. 10.

Edward John Hopkins, 1818–1901
Descant by L. David Miller, 1919–

John Ellerton, 1826–1893

Descant
4. Grant us thy peace through - out our earth - ly life,

Unison
1. Sav - ior, a - gain to thy dear name we raise
2. Grant us thy peace up - on our home-ward way;
3. Grant us thy peace, Lord, through the com - ing night;
4. Grant us thy peace through - out our earth - ly life,

Our balm in sor - row, and our stay in strife;

With one ac - cord our part - ing hymn of praise;
With thee be - gan, with thee shall end the day;
Turn thou for us its dark - ness in - to light;
Our balm in sor - row, and our stay in strife;

Then, when thy voice shall bid our con - flict cease,

We stand to bless thee ere our wor - ship cease;
Guard thou the lips from sin, the hearts from shame,
From harm and dan - ger keep thy chil - dren free,
Then, when thy voice shall bid our con - flict cease,

Call us, O Lord, to thine e - ter - nal peace. A - men.

Then, low - ly kneel - ing, wait thy word of peace.
That in this house have called up - on thy name.
For dark and light are both a - like to thee.
Call us, O Lord, to thine e - ter - nal peace. A - men.

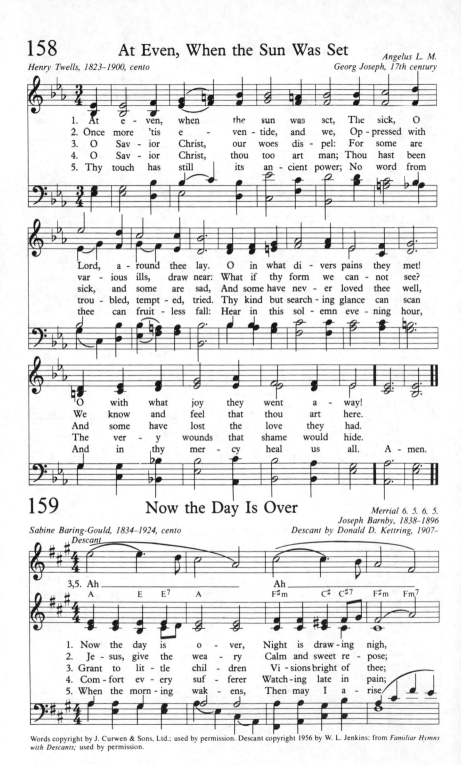

158 At Even, When the Sun Was Set

Angelus L. M.

Henry Twells, 1823–1900, cento

Georg Joseph, 17th century

1. At e - ven, when the sun was set, The sick, O
2. Once more 'tis e - ven - tide, and we, Op - pressed with
3. O Sav - ior Christ, our woes dis - pel: For some are
4. O Sav - ior Christ, thou too art man; Thou hast been
5. Thy touch has still its an - cient power; No word from

Lord, a - round thee lay. O in what di - vers pains they met!
var - ious ills, draw near: What if thy form we can - not see?
sick, and some are sad, And some have nev - er loved thee well,
trou - bled, tempt - ed, tried. Thy kind but search - ing glance can scan
thee can fruit - less fall: Hear in this sol - emn eve - ning hour,

O with what joy they went a - way!
We know and feel that thou art here.
And some have lost the love they had.
The ver - y wounds that shame would hide.
And in thy mer - cy heal us all. A - men.

159 Now the Day Is Over

Merrial 6. 5. 6. 5.
Joseph Barnby, 1838–1896
Descant by Donald D. Kettring, 1907–

Sabine Baring-Gould, 1834–1924, cento

Descant

3,5. Ah   Ah
    A   E   E⁷   A   F#m   C# C#7 F#m Fm7

1. Now the day is o - ver, Night is draw - ing nigh,
2. Je - sus, give the wea - ry Calm and sweet re - pose;
3. Grant to lit - tle chil - dren Vi - sions bright of thee;
4. Com - fort ev - ery suf - ferer Watch - ing late in pain;
5. When the morn - ing wak - ens, Then may I a - rise

Words copyright by J. Curwen & Sons, Ltd.; used by permission. Descant copyright 1956 by W. L. Jenkins; from *Familiar Hymns with Descants;* used by permission.

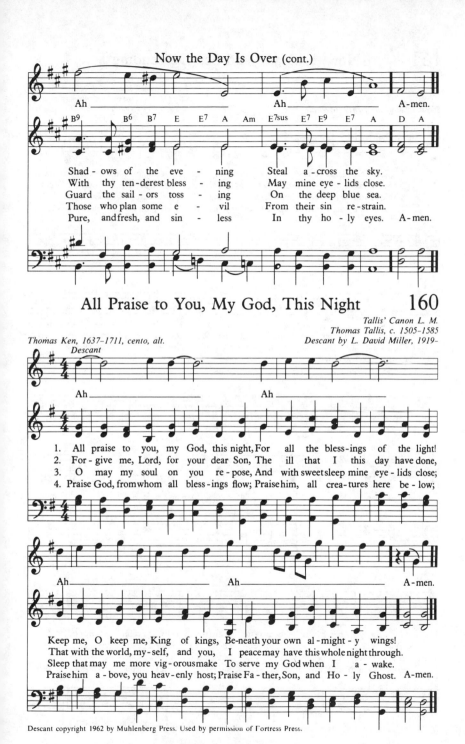

Ah _____ Ah _____ A-men.

Shad - ows of the eve - ning Steal a - cross the sky.
With thy ten - derest bless - ing May mine eye - lids close.
Guard the sail - ors toss - ing On the deep blue sea.
Those who plan some e - vil From their sin re - strain.
Pure, and fresh, and sin - less In thy ho - ly eyes. A-men.

All Praise to You, My God, This Night 160

Tallis' Canon L. M.
Thomas Tallis, c. 1505–1585
Descant by L. David Miller, 1919-

Thomas Ken, 1637–1711, cento, alt.

Descant

Ah _____ Ah _____

1. All praise to you, my God, this night, For all the bless - ings of the light!
2. For - give me, Lord, for your dear Son, The ill that I this day have done,
3. O may my soul on you re - pose, And with sweet sleep mine eye - lids close;
4. Praise God, from whom all bless - ings flow; Praise him, all crea - tures here be - low;

Ah _____ Ah _____ A-men.

Keep me, O keep me, King of kings, Be-neath your own al - might - y wings!
That with the world, my-self, and you, I peace may have this whole night through.
Sleep that may me more vig - orous make To serve my God when I a - wake.
Praise him a - bove, you heav - enly host; Praise Fa - ther, Son, and Ho - ly Ghost. A-men.

161   Now, on Land and Sea Descending

Vesper Hymn 8. 7. 8. 7. 8. 6. 8. 7.
John Stevenson, 'Selection
of Popular National Airs,' 1818

Samuel Longfellow, 1819–1892, alt.

1. Now, on land and sea de - scend-ing, Brings the night its peace pro-found;
2. Soon as dies the sun - set glo - ry, Stars of heaven shine out a - bove,
3. Now, our wants and bur - dens leav - ing To his care who cares for all,
4. As the dark - ness deep - ens o'er us, Lo! e - ter - nal stars a - rise;

Let our ves - per hymn be blend - ing With the ho - ly calm a - round.
Tell - ing still the an - cient sto - ry— Their Cre - a - tor's change - less love.
Cease we fear - ing, cease we griev - ing: At his touch our bur - dens fall.
Hope and faith and love rise glo - rious, Shin - ing in the spir - it's skies.

Ju - bi - la - te! Ju - bi - la - te! Ju - bi - la - te! A - men!

Let our ves - per hymn be blend - ing With the ho - ly calm a - round.
Tell - ing still the an - cient sto - ry— Their Cre - a - tor's change - less love.
Cease we fear - ing, cease we griev - ing: At his touch our bur - dens fall.
Hope and faith and love rise glo - rious, Shin - ing in the spir - it's skies. A-men.

164

Lancashire 7. 6. 7. 6. D.

Thomas Curtis Clark, 1877-1953

Henry Smart, 1813-1879

1. Where rest - less crowds are throng - ing A - long the cit - y ways,
2. In scenes of want and sor - row And haunts of fla - grant wrong,
3. O Christ, be - hold thy peo - ple— They press on ev - er - y hand!

Where pride and greed and tur - moil Con - sume the fe - vered days,
In homes where kind - ness fal - ters, And strife and fear are strong,
Bring light to all the cit - ies Of our be - lov - ed land.

Where vain am - bi - tions ban - ish All thoughts of praise and prayer,
In bus - y street of bar - ter, In lone - ly thor-ough-fare,
May all our bit - ter striv - ing Give way to vi - sions fair

The peo - ple's spir - its wav - er: But thou, O Christ, art there.
The peo - ple's spir - its lan - guish: But thou, O Christ, art there.
Of righ-teous-ness and jus - tice: For thou, O Christ, art there. A - men.

163 In Adam We Have All Been One

The Saints' Delight C. M.
'Southern Harmony,' 1835

Martin H. Franzmann, 1907–

Harm. by Paul G. Bunjes, 1914–

1. In Ad-am we have all been one, One huge re-bel-lious man: We
2. We fled thee, and in los-ing thee We lost our broth-er too. Each
3. But thy strong love, it sought us still And sent thine on-ly Son, That
4. O thou who, when we loved thee not, Didst love and save us all, Thou

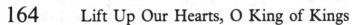

all have fled that eve-ning Voice That sought us as we ran.
sin-gly sought and claimed his own; Each man his broth-er slew.
we might hear his shep-herd's voice And, hear-ing him, be one.
great Good Shep-herd of man-kind, O hear us when we call. A-men.

5. Send us thy Spirit, teach us truth;
Thou Son, O set us free
From fancied wisdom, self-sought ways,
To make us one in thee.

6. Then shall our song united rise
To thine eternal throne,
Where with the Father evermore
And Spirit thou art one.

Words and harmonization from *Worship Supplement*, Concordia Publishing House, 1969. Used by permission.

164 Lift Up Our Hearts, O King of Kings

Truro L. M.

John H. B. Masterman, 1867–1933, cento, alt.

T. Williams, 'Psalmodia Evangelica,' 1789

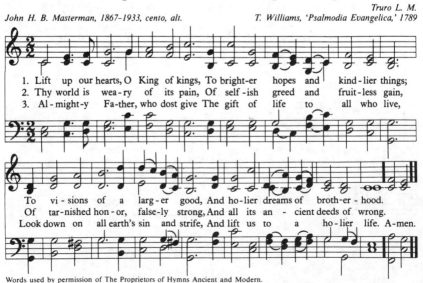

1. Lift up our hearts, O King of kings, To bright-er hopes and kind-lier things;
2. Thy world is wea-ry of its pain, Of self-ish greed and fruit-less gain,
3. Al-might-y Fa-ther, who dost give The gift of life to all who live,

To vi-sions of a larg-er good, And ho-lier dreams of broth-er-hood.
Of tar-nished hon-or, false-ly strong, And all its an-cient deeds of wrong.
Look down on all earth's sin and strife, And lift us to a ho-lier life. A-men.

Words used by permission of The Proprietors of Hymns Ancient and Modern.

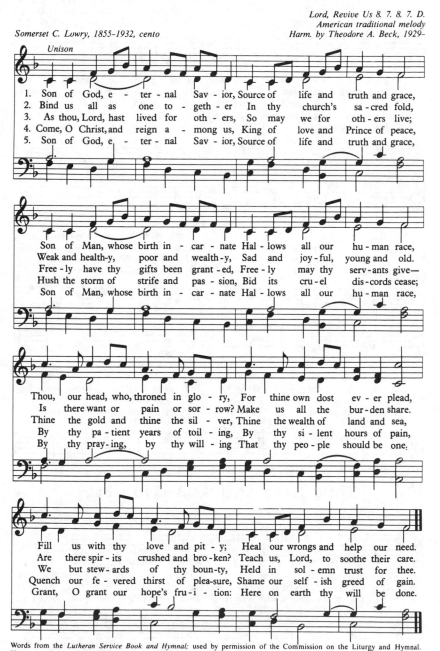

Son of God, Eternal Savior

Lord, Revive Us 8. 7. 8. 7. D.
American traditional melody
Harm. by Theodore A. Beck, 1929-

Somerset C. Lowry, 1855-1932, cento

Unison

1. Son of God, e - ter - nal Sav - ior, Source of life and truth and grace,
2. Bind us all as one to - geth - er In thy church's sa - cred fold,
3. As thou, Lord, hast lived for oth - ers, So may we for oth - ers live;
4. Come, O Christ, and reign a - mong us, King of love and Prince of peace,
5. Son of God, e - ter - nal Sav - ior, Source of life and truth and grace,

Son of Man, whose birth in - car - nate Hal - lows all our hu - man race,
Weak and health-y, poor and wealth-y, Sad and joy-ful, young and old.
Free - ly have thy gifts been grant - ed, Free - ly may thy serv - ants give—
Hush the storm of strife and pas - sion, Bid its cru - el dis - cords cease;
Son of Man, whose birth in - car - nate Hal - lows all our hu - man race,

Thou, our head, who, throned in glo - ry, For thine own dost ev - er plead,
Is there want or pain or sor - row? Make us all the bur - den share.
Thine the gold and thine the sil - ver, Thine the wealth of land and sea,
By thy pa - tient years of toil - ing, By thy si - lent hours of pain,
By thy pray - ing, by thy will - ing That thy peo - ple should be one.

Fill us with thy love and pit - y; Heal our wrongs and help our need.
Are there spir - its crushed and bro - ken? Teach us, Lord, to soothe their care.
We but stew - ards of thy boun - ty, Held in sol - emn trust for thee.
Quench our fe - vered thirst of plea-sure, Shame our self - ish greed of gain.
Grant, O grant our hope's fru - i - tion: Here on earth thy will be done.

Words from the *Lutheran Service Book and Hymnal*; used by permission of the Commission on the Liturgy and Hymnal.
Harmonization from *Worship Supplement*, Concordia Publishing House; used by permission.

166 Lord of All Nations, Grant Me Grace

Beatus Vir L. M.
Slovak hymn tune, 1561

Olive Wise Spannaus, 1916–

Harm. by Richard W. Hillert, 1923–

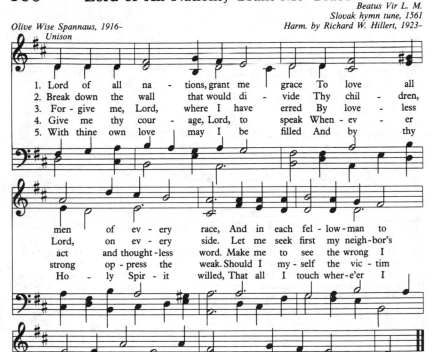

1. Lord of all na - tions, grant me grace To love all
2. Break down the wall that would di - vide Thy chil - dren,
3. For - give me, Lord, where I have erred By love - less
4. Give me thy cour - age, Lord, to speak When - ev - er
5. With thine own love may I be filled And by thy

men of ev - ery race, And in each fel - low - man to
Lord, on ev - ery side. Let me seek first my neigh - bor's
act and thought - less word. Make me to see the wrong I
strong op - press the weak. Should I my - self the vic - tim
Ho - ly Spir - it willed, That all I touch wher - e'er I

see My broth - er, loved, re - deemed by thee.
good In bonds of Chris - tian broth - er - hood.
do Will cru - ci - fy my Lord a - new.
be, Help me for - give, re - mem - bering thee.
be May be di - vine - ly touched by thee.

Words and harmonization from *A New Song*, © 1967 by Concordia Publishing House.

167 These Things Shall Be: A Loftier Race

Truro L. M.

J. Addington Symonds, 1840–1893, cento

T. Williams, 'Psalmodia Evangelica,' 1789

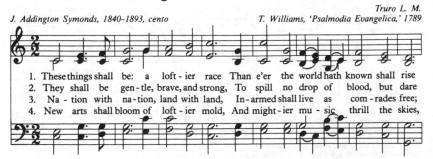

1. These things shall be: a loft - ier race Than e'er the world hath known shall rise
2. They shall be gen - tle, brave, and strong, To spill no drop of blood, but dare
3. Na - tion with na - tion, land with land, In - armed shall live as com - rades free;
4. New arts shall bloom of loft - ier mold, And might - ier mu - sic thrill the skies,

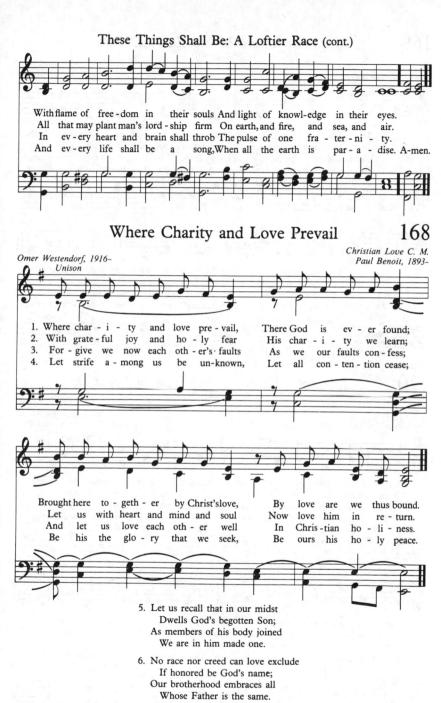

With flame of free-dom in their souls And light of knowl-edge in their eyes.
All that may plant man's lord-ship firm On earth, and fire, and sea, and air.
In ev-ery heart and brain shall throb The pulse of one fra-ter-ni-ty.
And ev-ery life shall be a song, When all the earth is par-a-dise. A-men.

Where Charity and Love Prevail 168

Omer Westendorf, 1916–

Christian Love C. M.
Paul Benoit, 1893–

Unison

1. Where char-i-ty and love pre-vail, There God is ev-er found;
2. With grate-ful joy and ho-ly fear His char-i-ty we learn;
3. For-give we now each oth-er's· faults As we our faults con-fess;
4. Let strife a-mong us be un-known, Let all con-ten-tion cease;

Brought here to-geth-er by Christ's love, By love are we thus bound.
Let us with heart and mind and soul Now love him in re-turn.
And let us love each oth-er well In Chris-tian ho-li-ness.
Be his the glo-ry that we seek, Be ours his ho-ly peace.

5. Let us recall that in our midst
   Dwells God's begotten Son;
   As members of his body joined
   We are in him made one.

6. No race nor creed can love exclude
   If honored be God's name;
   Our brotherhood embraces all
   Whose Father is the same.

169 In Christ There Is No East or West
(FIRST TUNE)

St. Peter C. M.

John Oxenham, 1852-1941

Alexander R. Reinagle, 1799-1877

1. In Christ there is no East or West, In him no South or North;
2. In him shall true hearts ev-ery-where Their high com-mu-nion find;
3. Join hands, then, broth-ers of the faith, What-e'er your race may be!
4. In Christ now meet both East and West, In him meet South and North;

But one great fel-low-ship of love Through-out the whole wide earth.
His serv-ice is the gold-en cord Close-bind-ing all man-kind.
Who serves my Fa-ther as a son Is sure-ly kin to me.
All Christ-ly souls are one in him Through-out the whole wide earth. A-men.

Words from *Bees in Amber*, by John Oxenham. Used by permission.

170 In Christ There Is No East or West
(SECOND TUNE)

McKee C. M.
American Negro melody
Arr. by Harry T. Burleigh, 1866-1949

John Oxenham, 1852-1941

1. In Christ there is no East or West, In him no South or North;
2. In him shall true hearts ev-ery-where Their high com-mu-nion find;
3. Join hands, then, broth-ers of the faith, What-e'er your race may be!
4. In Christ now meet both East and West, In him meet South and North;

But one great fel-low-ship of love Through-out the whole wide earth.
His serv-ice is the gold-en cord Close-bind-ing all man-kind.
Who serves my Fa-ther as a son Is sure-ly kin to me.
All Christ-ly souls are one in him Through-out the whole wide earth. A-men.

Words from *Bees in Amber*, by John Oxenham; used by permission. Music copyright, 1940, by Harry T. Burleigh; used by permission.

Through All the World

Conrad 14. 12. 12. 14.

Bryan Jeffery Leech, 1931–
Paul Liljestrand, 1931–

1. Through all the world let ev-ery na-tion sing to God the King. As Lord, may Christ pre-side where now he is de-fied And sov-ereign place his throne in lands not yet his own. Through all the world let ev-ery na-tion sing to God the King.

2. Through all the world let ev-ery man ex-press true righ-teous-ness. May Christ now be the norm to which all men con-form, His pas-sion cure the sin that fes-ters from with-in. Through all the world let ev-ery man ex-press true righ-teous-ness.

3. Through all the world let ev-ery man em-brace the gift of grace. May Christ's great light con-sume our dark-est cit-ies' gloom; May Christ's great love ef-face hos-til-i-ties of race. Through all the world let ev-ery man em-brace the gift of grace.

4. If all the world in ev-ery part shall hear and God re-vere, We must be moved to care and in his name to share The lib-er-at-ing word which must be told a-broad. Then all the world in ev-ery part shall hear and God re-vere.

172 God the Omnipotent! King, Who Ordainest

Sts. 1, 2, Henry F. Chorley, 1808–1872, alt.
Sts. 3, 4, John Ellerton, 1826–1893, alt.

Russian Hymn 11. 10. 11. 9.
Alexis F. Lvov, 1799–1870

1. God the Om-nip-o-tent! King, who or-dain-est
2. God the All-mer-ci-ful! earth hath for-sak-en
3. God the All-righ-teous One! man hath de-fied thee;
4. God the All-prov-i-dent! earth by thy chas-tening

Thun - - der thy clar-ion, the light-ning thy sword,
Thy ways all - ho - ly, and slight-ed thy word;
Yet to e - ter-ni - ty stand-eth thy word;
Yet shall to free-dom and truth be re-stored;

Show forth thy pit-y on high where thou reign-est:
Bid not thy wrath in its ter-rors a-wak-en:
False-hood and wrong shall not tar-ry be-side thee:
Through the thick dark-ness thy King-dom is has-tening:

Give to us peace in our time, O Lord.
Give to us peace in our time, O Lord.
Give to us peace in our time, O Lord.
Thou wilt give peace in thy time, O Lord. A - men.

Frank Mason North, 1850–1935

Germany L. M.
William Gardiner, 'Sacred Melodies,' 1815

1. Where cross the crowd - ed ways of life, Where sound the
2. In haunts of wretch - ed - ness and need, On shad - owed
3. From ten - der child - hood's help - less - ness, From wom - an's
4. The cup of wa - ter given for thee Still holds the

cries of race and clan, A - bove the noise of self - ish
thresh - olds dark with fears, From paths where hide the lures of
grief, man's bur - dened toil, From fam - ished souls, from sor - rows'
fresh - ness of thy grace; Yet long these mul - ti - tudes to

strife, We hear thy voice, O Son of Man.
greed, We catch the vi - sion of thy tears.
stress, Thy heart has nev - er known re - coil.
see The sweet com - pas - sion of thy face. A - men.

5. O Master, from the mountain side
    Make haste to heal these hearts of pain;
    Among these restless throngs abide,
    O tread the city's streets again;

6. Till sons of men shall learn thy love,
    And follow where thy feet have trod;
    Till glorious from thy heaven above
    Shall come the city of our God.

174   Christic for the World We Sing

174 Christ for the World We Sing

Samuel Wolcott, 1813–1886, alt.

Italian Hymn 6. 6. 4. 6. 6. 6. 4.
Felice de Giardini, 1716–1796

1. Christ for the world we sing; The world to Christ we bring
2. Christ for the world we sing; The world to Christ we bring
3. Christ for the world we sing; The world to Christ we bring
4. Christ for the world we sing; The world to Christ we bring

With lov - ing zeal— The poor and them that mourn, The faint and
With fer - vent prayer— The way - ward and the lost, By rest - less
With one ac - cord— With us the work to share, With us re -
With joy - ful song— The new - born souls whose days, Re - claimed from

o - ver-borne, Sin - sick and sor - row-worn, For Christ to heal.
pas - sions tossed, Re - deemed at count-less cost From dark de - spair.
proach to dare, With us the cross to bear, For Christ our Lord.
er - ror's ways, In - spired with hope and praise, To Christ be - long. A-men.

175   O God of Love, O King of Peace

Henry Williams Baker, 1821–1877, alt.

Quebec L. M.
Henry Baker, 1835–1910

1. O God of love, O King of peace, Make wars through-out the world to cease,
2. Re - mem-ber, Lord, your works of old, The won - ders that our fa-thers told,
3. Whom shall we trust but you, O Lord? Where rest but on your faith-ful word?
4. Where saints and an - gels dwell a - bove, All hearts are knit in ho - ly love;

The wrath of sin - ful man re - strain: Give peace, O God, give peace a - gain!
Re - mem-ber not our sin's dark stain: Give peace, O God, give peace a - gain!
None ev - er called on you in vain: Give peace, O God, give peace a - gain!
O bind us in that heav-enly chain: Give peace, O God, give peace a - gain! A-men.

Lead Us, O Father, in the Paths of Peace 176

William Henry Burleigh, 1812–1871

Langran 10. 10. 10. 10.
James Langran, 1835–1909

1. Lead us, O Fa - ther, in the paths of peace: With - out thy guid - ing
2. Lead us, O Fa - ther, in the paths of truth: Un-helped by thee, in
3. Lead us, O Fa - ther, in the paths of right: Blind - ly we stum - ble
4. Lead us, O Fa - ther, to thy heav-enly rest, How - ev - er rough and

hand we go a - stray, And doubts ap - pall, and sor - rows still in -
er - ror's maze we grope, While pas - sion stains, and fol - ly dims our
when we walk a - lone, In - volved in shad - ows of a dark-some
steep the path may be, Through joy or sor - row, as thou deem - est

crease; Lead us through Christ, the true and liv - ing way.
youth, And age comes on, un-cheered by faith or hope.
night; On - ly with thee we jour - ney safe - ly on.
best, Un - til our lives are per - fect - ed in thee. A - men.

175

177 Build Thou the City Splendid

Lancashire 7. 6. 7. 6. D.
Ernest K. Emurian, 1912-
Henry Smart, 1813-1879

1. Build thou the cit - y splen - did, And rear her tow - ers high,
2. Build thou the cit - y splen - did, That she may long en - dure;
3. Build thou the cit - y splen - did, Where all may dwell in peace,
4. Build thou the cit - y splen - did, A - dorned with beau - ty rare,
5. Build thou the cit - y splen - did, Up - on this bar - ren sod,

From firm foun - da - tions up - ward Un - til they pierce the sky.
With home - like hab - i - ta - tions And path - ways made se - cure.
And share in man's af - flu - ence As ben - e - fits in - crease;
And na - ture's gor - geous col - ors A - bun - dant ev - ery - where;
Where men may live to - geth - er With - in the love of God;

Make broad her streets and high - ways For church - es, stores, and schools;
Let there be full em - ploy - ment So all may work who will,
Where rac - es and re - li - gions Co - op - er - ate as one,
With wa - ters un - pol - lut - ed And air from poi - sons free,
So may they praise the Fa - ther, The God who gave them birth,

And leg - is - la - tive cham - bers Where e - qual jus - tice rules.
And in pro - duc - tive la - bor Their des - ti - nies ful - fill.
Ful - fill - ing the pe - ti - tion, "On earth Thy will be done."
So each may reach the full - ness De - creed for all by Thee.
That, lo! his ho - ly cit - y Is plant - ed here on earth. A - men.

Words used by permission of the author.

Georgia Harkness, 1891–

Donne secours 11. 10. 11. 10.
Genevan Psalter, 1551

1. Hope of the world, thou Christ of great com - pas - sion,
2. Hope of the world, God's gift from high - est heav - en,
3. Hope of the world, a - foot on dust - y high - ways,
4. Hope of the world, who by thy cross didst save us
5. Hope of the world, O Christ, o'er death vic - to - rious,

Speak to our fear - ful hearts by con - flict rent.
Bring - ing to hun - gry souls the bread of life,
Show - ing to wan - dering souls the path of light,
From death and dark de - spair, from sin and guilt,
Who by this sign didst con - quer grief and pain,

Save us, thy peo - ple, from con - sum - ing pas - sion,
Still let thy Spir - it un - to us be giv - en,
Walk thou be - side us lest the tempt - ing by - ways
We ren - der back the love thy mer - cy gave us;
We would be faith - ful to thy gos - pel glo - rious:

Who by our own false hopes and aims are spent.
To heal earth's wounds and end her bit - ter strife.
Lure us a - way from thee to end - less night.
Take thou our lives and use them as thou wilt.
Thou art our Lord! Thou dost for - ev - er reign! A - men.

179   Forgive, O Lord, Our Severing Ways

John Greenleaf Whittier, 1807–1892, cento, alt.

Cheltenham 8. 8. 8. 8.
James D. Shannon, 1936–

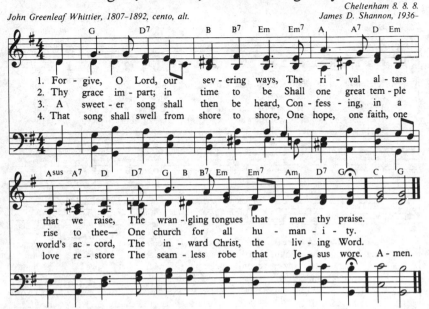

1. For - give, O Lord, our sev - ering ways, The ri - val al - tars
2. Thy grace im - part; in time to be Shall one great tem - ple
3. A sweet - er song shall then be heard, Con - fess - ing, in a
4. That song shall swell from shore to shore, One hope, one faith, one

that we raise, The wran - gling tongues that mar thy praise.
rise to thee— One church for all hu - man - i - ty.
world's ac - cord, The in - ward Christ, the liv - ing Word.
love re - store The seam - less robe that Je - sus wore. A - men.

180   Let There Be Light, Lord God of Hosts

William Merrill Vories, 1880–, alt.

Pentecost L. M.
William Boyd, 1847–1928

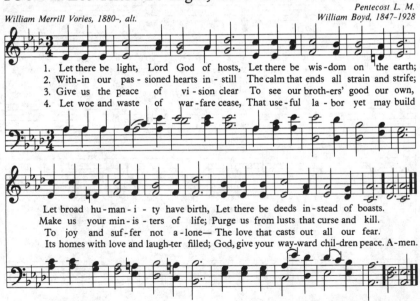

1. Let there be light, Lord God of hosts, Let there be wis - dom on the earth;
2. With - in our pas - sioned hearts in - still The calm that ends all strain and strife;
3. Give us the peace of vi - sion clear To see our broth - ers' good our own,
4. Let woe and waste of war - fare cease, That use - ful la - bor yet may build

Let broad hu - man - i - ty have birth, Let there be deeds in - stead of boasts.
Make us your min - is - ters of life; Purge us from lusts that curse and kill.
To joy and suf - fer not a - lone— The love that casts out all our fear.
Its homes with love and laugh - ter filled; God, give your way - ward chil - dren peace. A - men.

O Brother Man
181

John Greenleaf Whittier, 1807–1892, cento, alt.

Welwyn 11. 10. 11. 10.
Alfred Scott-Gatty, 1847–1918

1. O broth - er man, fold to your heart your broth - er;
2. For he whom Je - sus loved has tru - ly spo - ken:
3. Fol - low with rev - erent steps the great ex - am - ple
4. Then shall all shack - les fall; the storm - y clang - or

Where pit - y dwells, the peace of God is there;
The ho - lier wor - ship which he deigns to bless
Of him whose ho - ly work was do - ing good;
Of wild war mu - sic o'er the earth shall cease;

To wor - ship right - ly is to love each oth - er,
Re - stores the lost, and binds the spir - it bro - ken,
So shall the wide earth seem our Fa - ther's tem - ple,
Love shall tread out the bale - ful fire of an - ger,

Each smile a hymn, each kind - ly deed a prayer.
And feeds the wid - ow and the fa - ther - less.
Each lov - ing life a psalm of grat - i - tude.
And in its ash - es plant the tree of peace. A - men.

Music used by permission of the Abbot of Downside.

182   "Am I My Brother's Keeper?"

Brother's Keeper 7. 6. 7. 6. D.
Reginald Barrett-Ayres, 1920–
Arr. by David Hugh Jones, 1900–

Ian Ferguson, 1921–

1. "Am I my broth-er's keep-er?" The mut-tered cry was drowned
2. The rul-er called for wa-ter And thought his hands were clean.
3. As long as peo-ple hun-ger, As long as peo-ple thirst,

By A-bel's life-blood shout-ing In si-lence from the ground.
Christ count-ed less than or-der, The man than the ma-chine.
And ig-no-rance and ill-ness And war-fare do their worst,

For no man is an is-land di-vid-ed from the main;
The crowd cried, "Cru-ci-fy him." Their mal-ice would-n't budge,
As long as there's in-jus-tice In an-y of God's lands,

The bell that tolled for A-bel Tolled e-qual-ly for Cain.
So Pi-late called for wa-ter, And his-to-ry's his judge.
I am my broth-er's keep-er, I dare not wash my hands.

Come Forth, Ye Men of Every Race

Creation 11. 13. 11. 13. 8. 14. 8. 12.
Franz Joseph Haydn, 1732–1809
Arr. by Isaac B. Woodbury, 1819–1858

J. Holmes Smith, 1899–

1. Come forth, ye men of ev-ery race and na-tion! We are mak-ing God's new world for
2. A - wake, O sons of priv - i - lege and pow-er, For the dis - pos-sessed of earth to
3. Though ruth-less power may wield its weap-ons gor - y, We hold our-selves for thee all

all the sons of men: Our hearts u - nite in dar - ing ex - pec - ta - tion, For the
God for jus - tice cry! Let ea - ger hands re-store their right - ful dow - er, Lest the
loy - al - ties a - bove. Though storms of hate may rage in emp - ty glo - ry, In the

match - less Lord of life doth tread this earth a - gain. Be - hold, he comes as first he came
clam - or of our greed his Prov - i - dence de - ny. The last, the least, the lost are ours;
splen - dor of the dawn we see thy cross of love. With heal - ing rays it gleams a - far,

To write up - on the hearts of men in words of liv - ing flame His Spir - it of he -
To their e - man - ci - pa - tion we de - vote our ar - dent powers. While they are bound, can
And ra - di - ates its death-less hope from star to flam - ing star. We march with thee where

ro - ic love, That one re-demp-tive pur-pose through this age may move!
we be free? The knights of serv - ice choose the no - bler lib - er - ty.
mar - tyrs trod, Till all the sons of men be - come the sons of God. A-men.

184 Do You Know that the Lord Walks on Earth?

Sebastian Temple, 1928–

Do You Know Irregular
Sebastian Temple, 1928–

1. Do you know that the Lord walks on earth?
2. Do you know that he walks in dis - guise?
3. Do you know that the Lord thirsts so much?
4. Do you know he is cru - ci - fied each day?
5. Do you know that he wants to be free?

Do you know he is liv - - ing here now?
Do you know he's in crowds ev - ery - where?
Do you know that he's sit - - ting in jail?
Do you know that he suf - - fers and dies?
Do you know he wants help from you and me?

He is wait - ing for all men to rec - og - nize him here.
Ev - ery place that you go, you may find that he is there.
Ev - ery - where he is hun - gry and na - ked in the cold.
Ev - ery - where he is lone - ly and wait - ing for a call.
He needs our hands and feet and hearts to serve.

Do you know that the Lord walks on earth?
Do you know that the Lord's in dis - guise?
Do you know he's re - ject - ed with - out care?
Do you know he is sick and all a - lone?
Do you know he can on - ly work through men?

Words and music reprinted by permission of the Franciscan Communications Center, Los Angeles, Calif.

Father Eternal, Ruler of Creation

Old 124th 11. 10. 11. 10. 10.

Laurence Housman, 1865–1959

Genevan Psalter, 1551

1. Fa - ther e - ter - nal, rul - er of cre - a - tion, Spir - it of life, which moved ere form was made, Through the thick dark - ness cov - ering ev - ery na - tion, Light to man's blind - ness, O be thou our aid: Thy king - dom come, O Lord, thy will be done.

2. Rac - es and peo - ples, lo, we stand di - vid - ed, And shar - ing not our griefs, no joy can share; By wars and tu - mults love is mocked, de - rid - ed, His con - quering cross no king - dom wills to bear: Thy king - dom come, O Lord, thy will be done.

3. En - vious of heart, blind-eyed, with tongues con - found - ed, Na - tion by na - tion still goes un - for - given; In wrath and fear, by jeal - ou - sies sur - round - ed, Build - ing proud towers which shall not reach to heaven: Thy king - dom come, O Lord, thy will be done.

4. How shall we love thee, ho - ly, hid - den Be - ing, If we love not the world which thou hast made? O give us broth - er love for bet - ter see - ing Thy Word made flesh, and in a man - ger laid: Thy king - dom come, O Lord, thy will be done. A - men.

Words from *Enlarged Songs of Praise*. Used by permission of Oxford University Press.

186   Lord, We Pray for Golden Peace

Sebastian Temple, 1928–

Golden Peace Irregular with Refrain
Sebastian Temple, 1928–

1. Lord, we pray for gold - en peace,
2. Keep all men for - ev - er one,
3. Let your jus - tice reign su - preme And

Peace all o - ver the land. May all men dwell in
One in love and grace. Wipe a - way all
righ - teous - ness be done. Let good - ness rule the

lib - er - ty, Walk - ing hand in hand.
war and strife, Give free - dom to each race.
hearts of men And e - vil be o - ver - come.

Refrain

Ban - ish fear and ig - no - rance, Hun - ger, thirst, and

pain; Ban - ish hate and pov - er - ty, Let

no man live in vain, Let no man live in vain.

Gilbert Keith Chesterton, 1874–1936

Llangloffan 7. 6. 7. 6. D.
Welsh traditional melody
Harm. by David Evans, 1874–1948

1. O God of earth and al - tar, Bow down and hear our cry;
2. From all that ter - ror teach - es, From lies of tongue and pen;
3. Tie in a liv - ing teth - er The prince and priest and thrall;

Our earth - ly rul - ers fal - ter, Our peo - ple drift and die;
From all the eas - y speech - es That com - fort cru - el men;
Bind all our lives to - geth - er, Smite us and save us all;

The walls of gold en - tomb us, The swords of scorn di - vide;
From sale and prof - a - na - tion Of hon - or and the sword;
In ire and ex - ul - ta - tion A - flame with faith, and free,

Take not thy thun - der from us, But take a - way our pride.
From sleep and from dam - na - tion, De - liv - er us, good Lord!
Lift up a liv - ing na - tion, A sin - gle sword to thee. A-men.

Words used by permission of Oxford University Press. Music from *The Revised Church Hymnary;* used by permission of Oxford University Press.

188 God Save America! New World of Glory

Russian Hymn 11. 10. 11. 10.

William G. Ballantine, 1848–1937

Alexis F. Lvov, 1799–1870

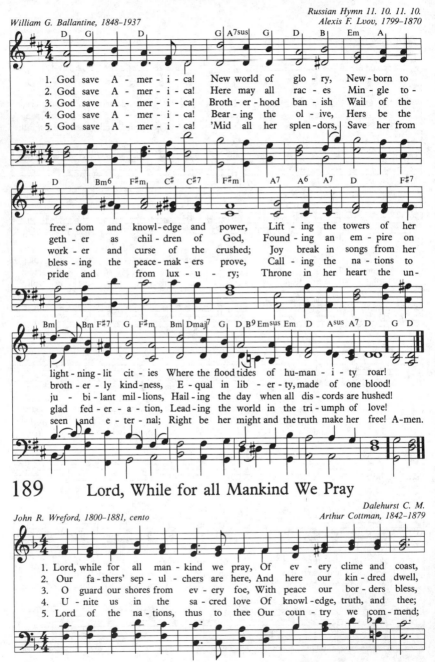

1. God save A - mer - i - ca! New world of glo - ry, New - born to
2. God save A - mer - i - ca! Here may all rac - es Min - gle to -
3. God save A - mer - i - ca! Broth - er - hood ban - ish Wail of the
4. God save A - mer - i - ca! Bear - ing the ol - ive, Hers be the
5. God save A - mer - i - ca! 'Mid all her splen - dors, Save her from

free - dom and knowl - edge and power, Lift - ing the towers of her
geth - er as chil - dren of God, Found - ing an em - pire on
work - er and curse of the crushed; Joy break in songs from her
bless - ing the peace - mak - ers prove, Call - ing the na - tions to
pride and from lux - u - ry; Throne in her heart the un -

light - ning - lit cit - ies Where the flood tides of hu - man - i - ty roar!
broth - er - ly kind - ness, E - qual in lib - er - ty, made of one blood!
ju - bi - lant mil - lions, Hail - ing the day when all dis - cords are hushed!
glad fed - er - a - tion, Lead - ing the world in the tri - umph of love!
seen and e - ter - nal; Right be her might and the truth make her free! A - men.

189 Lord, While for all Mankind We Pray

Dalehurst C. M.

John R. Wreford, 1800–1881, cento

Arthur Cottman, 1842–1879

1. Lord, while for all man - kind we pray, Of ev - ery clime and coast,
2. Our fa - thers' sep - ul - chers are here, And here our kin - dred dwell,
3. O guard our shores from ev - ery foe, With peace our bor - ders bless,
4. U - nite us in the sa - cred love Of knowl - edge, truth, and thee;
5. Lord of the na - tions, thus to thee Our coun - try we com - mend;

O hear us for our na-tive land, The land we love the most.
Our chil-dren too; how should we love An-oth-er land so well?
With pros-perous times our cit-ies crown, Our fields with plen-teous-ness.
And let our hills and val-leys shout The songs of lib-er-ty.
Be thou her ref-uge and her trust, Her ev-er-last-ing friend. A-men.

O God, Beneath Thy Guiding Hand 190

Duke Street L. M.
John Hatton, ?–1793

Leonard Bacon, 1802–1881, cento

1. O God, be-neath thy guid-ing hand Our ex-iled
2. Thou heard'st, well pleased, the song, the prayer; Thy bless-ing
3. Laws, free-dom, truth, and faith in God Came with those
4. And here thy name, O God of love, Their chil-dren's

fa-thers crossed the sea, And when they trod the
came, and still its power Shall on-ward through all
ex-iles o'er the waves, And where their pil-grim
chil-dren shall a-dore, Till these e-ter-nal

win-try strand, With prayer and psalm they wor-shiped thee.
ag-es bear The mem-ory of that ho-ly hour.
feet have trod, The God they trust-ed guards their graves.
hills re-move, And spring a-dorns the earth no more. A-men.

187

Mine Eyes Have Seen the Glory

Battle Hymn of the Republic
15. 15. 15. 6. with Refrain
American camp meeting tune

Julia Ward Howe, 1819-1910, cento

1. Mine eyes have seen the glo-ry of the com-ing of the Lord;
2. I have seen him in the watch-fires of a hun-dred cir-cling camps;
3. He has sound-ed forth the trum-pet that shall nev-er call re-treat;
4. In the beau-ty of the lil-ies Christ was born a-cross the sea,

He is tram-pling out the vin-tage where the grapes of wrath are stored;
They have build-ed him an al-tar in the eve-ning dews and damps;
He is sift-ing out the hearts of men be-fore his judg-ment seat;
With a glo-ry in his bos-om that trans-fig-ures you and me;

He hath loosed the fate-ful light-ning of his ter-ri-ble swift sword;
I can read his righ-teous sen-tence by the dim and flar-ing lamps;
O be swift, my soul, to an-swer him; be ju-bi-lant, my feet!
As he died to make men ho-ly, let us die to make men free!

Refrain

His truth is march-ing on.
His day is march-ing on.
Our God is march-ing on.
While God is march-ing on.

Glo-ry! glo-ry! Hal-le-

Mine Eyes Have Seen the Glory (cont.)

lu - jah! Glo - ry! glo - ry! Hal - le - lu - jah!

Glo - ry! glo - ry! Hal - le - lu - jah! His truth is march - ing on.

Lord, Guard and Guide the Men Who Fly   192

Mary C. D. Hamilton, alt.

Quebec L. M.
Henry Baker, 1835-1910

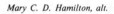

1. Lord, guard and guide the men who fly Through the great spac - es of the sky;
2. You who sup - port with ten - der might The bal - anced birds in all their flight,
3. Con - trol their minds with in - stinct fit When - e'er, ad - ven - tur - ing, they quit
4. A - loft in sol - i - tudes of space, Up - hold them with your sav - ing grace.

Be with them tra - vers - ing the air In dark - ening storms or sun - shine fair.
Lord of the tem - pered winds, be near, That, hav - ing you, they know no fear.
The firm se - cur - i - ty of land; Grant stead - fast eye and skill - ful hand.
O God, pro - tect the men who fly Through lone - ly ways be - neath the sky. A - men.

193   My Country, 'Tis of Thee

America 6. 6. 4. 6. 6. 6. 4.

Samuel F. Smith, 1808–1895, cento

'Thesaurus Musicus,' 1740

1. My coun - try, 'tis of thee, Sweet land of lib - er - ty, Of thee I sing; Land where my fa - thers died, Land of the pil - grims' pride, From ev - ery moun - tain - side Let free - dom ring.
2. My na - tive coun - try, thee, Land of the no - ble free, Thy name I love; I love thy rocks and rills, Thy woods and tem - pled hills; My heart with rap - ture thrills Like that a - bove.
3. Let mu - sic swell the breeze, And ring from all the trees Sweet free - dom's song; Let mor - tal tongues a - wake; Let all that breathe par - take; Let rocks their si - lence break, The sound pro - long.
4. Our fa - thers' God, to thee, Au - thor of lib - er - ty, To thee we sing; Long may our land be bright With free - dom's ho - ly light; Pro - tect us by thy might, Great God, our King. A - men.

194   God Bless Our Native Land

Sts. 1, 2, Siegfried A. Mahlmann, 1771–1826
St. 1 tr. by Charles T. Brooks, 1813–1883, alt.
St. 2 tr. by John S. Dwight, 1813–1893
St. 3, William Edward Hickson, 1803–1870

1. God bless our native land;
   Firm may she ever stand
     Through storm and night:
   When the wild tempests rave,
   Ruler of wind and wave,
   O God, our country save
     By your great might.

2. For her our prayer shall rise
   To God above the skies;
     On him we wait;
   Lord, you are ever nigh,
   Guarding with watchful eye,
   To you aloud we cry,
     God save the State!

3. Not for this land alone,
   But be God's mercies shown
     From shore to shore;
   And may the nations see
   That men should brothers be,
   And form one family
     The wide world o'er. Amen.

This hymn may be sung to the tune *America*, Hymn 193, above.

Not Alone for Mighty Empire

William Pierson Merrill, 1867–1954, alt.

Austrian Hymn 8. 7. 8. 7. D.
Franz Joseph Haydn, 1732–1809

1. Not a-lone for might-y em-pire Stretch-ing far o'er land and sea,
2. Not for bat-tle-ships and for-tress, Not for con-quests of the sword,
3. For the ar-mies of the faith-ful, Souls that passed and left no name;
4. God of jus-tice, save the peo-ple From the clash of race and creed,

Not a-lone for boun-teous har-vests, Lift we up our hearts to thee.
But for con-quests of the spir-it Give we thanks to thee, O Lord;
For the glo-ry that il-lu-mines Pa-triot lives of death-less fame;
From the strife of class and fac-tion— Make our na-tion free in-deed;

Stand-ing in the liv-ing pres-ent, Mem-o-ry and hope be-tween,
For the price-less gift of free-dom, For the home, the church, the school,
For our proph-ets and a-pos-tles, Loy-al to the liv-ing Word—
Keep her faith in sim-ple man-hood Strong as when her life be-gan,

Lord, we would with deep thanks-giv-ing Praise thee more for things un-seen.
For the o-pen door to man-hood, In a land the peo-ple rule.
For all he-roes of the Spir-it, Give we thanks to thee, O Lord.
Till it find its full fru-i-tion In the broth-er-hood of man! A-men.

196 Eternal Father, Strong to Save

Sts. 1–3, William Whiting, 1825–1878, cento, alt.
St. 4, Mary C. D. Hamilton

Melita 8. 8. 8. 8. 8. 8.
John B. Dykes, 1823–1876

1. E - ter - nal Fa - ther, strong to save, Whose arm hath bound the
2. O Christ! whose voice the wa - ters heard And hushed their rag - ing
3. Most Ho - ly Spir - it! who didst brood Up - on the cha - os
4. Lord, guard and guide the men who fly Through the great spac - es

rest - less wave, Who bidd'st the might - y o - cean deep
at thy word, Who walk - edst on the foam - ing deep,
dark and rude, And bid its an - gry tu - mult cease,
in the sky. Be with them al - ways in the air,

Its own ap - point - ed lim - its keep, O hear us when we
And calm a - midst its rage didst sleep, O hear us when we
And give, for wild con - fu - sion, peace, O hear us when we
In dark - ening storms or sun - light fair. O hear us when we

cry to thee For those in per - il on the sea!
cry to thee For those in per - il on the sea!
cry to thee For those in per - il on the sea!
lift our prayer For those in per - il in the air! A - men.

192

5. Eternal Father, grant, we pray,
   To all Marines, both night and day,
   The courage, honor, strength, and skill
   Their land to serve, thy law fulfill;
   Be thou the shield forevermore
   From every peril to the Corps.
   J. E. Seim, 1966

6. Lord, stand beside the men who build,
   And give them courage, strength, and skill.
   O grant them peace of heart and mind,
   And comfort loved ones left behind.
   Lord, hear our prayer for all Seabees,
   Where'er they be on land or sea.
   R. J. Dietrich, 1960, alt.

7. Lord God, our power evermore,
   Whose arm doth reach the ocean floor,
   Dive with our men beneath the sea;
   Traverse the depths protectively.
   O hear us when we pray, and keep
   Them safe from peril in the deep.
   David B. Miller, 1965

8. O God, protect the women who,
   In service, faith in thee renew;
   O guide devoted hands of skill
   And bless their work within thy will;
   Inspire their lives that they may be
   Examples fair on land and sea.
   Lines 1-4, Merle E. Strickland, 1972,
   and adapted by James D. Shannon, 1973.
   Lines 5-6, Beatrice M. Truitt, 1948

9. Creator, Father, who dost show
   Thy splendor in the ice and snow,
   Bless those who toil in summer light
   And through the cold antarctic night,
   As they thy frozen wonders learn;
   Bless those who wait for their return.
   L. E. Vogel, 1965

10. Eternal Father, Lord of hosts,
    Watch o'er the men who guard our coasts.
    Protect them from the raging seas
    And give them light and life and peace.
    Grant them from thy great throne above
    The shield and shelter of thy love.
    Author and date unknown

11. Eternal Father, King of birth,
    Who didst create the heaven and earth,
    And bid the planets and the sun
    Their own appointed orbits run:
    O hear us when we seek thy grace
    For those who soar through outer space.
    J. E. Volonte, 1961

12. Creator, Father, who first breathed
    In us the life that we received,
    By power of thy breath restore
    The ill, and men with wounds of war.
    Bless those who give their healing care,
    That life and laughter all may share.
    Galen H. Meyer, 1969
    Adapted by James D. Shannon, 1970

13. God, who dost still the restless foam,
    Protect the ones we love at home.
    Provide that they should always be
    By thine own grace both safe and free.
    O Father, hear us when we pray
    For those we love so far away.
    Hugh Taylor, date unknown

14. Lord, guard and guide the men who fly
    And those who on the ocean ply;
    Be with our troops upon the land,
    And all who for their country stand:
    Be with these guardians day and night
    And may their trust be in thy might.
    Author unknown, about 1955

15. O Father, King of earth and sea,
    We dedicate this ship to thee.
    In faith we send her on her way;
    In faith to thee we humbly pray:
    O hear from heaven our sailor's cry
    And watch and guard her from on high!

16. And when at length her course is run,
    Her work for home and country done,
    Of all the souls that in her sailed
    Let not one life in thee have failed;
    But hear from heaven our sailor's cry,
    And grant eternal life on high!
    Stanzas 15, 16, author and date unknown

Bless Thou the Astronauts Who Face

Ernest K. Emurian, 1912–

Melita 8. 8. 8. 8. 8. 8.
John B. Dykes, 1823–1876

1. Bless Thou the as - tro - nauts who face The vast im - men - si -
2. How ex - cel - lent in all the earth Thy name, O God, who
3. We still up - on thy laws de - pend As our do - min - ions
4. Give all men, for all time to be, The bless - ing of tran -

ties of space; And may they know, in air, on land,
gave it birth; When first up - on the moon man trod,
thus ex - tend, While from the na - tions tri - umph rings
quil - li - ty, As gal - ax - ies and qua - sars share

Thou hold - est them with - in thy hand. O may the small step
How ex - cel - lent thy name, O God. The heavens thy glo - ry
When we mount up with ea - gles' wings. Grant on each plan - et,
The knowl - edge that our God is there! May fu - ture ae - ons

each doth take Aid oth - ers gi - ant leaps to make.
doth de - clare; Wher - e'er we are, Lo! thou art there.
far and near, To all thy glo - ry may ap - pear.
call to mind, "We came in peace for all man - kind." A - men.

God of Our Fathers, Whose Almighty Hand 198

Daniel C. Roberts, 1841–1907

National Hymn 10. 10. 10. 10.
George William Warren, 1828–1902

Trumpets, before each stanza
(Optional)

1. God of our fa - thers, whose al - might - y
2. Thy love di - vine hath led us in the
3. From war's a - larms, from dead - ly pes - ti -
4. Re - fresh thy peo - ple on their toil - some

hand   Leads forth in beau - ty all the star - ry band
past;   In this free land by thee our lot is cast;
lence,   Be thy strong arm our ev - er sure de - fense;
way,   Lead us from night to nev - er - end - ing day;

Of shin - ing worlds in splen - dor through the skies,
Be thou our rul - er, guard - ian, guide, and stay;
Thy true re - li - gion in our hearts in - crease,
Fill all our lives with love and grace di - vine,

Our grate - ful songs be - fore thy throne a - rise.
Thy word our law, thy paths our cho - sen way.
Thy boun - teous good - ness nour - ish us in peace.
And glo - ry, laud, and praise be ev - er thine. A - men.

199 O God of Truth, the Power of Nations Free

Toulon 10. 10. 10. 10.

Daniel B. Merrick, Jr., 1926–

Abridged from Genevan Psalter, 1551

1. O God of truth, the power of na - tions free;
2. Armed by thy might, our fa - thers set us free.
3. Fix high our pur - pose in this fate - ful hour;
4. Thus let us fal - ter not at du - ty's call,

Source of all wis - dom, strength, and lib - er - ty;
Bind us to them in faith and loy - al - ty;
Save from the shame that blights the gift of power;
Which bids us seek a broth - er - hood for all,

Giv - er of faith, on whom our hopes de - pend:
Set high our aims, that jus - tice may pre - vail;
For - give our fool - ish pride, we hum - bly pray,
Build - ing through all the com - ing years with thee

Hear us as hymns of praise to thee as - cend.
Fill us with love, and hope that can - not fail.
Yet grant us cour - age e - qual to our day.
A com - mon - wealth u - nit - ed, strong and free. A - men.

O Beautiful for Spacious Skies

Katherine Lee Bates, 1859-1929

Materna C. M. D.
Samuel A. Ward, 1848-1903

1. O beau-ti-ful for spa-cious skies, For am-ber waves of grain,
2. O beau-ti-ful for pil-grim feet, Whose stern, im-pas-sioned stress
3. O beau-ti-ful for he-roes proved In lib-er-at-ing strife,
4. O beau-ti-ful for pa-triot dream That sees, be-yond the years,

For pur-ple moun-tain maj-es-ties A-bove the fruit-ed plain!
A thor-ough-fare for free-dom beat A-cross the wil-der-ness!
Who more than self their coun-try loved, And mer-cy more than life!
Thine al-a-bas-ter cit-ies gleam, Un-dimmed by hu-man tears!

A-mer-i-ca! A-mer-i-ca! God shed his grace on thee,
A-mer-i-ca! A-mer-i-ca! God mend thine ev-ery flaw,
A-mer-i-ca! A-mer-i-ca! May God thy gold re-fine,
A-mer-i-ca! A-mer-i-ca! God shed his grace on thee,

And crown thy good with broth-er-hood From sea to shin-ing sea!
Con-firm thy soul in self-con-trol, Thy lib-er-ty in law!
Till all suc-cess be no-ble-ness And ev-ery gain di-vine!
And crown thy good with broth-er-hood From sea to shin-ing sea! A-men.

201   O Say, Can You See

Francis Scott Key, 1779-1843,
cento, alt.

National Anthem Irregular
Ascribed to John Stafford Smith, 1750-1836

1. O say, can you see, by the dawn's ear-ly light,
2. On the shore dim-ly seen through the mists of the deep,
3. O thus be it ev-er when free men shall stand

What so proud-ly we hailed at the twi-light's last gleam-ing,
Where the foe's haugh-ty host in dread si-lence re-pos-es,
Be-tween their loved homes and the war's des-o-la-tion;

Whose broad stripes and bright stars, through the per-il-ous fight,
What is that which the breeze, o'er the tow-er-ing steep
Blest with vic-to-ry and peace, may the heaven-res-cued land

O'er the ram-parts we watched were so gal-lant-ly stream-ing?
As it fit-ful-ly blows, half con-ceals, half dis-clos-es?
Praise the Power that has made and pre-served us a na-tion.

202 Great God, We Sing That Mighty Hand

Wareham L. M.

Philip Doddridge, 1702-1751, alt.

William Knapp, 1698-1768

1. Great God, we sing that might-y hand By which sup-
2. By day, by night, at home, a - broad, Still are we
3. With grate - ful hearts the past we own; The fu - ture,
4. In scenes ex - alt - ed or de - pressed You are our
5. When death shall in - ter - rupt our songs And seal in

port - ed still we stand; The o - pening year your
guard - ed by our God: By his in - ces - sant
all to us un - known, We to your guard - ian
joy, and you our rest; Your good - ness all our
si - lence mor - tal tongues, Our help - er, God, in

mer - cy shows; That mer - cy crowns it till it close.
boun - ty fed, By his un - err - ing coun - sel led.
care com - mit And, peace - ful, leave be - fore your feet.
hopes shall raise, A - dored through all our chang - ing days.
whom we trust, In bet - ter worlds our souls shall boast. A-men.

203 O Lord of Hosts, Almighty King

Quebec L. M.

Oliver Wendell Holmes, 1809-1894

Henry Baker, 1835-1910

1. O Lord of hosts, al - might-y King, Be - hold the sac - ri - fice we bring:
2. Wake in our breasts the liv - ing fires, The ho - ly faith that warmed our sires;
3. Be thou a pil - lared flame to show The mid - night snare, the si - lent foe;
4. God of all na - tions, sov-ereign Lord, In thy dread name we draw the sword,
5. From trea-son's rent, from mur-der's stain, Guard thou its folds till peace shall reign,

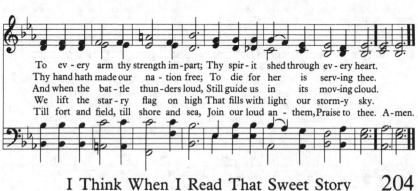

To ev - ery arm thy strength im-part; Thy spir- it shed through ev-ery heart.
Thy hand hath made our na - tion free; To die for her is serv-ing thee.
And when the bat - tle thun-ders loud, Still guide us in its mov-ing cloud.
We lift the star - ry flag on high That fills with light our storm-y sky.
Till fort and field, till shore and sea, Join our loud an - them, Praise to thee. A-men.

I Think When I Read That Sweet Story 204

Luke Irregular
Greek traditional melody
Arr. by William B. Bradbury, 1816–1868
Harm. by C. Winfred Douglas, 1867–1944

Jemima Luke, 1813–1906, cento, alt.

1. I think when I read that sweet sto - ry of old, When
2. I wish that his hands had been placed on my head, That his
3. Yet still to his foot - stool in prayer I may go, And

Je - sus was here a - mong men, How he called lit - tle chil - dren as
arms had been thrown a-round me, And that I might have seen his kind
know that I share in his love; And if I now ear - nest - ly

lambs to his fold: I should like to have been with them then.
look when he said, "Let the lit - tle ones come un - to me."
serve him be - low, I shall see him and serve him a - bove. A - men.

Harmonization used by permission of The Church Pension Fund.

I Love to Tell the Story

Arabella Catherine Hankey, 1834–1911, cento
Refrain by William G. Fischer, 1835–1912

Hankey 7. 6. 7. 6. D. with Refrain
William G. Fischer, 1835–1912

1. I love to tell the sto - ry Of un - seen things a - bove, Of Je - sus and his glo - ry, Of Je - sus and his love. I love to tell the sto - ry, Be - cause I know 'tis true; It sat - is - fies my long - ings As noth - ing else could do.

2. I love to tell the sto - ry; 'Tis plea - sant to re - peat What seems, each time I tell it, More won - der - ful - ly sweet. I love to tell the sto - ry, For some have nev - er heard The mes - sage of sal - va - tion From God's own ho - ly Word.

3. I love to tell the sto - ry; For those who know it best Seem hun - ger - ing and thirst-ing To hear it, like the rest. And when, in scenes of glo - ry, I sing the new, new song, 'Twill be the old, old sto - ry That I have loved so long.

Refrain

I love to tell the sto - ry, 'Twill be my theme in glo - ry To tell the old, old sto - ry Of Je - sus and his love. A - men.

Sing Them Over Again to Me 206

Wonderful Words 8. 6. 8. 6. 6. 6. with Refrain
Philip P. Bliss, 1838–1876
Harm. for 'The Hymnbook,' 1955

Philip P. Bliss, 1838–1876

1. Sing them o - ver a - gain to me, Won - der - ful words of life; Let me more of their beau - ty see, Won - der - ful words of life. Words of life and beau - ty Teach me faith and du - ty:
2. Christ, the bless - ed One, gives to all Won - der - ful words of life; Sin - ner, list to the lov - ing call, Won - der - ful words of life. All so free - ly giv - en, Woo - ing us to heav - en:
3. Sweet - ly ech - o the gos - pel call, Won - der - ful words of life; Of - fer par - don and peace to all, Won - der - ful words of life. Je - sus, on - ly Sav - ior, Sanc - ti - fy for - ev - er:

Refrain

Beau - ti - ful words, won - der - ful words, Won - der - ful words of life,

Beau - ti - ful words, won - der - ful words, Won - der - ful words of life. A - men.

Tell Me the Old, Old Story

Evangel 7. 6. 7. 6. D. with Refrain

Arabella Catherine Hankey, 1834–1911, cento

William H. Doane, 1832–1915

1. Tell me the old, old sto-ry Of un-seen things a - bove, Of Je-sus and his glo-ry, Of Je-sus and his love. Tell me the sto-ry sim-ply, As to a lit-tle child, For I am weak and wea-ry, And help-less and de - filed.
2. Tell me the sto-ry slow-ly, That I may take it in— That won-der-ful re - demp-tion, God's rem-e - dy for sin. Tell me the sto-ry of - ten, For I for-get so soon; The ear-ly dew of morn-ing Has passed a - way at noon.
3. Tell me the sto-ry soft-ly, With ear-nest tones and grave; Re - mem-ber, I'm the sin - ner Whom Je-sus came to save. Tell me the sto-ry al - ways, If you would real-ly be, In an-y time of trou-ble, A com-fort-er to me.

Refrain

Tell me the old, old sto-ry, Tell me the old, old sto-ry, Tell me the old, old sto-ry Of Je-sus and his love. A-men.

Stories of Jesus 8. 4. 8. 4. 5. 4. 5. 4.

William H. Parker, 1845-1929, cento

Frederic A. Challinor, 1866-1952

1. Tell me the sto - ries of Je - sus I love to hear;
2. First let me hear how the chil - dren Stood round his knee,
3. In - to the cit - y I'd fol - low The chil - dren's band,

Things I would ask him to tell me If he were here:
And I shall fan - cy his bless - ing Rest - ing on me;
Wav - ing a branch of the palm tree High in my hand;

Scenes by the way - side, Tales of the sea,
Words full of kind - ness, Deeds full of grace,
One of his her - alds, Yes, I would sing

Sto - ries of Je - sus, Tell them to me.
All in the love - light Of Je - sus' face.
Loud - est ho - san - nas, "Je - sus is King!" A - men.

We've a Story to Tell to the Nations

Message 10. 8. 8. 7. 7. with Refrain
Henry Ernest Nichol, 1862-1928
Henry Ernest Nichol, 1862-1928, alt.

1. We've a sto-ry to tell to the na-tions That shall turn their hearts to the right, A sto-ry of truth and mer-cy, A sto-ry of peace and light, A sto-ry of peace and light.
2. We've a song to be sung to the na-tions That shall lift their hearts to the Lord, A song that shall con-quer e-vil And shat-ter the spear and sword, And shat-ter the spear and sword.
3. We've a mes-sage to give to the na-tions, That the Lord who reign-eth a-bove Hath sent us his Son to save us, And show us that God is love, And show us that God is love.
4. We've a Sav-ior to show to the na-tions, Who the path of sor-row hath trod, That all of the world's great peo-ples Might come to the truth of God, Might come to the truth of God.

Refrain

For the dark-ness shall turn to dawn-ing, And the dawn-ing to noon-day bright,

Words and music copyright. Used by permission of H. E. Nichol, Kirkella, Hull, England.

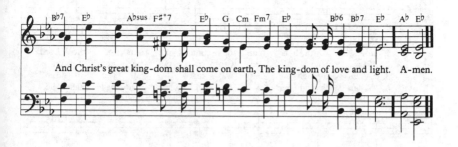

And Christ's great king-dom shall come on earth, The king-dom of love and light. A-men.

Break Thou the Bread of Life 210

Mary A. Lathbury, 1841–1913, cento

Bread of Life 6. 4. 6. 4. D.
William F. Sherwin, 1826–1888

1. Break thou the bread of life, Dear Lord, to me, As thou didst
2. Bless thou the truth, dear Lord, Now un-to me, As thou didst

break the loaves Be-side the sea; Be-yond the sa-cred page
bless the bread By Gal-i-lee; Then shall all bond-age cease,

I seek thee, Lord; My spir-it pants for thee, O liv-ing Word!
All fet-ters fall; And I shall find my peace, My All in All. A-men.

211

How Firm a Foundation

Anonymous in Rippon's
'Selection of Hymns,' 1787, cento, alt.

Foundation 11. 11. 11. 11.
American traditional melody

1. How firm a foun - da - tion, you saints of the Lord,
2. "Fear not, I am with you; O be not dis - mayed,
3. "When through the deep wa - ters I call you to go,
4. "When through fier - y tri - als your path - way shall lie,
5. "The soul that on Je - sus has leaned for re - pose,

Is laid for your faith in his ex - cel - lent Word!
For I am your God, and will still give you aid;
The riv - ers of sor - row shall not o - ver - flow;
My grace, all - suf - fi - cient, shall be your sup - ply,
I will not, I will not de - sert to his foes;

What more can he say than to you he has said,
I'll strength - en you, help you, and cause you to stand,
For I will be with you your trou - bles to bless,
The flame shall not hurt you; I on - ly de - sign
That soul, though all hell should en - deav - or to shake,

To you who for ref - uge to Je - sus have fled?
Up - held by my righ - teous, om - nip - o - tent hand.
And sanc - ti - fy to you your deep - est dis - tress.
Your dross to con-sume, and your gold to re - fine.
I'll nev - er, no, nev - er, no, nev - er for - sake!" A - men.

208

O Word of God Incarnate

Munich 7. 6. 7. 6. D.
'Neuvermehrtes Meiningisches Gesangbuch,' 1693
Arr. by Felix Mendelssohn, 1809–1847

William Walsham How, 1823–1897

212

1. O Word of God in-car-nate, O Wis-dom from on high,
2. The church from her dear Mas-ter Re-ceived the gift di-vine,
3. It float-eth like a ban-ner Be-fore God's host un-furled;
4. O make thy church, dear Sav-ior, A lamp of pur-est gold,

O Truth un-changed, un-chang-ing, O Light of our dark sky,
And still that light she lift-eth O'er all the earth to shine.
It shin-eth like a bea-con A-bove the dark-ling world.
To bear be-fore the na-tions Thy true light, as of old.

We praise thee for the ra-diance That from the hal-lowed page,
It is the gold-en cas-ket, Where gems of truth are stored;
It is the chart and com-pass That o'er life's surg-ing sea,
O teach thy wan-dering pil-grims By this their path to trace,

A lan-tern to our foot-steps, Shines on from age to age.
It is the heaven-drawn pic-ture Of Christ, the liv-ing Word.
'Mid mists and rocks and quick-sands, Still guides, O Christ, to thee.
Till, clouds and dark-ness end-ed, They see thee face to face. A-men.

213   The Spirit Breathes Upon the Word

Belmont C. M.

William Cowper, 1731–1800   *Arr. from William Gardiner, 'Sacred Melodies,' 1812*

1. The Spir - it breathes up - on the Word And brings the truth to sight;
2. A glo - ry gilds the sa - cred page, Maj-es - tic, like the sun:
3. The hand that gave it still sup - plies The gra - cious light and heat:
4. Let ev - er - last - ing thanks be thine For such a bright dis - play,
5. My soul re - joic - es to pur - sue The steps of him I love,

Pre - cepts and prom - is - es af - ford A sanc - ti - fy - ing light.
It gives a light to ev - ery age; It gives, but bor - rows none.
His truths up - on the na - tions rise; They rise, but nev - er set.
As makes a world of dark-ness shine With beams of heav - enly day.
Till glo - ry break up-on my view In bright-er worlds a - bove. A-men.

214   Unto Us a Child Is Born

Unto Us Irregular with Refrain
Lucien Deiss, 1921–

Lucien Deiss, 1921–

Refrain

Un - to us a child is born, Un - to

Fine

us a son is giv - en. E - ter - nal is his sway.

1. The people who walk in darkness have seen a great light;
2. For the yoke of his burden, and the bar on his shoul - der,
3. For to us a child is born, to our race a son is giv - en;
4. Ever wider shall his do - minion be over his king - dom;

For men a - - biding in the land of death, a new
And the rod of the op - pressor you have broken, as on the
His shoulders will bear the scepter of his reign, and his
Upon the throne of David, in a

splen - dor has ap - peared; To them you have brought a - bun - dant
day of Ma - di - an; For ev - ery boot that tramped in
name shall be called: Counselor of mar - vel - ous
peace that nev - er ends. He has estab - lished it and made it

joy. Before you they re - joice, as with the joy at
bat - tle, For every cloak that rolled in blood, will be set a -
deeds, Mighty War - - rior of God, everlasting
firm, Based on justice and on right: both now and for-

D.C.

harvest, as men re - joice when di - vid - ing spoils.
side, will go to feed the blaz - ing fire.
Father of nations, and royal Prince of Peace.
ever the Lord of hosts will do these might - y deeds.

215   Ye Watchers and Ye Holy Ones

Athelstan Riley, 1858-1945

Lasst uns erfreuen 8. 8. 4. 4. 8. 8. with Alleluias
Cologne, 'Geistliche Kirchengesänge,' 1623

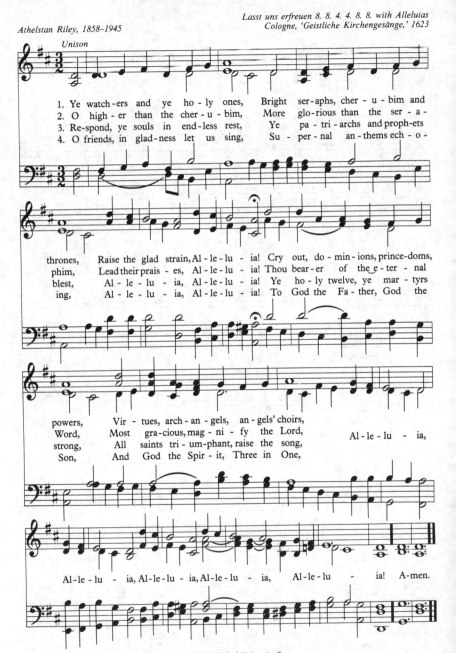

1. Ye watch-ers and ye ho-ly ones, Bright ser-aphs, cher-u-bim and thrones, Raise the glad strain, Al-le-lu-ia! Cry out, do-min-ions, prince-doms, powers, Vir-tues, arch-an-gels, an-gels' choirs, Al-le-lu-ia, Al-le-lu-ia, Al-le-lu-ia, Al-le-lu-ia, Al-le-lu-ia! A-men.

2. O high-er than the cher-u-bim, More glo-rious than the ser-a-phim, Lead their prais-es, Al-le-lu-ia! Thou bear-er of the e-ter-nal Word, Most gra-cious, mag-ni-fy the Lord,

3. Re-spond, ye souls in end-less rest, Ye pa-tri-archs and proph-ets blest, Al-le-lu-ia, Al-le-lu-ia! Ye ho-ly twelve, ye mar-tyrs strong, All saints tri-um-phant, raise the song,

4. O friends, in glad-ness let us sing, Su-per-nal an-thems ech-o-ing, Al-le-lu-ia, Al-le-lu-ia! To God the Fa-ther, God the Son, And God the Spir-it, Three in One,

Words from *The English Hymnal.* Used by permission of Oxford University Press.

Watchman, Tell Us of the Night

John Bowring, 1792–1872, alt.

St. George's Windsor 7. 7. 7. 7. D.
George J. Elvey, 1816–1893

1. Watch-man, tell us of the night, What its signs of prom-ise are.
2. Watch-man, tell us of the night; High-er yet that star as-cends.
3. Watch-man, tell us of the night, For the morn-ing seems to dawn.

Trav-eler, o'er yon moun-tain's height See that glo-ry-beam-ing star!
Trav-eler, bless-ed-ness and light, Peace and truth, its course por-tends.
Trav-eler, dark-ness takes its flight; Doubt and ter-ror are with-drawn.

Watch-man, does its beau-teous ray Aught of joy or hope fore-tell?
Watch-man, will its beams a-lone Gild the spot that gave them birth?
Watch-man, let your wan-derings cease; Has-ten to your qui-et home.

Trav-eler, yes; it brings the day, Prom-ised day of Is-ra-el.
Trav-eler, ag-es are its own, And it bursts o'er all the earth!
Trav-eler, lo, the Prince of Peace, Lo, the Son of God, is come! A-men.

213

Come, Thou Long-expected Jesus

Hyfrydol 8. 7. 8. 7. D.

Charles Wesley, 1707–1788

Rowland Hugh Prichard, 1811–1887

1. Come, thou long - ex - pect - ed Je - sus, Born to set thy peo - ple free;
2. Born thy peo - ple to de - liv - er, Born a child and yet a King,

From our fears and sins re - lease us; Let us find our rest in thee.
Born to reign in us for - ev - er, Now thy gra - cious king - dom bring.

Is - rael's Strength and Con - so - la - tion, Hope of all the earth thou art;
By thine own e - ter - nal Spir - it Rule in all our hearts a - lone;

Dear De - sire of ev - ery na - tion, Joy of ev - ery long - ing heart.
By thine all - suf - fi - cient mer - it Raise us to thy glo - rious throne. A - men.

O Come, O Come, Emmanuel

Anonymous, c. 12th century, cento
Tr. by John Mason Neale, 1818-1866, alt.

Veni Emmanuel 8. 8. 8. 8. 8. 8.
French, 'Processionale,' 15th century
Arr. by Thomas Helmore, 1811-1890

1. O come, O come, Emmanuel, And ransom captive Israel, That mourns in lonely exile here, Until the Son of God appear.

2. O come, thou Rod of Jesse, free Thine own from Satan's tyranny; From depths of hell thy people save And give them victory o'er the grave.

3. O come, thou Day-spring, come and cheer Our spirits by thine advent here; And drive away the shades of night, And pierce the clouds and bring us light!

4. O come, thou Key of David, come, And open wide our heavenly home; Make safe the way that leads on high, And close the path to misery.

Refrain

Rejoice! Rejoice! Emmanuel Shall come to thee, O Israel! Amen.

219   Wake, Awake, for Night Is Flying

Sleepers, Wake 8. 9. 8. 8. 9. 8. 6. 6. 4. 4. 4. 8.

Philipp Nicolai, 1556-1608
Tr. by Catherine Winkworth, 1827-1878, alt.

Philipp Nicolai, 1556-1608
Harm. by Johann Sebastian Bach, 1685-1750

1. Wake, a-wake, for night is fly - ing; The watch-men on the
2. Zi - on hears the watch-men sing - ing; Her heart with deep de-
3. Now let all the heavens a - dore thee, And men and an-gels sing

heights are cry - ing, A - wake, Je - ru - sa - lem, a - rise!
light is spring - ing, She wakes, she ris - es from her gloom,
be - fore thee With harp and cym - bal's clear - est tone;

Mid-night's sol - emn hour is toll - ing; His char - iot wheels are
For her Lord comes down all glo - rious, In grace ar - rayed, by
Of one pearl each shin - ing por - tal, Where we shall join the

near - er roll - ing; He comes! O Church, lift up thine eyes!
truth vic - to - rious; Her star is risen, her light is come!
choirs im - mor - tal In prais - es round thy glo - rious throne;

216

Rise up, with will - ing feet Go forth, the Bride - groom meet:
Ah, come thou bless - ed One, God's own be - lov - ed Son,
No vis - ion ev - er brought, No ear hath ev - er caught

Hal - le - lu - jah! Lo, great and small, We an - swer all;
Hal - le - lu - jah! We haste a - long, An ea - ger throng,
Such great glo - ry! There - fore will we, e - ter - nal - ly,

We fol - low where thy voice shall call.
And glad - some join the ad - vent song.
Sing hymns of joy and praise to thee. A - men.

220   Lo, How a Rose E'er Blooming

Anonymous German carol, 16th century, cento
Tr. by Theodore Baker, 1851-1934

Praetorius 7. 6. 7. 6. 6. 7. 6.
Cologne, 'Geistliche Kirchengesäng,' 1599

1. Lo, how a rose e'er bloom-ing From ten - der stem hath sprung,
2. I - sa - iah 'twas fore - told it, The rose I have in mind;

Of Jes - se's lin - eage com - ing, As men of old have sung.
With Mar - y we be - hold it, The vir - gin moth - er kind.

It came, a flower - et bright, A - mid the cold of
To show God's love a - right She bore to men a

win - ter When half spent was the night.
Sav - ior, When half spent was the night. A - men.

Hail, Holy Queen, Enthroned Above

Ascribed to Hermanus Contractus, 1013–1054
Tr. in 'Roman Hymnal,' New York, 1884

Salve Regina 8. 4. 8. 4. with Refrain
Hildesheim melody, 1736
Harm. by Nicola A. Montani, 1880–1948

1. Hail, ho - ly queen, en - throned a - bove, O Ma - ri - a!
2. Our life, our sweet - ness here be - low, O Ma - ri - a!

Hail, Moth-er of mer - cy and of love! O Ma - ri - a!
Our hope in sor - row and in woe, O Ma - ri - a!

Refrain

Tri - umph, all ye cher - u - bim, Sing with us, ye

ser - a - phim, Heaven and earth re - sound the hymn:

Sal - ve, Sal - ve, Sal - ve Re - gi - na!

Harmonization from *The St. Gregory Hymnal.* Used by permission of the Gregorian Institute of America.

Daily, Daily Sing to Mary

Ascribed to Bernard of Cluny, 12th century
Tr. by Henry Bittleston, 1818–1886, cento

Sunrise 8. 7. 8. 7. D.
Trier, 'Gesangbuch,' 1695

1. Dai - ly, dai - ly sing to Mar - y, Sing, my soul, her prais - es due;
2. She is might - y to de - liv - er; Call her, trust her lov - ing - ly;
3. Sing, my tongue, the Vir - gin's tro - phies, Who for us her Mak - er bore;

All her feasts, her ac - tions, hon - or With the heart's de - vo - tion true.
When the temp - est rag - es round thee, She will calm the trou - bled sea.
For the curse of old in - flict - ed Peace and bless - ing to re - store.

Lost in won-dering con - tem - pla - tion Be her maj - es - ty con - fessed.
Gifts of heav - en she has giv - en, No - ble La - dy, to our race;
Sing in songs of praise un - end - ing, Sing the world's ma - jes - tic queen.

Call her Moth - er, call her Vir - gin, Hap - py Moth - er, Vir - gin blest.
She, the queen who decks her sub - jects With the lights of God's own grace.
Wea - ry not, nor faint in tell - ing All the gifts she gives to men.

Sicilian Mariners 5. 5. 7. 5. 5. 10.
Sicilian melody, alt.

Melvin Farrell, 1930–

1. Vir - gin, full of grace, Pur - est of our race,
2. Mar - y, plead for us, In - ter - cede for us;
3. Queen of saints a - bove, Won - drous in your love,
4. Star of o - cean bright, Splen - dor in the night,

Hear your chil - dren, O Mar - y!
Hope of sin - ners, O Mar - y!
Rise to shield us, O Mar - y!
Guide us home - ward, O Mar - y!

Maid - en of glad - ness, Ban - ish our sad - ness:
You are the por - tal To life im - mor - tal:
Show us, O Moth - er, Je - sus, our Broth - er:
Help, we im - plore you, Your sons be - fore you:

Pray for us, O pray for us, O Mar - y!

224 Mary, We Greet Thee, Mother and Queen

11th century Latin office hymn, cento
Tr. by Melvin Farrell, 1930–

Salve Regina 13. 11. 11. 20.
Gregorian Mode V
Harm. by Albert de Klerk, 1917–

Mar - y, we greet thee, Moth - er and Queen all - mer - ci - ful:

Our life, our com - fort, and our hope, we hail thee. To thee we ex - iles,

chil - dren of Eve, lift our voic - es. To thee we send our sighs

while, mourn - ing and weep - ing, we pass through this vale of sor - row.

Haste, then, we pray; O our in-ter-ces-sor, look with pit-y, with eyes of love and ten-der-ness, up-on us sin - ners.

And, Moth - er, when this earth-ly ex - ile shall be end-ed, show us thy womb's most bless-ed fruit, thy Je - sus. O clem-ent,

O lov - ing, O gra-cious Vir-gin Mar - y.

225   Immaculate Mary, Your Praises We Sing

Anonymous
A. Police, 'Parochial Hymn Book,' Boston, 1897, alt.

L'Heure était venue 6. 5. 6. 5. with Refrain
French traditional melody (Lourdes)
Harm. by Lawrence D. Gagnier, 1921-

1. Im - mac - u - late Mar - y, your prais - es we sing;
2. In heav - en the bless - ed your glo - ry pro - claim;
3. We pray you, O Moth - er, may God's will be done;
4. We pray for our Moth - er, the church up - on earth;

You reign now with Christ, our Re - deem - er and King.
On earth we, your chil - dren, in - voke your fair name.
We pray for his glo - ry; may his king - dom come.
And bless, ho - ly Mar - y, the land of our birth.

Refrain

A - ve, a - ve, a - ve, Ma - ri - a!

A - ve, a - ve, Ma - ri - - - a!

Be Joyful, Mary, Heavenly Queen

Anonymous, 17th century, cento
Tr. anonymous, 17th century, alt.

Regina coeli jubila 8. 5. 8. 4. 7.
Leisentritt, 'Gesangbuch,' 1584, alt.

1. Be joy - ful, Mar - y, heav - enly queen, be joy - ful, Mar - y! Your grief is changed to joy se - rene, al - le - lu - ia! Re - joice, re - joice, O Mar - y!
2. The Son you bore by heav - en's grace, be joy - ful, Mar - y! Did by his death our guilt e - rase, al - le - lu - ia! Re - joice, re - joice, O Mar - y!
3. The Lord has ris - en from the dead, be joy - ful, Mar - y! He rose in glo - ry as he said, al - le - lu - ia! Re - joice, re - joice, O Mar - y!
4. Then pray to God, O Vir - gin fair, be joy - ful, Mar - y! That he our souls to heav - en bear, al - le - lu - ia! Re - joice, re - joice, O Mar - y!

227 The God Whom Earth and Sea and Sky

Eisenach L. M.
Ascribed to Venantius Fortunatus, 530–609, cento
Tr. by John Mason Neale, 1818–1866, alt.
Johann Hermann Schein, 1586–1630
Harm. by Johann Sebastian Bach, 1685–1750

1. The God whom earth and sea and sky
   A - dore and laud and mag - ni - fy,
   Whose might they own, whose praise they tell,
   In Mar - y's bod - y deigned to dwell.

2. O Moth - er blest! the cho - sen shrine
   Where - in the Ar - chi - tect di - vine,
   Whose hand con - tains the earth and sky,
   Came down in hid - den guise to lie.

3. Blest in the mes - sage Gab - riel brought;
   Blest in the work the Spir - it wrought;
   Most blest, to bring to hu - man birth
   The long de - sired of all the earth.

4. O Lord, the Vir - gin - born, to thee
   E - ter - nal praise and glo - ry be,
   Whom with the Fa - ther we a - dore,
   And Ho - ly Spir - it ev - er - more.

226

My Soul Magnifies the Lord

Magnificat Irregular
Ewald J. Bash, 1924–
Harm. by David Hugh Jones, 1900–

Luke 1:39–55

1. My soul mag-ni-fies the Lord, and my spir-it re-joic-es in God:
2. His mer-cy is on those who wor-ship him; his chil-dren in each gen-e-ra-tion.
3. He has helped his serv-ant Is-ra-el, in re-mem-brance of his mer-cy,

For he has re-gard-ed the low-li-ness of this poor maid-en.
And strong is his arm as he scat-ters the proud in the van-i-ty of their hearts.
As he spake to our fa-thers, to A-bra-ham and to his chil-dren for-ev-er.

Be-hold, all peo-ples in ev-ery age from this time shall call me bless-ed.
He has put down the might-y from their seats, and ex-alt-ed them of low de-gree.
Glo-ry to the Fa-ther, and to the Son, and to the Ho-ly Spir-it.

For he that is might-y does great things to me, and ho-ly is his name.
He has filled the hun-gry with good things, and the rich are sent emp-ty a-way.
As it was and is and ev-er shall be world with-out end. A-men.

229   Joy to the World! the Lord Is Come

Antioch C. M.
George Frederick Handel, 1685-1759
Arr. by Lowell Mason, 1792-1872
Descant by Donald D. Kettring, 1907-

Isaac Watts, 1674-1748, cento, alt.

1. Joy to the world! the Lord is come: Let earth re-
2. Joy to the earth! the Sav - ior reigns: Let men their
3. He rules the world with truth and grace, And makes the

Descant: 3. with truth and grace, And makes

ceive her King; Let ev - ery heart pre - pare him room,
songs em - ploy; While fields and floods, rocks, hills, and plains
na - tions prove The glo - ries of his righ - teous - ness,

Descant: the na-tions prove The glo - ries of his righ-teous-ness,

And heaven and na - ture sing, And heaven and na - ture
Re - peat the sound - ing joy, Re - peat the sound - ing
And won - ders of his love, And won - ders of his

Descant: And won - ders of his love, And won - ders

And heaven and na - ture sing, And
Re - peat the sound - ing joy, Re -
And won - ders of his love, And

Joy to the World! the Lord Is Come (cont.)

of his love, And won-ders, won - ders of his love. A - men.

A7 D G D Em D A7 D G D

sing, And heaven, and heaven and na - ture sing.
joy, Re - peat, re - peat the sound-ing joy.
love, And won - ders, won - ders of his love. A - men.

heaven and na - ture sing.
peat the sound - ing joy,
won - ders of his love,

Silent Night! Holy Night   230

Joseph Mohr, 1792–1848, cento
Sts. 1–3, tr. by John Freeman Young, 1820–1885, alt.
St. 4, tr. anonymous, alt.

Stille Nacht Irregular
Franz Gruber, 1787–1863

Bb Eb Bb Eb Bb F7 Bb Eb

1. Si - lent night! ho - ly night! All is calm, all is bright Round yon
2. Si - lent night! ho - ly night! Shep-herds quake at the sight, Glo - ries
3. Si - lent night! ho - ly night! Son of God, love's pure light Ra - diant
4. Si - lent night! ho - ly night! Won-drous Star, lend your light; With the

Eb Eb Bb Eb Bb Eb Bb Eb Bb

vir - gin moth - er and Child! Ho - ly In - fant, so ten - der and mild,
stream from heav - en a - far, Heav-enly hosts sing: "Al - le - lu - ia,
beams from your ho - ly face, With the dawn of re - deem - ing grace,
an - gels let us sing Al - le - lu - ia to our King;

F7 F Bb F7 Bb Eb Bb

Sleep in heav - en - ly peace, Sleep in heav - en - ly peace.
Christ the Sav - ior is born, Christ the Sav - ior is born."
Je - sus, Lord, at your birth, Je - sus, Lord, at your birth.
Christ the Sav - ior is born, Christ the Sav - ior is born. A - men.

229

231 Hark, the Herald Angels Sing

Mendelssohn 7. 7. 7. 7. D. with Refrain
Felix Mendelssohn, 1809–1847
Arr. by William H. Cummings, 1831–1915
Descant by Donald D. Kettring, 1907–

Charles Wesley, 1707–1788, cento, alt.

Descant
3. Hail! _____ hail, _____ right-teous-ness!

1. Hark, the her - ald an - gels sing, "Glo - ry to the new-born King;
2. Christ, by high - est heaven a - dored; Christ, the Ev - er - last - ing Lord!
3. Hail the heaven-born Prince of peace! Hail the Sun of right-teous-ness!

Light _____ to all he brings, Risen with heal - ing in his wings.

Peace on earth, and mer - cy mild, God and sin - ners rec - on - ciled!"
Late in time be - hold him come To the earth from heav - en's home;
Light and life to all he brings, Risen with heal - ing in his wings.

his glo - ry by, _____ no more may

Joy - ful, all ye na - tions, rise, Join the tri - umph of the skies;
Veiled in flesh the God - head see; Hail th' in - car - nate De - i - ty,
Mild he lays his glo - ry by, Born that man no more may die,

die, Born to raise the sons of earth, Hark! the

With th' an - gel - ic host pro - claim, "Christ is born in Beth - le - hem!"
Pleased as man with men to dwell, Je - sus, our Em - man - u - el.
Born to raise the sons of earth, Born to give them sec - ond birth.

Hark, the Herald Angels Sing (cont.)

Refrain

her - - ald an-gels sing, "Glo - ry to the new-born King!" A-men.

Hark, the her - ald an-gels sing, "Glo - ry to the new-born King!" A-men.

Let All Mortal Flesh Keep Silence 232

Liturgy of St. James
Tr. by Gerard Moultrie, 1829-1885

Picardy 8. 7. 8. 7. 8. 7.
French traditional melody

Unison

1. Let all mor-tal flesh keep si - lence, And with fear and trem - bling stand;
2. King of kings, yet born of Mar - y, As of old on earth he stood,
3. Rank on rank the host of heav-en Spreads its van-guard on the way,
4. At his feet the six - winged ser-aph; Cher - u - bim, with sleep-less eye,

Pon - der noth-ing earth - ly - mind - ed, For with bless - ing in his hand
Lord of lords, in hu - man ves - ture— In the bod - y and the blood—
As the Light of Light de - scend - eth From the realms of end - less day,
Veil their fac - es to the pres - ence, As with cease - less voice they cry,

Christ our God to earth de - scend - eth, Our full hom - age to de - mand.
He will give to all the faith - ful His own self for heav - enly food.
That the powers of hell may van - ish As the dark-ness clears a - way.
Al - le - lu - ia, Al - le - lu - ia, Al - le - lu - ia, Lord Most High! A-men.

231

233 I Wonder as I Wander, Out Under the Sky

As I Wander Irregular
American traditional melody
Arr. by John Jacob Niles, 1892–

Spiritual

1. I won - der as I wan - der, out un - der the sky, How
2. When Mar - y birthed Je - sus, 'twas in a cow's stall, With
3. If Je - sus had want - ed for an - y wee thing, A

Je - sus the Sav - ior did come for to die, For poor on' - ry peo - ple like
wise men and farm - ers and shep - herds and all. But high from the heav - ens a
star in the sky or a bird on the wing, Or all of God's an - gels in

you and like I— I won - der as I wan - der, out un - der the sky.
star's light did fall, And the prom - ise of ag - es it then did re - call.
heaven for to sing, He sure - ly could have had it, 'cause he was the King.

The Coming of Our God 234

Charles Coffin, 1676–1749
Tr. by Robert Campbell, 1814–1868, alt.

Optatus votis S. M.
Anonymous
Harm. by George R. Woodward, 1848–1934

1. The com-ing of our God Our thoughts must now em-ploy;
2. The co-e-ter-nal Son A maid-en's off-spring see;
3. Daugh-ter of Zi-on, rise To greet thine in-fant King;
4. In glo-ry from his throne A-gain will Christ de-scend;

Then let us meet him on the road With songs of ho-ly joy.
A serv-ant's form Christ put-teth on, To set his peo-ple free.
Nor let thy stub-born heart de-spise The par-don he doth bring.
And sum-mon all that are his own To joys that nev-er end.

5. Let deeds of darkness fly
   Before the approaching morn,
   For unto sin 'tis ours to die
   And serve the Virgin-born.

6. Our joyful praises sing
   To Christ, who set us free;
   Like tribute to the Father bring,
   And, Holy Ghost, to thee.

The Baby Is Born 235

Peter D. Smith, 1938–

Mary's View Irregular
Peter D. Smith, 1938–

1. The ba-by is born, I'm tired, I'm worn. Cry ba-by, cry.
2. You're born to save man: As God's Son you can. Cry ba-by, cry.
3. So soon you will grow, Your Fa-ther's will, know. Cry ba-by, cry.
4. You're hu-man, you're real, God's prom-ise to seal. Cry ba-by, cry.
5. But now you must sleep, Your mis-sion will keep. Sleep ba-by, sleep.

236   The Snow Lay on the Ground

Venite adoremus 6. 4. 6. 4. D. with Refrain

Anglo-Irish traditional carol
18th century (?), alt.

English traditional melody
Harm. by Leo Sowerby, 1895-1968

1. The snow lay on the ground, The stars shone bright, When
2. 'Twas Mar-y, daugh-ter pure Of ho-ly Anne, That
3. Saint Jo-seph, too, was by To tend the child; To
4. And thus that man-ger poor Be-came a throne, For

Christ our Lord was born On Christ-mas night.
brought in-to this world The God made man.
guard him, and pro-tect His moth-er mild:
he whom Mar-y bore Was God the Son.

Ve - ni - te a - do - re - mus Do - mi - num; Ve -
She laid him in a stall At Beth - le - hem; The
The an - gels hov - ered round, And sang this song, Ve -
O come, then, let us join The heav - enly host, To

ni - te a - do - re - mus Do - mi - num.
ass and ox - en shared The roof with them.
ni - te a - do - re - mus Do - mi - num.
praise the Fa - ther, Son, And Ho - ly Ghost.

Harmonization used by permission of Ronald Stalford, Executor, Estate of Leo Sowerby.

The Snow Lay on the Ground (cont.)

Refrain

Ve - ni - te a - do - re - mus Do - mi - num, Ve-

ni - te a - do - re - mus Do - mi - num. A - men.

I Am So Glad Each Christmas Eve 237

Marie Wexelsen, 1832–1911, cento
Tr. by Peter Andrew Sveeggen, 1881–1959

Christmas Eve C. M.
Peder Knudsen, 1819–1863

1. I am so glad each Christ-mas Eve, The night of Je - sus' birth!
2. The lit - tle child in Beth - le - hem, He was a King in - deed!
3. He dwells a - gain in heav - en's realm, The Son of God to - day;
4. I am so glad on Christ-mas Eve! His prais - es then I sing;
5. And so I love each Christ-mas Eve, And I love Je - sus too;

Then like the sun the star shone forth, And an - gels sang on earth.
For he came down from heaven a - bove To help a world in need.
And still he loves his lit - tle ones And hears them when they pray.
He o - pens then for ev - ery child The pal - ace of the King.
And that he loves me ev - ery day I know so well is true.

Words and music from the *Lutheran Service Book and Hymnal*. Used by permission of the Commission on the Liturgy and Hymnal.

238   There's a Star in the East

Rise Up Irregular
American Negro melody
Arr. by David Hugh Jones, 1900–

Spiritual

There's a star in the east on Christ-mas morn; Rise up, shep-herd, and fol - low. It will lead to the place where the Sav - ior is born; Rise up, shep-herd, and fol - low. Leave your sheep and leave your lambs; Rise up, shep-herd, and fol - low. Leave your ewes and leave your rams; Rise up, shep-herd, and fol - low. Fol - low, fol - low, Rise up, shep-herd, and

fol - low. Fol-low the star of Beth-le-hem; Rise up, shep-herd, and fol-low.

Once in Royal David's City 239

Irby 8. 7. 8. 7. 8. 7.

Cecil Frances Alexander, 1818-1895, cento

Henry J. Gauntlett, 1805-1876

1. Once in roy - al Da - vid's cit - y Stood a low - ly cat - tle shed,
2. He came down to earth from heav - en Who is God and Lord of all,
3. Je - sus is our child - hood's pat - tern, Day by day like us he grew;
4. And our eyes at last shall see him, Through his own re - deem - ing love;

Where a moth - er laid her ba - by In a man - ger for his bed:
And his shel - ter was a sta - ble, And his cra - dle was a stall:
He was lit - tle, weak, and help - less, Tears and smiles like us he knew:
For that child so dear and gen - tle Is our Lord in heaven a - bove,

Mar - y was that moth - er mild, Je - sus Christ, her lit - tle child.
With the poor, and mean, and low - ly, Lived on earth our Sav - ior ho - ly.
And he feel - eth for our sad - ness, And he shar - eth in our glad - ness.
And he leads his chil - dren on To the place where he is gone. A-men.

While Shepherds Watched Their Flocks

Christmas 8. 6. 8. 6. 6.
George Frederick Handel, 1685-1759
Arr. by David Weyman, 'Melodia
Sacra,' 1815

Nahum Tate, 1652–1715, cento, alt.

1. While shep-herds watched their flocks by night, All seat-ed on the
2. "Fear not," said he, for might-y dread Had seized their trou-bled
3. "To you, in Da - vid's town this day, Is born of Da - vid's
4. "The heav-enly Babe you there shall find To hu - man view dis -
5. "All glo - ry be to God on high, And to the earth be

ground, The an - gel of the Lord came down, And
mind; "Glad ti - dings of great joy I bring To
line The Sav - ior, who is Christ the Lord, And
played, All mean - ly wrapped in swath - ing bands, And
peace: Good will hence - forth, from heaven to men, Be -

glo - ry shone a - round, And glo - ry shone a - round.
you and all man - kind, To you and all man - kind.
this shall be the sign: And this shall be the sign:
in a man - ger laid, And in a man - ger laid."
gin and nev - er cease! Be - gin and nev - er cease!" A-men.

In Bethlehem 'Neath Starlit Skies

Waits' Carol 8. 8. 8. 8. 8. with Alleluias

Grace M. Stutsman, 1886-1970

Grace M. Stutsman, 1886-1970

Unison

1. In Beth - le - hem 'neath star - lit skies, Al - le - lu - ia, Al - le - lu - ia!
2. The hos - tel rang with song and shout; Al - le - lu - ia, Al - le - lu - ia!
3. And so, good friends, we wish you well; Al - le - lu - ia, Al - le - lu - ia!

A babe with - in a man - ger lies. Al - le - lu - ia, Al - le - lu - ia!
Yet none there were who looked with - out. Al - le - lu - ia, Al - le - lu - ia!
To you we sing this glad no - el. Al - le - lu - ia, Al - le - lu - ia!

No room in - side the hos - tel there For Jo - seph or Ma - don - na fair;
But ah! with - in that sta - ble old The beasts a won - drous sight be - hold:
Our sweet - est car - ols gai - ly ring To wel - come Christ, the in - fant King;

No one to light - en their de - spair. Al - le - lu - ia, Al - le - lu - ia!
Three wise men bear - ing gifts of gold! Al - le - lu - ia, Al - le - lu - ia!
To you the joy - ous news we bring. Al - le - lu - ia, Al - le - lu - ia!

Joseph Dearest, Joseph Mine

Anonymous German carol, c. 1500, cento
Tr. by Percy Dearmer, 1867–1936

Resonet in laudibus 7. 8. 8. 4. 7. with Refrain
German traditional carol, 15th century
Harm. by Ralph Vaughan Williams, 1872–1958

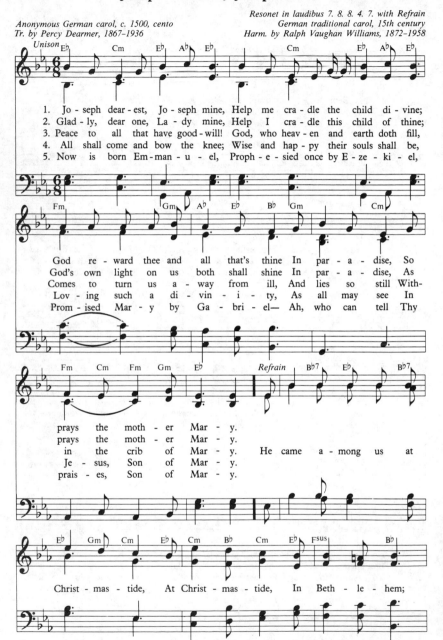

1. Jo - seph dear - est, Jo - seph mine, Help me cra - dle the child di - vine;
2. Glad - ly, dear one, La - dy mine, Help I cra - dle this child of thine;
3. Peace to all that have good - will! God, who heav - en and earth doth fill,
4. All shall come and bow the knee; Wise and hap - py their souls shall be,
5. Now is born Em - man - u - el, Proph - e - sied once by E - ze - ki - el,

God re - ward thee and all that's thine In par - a - dise, So
God's own light on us both shall shine In par - a - dise, As
Comes to turn us a - way from ill, And lies so still With-
Lov - ing such a di - vin - i - ty, As all may see In
Prom - ised Mar - y by Ga - bri - el— Ah, who can tell Thy

prays the moth - er Mar - y.
prays the moth - er Mar - y.
in the crib of Mar - y.
Je - sus, Son of Mar - y.
prais - es, Son of Mar - y.

Refrain

He came a - mong us at
Christ - mas - tide, At Christ - mas - tide, In Beth - le - hem;

Joseph Dearest, Joseph Mine (cont.)

Men shall bring him from far and wide Love's di - a - dem.

Je - sus, Je - sus, Lo, he comes, and loves, and saves, and frees us!

Still, Still, Still

243

Still, Still, Still 3. 6. 9. 8. 3. 6.

Austrian traditional carol
Tr. by George K. Evans, 1917–

Austrian traditional melody
Arr. by Walter Ehret, 1918–

1. Still, still, still, He sleeps this night so chill! The
2. Sleep, sleep, sleep, He lies in slum - ber deep While

Vir - gin's ten - der arms en - fold - ing, Warm and safe the Child are hold-ing.
an - gel hosts from heaven come wing-ing, Sweet-est songs of joy are sing-ing.

Still, still, still, He sleeps this night so chill.
Sleep, sleep, sleep, He lies in slum - ber deep.

Go, Tell It on the Mountain

Go Tell It 7. 6. 7. 6. with Refrain
American Negro melody
Arr. by John W. Work III, 1901–1967

Spiritual, cento
Adapted by John W. Work III, 1901–1967

Go, tell it on the moun-tain, O-ver the hills and ev-ery-where,

Go, tell it on the moun-tain That Je-sus Christ is born.

1. While shep-herds kept their watch-ing O'er si-lent flocks by night,
2. The shep-herds feared and trem-bled When lo! a-bove the earth
3. Down in a low-ly man-ger The hum-ble Christ was born,

Be-hold through-out the heav-ens There shone a ho-ly light.
Rang out the an-gel cho-rus That hailed our Sav-ior's birth.
And God sent us sal-va-tion That bless-ed Christ-mas morn.

Of the Father's Love Begotten   245

Aurelius Clemens Prudentius, 348–413, cento
Tr. by John Mason Neale, 1818–1866 and
Henry Williams Baker, 1821–1877

Divinum mysterium 8. 7. 8. 7. 8. 7. 7.
Plainsong, Mode V, 13th century
Arr. by C. Winfred Douglas, 1867–1944

1. Of the Fa-ther's love be-got-ten, Ere the worlds be-gan to be, He is Al-pha and O-meg-a, He the Source, the End-ing he, Of the things that are, that have been, And that fu-ture years shall see, Ev-er-more and ev-er-more!

2. O ye heights of heaven, a-dore him; An-gel hosts, his prais-es sing; Powers, do-min-ions, bow be-fore him, And ex-tol our God and King; Let no tongue on earth be si-lent, Ev-ery voice in con-cert ring, Ev-er-more and ev-er-more!

3. Christ, to thee with God the Fa-ther, And, O Ho-ly Ghost, to thee, Hymn and chant and high thanks-giv-ing And un-wea-ried prais-es be: Hon-or, glo-ry, and do-min-ion, And e-ter-nal vic-to-ry, Ev-er-more and ev-er-more! A-men.

Good Christian Men, Rejoice

German-Latin carol, 14th century, cento
Tr. by John Mason Neale, 1818–1866, alt.

In dulci jubilo 6. 6. 7. 7. 7. 8. 5. 5.
German traditional melody, 14th century, alt.

1. Good Chris-tian men, re - joice With heart and soul and voice;
2. Good Chris-tian men, re - joice With heart and soul and voice;
3. Good Chris-tian men, re - joice With heart and soul and voice;

Now give heed to what we say: Je - sus Christ is born to - day;
Now we hear of end - less bliss; Je - sus Christ was born for this!
Now we need not fear the grave; Je - sus Christ was born to save!

Ox and ass be - fore him bow, And he is in the man - ger now.
He un - bars the heav-enly door, And man is bless - ed ev - er - more.
Calls you one and calls you all To gain his ev - er - last - ing hall.

Christ is born to - day! Christ is born to - day!
Christ was born for this! Christ was born for this!
Christ was born to save! Christ was born to save!

God Rest You Merry, Gentlemen 247

God Rest Ye Merry, Irregular with Refrain
English traditional melody, 18th century
Harm. 'Christmas Carols Old and New,' 1871

English carol, 18th century, cento, alt.

1. God rest you mer - ry, gen - tle - men, Let noth - ing you dis - may.
2. From God, our heav - enly Fa - ther, A bless - ed an - gel came,
3. "Fear not, then," said the an - gel, "Let noth - ing you af - fright;
4. Now to the Lord sing prais - es, All you with - in this place,

Re - mem - ber, Christ our Sav - ior Was born on Christ - mas Day,
And un - to cer - tain shep - herds Brought ti - dings of the same:
This day is born a Sav - ior, Of a pure vir - gin bright,
And with true love and broth - er - hood Each oth - er now em - brace;

To save us all from Sa - tan's power When we were gone a - stray.
How that in Beth - le - hem was born The Son of God by name.
To free all those who trust in him From Sa - tan's power and might."
This ho - ly tide of Christ - mas All oth - er doth de - face.

Refrain

O ti - dings of com - fort and joy, com - fort and joy;

O ti - - dings of com - fort and joy!

248   The True Light That Enlightens Man

Michael Row Irregular with Refrain
American Negro melody
John Ylvisaker, 1937–   , alt.   *Arr. by Paul Abels, 1937–*

1. The true light that en-light-ens man, Al - le - lu - ia! Came to
2. And to all who be-lieve in him, Al - le - lu - ia! Free-dom
3. Word made flesh has dwelt with man, Al - le - lu - ia! We shall
4. For the law through Mo - ses came, Al - le - lu - ia! Grace and

earth from God's right hand, Al - le - lu - ia!
gave from bonds of sin, Al - le - lu - ia!
live with him a - gain, Al - le - lu - ia!
truth in Je - sus' name, Al - le - lu - ia!

Glo - ry be to thee, O Lord, Al - le - lu - ia!

Praise to thee, O Son of God, Al - le - lu - ia!

Gentle Mary Laid Her Child

Joseph Simpson Cook, 1859–1933

Tempus adest floridum 7. 6. 7. 6. D.
'Piae Cantiones,' 1582
Arr. by Ernest C. MacMillan, 1893–

1. Gen - tle Mar - y laid her child Low - ly in a man - ger;
2. An - gels sang a - bout his birth, Wise Men sought and found him;
3. Gen - tle Mar - y laid her child Low - ly in a man - ger;

There he lay, the un - de - filed, To the world a stran - ger.
Heav - en's star shone bright - ly forth, Glo - ry all a - round him.
He is still the un - de - filed, But no more a stran - ger.

Such a babe in such a place, Can he be the Sav - ior?
Shep - herds saw the won - drous sight, Heard the an - gels sing - ing;
Son of God of hum - ble birth, Beau - ti - ful the sto - ry;

Ask the saved of all the race, Who have found his fa - vor.
All the plains were lit that night, All the hills were ring - ing.
Praise his name in all the earth, Hail! the King of glo - ry! A-men.

250   Angels We Have Heard on High

Gloria 7. 7. 7. 7. with Refrain
French carol, 18th century, cento
Tr. in 'Crown of Jesus,' 1862, alt.
French carol melody
Arr. by Edward Shippen Barnes, 1887–1958

1. An - gels we have heard on high, Sing - ing sweet - ly through the night,
2. Shep - herds, why this ju - bi - lee? Why these songs of hap - py cheer?
3. Come to Beth - le - hem and see Him whose birth the an - gels sing;

And the moun - tains in re - ply Ech - o - ing their brave de - light.
What great bright-ness did you see? What glad ti - dings did you hear?
Come, a - dore on bend - ed knee Christ, the Lord, the new - born King.

Glo - - - - - - - ri - a

in ex - cel - sis De - o, Glo - - - - - - - -

- - - - ri - a in ex - cel - sis De - o.

Polish traditional carol
Para. by Edith M. G. Reed, 1885-1933

W zlobie lezy 4. 4. 7. 4. 4. 7. 4. 4. 4. 4. 7.
Polish carol
Harm. by David Hugh Jones, 1900–

1. In - fant ho - ly, In - fant low - ly, For his bed a cat - tle stall;
2. Flocks were sleep-ing; Shep-herds keep-ing Vig - il till the morn-ing new

Ox - en low - ing, Lit - tle know-ing Christ the Babe is Lord of all.
Saw the glo - ry, Heard the sto - ry, Ti - dings of a gos - pel true.

Swift are wing - ing An - gels sing - ing, No - els ring-ing,
Thus re - joic - ing, Free from sor - row, Prais - es voic-ing,

Ti - dings bring - ing: Christ the Babe is Lord of all.
Greet the mor - row: Christ the Babe was born for you. A - men.

Words from *Kingsway Carol Book;* used by permission of the publishers, Evans Brothers Limited. Music copyright 1955 by John Ribble; from *The Hymnbook;* used by permission.

252　Away in a Manger, No Crib for His Bed

Anonymous American
Sts. 1, 2, c. 1884, alt.
St. 3, c. 1892, alt.

Mueller 11. 11. 11. 11.
James R. Murray, 1841–1905
Descant by L. David Miller, 1919–

Descant

3. Ah _____ Ah ___

1. A - way　in　a　man - ger, no　crib　for　his　bed, The　lit - tle Lord
2. The cat - tle are low - ing, the　poor Ba - by wakes, But　lit - tle Lord
3. Be near　me, Lord Je - sus; I　ask　you　to　stay Close　by　me for -

Ah ___

Je - sus　laid down his sweet head. The　stars　in　the　sky　looked
Je - sus,　no　cry - ing　he　makes.　I　love　you, Lord Je - sus, look
ev - er　and love　me, I　pray. Bless all　the dear chil - dren in

Ah ___ A - men.

down where he lay, The　lit - tle Lord Je - sus, a - sleep on the hay.
down from the sky And stay　by　my side un - til morn - ing is nigh.
your ten - der care, And take　us　to heav - en　to live with you there. A - men.

Descant copyright 1962 by Muhlenberg Press. Used by permission of Fortress Press.

Anonymous German carol, 17th century
Tr. by Theodore Baker, 1851–1934, alt.

Jüngst 8. 8. 4. 3. 3. 3. 8. 8.
Trier, 'Gesangbuch,' 1871
Arr. by Hugo Jüngst, 1853–1923, alt.

1. While by my sheep I watched at night,
2. There has been born, so he did say,
3. There does he lie, in man - ger mean,
4. Lord, ev - er - more to me be nigh,

Glad ti - dings brought an an - gel bright.
In Beth - le - hem a child to - day.
Who shall re - deem the world from sin.
Then shall my heart be filled with joy.

How great my joy, great my joy, joy, joy, joy, joy, joy, joy!

Praise we the Lord in heaven on high! Praise we the Lord in heaven on high!
Be - ne - di - ca - mus Do - mi - no! Be - ne - di - ca - mus Do - mi - no!

O Little Town of Bethlehem

St. Louis 8. 6. 8. 6. 7. 6. 8. 6.

Phillips Brooks, 1835–1893, cento

Lewis H. Redner, 1831–1908

1. O lit-tle town of Beth-le-hem, How still we see thee lie;
2. For Christ is born of Mar-y; And gath-ered all a-bove,
3. How si-lent-ly, how si-lent-ly The won-drous gift is given!
4. O ho-ly Child of Beth-le-hem, De-scend to us, we pray;

A-bove thy deep and dream-less sleep The si-lent stars go by.
While mor-tals sleep, the an-gels keep Their watch of won-dering love.
So God im-parts to hu-man hearts The bless-ings of his heaven.
Cast out our sin, and en-ter in, Be born in us to-day.

Yet in thy dark streets shin-eth The ev-er-last-ing Light;
O morn-ing stars, to-geth-er Pro-claim the ho-ly birth;
No ear may hear his com-ing, But in this world of sin,
We hear the Christ-mas an-gels The great glad ti-dings tell;

The hopes and fears of all the years Are met in thee to-night.
And prais-es sing to God the King, And peace to men on earth.
Where meek souls will re-ceive him, still The dear Christ en-ters in.
O come to us, a-bide with us, Our Lord Em-man-u-el. A-men.

Alternative tune: *Forest Green*, Hymn 85.

John Francis Wade, c. 1711-1786, cento
Tr. by Frederick Oakeley, 1802-1880, alt.

Adeste fideles Irregular with Refrain
John Francis Wade, c. 1711-1786

1. O come, all ye faith - ful, joy - ful and tri - um-phant, O come ye, O
2. Sing, choirs of an - gels, sing in ex - ul - ta - tion; O sing, all ye
3. Yea, Lord, we greet thee, born this hap - py morn - ing: Je - sus, to

come ye to Beth - le - hem! Come and be - hold him, born the King of
cit - i - zens of heaven a - bove! Glo - ry to God, all glo - ry in the
thee be all glo - ry given; Word of the Fa - ther, now in flesh ap-

Refrain

an - gels!
high - est: O come, let us a - dore him, O come, let us a-
pear - ing:

dore him, O come, let us a - dore him, Christ the Lord! A-men.

O Holy Night

Ascribed to Cappeau de Roquemaure
Tr. by John S. Dwight, 1813–1893

Holy Night 11. 10. 11. 10. D.
Adolphe Adam, 1803–1856

1. O ho-ly night! the stars are bright-ly shin - ing,
2. Led by the light of faith se - rene-ly beam - ing,
3. Tru-ly he taught us to love one an - oth - er;

It is the night of the dear Sav-ior's birth. Long lay the
With glow-ing hearts by his cra-dle we stand; So led by
His law is love, and his gos-pel is peace; Chains shall he

world in sin and er - ror pin - ing, Till he ap-
light of a star sweet-ly gleam - ing, Here came the
break, for the slave is our broth - er, And in his

peared and the soul felt its worth. A thrill of hope the
wise men from O - ri - ent land. The King of kings lay
name all op - pres - sion shall cease. Sweet hymns of joy in

O Holy Night (cont.)

wea - ry soul re - joic - es, For yon - der breaks a new and glo - rious morn;
thus in low - ly man - ger, In all our tri - als born to be our friend;
grate - ful cho - rus raise we, Let all with - in us praise his ho - ly name;

Fall on your knees, Oh, hear the an - gel voic - es! O night di -
He knows our need, To our weak - ness is no stran - ger. Be - hold your
Christ is the Lord, Oh, praise his name for - ev - er! His power and

vine, O night when Christ was born! O night, O ho - ly
King, be - fore him low - ly bend! Be - hold your King, be-
glo - ry ev - er - more pro - claim! His

night, O night di - vine!
fore him low - ly bend!
power and glo - ry ev - er - more pro - claim.

255

It Came Upon the Midnight Clear

Carol C. M. D.

Edmund H. Sears, 1810–1876, cento, alt.

Richard Storrs Willis, 1819–1900

1. It came up-on the mid-night clear, That glo-rious song of old,
2. Still through the clo-ven skies they come, With peace-ful wings un-furled,
3. And ye, be-neath life's crush-ing load, Whose forms are bend-ing low,
4. For lo, the days are has-tening on, By proph-et bards fore-told,

From an-gels bend-ing near the earth To touch their harps of gold;
And still their heav-enly mu-sic floats O'er all the wea-ry world:
Who toil a-long the climb-ing way With pain-ful steps and slow,
When with the ev-er-cir-cling years Comes round the age of gold;

"Peace on the earth, good will to men, From heaven's all-gra-cious King":
A-bove its sad and low-ly plains They bend on hov-ering wing,
Look now, for glad and gold-en hours Come swift-ly on the wing:
When peace shall o-ver all the earth Its an-cient splen-dors fling,

The world in sol-emn still-ness lay, To hear the an-gels sing.
And ev-er o'er its Ba-bel sounds The bless-ed an-gels sing.
O rest be-side the wea-ry road, And hear the an-gels sing.
And the whole world send back the song Which now the an-gels sing. A-men.

Bring a Torch, Jeannette, Isabella! 258

Bring a Torch Irregular

French traditional carol, 17th century, cento
Tr. by E. Cuthbert Nunn, 1868-1914

Arr. from Marc-Antoine Charpentier, 1634-1702
Harm. by E. Cuthbert Nunn, 1868-1914

1. Bring a torch, Jeannette, Isabella! Bring a torch, to the cradle run! It is Jesus, good folk of the village; Christ is born and Mary's calling. Ah! ah! beautiful is the mother! Ah! ah! beautiful is her son!

2. It is wrong when the child is sleeping, It is wrong to talk so loud; Silence, all, as you gather around, Lest your noise should waken Jesus. Hush! hush! see how fast he slumbers; Hush! hush! see how fast he sleeps!

3. Softly to the little stable, Softly for a moment come; Look and see how charming is Jesus, How he is white, his cheeks are rosy. Hush! hush! see how the child is sleeping; Hush! hush! see how he smiles in dreams.

Angels, from the Realms of Glory

Regent Square 8. 7. 8. 7. 8. 7.
Henry Smart, 1813–1879
Descant by L. David Miller, 1919–

James Montgomery, 1771–1854, cento

1. An - gels, from the realms of glo - ry, Wing your flight o'er
2. Shep - herds, in the fields a - bid - ing, Watch - ing o'er your
3. Sag - es, leave your con - tem - pla - tions, Bright - er vi - sions
4. Saints, be - fore the al - tar bend - ing, Watch - ing long in

all the earth; Ye who sang cre - a - tion's sto - ry
flocks by night, God with man is now re - sid - ing,
beam a - far; Seek the great De - sire of na - tions;
hope and fear, Sud - den - ly the Lord, de - scend - ing,

Now pro - claim Mes - si - ah's birth: Come and wor - ship,
Yon - der shines the in - fant Light: Come and wor - ship,
Ye have seen his na - tal star: Come and wor - ship,
In his tem - ple shall ap - pear: Come and wor - ship,

Descant copyright 1962 by Muhlenberg Press. Used by permission of Fortress Press.

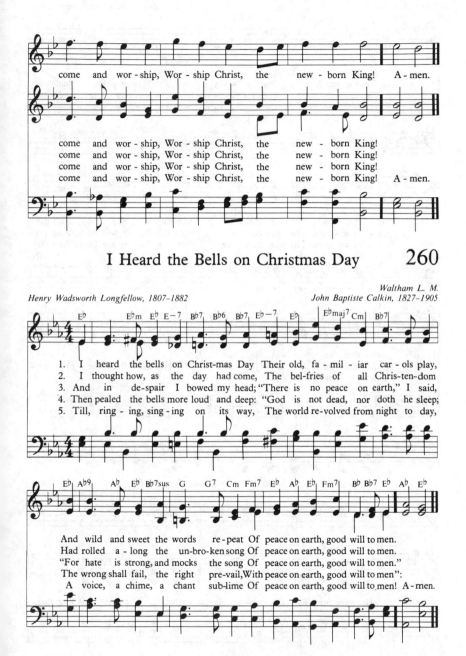

come and wor - ship, Wor - ship Christ, the new - born King! A - men.

come and wor - ship, Wor - ship Christ, the new - born King!
come and wor - ship, Wor - ship Christ, the new - born King!
come and wor - ship, Wor - ship Christ, the new - born King!
come and wor - ship, Wor - ship Christ, the new - born King! A - men.

I Heard the Bells on Christmas Day 260

Waltham L. M.

Henry Wadsworth Longfellow, 1807–1882

John Baptiste Calkin, 1827–1905

1. I heard the bells on Christ-mas Day Their old, fa - mil - iar car - ols play,
2. I thought how, as the day had come, The bel-fries of all Chris-ten-dom
3. And in de-spair I bowed my head; "There is no peace on earth," I said,
4. Then pealed the bells more loud and deep: "God is not dead, nor doth he sleep;
5. Till, ring - ing, sing - ing on its way, The world re-volved from night to day,

And wild and sweet the words re-peat Of peace on earth, good will to men.
Had rolled a - long the un-bro-ken song Of peace on earth, good will to men.
"For hate is strong, and mocks the song Of peace on earth, good will to men."
The wrong shall fail, the right pre-vail, With peace on earth, good will to men":
A voice, a chime, a chant sub-lime Of peace on earth, good will to men! A - men.

261   The Virgin Mary Had a Baby Boy

Baby Boy 10. 10. 10. 9. with Refrain
West Indies carol
Arr. by David Hugh Jones, 1900–

West Indies carol
Unison

1. The Vir-gin Mar-y had a ba-by boy, The Vir-gin Mar-y had a
2. The an-gels sang when the ba-by was born, The an-gels sang when the
3. The wise men saw where the ba-by was born, The wise men saw where the

ba - by boy, The Vir - gin Mar - y had a ba - by boy, And they
ba - by was born, The an - gels sang when the ba - by was born, And pro -
ba - by was born, The wise men saw where the ba - by was born, And they

say that his name was Je - sus.
claimed him the Sav - ior Je - sus.   He come from the glo - ry—
saw that his name was Je - sus.

He come from the glo - ri - ous king-dom; Oh, yes! be - liev - er.

He come from the glo - ry— He come from the glo - ri - ous king-dom.

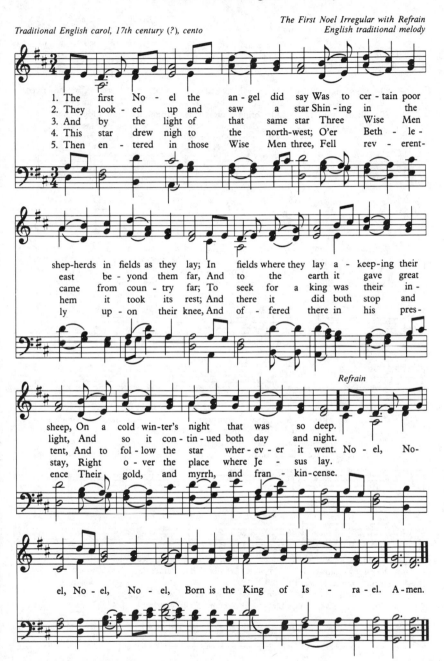

Traditional English carol, 17th century (?), cento

The First Noel Irregular with Refrain
English traditional melody

1. The first No - el the an - gel did say Was to cer - tain poor
2. They look - ed up and saw a star Shin - ing in the
3. And by the light of that same star Three Wise Men
4. This star drew nigh to the north-west; O'er Beth - le -
5. Then en - tered in those Wise Men three, Fell rev - erent-

shep-herds in fields as they lay; In fields where they lay a - keep-ing their
east be - yond them far, And to the earth it gave great
came from coun - try far; To seek for a king was their in -
hem it took its rest; And there it did both stop and
ly up - on their knee, And of - fered there in his pres-

Refrain

sheep, On a cold win-ter's night that was so deep.
light, And so it con - tin - ued both day and night.
tent, And to fol - low the star wher - ev - er it went. No - el, No-
stay, Right o - ver the place where Je - sus lay.
ence Their gold, and myrrh, and fran - kin-cense.

el, No - el, No - el, Born is the King of Is - ra - el. A-men.

263 Good King Wenceslas Looked Out

John Mason Neale, 1818–1866, *cento, alt.*

Tempus adest floridum 7. 6. 7. 6. D.
'Piae Cantiones,' 1582

1. Good King Wen - ces - las looked out On the Feast of Ste - phen,
2. "Hith - er, page, and stand by me, If you know it, tell - ing;
3. "Bring me food and bring me wine, Bring me pine logs hith - er.
4. "Sire, the night is dark - er now, And the wind blows strong - er;
5. In his mas - ter's steps he trod, Where the snow lay dint - ed;

When the snow lay round a - bout, Deep and crisp and e - ven.
Yon - der peas - ant, who is he? Where and what his dwell - ing?"
You and I will see him dine When we bear them thith - er."
Fails my heart, I know not how; I can go no long - er."
Heat was in the ver - y sod Which the saint had print - ed.

Bright - ly shown the moon that night, Tho' the frost was cru - el,
"Sire, he lives a good league hence, Un - der - neath the moun - tain;
Page and mon - arch, forth they went, Forth they went to - geth - er;
"Mark my foot - steps, my good page; Tread now in them bold - ly;
There - fore, Chris - tian men, be sure, Wealth or rank pos - sess - ing,

When a poor man came in sight, Gath - er - ing win - ter fu - el.
Right a - gainst the for - est fence, By Saint Ag - nes' foun - tain."
Through the cold wind's wild la - ment And the bit - ter weath - er.
You shall find the win - ter's rage Freeze your blood less cold - ly."
You who now will bless the poor Shall your - selves find bless - ing.

We Three Kings of Orient Are

264

Kings of Orient 8. 8. 8. 6. with Refrain

John H. Hopkins, Jr., 1820–1891, alt.

John H. Hopkins, Jr., 1820–1891, alt.

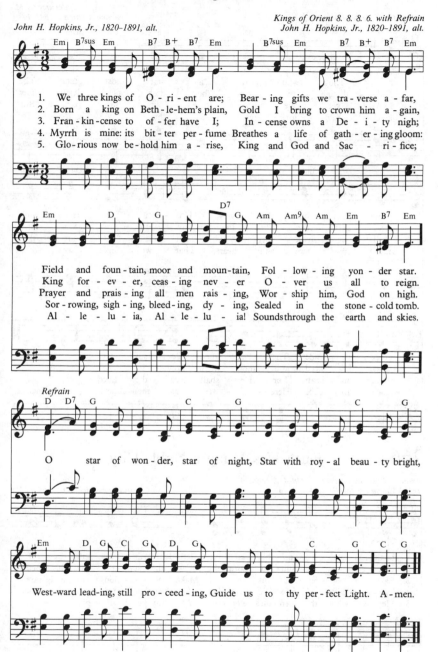

1. We three kings of O - ri - ent are; Bear - ing gifts we tra - verse a - far,
2. Born a king on Beth - le - hem's plain, Gold I bring to crown him a - gain,
3. Fran - kin - cense to of - fer have I; In - cense owns a De - i - ty nigh;
4. Myrrh is mine: its bit - ter per - fume Breathes a life of gath - er - ing gloom:
5. Glo - rious now be - hold him a - rise, King and God and Sac - ri - fice;

Field and foun - tain, moor and moun - tain, Fol - low - ing yon - der star.
King for - ev - er, ceas - ing nev - er O - ver us all to reign.
Prayer and prais - ing all men rais - ing, Wor - ship him, God on high.
Sor - row - ing, sigh - ing, bleed - ing, dy - ing, Sealed in the stone - cold tomb.
Al - le - lu - ia, Al - le - lu - ia! Sounds through the earth and skies.

Refrain

O star of won - der, star of night, Star with roy - al beau - ty bright,

West - ward lead - ing, still pro - ceed - ing, Guide us to thy per - fect Light. A - men.

263

265   O Thou Who by a Star Didst Guide

John Mason Neale, 1818–1866, cento

Dalehurst C. M.
Arthur Cottman, 1842–1879

1. O Thou who by a star didst guide The Wise Men on their way, Un - til it came and stood be - side The place where Je - sus lay,
2. Al - though by stars thou dost not lead Thy serv - ants now be - low, Thy Ho - ly Spir - it, when they need, Will show them how to go.
3. As yet we know thee but in part; But still we trust thy Word, That bless - ed are the pure in heart, For they shall see the Lord.
4. O Sav - ior, give us then thy grace To make us pure in heart, That we may see thee face to face Here - af - ter, as thou art. A - men.

266   Earth Has Many a Noble City

Aurelius Clemens Prudentius, 348–413, cento
Tr. by Edward Caswall, 1814–1878, alt.

Stuttgart 8. 7. 8. 7.
Christian Friedrich Witt, 1660–1716

1. Earth has man - y a no - ble cit - y; Beth-lehem, thou dost all ex - cel:
2. Fair - er than the sun at morn - ing Was the star that told his birth,
3. East - ern sag - es at his cra - dle Make ob - la - tions rich and rare;
4. Sa - cred gifts of mys - tic mean - ing: In - cense doth their God dis - close,
5. Je - su, whom the Gen - tiles wor-shiped At thy glad E - piph - a - ny,

Out of thee the Lord from heav-en Came to rule his Is - ra - el.
To the world its God an-nounc-ing Seen in flesh-ly form on earth.
See them give, in deep de - vo-tion, Gold and fran - kin - cense and myrrh.
Gold the King of kings pro-claim-eth, Myrrh his sep - ul - cher fore-shows.
Un - to thee, with God the Fa - ther And the Spir - it, glo - ry be. A-men.

As with Gladness Men of Old 267

Dix 7. 7. 7. 7. 7. 7.
Adapted from Conrad Kocher, 1786–1872
by William H. Monk, 1823–1889

William Chatterton Dix, 1837-1898, cento, alt.

1. As with glad-ness men of old Did the guid-ing star be-hold;
2. As with joy - ful steps they sped, Sav - ior, to your low - ly bed,
3. As they of - fered gifts most rare At your cra - dle rude and bare,
4. Ho - ly Je - sus, ev - ery day Keep us in the nar - row way;

As with joy they hailed its light, Lead-ing on-ward, beam-ing bright;
There to bend the knee be - fore You whom heaven and earth a - dore,
So may we with ho - ly joy, Pure, and free from sin's al - loy,
And, when earth-ly things are past, Bring our ran-somed souls at last

So, Lord Je - sus, may we too Ev - er-more be led to you.
So may we with will - ing feet Ev - er seek your mer - cy seat.
All our cost-liest trea - sures bring, Christ, to you, our heav-enly King.
Where they need no star to guide, Where no clouds your glo - ry hide. A-men.

268 Brightest and Best of the Sons of the Morning

Reginald Heber, 1783–1826, cento

Morning Star 11. 10. 11. 10.
James P. Harding, c. 1850–1911

1. Bright - est and best of the sons of the morn - ing,
2. Cold on his cra - dle the dew - drops are shin - ing;
3. Say, shall we yield him, in cost - ly de - vo - tion,
4. Vain - ly we of - fer each am - ple ob - la - tion;

Dawn on our dark - ness and lend us thine aid;
Low lies his head with the beasts of the stall;
O - dors of E - dom and of - ferings di - vine,
Vain - ly with gifts would his fa - vor se - cure;

Star of the East, the ho - ri - zon a - dorn - ing,
An - gels a - dore him in slum - ber re - clin - ing,
Gems of the moun - tain and pearls of the o - cean,
Rich - er by far is the heart's ad - o - ra - tion;

Guide where our in - fant Re - deem - er is laid.
Mak - er and Mon - arch and Sav - ior of all.
Myrrh from the for - est and gold from the mine?
Dear - er to God are the prayers of the poor. A - men.

What Star Is This, with Beams So Bright 269

Puer nobis nascitur L. M.
'Piae Cantiones,' 1582

Charles Coffin, 1676–1749, cento
Tr. by John Chandler, 1806–1876, alt.

Adapted by Michael Praetorius, 1571–1621
Harm. by George R. Woodward, 1848–1934

1. What star is this, with beams so bright, More love - ly than the noon - day light? 'Tis sent to announce a new - born king, Glad ti - dings of our God to bring.

2. 'Tis now ful - filled what God de - creed, "From Ja - cob shall a star pro - ceed"; And lo! the east - ern sag - es stand, To read in heaven the Lord's com - mand.

3. O Je - sus, while the star of grace Im - pels us on to seek thy face, Let not our sloth - ful hearts re - fuse The guid - ance of thy light to use.

4. To God the Fa - ther, heav - enly Light, To Christ, re - vealed in earth - ly night, To God the Ho - ly Ghost we raise An end - less song of thank - ful praise! A - men.

Arrangement of music from *The Cowley Carol Book.* Used by permission of A. R. Mowbray & Co. Ltd.

There's a Song in the Air

Christmas Song 6. 6. 6. 6. 12. 12.

Josiah G. Holland, 1819–1881, alt.

Karl P. Harrington, 1861–1953

1. There's a song in the air! There's a star in the sky! There's a moth-er's deep prayer And a ba-by's low cry! And the star rains its fire while the beau-ti-ful sing, For the man-ger of Beth-le-hem cra-dles a King!

2. There's a tu-mult of joy O'er the won-der-ful birth, For the Vir-gin's sweet boy Is the Lord of the earth. Yes the star rains its fire while the beau-ti-ful sing, For the man-ger of Beth-le-hem cra-dles a King!

3. In the light of that star Lie the ag-es im-pearled; And that song from a-far Has swept o-ver the world. Ev-ery hearth is a-flame, and the beau-ti-ful sing In the homes of the na-tions that Je-sus is King!

4. We re-joice in the light, And we ech-o the song That comes down through the night From the heav-en-ly throng. Yes we shout to the love-ly e-van-gel they bring, And we greet in his cra-dle our Sav-ior and King!

The Wise May Bring Their Learning 271

Anonymous
'Book of Praise for Children,' 1881

Christmas Morn 7. 6. 7. 6. D.
Edward J. Hopkins, 1818-1901

1. The wise may bring their learn-ing, The rich may bring their wealth,
2. We'll bring him hearts that love him; We'll bring him thank-ful praise,
3. We'll bring the lit-tle du-ties We have to do each day;

And some may bring their great-ness, And some bring strength and health;
And young souls meek-ly striv-ing To walk in ho-ly ways;
We'll try our best to please him, At home, at school, at play;

We, too, would bring our trea-sures To of-fer to the King;
And these shall be the trea-sures We of-fer to the King,
And bet-ter are these trea-sures To of-fer to our King

We have no wealth or learn-ing: What shall we chil-dren bring?
And these are gifts that e-ven The poor-est child may bring.
Than rich-est gifts with-out them—Yet these a child may bring.

Words and music from the *Lutheran Service Book and Hymnal.* Used by permission of the Commission on the Liturgy and Hymnal.

What Child Is This, Who, Laid to Rest

Greensleeves 8. 7. 8. 7. 6. 8. 6. 7.

William Chatterton Dix, 1837-1898

English traditional melody

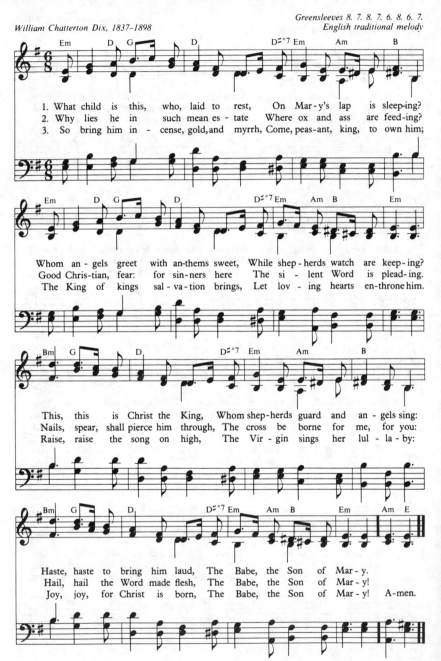

1. What child is this, who, laid to rest, On Mar-y's lap is sleep-ing?
2. Why lies he in such mean es - tate Where ox and ass are feed-ing?
3. So bring him in - cense, gold, and myrrh, Come, peas-ant, king, to own him;

Whom an - gels greet with an-thems sweet, While shep - herds watch are keep-ing?
Good Chris-tian, fear: for sin-ners here The si - lent Word is plead-ing.
The King of kings sal - va-tion brings, Let lov - ing hearts en-throne him.

This, this is Christ the King, Whom shep-herds guard and an - gels sing:
Nails, spear, shall pierce him through, The cross be borne for me, for you:
Raise, raise the song on high, The Vir - gin sings her lul - la - by:

Haste, haste to bring him laud, The Babe, the Son of Mar - y.
Hail, hail the Word made flesh, The Babe, the Son of Mar - y!
Joy, joy, for Christ is born, The Babe, the Son of Mar - y! A-men.

Emily E. S. Elliott, 1836–1897, cento, alt.

Margaret (Matthews) Irregular
Timothy R. Matthews, 1826–1910

1. Thou didst leave thy throne and thy king - ly crown When thou cam - est to earth for me; But in Beth - le - hem's home there was found no room For thy ho - ly na - tiv - i - ty. O come to my heart, Lord Je - sus: There is room in my heart for thee!

2. Heav - en's arch - es rang when the an - gels sang, Pro - claim - ing thy roy - al de - gree; But in low - ly birth didst thou come to earth, And in great hu - mil - i - ty. O come to my heart, Lord Je - sus: There is room in my heart for thee!

3. Thou cam - est, O Lord, with the liv - ing Word That should set thy peo - ple free; But with mock - ing scorn and with crown of thorn They bore thee to Cal - va - ry. O come to my heart, Lord Je - sus: There is room in my heart for thee!

4. When the heavens shall ring, and the an - gels sing At thy com - ing to vic - to - ry, Let thy voice call me home, say - ing, "Yet there is room, There is room at my side for thee." And my heart shall re - joice, Lord Je - sus: There is room in my heart for thee! A - men.

274   One Day When Heaven Was Filled

Chapman 11. 10. 11. 10. with Refrain

J. Wilbur Chapman, 1859–1918

Charles H. Marsh, 1885–1956

1. One day when heav - en was filled with his prais - es, One day when
2. One day they led him up Cal - va - ry's moun - tain, One day they
3. One day they left him a - lone in the gar - den, One day he
4. One day the grave could con - ceal him no lon - ger, One day the
5. One day the trum - pet will sound for his com - ing, One day the

sin was as black as could be, Je - sus came forth to be
nailed him to die on the tree; Suf - fer - ing an - guish, de -
rest - ed, from suf - fer - ing free; An - gels came down o'er his
stone rolled a - way from the door; Then he a - rose, o - ver
skies with his glo - ry will shine; Won - der - ful day, my be -

born of a vir - gin, Dwelt a - mong men: my ex - am - ple is he!
spised and re - ject - ed, Bear - ing our sins, my Re - deem - er is he!
tomb to keep vig - il; Hope of the hope - less, my Sav - ior is he!
death he has con - quered; Now is as - cend - ed, my Lord ev - er - more!
lov - ed ones bring - ing; Glo - ri - ous Sav - ior, this Je - sus is mine!

Refrain

Liv - ing, he loved me; dy - ing, he saved me; Bur - ied, he

car - ried my sins far a - way; Ris - ing, he jus - ti - fied

free - ly for - ev - er: One day he's com - ing— oh, glo - ri - ous day!

Fairest Lord Jesus 275

St. Elizabeth 5. 6. 8. 5. 5. 8.

Anonymous, 'Münster Gesangbuch,' 1677, cento
Tr. anonymous, 1850

Leipzig, 'Schlesische Volkslieder,' 1842
Arr. by Richard Storrs Willis, 1819–1900

1. Fair - est Lord Je - sus, Rul - er of all na - ture,
2. Fair are the mead - ows, Fair - er still the wood - lands,
3. Fair is the sun - shine, Fair - er still the moon - light,

O thou of God and man the Son, Thee will I cher - ish,
Robed in the bloom - ing garb of spring: Je - sus is fair - er,
And all the twin - kling star - ry host: Je - sus shines bright - er,

Thee will I hon - or, Thou, my soul's glo - ry, joy, and crown.
Je - sus is pur - er, Who makes the woe - ful heart to sing.
Je - sus shines pur - er, Than all the an - gels heaven can boast. A - men.

276   It Fell Upon a Summer Day

Childhood 8. 8. 8. 6.

Stopford Augustus Brooke, 1832-1916, cento

Henry Walford Davies, 1869-1941

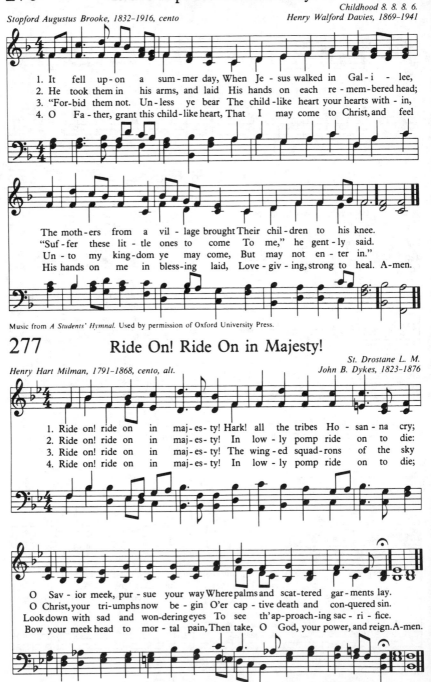

1. It fell up-on a sum-mer day, When Je - sus walked in Gal - i - lee,
2. He took them in his arms, and laid His hands on each re - mem-bered head;
3. "For-bid them not. Un - less ye bear The child -like heart your hearts with - in,
4. O Fa - ther, grant this child-like heart, That I may come to Christ, and feel

The moth-ers from a vil - lage brought Their chil - dren to his knee.
"Suf - fer these lit - tle ones to come To me," he gent - ly said.
Un - to my king-dom ye may come, But may not en - ter in."
His hands on me in bless-ing laid, Love - giv - ing, strong to heal. A-men.

Music from *A Students' Hymnal*. Used by permission of Oxford University Press.

277   Ride On! Ride On in Majesty!

St. Drostane L. M.

Henry Hart Milman, 1791-1868, cento, alt.

John B. Dykes, 1823-1876

1. Ride on! ride on in maj - es - ty! Hark! all the tribes Ho - san - na cry;
2. Ride on! ride on in maj - es - ty! In low - ly pomp ride on to die:
3. Ride on! ride on in maj - es - ty! The wing - ed squad-rons of the sky
4. Ride on! ride on in maj - es - ty! In low - ly pomp ride on to die;

O Sav - ior meek, pur - sue your way Where palms and scat-tered gar-ments lay.
O Christ, your tri-umphs now be - gin O'er cap - tive death and con-quered sin.
Look down with sad and won-dering eyes To see th'ap-proach-ing sac - ri - fice.
Bow your meek head to mor - tal pain, Then take, O God, your power, and reign. A-men.

All Hail the Power of Jesus' Name! 278

Sts. 1–3, Edward Perronet, 1726–1792, cento, alt.
St. 4, John Rippon, 1751–1836

Coronation C. M.
Oliver Holden, 1765–1844
Descant by L. David Miller, 1919–

1. All hail the power of Je - sus' name! Let an - gels pros - trate fall;
2. You cho - sen seed of Is - rael's race, You ran - somed from the Fall,
3. Let ev - ery kin - dred, ev - ery tribe, On this ter - res - trial ball,
4. O that with yon - der sa - cred throng We at his feet may fall!

Bring forth the roy - al di - a - dem, And crown him Lord of all;
Hail him who saves you by his grace, And crown him Lord of all;
To him all maj - es - ty as - cribe, And crown him Lord of all;
We'll join the ev - er - last - ing song, And crown him Lord of all;

Bring forth the roy - al di - a - dem, And crown him Lord of all!
Hail him who saves you by his grace, And crown him Lord of all!
To him all maj - es - ty as - cribe, And crown him Lord of all!
We'll join the ev - er - last - ing song, And crown him Lord of all! A-men.

279 Hosanna, Loud Hosanna

Ellacombe 7. 6. 7. 6. D.
'Gesangbuch der h. w.
kath. Hofkapelle,' Württemberg, 1784

Jeannette Threlfall, 1821–1880, cento

1. Ho - san - na, loud ho - san - na The lit - tle chil - dren sang;
2. From Ol - i - vet they fol - lowed Mid an ex - ult - ant crowd,
3. "Ho - san - na in the high - est!" That an - cient song we sing,

Through pil - lared court and tem - ple The joy - ful an - them rang;
The vic - tor palm branch wav - ing, And chant - ing clear and loud;
For Christ is our Re - deem - er, The Lord of heaven our King.

To Je - sus, who had blessed them Close fold - ed to his breast,
The Lord of men and an - gels Rode on in low - ly state,
O may we ev - er praise him With heart and life and voice,

The chil - dren sang their prais - es, The sim - plest and the best.
Nor scorned that lit - tle chil - dren Should on his bid - ding wait.
And in his bliss - ful pres - ence E - ter - nal - ly re - joice. A - men.

When Jesus Left His Father's Throne 280

Kingsfold C. M. D.

James Montgomery, 1771–1854,
cento, alt.

Melody coll. by Lucy Broadwood, 1858–1929
Harm. and arr. by Ralph Vaughan Williams, 1872–1958

1. When Jesus left his Father's throne, He chose an humble birth;
2. Sweet were his words and kind his look When mothers round him pressed;
3. When Jesus into Zion rode, The children sang around;

Like us, unhonored and unknown, He came to dwell on earth.
Their infants in his arms he took, And on his bosom blessed.
For joy they plucked the palms and strewed Their garments on the ground.

Like him may we be found below, In wisdom's path of peace;
Safe from the world's alluring harms, Beneath his watchful eye,
Hosanna our glad voices raise, Hosanna to our King!

Like him in grace and knowledge grow, As years and strength increase.
Thus in the circle of his arms May we forever lie.
Should we forget our Savior's praise, The stones themselves would sing.

Music from *The English Hymnal.* Used by permission of Oxford University Press.

277

All Glory, Laud, and Honor

Theodulph of Orleans, c. 750–821, cento
Tr. by John Mason Neale, 1818–1866

St. Theodulph 7. 6. 7. 6. D.
Melchior Teschner, 1584–1635

1. All glo - ry, laud, and hon - or To thee, Re - deem - er, King,
2. Thou art the King of Is - rael, Thou Da - vid's roy - al Son,
3. Thou didst ac - cept their prais - es; Ac - cept the prayers we bring,

To whom the lips of chil - dren Made sweet ho - san - nas ring!
Who in the Lord's name com - est, The King and bless - ed One!
Who in all good de - light - est, Thou good and gra - cious King!

The peo - ple of the He - brews With palms be - fore thee went;
To thee, be - fore thy pas - sion, They sang their hymns of praise;
All glo - ry, laud, and hon - or To thee, Re - deem - er, King,

Our praise and prayer and an - thems Be - fore thee we pre - sent.
To thee, now high ex - alt - ed, Our mel - o - dy we raise.
To whom the lips of chil - dren Made sweet ho - san - nas ring! A - men.

Hosanna to the Living Lord!

Reginald Heber, 1783–1826, cento, alt.

Hosanna 8. 8. 8. 8. 4. 7.
John B. Dykes, 1823–1876

1. Ho - san - na to the liv - ing Lord! Ho - san - na
2. Ho - san - na, Lord! thine an - gels cry; Ho - san - na,
3. O Sav - ior, with pro - tect - ing care A - bide in
4. But chief - est, in our cleans - ed breast, E - ter - nal,

to the in - car - nate Word! To Christ, Cre - a - tor, Sav - ior, King,
Lord! thy saints re - ply. A - bove, be - neath us, and a - round,
this thy house of prayer, Where we thy part - ing prom - ise claim,
bid thy Spir - it rest; And make our se - cret soul to be

Let earth, let heaven ho - san - na sing! Ho - san - na,
The dead and liv - ing swell the sound. Ho - san - na,
As - sem - bled in thy sa - cred name. Ho - san - na,
A tem - ple pure and wor - thy thee! Ho - san - na,

Lord! Ho - san - na in the high - est!
Lord! Ho - san - na in the high - est!
Lord! Ho - san - na in the high - est!
Lord! Ho - san - na in the high - est! A - men.

Words and music from the *Lutheran Service Book and Hymnal.* Used by permission of the Commission on the Liturgy and Hymnal.

283   'Tis Midnight, and on Olive's Brow

Olive's Brow L. M.

William B. Tappan, 1794–1849, alt.

William B. Bradbury, 1816–1868

1. 'Tis mid - night, and on Ol - ive's brow The star is dimmed that late - ly shone; 'Tis mid - night, in the gar - den now The suf - fering Sav - ior prays a - lone.
2. 'Tis mid - night, and from all re - moved, Im - man - uel wres - tles lone with fears; E'en that dis - ci - ple whom he loved Heeds not his Mas - ter's grief and tears.
3. 'Tis mid - night, and for oth - ers' guilt The Man of Sor - rows weeps in blood; Yet he that has in an - guish knelt Is not for - sak - en by his God.
4. 'Tis mid - night, and from heav - enly plains Is borne the song that an - gels know; Un - heard by mor - tals are the strains That sweet - ly soothe the Sav - ior's woe. A - men.

284   O Perfect Life of Love

Gorton S. M.
Ludwig van Beethoven, 1770–1827
Arr. by John Ebenezer West, 1863–1929

Henry Williams Baker, 1821–1877, cento

1. O per - fect life of love, All, all is fin - ished now;
2. No work is left un - done Of all the Fa - ther willed;
3. No pain that we can share But he has felt its smart;
4. In per - fect love he dies; For me he dies, for me!
5. Yet work, O Lord, in me, As thou for me hast wrought;

O Perfect Life of Love (cont.)

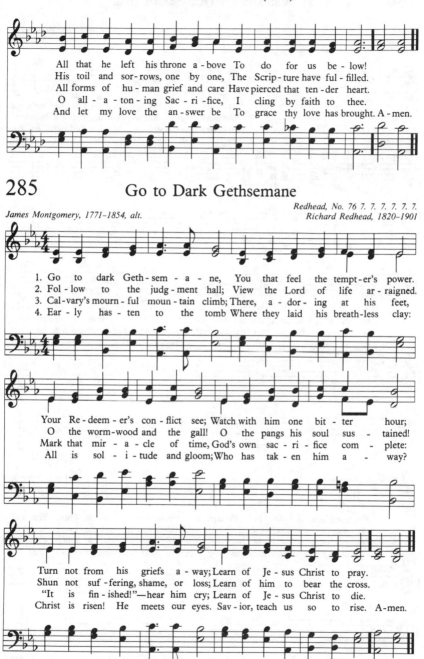

All that he left his throne a-bove To do for us be-low!
His toil and sor-rows, one by one, The Scrip-ture have ful-filled.
All forms of hu-man grief and care Have pierced that ten-der heart.
O all-a-ton-ing Sac-ri-fice, I cling by faith to thee.
And let my love the an-swer be To grace thy love has brought. A-men.

285   Go to Dark Gethsemane

James Montgomery, 1771–1854, alt.

Redhead, No. 76 7. 7. 7. 7. 7. 7.
Richard Redhead, 1820–1901

1. Go to dark Geth-sem-a-ne, You that feel the tempt-er's power.
2. Fol-low to the judg-ment hall; View the Lord of life ar-raigned.
3. Cal-vary's mourn-ful moun-tain climb; There, a-dor-ing at his feet,
4. Ear-ly has-ten to the tomb Where they laid his breath-less clay:

Your Re-deem-er's con-flict see; Watch with him one bit-ter hour;
O the worm-wood and the gall! O the pangs his soul sus-tained!
Mark that mir-a-cle of time, God's own sac-ri-fice com-plete:
All is sol-i-tude and gloom; Who has tak-en him a-way?

Turn not from his griefs a-way; Learn of Je-sus Christ to pray.
Shun not suf-fering, shame, or loss; Learn of him to bear the cross.
"It is fin-ished!"—hear him cry; Learn of Je-sus Christ to die.
Christ is risen! He meets our eyes. Sav-ior, teach us so to rise. A-men.

286   It Was on a Friday Morning

Friday Morning Irregular
Sydney Carter, 1915–
Harm. by John Farmer

Sydney Carter, 1915–

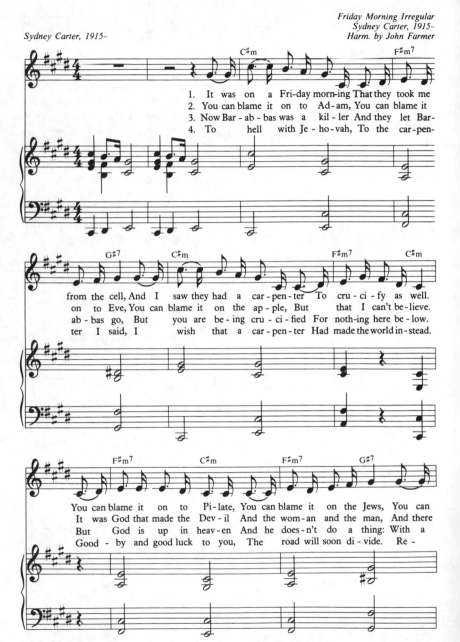

1. It was on a Fri-day morn-ing That they took me from the cell, And I saw they had a car-pen-ter To cru-ci-fy as well. You can blame it on to Pi-late, You can blame it on the Jews, You can

2. You can blame it on to Ad-am, You can blame it on to Eve, You can blame it on the ap-ple, But that I can't be-lieve. It was God that made the Dev-il And the wom-an and the man, And there

3. Now Bar-ab-bas was a kil-ler And they let Bar-ab-bas go, But you are be-ing cru-ci-fied For noth-ing here be-low. But God is up in heav-en And he does-n't do a thing: With a

4. To hell with Je-ho-vah, To the car-pen-ter I said, I wish that a car-pen-ter Had made the world in-stead. Good-by and good luck to you, The road will soon di-vide. Re-

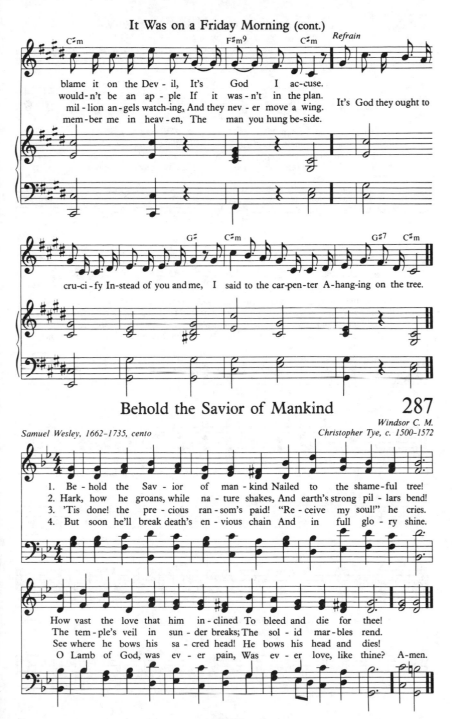

It Was on a Friday Morning (cont.)

blame it on the Dev - il, It's God I ac-cuse.
would - n't be an ap - ple If it was - n't in the plan.
mil - lion an-gels watch-ing, And they nev - er move a wing.
mem - ber me in heav - en, The man you hung be-side.

Refrain

It's God they ought to

cru-ci - fy In-stead of you and me, I said to the car-pen-ter A-hang-ing on the tree.

Behold the Savior of Mankind   287

Windsor C. M.

Samuel Wesley, 1662-1735, cento

Christopher Tye, c. 1500-1572

1. Be - hold the Sav - ior of man - kind Nailed to the shame - ful tree!
2. Hark, how he groans, while na - ture shakes, And earth's strong pil - lars bend!
3. 'Tis done! the pre - cious ran - som's paid! "Re - ceive my soul!" he cries.
4. But soon he'll break death's en - vious chain And in full glo - ry shine.

How vast the love that him in - clined To bleed and die for thee!
The tem - ple's veil in sun - der breaks; The sol - id mar - bles rend.
See where he bows his sa - cred head! He bows his head and dies!
O Lamb of God, was ev - er pain, Was ev - er love, like thine? A-men.

288 There Is a Green Hill Far Away

Cecil Frances Alexander, 1818–1895, cento

Green Hill C. M. with Refrain
George C. Stebbins, 1846–1945

1. There is a green hill far a-way, With-out a cit-y wall,
2. We may not know, we can-not tell, What pains he had to bear;
3. He died that we might be for-given, He died to make us good,
4. There was no oth-er good e-nough To pay the price of sin;

Where the dear Lord was cru-ci-fied, Who died to save us all.
But we be-lieve it was for us He hung and suf-fered there.
That we might go at last to heaven, Saved by his pre-cious blood.
He on-ly could un-lock the gate Of heaven and let us in.

Refrain

O dear-ly, dear-ly has he loved, And we must love him too,

And trust in his re-deem-ing blood, And try his works to do. A-men.

Near the Cross Was Mary Weeping

289

Stabat Mater 8. 8. 7. 8. 8. 7.

Latin sequence, 13th century, cento
Tr. by James Waddell Alexander, 1804–1859, cento, alt.

Traditional melody
Arr. by Conrad Kocher, 1786–1872

1. Near the cross was Mar-y weep-ing, There her mourn-ful sta-tion keep-ing, Gaz-ing on her dy-ing Son. There with speech-less grief op-press-ed, An-guish-strick-en and dis-tress-ed, Through her soul the sword had gone.
2. Who up-on that Suf-fer-er gaz-ing, Bowed in sor-row so a-maz-ing, Would not with his moth-er mourn? 'Twas our sins brought him from heav-en; These the cru-el nails had driv-en; All his griefs for us were borne.
3. When no eye its pit-y gave us, When there was no arm to save us, He his love and power dis-played; By his stripes he wrought our heal-ing; By his death, our life re-veal-ing, He for us the ran-som paid.
4. Je-sus, may thy love con-strain us That from sin we may re-frain us, In thy griefs may deep-ly grieve. Thee our best af-fec-tions giv-ing, To thy glo-ry ev-er liv-ing, May we in thy glo-ry live. A-men.

285

290 Must Jesus Bear the Cross Alone

Thomas Shepherd, 1665–1739, cento, alt.

Maitland C. M.
George N. Allen, 1812–1877

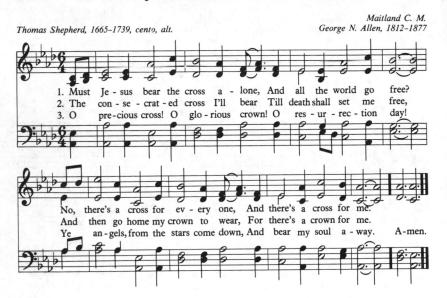

1. Must Je - sus bear the cross a - lone, And all the world go free?
2. The con - se - crat - ed cross I'll bear Till death shall set me free,
3. O pre - cious cross! O glo - rious crown! O res - ur - rec - tion day!

No, there's a cross for ev - ery one, And there's a cross for me.
And then go home my crown to wear, For there's a crown for me.
Ye an - gels, from the stars come down, And bear my soul a - way. A - men.

291 O Come and Mourn with Me Awhile!

St. Cross L. M.
John B. Dykes, 1823–1876

Frederick William Faber, 1814–1863, cento

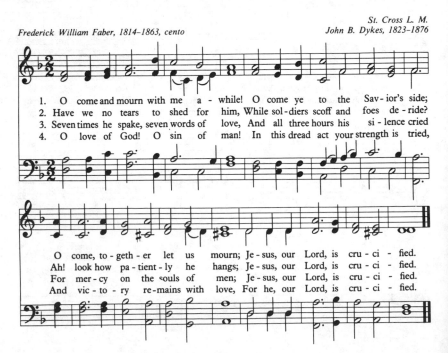

1. O come and mourn with me a - while! O come ye to the Sav - ior's side;
2. Have we no tears to shed for him, While sol - diers scoff and foes de - ride?
3. Seven times he spake, seven words of love, And all three hours his si - lence cried
4. O love of God! O sin of man! In this dread act your strength is tried,

O come, to - geth - er let us mourn; Je - sus, our Lord, is cru - ci - fied.
Ah! look how pa - tient - ly he hangs; Je - sus, our Lord, is cru - ci - fied.
For mer - cy on the souls of men; Je - sus, our Lord, is cru - ci - fied.
And vic - to - ry re - mains with love, For he, our Lord, is cru - ci - fied.

Ah, Holy Jesus, How Hast Thou Offended 292

Johann Heermann, 1585–1647, cento
Tr. by Robert Bridges, 1844–1930

Herzliebster Jesu 11. 11. 11. 5.
Johann Crüger, 1598–1662

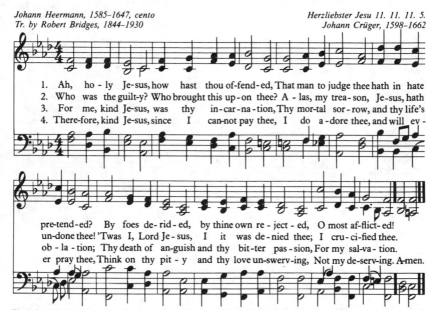

1. Ah, ho-ly Je-sus, how hast thou of-fend-ed, That man to judge thee hath in hate
2. Who was the guilt-y? Who brought this up-on thee? A-las, my trea-son, Je-sus, hath
3. For me, kind Je-sus, was thy in-car-na-tion, Thy mor-tal sor-row, and thy life's
4. There-fore, kind Je-sus, since I can-not pay thee, I do a-dore thee, and will ev-

pre-tend-ed? By foes de-rid-ed, by thine own re-ject-ed, O most af-flict-ed!
un-done thee! 'Twas I, Lord Je-sus, I it was de-nied thee; I cru-ci-fied thee.
ob-la-tion; Thy death of an-guish and thy bit-ter pas-sion, For my sal-va-tion.
er pray thee, Think on thy pit-y and thy love un-swerv-ing, Not my de-serv-ing. A-men.

Words from *The Yattendon Hymnal*, ed. by Robert Bridges and H. Ellis Wooldridge. Used by permission of Oxford University Press.

In the Cross of Christ I Glory 293

John Bowring, 1792–1872

Rathbun 8. 7. 8. 7.
Ithamar Conkey, 1815–1867

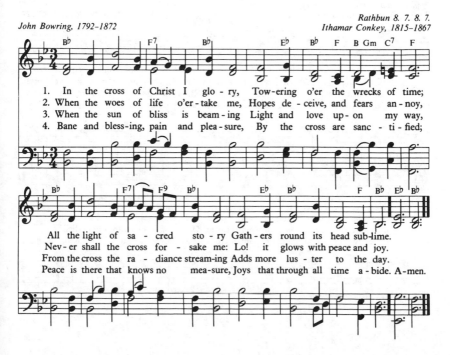

1. In the cross of Christ I glo-ry, Tow-ering o'er the wrecks of time;
2. When the woes of life o'er-take me, Hopes de-ceive, and fears an-noy,
3. When the sun of bliss is beam-ing Light and love up-on my way,
4. Bane and bless-ing, pain and plea-sure, By the cross are sanc-ti-fied;

All the light of sa-cred sto-ry Gath-ers round its head sub-lime.
Nev-er shall the cross for-sake me: Lo! it glows with peace and joy.
From the cross the ra-diance stream-ing Adds more lus-ter to the day.
Peace is there that knows no mea-sure, Joys that through all time a-bide. A-men.

294 Alas! and Did My Savior Bleed

Martyrdom C. M.
Scotch traditional melody
Arr. by Hugh Wilson, 1764–1824
and Robert Archibald Smith, 1780–1829

Isaac Watts, 1674–1748, cento, alt.

1. A - las! and did my Sav - ior bleed, And did my Sov - ereign die!
2. Was it for sins that I have done He suf - fered on the tree?
3. Well might the sun in dark - ness hide, And shut his glo - ries in,
4. Thus might I hide my blush - ing face While his dear cross ap - pears;
5. But drops of grief can ne'er re - pay The debt of love I owe;

Would he de - vote that sa - cred head For sin - ners such as I!
A - maz - ing pit - y! grace un - known! And love be - yond de - gree!
When God, the might - y Mak - er, died For man the crea-ture's sin.
Dis - solve my heart in thank - ful - ness, And melt mine eyes to tears.
Here, Lord, I give my - self a - way; 'Tis all that I can do. A-men.

295 My God, I Love Thee, Not Because

Francis Xavier, 1506–1552, cento
Tr. by Edward Caswall, 1814–1878, alt.

St. James C. M.
Raphael Courteville, c. 1677–1772

1. My God, I love thee, not be - cause I hope for heaven there-by;
2. But, O my Je - sus, thou didst me Up - on the cross em-brace;
3. Then why, O bless - ed Je - sus Christ, Should I not love thee well;
4. E'en so I love thee, and will love, And in thy praise will sing,

Nor yet be - cause, if I love not, I must for - ev - er die.
For me didst bear the nails and spear And man - i - fold dis - grace.
Not for the sake of win - ning heaven, Or of es - cap - ing hell?
Sole - ly be - cause thou art my God And my e - ter - nal King. A-men.

288

O Sacred Head, Now Wounded

Bernard of Clairvaux, c. 1091–1153
Tr. into German by Paul Gerhardt, 1607–1676, cento
Tr. from German by James Waddell Alexander, 1804–1859

Passion Chorale 7. 6. 7. 6. D.
Melody by Hans Leo Hassler, 1564–1612
Harm. by Johann Sebastian Bach, 1685–1750

1. O sa - cred Head, now wound - ed, With grief and shame weighed down;
2. What thou, my Lord, hast suf - fered Was all for sin - ners' gain:
3. What lan - guage shall I bor - row To thank thee, dear - est Friend,

Now scorn - ful - ly sur - round - ed With thorns, thine on - ly crown;
Mine, mine was the trans - gres - sion, But thine the dead - ly pain.
For this thy dy - ing sor - row, Thy pit - y with - out end?

O sa - cred Head, what glo - ry, What bliss till now was thine!
Lo, here I fall, my Sav - ior! 'Tis I de - serve thy place;
O make me thine for - ev - er; And should I faint - ing be,

Yet, though de - spised and gor - y, I joy to call thee mine.
Look on me with thy fa - vor, Vouch-safe to me thy grace.
Lord, let me nev - er, nev - er, Out - live my love to thee. A - men.

297
On a Hill Far Away

George Bennard, 1873-1958

Old Rugged Cross Irregular with Refrain
George Bennard, 1873-1958

1. On a hill far a - way stood an old rug - ged cross, The em - blem of suf - fering and shame; And I love that old cross where the dear - est and best For a world of lost sin - ners was slain.
2. Oh, that old rug - ged cross, so de - spised by the world, Has a won - drous at - trac - tion for me; For the dear Lamb of God left his glo - ry a - bove To bear it to dark Cal - va - ry.
3. In the old rug - ged cross, stained with blood so di - vine, A won - drous beau - ty I see; For 'twas on that old cross Je - sus suf - fered and died To par - don and sanc - ti - fy me.
4. To the old rug - ged cross I will ev - er be true, Its shame and re - proach glad - ly bear; Then he'll call me some - day to my home far a - way, Where his glo - ry for - ev - er I'll share.

Refrain
So I'll cher - ish the old rug - ged cross, the cross, Till my tro - phies at last I lay down; I will cling to the old rug - ged cross, the old rug - ged cross, And ex - change it some - day for a crown.

Were You There

Were You There 10. 10. 13. 10.
American Negro melody

Spiritual, cento

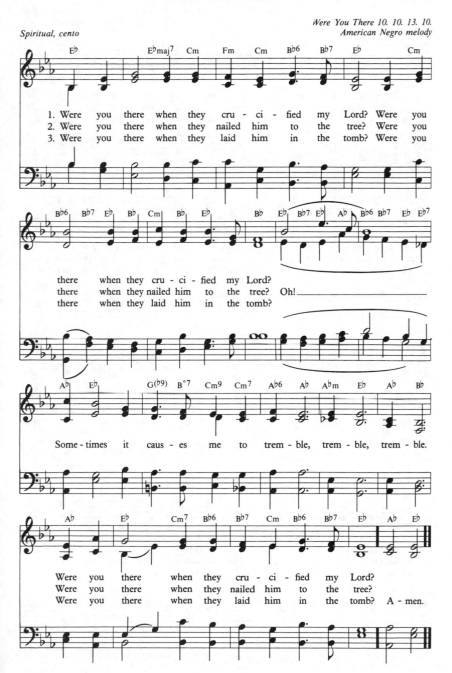

1. Were you there when they cru-ci-fied my Lord? Were you there when they cru-ci-fied my Lord? Sometimes it causes me to trem-ble, trem-ble, trem-ble. Were you there when they cru-ci-fied my Lord?

2. Were you there when they nailed him to the tree? Were you there when they nailed him to the tree? Oh!_____ Sometimes it causes me to trem-ble, trem-ble, trem-ble. Were you there when they nailed him to the tree?

3. Were you there when they laid him in the tomb? Were you there when they laid him in the tomb? Sometimes it causes me to trem-ble, trem-ble, trem-ble. Were you there when they laid him in the tomb? A-men.

299   The Roman Soldier Knew Not Why

Roman Soldier 8. 8. 8. 8. 8. 8. 8. with Refrain

Alice Jane Schneider, 1918–

Kent E. Schneider, 1945–

1. The Ro-man sol-dier knew not why It trou-bled him to cru-ci-fy The man from Gal-i-lee un-til The skies grew dark, quakes shook the hills, And as the fig-ure slumped in death The sol-dier spoke be-neath his breath:

2. Of what can we be tru-ly sure? Time shows that lit-tle does en-dure. Both rules and rul-ers come and go, Yet this un-shak-en truth we know: Still stands the cross in hope and shame ac-knowl-edg-ing the Chris-tians' claim:

3. Be-side his cross we kneel and pray, To share his love and life each day. As Christ has died that we may live, To him our lives we ful-ly give; In u-ni-ty we gath-er to ac-claim our faith and hope a-new:

Refrain

"It's true he is the

Son of God, The man from Gal - i - lee: This Je - sus was the

Prom-ised One, The Christ of Proph - e - cy!" -cy!"

When I Survey the Wondrous Cross 300

Hamburg L. M.

Isaac Watts, 1674–1748, cento

Arr. by Lowell Mason, 1792–1872

1. When I sur - vey the won-drous cross On which the Prince of glo - ry died,
2. For - bid it, Lord, that I should boast, Save in the death of Christ my God:
3. See, from his head, his hands, his feet, Sor - row and love flow min - gled down:
4. Were the whole realm of na - ture mine, That were a pres - ent far too small;

My rich-est gain I count but loss And pour con - tempt on all my pride.
All the vain things that charm me most, I sac - ri - fice them to his blood.
Did e'er such love and sor - row meet, Or thorns com - pose so rich a crown?
Love so a - maz - ing, so di - vine, De-mands my soul, my life, my all. A-men.

301 Lord Christ, When First Thou Cam'st

Mit Freuden zart 8. 7. 8. 7. 8. 8. 7.

Walter Russell Bowie, 1882–1969

Bohemian Brethren, 1566

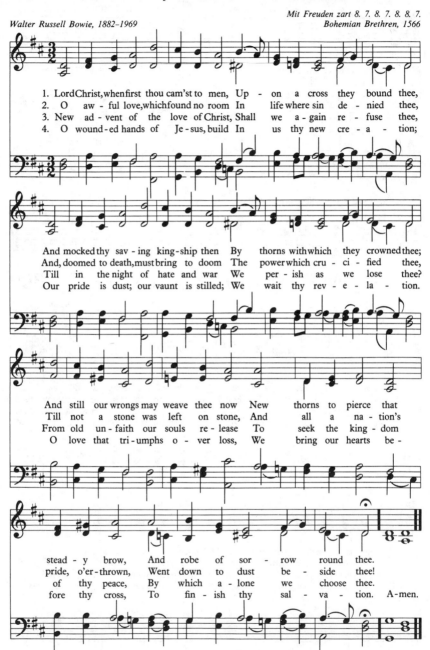

1. Lord Christ, when first thou cam'st to men, Upon a cross they bound thee,
And mocked thy saving kingship then By thorns with which they crowned thee;
And still our wrongs may weave thee now New thorns to pierce that steady brow,
And robe of sorrow round thee.

2. O awful love, which found no room In life where sin denied thee,
And, doomed to death, must bring to doom The power which crucified thee,
Till not a stone was left on stone, And all a nation's pride, o'erthrown,
Went down to dust beside thee!

3. New advent of the love of Christ, Shall we again refuse thee,
Till in the night of hate and war We perish as we lose thee?
From old unfaith our souls release To seek the kingdom of thy peace,
By which alone we choose thee.

4. O wounded hands of Jesus, build In us thy new creation;
Our pride is dust; our vaunt is stilled; We wait thy revelation.
O love that triumphs over loss, We bring our hearts before thy cross,
To finish thy salvation. A-men.

Ascribed to Wipo of Burgundy, d. c. 1050
Tr. by Jane E. Leeson, 1807-1882, cento
Alt. by Irvin Udulutsch, 1920-

Victimae Paschali 7. 7. 7. 7. D.
Traditional melody
Harm. by David Kraehenbuehl, 1923-

1. Christ the Lord is risen to - day; Chris-tians, haste your vows to pay:
2. Christ, the Vic - tim un - de - filed, Man to God has rec - on - ciled;
3. Christ, who once for sin - ners bled, Now the first - born from the dead,

Of - fer him your prais - es meet At the Pas - chal Vic - tim's feet.
When in strange and aw - ful strife Met to - geth - er death and life;
Throned in end - less might and power, Lives and reigns for - ev - er - more.

For the sheep the Lamb has bled, Sin - less in the sin - ner's stead;
Chris - tians, on this hap - py day Haste with joy your vows to pay.
Hail, e - ter - nal Hope on high! Hail, O King of vic - to - ry!

Christ the Lord is risen on high, Now he lives no more to die!
Christ the Lord is risen on high, Now he lives no more to die!
Hail, the Prince of life a - dored! Help and save us, gra - cious Lord.

Harmonization used by permission of David Kraehenbuehl.

303　　I Serve a Risen Savior

Alfred H. Ackley, 1887–1960

Ackley 13. 13. 13. 11. with Refrain
Alfred H. Ackley, 1887–1960

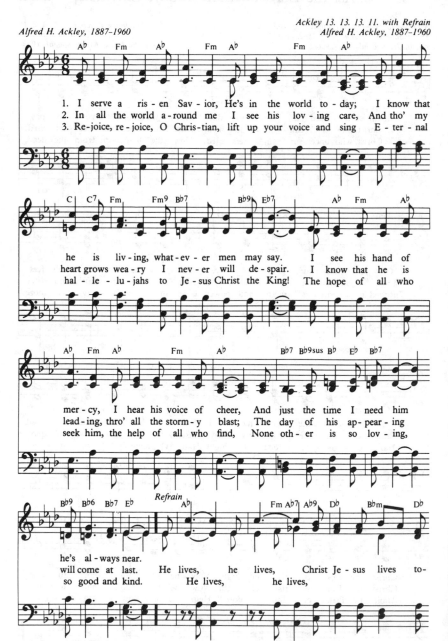

1. I serve a ris - en Sav - ior, He's in the world to - day;　I know that
2. In all the world a - round me　I see his lov - ing care, And tho' my
3. Re - joice, re - joice, O Chris - tian, lift up your voice and sing　E - ter - nal

he is liv - ing, what - ev - er men may say.　I see his hand of
heart grows wea - ry　I nev - er will de - spair.　I know that he is
hal - le - lu - jahs to Je - sus Christ the King!　The hope of all who

mer - cy, I hear his voice of　cheer, And just the time I need him
lead - ing, thro' all the storm - y　blast; The day of his ap - pear - ing
seek him, the help of all who find,　None oth - er is so lov - ing,

Refrain

he's al - ways near.　He lives,　he lives,　Christ Je - sus lives to-
will come at last.　He lives,　he lives,
so good and kind.　He lives,　he lives,

304   Come, Christians, Join to Sing

Spanish Chant 6. 6. 6. 6. D.
Source unknown
Harm. by David Evans, 1874–1948
Descant by Donald D. Kettring, 1907–

Christian Henry Bateman, 1813–1889, cento, alt.

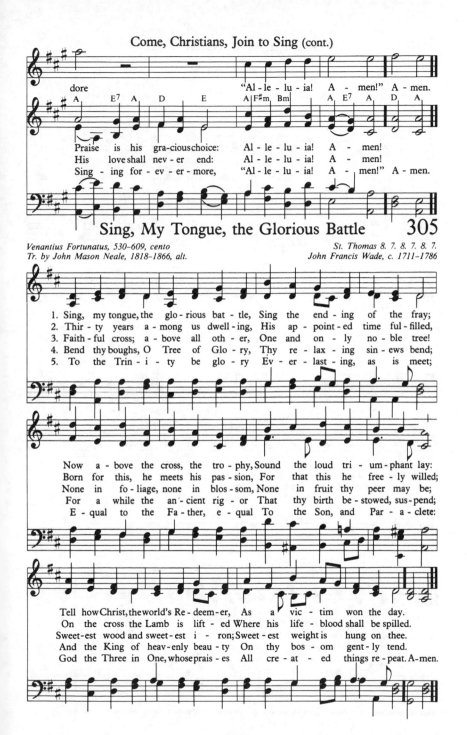

dore "Al - le - lu - ia! A - men!" A - men.

Praise is his gra-cious choice: Al - le - lu - ia! A - men!
His love shall nev - er end: Al - le - lu - ia! A - men!
Sing - ing for - ev - er - more, "Al - le - lu - ia! A - men!" A - men.

Sing, My Tongue, the Glorious Battle   305

Venantius Fortunatus, 530-609, cento
Tr. by John Mason Neale, 1818-1866, alt.

St. Thomas 8. 7. 8. 7. 8. 7.
John Francis Wade, c. 1711-1786

1. Sing, my tongue, the glo - rious bat - tle, Sing the end - ing of the fray;
2. Thir - ty years a - mong us dwell - ing, His ap - point - ed time ful - filled,
3. Faith - ful cross; a - bove all oth - er, One and on - ly no - ble tree!
4. Bend thy boughs, O Tree of Glo - ry, Thy re - lax - ing sin - ews bend;
5. To the Trin - i - ty be glo - ry Ev - er - last - ing, as is meet;

Now a - bove the cross, the tro - phy, Sound the loud tri - um - phant lay:
Born for this, he meets his pas - sion, For that this he free - ly willed;
None in fo - liage, none in blos - som, None in fruit thy peer may be;
For a while the an - cient rig - or That thy birth be - stowed, sus - pend;
E - qual to the Fa - ther, e - qual To the Son, and Par - a - clete:

Tell how Christ, the world's Re - deem - er, As a vic - tim won the day.
On the cross the Lamb is lift - ed Where his life - blood shall be spilled.
Sweet - est wood and sweet - est i - ron; Sweet - est weight is hung on thee.
And the King of heav - enly beau - ty On thy bos - om gent - ly tend.
God the Three in One, whose prais - es All cre - at - ed things re - peat. A-men.

Jesus Christ Is Risen Today

Bohemian Latin carol, 14th century, cento
St. 1, tr. in 'Lyra Davidica,' 1708
St. 2, John Arnold's 'Compleate Psalmist,' 1749
St. 3, Charles Wesley, 1707-1788, alt.

Llanfair 7. 7. 7. 7. with Alleluias
Robert Williams, c. 1781-1821
Harm. by David Evans, 1874-1948

1. Je - sus Christ is risen to - day, Al - le - lu - ia!
2. Hymns of praise then let us sing, Al - le - lu - ia!
3. Sing we to our God a - bove, Al - le - lu - ia!

Our tri - um - phant ho - ly day, Al - le - lu - ia!
Un - to Christ, our heav - enly King, Al - le - lu - ia!
Praise e - ter - nal as his love; Al - le - lu - ia!

Who did once, up - on the cross, Al - le - lu - ia!
Who en - dured the cross and grave, Al - le - lu - ia!
Praise him, all you heav - enly host, Al - le - lu - ia!

Suf - fer to re - deem our loss. Al - le - lu - ia!
Sin - ners to re - deem and save. Al - le - lu - ia!
Fa - ther, Son, and Ho - ly Ghost. Al - le - lu - ia! A - men.

Harmonization from *The Revised Church Hymnary.* Used by permission of Oxford University Press.

The Day of Resurrection!

John of Damascus, c. 696–c. 754
Tr. by John Mason Neale, 1818–1866, alt.

Lancashire 7. 6. 7. 6. D.
Henry Smart, 1813–1879

1. The day of res - ur - rec - tion! Earth, tell it out a - broad!
2. Our hearts be pure from e - vil, That we may see a - right
3. Now let the heavens be joy - ful, Let earth her song be - gin;

The Pass - o - ver of glad - ness, The Pass - o - ver of God!
The Lord in rays e - ter - nal Of res - u - rec - tion light,
Let all the world keep tri - umph, And all that is there - in;

From death to life e - ter - nal, From this world to the sky,
And, lis - tening to his ac - cents, May hear, so calm and plain,
Let all things seen and un - seen Their notes of glad - ness blend,

Our Christ has brought us o - ver With hymns of vic - to - ry.
His own "All hail!" and, hear - ing, May raise the vic - tor strain.
For Christ the Lord has ris - en, Our joy that has no end. A - men.

308   I Danced in the Morning

Sydney Carter, 1915-

Lord of the Dance Irregular with Refrain
American Shaker melody
Arr. and adapted by Sydney Carter, 1915-

1. I danced in the morn-ing when the world was be-gun, And I danced in the moon and the stars and the sun And I came down from heav-en and I danced on the earth— At Beth-le-hem I had my birth.

2. I danced for the scribe and the Phar-i-see, But they would not dance and they would-n't fol-low me; I danced for the fish-er-men, for James and John— They came with me and the dance went on.

3. I danced on the Sab-bath and I cured the lame; The ho-ly peo-ple said it was a shame; They whipped and they stripped and they hung me high, And they left me there on a cross to die.

4. I danced on a Fri-day when the sky turned black. It's hard to dance with the dev-il on your back; They bur-ied my bod-y and they thought I'd gone. But I am the dance and I still go on.

I Danced in the Morning (cont.)

Refrain

Dance, then, wher - ev - er you may be,
I am the Lord of the dance, said he, And I'll
lead you all, wher - ev - er you may be, And I'll
lead you all in the dance, said he. dance, said he.

Sts. 1–4. *St. 5.*

Melody for St. 5

5. They cut me down and I leap up high— I am the
life that - 'll nev - er, nev - er die; I'll live in you if you'll
(Refrain)
live in me— I am the Lord of the dance, said he.

309 Christ Arose on Easter Morn

Margaret (Holt) 7. 6. 7. 6. with Refrain
Ernest K. Emurian, 1912–
Ernest K. Emurian, 1912–

1. Christ a - rose on Eas - ter morn,
2. Since his pow - er can - not fail, Sing we hal - le -
3. He whom heaven and earth a - dore

Faith and hope were then re - born.
lu - jah! Sin and death can - not pre - vail.
Lives and reigns for - ev - er - more.

Refrain

Sing we hal - le - lu - jah! Sing we now this glad re - frain,

Prais - ing him who rose a - gain, Life e - ter - nal

to at - tain, Sing we hal - le - lu - jah!

Victory 8. 8. 8. with Alleluias
Cologne, 'Symphonia Sirenum,' 1695, cento
Tr. by Francis Pott, 1832–1909
Giovanni Pierluigi da Palestrina, 1525–1594
Arr. by William H. Monk, 1823–1889

Al - le - lu - ia! Al - le - lu - ia! Al - le - lu - ia!

1. The strife is o'er, the bat - tle done; The vic - to - ry of
2. The powers of death have done their worst, But Christ their le - gions
3. The three sad days are quick - ly sped; He ris - es glo - rious
4. Lord, by the stripes which wound - ed thee, From death's dread sting thy

life is won; The song of tri - umph has be - gun.
hath dis - persed; Let shouts of ho - ly joy out - burst.
from the dead: All glo - ry to our ris - en Head!
serv - ants free, That we may live and sing to thee.

Al - le - lu - ia! A - men.

311 Hail the Day That Sees Him Rise

Charles Wesley, 1707–1788, cento, alt.

Ascension 7. 7. 7. 7. with Alleluias
William H. Monk, 1823–1889

1. Hail the day that sees him rise,
2. There the glo - rious tri - umph waits;
3. See! he lifts his hands a - bove;
4. Lord be - yond our mor - tal sight,

Al - le - lu - ia!

Glo - rious, to his na - tive skies;
Lift your heads, e - ter - nal gates!
See! he shows the prints of love:
Raise our hearts to reach thy height,

Al - le - lu - ia!

Christ, a - while to mor - tals given,
Wide un - fold the ra - diant scene;
Hark! his gra - cious lips be - stow
There thy face un - cloud - ed see,

Al - le - lu - ia!

En - ters now the high - est heaven!
Take the King of glo - ry in!
Bless - ings on his church be - low.
Find our heaven of heavens in thee.

Al - le - lu - ia!

A - men.

Alternative tune: *Llanfair*, Hymn 317.

Low in the Grave He Lay

Christ Arose 6. 5. 6. 4. with Refrain

Robert Lowry, 1826–1899

Robert Lowry, 1826–1899

1. Low in the grave he lay, Je - sus my Sav - ior! Wait - ing the com-ing day,
2. Vain - ly they watch his bed, Je - sus my Sav - ior! Vain - ly they seal the dead,
3. Death can-not keep his prey, Je - sus my Sav - ior! He tore the bars a - way,

Je - sus my Lord! Up from the grave he a - rose, With a
He a - rose,

might-y tri-umph o'er his foes; He a - rose a vic - tor from the
He a - rose!

dark do-main, And he lives for - ev - er with his saints to reign. He a-

rose! He a - rose! Hal - le - lu - jah! Christ a - rose!
He a - rose! He a - rose!

307

313   Come, You Faithful, Raise the Strain

John of Damascus, c. 696–c. 754
Tr. by John Mason Neale, 1818–1866, alt.

St. Kevin 7. 6. 7. 6. D.
Arthur S. Sullivan, 1842–1900

1. Come, you faith-ful, raise the strain Of tri-umph-ant glad-ness;
2. 'Tis the spring of souls to-day; Christ has burst his pris-on,
3. Now the queen of sea-sons, bright With the day of splen-dor,
4. Nei-ther might the gates of death, Nor the tomb's dark por-tal,

God has brought his Is-ra-el In-to joy from sad-ness;
And from three days' sleep in death As a sun has ris-en;
With the roy-al feast of feasts, Comes its joy to ren-der;
Nor the watch-ers, nor the seal Hold you as a mor-tal;

Loosed from Phar-aoh's bit-ter yoke Ja-cob's sons and daugh-ters;
All the win-ter of our sins, Long and dark, is fly-ing.
Comes to glad Je-ru-sa-lem, Who with true af-fec-tion
But to-day a-midst the Twelve You did stand, be-stow-ing

Led them with un-moist-ened foot Through the Red Sea wa-ters.
From his light, to whom we give All our praise un-dy-ing.
Wel-comes in un-wea-ried strains Je-sus' res-ur-rec-tion.
Your own peace which ev-er-more Pass-es hu-man know-ing. A-men.

308

O Sons and Daughters, Let Us Sing! 314

Jean Tisserand, ?–1494, cento
Tr. by John Mason Neale, 1818–1866, alt.

O filii et filiae 8. 8. 8. with Alleluias
French melody, 16th century

Al - le - lu - ia! Al - le - lu - ia! Al - le - lu - ia! Al - le - lu - ia!

1. O sons and daugh - ters, let us sing!
2. That Eas - ter morn, at break of day,
3. An an - gel clad in white they see,
4. How blest are they who have not seen,
5. On this most ho - ly day of days

The King of heaven, the glo - rious King, O'er death to - day rose
The faith - ful wom - en went their way To seek the tomb where
Who sat, and spake un - to the three, "Your Lord doth go to
And yet whose faith hath con - stant been, For they e - ter - nal
Our hearts and voic - es, Lord, we raise To thee, in ju - bi -

tri - umph - ing.
Je - sus lay.
Gal - i - lee." Al - le - lu - ia! Al - le - lu - ia!
life shall win.
lee and praise. A - men.

309

315   Christ the Lord Is Risen From

Calypso Easter Carol 6. 5. 6. 5. with Alleluias

Richard K. Avery, 1934–
Donald S. Marsh, 1923–

Richard K. Avery, 1934–
Donald S. Marsh, 1923–

1. Christ the Lord is ris - en From his three-day tomb, Gone is all our sor - row, Gone is all our gloom.
2. Christ the Lord is ris - en, O - ver-com-ing doom, For this task was tak - en From his moth-er's womb.
3. Christ the Lord is ris - en, Like the lil - ies bloom, And his ris - en Spir - it Fills this ho - ly room.

Refrain

Hal-le-lu - jah! Hal-le-lu - jah! Hal-le-lu - jah! Hal-le-lu - jah!

Hal-le-lu - jah!

*Percussion

Christ, Whose Glory Fills the Skies 316

Charles Wesley, 1707–1788, alt.

Lux prima 7. 7. 7. 7. 7. 7.
Charles Gounod, 1818–1893

1. Christ, whose glo - ry fills the skies, Christ, the true, the on - ly Light,
2. Dark and cheer-less is the morn Un - ac - com - pa - nied by thee;
3. Vis - it, then, this soul of mine; Pierce the gloom of sin and grief;

Sun of Righ-teous - ness, a - rise, Tri - umph o'er the shades of night;
Joy-less is the day's re - turn Till thy mer-cy's beams I see;
Fill me, Ra - dian - cy di - vine; Scat - ter all my un - be - lief;

Day-spring from on high, be near; Day - star, in my heart ap - pear.
Till they in - ward light im-part, Cheer my eyes and warm my heart.
More and more thy - self dis-play, Shin - ing to the per - fect day. A - men.

317 Let the Earth Rejoice and Sing

Llanfair 7. 7. 7. 7. with Alleluias
Robert Williams, c. 1781–1821
Harm. by John Roberts, 1822–1877

Melvin Farrell, 1930–

1. Let the earth re - joice and sing, Al - le - lu - ia!
2. He who died up - on a tree Al - le - lu - ia!
3. Je - sus, Lord, all hail to thee; Al - le - lu - ia!
4. Je - sus, Vic - tor, hear our prayer, Al - le - lu - ia!
5. While in heav - en thou dost gaze Al - le - lu - ia!

At the tri - umph of our King. Al - le - lu - ia!
Now shall reign e - ter - nal - ly. Al - le - lu - ia!
On this day of vic - to - ry Al - le - lu - ia!
In thy tri - umph let us share, Al - le - lu - ia!
On thy church who sings thy praise, Al - le - lu - ia!

He as - cends from mor - tal sight, Al - le - lu - ia!
He who saved our fal - len race Al - le - lu - ia!
Thou didst shat - ter Sa - tan's might, Al - le - lu - ia!
Lift our minds and hearts a - bove, Al - le - lu - ia!
Fas - ten all our hope in thee, Al - le - lu - ia!

Reigns now at our Fa - ther's right. Al - le - lu - ia!
Takes in heaven his right - ful place. Al - le - lu - ia!
Ris - ing glo - rious from the fight. Al - le - lu - ia!
Strength-en all men in thy love. Al - le - lu - ia!
Till thy face un - veiled we see. Al - le - lu - ia!

That Easter Day with Joy Was Bright 318

Puer nobis nascitur L. M.

Sts. 1, 2, 3, Latin office hymn, pre-8th century   'Piae Cantiones,' 1582
Sts. 4, 5, Latin office hymn, pre-10th century   Adapted by Michael Praetorius, 1571-1621
Tr. by John Mason Neale, 1818-1866, alt.   Harm. by George R. Woodward, 1848-1934

1. That Eas - ter Day with joy was bright, The sun shone
2. His ris - en flesh with ra - diance glowed; His wound - ed
3. O Je - sus, King of gen - tle - ness, Do thou thy-
4. O Lord of all, with us a - bide In this our
5. All praise, O ris - en Lord, we give To thee, who,

out with fair - er light, When, to their long - ing eyes re-
hands and feet he showed; Those scars their sol - emn wit - ness
self our hearts pos - sess, That we may give thee all our
joy - ful Eas - ter - tide; From ev - ery weap - on death can
dead, a - gain dost live; To God the Fa - ther e - qual

stored, The a - pos - tles saw their ris - en Lord.
gave That Christ was ris - en from the grave.
days The will - ing trib - ute of our praise.
wield Thine own re - deemed for - ev - er shield.
praise, And God the Ho - ly Ghost, we raise. A - men.

319   Christ the Lord Is Risen Today, Sons

Easter Hymn 7. 7. 7. 7. with Alleluias
'Lyra Davidica,' 1708
Charles Wesley, 1707–1788, cento, alt.   Descant by *L. David Miller, 1919–*

1. Christ the Lord is risen to-day,   Al - le - lu - ia!
2. Lives a-gain our glo-rious King!   Al - le - lu - ia!
3. Love's re-deem-ing work is done,   Al - le - lu - ia!
4. Soar we now where Christ has led,   Al - le - lu - ia!

Sons of men and an-gels say;   Al - le - lu - ia!
Where, O death, is now your sting?   Al - le - lu - ia!
Fought the fight, the bat-tle won;   Al - le - lu - ia!
Fol-lowing our ex-alt-ed Head;   Al - le - lu - ia!

Raise your joys and tri-umphs high;   Al - le - lu - ia!
Once he died, our souls to save;   Al - le - lu - ia!
Death in vain for-bids him rise;   Al - le - lu - ia!
Made like him, like him we rise;   Al - le - lu - ia!

Ah _____ Al - le - lu - ia! A-men.

Sing, you heavens, and earth, re - ply. Al - le - lu - ia!
Where your vic - to - ry, O grave? Al - le - lu - ia!
Christ has o - pened par - a - dise. Al - le - lu - ia!
Ours the cross, the grave, the skies! Al - le - lu - ia! A-men.

Rejoice, the Lord Is King 320

Charles Wesley, 1707–1788, cento

Darwall's 148th 6. 6. 6. 6. 8. 8.
John Darwall, 1731–1789

1. Re - joice, the Lord is King! Your Lord and King a - dore!
2. The Lord, our Sav - ior, reigns, The God of truth and love;
3. His king - dom can - not fail, He rules o'er earth and heaven;
4. He all his foes shall quell, Shall all our sins de - stroy,

Re - joice, give thanks, and sing, And tri - umph ev - er - more:
When he had purged our stains, He took his seat a - bove:
The keys of death and hell Are to our Je - sus given:
And ev - ery bos - om swell With pure se - raph - ic joy:

Lift up your heart, lift up your voice! Re-joice, a-gain I say, re - joice! A-men.

315

Alleluia! Sing to Jesus!

Hyfrydol 8. 7. 8. 7. D.

William Chatterton Dix, 1837–1898, cento

Rowland Hugh Prichard, 1811–1887

1. Al - le - lu - ia! sing to Je - sus!
2. Al - le - lu - ia! Bread of Heav - en,
3. Al - le - lu - ia! King e - ter - nal,

His the scep - ter, his the throne;
Here on earth our food and stay!
You are Lord of lords a - lone.

Al - le - lu - ia! his the tri - umph,
Al - le - lu - ia! here the sin - ful
Al - le - lu - ia! born of Mar - y,

His the vic - to - ry a - lone;
Turn to you from day to day:
Earth's your foot - stool, heav - en your throne:

Alleluia! Sing to Jesus! (cont.)

Hark! the songs of peace - ful Zi - on
In - ter - ces - sor, friend of sin - ners,
You with - in the veil have en - tered,

Thun - der like a might - y flood;
Earth's Re - deem - er, plead for us
Robed in flesh, our great High Priest;

Je - sus out of ev - ery na - tion
Where the voic - es of the bless - ed
You on earth are Priest and Vic - tim

Has re - deemed us by his blood.
Join the chant vic - to - ri - ous.
In the Eu - cha - ris - tic feast.

322 King of Kings Is He Anointed

Catherine Maguire, 1910–

Christ the King 8. 6. 8. 6. 8. 7. 8. 5. 8. 5.
Margaret Leddy, 1909–1960

1. King of kings is he a - noint - ed; Let all men a - dore him;
2. Son of God and yet our broth - er, Let all men a - dore him;

Lord a - bove all lords ap - point - ed, Let us bow be - fore him.
Son of Mar - y our sweet moth - er, Let us bow be - fore him.

Christ who leads us, Christ who loves us, Christ our rul - er from his birth,
Christ who made us, Christ who saves us, Christ who can all foes de - fy,

He shall tri - umph, he shall tri - umph, O - ver all the earth.
He shall tri - umph, he shall tri - umph, From his throne on high;

King of kings is he ap - point - ed O - ver all the earth.
Son of God and yet our broth - er, From his throne on high.

Lord, Enthroned in Heavenly Splendor
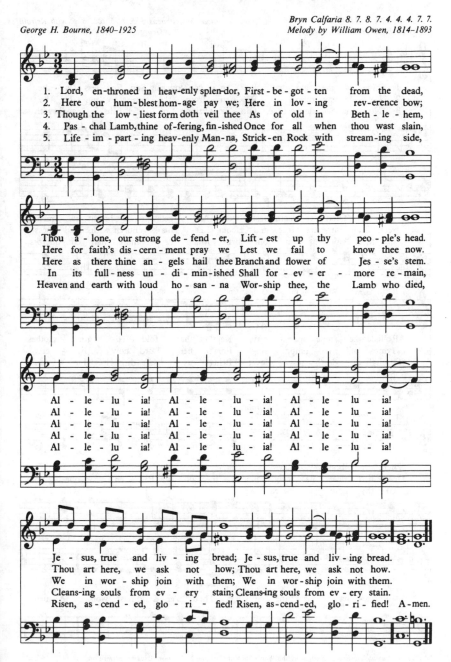

323

Bryn Calfaria 8. 7. 8. 7. 4. 4. 4. 7. 7.

George H. Bourne, 1840–1925

Melody by William Owen, 1814–1893

1. Lord, en-throned in heav-enly splen-dor, First - be - got - ten from the dead,
2. Here our hum-blest hom-age pay we; Here in lov - ing rev-erence bow;
3. Though the low - liest form doth veil thee As of old in Beth - le - hem,
4. Pas - chal Lamb, thine of-fering, fin-ished Once for all when thou wast slain,
5. Life - im - part - ing heav-enly Man-na, Strick-en Rock with stream-ing side,

Thou a - lone, our strong de - fend - er, Lift - est up thy peo - ple's head.
Here for faith's dis - cern - ment pray we Lest we fail to know thee now.
Here as there thine an - gels hail thee Branch and flow-er of Jes - se's stem.
In its full - ness un - di - min-ished Shall for - ev - er - more re - main,
Heaven and earth with loud ho - san - na Wor-ship thee, the Lamb who died,

Al - le - lu - ia! Al - le - lu - ia! Al - le - lu - ia!
Al - le - lu - ia! Al - le - lu - ia! Al - le - lu - ia!
Al - le - lu - ia! Al - le - lu - ia! Al - le - lu - ia!
Al - le - lu - ia! Al - le - lu - ia! Al - le - lu - ia!
Al - le - lu - ia! Al - le - lu - ia! Al - le - lu - ia!

Je - sus, true and liv - ing bread; Je - sus, true and liv - ing bread.
Thou art here, we ask not how; Thou art here, we ask not how.
We in wor - ship join with them; We in wor - ship join with them.
Cleans-ing souls from ev - ery stain; Cleans-ing souls from ev - ery stain.
Risen, as - cend - ed, glo - ri - fied! Risen, as - cend-ed, glo - ri - fied! A - men.

324 Thine Is the Glory

Edmond Budry, 1854–1932
Tr. by R. Birch Hoyle, 1875–1939

Judas Maccabaeus 5. 5. 6. 5. 6. 5. 6. 5. with Refrain
George Frederick Handel, 1685–1759

1. Thine is the glo - ry, Ris - en, con - quering Son, End - less is the
2. Lo! Je - sus meets us. Ris - en from the tomb, Lov - ing - ly he
3. No more we doubt thee, Glo - rious Prince of life! Life is naught with -

vic - tory Thou o'er death hast won. An - gels in bright rai - ment
greets us, Scat - ters fear and gloom. Let his church with glad - ness
out thee; Aid us in our strife; Make us more than con - querors,

Rolled the stone a - way, Kept the fold - ed grave - clothes
Hymns of tri - umph sing, For her Lord now liv - eth;
Through thy death - less love; Bring us safe through Jor - dan

Refrain

Where thy bod - y lay.
Death hath lost its sting. Thine is the glo - ry, Ris - en, con - quering Son;
To thy home a - bove.

End - less is the vic - tory Thou o'er death hast won. A - men.

Words from *Cantate Domino*. Copyright by the World Student Christian Federation. Used by permission.

Crown Him with Many Crowns

Diademata S. M. D.
George J. Elvey, 1816–1893
Descant by L. David Miller, 1919-

Matthew Bridges, 1800–1894, cento, alt.

Descant

Ah

1. Crown him with man-y crowns, The Lamb up-on his throne;
2. Crown him the Lord of love; Be-hold his hands and side,
3. Crown him the Lord of peace, Whose power a scep-ter sways
4. Crown him the Lord of years, The Po-ten-tate of time,

Ah

Hark! how the heav-enly an-them drowns All mu-sic but its own.
Rich wounds yet vis-i-ble a-bove In beau-ty glo-ri-fied.
From pole to pole, that wars may cease, And all be prayer and praise.
Cre-a-tor of the roll-ing spheres, In-ef-fa-bly sub-lime.

Ah

A-wake, my soul, and sing Of him who died for me,
No an-gel in the sky Can ful-ly bear that sight,
His reign shall know no end, And round his pierc-ed feet
All hail, Re-deem-er, hail! For you have died for me;

Ah

And hail him as our match-less King Through all e-ter-ni-ty.
But down-ward bends his won-dering eye At mys-ter-ies so bright.
Fair flowers of par-a-dise ex-tend Their fra-grance ev-er sweet.
Your praise and glo-ry shall not fail Through-out e-ter-ni-ty.

326 While the Stone Was Sealed by the Jews

Tou Lithou Irregular
Orthodox traditional melody, tone 1

While the stone was sealed by the Jews, and the soldiers

kept guard over thy most pure bod - y, thou didst rise

on the third day, O Sav - ior, grant - ing life to the world.

For which cause the heavenly powers cried aloud unto

thee, O Giv - er of life: Glory to thy resurrection, O

Christ! Glo - ry to thy king - dom! Glory to thy prov -

i - dence, O thou who alone lovest man - kind.

Hote Katelthes Irregular
Orthodox traditional melody, tone 2

When thou didst condescend unto death, O Life im - mor -

tal, thou didst slay hell with the lightning flash of

thy di - vin - i - ty. When al - so thou didst raise

up the dead from the in - fer - nal re - gions, all the pow-

ers of heav - en cried a - loud: O Life - Giv - er, Christ

our God, glo - ry to thee.

328   # Let the Heavens Rejoice

Euphorainestho Irregular
Orthodox traditional melody, tone 3

Let the heav - ens re - joice and let the earth be glad,
for the Lord hath showed strength with his arm. He
hath tram - pled down death by death: he is be - come the
first - born of the dead: from the pit of hell he hath
de - liv - ered us, and grant - ed un - to the world great
mer - cy.

329   # When the Women Disciples of the Lord

To Phaidron Irregular
Orthodox traditional melody, tone 4

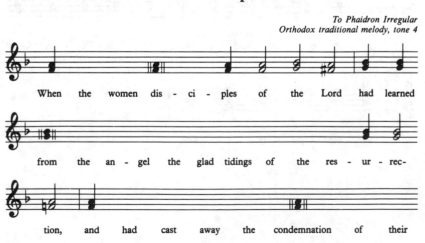

When the women dis - ci - ples of the Lord had learned
from the an - gel the glad tidings of the res - ur - rec-
tion, and had cast away the condemnation of their

fore - fa - thers, they spake exultingly to the a - pos-

tles: Death is no more: Christ God is ris - en, grant

un - to the world great mer - cy.

The Word, Who with the Father 330

Ton Synarchon Logon Irregular
Orthodox traditional melody, tone 5

The Word, who with the Father and the Spirit hath no

be - gin - ning, and who, for our salvation, was born of

a vir - gin, let us faith - ful believers hymn and wor -

ship: for he was pleased to ascend the cross in the

flesh, and to en - dure death, and to raise the dead

by his glo - ri - ous res - ur - rec - tion.

331 The Angelic Powers Were in Thy Tomb

Angelikai Dynameis Irregular
Orthodox traditional melody, tone 6

The angelic powers were in thy tomb, and the guards be-came as dead men, and Mar-y stood by the grave, seek-ing thy most pure bod - y. Thou hast captured hell without be - ing tempt - ed by it: thou didst meet the Vir - gin, grant - ing life. Thou that hast ris - en from the dead, O Lord, glo - ry to thee.

332 By Thy Cross Thou Didst Destroy Death

Katelysas Irregular
Orthodox traditional melody, tone 7

By thy cross thou didst de - stroy death; to the thief thou hast opened par - a - dise: for the myrrh - bear - ing

326

By Thy Cross Thou Didst Destroy Death (cont.)

women thou hast changed lamentation in - to joy, and

didst command them to announce unto thine a - pos - tles

that thou art ris - en from the dead, O Christ our God,

grant - ing to the world great mer - cy.

Thou Didst Descend from on High

333

Ex Hypsous Katelthes Irregular
Orthodox traditional melody, tone 8

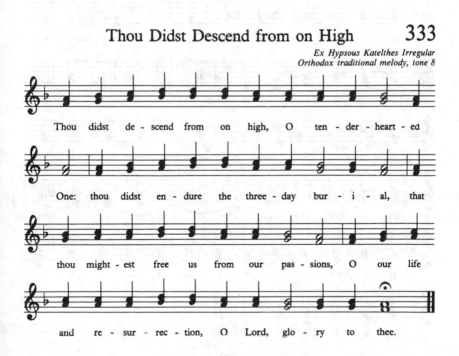

Thou didst de - scend from on high, O ten - der - heart - ed

One: thou didst en - dure the three - day bur - i - al, that

thou might - est free us from our pas - sions, O our life

and re - sur - rec - tion, O Lord, glo - ry to thee.

334   Let Us, Who Mystically Represent

Greek hymn, 6th century
Tr. anonymous

Cherubic Hymn Irregular
Orthodox traditional melody

Let us, who mys - ti - cally rep - re - sent the cher-
u - bim, rep - re - sent the cher - u - bim, and who
sing the thrice - ho - ly hymn to the life - cre -
at - ing Trin - i - ty, to the life - cre - at - ing Trin -
i - ty, now lay a - side all earth - ly cares,
now lay a - side all earth - ly cares, now lay a -
side all earth - ly cares. A - men. That we may
re - ceive the King of all, who comes in - vis - i-
bly up - borne by the an - gel - ic hosts.
Al - le - lu - ia, Al - le - lu - ia, Al - le - lu-
ia, Al - le - lu - ia.

When Thou, O Lord, Wast Baptized 335

En Iordane Irregular
Orthodox traditional melody

When thou, O Lord, wast baptized in the Jor-dan, the wor-ship of the Trinity was made man-i-fest! For the voice of the Fa-ther bare wit-ness to thee, and called thee his be-lov-ed Son! And the Spir-it, in the form of a dove, con-firmed the truth-ful-ness of his word, O Christ our God, who hast re-vealed thy-self and hast enlightened the world, glo-ry to thee!

Thy Nativity, O Christ Our God 336

He Genesis Sou Irregular
Orthodox traditional melody

Thy nativity, O Christ our God, has shone to the world the light of wis-dom! For by it, those who wor-shiped the stars were taught by a star to adore thee, the Sun of righ-teous-ness, and to know thee, the O-ri-ent from on high, O Lord, glo-ry to thee!

O Gladsome Light of Holy Glory

Greek hymn, 2d century
Tr. anonymous

Phos Hilaron Irregular
Orthodox traditional melody

O glad-some light of ho-ly glo - ry, Ho-ly Im -

mor-tal One, heav-enly Fa - ther, Di-vine E - ter-nal One.

Bles-sed Je - - su - - us Christ, we come un-to thy

light. To the glo-ry of the set - ting sun be-hold-ing rays of

eve-ning light, we praise thee, O Fa - ther, and Son, and

Ho - ly Spir - it. Wor-thy is thy

name, of praise and ex - al - ta - - - - - tion, with

O Gladsome Light of Holy Glory (cont.)

voic-es raised on high, O Son of God, who gives of the

pre-cious gift of life to all man - kind. And thus the world pro - claims

thee, with glo - ry to thy ho - ly name.

O Christ Has Risen from the Dead   338

Christos Aneste Irregular
Orthodox traditional melody

O Christ has ris - en from the dead, and

through death and by death has tram - pled, tram - pled, up - on

death, and thus be - stowed up - on those in the tombs the gift

of life, of e - ter - nal life.

Thy Mystical Supper, O Son of God

Ton Koinonikon Irregular
Orthodox traditional melody

Thy mystical supper, O Son of God, ac - cept me to - day
as a com - mu - ni - cant; for I will not reveal thy
mystery to thine en - e - mies, neither like Judas will I
give thee a kiss, but like the thief will I con - fess
thee; re - mem - ber me, O Lord, in thy king - dom,
re - mem - ber me, O Lord, in thy king - dom.

O Jesus, We Adore Thee

340

John Rodgers, 1917–
Refrain from the 'Raccolta'

O Sacrament Most Holy 13. 13. with Refrain
Fulda, 'Gesangbuch,' 1891
Harm. by John Rodgers, 1917–

Unison

1. O Je - sus, we a - dore thee, who in thy love di - vine Con -
2. O Je - sus, we a - dore thee, our vic - tim and our priest, Whose
3. O Je - sus, we a - dore thee, our Sav - ior and our King, And

ceal thy might - y God - head in forms of bread and wine.
pre - cious blood and bod - y be - come our sa - cred feast.
with the saints and an - gels an hum - ble hom - age bring.

O Sac - ra - ment most ho - ly, O Sac - ra - ment di - vine, All

praise and all thanks - giv - ing be ev - ery mo - ment thine!

Words and music published by The Liturgical Press. Copyrighted by The Order of St. Benedict, Inc., Collegeville, Minnesota.
Used by permission.

333

341   What You Gave Us for Our Taking

Tua munera fuerunt 8. 8. 7. 7.
Anonymous Latin hymn
Tr. by John Julian Ryan, 1898– , alt.
Source unknown
Harm. by David Kraehenbuehl, 1923–

1. What you gave us for our tak-ing Now as works of hu-man mak-ing
2. These our gifts, by Christ made roy-al, Come from hearts con-trite and loy-al;
3. May this bread and may this wine, then, Born of earth, be made di-vine, when
4. So may foods that quench and nour-ish Change to make the spir-it flour-ish,

Let us, Lord, give back to you, Let us, Lord, give back to you.
Take them, Fa-ther, with our love, Take them, Fa-ther, with our love.
They be-come Christ's sac-ri-fice, They be-come Christ's sac-ri-fice.
Pledge of heav-en's feast of joy, Pledge of heav-en's feast of joy.

342   Beneath the Forms of Outward Rite

Belmont C. M.
Adapted from William Gardiner's
James A. Blaisdell, 1867–1957
'Sacred Melodies,' 1812

1. Be-neath the forms of out-ward rite Thy sup-per, Lord, is spread
2. The bread is al-ways con-se-crate Which men di-vide with men;
3. The bless-ed cup is on-ly passed True mem-o-ry of thee,
4. O Mas-ter, through these sym-bols shared, Thine own dear self im-part,

In ev-ery qui-et up-per room Where faint-ing souls are fed.
And ev-ery act of broth-er-hood Re-peats thy feast a-gain.
When life a-new pours out its wine With rich suf-fi-cien-cy.
That in our dai-ly life may flame The pas-sion of thy heart. A-men.

At the Lamb's High Feast We Sing

343

Latin office hymn, 17th century
Tr. by Robert Campbell, 1814–1868, alt.

Sonne der Gerechtigkeit 7. 7. 7. 7. 4.
Bohemian Brethren, 1566
Harm. by Jan O. Bender, 1909–

Unison

1. At the Lamb's high feast we sing Praise to our vic-
2. Praise we him, whose love di - vine Gives his sa - cred
3. Might - y Vic - tim from the sky, Hell's fierce powers be-
4. Now no more can death ap - pall, Now no more the

to rious King, Who has washed us in the tide
blood for wine, Gives his bod - y for the feast,
neath thee lie; Thou hast con - quered in the fight,
grave en - thrall; Thou hast o - pened par - a - dise,

Flow - ing from his pierc - ed side. Al - le - lu - ia!
Christ the Vic - tim, Christ the Priest. Al - le - lu - ia!
Thou hast brought us life and light. Al - le - lu - ia!
And in thee thy saints shall rise. Al - le - lu - ia!

5. Easter triumph, Easter joy,
Sin alone can this destroy;
From sin's power do thou set free
Souls newborn, O Lord, in thee.
Alleluia!

6. Hymns of glory, songs of praise,
Father, unto thee we raise:
Risen Lord, all praise to thee
With the Spirit ever be.
Alleluia!

344   Take Our Bread, We Ask You

Take Our Bread Irregular
Joseph Wise, 1939–
Harm. by G. Miller, 1936–

Joseph Wise, 1939–

Take our bread, we ask you; take our hearts, we love you.

Take our lives, O Fa-ther: we are yours, we are

yours.   1. Yours as we stand at the ta-ble

you set; Yours as we eat the bread our hearts can't

for-get.   We are the sign of your life with us

345   O King of Might and Splendor

Crüger 7. 6. 7. 6. D.
Johann Crüger, 1598–1662
Arr. by William H. Monk, 1823–1899
Harm. by Gregory Murray, 1905–

'Manuale cantus sancti,' Ratisbon, 19th century
Tr. by Gregory Murray, 1905–

1. O King of might and splen - dor, Cre - a - tor most a - dored,
2. Thy bod - y thou hast giv - en, Thy blood thou hast out-poured,

This sac - ri - fice we ren - der To thee as sov-ereign Lord.
That sin might be for - giv - en, O Je - sus, lov - ing Lord.

May these our gifts be pleas - ing Un - to thy Maj - es - ty,
As now with love most ten - der Thy death we cel - e - brate,

Man - kind from sin re - leas - ing Who have of - fend - ed thee.
Our lives in self - sur - ren - der To thee we con - se - crate.

Words and harmonization from *The Westminster Hymnal.* Used by permission of A. Gregory Murray and Search Press, Ltd.

Humbly Let Us Voice Our Homage   346

Thomas Aquinas, 1227-1274, cento
Tr. by Melvin Farrell, 1930-

St. Thomas 8. 7. 8. 7. 8. 7.
John F. Wade, c. 1711-1786

1. Hum-bly let us voice our hom-age For so great a
2. Glo-ry, hon-or, ad-o-ra-tion Let us sing with

sac-ra-ment: Let all for-mer rites sur-ren-der
one ac-cord! Praised be God, al-might-y Fa-ther;

To the Lord's new tes-ta-ment; What our sens-es
Praised be Christ, his Son, our Lord; Praised be God the

fail to fath-om Let us grasp through faith's con-sent!
Ho-ly Spir-it; Tri-une God-head be a-dored! A-men.

Humbly We Adore Thee

Ascribed to Thomas Aquinas, 1227–1274
Tr. by Melvin Farrell, 1930–

Adoro te devote 11. 11. 12. 12.
Paris, 'Processionale,' 1697

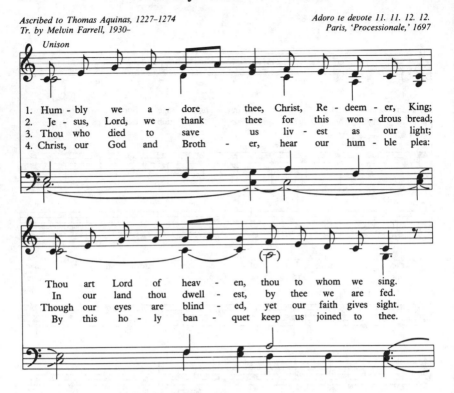

1. Hum - bly we a - dore thee, Christ, Re - deem - er, King;
2. Je - sus, Lord, we thank thee for this won - drous bread;
3. Thou who died to save us liv - est as our light;
4. Christ, our God and Broth - er, hear our hum - ble plea:

Thou art Lord of heav - en, thou to whom we sing.
In our land thou dwell - est, by thee we are fed.
Though our eyes are blind - ed, yet our faith gives sight.
By this ho - ly ban - quet keep us joined to thee.

5. Hail, thou Word incarnate, born from Mary's womb;
   Hail, thou Strength immortal, risen from the tomb.
   Share with us thy victory, Savior ever blest:
   Live more fully in our hearts; be our constant guest.

6. Faith alone reveals here bread of paradise;
   Faith alone may witness Jesus' sacrifice.
   Therefore, Lord, as once of old Thomas gained his sight,
   Now increase our feeble faith: shed thy healing light.

7. Christ, at his last supper, breaking bread, decreed:
   "This, my body, take and eat"—heavenly food indeed!
   Then he blessed the cup of wine—"Take ye this," he said:
   "Drink the chalice of my blood, soon for sinners shed."

8. Now with glad thanksgiving, praise Christ glorified;
   He in us is present; we in him abide.
   Members of his body, we in him are one;
   Hail this sacred union, heaven on earth begun!

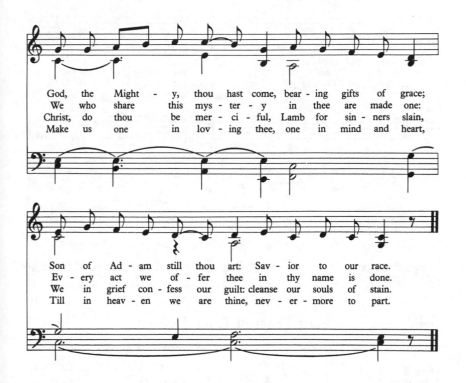

God, the Might - y, thou hast come, bear - ing gifts of grace;
We who share this mys - ter - y in thee are made one:
Christ, do thou be mer - ci - ful, Lamb for sin - ners slain,
Make us one in lov - ing thee, one in mind and heart,

Son of Ad - am still thou art: Sav - ior to our race.
Ev - ery act we of - fer thee in thy name is done.
We in grief con - fess our guilt: cleanse our souls of stain.
Till in heav - en we are thine, nev - er - more to part.

348 Draw Nigh and Take the Body of the Lord

Anonymous, Bangor 'Antiphoner,' 7th century
Tr. by John Mason Neale, 1818–1866, cento

Lammas 10. 10.
Arthur H. Brown, 1830–1926

1. Draw nigh and take the bod - y of the Lord,
2. Saved by that bod - y and that ho - ly blood,
3. Sal - va - tion's giv - er, Christ, the on - ly Son,
4. Of - fered was he for great - est and for least,

And drink the ho - ly blood for you out - poured.
With souls re - freshed, we ren - der thanks to God.
By his dear cross and blood the vic - tory won.
Him - self the vic - tim, and him - self the priest.

349 Blest Feast of Love Divine!

Thatcher S. M.
Edward Denny, 1796–1889, cento, alt.
Arr. from George Frederick Handel, 1685–1759

1. Blest feast of love di - vine! 'Tis grace that makes us free
2. That blood which flowed for sin, In sym - bol here we see,
3. O if this glimpse of love Be so di - vine - ly sweet,
4. To see thee face to face, Thy per - fect like - ness wear,

To feed up - on this bread and wine, In mem - ory, Lord, of thee!
And feel the bless - ed pledge with - in, That we are loved of thee!
What will it be, O Lord, a - bove, Thy glad-dening smile to meet!
And all thy ways of won - drous grace Through end - less years de-clare! A-men.

Jesus, My Lord, My God, My All

350

Jesus, My Lord, My God L. M. with Refrain

Frederick William Faber, 1814–1863, cento

English traditional melody

1. Je - sus, my Lord, my God, my All! How can I love thee as I ought? And how re - vere this won - drous gift, So far sur - pass - ing hope or thought?

2. Had I but Mar - y's sin - less heart, To love thee with, my dear - est King; O! with what bursts of fer - vent praise, Thy good-ness, Je - sus, would I sing.

3. O! see up - on the al - tar placed The vic - tim of di - vin - est love! Let all the earth be - low a - dore, And join the choirs of heaven a - bove.

4. Je - sus, dear pas - tor of the flock, We crowd in love a - bout thy feet; Our voic - es yearn to praise thee, Lord, And joy - ful - ly thy pres - ence greet.

Refrain

Sweet Sac - ra - ment, we thee a - dore; O! make us love thee more and more; O! make us love thee more and more.

351   For the Bread, Which Thou Hast Broken

Agape 8. 7. 8. 7.

Louis F. Benson, 1855–1930   *Charles J. Dickinson, 1822–1883*

1. For the bread, which thou hast bro-ken; For the
2. By this pledge that thou dost love us, By thy
3. With our saint-ed ones in glo-ry Seat-ed
4. In thy serv-ice, Lord, de-fend us; In our

wine, which thou hast poured; For the words, which thou hast
gift of peace re-stored, By thy call to heaven a-
at our Fa-ther's board, May the church that wait-eth
hearts keep watch and ward; In the world where thou dost

spo-ken— Now we give thee thanks, O Lord.
bove us, Hal-low all our lives, O Lord.
for thee Keep love's tie un-bro-ken, Lord.
send us Let thy king-dom come, O Lord. A-men.

352   According to Thy Gracious Word

Martyrdom C. M.
Scotch traditional melody
Arr. by Hugh Wilson, 1764–1824, and
Robert Archibald Smith, 1780–1829

James Montgomery, 1771–1854, cento

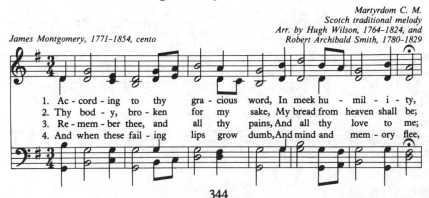

1. Ac-cord-ing to thy gra-cious word, In meek hu-mil-i-ty,
2. Thy bod-y, bro-ken for my sake, My bread from heaven shall be;
3. Re-mem-ber thee, and all thy pains, And all thy love to me;
4. And when these fail-ing lips grow dumb, And mind and mem-ory flee,

This will I do, my dy-ing Lord, I will re - mem-ber thee.
Thy tes-ta-men-tal cup I take, And thus re - mem-ber thee:
Yea, while a breath, a pulse re-mains, Will I re - mem-ber thee.
When thou shalt in thy king-dom come, Je-sus, re - mem-ber me. A-men.

Bread of the World in Mercy Broken 353

Reginald Heber, 1783–1826

Eucharistic Hymn 9. 8. 9. 8.
John S. B. Hodges, 1830–1915

1. Bread of the world in mer - cy bro - ken, Wine of the soul in
2. Look on the heart by sor - row bro - ken, Look on the tears by

mer - cy shed, By whom the words of life were spo - ken,
sin - ners shed; And be your feast to us the to - ken

And in whose death our sins are dead:
That by your grace our souls are fed. A - men.

354 Here at Thy Table, Lord

May Pierpont Hoyt, 19th century

Bread of Life 6. 4. 6. 4. D.
William F. Sherwin, 1826–1888

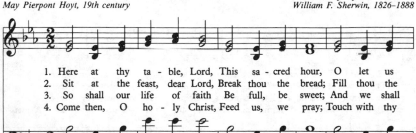

1. Here at thy ta - ble, Lord, This sa - cred hour, O let us
2. Sit at the feast, dear Lord, Break thou the bread; Fill thou the
3. So shall our life of faith Be full, be sweet; And we shall
4. Come then, O ho - ly Christ, Feed us, we pray; Touch with thy

feel thee near, In lov - ing power, Call - ing our thoughts a - way
cup that brings Life to the dead: That we may find in thee
find our strength For each day meet; Fed by thy liv - ing bread,
pierc - ed hand Each com - mon day, Mak - ing this earth - ly life

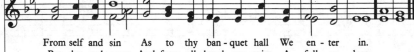

From self and sin As to thy ban - quet hall We en - ter in.
Par - don and peace, And from all bond - age win A full re - lease.
All hun - ger past, We shall be sat - is - fied, And saved at last.
Full of thy grace, Till in the home of heaven We find our place. A - men.

355 Be Known to Us in Breaking Bread

James Montgomery, 1771–1854, cento, alt.

St. Flavian C. M.
Day's Psalter, 1562

F   Csus   C   F   Dm   Gm7   C   F   Bb   F   Bb   Gm   A

1. Be known to us in break - ing bread, But do not then de - part;
2. Re - main with us in love di - vine; Your bod - y and your blood,

Sav - ior, a - bide with us, and spread Your Ta - ble in our heart.
That liv - ing bread, that heav - en - ly wine, Be our im - mor - tal food. A - men.

The King of Heaven His Table Spreads 356

Dundee (French) C. M.
Philip Doddridge, 1702-1751, cento
Scottish Psalter, 1615

1. The King of heaven his ta - ble spreads, And
2. Par - don and peace to dy - ing men And
3. Mil - lions of souls, in glo - ry now, Were
4. All things are read - y, come a - way, Nor

bless - ings crown the board; Not par - a - dise, with
end - less life are given, Through the rich blood that
fed and feast - ed here; And mil - lions more, still
weak ex - cus - es frame. Come to your plac - es

all its joys, Could such de - light af - ford.
Je - sus shed, To raise our souls to heaven.
on the way, A - round the board ap - pear.
at the feast, And bless the found - er's name. A - men.

357 Here, O My Lord, I See Thee Face to Face

Morecambe 10. 10. 10. 10.

Horatius Bonar, 1808-1889, cento

Frederick C. Atkinson, 1841-1897

1. Here, O my Lord, I see thee face to face;
   Here would I touch and han-dle things un-seen,
   Here grasp with firm-er hand e-ter-nal grace,
   And all my wea-ri-ness up-on thee lean.

2. Here would I feed up-on the bread of God,
   Here drink with thee the roy-al wine of heaven;
   Here would I lay a-side each earth-ly load,
   Here taste a-fresh the calm of sin for-given.

3. This is the hour of ban-quet and of song;
   This is the heav-enly Ta-ble spread for me:
   Here let me feast, and, feast-ing, still pro-long
   The brief, bright hour of fel-low-ship with thee.

4. I have no help but thine, nor do I need
   An-oth-er arm save thine to lean up-on:
   It is e-nough, my Lord, e-nough in-deed;
   My strength is in thy might, thy might a-lone. A-men.

Lord, Who at Your First Eucharist Did Pray 358

William Harry Turton, 1856–1938, cento, alt.

Unde et memores 10. 10. 10. 10. 10. 10.
William H. Monk, 1823–1889, alt.

1. Lord, who at your first Eu - cha - rist did pray That all your church might
2. For all your church, O Lord, we in - ter - cede. Make all our sad di -
3. We pray to you for wan-derers from your fold. O bring them back, good

be for - ev - er one, Grant us at ev - ery Eu - cha - rist to say
vi - sions soon to cease; Draw us the near - er each to each, we plead,
Shep-herd of the sheep, Back to the faith which saints be - lieved of old,

With long - ing heart and soul, "Your will be done." O may we all one
By draw - ing all to you, O Prince of Peace. Thus may we all one
Back to the church which still that faith shall keep. Soon may we all one

bread, one bod - y be, Through this blest sac - ra - ment of u - ni - ty.
bread, one bod - y be, Through this blest sac - ra - ment of u - ni - ty.
bread, one bod - y be, Through this blest sac - ra - ment of u - ni - ty.

359   O Living Bread from Heaven

Johann Rist, 1607–1667, cento
Tr. by Catherine Winkworth, 1827–1878

Aurelia 7. 6. 7. 6. D.
Samuel S. Wesley, 1810–1876

1. O liv - ing Bread from heav - en, How hast thou fed thy guest!
2. My Lord, thou here hast led me With - in thy ho - liest ' place,
3. Thou giv - est all I want - ed, The food can death de - stroy;
4. Lord, grant me that, thus strength-ened With heav - enly food, while here

The gifts thou now hast giv - en Have filled my heart with rest.
And there thy - self hast fed me With trea - sures of thy grace;
And thou hast free - ly grant - ed The cup of end - less joy.
My course on earth is length-ened, I serve with ho - ly fear;

O won - drous food of bless - ing, O cup that heals our woes,
And thou hast free - ly giv - en What earth could nev - er buy,
Ah, Lord, I do not mer - it The fa - vor thou hast shown,
And when thou call'st my spir - it To leave this world be - low,

My heart, this gift pos - sess - ing, In thank - ful song o'er-flows!
The Bread of Life from heav - en, That now I shall not die.
And all my soul and spir - it Bow down be - fore thy throne.
I en - ter, through thy mer - it, Where joys un - min - gled flow. A - men.

Words and music from the *Lutheran Service Book and Hymnal.* Used by permission of Commission on the Liturgy and Hymnal.

Let Us Break Bread Together

Break Bread Together 7. 3. 7. 3. with Refrain
American Negro melody

Spiritual

1. Let us break bread to - geth - er On our knees, on our knees;
2. Let us drink wine to - geth - er On our knees, on our knees;
3. Let us praise God to - geth - er On our knees, on our knees;

Let us break bread to - geth - er On our knees, on our knees.
Let us drink wine to - geth - er On our knees, on our knees.
Let us praise God to - geth - er On our knees, on our knees.

Refrain

When I fall on my knees, with my face to the ris - ing

sun, O Lord, have mer - cy on me. A - men.

361 Come, Let's Share in the Banquet

Sebastian Temple, 1928–

Banquet of the Lord 10. 7. 10. 7. with Refrain
Sebastian Temple, 1928–

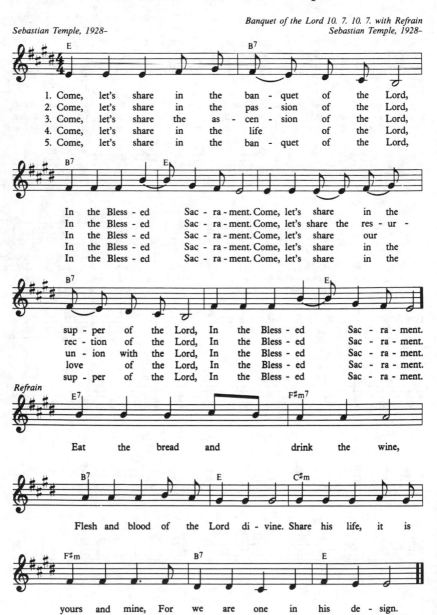

1. Come, let's share in the ban - quet of the Lord,
2. Come, let's share in the pas - sion of the Lord,
3. Come, let's share the as - cen - sion of the Lord,
4. Come, let's share in the life of the Lord,
5. Come, let's share in the ban - quet of the Lord,

In the Bless - ed Sac - ra - ment. Come, let's share in the
In the Bless - ed Sac - ra - ment. Come, let's share the res - ur -
In the Bless - ed Sac - ra - ment. Come, let's share our
In the Bless - ed Sac - ra - ment. Come, let's share in the
In the Bless - ed Sac - ra - ment. Come, let's share in the

sup - per of the Lord, In the Bless - ed Sac - ra - ment.
rec - tion of the Lord, In the Bless - ed Sac - ra - ment.
un - ion with the Lord, In the Bless - ed Sac - ra - ment.
love of the Lord, In the Bless - ed Sac - ra - ment.
sup - per of the Lord, In the Bless - ed Sac - ra - ment.

Refrain

Eat the bread and drink the wine,

Flesh and blood of the Lord di - vine. Share his life, it is

yours and mine, For we are one in his de - sign.

Words and music reprinted by permission of the Franciscan Communications Center, Los Angeles, Calif.

If We Eat of the Lord

362

Sebastian Temple, 1928-

If We Eat 6. 6. 7. D.
Sebastian Temple, 1928-

1. If we eat of the Lord And we
2. The Lord tells us his plans; Lis - ten
3. "This com - mand," says the Lord, "I give
4. "From this ban - quet of life Bring my
5. If we eat of the Lord And we

drink of the Lord, Like the Lord we shall all
to his com - mands: "To the Fa - ther come through
spe - cially to you: Love each man as I love
love to the world; Be a sign for all to
drink of the Lord, Like the Lord we shall all

be. Then we live with his life, And we
me; Share this ban quet of love, Eat my
you. By this sign all will know What I
see, That I bring man my peace Through the
be. Then we live with his life, And we

share in his love, And his truth will make us free.
flesh, drink my blood, Do this in my mem - o - ry."
have to be - stow; Through this love, man I re - new.
break - ing of bread, That I come to make him free."
share in his love, And his truth will make us free.

363   We Come Before Our God and King

Eisenach 8. 8. 8. 8. 8. 8.
Johann Hermann Schein, 1586–1630
Harm. by Eugene Englert, 1931–

Eugene Lindusky, 1924–

1. We come be-fore our God and King; Our hum-ble bread and
2. We place our-selves be-fore your throne: Take all we are and

wine we bring. Though now the fruit of field and vine, They
all we own. Our hearts, our lives are yours by right, Then

soon shall be a gift di-vine, For when the sa-cred
make them pleas-ing in your sight. U-nite them all with

words are done, Our gift will be your on-ly Son.
Christ, your Son, That he and we may be as one.

One Table Spread

Dalton E. McDonald, 1910–

Mannitto 10. 4. 10. 4. 12. 10.
Donald D. Kettring, 1907–

One ta-ble spread through-out the whole wide earth— The King's own feast!

From ev-ery na-tion men shall come to share, From west and east.

All now is read-y, and our Host in-vites us in:

"Both bad and good are guests. Let us be-gin." A - men.

365

All Hail, Adored Trinity

Anonymous Latin, before 11th century
Tr. by John D. Chambers, 1805-1893, cento, alt.

Old 'Hundredth L. M.
Louis Bourgeois, c. 1510-1561

1. All hail, a - dor - ed Trin - i - ty; All
2. Three Per - sons praise we ev - er - more, And
3. O Trin - i - ty, O U - ni - ty, Be

praise, e - ter - nal U - ni - ty: O God the Fa - ther,
thee the e - ter - nal One a - dore: In thy sure mer - cy
pres - ent as we wor - ship thee; And to the an - gels'

God the Son, And God the Spir - it, ev - er One.
ev - er kind, May we our true pro - tec - tion find.
songs in light Our prayers and prais - es now u - nite.

366

Breathe on Me, Breath of God

Edwin Hatch, 1835-1889, alt.

Trentham S. M.
Robert Jackson, 1842-1914

1. Breathe on me, breath of God, Fill me with life a - new, That I may
2. Breathe on me, breath of God, Un - til my heart is pure, Un - til with
3. Breathe on me, breath of God, Till I am whol - ly thine, Un - til this
4. Breathe on me, breath of God, So shall I nev - er die, But live with

Breathe on Me, Breath of God (cont.)

love what you would love And do what you would do.
you I will one will, To do and to en - dure.
earth - ly part of me Glows with your fire di - vine.
you the per - fect life Of your e - ter - ni - ty. A - men.

Spirit of God, Descend Upon My Heart 367

Morecambe 10. 10. 10. 10.

Ascribed to George Croly, 1780–1860, alt. *Frederick C. Atkinson, 1841–1897*

1. Spir - it of God, de - scend up - on my heart; Wean it from earth;through
2. I ask no dream, no proph - et ec - sta - sies, No sud - den rend - ing
3. Have you not bid us love you, God and King? All, all your own, soul,
4. Teach me to feel that you are al - ways nigh; Teach me the strug - gles
5. Teach me to love you as your an - gels love, One ho - ly pas - sion

all its puls - es move; Stoop to my weak - ness, might - y as you are,
of the veil of clay, No an - gel vis - i - tant, no o - pening skies;
heart, and strength, and mind; I see your cross—there teach my heart to cling:
of the soul to bear, To check the ris - ing doubt, the reb - el sigh;
fill - ing all my frame; The bap - tism of the heaven - de - scend - ed Dove,

And make me love you as I ought to love.
But take the dim - ness of my soul a - way.
O let me seek you, and O let me find!
Teach me the pa - tience of un - an - swered prayer.
My heart an al - tar, and your love the flame. A - men.

357

368 God, Father, Praise and Glory

Anonymous
Mainz, 'Gesangbuch,' 1833
Tr. by John Rothensteiner, ?-1936, alt.

Gott Vater sei gepriesen 7. 6. 7. 6. with Refrain
Mainz, 'Gesangbuch,' 1833
Harm. by George Higdon, 1907-

1. God, Fa - ther, praise and glo - ry Thy chil - dren bring to thee.
2. And thou, Lord co - e - ter - nal, God's sole be - got - ten Son,
3. O Ho - ly Ghost, Cre - a - tor, Thou gift of God Most High,

Thy grace and peace to man - kind Shall now for - ev - er be.
O Je - sus, King a - noint - ed, Who hast re - demp - tion won.
Life, love, and ho - ly wis - dom, Our weak - ness now sup - ply.

Refrain

O most ho - ly Trin - i - ty, Un - di - vid - ed U - ni - ty;

Ho - ly God, might - y God, God im - mor - tal, be a - dored.

358

Come, Holy Ghost, Creator Blest 369

Ascribed to Rhabanus Maurus, 776–856, cento
Tr. by Edward Caswall, 1814–1878, alt.

Veni Creator L. M.
Arr. from Louis Lambillotte, 1796–1855
Harm. by Lawrence D. Gagnier, 1921–

1. Come, Holy Ghost, Creator blest, And in our hearts take up thy rest; Come with thy grace and heavenly aid, To fill the hearts which thou hast made.

2. O Comfort blest, to thee we cry, Thou heavenly gift of God Most High; Thou font of life, and fire of love, And sweet anointing from above.

3. Praise be to thee, Father and Son, And Holy Spirit, Three in One; And may the Son on us bestow The gifts that from the Spirit flow.

O Holy Spirit, Come to Us

Anonymous Latin hymn, cento
Tr. by Melvin Farrell, 1930–

Tallis' Ordinal C. M.
Thomas Tallis, c. 1505–1585

1. O Ho - ly Spir - it, come to us, The chil - dren thou hast made: In - flame our hearts and rule our minds With thine un - fail - ing aid.

2. Thou art our source of strength and might, Great gift from God a - bove: Thou art the font of truth and light, The flame of hope and love.

3. We thank thee for thy gifts of grace, O Prom - ised One of God: Thy won - drous life be - comes our own, Thy strength, our staff and rod.

4. Then come, great Spir - it, to thy sons; Our hearts make pure and strong. Di - rect our wea - ry steps to thee, And turn our wills from wrong.

5. O mighty Counsel, hear our prayer:
And teach us trust in thee;
For in thy love we place our hope
To live eternally.

6. Show us the Father and the Son,
O Spirit, we implore,
That in the Godhead we may live
Both now and evermore.

Holy Ghost, with Light Divine 371

Andrew Reed, 1787-1862, cento

Gottschalk 7. 7. 7. 7.
Louis M. Gottschalk, 1829-1869
Arr. by Edwin P. Parker, 1836-1925

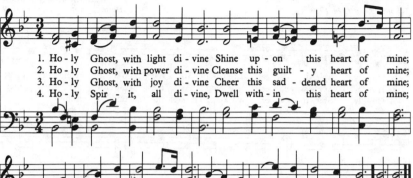

1. Ho-ly Ghost, with light di-vine Shine up-on this heart of mine;
2. Ho-ly Ghost, with power di-vine Cleanse this guilt-y heart of mine;
3. Ho-ly Ghost, with joy di-vine Cheer this sad-dened heart of mine;
4. Ho-ly Spir-it, all di-vine, Dwell with-in this heart of mine;

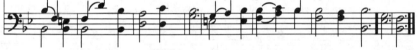

Chase the shades of night a-way, Turn my dark-ness in-to day.
Long has sin, with-out con-trol, Held do-min-ion o'er my soul.
Bid my man-y woes de-part, Heal my wound-ed, bleed-ing heart.
Cast down ev-ery i-dol throne, Reign su-preme, and reign a-lone. A-men.

Come, Holy Spirit, Heavenly Dove 372

Isaac Watts, 1674-1748, cento, alt.

St. Agnes C. M.
John B. Dykes, 1823-1876

1. Come, Ho-ly Spir-it, heav-enly Dove, With your life-giv-ing powers;
2. In vain we tune our for-mal songs, In vain we strive to rise;
3. Dear Lord, and shall we ev-er live At this poor dy-ing rate?
4. Come, Ho-ly Spir-it, heav-enly Dove, With your life-giv-ing powers;

Kin-dle a flame of sa-cred love In these cold hearts of ours.
Ho-san-nas lan-guish on our tongues, And our de-vo-tion dies.
Our love so faint, so cold to you, And yours to us so great!
Come, shed a-broad the Sav-ior's love, And that shall kin-dle ours. A-men.

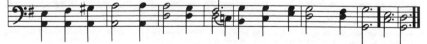

Holy Spirit, Ever Dwelling

In Babilone 8. 7. 8. 7. D.
Dutch traditional melody
Harm. by Carl F. Schalk, 1929–

Timothy Rees, 1874–1939

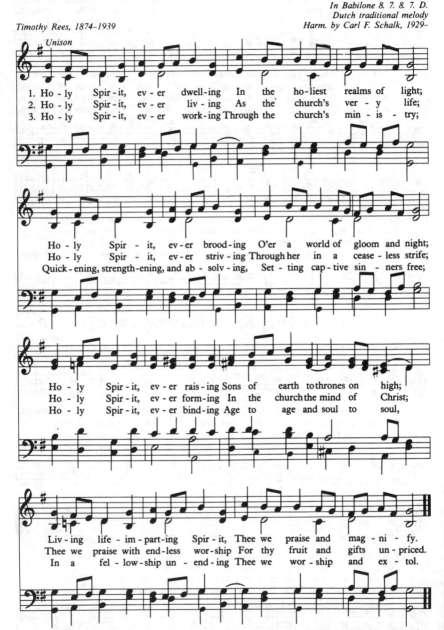

Unison

1. Ho - ly Spir - it, ev - er dwell-ing In the ho - liest realms of light;
2. Ho - ly Spir - it, ev - er liv - ing As the church's ver - y life;
3. Ho - ly Spir - it, ev - er work-ing Through the church's min - is - try;

Ho - ly Spir - it, ev - er brood-ing O'er a world of gloom and night;
Ho - ly Spir - it, ev - er striv - ing Through her in a cease - less strife;
Quick - ening, strength-ening, and ab - solv - ing, Set - ting cap - tive sin - ners free;

Ho - ly Spir - it, ev - er rais - ing Sons of earth to thrones on high;
Ho - ly Spir - it, ev - er form-ing In the church the mind of Christ;
Ho - ly Spir - it, ev - er bind-ing Age to age and soul to soul,

Liv - ing life - im - part-ing Spir - it, Thee we praise and mag - ni - fy.
Thee we praise with end-less wor - ship For thy fruit and gifts un - priced.
In a fel - low-ship un - end - ing Thee we wor - ship and ex - tol.

Words from *Mirfield Mission Hymn Book;* used by permission of A. R. Mowbray & Co. Ltd. Harmonization from *A New Song,*
© 1967 by Concordia Publishing House; used by permission.

Holy Spirit, Truth Divine

374

Vienna 7. 7. 7. 7.

Samuel Longfellow, 1819-1892, cento, alt.

Justin Heinrich Knecht, 1752-1817

1. Ho - ly Spir - it, truth di - vine, Dawn up - on this soul of mine;
2. Ho - ly Spir - it, love di - vine, Glow with - in this heart of mine;
3. Ho - ly Spir - it, power di - vine, Fill and nerve this will of mine;
4. Ho - ly Spir - it, right di - vine, King with - in my con-science reign;

Word of God, and in - ward light, Wake my spir - it, clear my sight.
Kin - dle ev - ery high de - sire; Per - ish self in your pure fire.
By you may I strong-ly live, Brave - ly bear, and no - bly strive.
Be my law, and I shall be Firm - ly bound, for - ev - er free. A-men.

Amazing Grace! How Sweet the Sound

375

Amazing Grace C. M.
American traditional melody
Arr. by Edwin O. Excell, 1851-1921

John Newton, 1725-1807, cento

1. A - maz - ing grace! How sweet the sound That saved a wretch like me!
2. 'Twas grace that taught my heart to fear, And grace my fears re - lieved;
3. Through man - y dan - gers, toils, and snares I have al - read - y come;
4. The Lord has prom-ised good to me; His word my hope se - cures;

I once was lost, but now am found, Was blind, but now I see.
How pre - cious did that grace ap - pear The hour I first be - lieved!
'Tis grace has brought me safe thus far, And grace will lead me home.
He will my shield and por - tion be As long as life en - dures. A-men.

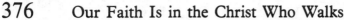

376   Our Faith Is in the Christ Who Walks

Thomas Curtis Clark, 1877-1953

Quebec L. M.
Henry Baker, 1835-1910

1. Our faith is in the Christ who walks With men to-day, in street and mart;
2. His gos-pel calls for liv-ing men, With sing-ing blood and minds a-lert;
3. We serve no God whose work is done, Who rests with-in his fir-ma-ment;
4. God was and is and e'er shall be; Christ lived and loved and loves us still;

The con-stant friend who thinks and talks With those who seek him with the heart.
Strong men, who fall to rise a-gain, Who strive and bleed, with cour-age girt.
Our God, his la-bors but be-gun, Toils ev-er-more, with power un-spent.
And man goes for-ward, proud and free, God's pres-ent pur-pose to ful-fill. A-men.

377   By the Babylonian Rivers

Babylonian Rivers 8. 7. 8. 7.
Latvian melody
Arr. by Ewald J. Bash, 1924–
Harm. by David Hugh Jones, 1900–

Ewald J. Bash, 1924–

1. By the Bab-y-lo-nian riv-ers We sat down in grief and wept;
2. There our cap-tors in de-ri-sion Did re-quire of us a song;
3. How shall we sing the Lord's song In a strange and bit-ter land?
4. Let thy cross be ben-e-dic-tion For men bound in tyr-an-ny;

Hanged our harps up-on a wil-low, Mourned for Zi-on when we slept.
So we sat with star-ing vi-sion, And the days were hard and long.
Can our voic-es veil the sor-row? Lord God, help thy ho-ly band.
By the power of res-ur-rec-tion Loose them from cap-tiv-i-ty.

Brightly Beams Our Father's Mercy

Philip P. Bliss, 1838–1876, alt.

Lower Lights 8. 7. 8. 7. with Refrain
Philip P. Bliss, 1838–1876

1. Bright - ly beams our Fa - ther's mer - cy From his light-house ev - er - more;
2. Dark the night of sin has set - tled, Loud the an - gry bil - lows roar;
3. Trim your fee - ble lamp, my broth - er! Some poor sea - man, tem - pest-tossed,

But to us he gives the keep - ing Of the lights a - long the shore.
Ea - ger eyes are watch-ing, long - ing, For the lights a - long the shore.
Try - ing now to make the har - bor, In the dark - ness may be lost.

Refrain

Let the low - er lights be burn - ing! Send a

gleam a - cross the wave! Some poor faint - ing, strug - gling

sea - man You may res - cue, you may save. A - men.

365

And I Couldn't Hear Nobody Pray

Nobody Pray Irregular with Refrain
American Negro melody
Arr. by David Hugh Jones, 1900–

And I Couldn't Hear Nobody Pray (cont.)

And my Sav - ior,
In - to Ca - naan,
With my Je - sus,

pray, I could-n't hear no-bod-y pray, I pray.

Be Firm and Be Faithful

380

Lyons 11. 11. 11. 11.
J. Michael Haydn, 1737–1806
Arr. by William Gardiner, 1770–1853

Anonymous

1. Be firm and be faith-ful; de - sert not the right; The brave be-come bold - er the
2. If scorn be thy por-tion, if ha - tred and loss, If stripes or a pris - on, re -

dark - er the night. Then up and be do - ing, Though cow-ards may fail; Thy
mem - ber the cross. God watch-es a - bove thee, and he will re-quite; For -

du - ty pur - su - ing, dare all and pre - vail.
sake those that love thee, but nev - er the right.

From the *Christian Science Hymnal.*

367

Nobody Knows the Trouble I've Seen

Nobody Knows Irregular with Refrain
American Negro melody
Arr. by David Hugh Jones, 1900–

Spiritual

No - bod - y knows the trou - ble I've seen, No - bod - y knows but Je - sus, Oh,

no - bod - y knows the trou - ble I've seen, Glo - ry hal - le - lu - jah!

1. Some - times I'm up, some - times I'm down, Oh, yes, Lord!
2. Al - though you see me going a - long so, Oh, yes, Lord!
3. What makes old Sa - tan hate me so? Oh, yes, Lord!

After St. 3, D.C. al Fine

Some - times I'm al - most to the ground, Oh, yes, Lord!
I have my trou - bles here be - low, Oh, yes, Lord!
'Cause he got me once and let me go. Oh, yes, Lord! Oh,

Be Still, My Soul

382

Katherine von Schlegel, 1697-?, cento
Tr. by Jane L. Borthwick, 1813-1897, alt.

Finlandia 10. 10. 10. 10. 10. 10.
Jan Sibelius, 1865-1957
Arr. for 'The Hymnal,' 1933

1. Be still, my soul: the Lord is on your side; Bear pa-tient-ly the cross of grief or pain; Leave to your God to or-der and pro-vide; In ev-ery change he faith-ful will re-main. Be still, my soul: your best, your heav-enly friend Through thorn-y ways leads to a joy-ful end.

2. Be still, my soul: your God does un-der-take To guide the fu-ture as he has the past. Your hope, your con-fi-dence, let noth-ing shake; All now mys-te-rious shall be bright at last. Be still, my soul: the waves and winds still know His voice who ruled them while he dwelt be-low.

3. Be still, my soul: the hour is has-tening on When we shall be for-ev-er with the Lord, When dis-ap-point-ment, grief, and fear are gone, Sor-row for-got, love's pur-est joys re-stored. Be still, my soul: when change and tears are past, All safe and bless-ed we shall meet at last. A-men.

383 Christian, Do You See Them

John Mason Neale, 1818–1866, alt.

St. Andrew of Crete 6. 5. 6. 5. D.
John B. Dykes, 1823–1876

1. Chris - tian, do you see them On the ho - ly ground,
2. Chris - tian, do you feel them, How they work with - in,
3. Chris - tian, do you hear them, How they speak so fair?
4. "Well I know your trou - ble, O my serv - ant true.

How the powers of dark - ness Com - pass you a - round?
Striv - ing, tempt - ing, lur - ing, Goad - ing in - to sin?
"Al - ways fast and vig - il? Al - ways watch and prayer?"
You are ver - y wea - ry— I was wea - ry too.

Chris - tian, up and smite them, Count - ing gain but loss,
Chris - tian, nev - er trem - ble, Nev - er be down - cast;
Chris - tian, an - swer bold - ly: "While I breathe, I pray."
But that toil shall make you Some - day all my own,

In the strength that's prom - ised In the ho - ly cross.
Gird your - self for bat - tle, Watch and pray and fast.
Peace shall fol - low bat - tle, Night shall end in day.
And the end of sor - row Shall be near my throne." A - men.

When Upon Life's Billows   384

Blessings 11. 11. 11. 11. with Refrain

Johnson Oatman, Jr., 1856–1926

Edwin O. Excell, 1851–1921

1. When up-on life's bil-lows you are tem-pest-tossed, When you are dis-
2. Are you ev-er bur-dened with a load of care? Does the cross seem
3. When you look at oth-ers with their lands and gold, Think that Christ has
4. So, a-mid the con-flict, wheth-er great or small, Do not be dis-

cour-aged, think-ing all is lost, Count your man-y bless-ings, name them
heav-y you are called to bear? Count your man-y bless-ings, ev-ery
prom-ised you his wealth un-told; Count your man-y bless-ings, mon-ey
cour-aged, God is o-ver all; Count your man-y bless-ings, an-gels

one by one, And it will sur-prise you what the Lord hath done.
doubt will fly, And you will be sing-ing as the days go by.
can-not buy Your re-ward in heav-en, nor your home on high.
will at-tend, Help and com-fort give you to your jour-ney's end.

Refrain

Count your bless-ings, Name them one by one; Count your
Count your man-y bless-ings, Name them one by one; Count your man-y

bless-ings, See what God hath done; Count your bless-ings,
bless-ings, See what God hath done; Count your man-y bless-ings,

Name them one by one; Count your man-y bless-ings, See what God hath done.

385 Forty Days and Forty Nights

Posen 7. 7. 7. 7.

George C. Strattner, 1650–1705

George C. Strattner, 1650–1705

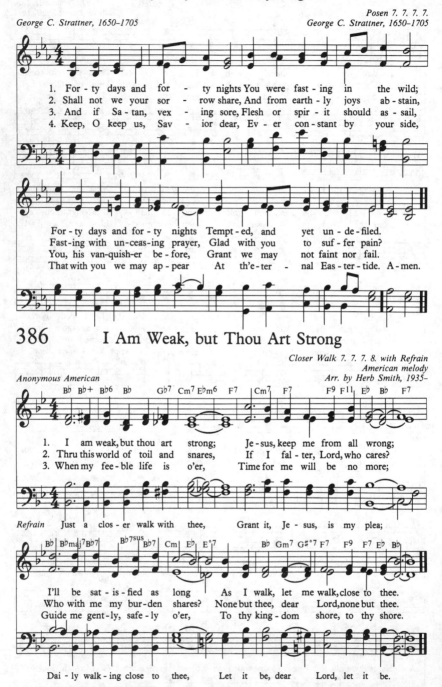

1. For - ty days and for - ty nights You were fast - ing in the wild;
2. Shall not we your sor - row share, And from earth - ly joys ab - stain,
3. And if Sa - tan, vex - ing sore, Flesh or spir - it should as - sail,
4. Keep, O keep us, Sav - ior dear, Ev - er con - stant by your side,

For - ty days and for - ty nights Tempt - ed, and yet un - de - filed.
Fast - ing with un - ceas - ing prayer, Glad with you to suf - fer pain?
You, his van - quish - er be - fore, Grant we may not faint nor fail.
That with you we may ap - pear At th'e - ter - nal Eas - ter - tide. A - men.

386 I Am Weak, but Thou Art Strong

Closer Walk 7. 7. 7. 8. with Refrain
American melody

Anonymous American

Arr. by Herb Smith, 1935-

1. I am weak, but thou art strong; Je - sus, keep me from all wrong;
2. Thru this world of toil and snares, If I fal - ter, Lord, who cares?
3. When my fee - ble life is o'er, Time for me will be no more;

Refrain Just a clos - er walk with thee, Grant it, Je - sus, is my plea;

I'll be sat - is - fied as long As I walk, let me walk, close to thee.
Who with me my bur - den shares? None but thee, dear Lord, none but thee.
Guide me gent - ly, safe - ly o'er, To thy king - dom shore, to thy shore.

Dai - ly walk - ing close to thee, Let it be, dear Lord, let it be.

James Montgomery, 1771-1854
Alt. by Frances A. Hutton, 1811-1877
and Godfrey Thring, 1823-1903

Penitence 6. 5. 6. 5. D.
Spencer Lane, 1843-1903

1. In the hour of tri - al, Je - sus, plead for me,
2. With for - bid - den plea - sures Would this vain world charm,
3. Should thy mer - cy send me Sor - row, toil, or woe,
4. When my last hour com - eth, Fraught with strife and pain,

Lest by base de - ni - al I de - part from thee;
Or its sor - did trea - sures Spread to work me harm;
Or should pain at - tend me On my path be - low,
When my dust re - turn - eth To the dust a - gain;

When thou seest me wa - ver, With a look re - call,
Bring to my re - mem - brance Sad Geth - sem - a - ne,
Grant that I may nev - er Fail thy hand to see;
On thy truth re - ly - ing, Through that mor - tal strife,

Nor for fear or fa - vor Suf - fer me to fall.
Or, in dark - er sem - blance, Cross-crowned Cal - va - ry.
Grant that I may ev - er Cast my care on thee.
Je - sus, take me, dy - ing, To e - ter - nal life. A - men.

388 And Are We Yet Alive

Dennis S. M.

Johann G. Nägeli, 1773–1836

Arr. by Lowell Mason, 1792–1872

Charles Wesley, 1707–1788, cento, alt.

1. And are we yet a - live, And see each oth - er's face? Glo - ry and thanks to Je - sus give For his al - might - y grace.

2. What trou - bles have we seen, What might - y con - flicts past, Fight - ings with - out, and fears with - in, Since we as - sem - bled last!

3. Yet out of all the Lord Hath brought us by his love; And still he doth his help af - ford, And hides our life a - bove.

4. Then let us make our boast Of his re - deem - ing power, Which saves us to the ut - ter - most, Till we can sin no more.

5. Let us take up the cross, Till we the crown ob - tain, And glad - ly reck - on all things loss, So we may Je - sus gain. A - men.

374

Just as I Am, Without One Plea 389

Woodworth L. M.

Charlotte Elliott, 1789–1871, cento

William B. Bradbury, 1816–1868

1. Just as I am, with-out one plea But that thy blood was shed for me
2. Just as I am, though tossed a - bout With man-y a con-flict, man-y a doubt,
3. Just as I am, thou wilt re - ceive, Wilt wel-come, par-don, cleanse, re - lieve;
4. Just as I am, thy love un-known Has bro - ken ev - ery bar - rier down;

And that thou biddest me come to thee, O Lamb of God, I come, I come!
Fight-ings and fears with-in, with-out, O Lamb of God, I come, I come!
Be - cause thy prom - ise I be - lieve, O Lamb of God, I come, I come!
Now to be thine, yea, thine a - lone, O Lamb of God, I come, I come! A-men.

Father, Now Thy Sinful Child 390

Herrnhut 7. 7. 7. 7. (Trochaic)
J. Thommen, 'Erbaulicher
musikalischer Christenschatz,' 1745

Josiah Conder, 1789–1855, alt.

1. Fa - ther, now thy sin - ful child Through thy love is rec - on-ciled.
2. Lord, for - give me, day by day, Debts I can - not hope to pay,
3. Par - don, Lord, and are there those Who my debt-ors are, or foes?
4. Much for - giv - en, may I learn Love for ha - tred to re - turn;

By thy par - doning grace I live; Dai - ly still I cry, For - give.
Du - ties I have left un - done, E - vils I have failed to shun.
I, who by for - give - ness live, Here their tres-pass - es for - give.
Then as-sured my heart shall be Thou, my God, hast par-doned me. A-men.

391 Out of My Bondage, Sorrow, and Night

Jesus, I Come 8. 8. 9. 6. 9. 9. 9. 6.

William T. Sleeper, 1819–1904

George C. Stebbins, 1846–1945

1. Out of my bond-age, sor-row, and night, Je - sus, I come, Je - sus, I come;
2. Out of my shame-ful fail - ure and loss, Je - sus, I come, Je - sus, I come;
3. Out of un - rest and ar - ro-gant pride, Je - sus, I come, Je - sus, I come;
4. Out of the fear and dread of the tomb, Je - sus, I come, Je - sus, I come;

In - to thy free-dom, glad-ness, and light, Je - sus, I come to thee; Out of my
In - to the glo-rious gain of thy cross, Je - sus, I come to thee; Out of earth's
In - to thy bless - ed will to a - bide, Je - sus, I come to thee; Out of my -
In - to the joy and light of thy home, Je - sus, I come to thee; Out of the

sick - ness in - to thy health, Out of my want and in - to thy wealth,
sor - rows in - to thy balm, Out of life's storms and in - to thy calm,
self to dwell in thy love, Out of de - spair in-to rap-tures a - bove,
depths of ru - in un-told, In - to the peace of thy shel - ter-ing fold,

Out of my sin and in - to thy-self, Je - sus, I come to thee.
Out of dis-tress to ju - bi-lant psalm, Je - sus, I come to thee.
Up - ward for aye on wings like a dove, Je - sus, I come to thee.
Ev - er thy glo-rious face to be-hold, Je - sus, I come to thee. A-men.

376

Sinners Jesus Will Receive

392

Erdmann Neumeister, 1671-1756, cento
Tr. by Emma F. Bevan, 1827-1909, alt.

Neumeister 7. 7. 7. 7. with Refrain
James McGranahan, 1840-1907

1. Sin - ners Je - sus will re - ceive; Sound this word of grace to all
2. Come, and he will give you rest; Trust him, for his word is plain;
3. Now my heart con-demns me not, Pure be - fore the law I stand;
4. Christ re - ceiv - eth sin - ful men, E - ven me with all my sin;

Who the heav - enly path - way leave, All who lin - ger, all who fall.
He will take the sin - ful - est; Christ re - ceiv - eth sin - ful men.
He who cleansed me from all spot, Sat - is - fied its last de - mand.
Purged from ev - ery spot and stain, Heaven with him I en - ter in.

Refrain

Sing it o'er and o'er a - gain; Christ re-
Sing it o'er a-gain, sing it o'er a-gain; Christ re-

ceiv - eth sin - ful men; Make the mes sage
ceiv-eth sin-ful men, Christ re-ceiv-eth sin-ful men; Make the message plain,

clear and plain: Christ re - ceiv - eth sin - ful men.
make the message plain:

Years I Spent in Vanity and Pride

William R. Newell, 1868-1956

Calvary 9. 9. 9. 4. with Refrain
Daniel B. Towner, 1850-1919

1. Years I spent in van - i - ty and pride, Car - ing not my Lord was
2. By God's Word at last my sin I learned; Then I trem-bled at the
3. Now I've given to Je - sus ev - ery - thing; Now I glad - ly own him
4. O the love that drew sal - va-tion's plan! O the grace that brought it

cru - ci - fied, Know-ing not it was for me he died On Cal - va - ry.
law I'd spurned, Till my guilt - y soul im - plor - ing turned To Cal - va - ry.
as my King; Now my rap-tured soul can on - ly sing Of Cal - va - ry.
down to man! O the might - y gulf that God did span At Cal - va - ry!

Refrain

Mer - cy there was great, and grace was free; Par - don there was mul - ti -

plied to me; There my bur-dened soul found lib - er - ty, At Cal - va - ry.

It's Me, O Lord

It's Me 9. 7. 9. 7. with Refrain
American Negro melody
Arr. by David Hugh Jones, 1900-

Spiritual

It's me, it's me, it's me, O Lord, Stand-ing in the need of prayer;

It's me, it's me, it's me, O Lord, Stand-ing in the need of prayer.

Not my moth-er nor my fa-ther, but it's me, O Lord, Stand-ing in the need of prayer;

Not my broth-er nor my sis-ter, but it's me, O Lord, Stand-ing in the need of prayer.

395 Marvelous Grace of Our Loving Lord

Julia H. Johnston, 1849–1919

Marvelous Grace 9. 9. 9. 9. with Refrain
Daniel B. Towner, 1850–1919

1. Mar - vel-ous grace of our lov - ing Lord, Grace that ex - ceeds our
2. Sin and de - spair, like the sea waves cold, Threat - en the soul with
3. Dark is the stain that we can - not hide. What can a - vail to
4. Mar - vel-ous, in - fi - nite, match-less grace, Free - ly be - stowed on

sin and our guilt, Yon - der on Cal - va - ry's mount out - poured,
in - fi - nite loss; Grace that is great - er, yes, grace un - told,
wash it a - way? Look! there is flow - ing a crim - son tide;
all who be - lieve; You that are long - ing to see his face,

There where the blood of the Lamb was spilt.
Points to the ref - uge, the might - y cross. Grace, grace,
Whit - er than snow you may be to - day. Mar - vel - ous grace,
Will you this mo - ment his grace re - ceive?

God's grace, Grace that will par - don and cleanse with - in; Grace,
in - fi - nite grace, Mar - vel-ous

grace, God's grace, Grace that is great - er than all our sin.
grace, in - fi - nite grace.

Yes, I Shall Arise

396

I Shall Arise 9. 10. with Refrain
Lucien Deiss, 1921–

Lucien Deiss, 1921–
Unison   *Refrain*

Yes, I shall a - rise and re - turn to my Fa - ther!

1. To you, O Lord, I lift up my soul: In you,
2. Look down on me, have mer - cy, O Lord; For - give
3. My heart and soul shall yearn for your face; Be gra -
4. Do not with - hold your good - ness from me; O Lord,

O my God, I place all my trust.
me my sins, be - hold all my grief.
cious to me and an - swer my plea.
may your love be deep in my soul.

5. To you I pray; have pity on me;
   My God, I have sinned against your great love.

6. Mercy I cry, O Lord, wash me clean;
   And whiter than snow my spirit shall be.

7. Give me again the joy of your help;
   Now open my lips, your praise I will sing.

8. Happy is he, forgiven by God;
   His sins blotted out, his guilt is no more.

9. You are my joy, my refuge and strength;
   Let all upright hearts give praise to the Lord.

10. My soul will sing, my heart will rejoice;
    The blessings of God will fill all my days.

397   There Is a Fountain Filled with Blood

Cleansing Fountain C. M. D.
American traditional melody
Arr. from Lowell Mason, 1792–1872

William Cowper, 1731–1800, cento, alt.

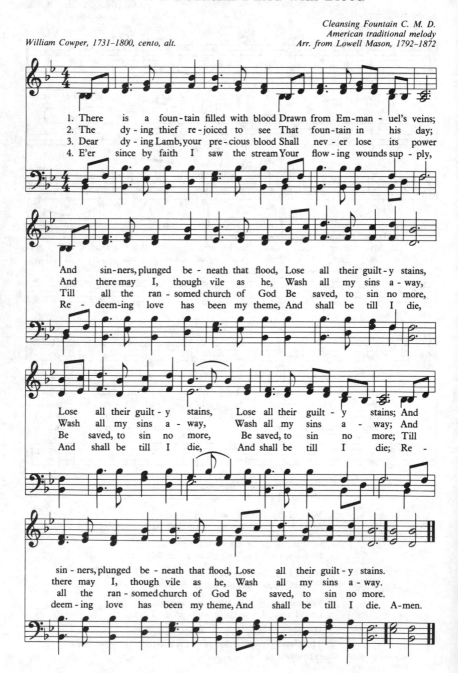

1. There is a foun-tain filled with blood Drawn from Em-man-uel's veins;
2. The dy-ing thief re-joiced to see That foun-tain in his day;
3. Dear dy-ing Lamb, your pre-cious blood Shall nev-er lose its power
4. E'er since by faith I saw the stream Your flow-ing wounds sup-ply,

And sin-ners, plunged be-neath that flood, Lose all their guilt-y stains,
And there may I, though vile as he, Wash all my sins a-way,
Till all the ran-somed church of God Be saved, to sin no more,
Re-deem-ing love has been my theme, And shall be till I die,

Lose all their guilt-y stains, Lose all their guilt-y stains; And
Wash all my sins a-way, Wash all my sins a-way; And
Be saved, to sin no more, Be saved, to sin no more; Till
And shall be till I die, And shall be till I die; Re-

sin-ners, plunged be-neath that flood, Lose all their guilt-y stains.
there may I, though vile as he, Wash all my sins a-way.
all the ran-somed church of God Be saved, to sin no more.
deem-ing love has been my theme, And shall be till I die. A-men.

Cleansing 7. 7. 7. 5. 7. 7. 7. 7.

Fanny J. Crosby, 1823–1915, alt.

William H. Doane, 1832–1915

Duet

1. "Tho' your sins be as scar-let, They shall be as white as snow; as snow;
2. Hear the voice that en-treats you: O re-turn you un-to God! to God!
3. He'll for-give your trans-gres-sions, And re-mem-ber them no more; no more;

Quartet

Tho' they be red like crim-son, They shall be as wool";
He is of great com-pas-sion, And of won-drous love;
"Look un-to me, you peo-ple," Says the Lord your God;

1. Tho' they be red

Duet   **Quartet**

"Tho' your sins be as scar-let, Tho' your sins be as scar-let,
Hear the voice that en-treats you, Hear the voice that en-treats you,
He'll for-give your trans-gres-sions, He'll for-give your trans-gres-sions,

They shall be as white as snow, They shall be as white as snow."
O re-turn you un-to God! O re-turn you un-to God!
And re-mem-ber them no more, And re-mem-ber them no more. A-men.

399   Wonderful Grace of Jesus

Wonderful Grace 7. 6. 7. 6. 7. 6. 11. with Refrain
Haldor Lillenas, 1885-1959
Haldor Lillenas, 1885-1959

1. Won - der - ful grace of Je - sus, Great - er than all my sin:
2. Won - der - ful grace of Je - sus, Reach - ing to all the lost,
3. Won - der - ful grace of Je - sus, Reach - ing the most de - filed,

How shall my tongue de - scribe it, Where shall its praise be - gin?
By it I have been par - doned, Saved to the ut - ter - most;
By its trans - form - ing pow - er, Mak - ing him God's dear child,

Tak - ing a - way my bur - den, Set - ting my spir - it free;
Chains have been torn a - sun - der, Giv - ing me lib - er - ty;
Pur - chas - ing peace and heav - en, For all e - ter - ni - ty;

For the won - der - ful grace of Je - sus reach - es me.
For the won - der - ful grace of Je - sus reach - es me.
And the won - der - ful grace of Je - sus reach - es me.

Refrain

the match - less grace of Je - sus,
Won - der - ful the match - less grace of Je - - sus, Deep - er than the

Wonderful Grace of Jesus (cont.)

the roll-ing sea; Won - der - ful
might-y roll-ing sea; High - er than the moun-tain,

grace, all - suf - fi - cient for
spar-kling like a foun-tain, All - suf - fi - cient grace for e - ven

me, for e - ven me, Broad - er than the scope of my trans-
me,   trans-

gres - sions, Great - er far than all my sin and shame;
gres - sions, sing it!   my sin and shame;

O mag - ni - fy the pre - cious name of Je - sus, Praise his name!

400 Dear Lord and Father of Mankind

Rest 8. 6. 8. 8. 6.

John Greenleaf Whittier, 1807–1892, cento

Frederick C. Maker, 1844–1927

1. Dear Lord and Fa - ther of man - kind, For - give our fool - ish ways;
2. In sim - ple trust like theirs who heard, Be - side the Syr - ian sea,
3. O Sab - bath rest by Gal - i - lee, O calm of hills a - bove,
4. Drop thy still dews of qui - et - ness, Till all our striv - ings cease;
5. Breathe through the heats of our de - sire Thy cool - ness and thy balm;

Re - clothe us in our right - ful mind, In pur - er lives thy
The gra - cious call - ing of the Lord, Let us, like them, with -
Where Je - sus knelt to share with thee The si - lence of e -
Take from our souls the strain and stress, And let our or - dered
Let sense be dumb, let flesh re - tire; Speak through the earth - quake,

serv - ice find, In deep - er rev - erence, praise.
out a word Rise up and fol - low thee.
ter - ni - ty, In - ter - pret - ed by love!
lives con - fess The beau - ty of thy peace.
wind, and fire, O still, small voice of calm! A - men.

Music by courtesy of The Psalms & Hymns Trust, London.

401 O Lord, I Am Not Worthy

Sts. 1, 2, anonymous
St. 3 from the 'Raccolta'

Non dignus 7. 6. 7. 6.
Traditional Catholic melody

1. O Lord, I am not wor - thy That thou shouldst come to me,
2. And hum - bly I'll re - ceive thee, The bride - groom of my soul,
3. O Sac - ra - ment most ho - ly! O Sac - ra - ment di - vine!

O Lord, I Am Not Worthy (cont.)

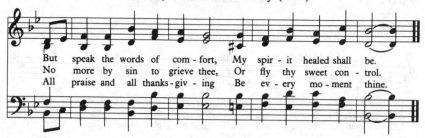

But speak the words of com - fort, My spir - it healed shall be.
No more by sin to grieve thee, Or fly thy sweet con - trol.
All praise and all thanks - giv - ing Be ev - ery mo - ment thine.

Lord, I Hear of Showers of Blessing 402

Even Me 8. 7. 8. 7. 3. 3. 7.

Elizabeth Codner, 1824-1919, cento

William B. Bradbury, 1816-1868

1. Lord, I hear of showers of bless - ing Thou art scat - tering full and free;
2. Pass me not, O gra - cious Fa - ther, Sin - ful though my heart may be;
3. Pass me not, O ten - der Sav - ior, Let me love and cling to thee;
4. Love of God, so pure and change-less, Blood of Christ, so rich, so free,

Showers, the thirst - y land re - fresh - ing; Let some drops now fall on me,
Thou mightst leave me, but the rath - er Let thy mer - cy light on me,
I am long - ing for thy fa - vor; Whilst thou'rt call - ing, O call me,
Grace of God, so strong and bound - less, Mag - ni - fy them all in me,

E - ven me, E - ven me, Let some drops now fall on me.
E - ven me, E - ven me, Let thy mer - cy light on me.
E - ven me, E - ven me, Whilst thou'rt call - ing, O call me.
E - ven me, E - ven me, Mag - ni - fy them all in me. A-men.

387

403

Turn Back, O Man

Clifford Bax, 1886–1962, alt.

Old 124th 10. 10. 10. 10. 10.
Genevan Psalter, 1551

1. Turn back, O man, for - swear your fool - ish ways. Old now is
2. Earth might be fair and all men glad and wise. Age af - ter
3. Earth shall be fair, and all her peo - ple one: Nor till that

earth, and none may count her days, Yet you, her child, whose
age their trag - ic em - pires rise, Built while they dream, and
hour shall God's whole will be done. Now, e - ven now, once

head is crowned with flame, Still will not hear your in - ner God pro -
in that dream - ing weep: Would man but wake from out his haunt - ed
more from earth to sky, Peals forth in joy man's old, un - daunt - ed

claim— "Turn back, O man, for - swear your fool - ish ways."
sleep, Earth might be fair and all men glad and wise.
cry— "Earth shall be fair, and all her folk be one!" A - men.

Come, Every Soul by Sin Oppressed 404

Trust C. M. with Refrain
John Hart Stockton, 1813-1877
Refrain by Ira D. Sankey, 1840-1908

John Hart Stockton, 1813-1877, cento, alt.

1. Come, ev - ery soul by sin op-pressed, There's mer - cy with the Lord,
2. For Je - sus shed his pre - cious blood Rich bless-ings to be - stow;
3. Yes, Je - sus is the truth, the way, That leads you in - to rest;
4. Come, then, and join this ho - ly band, And on to glo - ry go,

And he will sure - ly give you rest By trust - ing in his word.
Plunge now in - to the crim - son flood That wash - es white as snow.
Be - lieve in him with - out de - lay And you are ful - ly blest.
To dwell in that ce - les - tial land Where joys im - mor - tal flow.

Refrain

On - ly trust him, on - ly trust him, on - ly trust him now;

He will save you, he will save you, he will save you now.

405   I Heard the Voice of Jesus Say

Horatius Bonar, 1808–1889, alt.

Vox dilecti C. M. D.
John B. Dykes, 1823–1876

1. I heard the voice of Je-sus say, "Come un-to me and rest;
2. I heard the voice of Je-sus say, "Be-hold, I free-ly give
3. I heard the voice of Je-sus say, "I am this dark world's light;

Lay down, O wea-ry one, lay down Your head up-on my breast."
The liv-ing wa-ter; thirst-y one, Stoop down and drink and live."
Look un-to me, your morn shall rise, And all your day be bright."

I came to Je-sus as I was, Wea-ry and worn and sad;
I came to Je-sus, and I drank Of that life-giv-ing stream;
I looked to Je-sus, and I found In him my star, my sun;

I found in him a rest-ing place, And he has made me glad.
My thirst was quenched, my soul re-vived, And now I live in him.
And in that light of life I'll walk Till trav-eling days are done. A-men.

390

St. Crispin L. M.

Cornelius Elven, 1797–1873, cento, alt.

George J. Elvey, 1816–1893

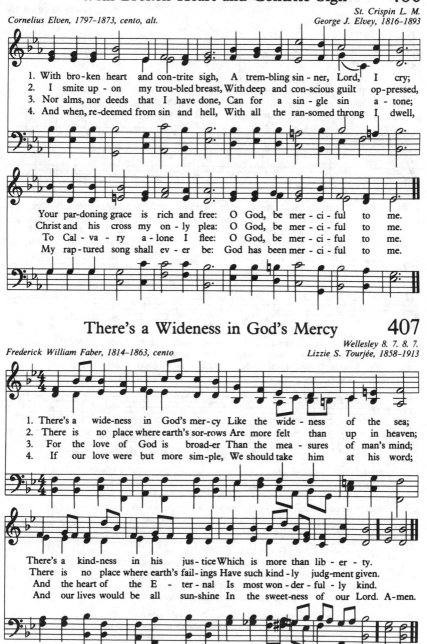

1. With bro-ken heart and con-trite sigh, A trem-bling sin - ner, Lord, I cry;
2. I smite up - on my trou-bled breast, With deep and con-scious guilt op-pressed,
3. Nor alms, nor deeds that I have done, Can for a sin - gle sin a - tone;
4. And when, re-deemed from sin and hell, With all the ran-somed throng I dwell,

Your par-doning grace is rich and free: O God, be mer - ci - ful to me.
Christ and his cross my on - ly plea: O God, be mer - ci - ful to me.
To Cal - va - ry a - lone I flee: O God, be mer - ci - ful to me.
My rap-tured song shall ev - er be: God has been mer - ci - ful to me.

There's a Wideness in God's Mercy 407

Wellesley 8. 7. 8. 7.

Frederick William Faber, 1814–1863, cento

Lizzie S. Tourjée, 1858–1913

1. There's a wide-ness in God's mer-cy Like the wide - ness of the sea;
2. There is no place where earth's sor-rows Are more felt than up in heaven;
3. For the love of God is broad-er Than the mea - sures of man's mind;
4. If our love were but more sim-ple, We should take him at his word;

There's a kind-ness in his jus-tice Which is more than lib - er - ty.
There is no place where earth's fail-ings Have such kind-ly judg-ment given.
And the heart of the E - ter-nal Is most won-der - ful-ly kind.
And our lives would be all sun-shine In the sweet-ness of our Lord. A-men.

Alternative tune: *In Babilone*, Hymn 373.

408 Forgive Us, Lord, for Shallow Thankfulness

Sursum corda 10. 10. 10. 10.

William Watkins Reid, 1890–

Alfred M. Smith, 1879–1971

1. For - give us, Lord, for shal - low thank - ful - ness,
2. Teach us to thank thee, Lord, for love and grace,
3. For - give us, Lord, for self - ish thanks and praise,
4. Teach us, O Lord, true thank - ful - ness di - vine,

For dull con - tent with warmth and shel - tered care,
For life and vi - sion and a pur - pose clear,
For word that speaks at var - i - ance with deed;
That gives as Christ gave, nev - er count - ing cost,

For songs of praise for food and har - vest press,
For Christ, thy Son, and for each hu - man face
For - give our thanks for walk - ing pleas - ant ways
That knows no bar - ri - er of "mine" and "thine,"

While of thy rich - er gifts we're un - a - ware.
That shows thy mes - sage ev - er new and near.
Un - mind - ful of a bro - ken broth - er's need.
As - sured that on - ly what's with - held is lost. A - men.

5. Forgive us, Lord, for feast that knows not fast,
   For joy in things the while we starve the soul,
   For walls and wars that hide thy mercies vast
   And mar our vision of the kingdom goal.

6. Open our eyes to glimpse thy love's intent,
   Our minds and hearts to plumb its depth and height;
   May thankfulness be days in service spent,
   Reflection of Christ's life and love and light.

I Will Sing the Wondrous Story

Wondrous Story 8. 7. 8. 7. with Refrain

Francis H. Rowley, 1854–1952

Peter P. Bilhorn, 1861–1936

1. I will sing the won-drous sto - ry Of the Christ who died for me,
2. I was lost, but Je - sus found me, Found the sheep that went a - stray,
3. I was bruised, but Je - sus healed me; Faint was I from man-y a fall;
4. Days of dark-ness still come o'er me, Sor-row's paths I of - ten tread,
5. He will keep me till the riv - er Rolls its wa - ters at my feet;

How he left his home in glo - ry For the cross of Cal - va - ry.
Threw his lov - ing arms a - round me, Drew me back in - to his way.
Sight was gone, and fears pos-sessed me, But he freed me from them all.
But the Sav - ior still is with me; By his hand I'm safe - ly led.
Then he'll bear me safe - ly o - ver, Where the loved ones I shall meet.

Refrain

Yes, I'll sing the won-drous sto - ry Of the
Yes, I'll sing the won-drous sto-ry

Christ who died for me, Sing it with the saints in
Of the Christ who died for me, Sing it with

glo - ry, Gath-ered by the crys-tal sea.
the saints in glo-ry, Gath-ered by the crys-tal sea.

410   Pass Me Not, O Gentle Savior

Pass Me Not 8. 5. 8. 5. with Refrain

Fanny J. Crosby, 1823–1915   *William H. Doane, 1832–1915*

1. Pass me not, O gen - tle Sav - ior, Hear my hum - ble cry;
2. Let me at thy throne of mer - cy Find a sweet re - lief;
3. Trust - ing on - ly in thy mer - it, Would I seek thy face;
4. Thou the Spring of all my com - fort, More than life to me,

While on oth - ers thou art smil - ing, Do not pass me by.
Kneel - ing there in deep con - tri - tion, Help my un - be - lief.
Heal my wound - ed, bro - ken spir - it, Save me by thy grace.
Whom have I on earth be - side thee? Whom in heaven but thee?

Refrain

Sav - ior, Sav - ior, hear my hum - ble cry; While on oth - ers
thou art call - ing, Do not pass me by. A - men.

Rescue the Perishing, Care for the Dying 411

Fanny J. Crosby, 1823–1915

Rescue 11. 10. 11. 10. with Refrain
William H. Doane, 1832–1915

1. Res - cue the per - ish - ing, care for the dy - ing, Snatch them in pit - y from
2. Though they are slight-ing him, still he is wait-ing, Wait - ing the pen - i - tent
3. Down in the hu - man heart, crushed by the tempt-er, Feel - ings lie bur-ied that
4. Res - cue the per - ish - ing, du - ty de-mands it; Strength for thy la - bor the

sin and the grave; Weep o'er the err - ing one, lift up the fall - en,
child to re - ceive; Plead with them ear - nest - ly, plead with them gent - ly;
grace can re - store; Touched by a lov - ing hand, wak - ened by kind - ness,
Lord will pro - vide; Back to the nar - row way pa - tient - ly win them;

Refrain

Tell them of Je - sus the might - y to save.
He will for - give if they on - ly be - lieve.
Chords that were bro - ken will vi - brate once more. Res-cue the per - ish - ing,
Tell the poor wan-derer a Sav - ior has died.

care for the dy - ing; Je - sus is mer - ci - ful, Je - sus will save. A - men.

395

412

Have You Been to Jesus

Washed in the Blood 11. 9. 11. 9. with Refrain

Elisha A. Hoffman, 1839-1929

Elisha A. Hoffman, 1839-1929

1. Have you been to Je - sus for the cleans - ing power? Are you washed in the blood of the Lamb? Are you ful - ly trust - ing in his grace this hour? Are you washed in the blood of the Lamb?
2. Are you walk - ing dai - ly by the Sav - ior's side? Are you washed in the blood of the Lamb? Do you rest each mo - ment in the Cru - ci - fied? Are you washed in the blood of the Lamb?
3. When the Bride-groom com - eth will your robes be white, Pure and white in the blood of the Lamb? Will your soul be read - y for the man - sions bright, And be washed in the blood of the Lamb?
4. Lay a - side the gar - ments that are stained with sin, And be washed in the blood of the Lamb; There's a foun - tain flow - ing for the soul un - clean: O be washed in the blood of the Lamb.

Refrain

Are you washed in the blood, In the soul - cleans - ing

Are you washed in the blood,

Give Me, O Lord, an Understanding Heart 413

Penitentia 10. 10. 10. 10.

James J. Rome, 1858-1920

Edward Dearle, 1806-1891

1. Give me, O Lord, an un-der-stand-ing heart, That I may learn to know my-self in thee, To spurn the wrong and choose the bet-ter part And thus from sin-ful bond-age be set free.

2. Give me, O Lord, a meek and con-trite heart, That I may learn to quell all self-ish pride, Bow-ing be-fore thee, see thee as thou art And 'neath thy shel-ter-ing pres-ence safe-ly hide.

3. Give me, O Lord, a gen-tle, lov-ing heart, That I may learn to be more ten-der, kind, And with thy heal-ing touch, each wound and smart With Christ-ly bands of love and truth to bind.

414
Softly and Tenderly

Thompson 11. 7. 11. 7. with Refrain
Will L. Thompson, 1847–1909
Will L. Thompson, 1847–1909

398

O Dearest Lord, by All Adored

St. 1, Maurice F. Bell, 1862–1947
St. 2, Nikolaus Decius, 1490?–1541
Tr. by William Ball, 1784–1869, alt.

Mit Freuden zart 8. 7. 8. 7. 8. 8. 7.
Bohemian Brethren, 1566

1. O dear-est Lord, by all a-dored, Our tres-pass-es con-fess-ing,
To thee this day thy chil-dren pray, The ho-ly Faith pro-fess-ing! Ac-cept, O King, the gifts we bring, Our songs of praise, the prayers we raise; And grant us, Lord, thy bless-ing.

2. To God on high be thanks and praise, Who deigns our bonds to sev-er;
His care shall guide us all our days, And harm shall reach us nev-er. On him we rest with faith as-sured; Of all that live he is the Lord, For-ev-er and for-ev-er.

Stanza 1 from *The English Hymnal.* Used by permission of Oxford University Press.

416 I Was Sinking Deep in Sin

Love Lifted Me 7. 6. 7. 6. 7. 6. 7. 4. with Refrain

James Rowe, 1865-1933 *Howard E. Smith, 1863-1918*

1. I was sink-ing deep in sin, Far from the peace-ful shore, Ver - y deep-ly
2. All my heart to him I give, Ev - er to him I'll cling, In his bless - ed
3. Souls in dan - ger, look a - bove, Je - sus com-plete - ly saves; He will lift you

stained with - in, Sink - ing to rise no more; But the Mas - ter of the sea
pres - ence live, Ev - er his prais - es sing. Love so might - y and so true
by his love Out of the an - gry waves. He's the Mas - ter of the sea,

Heard my de-spair-ing cry, From the wa-ters lift-ed me, Now safe am I.
Mer - its my soul's best songs; Faith-ful, lov - ing serv - ice, too, To him be-longs.
Bil - lows his will o - bey; He your Sav - ior wants to be— Be saved to-day.

Refrain

Love lift - ed me! Love lift - ed me! When noth - ing
e - ven me! e - ven me!

else could help, Love lift - ed me. Love lift - ed me.

Am I a Soldier of the Cross 417

Isaac Watts, 1674–1748, cento, alt.

Arlington C. M.
Thomas A. Arne, 1710–1778

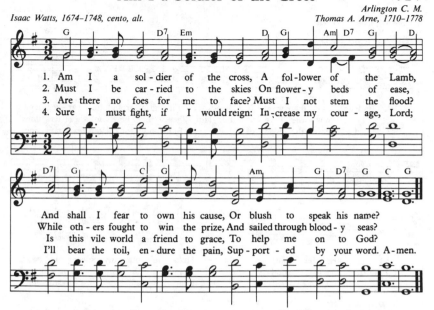

1. Am I a sol-dier of the cross, A fol-lower of the Lamb,
2. Must I be car-ried to the skies On flower-y beds of ease,
3. Are there no foes for me to face? Must I not stem the flood?
4. Sure I must fight, if I would reign: In-crease my cour-age, Lord;

And shall I fear to own his cause, Or blush to speak his name?
While oth-ers fought to win the prize, And sailed through blood-y seas?
Is this vile world a friend to grace, To help me on to God?
I'll bear the toil, en-dure the pain, Sup-port-ed by your word. A-men.

Fight the Good Fight with All Thy Might 418

John S. B. Monsell, 1811–1875

Pentecost L. M.
William Boyd, 1847–1928

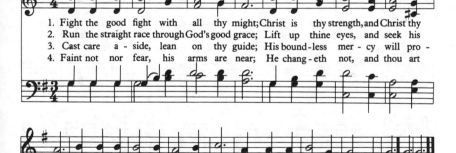

1. Fight the good fight with all thy might; Christ is thy strength, and Christ thy
2. Run the straight race through God's good grace; Lift up thine eyes, and seek his
3. Cast care a-side, lean on thy guide; His bound-less mer-cy will pro-
4. Faint not nor fear, his arms are near; He chang-eth not, and thou art

right: Lay hold on life, and it shall be Thy joy and crown e-ter-nal-ly.
face; Life with its way be-fore us lies; Christ is the path, and Christ the prize.
vide; Trust, and thy trust-ing soul shall prove Christ is its life, and Christ its love.
dear; On-ly be-lieve, and thou shalt see That Christ is all in all to thee. A-men.

419   Guide Me, O Thou Great Jehovah

William Williams, 1717–1791, cento
Tr. St. 1, Peter Williams, 1772–1796
Tr. Sts. 2, 3, William Williams, 1717–1791, alt.

Zion 8. 7. 8. 7. 8. 7.
Thomas Hastings, 1784–1872

1. Guide me, O thou great Je - ho - vah, Pil - grim through this bar - ren land.
2. O - pen now the crys - tal foun-tain, Whence the heal - ing wa - ters flow;
3. When I tread the edge of Jor - dan, Bid my anx - ious fears sub-side;

I am weak, but thou art might - y; Hold me with thy power - ful hand:
Let the fier - y, cloud - y pil - lar Lead me all my jour - ney through:
Bear me through the swell-ing cur - rent; Land me safe on Ca - naan's side:

Bread of heav - en, Feed me till I want no more.
Strong De - liv - er - er, Be thou still my strength and shield.
Songs of prais - es I will ev - er give to thee.

Bread of heav - en, Feed me till I want no more.
Strong De - liv - er - er, Be thou still my strength and shield.
Songs of prais - es I will ev - er give to thee. A - men.

Alternative tune: *Cwm Rhondda*, Hymn 440.

Rise Up, O Men of God! 420

Festal Song S. M.
William Pierson Merrill, 1867–1954
William H. Walter, 1825–1893

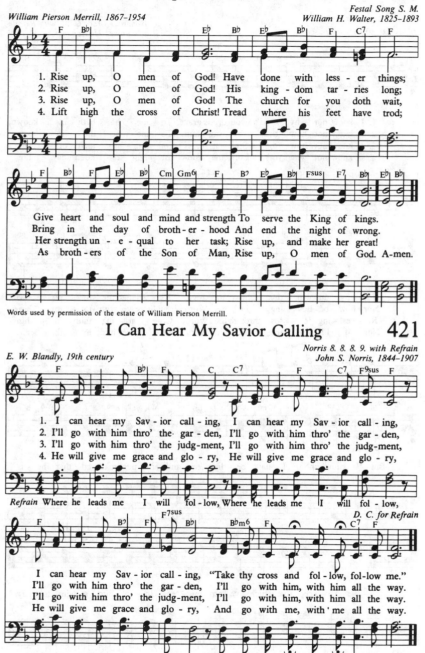

1. Rise up, O men of God! Have done with less-er things;
2. Rise up, O men of God! His king-dom tar-ries long;
3. Rise up, O men of God! The church for you doth wait,
4. Lift high the cross of Christ! Tread where his feet have trod;

Give heart and soul and mind and strength To serve the King of kings.
Bring in the day of broth-er-hood And end the night of wrong.
Her strength un-e-qual to her task; Rise up, and make her great!
As broth-ers of the Son of Man, Rise up, O men of God. A-men.

I Can Hear My Savior Calling 421

Norris 8. 8. 8. 9. with Refrain
E. W. Blandly, 19th century
John S. Norris, 1844–1907

1. I can hear my Sav-ior call-ing, I can hear my Sav-ior call-ing,
2. I'll go with him thro' the gar-den, I'll go with him thro' the gar-den,
3. I'll go with him thro' the judg-ment, I'll go with him thro' the judg-ment,
4. He will give me grace and glo-ry, He will give me grace and glo-ry,

Refrain Where he leads me I will fol-low, Where he leads me I will fol-low,

I can hear my Sav-ior call-ing, "Take thy cross and fol-low, fol-low me."
I'll go with him thro' the gar-den, I'll go with him, with him all the way.
I'll go with him thro' the judg-ment, I'll go with him, with him all the way.
He will give me grace and glo-ry, And go with me, with me all the way.

D. C. for Refrain

Where he leads me I will fol-low, I'll go with him, with him all the way.

422 I Know Not Why God's Wondrous Grace

Wondrous Grace C. M. with Refrain

Daniel W. Whittle, 1840–1901, cento

James McGranahan, 1840–1907

1. I know not why God's won-drous grace To me he hath made known,
2. I know not how this sav - ing faith To me he did im - part,
3. I know not how the Spir - it moves, Con - vinc - ing men of sin,
4. I know not when my Lord may come, At night or noon - day fair,

Nor why, un - wor - thy, Christ in love Re - deemed me for his own.
Nor how be - liev - ing in his Word Wrought peace with - in my heart.
Re - veal - ing Je - sus through the Word, Cre - at - ing faith in him.
Nor if I'll walk the vale with him, Or "meet him in the air."

Refrain

But "I know whom I have be - liev - ed, and am per - suad - ed that he is

a - ble To keep that which I've com - mit - ted Un - to him a - gainst that day."

Lord of the Worlds Above

Isaac Watts, 1674-1748, cento, alt.

Darwall's 148th 6. 6. 6. 6. 8. 8.
John Darwall, 1731-1789

1. Lord of the worlds a-bove, How pleas-ant and how fair
The dwell-ings of thy love, Thine earth-ly tem-ples, are! To thine a-bode my heart as-pires, With warm de-sires to see my God.

2. O hap-py souls that pray Where God ap-points to hear!
O hap-py men that pay Their con-stant serv-ice there! They praise thee still; and hap-py they That love the way to Zi-on's hill.

3. They go from strength to strength, Through this dark vale of tears,
Till each ar-rives at length, Till each in heaven ap-pears: O glo-rious seat, when God, our King, Shall thith-er bring our will-ing feet!

4. God is our Sun and Shield, Our Light and our De-fense;
With gifts his hands are filled: We draw our bless-ings thence. Thrice hap-py he, O God of hosts, Whose spir-it trusts a-lone in thee! A-men.

424

I Need Thee Every Hour

Annie S. Hawks, 1835–1918
Refrain by Robert Lowry, 1826–1899

Need 6. 4. 6. 4. with Refrain
Robert Lowry, 1826–1899

1. I need thee ev - ery hour, Most gra - cious Lord;
2. I need thee ev - ery hour; Stay thou near - by;
3. I need thee ev - ery hour In joy or pain;
4. I need thee ev - ery hour; Teach me thy will,
5. I need thee ev - ery hour, Most Ho - ly One;

No ten - der voice like thine Can peace af - ford.
Temp - ta - tions lose their power When thou art nigh.
Come quick - ly, and a - bide Or life is vain.
And thy rich prom - is - es In me ful - fill.
O make me thine in - deed, Thou bless - ed Son.

Refrain

I need thee, O I need thee; Ev - ery hour I need thee;

O bless me now, my Sav - ior, I come to thee. A - men.

I Sought the Lord and Afterward I Knew 425

Anonymous
'Holy Songs, Carols and Sacred Ballads,' 1880, Boston

Wachusett 10. 10. 10. 6.
Katherine K. Davis, 1892-

Unison

1. I sought the Lord, and af - ter - ward I knew
2. Thou didst reach forth thy hand and mine en - fold;
3. I find, I walk, I love, but oh, the whole

He moved my soul to seek him, seek - ing me.
I walked and sank not on the storm - vexed sea.
Of love is but my an - swer, Lord, to thee!

It was not I that found, O Sav - ior true;
'Twas not so much that I on thee took hold
For thou wert long be - fore - hand with my soul;

No, I was found of thee.
As thou, dear Lord, on me.
Al - ways thou lov - edst me. A - men.

Jesus Walked This Lonesome Valley

Lonesome Valley 8. 8. 9. 8. D.
American traditional melody
Arr. by David Hugh Jones, 1900–

Spiritual

1. Je - sus walked this lone - some val - ley, He had to
   We must walk this lone - some val - ley, We have to
2. You must go and stand your tri - al, You have to
   We must go and stand our tri - al, We have to

walk it by him - self, Oh, No - bod - y else could walk it
walk it by our - selves, Oh, No - bod - y else can walk it
stand it by your - self, Oh, No - bod - y else can stand it
stand it by our - selves, Oh, No - bod - y else can stand it

for him, He had to walk it by him - self.
for us, We have to walk it by our - selves.
for you, You have to stand it by your - self.
for us, We have to stand it for our - selves.

Lead On, O King Eternal

Ernest W. Shurtleff, 1862-1917, alt.

Lancashire 7. 6. 7. 6. D.
Henry Smart, 1813-1879

1. Lead on, O King e - ter - nal, The day of march has come;
2. Lead on, O King e - ter - nal, Till sin's fierce war shall cease,
3. Lead on, O King e - ter - nal, We fol - low, not with fears,

Hence - forth in fields of con - quest Your tents shall be our home.
And ho - li - ness shall whis - per The sweet a - men of peace.
For glad - ness breaks like morn - ing Wher - e'er your face ap - pears.

Through days of prep - a - ra - tion Your grace has made us strong,
For not with swords' loud clash - ing, Nor roll of stir - ring drums,
Your cross is lift - ed o'er us; We jour - ney in its light;

And now, O King e - ter - nal, We lift our bat - tle song.
But deeds of love and mer - cy, The heav - enly king - dom comes.
The crown a - waits the con - quest; Lead on, O God of might. A - men.

O Jesus, I Have Promised

John E. Bode, 1816–1874, cento, alt.

Angel's Story 7. 6. 7. 6. D.
Arthur H. Mann, 1850–1929

1. O Je - sus, I have prom - ised To serve you to the end;
2. O let me feel you near me! The world is ev - er near;
3. O let me hear you speak - ing In ac - cents clear and still,
4. O Je - sus, you have prom - ised To all who fol - low you

Now be for - ev - er near me, My mas - ter and my friend:
I see the sights that daz - zle, The tempt - ing sounds I hear;
A - bove the storms of pas - sion, The mur - murs of self - will!
That where you are in glo - ry Your serv - ant shall be too;

I shall not fear the bat - tle If you are by my side,
My foes are ev - er near me, A - round me and with - in;
O speak to re - as - sure me, To has - ten or con - trol!
And, Je - sus, I have prom - ised To serve you to the end;

Nor wan - der from the path - way If you will be my guide.
But, Je - sus, draw now near - er, And shield my soul from sin.
O speak, and make me lis - ten, O Guard - ian of my soul!
O give me grace to fol - low, My mas - ter and my friend! A - men.

Music used by permission of E. R. Goodliffe.

O Morning Star, How Fair and Bright 429

Philipp Nicolai, 1556–1608, cento
Tr. by Catherine Winkworth, 1827–1878, alt.

Frankfort 8. 8. 7. 8. 8. 7. 4. 8. 4. 8.
Philipp Nicolai, 1556–1608
Harm. by Johann Sebastian Bach, 1685–1750

1. O Morn - ing Star, how fair and bright Thou beam - est forth in
truth and light! O Sov-ereign meek and low - ly! Thou root of Jes - se,
Da - vid's Son, My Lord and Mas - ter, thou hast won My heart to serve thee
sole - ly! Thou art ho - ly, Fair and glo - rious, all - vic - to - rious,
Rich in bless - ing, Rule and might o'er all pos - sess - ing.

2. Thou heav - enly Bright - ness! Light di - vine! O deep with - in my
heart now shine, And make thee there an al - tar! Fill me with joy and
strength to be Thy mem-ber, ev - er joined to thee In love that can - not
fal - ter; Toward thee long - ing Doth pos - sess me; turn and bless me;
Here in sad - ness Eye and heart long for thy glad - ness! A - men.

430   Onward, Christian Soldiers

St. Gertrude 6. 5. 6. 5. D. with Refrain

Sabine Baring-Gould, 1834–1924, cento

Arthur S. Sullivan, 1842–1900

1. On-ward, Chris-tian sol-diers, March-ing as to war, With the cross of Je - sus Go - ing on be - fore: Christ the roy - al mas - ter Leads a - gainst the foe; For - ward in - to bat - tle, See, his ban-ners go.

2. Like a might - y ar - my Moves the church of God; Broth-ers, we are tread - ing Where the saints have trod; We are not di - vid - ed, All one bod - y we, One in hope and doc - trine, One in char - i - ty.

3. Crowns and thrones may per - ish, King-doms rise and wane, But the church of Je - sus Con-stant will re - main; Gates of hell can nev - er 'Gainst that church pre - vail; We have Christ's own prom - ise, And that can - not fail.

4. On - ward, then, ye peo-ple, Join our hap - py throng, Blend with ours your voic - es In the tri - umph song; Glo - ry, laud, and hon - or Un - to Christ the King; This through count - less ag - es Men and an - gels sing.

Refrain

On - ward, Chris - tian sol - diers, March - ing as to war, With the cross of Je - sus Go - ing on be - fore. A-men.

Open My Eyes, that I May See

Clara H. Scott, 1841–1897

Open My Eyes 8. 8. 9. 8. with Refrain
Clara H. Scott, 1841–1897

1. O - pen my eyes, that I may see Glimps-es of truth thou hast for me;
2. O - pen my ears, that I may hear Voic - es of truth thou send-est clear;
3. O - pen my mouth, and let me bear Glad - ly the warm truth ev - ery-where;

Place in my hands the won-der-ful key That shall un-clasp, and set me free.
And while the wave notes fall on my ear, Ev - ery-thing false will dis - ap - pear.
O - pen my heart, and let me pre-pare Love with thy chil-dren thus to share.

Refrain

Si - lent - ly now I wait for thee, Read - y, my God, thy will to see;

O - pen my eyes, il - lu - mine me, Spir - it di - vine! A - men.

432   You Can Live While You're Dyin'

Robert Edwin, 1946–

With Joy Irregular with Refrain
Robert Edwin, 1946–

Webb 7. 6. 7. 6. D.

George Duffield, Jr., 1818–1888, cento, alt.

George J. Webb, 1803–1887

1. Stand up, stand up for Je - sus, You sol - diers of the cross;
2. Stand up, stand up for Je - sus, The trum - pet call o - bey;
3. Stand up, stand up for Je - sus, Stand in his strength a - lone;
4. Stand up, stand up for Je - sus, The strife will not be long;

Lift high his roy - al ban - ner, It must not suf - fer loss:
Forth to the might - y con - flict In this his glo - rious day:
The arm of flesh will fail you, You dare not trust your own:
This day the noise of bat - tle, The next the vic - tor's song:

From vic - tory un - to vic - tory His ar - my shall he lead,
You who are men now serve him A - gainst un - num-bered foes;
Put on the gos - pel ar - mor, Each piece put on with prayer;
To him that wins the bat - tle A crown of life shall be;

Till ev - ery foe is van-quished And Christ is Lord in - deed.
Let cour - age rise with dan - ger, And strength to strength op - pose.
Where du - ty calls, or dan - ger, Be nev - er want - ing there.
He with the King of glo - ry Shall reign e - ter - nal - ly. A - men.

The Light of God Is Falling 434

Greenland 7. 6. 7. 6. D.
J. Michael Haydn, 1737–1806
Arr. by Christian I. Latrobe, 1758–1836
and Benjamin Jacobs, 1778–1829

Louis F. Benson, 1855–1930

1. The light of God is fall-ing Up-on life's com-mon way;
2. Who shares his life's pure plea-sures, And walks the hon-est road,
3. Where hu-man lives are throng-ing In toil and pain and sin,
4. Thy ran-somed host in glo-ry, All souls that sin and pray,

The Mas-ter's voice still call-ing, "Come, walk with me to-day";
Who trades with heap-ing mea-sures, And lifts his broth-er's load,
While clois-tered hearts are long-ing To bring the king-dom in,
Turn toward the cross that bore thee; "Be-hold the man!" they say;

No du-ty can seem low-ly To him who lives with thee,
Who turns the wrong down blunt-ly, And lends the right a hand,
O Christ, the el-der broth-er Of proud and beat-en men,
And while thy church is plead-ing For all who would do good,

And all of life grows ho-ly, O Christ of Gal-i-lee!
He dwells in God's own coun-try, He tills the Ho-ly Land.
When they have found each oth-er, Thy king-dom will come then!
We hear thy true voice lead-ing Our song of broth-er-hood. A-men.

435 There's a Royal Banner Given for Display

Daniel W. Whittle, 1840–1901

Royal Banner 11. 7. 11. 7. with Refrain
James McGranahan, 1840–1907

1. There's a roy - al ban - ner giv - en for dis - play To the sol - diers of the King; As an en - sign fair we lift it up to - day, While as ran - somed ones we sing.
2. Though the foe may rage and gath - er as the flood, Let the stan - dard be dis - played; And be - neath its folds, as sol - diers of the Lord, For the truth be not dis - mayed!
3. O - ver land and sea, wher - ev - er man may dwell, Make the glo - rious ti - dings known; Of the crim - son ban - ner now the sto - ry tell, While the Lord shall claim his own!
4. When the glo - ry dawns 'tis draw - ing ver - y near; It is has - tening day by day; Then be - fore our King the foe shall dis - ap - pear, And the cross the world shall sway!

Refrain

March - ing on, march - ing on, on, on, For Christ count ev - ery - thing but loss! ev - ery - thing, ev - ery - thing but loss! And to crown him King, we'll toil and sing 'Neath the ban - ner of the cross! Be - neath

Christ of the Upward Way

Walter J. Mathams, 1853–1932, cento

Sursum corda 6. 4. 6. 4. 10. 10.
George Lomas, 1834–1884

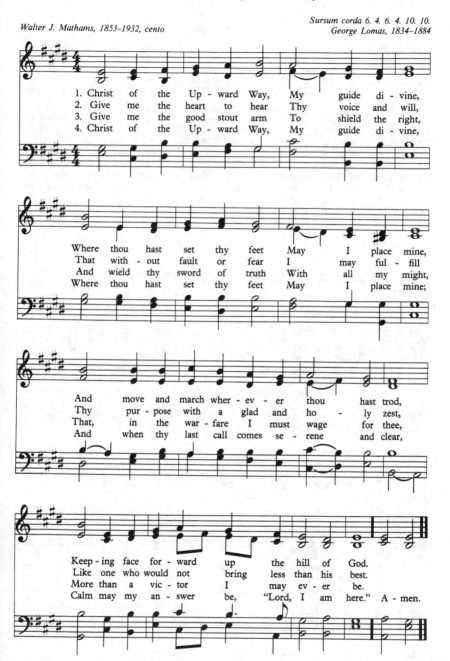

1. Christ of the Up - ward Way, My guide di - vine,
2. Give me the heart to hear Thy voice and will,
3. Give me the good stout arm To shield the right,
4. Christ of the Up - ward Way, My guide di - vine,

Where thou hast set thy feet May I place mine,
That with - out fault or fear I may ful - fill
And wield thy sword of truth With all my might,
Where thou hast set thy feet May I place mine;

And move and march wher - ev - er thou hast trod,
Thy pur - pose with a glad and ho - ly zest,
That, in the war - fare I must wage for thee,
And when thy last call comes se - rene and clear,

Keep - ing face for - ward up the hill of God.
Like one who would not bring less than his best.
More than a vic - tor I may ev - er be.
Calm may my an - swer be, "Lord, I am here." A - men.

419

437   Faith of Our Fathers! Living Still

St. Catherine 8. 8. 8. 8. 8. 8.
Henri F. Hemy, 1818–1888
Alt. by James G. Walton, 1821–1905
Descant by L. David Miller, 1919–

Frederick William Faber, 1814–1863, cento, alt.

1. Faith of our fa - thers! liv - ing still In spite of
2. Faith of our fa - thers! God's great power Shall win all
3. Faith of our fa - thers! we will love Both friend and

dun - geon, fire, and sword, O how our hearts beat high with joy
na - tions un - to thee; And through the truth that comes from God
foe in all our strife, And preach thee, too, as love knows how

When - e'er we hear that glo - rious word: Faith of our
Man - kind shall then be tru - ly free: Faith of our
By kind - ly words and vir - tuous life: Faith of our

fa-thers, ho - ly faith! We will be true to thee till death.

fa-thers, ho - ly faith! We will be true to thee till death.
fa-thers, ho - ly faith! We will be true to thee till death.
fa-thers, ho - ly faith! We will be true to thee till death. A - men.

Spirit Divine, Attend Our Prayer 438

Andrew Reed, 1787–1862
Recast by Samuel Longfellow, 1819–1892, alt.

Gräfenberg C. M.
Johann Crüger, 1598–1662

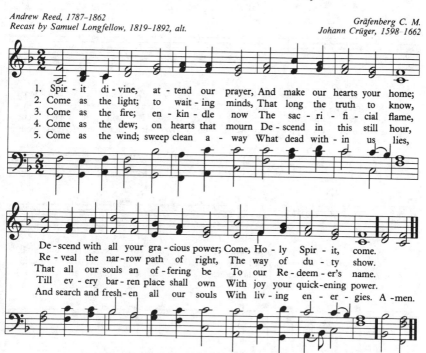

1. Spir - it di - vine, at - tend our prayer, And make our hearts your home;
2. Come as the light; to wait - ing minds, That long the truth to know,
3. Come as the fire; en - kin - dle now The sac - ri - fi - cial flame,
4. Come as the dew; on hearts that mourn De - scend in this still hour,
5. Come as the wind; sweep clean a - way What dead with - in us lies,

De - scend with all your gra - cious power; Come, Ho - ly Spir - it, come.
Re - veal the nar - row path of right, The way of du - ty show.
That all our souls an of - fering be To our Re - deem - er's name.
Till ev - ery bar - ren place shall own With joy your quick-ening power.
And search and fresh - en all our souls With liv - ing en - er - gies. A - men.

Come, All Ye Sons of God

Back to Zion 13. 13. 13. 14.
Orson Pratt Huish, 1851–1932
Arr. by David Hugh Jones, 1900–

Thomas Davenport, 1815–1888

1. Come, all ye sons of God, who have re - ceived the priest - hood,
2. Come, all ye scat - tered sheep, and lis - ten to your Shep - herd,
3. Re - pent and be bap - tized, and have your sins re - mit - ted,
4. And when your grief is o'er and end - ed your af - flic - tion,

Go spread the gos - pel wide and gath - er in his peo - ple;
While you the bless - ings reap, which long have been pre - dict - ed;
And get the Spir - it's zeal; O then you'll be u - nit - ed;
Your spir - its then will soar to a - wait the res - ur - rec - tion;

The lat - ter - day work has be - gun, to gath - er scat - tered
By proph - ets long it's been fore - told He'll gath - er you in -
Go cast up - on him all your care; He will re - gard your
And then his pres - ence you'll en - joy, in heav - enly bliss your

Is - rael in And bring them back to Zi - on to praise the Lamb.
to his fold And bring you home to Zi - on to praise the Lamb.
hum - ble prayer And bring you home to Zi - on to praise the Lamb.
time em - ploy, A thou - sand years in Zi - on to praise the Lamb.

God of Grace and God of Glory

440

Cwm Rhondda 8. 7. 8. 7. 8. 7.

Harry Emerson Fosdick, 1878–1969

John Hughes, 1873–1932

1. God of grace and God of glory, On thy people
   pour thy power; Crown thine an - cient church's sto - ry; Bring her bud to
   glo - rious flower. Grant us wis - dom, grant us cour - age,
   For the fac - ing of this hour, For the fac - ing of this hour.

2. Lo! the hosts of e - vil round us Scorn thy Christ, as -
   sail his ways! From the fears that long have bound us Free our hearts to
   faith and praise. Grant us wis - dom, grant us cour - age,
   For the liv - ing of these days, For the liv - ing of these days.

3. Cure thy chil - dren's war - ring mad - ness, Bend our pride to
   thy con - trol; Shame our wan - ton, self - ish glad - ness, Rich in things and
   poor in soul. Grant us wis - dom, grant us cour - age,
   Lest we miss thy king - dom's goal, Lest we miss thy king - dom's goal.

4. Set our feet on loft - y plac - es; Gird our lives that
   they may be Ar - mored with all Christ - like grac - es In the fight to
   set men free. Grant us wis - dom, grant us cour - age,
   That we fail not man nor thee! That we fail not man nor thee!

5. Save us from weak res - ig - na - tion To the e - vils
   we de - plore; Let the gift of thy sal - va - tion Be our glo - ry
   ev - er - more. Grant us wis - dom, grant us cour - age,
   Serv - ing thee whom we a - dore, Serv - ing thee whom we a - dore. A - men.

423

Come, Come, Ye Saints

Come, Ye Saints 10. 6. 10. 6. 8. 8. 8. 6.

William Clayton, 1814–1879

Adapted from J. T. White, 'Sacred Harp,' 1844

1. Come, come, ye saints, no toil nor labor fear; But with joy
2. Why should we mourn or think our lot is hard? 'Tis not so;
3. We'll find the place which God for us prepared, Far away
4. And should we die before our journey's through, Happy day!

wend your way. Though hard to you this journey may appear,
all is right. Why should we think to earn a great reward,
in the west, Where none shall come to hurt or make afraid;
all is well! We then are free from toil and sorrow, too;

Grace shall be as your day. 'Tis better far for
If we now shun the fight? Gird up your loins; fresh
There the saints will be blessed. We'll make the air with
With the just we shall dwell! But if our lives are

us to strive Our useless cares from us to drive; Do
courage take; Our God will never us forsake; And
music ring, Shout praises to our God and King; A-
spared again To see the saints their rest obtain, O

Come, Come, Ye Saints (cont.)

this, and joy your hearts will swell— All is well! all is well!
soon we'll have this tale to tell— All is well! all is well!
bove the rest these words we'll tell— All is well! all is well!
how we'll make this cho-rus swell— All is well! all is well!

Have Thine Own Way, Lord! 442

Adelaide A. Pollard, 1862-1934

Surrender 5. 4. 5. 4. D.
George C. Stebbins, 1846-1945

1. Have thine own way, Lord! Have thine own way! Thou art the
2. Have thine own way, Lord! Have thine own way! Search me and
3. Have thine own way, Lord! Have thine own way! Wound-ed and
4. Have thine own way, Lord! Have thine own way! Hold o'er my

pot-ter; I am the clay. Mold me and make me Af-ter thy
try me, Mas-ter to-day! Whit-er than snow, Lord, Wash me just
wea-ry, Help me, I pray! Pow-er, all pow-er, Sure-ly is
be-ing Ab-so-lute sway! Fill with thy Spir-it Till all shall

will, While I am wait-ing, Yield-ed and still.
now, As in thy pres-ence Hum-bly I bow.
thine! Touch me and heal me, Sav-ior di-vine!
see Christ on-ly, al-ways, Liv-ing in me! A-men.

High on the Mountaintop

Joel H. Johnson, 1802–1883

Mountaintop 6. 6. 6. 6. 8. 8.
Ebenezer Beesley, 1840–1906

1. High on the moun-tain-top A ban-ner is un-furled.
2. For God re-mem-bers still His prom-ise made of old
3. His house shall there be reared His glo-ry to dis-play;
4. For there we shall be taught The law that will go forth,

Ye na-tions, now look up; It waves to all the world;
That he on Zi-on's hill Truth's stan-dard would un-fold!
And peo-ple shall be heard In dis-tant lands to say,
With truth and wis-dom fraught, To gov-ern all the earth.

In Des - er - et's sweet, peace - ful land,
Her light should there at - tract the gaze
"We'll now go up and serve the Lord,
For - ev - er there his ways we'll tread,

On Zi - on's mount be-hold it stand!
Of all the world in lat - ter days.
O - bey his truth and learn his word."
And save our - selves with all our dead.

I Sing a Song of the Saints of God 444

Grand Isle Irregular

Lesbia Scott, 1898–   , alt.

John Henry Hopkins, 1861–1945

Unison

1. I sing a song of the saints of God Pa-tient and brave and true,
2. They loved their Lord so dear, so dear, And his love made them strong;
3. They lived not on - ly in ag - es past, There are hun-dreds of thou-sands still;

Who toiled and fought and lived and died For the Lord they loved and
And they fol - lowed the right, for Je - sus' sake, The whole of their good lives
The world is bright with the joy - ous saints Who love to do Je - sus'

knew. And one was a doc - tor, and one was a queen, And
long. And one was a sol - dier, and one was a priest, And
will. You can meet them in school, or in lanes, or at sea, In

one was a shep-herd - ess on the green: They were all of them
one was slain by a fierce wild beast: And there's not an - y
church, or in trains, or in shops, or at tea; For the saints of

saints of God, and I mean, God help - ing, to be one too.
rea - son, no, not the least, Why I should-n't be one too.
God are just folk like me, And I mean to be one too.

445 More About Jesus I Would Know

Sweney L. M. with Refrain

Eliza E. Hewitt, 1851–1920

John R. Sweney, 1837–1899

1. More a-bout Je-sus I would know, More of his grace to oth-ers show;
2. More a-bout Je-sus let me learn, More of his ho-ly will dis-cern;
3. More a-bout Je-sus; in his word, Hold-ing com-mu-nion with my Lord,
4. More a-bout Je-sus; on his throne, Rich-es in glo-ry all his own;

More of his sav-ing full-ness see, More of his love who died for me.
Spir-it of God, my teach-er be, Show-ing the things of Christ to me.
Hear-ing his voice in ev-ery line, Mak-ing each faith-ful say-ing mine.
More of his king-dom's sure in-crease; More of his com-ing, Prince of Peace.

Refrain

More, more a-bout Je-sus, More, more a-bout Je-sus;

More of his sav-ing full-ness see, More of his love who died for me.

To Jesus Christ, Our Sovereign King 446

Ich glaub' an Gott 8. 7. 8. 7. with Refrain
Mainz, 'Gesangbuch,' 1870, alt.

Martin B. Hellriegel, 1890–   , alt.

Harm. by Robert Schaffer, 1921–

1. To Jesus Christ, our sovereign King, Who is the world's salvation, All praise and homage do we bring And thanks and adoration.

2. Your reign extend, O King benign, To every land and nation, For in your kingdom, Lord divine, Alone we find salvation.

3. To you and to your church, great King, We pledge our hearts' oblation; Until before your throne we sing In endless jubilation.

Refrain

Christ Jesus, Victor! Christ Jesus, Ruler! Christ Jesus, Lord and Redeemer!

Enter, O People of God

Francis Strahan, 1933–   , and
Richard Cross, 1932–

O Rouanez Karet Irregular with Refrain
Breton traditional melody
Harm. by Angelo A. della Picca, 1923–

1. En - ter, O peo - ple of God, glad - ly your voic - es
2. Je - sus, our God and our broth - er, of - fers him - self this
3. Ours is a her - i - tage ho - ly, ran - somed by sav - ing

raise, Of - fer your gifts to the Fa - ther,
day; He makes our gifts on the al - tar
blood; Mind - ful of this sa - cred ac - tion

sing - ing your songs of praise.
per - fect in ev - ery way. Peo - ple of God, sing
we join our hearts in love.

out with joy, Je - sus in - vites us all;

Come to the al - tar and eat there; Do not dis - dain his call.

Lord, Speak to Me, that I May Speak 448

Canonbury L. M.
Robert A. Schumann, 1810–1856
Arr. in J. Ireland Tucker's
'Hymnal with Tunes, Old and New,' 1872

Frances Ridley Havergal, 1836–1879, cento, alt.

1. Lord, speak to me, that I may speak In liv - ing ech - oes of your tone;
2. O lead me, Lord, that I may lead The wan - dering and the wa - vering feet;
3. O teach me, Lord, that I may teach The pre - cious things which you im - part;
4. O fill me with your full - ness, Lord, Un - til my ver - y heart o'er - flow
5. O use me, Lord, use e - ven me, Just as you will, and when, and where;

As you have sought, so let me seek Your err - ing chil - dren lost and lone.
O feed me, Lord, that I may feed Your hun - gering ones with man - na sweet!
And wing my words, that they may reach The hid - den depths of man - y a heart.
In kin - dling thought and glow - ing word, Your love to tell, your praise to show.
Un - til your bless - ed face I see, Your rest, your joy, your glo - ry share. A - men.

Sent Forth by God's Blessing

Ash Grove 6. 6. 11. 6. 6. 11. D.
Welsh traditional melody
Harm. by James Ritz, 1938–

Omer Westendorf, 1916–

1. Sent forth by God's bless - ing, Our true faith con -
2. With praise and thanks - giv - ing To God who is

fess - ing, The peo - ple of God from his dwell - ing take leave.
liv - ing, The tasks of our ev - ery - day life we em - brace.

God's sac - ri - fice end - ed, O now be ex -
Our faith ev - er shar - ing, In love ev - er

tend - ed The fruits of this Mass in all hearts who be - lieve.
car - ing, We claim as our broth - ers all men of each race.

The seed of his teach - ing, Our in - ner souls
One bread that has fed us, One light that has

reach - ing, Shall blos - som in ac - tion for God and for man.
led us U - nite us as one in his life that we share.

His grace shall in - cite us, His love shall u -
Then may all the liv - ing With praise and thanks -

nite us To fur - ther his king - dom by God's ho - ly plan.
giv - ing Give hon - or to Christ and his name that we bear.

450   The Voice of God Is Calling

John Haynes Holmes, 1879–1964

Meirionydd 7. 6. 7. 6. D.
William Lloyd, 1786–1852

1. The voice of God is call - ing Its sum-mons un - to men;
2. I hear my peo - ple cry - ing In cot and mine and slum;
3. We heed, O Lord, thy sum-mons, And an - swer: Here are we!
4. From ease and plen - ty save us, From pride of place ab - solve;

As once he spoke in Zi - on, So now he speaks a - gain:
No field or mart is si - lent, No cit - y street is dumb.
Send us up - on thine er - rand, Let us thy serv - ants be.
Purge us of low de - sire, Lift us to high re - solve;

Whom shall I send to suc - cor My peo - ple in their need?
I see my peo - ple fall - ing In dark - ness and de - spair.
Our strength is dust and ash - es, Our years a pass - ing hour;
Take us and make us ho - ly, Teach us thy will and way.

Whom shall I send to loos - en The bonds of shame and greed?
Whom shall I send to shat - ter The fet - ters which they bear?
But thou canst use our weak - ness To mag - ni - fy thy power.
Speak, and, be - hold! we an - swer; Com-mand, and we o - bey! A - men.

O Zion, Haste

Tidings 11. 10. 11. 10. with Refrain

Mary Ann Thomson, 1834–1923, cento, alt.

James Walch, 1837–1901

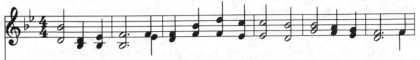

1. O Zi - on, haste, your mis - sion high ful - fill - ing, To tell to all the
2. Be - hold how man - y thou - sands still are ly - ing Bound in the dark - some
3. Pro - claim to ev - ery peo - ple, tongue, and na - tion That God, in whom they
4. Give of your sons to bear the mes - sage glo - rious; Give of your wealth to

world that God is Light, That he who made all na - tions is not will - ing
pris - on house of sin, With none to tell them of the Sav - ior's dy - ing,
live and move, is Love; Tell how he stooped to save his lost cre - a - tion,
speed them on their way; Pour out your soul for them in prayer vic - to - rious;

Refrain

One soul should per - ish, lost in shades of night.
Or of the life he died for them to win.
And died on earth that man might live a - bove.
And all ex - pend - ed Je - sus will re - pay.
Pub - lish glad ti - dings,

ti - dings of peace, Ti - dings of Je - sus, re - demp - tion and re - lease. A - men.

452 Living for Jesus a Life That Is True

Living 10. 10. 10. 10. with Refrain

Thomas O. Chisholm, 1866-1960

C. Harold Lowden, 1883-

1. Liv-ing for Je-sus a life that is true, Striv-ing to please him in all that I do; Yield-ing al - le-giance, glad-heart - ed and free, This is the path-way of bless-ing for me.
2. Liv-ing for Je-sus, who died in my place, Bear-ing on Cal - vary my sin and dis - grace; Such love con-strains me to an - swer his call, Fol - low his lead - ing and give him my all.
3. Liv-ing for Je-sus wher - ev - er I am, Do-ing each du - ty in his ho - ly name; Will-ing to suf - fer af - flic - tion and loss, Deem-ing each tri - al a part of my cross.
4. Liv-ing for Je-sus through earth's lit - tle while, My dear-est trea - sure, the light of his smile; Seek-ing the lost ones he died to re - deem, Bring-ing the wea - ry to find rest in him.

Refrain

O Je - sus, Lord and Sav - ior, I give my - self to thee, For thou, in thy a - tone-ment, Didst give thy-self for me; I own no oth - er Mas - ter, My heart shall be thy

throne; My life I give, hence-forth to live, O Christ, for thee a - lone.

We Are Climbing Jacob's Ladder 453

Jacob's Ladder 8. 8. 8. 5.
American Negro melody

Spiritual, cento

1. We are climb - ing Ja - cob's lad - der, We are climb - ing Ja - cob's lad - der, We are climb - ing Ja - cob's lad - der, Sol - diers of the cross.
2. Ev - ery round goes high - er, high - er, Ev - ery round goes high - er, high - er, Ev - ery round goes high - er, high - er, Sol - diers of the cross.
3. Sin - ner, do you love my Je - sus? Sin - ner, do you love my Je - sus? Sin - ner, do you love my Je - sus? Sol - diers of the cross.
4. If you love him, why not serve him? If you love him, why not serve him? If you love him, why not serve him? Sol - diers of the cross.
5. We are climb - ing high - er, high - er, We are climb - ing high - er, high - er, We are climb - ing high - er, high - er, Sol - diers of the cross. A - men.

Soldiers of Christ, Arise

Charles Wesley, 1707–1788, cento, alt.

Diademata S. M. D.
George J. Elvey, 1816–1893

1. Sol - diers of Christ, a - rise, And put your ar - mor on,
2. Stand, then, in his great might, With all his strength en - dued;
3. Leave no un - guard - ed place, No weak - ness of the soul;

Strong in the strength which God sup - plies Through his e - ter - nal Son;
And take, to arm you for the fight, The pan - o - ply of God:
Take ev - ery vir - tue, ev - ery grace, And for - ti - fy the whole.

Strong in the Lord of hosts, And in his might - y power;
That, hav - ing all things done, And all your con - flicts passed,
From strength to strength go on; Wres - tle, and fight, and pray;

Who in the strength of Je - sus trusts Is more than con - quer - or.
You may o'er - come, through Christ a - lone, And stand com - plete at last.
Tread all the powers of dark - ness down, And win the well - fought day. A - men.

The Son of God Goes Forth to War

All Saints New C. M. D.
Reginald Heber, 1783–1826
Henry S. Cutler, 1824–1902

1. The Son of God goes forth to war, A king-ly crown to gain;
   His blood-red ban-ner streams a-far: Who fol-lows in his train?
   Who best can drink his cup of woe, Tri-um-phant o-ver pain,
   Who pa-tient bears his cross be-low, He fol-lows in his train.

2. The mar-tyr first, whose ea-gle eye Could pierce be-yond the grave,
   Who saw his Mas-ter in the sky, And called on him to save;
   Like him, with par-don on his tongue In midst of mor-tal pain,
   He prayed for them that did the wrong: Who fol-lows in his train?

3. A glo-rious band, the cho-sen few On whom the Spir-it came,
   Twelve val-iant saints, their hope they knew, And mocked the cross and flame:
   They met the ty-rant's bran-dished steel, The li-on's gor-y mane;
   They bowed their necks the death to feel: Who fol-lows in their train?

4. A no-ble ar-my, men and boys, The ma-tron and the maid,
   A-round the Sav-ior's throne re-joice, In robes of light ar-rayed:
   They climbed the steep as-cent of heaven Through per-il, toil, and pain:
   O God, to us may grace be given To fol-low in their train! A-men.

456 God Send Us Men Whose Aim 'Twill Be

Melrose L. M.

Frederick J. Gillman, 1866-1949, alt.

Frederick C. Maker, 1844-1927

1. God send us men whose aim 'twill be,
2. God send us men alert and quick
3. God send us men of steadfast will,
4. God send us men with hearts ablaze,

Not to defend some ancient creed,
His lofty precepts to translate,
Patient, courageous, strong and true,
All truth to love, all wrong to hate;

But to live out the laws of Christ
Until the laws of Christ become
With vision clear and mind equipped
These are the patriots nations need;

In every thought and word and deed.
The laws and habits of the state.
His will to learn, his work to do.
These are the bulwarks of the state. A - men.

440

My Hope Is Built on Nothing Less 457

Edward Mote, 1797-1874, cento, alt.

Solid Rock L. M. with Refrain
William B. Bradbury, 1816-1868

1. My hope is built on noth-ing less Than Je - sus' blood and
2. When dark-ness veils his love-ly face, I rest on his un-
3. His oath, his cov-e - nant, his blood, Sup-port me in the
4. When he shall come with trum-pet sound, O may I then in

righ-teous-ness; I dare not trust the sweet-est frame, But
chang-ing grace; In ev - ery high and storm-y gale, My
whelm-ing flood; When all a-round my soul gives way, He
him be found; Dressed in his righ-teous-ness a - lone, Fault-

Refrain

whol-ly lean on Je - sus' name.
an-chor holds with-in the veil.   On Christ, the sol - id Rock, I stand; All
then is all my hope and stay.
less to stand be-fore the throne.

oth-er ground is sink-ing sand, All oth-er ground is sink-ing sand. A - men.

Jesus, Keep Me Near the Cross

Fanny J. Crosby, 1823-1915

Near the Cross 7. 6. 7. 6. with Refrain
William H. Doane, 1832-1915

1. Je - sus, keep me near the cross; There a pre-cious foun-tain, Free to all, a
2. Near the cross, a trem-bling soul, Love and mer - cy found me; There the bright and
3. Near the cross! O Lamb of God, Bring its scenes be - fore me; Help me walk from
4. Near the cross I'll watch and wait, Hop-ing, trust-ing ev - er, Till I reach the

heal - ing stream, Flows from Cal - vary's moun-tain.
morn-ing Star Sheds its beams a - round me.
day to day With its shad - ows o'er me. In the cross, in the cross, Be my glo-ry
gold - en strand Just be - yond the riv - er.

ev - er, Till my rap-tured soul shall find Rest be-yond the riv - er. A - men.

459 From You All Skill and Science Flow

Charles Kingsley, 1819-1875, cento, alt.

St. Peter C. M.
Alexander R. Reinagle, 1799-1877

1. From you all skill and sci - ence flow, All pit - y, care, and love,
2. And part them, Lord, to each and all, As each and all shall need,
3. And has - ten, Lord, that per - fect day When pain and death shall cease,
4. When ev - er blue the sky shall gleam, And ev - er green the sod;

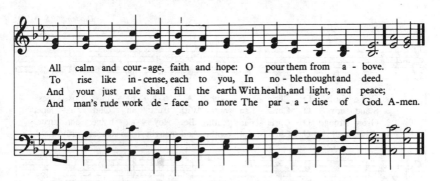

All calm and cour-age, faith and hope: O pour them from a - bove.
To rise like in-cense, each to you, In no - ble thought and deed.
And your just rule shall fill the earth With health, and light, and peace;
And man's rude work de - face no more The par - a - dise of God. A-men.

More Love to Thee, O Christ   460

More Love to Thee 6. 4. 6. 4. 6. 6. 4. 4.

Elizabeth P. Prentiss, 1818-1878, cento   *William H. Doane, 1832-1915*

1. More love to thee, O Christ, More love to thee! Hear thou the
2. Once earth - ly joy I craved, Sought peace and rest; Now thee a -
3. Then shall my lat - est breath Whis - per thy praise; This be the

prayer I make On bend - ed knee; This is my ear - nest plea,
lone I seek; Give what is best: This all my prayer shall be,
part - ing cry My heart shall raise; This still its prayer shall be,

More love, O Christ, to thee, More love to thee, More love to thee! A-men.

443

Come Forth, O Christian Youth

Mary Ellen Jackson, 1926–

Diademata S. M. D.
George J. Elvey, 1816–1893

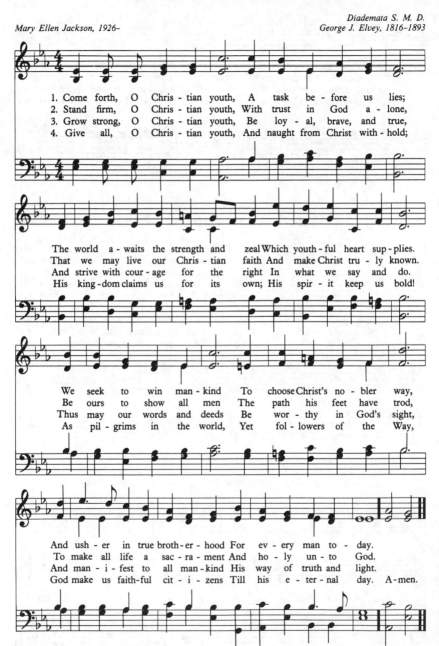

1. Come forth, O Chris-tian youth, A task be-fore us lies;
2. Stand firm, O Chris-tian youth, With trust in God a-lone,
3. Grow strong, O Chris-tian youth, Be loy-al, brave, and true,
4. Give all, O Chris-tian youth, And naught from Christ with-hold;

The world a-waits the strength and zeal Which youth-ful heart sup-plies.
That we may live our Chris-tian faith And make Christ tru-ly known.
And strive with cour-age for the right In what we say and do.
His king-dom claims us for its own; His spir-it keep us bold!

We seek to win man-kind To choose Christ's no-bler way,
Be ours to show all men The path his feet have trod,
Thus may our words and deeds Be wor-thy in God's sight,
As pil-grims in the world, Yet fol-lowers of the Way,

And ush-er in true broth-er-hood For ev-ery man to-day.
To make all life a sac-ra-ment And ho-ly un-to God.
And man-i-fest to all man-kind His way of truth and light.
God make us faith-ful cit-i-zens Till his e-ter-nal day. A-men.

Jesus, I My Cross Have Taken

Ellesdie 8. 7. 8. 7. D.
Wolfgang Amadeus Mozart, 1756–1791
Arr. by Hubert P. Main, 1839–1925

Henry Francis Lyte, 1793–1847, cento

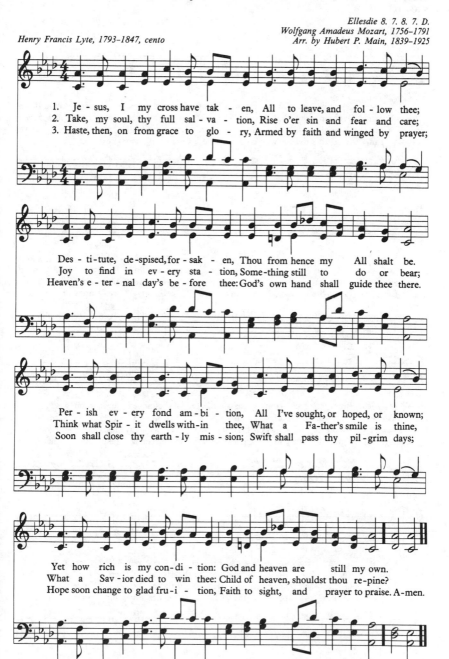

1. Je - sus, I my cross have tak - en, All to leave, and fol - low thee;
2. Take, my soul, thy full sal - va - tion, Rise o'er sin and fear and care;
3. Haste, then, on from grace to glo - ry, Armed by faith and winged by prayer;

Des - ti-tute, de-spised, for - sak - en, Thou from hence my All shalt be.
Joy to find in ev - ery sta - tion, Some-thing still to do or bear;
Heaven's e - ter - nal day's be - fore thee: God's own hand shall guide thee there.

Per - ish ev - ery fond am - bi - tion, All I've sought, or hoped, or known;
Think what Spir - it dwells with - in thee, What a Fa-ther's smile is thine,
Soon shall close thy earth - ly mis - sion; Swift shall pass thy pil - grim days;

Yet how rich is my con-di - tion: God and heaven are still my own.
What a Sav - ior died to win thee: Child of heaven, shouldst thou re-pine?
Hope soon change to glad fru-i - tion, Faith to sight, and prayer to praise. A-men.

463 Love Divine, All Loves Excelling

Charles Wesley, 1707–1788

Beecher 8. 7. 8. 7. D.
John Zundel, 1815–1882

1. Love di - vine, all loves ex - cel - ling, Joy of heaven, to earth come down,
2. Breathe, O breathe thy lov - ing Spir - it In - to ev - ery trou - bled breast!
3. Come, Al - might - y to de - liv - er, Let us all thy life re - ceive;
4. Fin - ish, then, thy new cre - a - tion; Pure and spot - less let us be;

Fix in us thy hum - ble dwell - ing, All thy faith - ful mer - cies crown!
Let us all in thee in - her - it, Let us find the prom - ised rest;
Sud - den - ly re - turn, and nev - er, Nev - er - more thy tem - ples leave.
Let us see thy great sal - va - tion Per - fect - ly re - stored in thee:

Je - sus, thou art all com - pas - sion, Pure, un - bound - ed love thou art;
Take a - way the love of sin - ning; Al - pha and O - meg - a be;
Thee we would be al - ways bless - ing, Serve thee as thy hosts a - bove,
Changed from glo - ry in - to glo - ry, Till in heaven we take our place,

Vis - it us with thy sal - va - tion, En - ter ev - ery trem - bling heart.
End of faith, as its Be - gin - ning, Set our hearts at lib - er - ty.
Pray and praise thee with - out ceas - ing, Glo - ry in thy per - fect love.
Till we cast our crowns be - fore thee, Lost in won - der, love, and praise. A - men.

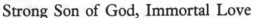

Strong Son of God, Immortal Love 464

St. Crispin L. M.
Alfred Tennyson, 1809–1892, cento
George J. Elvey, 1816–1893

1. Strong Son of God, im-mor-tal love, Whom we, that have not seen thy face,
2. Thou seem-est hu-man and di-vine, The high-est, ho-liest man-hood, thou.
3. Our lit-tle sys-tems have their day; They have their day and cease to be;
4. Let knowl-edge grow from more to more, But more of rev-erence in us dwell;

By faith, and faith a-lone, em-brace, Be-liev-ing where we can-not prove:
Our wills are ours, we know not how; Our wills are ours, to make them thine.
They are but bro-ken lights of thee, And thou, O Lord, art more than they.
That mind and soul, ac-cord-ing well, May make one mu-sic as be-fore. A-men.

O for a Closer Walk with God 465

Beatitudo C. M.
William Cowper, 1731–1800, cento
John B. Dykes, 1823–1876

1. O for a clos-er walk with God, A calm and heav-enly frame,
2. Re-turn, O ho-ly Dove, re-turn, Sweet mes-sen-ger of rest!
3. The dear-est i-dol I have known, What-e'er that i-dol be,
4. So shall my walk be close with God, Calm and se-rene my frame;

A light to shine up-on the road That leads me to the Lamb!
I hate the sins that made thee mourn And drove thee from my breast.
Help me to tear it from thy throne, And wor-ship on-ly thee.
So pur-er light shall mark the road That leads me to the Lamb. A-men.

447

466   We Are Living, We Are Dwelling

Blaenhafren 8. 7. 8. 7. D.
Welsh traditional melody

Arthur Cleveland Coxe, 1818–1896

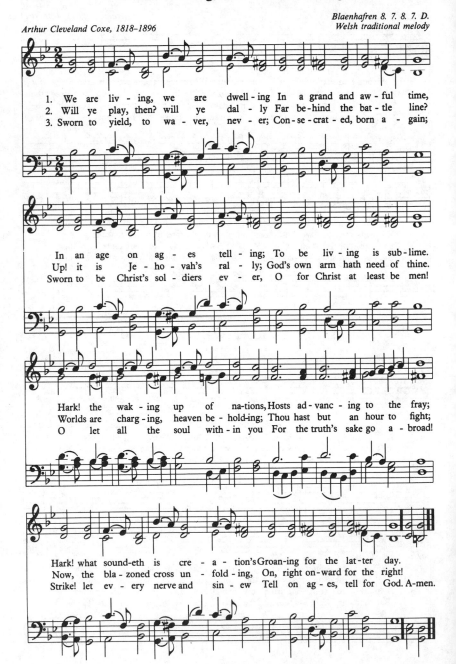

1. We are liv - ing, we are dwell - ing In a grand and aw - ful time,
2. Will ye play, then? will ye dal - ly Far be - hind the bat - tle line?
3. Sworn to yield, to wa - ver, nev - er; Con - se - crat - ed, born a - gain;

In an age on ag - es tell - ing; To be liv - ing is sub - lime.
Up! it is Je - ho - vah's ral - ly; God's own arm hath need of thine.
Sworn to be Christ's sol - diers ev - er, O for Christ at least be men!

Hark! the wak - ing up of na - tions, Hosts ad - vanc - ing to the fray;
Worlds are charg - ing, heaven be - hold - ing; Thou hast but an hour to fight;
O let all the soul with - in you For the truth's sake go a - broad!

Hark! what sound - eth is cre - a - tion's Groan - ing for the lat - ter day.
Now, the bla - zoned cross un - fold - ing, On, right on - ward for the right!
Strike! let ev - ery nerve and sin - ew Tell on ag - es, tell for God. A - men.

448

Believing Fathers Oft Have Told

Meiringen 8. 6. 8. 6. 8. 8.

Archibald Hamilton Charteris, 1835–1908, alt.

Christian Gottlob Neefe, 1748–1798

1. Be - liev - ing fa - thers oft have told What things by
2. A - mid the world's con - fus - ed noise, Where we but
3. His church our shel - ter, he our guide, Our strength his
4. So by thy Spir - it mold us, Lord; In - spire our
5. We fain would serve thy church e'en now, With hearts from

God were done, When faith - ful men in days of old
dark - ly see, The Christ ap - peals, with sweet, clear voice:
heal - ing cross, We range our - selves up - on his side,
hearts to pray; Our hun - gry souls feed with thy word,
self set free, Striv - ing to make thy king - dom grow.

Their life - long bat - tle won: True broth - ers all, of
"My broth - ers, fol - low me, Like broth - ers true, of
Where none can suf - fer loss, Like broth - ers true, of
Teach all of us to say: "True broth - ers all, of
O God, so may it be, That, broth - ers true, with

one ac - cord, We hold one faith, we serve one Lord.
one ac - cord, To hold one faith, to serve one Lord."
one ac - cord, We hold one faith and serve one Lord.
one ac - cord, We hold one faith, we serve one Lord."
one ac - cord We hold the faith and serve the Lord! A - men.

468 **Sweet Is the Work, My God, My King**

Isaac Watts, 1674–1748, cento

Sweet Is the Work L. M.
John J. McClellan, 1874–1925

1. Sweet is the work, my God, my King, To praise thy
2. Sweet is the day of sa - cred rest. No mor - tal
3. My heart shall tri - umph in my Lord And bless his
4. But, O what tri - umph shall I raise To thy dear

name, give thanks and sing, To show thy love by
care shall seize my breast. O may my heart in
works and bless his word. Thy works of grace, how
name through end - less days, When in the realms of

morn - ing light And talk of all thy truth at night.
tune be found, Like Da - vid's harp of sol - emn sound!
bright they shine! How deep thy coun - sels, how di - vine!
joy I see Thy face in full fe - lic - i - ty.

469 **Jesus Calls Us: O'er the Tumult**

Cecil Frances Alexander, 1818–1895, cento, alt.

Galilee 8. 7. 8. 7.
William H. Jude, 1851–1922

1. Je - sus calls us: o'er the tu - mult Of our life's wild, rest - less sea,
2. Je - sus calls us from the wor - ship Of the vain world's gold - en store,
3. In our joys and in our sor - rows, Days of toil and hours of ease,
4. Je - sus calls us: by your mer - cies, Sav - ior, may we hear your call,

450

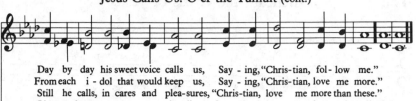

Day by day his sweet voice calls us, Say-ing, "Chris-tian, fol-low me."
From each i-dol that would keep us, Say-ing, "Chris-tian, love me more."
Still he calls, in cares and plea-sures, "Chris-tian, love me more than these."
Give our hearts to your o-be-dience, Serve and love you best of all. A-men.

Nearer, My God, to Thee 470

Sarah F. Adams, 1805-1848

Bethany 6. 4. 6. 4. 6. 6. 6. 4.
Lowell Mason, 1792-1872

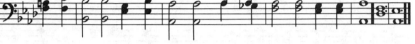

1. Near - er, my God, to thee, Near - er to thee! E'en though it
2. Though like the wan - der - er, The sun gone down, Dark - ness be
3. There let the way ap - pear, Steps un - to heaven: All that thou
4. Then, with my wak - ing thoughts Bright with thy praise, Out of my
5. Or if on joy - ful wing Cleav - ing the sky, Sun, moon, and

be a cross That rais - eth me; Still all my song shall be, Near - er, my
o - ver me, My rest a stone, Yet in my dreams I'd be Near - er, my
send - est me In mer - cy given: An - gels to beck - on me Near - er, my
ston - y griefs Beth - el I'll raise; So by my woes to be Near - er, my
stars for - got, Up - ward I fly, Still all my song shall be, Near - er, my

God, to thee, Near - er, my God, to thee, Near - er to thee! A - men.

451

471   Beneath the Cross of Jesus

St. Christopher 7. 6. 8. 6. 8. 6. 8. 6.

Elizabeth C. Clephane, 1830–1869

Frederick C. Maker, 1844–1927

1. Be - neath the cross of Je - sus I fain would take my stand—
2. Up - on the cross of Je - sus Mine eye at times can see
3. I take, O cross, thy shad - ow For my a - bid - ing place:

The shad - ow of a might - y rock With - in a wea - ry land;
The ver - y dy - ing form of one Who suf - fered there for me:
I ask no oth - er sun-shine than The sun - shine of his face;

A home with - in the wil - der - ness, A rest up - on the way,
And from my strick - en heart with tears Two won - ders I con-fess—
Con - tent to let the world go by, To know no gain nor loss:

From the burn-ing of the noon-tide heat And the bur - den of the day.
The won - ders of re-deem-ing love And my un-worth - i - ness.
My sin - ful self my on - ly shame, My glo - ry all, the cross. A-men.

Hear Us, O Lord

472

Unde et memores 10. 10. 10. 10. 10. 10.

John Shirley Anderson

William H. Monk, 1823-1889

1. Hear us, O Lord, as we thy serv-ants meet From man-y plac-es un-der-neath the skies, To lay our love and trib-ute at thy feet, And yield our-selves, a liv-ing sac-ri-fice; For thou, O Je-sus, art our hope a-lone, And one in thee we bow be-fore thy throne.

2. The word thou gav-est in the days of yore Has been pro-claimed a-far o'er land and sea; The gos-pel mes-sage rings from shore to shore, And hymns of praise as-cend un-ceas-ing-ly, From ris-ing un-til set-ting of the sun, Pro-claim-ing that the church in thee is one.

3. O Christ, the liv-ing and e-ter-nal Word, Un-chang-ing still through all the chang-ing years, No sweet-er name on earth was ev-er heard; No oth-er voice has power to calm our fears. Then speak once more to set thy peo-ple free, And make us one in love and one in thee.

4. A-round thy ta-ble we are met a-gain To break the bread and pour the sa-cred wine, Re-mem-ber-ing the sor-row and the pain, And all the mys-ter-y of love di-vine. O Word in-car-nate, God's e-ter-nal Son, Grant us thy grace, that all may yet be one.

5. Now make us one in serv-ing thee, O Lord: One in the hope of glo-ries yet to be, One in the proc-la-ma-tion of the word, One in the sa-cred gift of char-i-ty, One in the faith the fa-thers held of yore, One in the Love that lives for-ev-er-more. A-men.

473 March On, O Soul, with Strength

George T. Coster, 1835–1912, cento, alt.

Arthur's Seat 6. 6. 6. 6. 8. 8.
John Goss, 1800–1880

1. March on, O soul, with strength, Like those strong men of old
2. The sons of fa - thers we By whom our faith is taught
3. March on, O soul, with strength, As strong the bat - tle rolls;
4. Not long the con - flict: soon The ho - ly war shall cease;

Who 'gainst en - thron - ed wrong Stood con - fi - dent and bold;
To fear no ill, to fight The ho - ly fight they fought;
'Gainst lies and lusts and wrongs, Let cour - age rule our souls;
Faith's war - fare end - ed: won The home of end - less peace.

Who, thrust in prison or cast to flame,
He - ro - ic war - riors, ne'er from Christ
In keen - est strife, Lord, may we stand,
Look up! the vic - tor's crown at length!

Still made their glo - ry in your name.
By an - y lure or guile en - ticed.
Up - held and strength - ened by your hand.
March on, O soul, march on with strength. A - men.

O Jesus, You Are Standing

St. Hilda 7. 6. 7. 6. D.
Based on melody of Justin H. Knecht, 1752–1817

William Walsham How, 1823–1897, alt.

Edward Husband, 1843–1908

1. O Je - sus, you are stand - ing Out - side the fast-closed door,
2. O Je - sus, you are knock - ing, And lo! that hand is scarred,
3. O Je - sus, you are plead - ing In ac - cents meek and low,

In low - ly pa - tience wait - ing To pass the thresh-old o'er.
And thorns your brow en - cir - cle, And tears your face have marred,
"I died for you, my chil - dren, And will you treat me so?"

Shame on us, Chris - tian broth - ers, His name and sign who bear;
O love that pass - es knowl-edge, So pa - tient - ly to wait!
O Lord, with shame and sor - row We o - pen now the door;

O shame, thrice shame up - on us, To keep him stand - ing there!
O sin that has no e - qual, So fast to bar the gate!
Dear Sav - ior, en - ter, en - ter, And leave us nev - er - more! A - men.

475 Once to Every Man and Nation

James Russell Lowell, 1819–1891, alt., cento

Ebenezer 8. 7. 8. 7. D.

Thomas John Williams, 1869–1944

1. Once to ev - ery man and na - tion Comes the mo - ment to de - cide,
2. Then to side with truth is no - ble, When we share her wretch-ed crust,
3. Though the cause of e - vil pros-per, Yet 'tis truth a - lone is strong;

In the strife of truth with false-hood, For the good or e - vil side;
Ere her cause bring fame and prof - it, And 'tis pros-perous to be just;
Though her por - tion be the scaf - fold, And up - on the throne be wrong,

Some great cause, some new de - ci - sion, Of - fering each the bloom or blight,
Then it is the brave man choos-es While the cow-ard stands a - side,
Yet that scaf - fold sways the fu - ture, And, be - hind the dim un - known,

And the choice goes by for - ev - er 'Twixt that dark-ness and that light.
Till the mul - ti - tude make vir - tue Of the faith they had de - nied.
Stand-eth God with - in the shad - ow Keep-ing watch a - bove his own. A-men.

Give of Your Best to the Master

476

Barnard 8. 7. 8. 7. D.

Howard B. Grose, 1851-1938

Charlotte A. Barnard, 1820-1869

1. Give of your best to the Mas - ter; Give of the strength of your youth;
2. Give of your best to the Mas - ter; Give him first place in your heart;
3. Give of your best to the Mas - ter; Naught else is wor - thy his love;

Refrain: Give of your best to the Mas - ter; Give of the strength of your youth;

Throw your soul's fresh, glow-ing ar - dor In - to the bat - tle for truth.
Give him first place in your serv - ice, Con - se - crate ev - ery part.
He gave him - self for your ran - som, Gave up his glo - ry a - bove:

Clad in sal - va - tion's full ar - mor, Join in the bat - tle for truth.

Je - sus has set the ex - am - ple; Daunt-less was he, young and brave;
Give, and to you shall be giv - en; God his be - lov - ed Son gave;
Laid down his life with-out mur - mur, You from sin's ru - in to save;

Give him your loy - al de - vo - tion, Give him the best that you have.
Grate-ful - ly seek-ing to serve him, Give him the best that you have.
Give him your heart's ad - o - ra - tion, Give him the best that you have.

457

477   I Am Thine, O Lord

Fanny J. Crosby, 1823–1915, cento

I Am Thine 10. 7. 10. 7. with Refrain
William H. Doane, 1832–1915

1. I am thine, O Lord, I have heard thy voice, And it
2. O the pure de - light of a sin - gle hour That be -
3. Con - se - crate me now to thy serv - ice, Lord, By the

told thy love to me; But I long to rise in the arms of faith
fore thy throne I spend, When I kneel in prayer, and with thee, my God,
power of grace di - vine; Let my soul look up with a stead-fast hope,

And be clos - er drawn to thee.
I com - mune as friend with friend! Draw me near - er, near - er,
And my will be lost in thine.

bless - ed Lord, To the cross where thou hast died; Draw me near - er,

near - er, near - er, bless - ed Lord, To thy pre - cious, bleed - ing side. A - men.

Lord, I Want to Be a Christian

Be a Christian 8. 6. 8. 3. 3. 3. 8. 3.
American Negro melody

Spiritual, cento

1. Lord, I want to be a Chris-tian In my heart, in my heart,
2. Lord, I want to be more lov-ing In my heart, in my heart,
3. Lord, I want to be more ho-ly In my heart, in my heart,
4. Lord, I want to be like Je-sus In my heart, in my heart,

Lord, I want to be a Chris-tian In my heart.
Lord, I want to be more lov-ing In my heart.
Lord, I want to be more ho-ly In my heart.
Lord, I want to be like Je-sus In my heart.

In my heart, In my heart,
In my heart, In my heart,

Lord, I want to be a Chris-tian In my heart.
Lord, I want to be more lov-ing In my heart.
Lord, I want to be more ho-ly In my heart.
Lord, I want to be like Je-sus In my heart. A-men.

Savior, like a Shepherd Lead Us

'Hymns for the Young,' 1836, cento

Bradbury 8. 7. 8. 7. 8. 7.
William B. Bradbury, 1816–1868

1. Sav - ior, like a shep-herd lead us, Much we need thy ten - der care;
2. Thou hast prom-ised to re - ceive us, Poor and sin - ful though we be;
3. Ear - ly let us seek thy fa - vor; Ear - ly let us do thy will;

In thy plea - sant pas - tures feed us, For our use thy folds pre - pare.
Thou hast mer - cy to re - lieve us, Grace to cleanse and power to free.
Bless - ed Lord and on - ly Sav - ior, With thy love our bos - oms fill.

Bless - ed Je - sus, Bless - ed Je - sus, Thou hast bought us, thine we are;
Bless - ed Je - sus, Bless - ed Je - sus, Ear - ly let us turn to thee;
Bless - ed Je - sus, Bless - ed Je - sus, Thou hast loved us, love us still;

Bless - ed Je - sus, Bless - ed Je - sus, Thou hast bought us, thine we are.
Bless - ed Je - sus, Bless - ed Je - sus, Ear - ly let us turn to thee.
Bless - ed Je - sus, Bless - ed Je - sus, Thou hast loved us, love us still. A - men.

481 Take Thou Our Minds, Dear Lord

Hall 10. 10. 10. 10.

William Hiram Foulkes, 1877-1961

Calvin W. Laufer, 1874-1938

1. Take thou our minds, dear Lord, we hum-bly pray; Give us the
2. Take thou our hearts, O Christ, they are thine own; Come thou with-
3. Take thou our wills, Most High! Hold thou full sway; Have in our
4. Take thou our-selves, O Lord, heart, mind, and will; Through our sur-

mind of Christ each pass-ing day; Teach us to know the truth
in our souls and claim thy throne; Help us to shed a-broad
in-most souls thy per-fect way; Guard thou each sa-cred hour
ren-dered souls thy plans ful-fill. We yield our-selves to thee—

that sets us free; Grant us in all our thoughts to hon-or thee.
thy death-less love; Use us to make the earth like heaven a-bove.
from self-ish ease; Guide thou our or-dered lives as thou dost please.
time, tal-ents, all; We hear, and hence-forth heed, thy sov-ereign call. A-men.

482 O Master, Let Me Walk with Thee

Maryton L. M.

Washington Gladden, 1836-1918, cento

Henry Percy Smith, 1825-1898

1. O Mas-ter, let me walk with thee In low-ly paths of serv-ice free;
2. Help me the slow of heart to move By some clear, win-ning word of love;
3. Teach me thy pa-tience; still with thee In clos-er, dear-er com-pa-ny,
4. In hope that sends a shin-ing ray Far down the fu-ture's broad-ening way,

O Master, Let Me Walk with Thee (cont.)

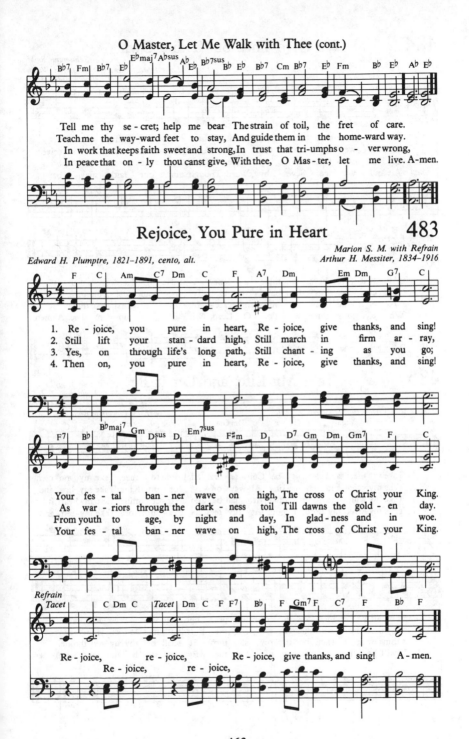

Tell me thy se - cret; help me bear The strain of toil, the fret of care.
Teach me the way-ward feet to stay, And guide them in the home-ward way.
In work that keeps faith sweet and strong, In trust that tri-umphs o - ver wrong,
In peace that on - ly thou canst give, With thee, O Mas - ter, let me live. A - men.

Rejoice, You Pure in Heart 483

Edward H. Plumptre, 1821–1891, cento, alt.

Marion S. M. with Refrain
Arthur H. Messiter, 1834–1916

1. Re - joice, you pure in heart, Re - joice, give thanks, and sing!
2. Still lift your stan - dard high, Still march in firm ar - ray,
3. Yes, on through life's long path, Still chant - ing as you go;
4. Then on, you pure in heart, Re - joice, give thanks, and sing!

Your fes - tal ban - ner wave on high, The cross of Christ your King.
As war - riors through the dark - ness toil Till dawns the gold - en day.
From youth to age, by night and day, In glad - ness and in woe.
Your fes - tal ban - ner wave on high, The cross of Christ your King.

Refrain
Re - joice, re - joice, Re - joice, give thanks, and sing! A - men.
Re - joice, re - joice,

463

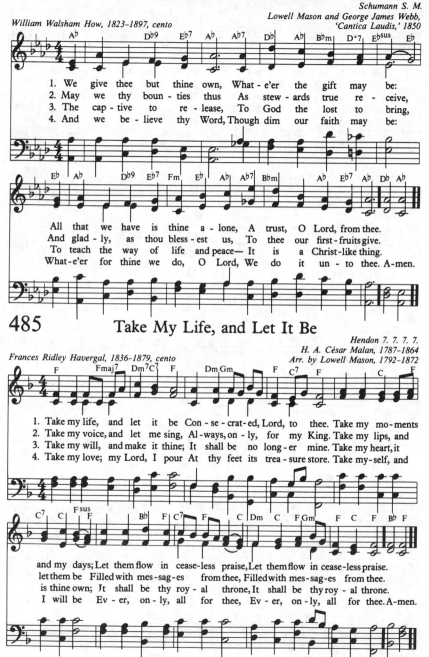

484

We Give Thee but Thine Own

Schumann S. M.

William Walsham How, 1823-1897, cento

*Lowell Mason and George James Webb,
'Cantica Laudis,' 1850*

1. We give thee but thine own, What-e'er the gift may be:
2. May we thy boun - ties thus As stew - ards true re - ceive,
3. The cap - tive to re - lease, To God the lost to bring,
4. And we be - lieve thy Word, Though dim our faith may be:

All that we have is thine a - lone, A trust, O Lord, from thee.
And glad - ly, as thou bless - est us, To thee our first - fruits give.
To teach the way of life and peace— It is a Christ-like thing.
What-e'er for thine we do, O Lord, We do it un - to thee. A-men.

485

Take My Life, and Let It Be

Hendon 7. 7. 7. 7.

*H. A. César Malan, 1787-1864
Arr. by Lowell Mason, 1792-1872*

Frances Ridley Havergal, 1836-1879, cento

1. Take my life, and let it be Con - se - crat - ed, Lord, to thee. Take my mo - ments
2. Take my voice, and let me sing, Al - ways, on - ly, for my King. Take my lips, and
3. Take my will, and make it thine; It shall be no long - er mine. Take my heart, it
4. Take my love; my Lord, I pour At thy feet its trea - sure store. Take my - self, and

and my days; Let them flow in cease-less praise, Let them flow in cease-less praise.
let them be Filled with mes-sag-es from thee, Filled with mes-sag-es from thee.
is thine own; Jt shall be thy roy - al throne, It shall be thy roy - al throne.
I will be Ev - er, on - ly, all for thee, Ev - er, on - ly, all for thee. A-men.

Be Thou My Vision, O Lord of My Heart   486

Anonymous Irish
Tr. by Mary Byrne, 1880–1931
Versified by Eleanor Hull, 1860–1935

Slane 10. 10. 9. 10.
Irish traditional melody
Harm. by David Evans, 1874–1948

1. Be thou my vi - sion, O Lord of my heart;
2. Be thou my wis - dom, and thou my true word;
3. Rich - es I heed not, nor man's emp - ty praise,
4. High King of heav - en, my vic - to - ry won,

Naught be all else to me, save that thou art—
I ev - er with thee and thou with me, Lord;
Thou mine in - her - i - tance, now and al - ways:
May I reach heav - en's joys, O bright heaven's Sun!

Thou my best thought, by day or by night,
Thou my great Fa - ther, I thy true son;
Thou and thou on - ly, first in my heart,
Heart of my own heart, what - ev - er be - fall,

Wak - ing or sleep - ing, thy pres - ence my light.
Thou in me dwell - ing, and I with thee one.
High King of heav - en, my trea - sure thou art.
Still be my vi - sion, O Rul - er of all. A - men.

All That I Am, All That I Do

All That I Am 8. 12. 12. 8. 5. 8. 12.
Sebastian Temple, 1928–
Harm. by Ann Margaret McNeil

Sebastian Temple, 1928–

1. All that I am, all that I do,
2. All that I dream, all that I pray,

All that I'll ev - er have, I of - fer now to you.
All that I'll ev - er make, I give to you to - day.

Take and sanc - ti - fy these gifts for your hon - or, Lord.

Know - ing that I love and serve you is e - nough re - ward.

Words and music reprinted by permission of the Franciscan Communications Center, Los Angeles, Calif.

All That I Am, All That I Do (cont.)

All that I am, all that I do,

All that I'll ev-er have, I of-fer now to you.

All that I dream, all that I pray,

All that I'll ev-er make, I give to you to-day.

488 Follow Christ and Love the World as He Did

Follow Christ Irregular
Sebastian Temple, 1928–

Sebastian Temple, 1928–

1. Fol - low Christ and love the world as he did, When he walked up - on the earth. Love each friend and en - e - my as he did; In God's eyes we have e - qual worth.

2. Fol - low Christ and serve the world as he did, When he min - is - tered to ev - ery - one. Serve each friend and en - e - my as he did So that the Fa - ther's will be done.

3. He said: "Love each oth - er as I loved you; By this all men will know you are mine. As I served you, so must you do: This new com - mand - ment I as - sign."

4. Fol - low Christ and love the world as he did, When he walked up - on the earth. Love each friend and en - e - my as he did; In God's eyes we have e - qual worth.

The Mass Is Ended 9. 9. 9. 9.
Sebastian Temple, 1928-

Sebastian Temple, 1928-

1. The Mass is end - ed, all go in
2. We wit - ness his love to ev - ery -
3. Thanks to the Fa - ther, who shows the
4. The Mass is end - ed, all go in

peace; We must di - min - ish,
one By our com - mu - nion
way, His life is with us
peace; We must di - min - ish,

and Christ in - crease. We take him
with Christ the Son. We take the
through - out each day. Let all our
and Christ in - crease. We take him

with us wher - e'er we go,
Mass to where men may be,
liv - ing and lov - ing be
with us wher - e'er we go,

That through our ac - tions his life may show.
So Christ may shine forth for all to see.
To praise and hon - or the Trin - i - ty.
That through our ac - tions his life may show.

Words and music reprinted by permission of the Franciscan Communications Center, Los Angeles, Calif.

490 He Who Would Valiant Be

John Bunyan, 1628–1688
Alt. by Percy Dearmer, 1867–1936

St. Dunstan's 6. 5. 6. 5. 6. 6. 6. 5.
C. Winfred Douglas, 1867–1944

1. He who would val - iant be 'Gainst all di - sas - ter,
2. Who so be - set him round With dis - mal sto - ries
3. Since, Lord, thou dost de - fend Us with thy Spir - it,

Let him in con - stan - cy Fol - low the Mas - ter.
Do but them - selves con - found— His strength the more is.
We know we at the end Shall life in - her - it.

There's no dis - cour - age - ment Shall make him once re - lent
No foes shall stay his might, Though he with gi - ants fight;
Then fan - cies, flee a - way! I'll fear not what men say;

His first a - vowed in - tent To be a pil - grim.
He will make good his right To be a pil - grim.
I'll la - bor night and day To be a pil - grim. A - men.

Words from *The English Hymnal;* used by permission of Oxford University Press. Music used by permission of The Church Pension Fund.

We Dedicate This Temple

Ernest K. Emurian, 1912–

Aurelia 7. 6. 7. 6. D.
Samuel S. Wesley, 1810–1876

491

1. We ded - i - cate this tem - ple, O Fa - ther, un - to thee,
2. We ded - i - cate this tem - ple To Christ, the Lord of love,
3. We ded - i - cate this tem - ple, O Spir - it from on high,
4. We ded - i - cate this tem - ple, This la - bor of our hands,

The God of an - cient ag - es, And ag - es yet to be;
Who brought God's rev - e - la - tion, The king - dom from a - bove;
To thee, in our thanks - giv - ing That thou art al - ways nigh;
To Fa - ther, Son, and Spir - it, Whose tem - ple ev - er stands

That here our hearts may wor - ship, And here our songs as - cend,
That we may learn his good - ness, His god - li - ness and grace,
To com - fort us in sor - row, To strength - en in dis - tress;
In hearts that learn to love thee, And minds that com - pre - hend;

In lov - ing ad - o - ra - tion And praise that knows no end.
Who holds all men and na - tions With - in his love's em - brace.
That we, through truth and mer - cy, May walk in ho - li - ness.
In wills em - powered to wit - ness Thy king - dom with - out end! A - men.

492   Come, We That Love the Lord

Isaac Watts, 1674–1748, cento, alt.
Refrain by Robert Lowry, 1826–1899

Marching to Zion S. M. with Refrain
Robert Lowry, 1826–1899

1. Come, we that love the Lord, And let our joys be known,
2. Let those re - fuse to sing Who nev - er knew our God;
3. The hill of Zi - on yields A thou-sand sa - cred sweets
4. Then let our songs a - bound, And ev - ery tear be dry;

Join in a song with sweet ac - cord, Join in a song with sweet ac - cord,
But chil - dren of the heav-enly King, But chil - dren of the heav-enly King,
Be - fore we reach the heav-enly fields, Be - fore we reach the heav-enly fields,
We're march-ing thro' Im - man - uel's ground, We're march-ing thro' Im - man - uel's ground,

And thus sur - round the throne, And thus sur - round the throne.
May speak their joys a - broad, May speak their joys a - broad.
Or walk the gold - en streets, Or walk the gold - en streets.
To fair - er worlds on high, To fair - er worlds on high.

And thus sur - round the throne, And thus sur - round the throne.

Refrain

We're march - ing to Zi - on, Beau - ti - ful, beau - ti - ful Zi - on;
We're march-ing on to Zi - on,

We're march-ing up-ward to Zi - on, The beau - ti - ful cit - y of God.
Zi - on, Zi - on,

Lord of the Church

493

Charterhouse 11. 10. 11. 10.
David Evans, 1874–1948

Frank von Christierson, 1900–

1. Lord of the church, we hear your ur-gent sum-mons: Now ev-ery
2. This is the king-dom goal for which we're striv-ing— The life in
3. Peace in our day for all the tribes and na-tions, The peace of
4. "Glo-ry to God"— the church in ju-bi-la-tion Of-fers to

Chris-tian to his serv-ant post— Lis-tening and work-ing,
Christ for all the sons of earth: Faith bring-ing free-dom
God in ev-ery heart and life; Peace from his love that
him un-end-ing prayer and praise, Serv-ice as com-rades

serv-ing God and giv-ing His best as mem-ber of God's might-y host.
and the life a-bun-dant, Jus-tice and hope, re-spect for each man's worth.
binds us all to-geth-er: In him must end our fu-tile, dead-ly strife.
in his loy-al le-gion— Our hopes, our lives tri-um-phant in his grace. A-men.

For All the Saints

Sine nomine 10. 10. 10. 4. 4.

William Walsham How, 1823–1897, cento

Ralph Vaughan Williams, 1872–1958

Unison

1. For all the saints who from their la-bors rest, Who thee by faith be-
2. Thou wast their rock, their for-tress, and their might; Thou, Lord, their Cap-tain
3. O may thy sol - diers, faith-ful, true, and bold, Fight as the saints who
4. O, blest com-mu - nion, fel-low-ship di - vine! We fee-bly strug-gle,

fore the world con-fessed, Thy name, O Je - sus, be for-ev - er blest.
in the well-fought fight; Thou, in the dark - ness drear, their one true light.
no - bly fought of old, And win with them the vic - tor's crown of gold.
they in glo - ry shine; Yet all are one in thee, for all are thine.

Al - le-lu - ia! Al - le-lu - ia! A-men.

5. And when the fight is fierce, the warfare long,
Steals on the ear the distant triumph song,
And hearts are brave again, and arms are strong.
Alleluia!
Alleluia!

6. From earth's wide bounds, from ocean's farthest
Through gates of pearl streams in the countless h
Singing to Father, Son, and Holy Ghost,
Alleluia!
Alleluia!

Music from *The English Hymnal.* Used by permission of Oxford University Press.

Built on the Rock the Church Shall Stand 495

Nicolai F. S. Grundtvig, 1783–1872, cento
Tr. by Carl Döving, 1867–1937, alt.

Kirken 8. 8. 8. 8. 8. 8. 8.
Ludvig M. Lindeman, 1812–1887

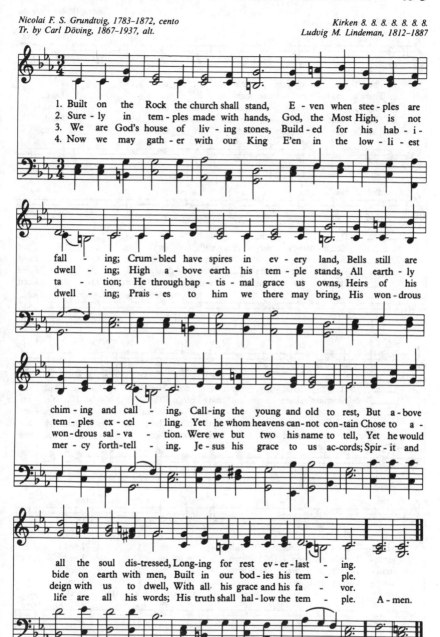

1. Built on the Rock the church shall stand, E-ven when stee-ples are fall - ing; Crum-bled have spires in ev-ery land, Bells still are chim-ing and call - ing, Call-ing the young and old to rest, But a-bove all the soul dis-tressed, Long-ing for rest ev-er-last - ing.

2. Sure-ly in tem-ples made with hands, God, the Most High, is not dwell - ing; High a-bove earth his tem-ple stands, All earth-ly tem-ples ex-cel - ling. Yet he whom heavens can-not con-tain Chose to a-bide on earth with men, Built in our bod-ies his tem - ple.

3. We are God's house of liv-ing stones, Build-ed for his hab-i-ta - tion; He through bap-tis-mal grace us owns, Heirs of his won-drous sal-va - tion. Were we but two his name to tell, Yet he would deign with us to dwell, With all his grace and his fa - vor.

4. Now we may gath-er with our King E'en in the low-li-est dwell - ing; Prais-es to him we there may bring, His won-drous mer-cy forth-tell - ing. Je-sus his grace to us ac-cords; Spir-it and life are all his words; His truth shall hal-low the tem - ple. A - men.

496   There's a Church Within Us, O Lord

Church Within Irregular

Kent E. Schneider, 1945-

Kent E. Schneider, 1945-

1. There's a church with-in us, O Lord,
2. There's po-ten-tial with-in us, O Lord;
3. There's a fire with-in us, O Lord;
4. There's some build-ing to be done, O Lord,
5. There's the church with-in us, O Lord,

There's a church with-in us, O Lord.
Some-thing's stir-ring with-in us, O Lord.
A new life's a-burn-in', O Lord.
There's some build-ing to be done, O Lord.
There's the church with-in us, O Lord.

Not a build-ing, but a soul, Not a por-tion, but a
Some-thing's strain-ing to have birth, To be vis-i-ble on
A fire for new life, Com-bat-ing pres-ent
Not with steel, not with stone, But with lives which are our
Not a build-ing, but one soul, Not a por-tion, but one

whole— There's a church with-in us, O Lord.
earth— There's po-ten-tial with-in us, O Lord.
strife— There's a fire with-in us, O Lord.
own— There's the church to be built, O Lord.
whole— We are your church in the world.

O Where Are Kings and Empires Now 497

St. Anne C. M.

Arthur Cleveland Coxe, 1818-1896, cento

Ascribed to William Croft, 1678-1727

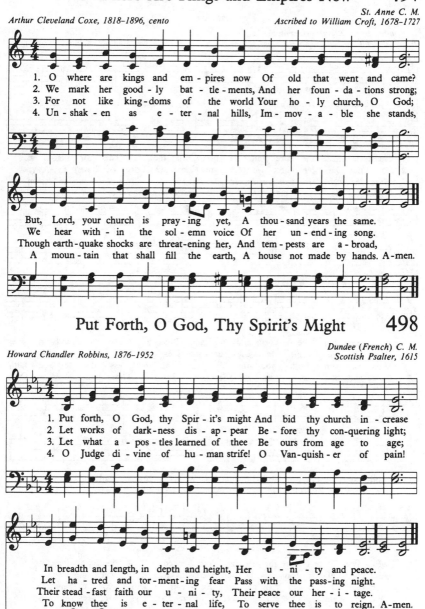

1. O where are kings and em-pires now Of old that went and came?
2. We mark her good-ly bat-tle-ments, And her foun-da-tions strong;
3. For not like king-doms of the world Your ho-ly church, O God;
4. Un-shak-en as e-ter-nal hills, Im-mov-a-ble she stands,

But, Lord, your church is pray-ing yet, A thou-sand years the same.
We hear with-in the sol-emn voice Of her un-end-ing song.
Though earth-quake shocks are threat-ening her, And tem-pests are a-broad,
A moun-tain that shall fill the earth, A house not made by hands. A-men.

Put Forth, O God, Thy Spirit's Might 498

Dundee (French) C. M.

Howard Chandler Robbins, 1876-1952

Scottish Psalter, 1615

1. Put forth, O God, thy Spir-it's might And bid thy church in-crease
2. Let works of dark-ness dis-ap-pear Be-fore thy con-quering light;
3. Let what a-pos-tles learned of thee Be ours from age to age;
4. O Judge di-vine of hu-man strife! O Van-quish-er of pain!

In breadth and length, in depth and height, Her u-ni-ty and peace.
Let ha-tred and tor-ment-ing fear Pass with the pass-ing night.
Their stead-fast faith our u-ni-ty, Their peace our her-i-tage.
To know thee is e-ter-nal life, To serve thee is to reign. A-men.

Words used by permission of Fleming H. Revell Company.

499 Christ Is Made the Sure Foundation

Latin office hymn, 7th century, cento
Tr. by John Mason Neale, 1818–1866, alt.

Regent Square 8. 7. 8. 7. 8. 7.
Henry Smart, 1813–1879
Descant by L. David Miller, 1919–

478

O Mary, Don't You Weep, Don't You Mourn 500

Mary, Don't You Weep Irregular with Refrain
American Negro melody
Arr. by David Hugh Jones, 1900–

Spiritual

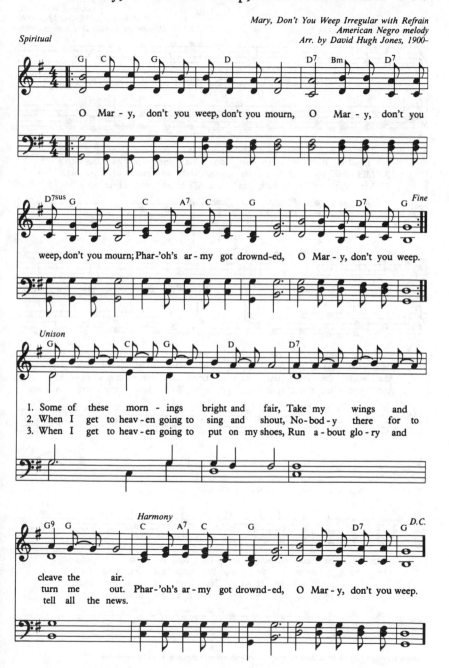

O Mar-y, don't you weep, don't you mourn, O Mar-y, don't you weep, don't you mourn; Phar-'oh's ar-my got drownd-ed, O Mar-y, don't you weep. *Fine*

Unison

1. Some of these morn-ings bright and fair, Take my wings and
2. When I get to heav-en going to sing and shout, No-bod-y there for to
3. When I get to heav-en going to put on my shoes, Run a-bout glo-ry and

Harmony

cleave the air.
turn me out. Phar-'oh's ar-my got drownd-ed, O Mar-y, don't you weep.
tell all the news.

D.C.

501 The Church's One Foundation

Aurelia 7. 6. 7. 6. D.
Samuel S. Wesley, 1810–1876
Descant by Donald D. Kettring, 1907–

Samuel J. Stone, 1839–1900, cento

Descant: 4. she hath un-ion With God the Three in One,

1. The church's one foun-da-tion Is Je-sus Christ her Lord;
2. E-lect from ev-ery na-tion, Yet one o'er all the earth,
3. 'Mid toil and trib-u-la-tion, And tu-mult of her war,
4. Yet she on earth hath un-ion With God the Three in One,

mys-tic sweet com-mu-nion With those whose rest is won:

She is his new cre-a-tion By wa-ter and the word:
Her char-ter of sal-va-tion One Lord, one faith, one birth;
She waits the con-sum-ma-tion Of peace for-ev-er-more;
And mys-tic sweet com-mu-nion With those whose rest is won:

hap-py, ho-ly! Give grace that we,

From heaven he came and sought her To be his ho-ly bride;
One ho-ly name she bless-es, Par-takes one ho-ly food,
Till with the vi-sion glo-rious Her long-ing eyes are blest,
O hap-py ones and ho-ly! Lord, give us grace that we,

Descant copyright 1956 by W. L. Jenkins; from *Familiar Hymns with Descants.* Used by permission.

480

The Church's One Foundation (cont.)

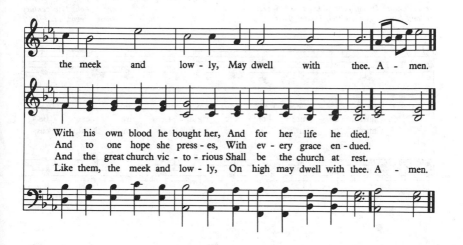

the meek   and   low - ly, May dwell   with   thee. A - men.

With his own blood he bought her, And for her life he died.
And to one hope she press - es, With ev - ery grace en - dued.
And the great church vic - to - rious Shall be the church at rest.
Like them, the meek and low - ly, On high may dwell with thee. A - men.

Our Church Proclaims God's Love and Care   502

Truro L. M.

Mabel Niedermeyer, 1899–   T. Williams, 'Psalmodia Evangelica,' 1789

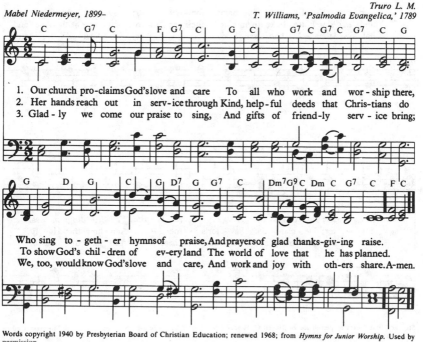

1. Our church pro-claims God's love and care   To all who work and wor - ship there,
2. Her hands reach out in serv-ice through Kind, help-ful deeds that Chris-tians do
3. Glad - ly we come our praise to sing, And gifts of friend-ly serv - ice bring;

Who sing to - geth - er hymns of praise, And prayers of glad thanks-giv-ing raise.
To show God's chil - dren of ev-ery land The world of love that he has planned.
We, too, would know God's love and care, And work and joy with oth-ers share. A-men.

503   Church, Rejoice! Raise Thy Voice

St. 1, Johann Daniel Herrnschmidt, 1675–1723
Tr. and Sts. 2, 3, Russell G. Holder, 1896–

Singt dem Herrn 3. 3. 7. 7. 7. 7. 7. 4. 4. 4. 4. 7.
Georg Joseph, 17th century
Alt. by Christian Gregor, 1723–1801

1. Church, re-joice! Raise thy voice, Sing Je-ho-vah's wor-thy praise; Ex-tol his name for-ev-er; Laud him, our God and Sav-ior; Pro-claim to ev-ery na-tion The ti-dings of sal-

2. Church, u-nite For the right; Let thy foes be-hold thy stand; Re-buke them for their er-ror; In-spire with hope and fer-vor; De-clare the Sav-ior's mer-it And how the Ho-ly

3. Church, go forth O'er the earth; Christ, thy head, has hal-lowed thee, A cho-sen bride for-ev-er, A-dorn-ed for our Sav-ior; Be strong and be not cheer-less, And may thy saints be

va - tion; Bear ye wit - ness To his great-ness; Spread the sto - ry
Spir - it By his pow - er, Ev - ery hour, Will di - rect us
fear - less; In all plac - es, With all rac - es, May that sto - ry

Of his glo - ry To the earth's re - mot - est bounds.
And pro - tect us In a world of sin and strife.
Of his glo - ry Be the hope of all the world. A - men.

Blest Be the Tie That Binds 504

Dennis S. M.
Johann G. Nägeli, 1773–1836
Arr. by Lowell Mason, 1792–1872

John Fawcett, 1739/40–1817, cento, alt.

1. Blest be the tie that binds Our hearts in Chris - tian love;
2. Be - fore our Fa - ther's throne We pour our ar - dent prayers;
3. We share each oth - er's woes, Each oth - er's bur - dens bear,
4. When we are called to part It gives us in - ward pain,

The fel - low - ship of kin - dred minds Is like to that a - bove.
Our fears, our hopes, our aims are one, Our com - forts and our cares.
And of - ten for each oth - er flows The sym - pa - thiz - ing tear.
But we shall still be joined in heart, And hope to meet a - gain. A - men.

505　O Church of God, Divided

Rotterdam 7. 6. 7. 6. D.

Marion Franklin Ham, 1867–1956

Berthold Tours, 1838–1897

1. O church of God, di - vid - ed And rent by end - less strife!
2. The sub - tle powers of dark - ness, Like foe - men in the night,
3. Dis - perse thy war - ring fac - tions, And bid their con - flicts cease;

Thy war - ring sects ob - scur - ing The way, the truth, the life;
Ad - vance up - on the strong - holds Of jus - tice, truth, and right;
Lift high the fall - en stan - dard Of Christ, the Prince of Peace;

A strick - en world, de - spair - ing, Is call - ing un - to thee.
The might - y sway of e - vil Pre - vails in ev - ery land.
One Lord, one faith, one spir - it, One God of all pro - claim.

O church of Christ's e - van - gel, What shall thine an - swer be?
O church of God's a - noint - ing, A - rise, and take thy stand!
Go forth, O church, u - nit - ed, To con - quer in his name! A - men.

Swing Low, Sweet Chariot

Swing Low Irregular with Refrain
American Negro melody
Arr. by David Hugh Jones, 1900–

Spiritual

Swing low, sweet char-i-ot, Com-ing for to car-ry me home,

Swing low, sweet char-i-ot, Com-ing for to car-ry me home.

1. I looked o-ver Jor-dan and what did I see,
2. If you get there be-fore I do,
3. I'm some-times up and some-times down,

Com-ing for to car-ry me home; Tell all my friends I'm
But still my soul feels

A band of an-gels

com-ing af-ter me,
com-ing too. Com-ing for to car-ry me home.
heav-en-ly bound.

507 Come, Ye Children of the Lord

Spanish Chant 7. 7. 7. 7. D.
Anonymous melody
Arr. by Benjamin Carr, 1768-1831

James H. Wallis, 1861-1940

1. Come, ye chil-dren of the Lord, Let us sing with one ac-cord.
2. O how joy-ful it will be When our Sav-ior we shall see!
3. All ar-rayed in spot-less white, We will dwell 'mid truth and light.

Let us raise a joy-ful strain To our Lord, who soon will reign
When in splen-dor he'll de-scend, Then all wick-ed-ness will end.
We will sing the songs of praise; We will shout in joy-ous lays.

On this earth, when it shall be Cleansed from all in-iq-ui-ty;
O what songs we then will sing To our Sav-ior, Lord and King!
Earth shall then be cleansed from sin. Ev-ery liv-ing thing there-in

When all men from sin will cease, And will live in love and peace.
O what love will then bear sway, When our fears shall flee a-way!
Shall in love and beau-ty dwell; Then with joy each heart will swell.

"Till He Come!" O Let the Words 508

Edward H. Bickersteth, 1825-1906

St. Petersburg 7. 7. 7. 7. 7. 7.
Dmitri S. Bortniansky, 1752-1825

1. "Till he come!" O let the words Linger on the trembling chords; Let the "little while" between In their golden light be seen; Let us think how heaven and home Lie beyond that "Till he come!"

2. When the weary ones we love Enter on their rest above, Seems the earth so poor and vast? All our life-joy overcast? Hush! be every murmur dumb. It is only "Till he come!"

3. Clouds and conflicts round us press; Would we have one sorrow less? All the sharpness of the cross, All that tells the world is loss— Death and darkness and the tomb— Only whisper "Till he come!"

4. See, the feast of love is spread, Drink the wine and break the bread— Sweet memorials— till the Lord Call us round his heavenly board; Some from earth, from glory some, Severed only "Till he come!" A-men.

Rejoice, Rejoice, Believers

Rejoice 7. 6. 7. 6. D.

Laurentius Laurenti, 1660–1722, cento
Tr. by Sarah B. Findlater, 1823–1907, alt.

J. A. Freylinghausen, 1670–1739
Adapted by Christian Gregor, 1723–1801

1. Re-joice, re-joice, be-liev - ers, And let your lights ap - pear;
2. See that your lamps are burn - ing; Re-plen-ish them with oil,
3. Our hope and ex-pec-ta - tion, O Je-sus, now ap - pear!

The eve-ning is ad-vanc - ing, And dark-er night is near;
And wait for your sal-va - tion, The end of earth-ly toil.
A-rise, thou Sun so longed for, O'er this be-night-ed sphere!

The Bride-groom is a-ris - ing, And soon he draw-eth nigh;
The watch-ers on the moun - tain Pro-claim the Bride-groom near.
With hearts and hands up-lift - ed, We plead, O Lord, to see

Up, pray, and watch, and wres - tle! At mid-night comes the cry.
Go meet him as he com - eth, With al-le-lu-ias clear.
The day of earth's re-demp - tion That brings us un-to thee. A-men.

Music used by permission of the Moravian Church in America.

I've Got a Robe, You've Got a Robe 510

Got a Robe 8. 8. 12. 9. with Refrain
American Negro melody
Arr. by David Hugh Jones, 1900–

Spiritual

1. I've got a robe, you've got a robe, All of God's chil-dren got a robe;
2. I've got a crown, you've got a crown, All of God's chil-dren got a crown;
3. I've got a shoes, you've got a shoes, All of God's chil-dren got a shoes;
4. I've got a harp, you've got a harp, All of God's chil-dren got a harp;
5. I've got a song, you've got a song, All of God's chil-dren got a song;

When I get to heav-en, goin' to put on my robe, Goin' to shout all o-ver God's
When I get to heav-en, goin' to put on my crown, Goin' to shout all o-ver God's
When I get to heav-en, goin' to put on my shoes, Goin' to walk all o-ver God's
When I get to heav-en, goin' to play on my harp, Goin' to play all o-ver God's
When I get to heav-en, goin' to sing a new song, Goin' to sing all o-ver God's

Refrain

hea-v'n. Hea-v'n, hea-v'n, Ev-'ry-bod-y talk-in' 'bout hea-v'n ain't

go-in' there, Hea-v'n, hea-v'n, Goin' to shout all o-ver God's hea-v'n.

489

511   Merciful Savior, Hear Our Humble Prayer

Old 124th 10. 10. 10. 10. 10.
Genevan Psalter, 1551, alt.
Harm. by Robert F. Crone

Melvin Farrell, 1930–

1. Mer - ci - ful Sav - ior, hear our hum - ble prayer,
2. Je - sus, all ho - ly, mer - ci - ful and just,
3. O gen - tle Sav - ior, Lamb for sin - ners slain,
4. Lord, at your pas - sion love did con - quer fear;

For all your serv - ants passed be - yond life's care;
Do you re - mem - ber man was made from dust;
Look on your broth - ers, cleanse their hearts of stain:
Now share that tri - umph with these souls so dear:

Though sin has touched them, yet their weak - ness spare.
Un - to your mer - cy we these souls en - trust.
Your cross has won them ev - er - last - ing gain.
Ban - ish their sor - rows, let your light ap - pear.

Refrain

O grant them par - don, Je - sus, Sav - ior blest,

And give their spir - its light and end - less rest.

Translation and harmonization © World Library Publications, Inc. Used by permission.

490

Jerusalem the Golden

Bernard of Cluny, 12th century, cento
Tr. by John Mason Neale, 1818-1866, alt.

Ewing 7. 6. 7. 6. D.
Alexander Ewing, 1830-1895

1. Je - ru - sa - lem the gold - en, With milk and hon - ey blest,
2. They stand, those halls of Zi - on, All ju - bi - lant with song,
3. There is the throne of Da - vid; And there, from care re - leased,
4. O sweet and bless - ed coun - try, The home of God's e - lect!

Be - neath your con - tem - pla - tion Sink heart and voice op - pressed.
And bright with man - y an an - gel, And all the mar - tyr throng.
The song of them that tri - umph, The shout of them that feast;
O sweet and bless - ed coun - try That ea - ger hearts ex - pect!

I know not, O I know not What joys a - wait us there,
The Prince is ev - er in them, The day - light is se - rene;
And they who with their Lead - er Have con - quered in the fight,
Je - sus, in mer - cy bring us To that dear land of rest,

What ra - dian - cy of glo - ry, What bliss be - yond com - pare!
The pas - tures of the bless - ed Are decked in glo - rious sheen.
For - ev - er and for - ev - er Are clad in robes of white.
Who are, with God the Fa - ther And Spir - it, ev - er blest. A - men.

513 When the Trumpet of the Lord Shall Sound

The Roll 15. 11. 15. 11. with Refrain

James M. Black, 1856–1938

James M. Black, 1856–1938

1. When the trum-pet of the Lord shall sound and time shall be no more, And the
2. On that bright and cloud-less morn-ing when the dead in Christ shall rise, And the
3. Let us la-bor for the Mas-ter from the dawn till set-ting sun, Let us

morn-ing breaks e-ter-nal, bright and fair; When the saved of earth shall gath-er
glo-ry of his res-ur-rec-tion share; When his cho-sen ones shall gath-er
tell of all his won-drous love and care; Then when all of life is o-ver

o-ver on the oth-er shore, And the roll is called up yon-der, I'll be there.
to their home be-yond the skies, And the roll is called up yon-der, I'll be there.
and our work on earth is done, And the roll is called up yon-der, We'll be there.

Refrain

When the roll is called up yon der, When the roll is
When the roll is called up yon-der, I'll be there, When the roll is

492

When the Trumpet of the Lord Shall Sound (cont.)

called up yon - der, When the roll is called up
called up yon - der, I'll be there,   When the roll is called up

yon - der, When the roll is called up yon - der, I'll be there.
yon - der,

I Love Your Kingdom, Lord 514

St. Thomas S. M.

Timothy Dwight, 1752–1817, cento, alt.   *Aaron Williams' 'The New Universal Psalmodist,' 1770*

1. I love your king - dom, Lord, The house of your a - bode, The
2. I love your church, O God! Her walls be - fore you stand Dear
3. For her my tears shall fall, For her my prayers as - cend, To
4. Be - yond my high - est joy I prize her heav - enly ways, Her
5. Sure as your truth shall last, To Zi - on shall be given The

church our blest Re - deem - er saved With his own pre - cious blood.
as the ap - ple of your eye, And grav - en on your hand.
her my cares and toils be given, Till toils and cares shall end.
sweet com - mu - nion, sol - emn vows, Her hymns of love and praise.
bright - est glo - ries earth can yield, And bright - er bliss of heaven. A - men.

515   He That Believes and Is Baptized

Thomas Hansen Kingo, 1634–1703
Tr. by George A. T. Rygh, 1860–1943, alt.

St. Paul 8. 7. 8. 7. 8. 8. 7.
'Etliche Cristliche Lyeder,' Wittenberg, 1524

1. He that be-lieves and is bap-tized Shall see the Lord's
   Bap-tized in-to the death of Christ, He is a new
2. With one ac-cord, O God, we pray; Grant us thy Ho-
   Look thou on our in-fir-mi-ty Through Je-sus' blood

sal-va-tion;
cre-a-tion; Through Christ's re-demp-tion he shall stand A-
ly Spir-it;
and mer-it; Grant us to grow in grace each day, That

mong the glo-rious heav-enly band Of ev-ery tribe and na-tion.
by this sac-ra-ment we may E-ter-nal life in-her-it. A-men.

Jesus, Friend So Kind and Gentle

Sicilian Mariners 8. 7. 8. 7. 8. 7.
Sicilian melody

Philip E. Gregory, 1886–

1. Je - sus, friend so kind and gen - tle, Lit - tle ones we
2. Thou who didst re - ceive the chil - dren To thy - self so
3. Grant to us a deep com - pas - sion For thy chil - dren

bring to thee; Grant to them thy dear - est bless - ing,
ten - der - ly, Give to all who teach and guide them
ev - ery - where. May we see our hu - man fam - ily

Let thine arms a - round them be; Now en - fold them
Wis - dom and hu - mil - i - ty, Vi - sion true to
Free from sor - row and de - spair, And be - hold thy

in thy good - ness, From all dan - ger keep them free.
keep them no - ble, Love to serve them faith - ful - ly.
king - dom glo - rious, In our world so bright and fair. A - men.

Words used by permission of the author.

517 O God, This Child from You Did Come

Shepherds' Pipes C. M. D.

Frank A. Brooks, Jr., 1935-

Annabeth McClelland Gay, 1925-

1. O God, this child from you did come, To you it shall re-turn;
2. Real acts of love and words of truth We hope to teach this child,
3. Of flesh and blood this child is made, In im-age of your-self.

But to our trust and love you chose To send it for some years.
And con-stant may our guid-ance be In like-ness of your Son.
To men we come; on earth we live— Our pur-pose clear, to serve.

Refrain

Be-cause we thank you for this life That to our lives has come,

To-geth-er we do pledge our-selves To help this child serve you. A-men.

Stand, Soldier of the Cross

518

Song 20 S. M.
Orlando Gibbons, 1583–1625
Harm. by Paul G. Bunjes, 1914–

Edward H. Bickersteth, 1825–1906

1. Stand, sol - dier of the cross, Your high al - le - giance claim, And vow to hold the world but loss For your Re - deem - er's name.
2. A - rise and be bap - tized To wash your sins a - way; Your league with God be sol - em - nized, Your faith con - fessed to - day.
3. No more your own, but Christ's, With all the saints of old, A - pos - tles, seers, e - van - ge - lists, And mar - tyr throngs en - rolled.
4. O bright the con - queror's crown, The song of tri - umph sweet, When faith casts ev - ery tro - phy down At our great Cap - tain's feet.
5. All glo - ry to the Son, Who comes to set us free, With Fa - ther, Spir - it, ev - er One, Through all e - ter - ni - ty. A - men.

519　　　**Maker of All, to You We Give**

North Park C. M.

Pamela-Rae Yeager Maloney, 1945–　　　　　　　*David L. Thorburn, 1936–*

1. Mak - er of all, to you we give Our praise for birth and life;
2. We ask to - day that you a - dopt This child in - to your church;
3. With grate - ful hearts we come to you. We pledge to raise this child
4. Cre - a - tor, Fa - ther! Glo - ry be To you and to your Son,

We thank you for this won - drous gift, A new and liv - ing soul.
Send now your Spir - it to be - come A pres - ent, con - stant guide.
In love and trust and hope, which is Our faith in Je - sus Christ.
Our Sav - ior, Broth - er; glo - ry be To Spir - it, who is Life.

Words used by permission of the author. Music used by permission of the composer.

520　　　**A Charge to Keep I Have**

Boylston S. M.

Charles Wesley, 1707–1788, alt.　　　　　　　*Lowell Mason, 1792–1872*

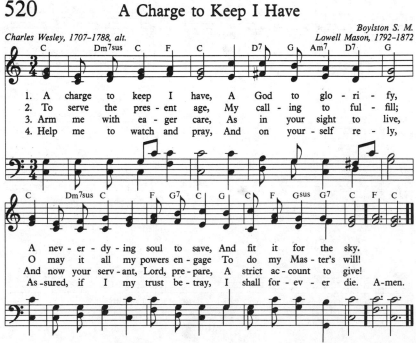

1. A charge to keep I have, A God to glo - ri - fy,
2. To serve the pres - ent age, My call - ing to ful - fill;
3. Arm me with ea - ger care, As in your sight to live,
4. Help me to watch and pray, And on your - self re - ly,

A nev - er - dy - ing soul to save, And fit it for the sky.
O may it all my powers en - gage To do my Mas - ter's will!
And now your serv - ant, Lord, pre - pare, A strict ac - count to give!
As - sured, if I my trust be - tray, I shall for - ev - er die. A - men.

For Christian Homes, O Lord, We Pray 521

Dutcher L. M.
John Sloat, 1932-
Harm. by David Hugh Jones, 1900-

Richard S. Armstrong, 1924-

1. For Chris - tian homes, O Lord, we pray, To keep us
2. U - nit - ed in a bond of love, We lift our
3. Pro - tect us and our loved ones dear From sor - row's
4. In faith we live by thine own grace, In faith serve
5. When thou dost call us all to rest, Then will we

con - stant in thy way, For all that home is
eyes to thee a - bove, Whence comes the strength and
bur - den, pain, and fear. Yet grant that when thy
our ap - point - ed place. And though the far - flung
know a home more blest, See all our care and

meant to be— A place where-in we dwell with thee.
will to live, The wish to share, the joy to give.
cross we bear, "Thy will be done" may be our prayer.
realms we roam, In faith our hearts are e'er at home.
sor - row cease, And find in Christ e - ter - nal peace. A - men.

Words and music copyright 1958 by David Hugh Jones. Used by permission.

499

O Perfect Love

Perfect Love 11. 10. 11. 10.
Joseph Barnby, 1838–1896

Dorothy Frances Gurney, 1858–1932

1. O per-fect Love, all hu-man thought tran-scend-ing,
2. O per-fect Life, be thou their full as-sur-ance
3. Grant them the joy which bright-ens earth-ly sor-row;

Low-ly we kneel in prayer be-fore thy throne,
Of ten-der char-i-ty and stead-fast faith,
Grant them the peace which calms all earth-ly strife,

That theirs may be the love which knows no end-ing,
Of pa-tient hope, and qui-et, brave en-dur-ance,
And to life's day the glo-rious un-known mor-row

Whom thou for-ev-er-more dost join in one.
With child-like trust that fears nor pain nor death.
That dawns up-on e-ter-nal love and life. A-men.

Our Father, by Whose Name

F. Bland Tucker, 1895–

Rhosymedre 6. 6. 6. 6. 8. 8. 8.
John David Edwards, 1806-1885

1. Our Fa - ther, by whose name All fa - ther - hood is known,
2. O Christ, thy - self a child With - in an earth - ly home,
3. O Spir - it, who dost bind Our hearts in u - ni - ty,

Who dost in love pro - claim Each fam - i - ly thine own,
With heart still un - de - filed, Thou didst to man - hood come;
Who teach - est us to find The love from self set free,

Bless thou all par - ents, guard - ing well, With con - stant love as
Our chil - dren bless, in ev - ery place, That they may all be -
In all our hearts such love in - crease, That ev - ery home, by

sen - ti - nel, The homes in which thy peo - ple dwell.
hold thy face, And know - ing thee may grow in grace.
this re - lease, May be the dwell - ing place of peace. A - men.

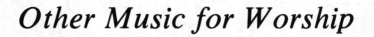

Other Music for Worship

Contents

O Worship the Lord 524

Porter 13. 8.
Robert Guy McCutchan, 1877–1958

O Worship the Lord 525

Source unknown

Praise the Lord! 526

Kent E. Schneider, 1945–

505

527   O Come, Let Us Sing Unto the Lord

From Psalm 95:1-7; 96:9, 13   *William Boyce, 1710-1779*

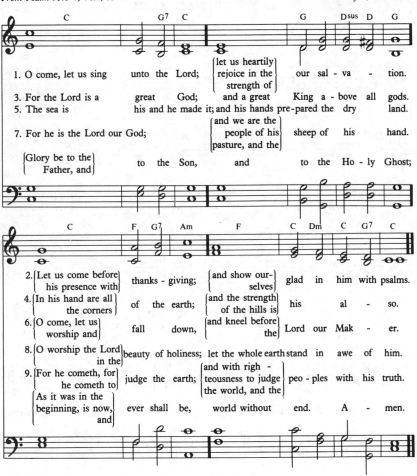

1. O come, let us sing   unto the Lord;   {let us heartily rejoice in the strength of}   our sal - va - tion.
3. For the Lord is a   great God;   and a great   King a - bove all   gods.
5. The sea is   his and he made it; and his hands pre-pared the dry   land.
7. For he is the Lord our God;   {and we are the people of his pasture, and the}   sheep of   his   hand.

{Glory be to the Father, and}   to   the   Son,   and   to   the   Ho - ly   Ghost;

2. {Let us come before his presence with}   thanks - giving;   {and show our-selves}   glad   in   him with psalms.
4. {In his hand are all the corners}   of   the   earth;   {and the strength of the hills is}   his   al - so.
6. {O come, let us worship and}   fall   down,   {and kneel before the}   Lord our Mak - er.
8. {O worship the Lord in the} beauty of holiness; let the whole earth stand in   awe   of   him.
9. {For he cometh, for he cometh to}   judge the earth;   {and with righ-teousness to judge the world, and the}   peo - ples with his truth.

As it was in the beginning, is now, and   ever shall   be,   world without   end.   A - men.

528   *Richard Tomlinson, 1822-?*   **529**   *Richard Goodson, 1655-1718*

From Psalm 100

William Byrd, c. 1543-1623

1. (O be joyful in the Lord,) all ye lands; (serve the Lord with gladness, and come before his) pres-ence with a song.

2. (Be ye sure that the Lord he is God; it is he that hath made us, and not) we our-selves; (we are his peo-ple and the) sheep of his pas-ture.

3. (O go your way in-to his gates with thanksgiving, and into his) courts with praise; (be thankful un-to him, and) speak— good of his name.

4. (For the Lord is gracious, his mer-cy is) ev-er-lasting; (and his truth endureth from generation to) gen-er-a-tion.

(Glory be to the Father, and) to the Son, and to the Ho-ly Ghost;

(As it was in the be-ginning, is now, and) ever shall be, world without end. A - men.

531

Oxford chant

532

William Russell, 1777-1813

533   Holy, Holy, Holy Lord, God of Power

Jan Vermulst, 1925–

Ho - ly, ho - ly, ho - ly Lord, God of power and might,

heav - en and earth are full of your glo - ry.

Ho - san - na in the high - est. Bless - ed is he who

comes in the name of the Lord. Ho - san - na in the high - est.

Holy, Holy, Holy Lord, God of Power   534

Noël Goemanne, 1926–

Holy, holy, holy Lord, God of power and might, heaven and earth are full of your glory. Hosanna in the highest. Blessed is he who comes in the name of the Lord. Hosanna in the highest.

535   Lead Me, Lord, in Thy Righteousness

Lead Me, Lord 10. 8. 9. 8.
Samuel S. Wesley, 1810-1876

From Psalm 5:8; 4:8

Lead me, Lord, lead me in thy righ-teous-ness; make thy way
plain be-fore my face. For it is thou, Lord, thou, Lord,
on-ly that mak — est me dwell in safe - ty. A-men.

536   Lord, for the Mercies of the Night

Farrant C. M.
Ascr. to Richard Farrant, c. 1530-1581

John Mason, ?-1694; alt.

1. Lord, for the mer-cies of the night Our hum-ble thanks we pay,
2. Let this day praise thee, O Lord God, And so let all our days;

Lord, for the Mercies of the Night (cont.)

And un-to thee we ded-i-cate The first-fruits of the day.
And O let heaven's e-ter-nal day Be thine e-ter-nal praise! A-men.

Holy, Holy, Holy Lord God of Hosts 537

Vincent Persichetti, 1915–

Ho - ly, ho - ly, ho - ly Lord God of

hosts, heaven and earth are full of thy glo - ry: Glo - ry be to

thee, O Lord Most High. A - men.

Music from *Hymns and Responses,* by Vincent Persichetti. © 1956 Elkan-Vogel, Inc. Used by permission.

538   Called to Create

Kent E. Schneider, 1945-   *Kent E. Schneider, 1945-*

Called to cre-ate the new world on earth. Called to re-late to man from his birth. Boxed up in box-es called now to be free and set in mo-tion our des-ti-ny.

Words and music copyright Kent Schneider 1969. Used by permission.

539   Create in Me a Clean Heart

Psalm 51:10-12   *Tonus regius*

1. Create in me a clean heart, O God; and renew a right spirit with-in me.
2. Cast me not away from your pres-ence; and take not your Ho-ly Spir-it from me.
3. Restore unto me the joy of your sal-va-tion; and uphold me with your free spir-it.

We Come Now to Worship

Roger Copeland, 1942–   Roger Copeland, 1942–

We come now to wor-ship and love the Lord our God; Keep si-lence, keep si-lence, keep si-lence be-fore him.

* Guitarist should play these chords as high on the fingerboard as possible to simulate the bell-like sounds intended. The 7th tone should be omitted from the D♭9 chords.

Words and music used by permission of Roger Copeland.

541 The Lord Is in His Holy Temple

Wolfgang Amadeus Mozart, 1756–1791
Adapted by Maurice C. Whitney

Habakkuk 2:20

The Lord is in his ho - ly tem - ple; Let all the earth keep si - lence, Keep si - lence be - fore him. A - men.

542 The Lord Is in His Holy Temple

Karl P. Harrington, 1861–1953

Habakkuk 2:20

The Lord is in his ho - ly tem-ple; Let all the earth keep si-lence be-fore him.

This Is the Day That the Lord Has Made 543

Thomas W. Holcombe, 1943–

This is the day that the Lord has made. ____

____ Let us re - joice and be glad in it. A - men.

OFFERTORY RESPONSES AND DOXOLOGIES

All Things Are Thine 544

Herr Jesu Christ, dich zu uns wend L. M.
'Pensum sacrum,' Görlitz, 1648
Harm. by Johann S. Bach, 1685–1750

John Greenleaf Whittier, 1807–1892

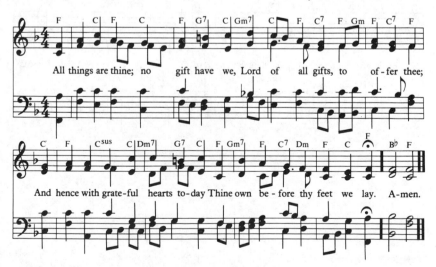

All things are thine; no gift have we, Lord of all gifts, to of - fer thee;

And hence with grate-ful hearts to-day Thine own be - fore thy feet we lay. A-men.

545   All Things Come of Thee, O Lord

From I Chronicles 29:14

Source unknown

All things come of thee, O Lord, and of thine own have we giv-en thee. A-men.

546   Bless Thou the Gifts

Samuel Longfellow, 1819–1892

Deus tuorum militum L. M.
Grenoble church melody

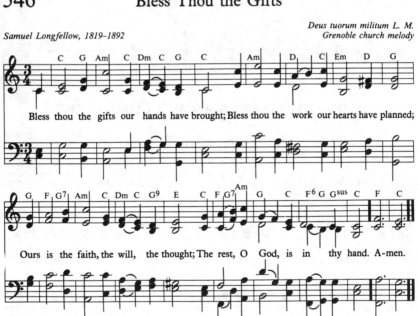

Bless thou the gifts our hands have brought; Bless thou the work our hearts have planned;

Ours is the faith, the will, the thought; The rest, O God, is in thy hand. A-men.

Praise God, from Whom All Blessings Flow 547

Port Jervis L. M.
Richard K. Avery, 1934–
and Donald S. Marsh, 1923–

Thomas Ken, 1637–1711

Music copyright 1967 by Richard K. Avery and Donald S. Marsh (ASCAP) from *Hymns Hot and Carols Cool.* Used by permission of Proclamation Productions, Inc., Orange Square, Port Jervis, N.Y.

548 Praise God, from Whom All Blessings Flow

Port Jervis L. M.
Richard K. Avery, 1934–
and Donald S. Marsh, 1923–
Arr. by Thomas W. Holcombe, 1943–

Praise God, from whom all bless-ings flow; Praise him, all peo - ple here be - low; Praise him a-bove, ye heav-enly host; Praise Fa-ther, Son, and Ho - ly Ghost. A - men, A - men, A - men, A - men, A - men, A - men.

Praise God, from Whom All Blessings Flow 549

Old Hundredth L. M.
Louis Bourgeois, c. 1510–1561, alt.
Thomas Ken, 1637–1711

Praise God, from whom all bless-ings flow; Praise him, all crea-tures here be-low;

Praise him a-bove, ye heav-enly host; Praise Fa-ther, Son, and Ho-ly Ghost. A-men.

AMENS

Twofold Amen 550

A - men, A - men.

Dresden

Threefold Amen 551

A-men, A-men, A - men.

Danish

Threefold Amen 552

Walter Henry Hall, 1862–1935

A-men, A-men, A - men.

553   Threefold Amen

Noël Goemanne, 1926–

A - men, A - men, A - men.

554   Threefold Amen

Thomas W. Holcombe, 1943–

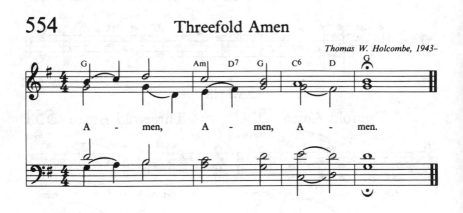

A - men, A - men, A - men.

555   Fourfold Amen

Oreste Ravanello, 1871–1938

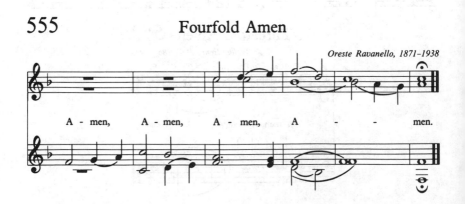

A - men, A - men, A - men, A - men.

The Great Amen

556

Joseph Roff, 1910–

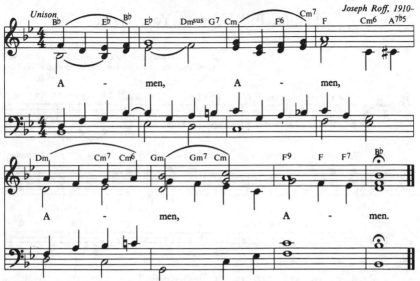

Sevenfold Amen

557

John Stainer, 1840–1901

558   Father, Fill Us with Your Love

Horsham 7. 7. 7. 7.
Melody coll. by Lucy Broadwood, 1858–1929
Harm. and arr. by Ralph Vaughan Williams, 1872–1958

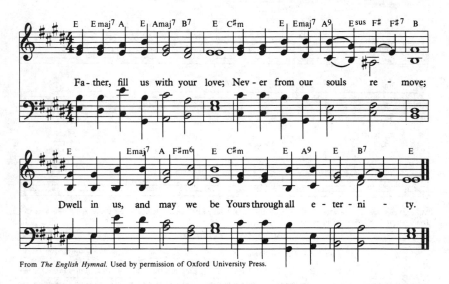

Fa-ther, fill us with your love; Nev-er from our souls re-move;
Dwell in us, and may we be Yours through all e-ter-ni-ty.

From *The English Hymnal.* Used by permission of Oxford University Press.

559   Hear Our Prayer, O Lord

George Whelpton, 1847–1930

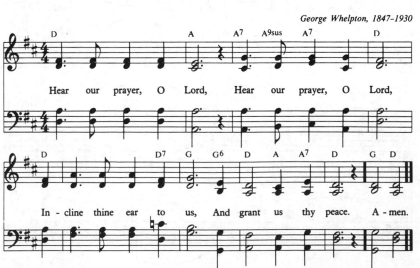

Hear our prayer, O Lord, Hear our prayer, O Lord,
In-cline thine ear to us, And grant us thy peace. A-men.

Lord, in Prayer Our Souls Arise 560

Thomas W. Holcombe, 1943-   Thomas W. Holcombe, 1943-

Lord, in prayer our souls a - rise to ven - ture where your

Spir - it flies: A - light, on us, O heav - enly Dove, and

help us all to live your love. A - men.

Almighty Father, Hear Our Prayer 561

Arr. from 'Elijah,' Felix Mendelssohn, 1809-1847

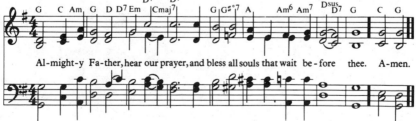

Al-might-y Fa-ther, hear our prayer, and bless all souls that wait be-fore thee. A-men.

562   Lord, Lead Us with Your Gentle Hand

Thomas W. Holcombe, 1943–

Thomas W. Holcombe, 1943–

Lord, lead us with your gen - tle hand, and

grant us your love and peace. A - men.

563   Lord, Who Lovest Little Children

Children's Prayer 8. 7.

Mira Rowland

Adapted from Francis Vincent Novello, 1781–1861

Lord, who lov - est lit - tle chil - dren, Hear us as we pray to thee. A-men.

Our Father, Who Art in Heaven

564

Calypso Lord's Prayer Irregular
West Indies traditional melody

Adapted by Ewald Bash, 1924–

Harm. by David Hugh Jones, 1900–

1. Our Fa-ther, who art in heav-en,
2. As in heav-en, so on the earth;
3. And for-give us, Fa-ther, all our debts;
4. And lead us not in-to temp - ta-tion;
5. For thine is the king-dom, pow-er, and glo-ry;
6. A-men, a-men, it shall be so;

Hal-low-ed be thy name;

Thy king-dom come, thy will be done.
Give us this day Our dai-ly bread.
As we for-give all our debt-ors.
But de-liv-er us from all e-vil.
For-ev-er and for-ev-er and ev-er.
A-men, a-men, it shall be so.

Hal-low-ed be thy name.

Words and melody adapted from *Edric Connor Collection of West Indian Spirituals and Folk Tunes* by permission of Boosey & Hawkes, Inc.

565

Lord's Prayer

Priest:
Let us pray: Taught by our Sav-ior's com-mand and formed by the word of God,

Priest and People:
we dare to say: Our Fa - ther who art in heav - en,

hal - lowed be thy name; thy king - dom come;

thy will be done on earth as it is in heav - en.

Give us this day our dai - ly bread; and for - give

us our tres - pass - es as we for-give those who tres-pass a - gainst us;

and lead us not in - to temp - ta - tion,

but de - liv - er us from e - vil.

Glory Be to the Father

566

Charles Meineke, 1782–1850

Glo - ry be to the Fa - ther and to the Son and to the Ho - ly Ghost; As it was in the be - gin - ning, is now, and ev - er shall be, world with - out end. A - men, A - men.

567

Glory Be to the Father

Old Scottish chant

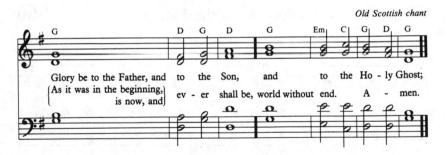

Glory be to the Father, and to the Son, and to the Ho - ly Ghost;
{As it was in the beginning,} ev - er shall be, world without end. A - men.
    is now, and}

568

Glory Be to the Father

Gloria Patri
Henry W. Greatorex, 1811–1858
Harm. by Thomas W. Holcombe, 1943–

Glo - ry be to the Fa - ther, and to the Son, and to the

Ho - ly Ghost; as it was in the be - gin - ning, is now, and ev - er

shall be, world with - out end. A - men, A - men.

Let the Words of My Mouth 569

Psalm 19:14

Joseph Barnby, 1838-1896

Let the words of my
mouth and the med-
itation } of my heart { be acceptable in
thy sight, O Lord,
my Strength and } my Re - deem - er. A-men.

Lord, Have Mercy Upon Us 570

George J. Elvey, 1816-1893

After each Commandment, except the Tenth

Lord, have mer-cy, have mer-cy up - on us, and in - cline our hearts to

After the Tenth Commandment

keep this law. Lord, have mer - cy, have mer - cy up - on us, and write all

these thy laws in our hearts, thy laws in our hearts, we be - seech thee.

571

May the Words of My Mouth

Alois Kaiser, 1840–1908

May the words of my mouth and the med - i - ta - tions of my heart be ac - cept - a - ble in your sight, O Lord, my Strength and my Re - deem - er. A - men.

From the *Union Hymnal*, copyright by the Central Conference of American Rabbis. Used by permission.

572

Let Thy Word Abide in Us

George Dyson, 1883–1964

Let thy Word a - bide in us, O Lord.

O Lord, Open Thou Our Eyes 573

From Psalm 119:18

John Camidge, 1735-1803

O Lord, o - pen thou our eyes, That we may be - hold won - drous things out of thy law.

Father of Mercies, in Thy Word 574

Anne Steele, 1716-1778

Gräfenberg C. M.
Johann Crüger, 1598-1662

Fa - ther of mer - cies, in thy Word What end - less glo - ry shines;

For - ev - er be thy name a - dored For these ce - les - tial lines. A - men.

Write These Words in Our Hearts 575

Source unknown

Write these words in our hearts, we be - seech thee, O Lord.

576

Glory Be to the Father

Proclamation
Richard K. Avery, 1934–
and Donald S. Marsh, 1923–

Glo - ry be to the Fa - ther, and the Son, and the Ho - ly Ghost;

As it was in the be - gin - ning, is now, and ev - er shall be,

world with - out end, A - men. As it was in the be - gin - ning, is

now, and ev - er shall be, world with-out end, A - men.

A - men, A - men, A - men, A - men,

A - men, A - men, A - men.

577 The Lord Bless You and Keep You

Arr. from Numbers 6:24–26

Peter C. Lutkin, 1858–1931

534

In the Name of Jesus 578

Moravian Liturgies, 1759

In the name of Je - - sus, A - - - - men.

Lord, Let Now Your Servant Depart 579

From Luke 2:29-32

Joseph Barnby, 1832-1896

1. Lord, let now your servant de - - - part in peace
2. For my eyes have seen
3. Which you have pre - pared
4. To be a light to lighten the Gentiles
5. Glory be to the Father, and to the Son,
6. As it was in the beginning, is now, and ever shall be,

ac - - - - cord - ing to your word.
your sal - - va - - tion,
before the face of all peo - ple;
and to be the glory of your peo - ple Is - ra - el.
and to the Ho - ly Ghost;
world without end, A - - men.

Peace, Peace, Peace, Go with You 580

Kent E. Schneider, 1945-

Peace, Peace, Peace go with you in - to all the world. A - men.

581   Through Him, with Him, in Him

Joseph Roff, 1910–

Through him, with him, in him, in the unity of the Holy Spirit,

all glory and honor is yours, al - might - y Fa - ther, for - ev - er and ev - er.

582   Send Us Forth Today

Thomas W. Holcombe, 1943–   *Thomas W. Holcombe, 1943–*

Send us forth to-day

Send us forth to-day

to do your will, O Lord, A - - - - men.

Send us forth to-day

Send us forth to-day

583   You Will Keep Him in Perfect Peace

Duke's Tune 8. 6.
Abridged from Andro Hart,
'The CL Psalmes of David,' 1615

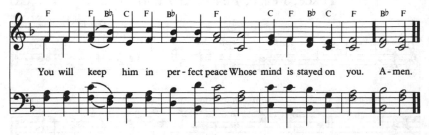

You will keep him in per - fect peace Whose mind is stayed on you. A - men.

Let All the Earth Cry Out to the Lord 584

Psalm 99 Irregular with Refrain
Stephen F. Somerville, 1931–

Psalm 99

Refrain

Let all the earth cry out to the Lord with joy, Give thanks to him and bless his name.

1. Let	all the earth cry out to the	Lord	with	joy,
2. Know	this:/the	Lord	is	God,
3. Go	in his gates with	songs	of	praise,
4. In - deed the		Lord	is	good,
5. Give	glory to the Father	and	the	Son,

with	gladness give your service	to	the	Lord,
he	made us,/we be -	long	to	him,
—	enter his	courts	with	hymns.
his	mercy	ev - er - last -		ing,
give	glory to the Holy Spirit,	with	them	one,

go	in before his face with joyful	hearts.
we	are his people/and the sheep of his	pas - ture.
Give	thanks to him/and bless his	name.
from	age to age endures his faithful - -	ness.
as	in the beginning,/so now, and evermore/	
	throughout eterni - ty.	

585

Lord, Have Mercy

Jan Vermulst, 1925–

Glory to God in the Highest

586

Text reprinted by permission of the International Committee on English in the Liturgy, Inc. Music © World Library Publications, Inc.; used by permission.

Continued on next page

Glory to God in the Highest (cont.)

God the Fa - ther Al - might - y. Lord Je - sus Christ, the on - ly - be - got - ten Son.

Lord God, Lamb of God, Son of the Fa - ther.

You, who take a - way the sins of the world, have mer - cy on us.

You, who take a - way the sins of the world, re - ceive our prayer.

540

Response to the Psalm After the First Reading

These seasonal common responses may be used instead of the proper responses. Where there are two or more responses for the same season, one may be used throughout the season or the alternate(s) may be used for variety.

587

ADVENT

For use with Psalm 25 (24)

Angelo A. della Picca, 1923–

To you, O Lord, I lift my soul.

588

ADVENT

For use with Psalm 85 (84)

Angelo A. della Picca, 1923–

Lord, let us see your kind - ness.

589

CHRISTMAS

For use with Psalm 98 (97)

Angelo A. della Picca, 1923–

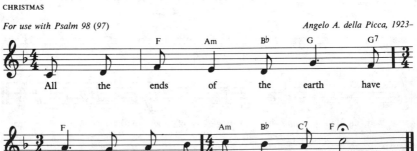

All the ends of the earth have

seen the sav - ing pow - er of God.

Response to the Psalm After the First Reading (cont.)

EPIPHANY

For use with Psalm 72 (71)　　　　　　　　　　　*Angelo A. della Picca, 1923-*

Lord, ev - ery na - tion on earth shall a - dore you.

LENT

For use with Psalm 51 (50)　　　　　　　　　　　*Angelo A. della Picca, 1923-*

Be mer - ci - ful, O Lord, for we have sinned.

LENT

For use with Psalm 91 (90)　　　　　　　　　　　*Angelo A. della Picca, 1923-*

Be with me, Lord, when I am in trou - ble.

LENT

For use with Psalm 130 (129)　　　　　　　　　　*Angelo A. della Picca, 1923-*

With the Lord there is

mer - cy, and full - ness of re - demp - tion.

594

EASTER

For use with Psalm 118 (117)

Angelo A. della Picca, 1923–

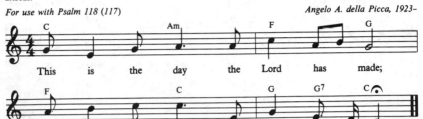

This is the day the Lord has made;

let us re - joice, re - joice and be glad.

595

ASCENSION

For use with Psalm 47 (46)

Angelo A. della Picca, 1923–

God mounts his throne to shouts of joy.

Alleluia

596

Angelo A. della Picca, 1923–

Al - le - lu - ia, al - le -

lu - ia, al - le - lu - ia,

597

Angelo A. della Picca, 1923–
Chant, from 'Liber usualis'

Al - le - lu - ia, al - le - lu - ia, al - le - lu - ia.

Alleluia (cont.)

598

Robert F. Twynham, 1930-

Al - le - lu - ia, al - le - lu - ia, al - le - lu - ia.

During Lent, one of the following should be substituted for the Alleluia.

599

Angelo A. della Picca, 1923-

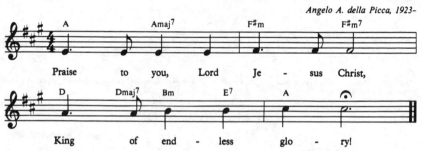

Praise to you, Lord Je - sus Christ, King of end - less glo - ry!

600

Angelo A. della Picca, 1923-

Praise and hon - or to you, Lord Je - sus Christ!

601

Angelo A. della Picca, 1923-

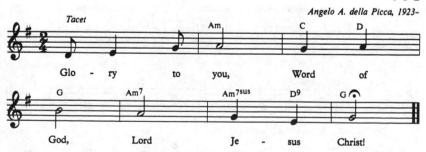

Glo - ry to you, Word of God, Lord Je - sus Christ!

602 Let Us Proclaim (A)

Joseph Roff, 1910–

Let us pro-claim the mys-ter-y of faith. Christ has died,

Christ is ris-en, Christ will come a-gain.

603 Let Us Proclaim (B)

Joseph Roff, 1910–

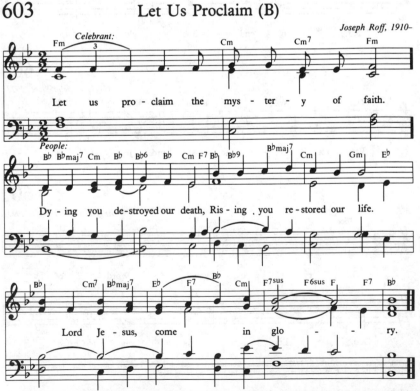

Let us pro-claim the mys-ter-y of faith.

Dy-ing you de-stroyed our death, Ris-ing you re-stored our life.

Lord Je-sus, come in glo-ry.

Lamb of God

Jan Vermulst, 1925–

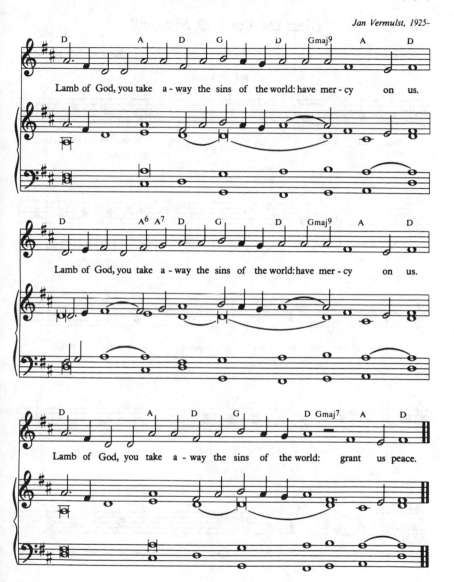

Lamb of God, you take a - way the sins of the world: have mer - cy on us.

Lamb of God, you take a - way the sins of the world: have mer - cy on us.

Lamb of God, you take a - way the sins of the world: grant us peace.

605 Bless the Lord, O My Soul

Orthodox traditional melody

FIRST ANTIPHON

Bless the Lord, O my soul. Bless - ed art thou,

O Lord. Bless the Lord, O my soul, and all that is

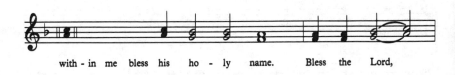

with - in me bless his ho - ly name. Bless the Lord,

O my soul, and for - get not all his ben - e - fits. Who

for - gives all thy sins, who heals all thy dis - eas-

es; who re - deems thy life from de - struc - tion,

Bless the Lord, O My Soul (cont.)

who crowns thee with mer - cy and com - pas - sion. The

Lord is com - pas - sion - ate and mer - ci - ful,

long - suf - fer - ing and of great mer - cy. Bless

the Lord, O my soul, and all that is with -

in me bless his ho - ly name. Bless - ed art thou, O Lord.

Glory to the Father

Orthodox traditional melody

SECOND ANTIPHON

Glo - ry to the Father, and to the Son, and to the
Holy Spirit, now and ever and unto ages of ag - es. A - men.

Only-begotten Son and Word of God, who art im - mor - tal, yet
didst deign for our salvation to be in - car - nate of
the holy mother of God and ever - vir - gin Mar - y and with -
out change be - came man, and was crucified, trampling
death by death: Do thou, O Christ our God, who art one
of the Holy Trin - i - ty, glorified with the Father and
the Ho - ly Spir - it, save us.

Orthodox traditional melody

THIRD ANTIPHON

In thy king - dom re - mem - ber us, O Lord,

when thou com - est into thy king - dom. Bless-

ed are the poor in spir - it, for theirs is the

kingdom of heav - en. Bless - ed are they that

mourn, for they shall be com - fort - ed.

Bless - ed are the meek, for they shall in - her - it

the earth. Bless - ed are they that hunger and thirst

for righ - teous - ness, for they shall be filled.

Continued on next page

In Thy Kingdom Remember Us, O Lord (cont.)

Bless - ed are the mer - ci - ful, for they shall

ob - tain mer - cy. Bless - ed are the pure in

heart, for they shall see God. Bless - ed are the

peace - mak - ers, for they shall be called the chil -

dren of God. Bless - ed are they that are persecut - ed

for righ - teous - ness' sake, for theirs is the kingdom

of heav - en. Bless - ed are ye, when men shall re -

vile you and per - se - cute you, and shall say all

manner of evil against you falsely, for my sake.

The Prokimenon

TONE 1: Let thy mercy, O Lord, be upon us, as we have set our hope on thee.
Rejoice in the Lord, O ye righteous; for it becomes the just to be thankful.

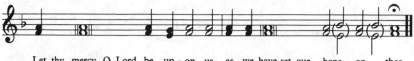

Let thy mercy, O Lord, be up - on us, as we have set our hope on thee.

TONE 2: The Lord is my strength and my song, and is become my salvation.
The Lord has chastened and corrected me; but hath not given me over unto death.

TONE 3: Sing praises unto our God, sing praises; sing praises unto our King, sing praises.
O clap your hands, all ye people; O sing unto God with the voice of melody.

TONE 4: How manifold are thy works, O Lord; in wisdom hast thou made them all.
Bless the Lord, O my soul; O Lord, my God, thou art exceedingly glorious.

TONE 5: Thou shalt keep us, O Lord; thou shalt preserve us from this generation henceforth and forever.
Save me, O Lord, for there is not one godly man left.

TONE 6: O Lord, save thy people, and bless thine inheritance.
Unto thee will I cry; O Lord, my Strength, keep not silent toward me.

TONE 7: The Lord shall give strength unto his people; the Lord shall give his people the blessing of peace.
Bring unto the Lord, O ye sons of God, bring young rams unto the Lord.

TONE 8: Pray unto the Lord our God, and render thanks.
In Jewry is God known; his name is great in Israel.

609

Mah-l'choo-s'cho

Traditional melody
Harm. by Wolf Hecker

Mah - l'choo - s' - cho ro - oo vo - ne - cho boh-kay - ah
yom lif - nay Moh - she ze ay - lee o - noo v' - om - roo.
Ah - doh - noi yim - loch l' - oh - lom vo - ed.

Harmony copyright by Wolf Hecker. Used by permission.

Leader: Thy children beheld thy sovereignty as thou didst cleave the sea before Moses; they exclaimed, "This is my God," and said, "The Lord shall reign forever and ever."

V' ne-e-mahr

Traditional melody
Harm. by Wolf Hecker.

V' ne-e-mahr kee fo-do Ah-doh-noi es Yah-ah-kohv oo-g'-o-loh mi-yahd cho-zok mi-me-noo, bo-rooch ah-to Ah-doh-noi go-ahl Yis-ro-ayl.

Leader: Thus also declared Jeremiah, thy prophet, "The Lord will surely redeem Jacob and rescue him from the hand of one stronger than he." Blessed art thou, Lord, who hast redeemed Israel.

611

Kiddush

Louis Lewandowski, 1821-1894
Freely adapted

Bo - rooch ah - to Ah - doh - noi eh - loh-

hay - noo me - lech ho - oh - lom boh - ray p' - ree hah - go-

fen. Bo - rooch ah - to Ah - doh - noi eh - loh-

hay - noo me - lech ho - oh - lom ah - sher ki - d'-

sho - noo b' - mitz - voh - sov v' - ro - tzo vo - noo v' - shah-

bahs ko - d' - shoh b' - ah - hah - vo oo - v'ro - tzohn hin - chee-

Kiddush (cont.)

lo - noo   zi- ko- rohn   l' - mah- ah - say   v' - ray -

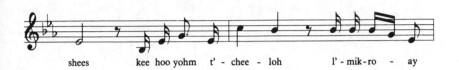

shees   kee hoo yohm   t' - chee - loh   l' - mik-ro   ay

koh - desh,   zay - cher   lee - tzee-ahs   Mitz - ro - yeem.   Kee

vo - noo vo - chahr - to v'oh - so - noo ki - dahsh - toh mi-

kol   ho - ah -   meem,   v' - shah - bahs kod - sh' - cho b'-

ah - hah-vo oo - v'ro - tzohn   hin - chahl - to - noo.   Bo-

rooch ah-to Ah-doh-noi   m' - kah - daysh hah-shah - bos.

557

Worship Resources

Contents

Order of Mass

Options are indicated by A, B, C, D.

INTRODUCTORY RITE

Joined together as Christ's people, we open the celebration by raising our voices in praise of God, who is present among us. This song should deepen our unity as it introduces the Mass we celebrate today.

Stand

Entrance Song

Select a psalm or a hymn from the hymn section, suitable to the season, feast, or part of the Mass. If there is no singing at the entrance, the Entrance Song proper is recited by the people or the lector, or the priest reads it after the Greeting.

After the Entrance Song, all make the sign of the cross.

PRIEST: In the name of the Father and of the Son + and of the Holy Spirit.

PEOPLE: **Amen.**

Greeting

The priest welcomes us in the name of the Lord. We show our union with God, our neighbor, and the priest by a united response to his greeting.

A

PRIEST: The grace of our Lord Jesus Christ and the love of God and the fellowship of the Holy Spirit be with you all.

PEOPLE: **And also with you.**

B

PRIEST: The grace and peace of God our Father and the Lord Jesus Christ be with you.

PEOPLE: **Blessed be God, the Father of our Lord Jesus Christ.**

Or,

And also with you.

C

PRIEST: The Lord be with you.

PEOPLE: **And also with you.**

BISHOP: Peace be with you.

PEOPLE: **And also with you.**

PENITENTIAL RITE

Before we hear the word of God, we acknowledge our sins humbly, ask for mercy, and accept his pardon.

After the introduction to the day's Mass, the priest invites the people to recall their sins and to repent of them in silence.

PRIEST: My brothers and sisters, to prepare ourselves to celebrate the sacred mysteries, let us call to mind our sins.

Then one of the following forms is used:

A

PRIEST
AND
PEOPLE:
> **I confess to almighty God,**
> **and to you, my brothers and sisters,**
> **that I have sinned through my own fault**
>
> *All strike their breast.*
>
> **in my thoughts and in my words,**
> **in what I have done,**
> **and in what I have failed to do;**
> **and I ask blessed Mary, ever virgin,**
> **all the angels and saints,**
> **and you, my brothers and sisters,**
> **to pray for me to the Lord our God.**

B

PRIEST:
> Lord, we have sinned against you:
> Lord, have mercy.

PEOPLE:
> **Lord, have mercy.**

PRIEST:
> Lord, show us your mercy and love,

PEOPLE:
> **And grant us your salvation.**

C

PRIEST*:
> You were sent to heal the contrite:
> Lord, have mercy.

PEOPLE:
> **Lord, have mercy.**

PRIEST*:
> You came to call sinners:
> Christ, have mercy.

PEOPLE:
> **Christ, have mercy.**

PRIEST*:
> You plead for us at the right hand of the Father:
> Lord, have mercy.

PEOPLE:
> **Lord, have mercy.**

*Or other minister.

562

Other invocations may be used.
At the end of any of the forms of the Penitential Rite:

PRIEST: May almighty God have mercy on us,
forgive us our sins,
and bring us to everlasting life.

PEOPLE: **Amen.**

Kyrie

Unless included in the Penitential Rite, the Kyrie is sung or said by all, with alternating parts for the choir or cantor and for the people.

PRIEST: Lord, have mercy.

PEOPLE: **Lord, have mercy.**

PRIEST: Christ, have mercy.

PEOPLE: **Christ, have mercy.**

PRIEST: Lord, have mercy.

PEOPLE: **Lord, have mercy.**

Gloria

As the church assembled in the Spirit, we praise and pray to the Father and the Lamb.

When the Gloria is sung or said, the priest or the cantors or everyone together may begin it.

Glory to God in the highest,
and peace to his people on earth.

Lord God, heavenly King,
almighty God and Father,
we worship you, we give you thanks,
we praise you for your glory.

Lord Jesus Christ, only Son of the Father,
Lord God, Lamb of God,
you take away the sin of the world:
have mercy on us;
you are seated at the right hand of the Father:
receive our prayer.

For you alone are the Holy One,
you alone are the Lord,
you alone are the Most High,

Jesus Christ,
with the Holy Spirit,
in the glory of God the Father. Amen.

Opening Prayer

The priest invites us to pray silently for a moment, and then, in our name, expresses the theme of the day's celebration and petitions God the Father through the mediation of Christ in the Holy Spirit.

PRIEST: Let us pray.

Priest and people pray silently for a while. Then the priest says the opening prayer and concludes:

. . . forever and ever.

PEOPLE: **Amen.**

LITURGY OF THE WORD

The proclamation of God's word is always centered on Christ, present through his word. Old Testament writings prepare for him; New Testament books speak of him directly. All of Scripture calls us to believe once more and to follow. After the reading, we reflect upon God's words and respond to them.

Sit   **First Reading**

At the end of the reading:

READER: This is the word of the Lord.

PEOPLE: **Thanks be to God.**

Psalm

The people repeat the response sung by the cantor or recited by the reader the first time and then after each verse.

Second Reading

At the end of the reading:

READER: This is the word of the Lord.

PEOPLE: **Thanks be to God.**

Stand   **Alleluia**

Jesus will speak to us in the Gospel. We rise now out of respect and prepare for his message with the Alleluia.

The people repeat the Alleluia after the cantor's Alleluia and then after the verse.

564

During Lent one of the following invocations is used as a response instead of the Alleluia:

A **Praise to you, Lord Jesus Christ, King of endless glory!**
B **Praise and honor to you, Lord Jesus Christ!**
C **Glory to you, Word of God, Lord Jesus Christ!**

Gospel

Before proclaiming the gospel, the deacon asks the priest:

DEACON: Father, give me your blessing.

The priest says:

PRIEST: The Lord be in your heart and on your lips, that you may worthily proclaim his gospel. In the name of the Father and of the Son + and of the Holy Spirit.

If there is no deacon, the priest says quietly:

Almighty God, cleanse my heart and my lips, that I may worthily proclaim your gospel.

DEACON*: The Lord be with you.

PEOPLE: **And also with you.**

DEACON*: A reading from the Holy Gospel according to _____ .

PEOPLE: **Glory to you, Lord.**

At the end of the reading:

DEACON*: This is the gospel of the Lord.

PEOPLE: **Praise to you, Lord Jesus Christ.**

Then the deacon (or the priest) kisses the book, saying quietly:

DEACON*: May the words of the Gospel wipe away our sins.

Sit   ### Homily

God's word is spoken again in the homily. The Holy Spirit speaking through the lips of the preacher explains and applies today's Bible readings to the needs of this particular congregation. He calls us to respond to Christ through the life we lead.

Stand   ### Profession of Faith

As a people, we express our acceptance of God's message in the Scriptures and the homily. We summarize our faith by proclaiming a creed handed down from the early church.

---

*Or priest.

All say the Profession of Faith on Sundays and solemnities.

ALL: **We believe in one God,**
the Father, the Almighty,
maker of heaven and earth,
of all that is seen and unseen.

We believe in one Lord, Jesus Christ,
the only Son of God,
eternally begotten of the Father,
God from God, Light from Light,
true God from true God,
begotten, not made, one in Being with the Father.
Through him all things were made.
For us men and for our salvation
he came down from heaven:

All bow at the following words up to "and became man."

by the power of the Holy Spirit
he was born of the Virgin Mary, and became man.
For our sake he was crucified under Pontius Pilate;
he suffered, died, and was buried.
On the third day he rose again
in fulfillment of the Scriptures;
he ascended into heaven
and is seated at the right hand of the Father.
He will come again in glory to judge the living and the dead,
and his kingdom will have no end.

We believe in the Holy Spirit, the Lord,
the giver of life,
who proceeds from the Father and the Son.
With the Father and the Son he is worshiped and glorified.
He has spoken through the prophets.
We believe in one holy catholic and apostolic church.
We acknowledge one baptism for the forgiveness of sins.
We look for the resurrection of the dead,
and the life of the world to come. Amen.

General Intercessions
(Prayer of the Faithful)

As a priestly people we unite with one another to pray for today's needs in the church and the world.

The several intentions of prayer are announced by the appropriate person, ordinarily not the priest himself. The intentions may be expressed simply as prayers for persons or things, e.g., "Let us pray for . . . that . . . ." The best way of ending each petition is with the expression, "Let us pray to the Lord," or, "We pray to the Lord."

Ordinarily the petitions should be relatively few in number, about five or six. Examples of such intentions in each category are: (1) *For the needs of the universal church,* e.g., for the pope, for the bishops, the pastors, and the priests of the church, for the missions, for the unity of Christians, for vocations. (2) *For the needs of the world,* e.g., for our civil leaders, for peace, for good weather, for public elections, for economic problems. (3) *For those in need or in trouble,* e.g., for those absent from the community, for those suffering persecution, for the unemployed, for the sick and infirm, for the dying, for prisoners, for exiles. (4) *For the assembly of the faithful,* e.g., for the members of this parish who are to be baptized, confirmed, married, ordained, for the pastor and the priests, for the parochial mission.

After the priest gives the introduction, the deacon or other minister sings or says the invocations.

PEOPLE: **Lord, hear our prayer.** (*Or other response, according to local custom.*)

At the end the priest says the concluding prayer.

PEOPLE: **Amen.**

LITURGY OF THE EUCHARIST

Made ready by reflection on God's word, we enter now into the eucharistic sacrifice itself, the Supper of the Lord. We celebrate the memorial which the Lord instituted at his last supper. We are God's new people, the redeemed brothers of Christ, gathered by him around his table. We are here to bless God and to receive the gift of Jesus' body and blood so that our faith and life may be transformed.

Sit   Offertory Song

The bread and the wine for the Eucharist, with our gifts for the church and the poor, are gathered and brought to the altar. We prepare our hearts by song or in silence as the Lord's table is being set. While the gifts of the people are brought forward to the priest and are placed on the altar, the Offertory Song is sung.

Before placing the bread on the altar, the priest says quietly:

PRIEST: Blessed are you, Lord, God of all creation.
Through your goodness we have this bread to offer,
which earth has given and human hands have made.
It will become for us the bread of life.

If there is no singing, the priest may say this prayer aloud, and the people may respond:

PEOPLE: **Blessed be God forever.**

When he pours wine and a little water into the chalice, the deacon (or the priest) says quietly:

DEACON: By the mystery of this water and wine
may we come to share in the divinity of Christ,
who humbled himself to share in our humanity.

Before placing the chalice on the altar, the priest says quietly:

PRIEST: Blessed are you, Lord, God of all creation.
Through your goodness we have this wine to offer,
fruit of the vine and work of human hands.
It will become our spiritual drink.

If there is no singing, the priest may say this prayer aloud, and the people may respond:

PEOPLE: **Blessed be God forever.**

The priest says quietly:

PRIEST: Lord God, we ask you to receive us and be pleased with the sacrifice we offer you with humble and contrite hearts.

Then he washes his hands, saying quietly:

PRIEST: Lord, wash away my iniquity; cleanse me from my sin.

Invitation to Prayer

PRIEST: Pray, brethren, that our sacrifice may be acceptable to God, the almighty Father.

PEOPLE: **May the Lord accept the sacrifice at your hands for the praise and glory of his name, for our good, and the good of all his church.**

Stand   **Prayer Over the Gifts**

The priest, speaking in our name, asks the Father to bless and accept these gifts.

At the end:

PEOPLE: **Amen.**

EUCHARISTIC PRAYER

We begin the eucharistic service of praise and thanksgiving, the center of the entire celebration, the central prayer of worship. At the priest's invitation we lift our hearts to God and unite with him in the words he addresses to the Father through Jesus Christ. Together we join Christ in his sacrifice, celebrating his memorial in the holy meal and acknowledging with him the wonderful works of God in our lives.

PRIEST: The Lord be with you.

PEOPLE: **And also with you.**

PRIEST: Lift up your hearts.

PEOPLE: **We lift them up to the Lord.**

PRIEST: Let us give thanks to the Lord our God.

PEOPLE: **It is right to give him thanks and praise.**

Preface
Sanctus

ALL: **Holy, holy, holy Lord, God of power and might,
heaven and earth are full of your glory.
    Hosanna in the highest.
Blessed is he who comes in the name of the Lord.
    Hosanna in the highest.**

Kneel

Memorial Acclamation

*After the words of institution, when the priest has replaced the
chalice on the altar and genuflected:*

PRIEST: Let us proclaim the mystery of faith.

PEOPLE: A
**Christ has died,
Christ is risen,
Christ will come again.**

B
**Dying you destroyed our death,
rising you restored our life.
Lord Jesus, come in glory.**

C
**When we eat this bread and drink this cup,
we proclaim your death, Lord Jesus,
until you come in glory.**

D
**Lord, by your cross and resurrection
you have set us free.
You are the Savior of the world.**

ORDER OF MASS

Doxology of the Eucharistic Prayer

PRIEST: Through him, with him, in him, in the unity of the Holy Spirit, all glory and honor is yours, almighty Father, forever and ever.

PEOPLE: **Amen.**

COMMUNION RITE

To prepare for the paschal meal, to welcome the Lord, we pray for forgiveness and exchange a sign of peace. Before eating Christ's body and drinking his blood, we must be one with him and with all our brothers and sisters in the church.

Stand   **Lord's Prayer**

PRIEST: Let us pray with confidence to the Father in the words our Savior gave us:

ALL: **Our Father, who art in heaven,
hallowed be thy name.
Thy kingdom come;
Thy will be done on earth as it is in heaven.
Give us this day our daily bread;
and forgive us our trespasses
as we forgive those who trespass against us.
And lead us not into temptation,
but deliver us from evil.**

PRIEST: Deliver us, Lord, from every evil, and grant us peace in our day. In your mercy keep us free from sin and protect us from all anxiety as we wait in joyful hope for the coming of our Savior, Jesus Christ.

PEOPLE: **For the kingdom, the power, and the glory are yours, now and forever.**

Sign of Peace

The church is a community of Christians joined by the Spirit in love. It needs to express, deepen, and restore its peaceful unity before eating the one body of the Lord and drinking from the one cup of salvation. We do this by a sign of peace.

The priest says the prayer for peace:

PRIEST: Lord Jesus Christ, you said to your apostles: I leave you peace, my peace I give you. Look not on our sins, but on the faith of your church, and grant us the peace and unity of your kingdom where you live forever and ever.

PEOPLE: **Amen.**

570

PRIEST: The peace of the Lord be with you always.

PEOPLE: **And also with you.**

DEACON*: Let us offer each other the sign of peace.

The people exchange a sign of peace and love, according to local custom.

Breaking of the Bread

Christians are gathered for the "breaking of the bread," another name for the Mass. In communion, though many we are made one body in the one bread, which is Christ.

The priest breaks the host over the paten and places a small piece in the chalice, saying quietly:

PRIEST: May this mingling of the body and blood of our Lord Jesus Christ bring eternal life to us who receive it.

Meanwhile the people sing (No. 604) or say:

PEOPLE: **Lamb of God, you take away the sins of the world:**
have mercy on us.
Lamb of God, you take away the sins of the world:
have mercy on us.
Lamb of God, you take away the sins of the world:
grant us peace.

The hymn may be repeated until the breaking of the bread is finished, but the last phrase is always "Grant us peace."

Communion

We pray in silence and then voice words of humility and hope as our final preparation before meeting Christ in the Eucharist.

Before communion, the priest says quietly one of the following prayers:

PRIEST: Lord Jesus Christ, Son of the living God,
by the will of the Father and the work of the Holy Spirit
your death brought life to the world.
By your holy body and blood
free me from all my sins and from every evil.
Keep me faithful to your teaching,
and never let me be parted from you.

---

*Or priest.

Or,

Lord Jesus Christ,
with faith in your love and mercy
I eat your body and drink your blood.
Let it not bring me condemnation,
but health in mind and body.

PRIEST: This is the Lamb of God,
who takes away the sins of the world.
Happy are those who are called to his supper.

Once only:

ALL: **Lord, I am not worthy to receive you,**
but only say the word and I shall be healed.

Before receiving communion, the priest says quietly:

PRIEST: May the body of Christ bring me to everlasting life.

And,

May the blood of Christ bring me to everlasting life.

He then gives communion to the people.

PRIEST: The body of Christ.

COMMUNICANT:

Amen.

Communion Song

The Communion Song is begun while the priest receives the body of Christ. The choir may sing during the communion processional. Or a song, preferably with refrain, may be sung by the cantor (or choir) and the people. A psalm or a hymn from the hymn section, suitable to the season, feast, or action of the Mass may be sung.

If there is no singing here, the Communion Song proper is said.

Sit   ### Silence After Communion

After communion there may be a period of silence, or a song of praise may be sung.

Stand   ### Prayer After Communion

The priest prays in our name that we may live the life of faith since we have been strengthened by Christ himself. Our Amen makes his prayer our own.

PRIEST: Let us pray.

Priest and people may pray silently for a while. Then the priest says the prayer after communion. At the end:

PEOPLE: **Amen.**

CONCLUDING RITE

We have heard God's word and eaten the body of Christ. Now it is time for us to leave, to do good works, to praise and bless the Lord in our daily lives.

Sit   *Brief announcements may be made.*

Stand   **Blessing**

PRIEST: The Lord be with you.

PEOPLE: **And also with you.**

PRIEST: May Almighty God bless you, the Father and the Son + and the Holy Spirit.

PEOPLE: **Amen.**

Dismissal

DEACON*: A Go in the peace of Christ.
           B The Mass is ended, go in peace.
           C Go in peace to love and serve the Lord.

PEOPLE: **Thanks be to God.**

---

*Or priest.

613   An Order of Worship, Protestant

PRELUDE

HYMN

OPENING SENTENCE OR CALL TO WORSHIP
(*See Nos. 736–740.*)

INVOCATION
(*See Nos. 741–760.*)

RESPONSE
(*See Nos. 524–543.*)

PRAYER OF CONFESSION
(*See Nos. 761–774.*)

ASSURANCE OF PARDON
(*See Nos. 775–781.*)

LORD'S PRAYER
(*See No. 727, or page 570.*)

HYMN

STATEMENT OF FAITH (optional)
(*See Nos. 728–729.*)

GLORIA PATRI
(*See Nos. 566–568, 576, 732.*)

ANTHEM (optional)

SCRIPTURE LESSON(S)
(*See Scripture Readings for the Year, Nos. 628–631; Selections from the Psalter, Nos. 632–684; Other Scripture Selections, Nos. 685–726.*)

PRAYER(S)

PRESENTATION OF OFFERINGS

RESPONSE
(*See Nos. 544–546.*)

Doxology
  (See Nos. 547–549.)

Sermon

Hymn

Benediction
  (See Nos. 823–832.)

Postlude

An Order of Worship, Protestant

LONGER FORM

**An Order of Worship for the Proclamation of the Word of God
and the Celebration of the Lord's Supper**

THE PREPARATION

The Greeting

Stand

MINISTER: The grace of the Lord Jesus Christ, and the love of God the Father, and the fellowship of the Holy Spirit, be with you all.

PEOPLE: **Amen.**

MINISTER: The Lord be with you.

PEOPLE: **And also with you.**

MINISTER: Let us pray.
Almighty God, to you all hearts are open, all desires known, and from you no secrets are hidden. Cleanse and inform our hearts and minds by the inspiration of your Holy Spirit, that we may truly love and worthily praise your holy name, through Christ our Lord.

PEOPLE: **Amen.**

An Act of Praise

A hymn or a psalm of praise may be sung, or the following ancient canticle of the church:

**Glory to God in the highest,
 and peace to his people on earth.**

**Lord God, heavenly King,
almighty God and Father,
 we worship you, and give you thanks,
 we praise you for your glory.**

**Lord Jesus Christ, only Son of the Father,
Lord God, Lamb of God,**

you take away the sin of the world:
   have mercy on us;
you are seated at the right hand of the Father:
   receive our prayer.

For you alone are the Holy One,
you alone are the Lord,
you alone are the Most High,
   Jesus Christ,
   with the Holy Spirit,
   in the glory of God the Father. Amen.

An Act of Penitence

The Bidding

MINISTER: God is the light and in him is no darkness at all.

If we say we have fellowship with him while we walk in darkness, we lie and do not live according to the truth.

But if we walk in the light, as he is in the light, we have fellowship with one another, and the blood of Jesus his Son cleanses us from all sin.

If we say we have no sin, we deceive ourselves, and the truth is not in us.

If we confess our sins, he is faithful and just, and will forgive our sins and cleanse us from all unrighteousness.

Let us humbly confess our sins to God, our heavenly Father.

The Confession

Kneel*

MINISTER
AND
PEOPLE:
Most holy and merciful Father, we confess to you and to one another, and to the whole communion of saints in heaven and earth, that we have sinned against you by what we have done, and by what we have left undone.

We have not loved you with our whole heart and mind and strength,
We have not loved our neighbors as ourselves,
We have not had in us the mind of Christ,
We have grieved your Holy Spirit.

---

*Or stand.

You alone know how often we have sinned and grieved you,
by wasting your gifts,
by wandering from your ways,
by forgetting your love.

Forgive us, we pray you, most merciful Father, and free us from
our sin.

Renew in us again the grace and strength of your Holy Spirit, for
the sake of Jesus Christ, your Son our Savior. Amen.

A Declaration of Pardon

MINISTER: The almighty and merciful Lord grant you true repentance, forgiveness of all your sins, time for amendment and newness of
life, and the grace and consolation of his Holy Spirit.

PEOPLE: **Amen.**

A doxology or a response of praise may be sung or said.

Sit   **THE PROCLAMATION OF THE WORD OF GOD**

Persons appointed may read:

An Old Testament Lesson

A New Testament Lesson

*After each lesson, a hymn, a psalm, an anthem, or a responsive
reading may be sung or said.*

Stand

MINISTER: **The Gospel**

Sit   **The Sermon**

At the conclusion of the sermon, there may follow:
A Hymn
*The Apostolic Creed (page 604 or No. 728) or the Nicene
Creed, or some other authorized*

Stand   **Affirmation of Faith**

MINISTER: Let us profess before God and one another our common faith.

The Nicene Creed

MINISTER
AND
PEOPLE:
    We believe in one God,
        the Father, the Almighty,
        maker of heaven and earth,
        of all that is seen and unseen.

We believe in one Lord, Jesus Christ,
 the only Son of God,
 eternally begotten of the Father,
 God from God, Light from Light,
 true God from true God,
 begotten, not made, one in Being with the Father.
Through him all things were made.
For us men and for our salvation
 he came down from heaven:
by the power of the Holy Spirit
 he was born of the Virgin Mary, and became man.
For our sake he was crucified under Pontius Pilate;
 he suffered, died, and was buried.
On the third day he rose again
 in fulfillment of the Scriptures;
 he ascended into heaven
  and is seated at the right hand of the Father.
He will come again in glory to judge the living and the dead,
 and his kingdom will have no end.

We believe in the Holy Spirit, the Lord,
 the giver of life,
who proceeds from the Father and the Son.
With the Father and the Son he is worshiped and glorified.
He has spoken through the prophets.
We believe in one holy catholic and apostolic church.
We acknowledge one baptism for the forgiveness of sins.
We look for the resurrection of the dead,
 and the life of the world to come. Amen.

The Peace

Minister and people shall exchange the greeting of peace:

MINISTER: The peace of the Lord be always with you.

PEOPLE: **And also with you.**

The Prayers

The minister or some person appointed shall lead the people in the following petitions and intercessions:

Stand*

In peace, in the peace of God from above, let us pray to the Lord:

---

* Or kneel.

For the peace of the whole world; and for the peace, unity, and faithful service of the churches of God in this and every land.

Hear us, O Lord.

For all Christian people, their ministers and teachers, that by word and example they may bring many to faith and obedience in Christ.

Hear us, O Lord.

For those in authority among the nations (and especially for the President, the Congress, and the Supreme Court of the United States), that they may govern with justice and promote peace and unity among all men.

Hear us, O Lord.

For all on whose labor we depend, especially those whose duty brings them into danger, that they may have courage and strength to serve the common good.

Hear us, O Lord.

For those who seek out knowledge, and guide our thought; for those who help us laugh and play, that truth and beauty may give joy to daily life.

Hear us, O Lord.

For all who suffer: the poor and lonely, the sick and afflicted, the tempted and the bereaved; for prisoners, and those who are oppressed, or persecuted, that they may be strengthened and delivered.

Hear us, O Lord.

For those who are enemies of the gospel of Christ, and who wrong their fellowmen, that they may be reconciled.

Hear us, O Lord.

For the dying, that they may rise to eternal life; and for the departed, that they may rest in peace.

Hear us, O Lord.

Here may be given the opportunity for members of the congregation to ask the prayers of the people for any special needs.

The minister may proceed:

Let us commit ourselves, one with another, to our God.

Lord, have mercy.

Let us ask of the Lord brotherly love by the help of his Holy Spirit, and for each one of us the grace of a holy life.

Lord, have mercy.

Let us remember before God all who are near and dear to us, those present and those absent, that we may love and serve one another in the bond of Christ.

Lord, have mercy.

Let us pray for our community (and nation), that in all things we may be honest and just, and free from prejudice, bitterness, strife, and fear.

Lord, have mercy.

Let us recall in thanksgiving those who have died in the faith. May God give them the crown of life in the day of resurrection, and judge them worthy with the righteous to enter into the joy of their Lord.

Lord, have mercy.

Let us give thanks for all his servants and witnesses of times past:

> Abraham, the father of believers,
> Moses, Samuel, Isaiah and all the prophets,
> John the Baptist, the forerunner,
> Mary, the mother of our Lord,
> Peter and Paul and all the apostles,
> Stephen the first martyr and all the martyrs and saints, in
> every age and in every land.

Lord, have mercy.

May the Lord God in his mercy give us with them hope in his salvation, and in the promise of eternal life in his kingdom.

Lord, have mercy.

The minister may conclude:

Heavenly Father, you have promised to hear what we ask in the name of your Son. We pray you, accept and fulfill our petitions, not as we ask in our ignorance and unworthiness, nor as we deserve in our sinfulness, but as you know and love us in your Son, Jesus Christ our Lord.

PEOPLE: **Amen.***

THE LORD'S SUPPER

The Offertory

Stand

MINISTER: Beloved in Christ, the Gospels tell us that on the first day of the week, the same day on which our Lord rose from the dead, he appeared to his disciples in the place where they were gathered, and was made known to them in the breaking of bread.

Come then to the joyful feast of the Lord. Let us prepare his table with offerings of our life and labor.

Sit *During the Offertory, a hymn, a psalm, or an anthem may be sung. Or the minister or some person appointed may read appropriate sentences from the Scriptures.*

Representatives of the congregation will receive and bring to the table the gifts of bread and wine, and other offerings of the people.

Stand *At the presentation, a doxology may be sung, or the following:*

MINISTER: You are worthy, our Lord and God, to receive glory and honor and power,

PEOPLE: **For you have created all things, and by your will they exist and were created.**

The Thanksgiving

The following Thanksgiving, or the Thanksgiving beginning on page 586, may be used:

MINISTER: The Lord be with you.

PEOPLE: **And also with you.**

MINISTER: Lift up your hearts.

PEOPLE: **We lift them up to the Lord.**

---

*If the service of the Word is used separately, without the observance of the Supper, it is appropriate to conclude it, after the Prayers, with the Lord's Prayer, an Offering, an Act of Thanksgiving, and a Dismissal or Benediction.

MINISTER: Let us give thanks to the Lord our God.

PEOPLE: **It is truly right so to do.**

MINISTER: We give you thanks, holy Father, almighty and eternal God, always and everywhere, through Jesus Christ your Son our Lord, by whom you made the world and all things living and beautiful.

We bless you for your continual love and care for every creature. We praise you for forming us in your image, and calling us to be your people. Though we rebelled against your love, you did not abandon us in our sin, but sent to us prophets and teachers to lead us into the way of salvation.

Above all, we give you thanks for the gift of Jesus your only Son, who is the way, the truth, and the life. In the fullness of time he took upon himself our nature; and by the obedience of his life, his suffering upon the cross, and his resurrection from the dead, he has delivered us from the way of sin and death.

We praise you that he now reigns with you in glory and ever lives to pray for us. We thank you for the Holy Spirit who leads us into truth, defends us in adversity, and unites us out of every people in one holy church.

Therefore with the whole company of saints in heaven and on earth, we worship and glorify you, God most holy, and we sing with joy:

MINISTER
AND
PEOPLE: **Holy, holy, holy Lord, God of power and might, heaven and earth are full of your glory. Hosanna in the highest.**

Kneel*

MINISTER: Holy Father, most glorious and gracious God, we give you thanks that our Savior Jesus Christ, before he suffered, gave us this memorial of his sacrifice, until his coming again:

For in the night when he was betrayed, he took bread. And when he had given thanks to you, he broke it, and gave it to his disciples, and said:
"Take, eat: This is my body which is given for you. Do this in remembrance of me."
In the same way also after supper, he took the cup. And when he had given you thanks, he gave it to them and said:

---

*Or stand.

583

"Drink this, all of you: This is my blood of the new covenant, which is poured out for you and many, for the forgiveness of sins. Do this, as often as you drink it, in remembrance of me."

MINISTER
AND
PEOPLE:
His death, O God, we proclaim. His resurrection we declare. His coming we await. Glory be to you, O Lord.

MINISTER: Heavenly Father, show forth among us the presence of your life-giving Word and Holy Spirit, to sanctify us and your whole church through these holy mysteries. Grant that all who share the communion of the body and blood of our Savior Jesus Christ may be one in him, and remain faithful in love and hope until that perfect feast with him in joy in his eternal kingdom.

MINISTER
AND
PEOPLE:
Gracious Father, accept with favor this our sacrifice of praise, which we now present with these holy gifts. We offer to you ourselves, giving you thanks for calling us to your service, as your own people, through the perfect offering of your Son Jesus our Lord;

By whom and with whom and in whom, in the unity of the Holy Spirit, all honor and glory be to you, Father Almighty, now and forever.

Amen.

MINISTER: As our Savior Christ has taught us, we dare to say:

MINISTER
AND
PEOPLE:
Our Father in heaven,
    holy be your name,
    your kingdom come,
    your will be done,
        on earth as in heaven.
Give us today our daily bread.
Forgive us our sins
    as we forgive those who sin against us.
Do not bring us to the test
    but deliver us from evil.
For the kingdom, the power, and the glory are yours
    now and forever.

The Breaking of Bread

After a period of silence, the ministers shall break the bread and pour the wine in preparation for the Communion, during which time the following may be said or sung:

584

*Stand**

MINISTER: The bread which we break, is it not a sharing in the body of Christ?

PEOPLE: **Because there is one bread, we who are many are one body, for we all partake of the one bread.**

MINISTER: The wine which we drink, is it not a sharing in the blood of Christ?

PEOPLE: **The cup which we bless is the communion in the blood of Christ.**

The Communion

Before the minister and the people receive the elements, the following may be said or sung:

MINISTER: Alleluia. Christ our Passover is sacrificed for us.

PEOPLE: **Therefore let us keep the feast. Alleluia.**

MINISTER: Blessed is he who comes in the name of the Lord.

PEOPLE: **Hosanna in the highest.**

MINISTER: The gifts of God for the people of God.

*Sit**

Then shall be said, either to the whole congregation or to each individual communicant, by the minister who gives the bread:

The body of Christ, the bread of heaven.

And by the minister who gives the wine:

The blood of Christ, the cup of salvation.

During the Communion time, silence may be kept, or hymns, psalms, and anthems may be sung.

An Act of Praise

Stand

A hymn or a psalm of doxology may be sung, or this canticle:

Nunc dimittis

**Now, Master, you have kept your word:
you let your servant go in peace.**

---

*Or kneel.

With my own eyes I have seen the salvation
  which you have prepared in the sight of every people:
a light to reveal you to the nations
  and the glory of your people Israel.

And the minister and the people may say this prayer of thanksgiving:

Almighty and everliving God, we give you thanks for receiving our sacrifice of praise and thanksgiving, and for feeding us with the spiritual food of the body and blood of our Savior Jesus Christ. Strengthen us ever with your Holy Spirit, that we may serve you in faith and love, by word and deed, until we come to the joy of your eternal kingdom; through the same Jesus Christ our Lord, who lives and reigns with you and the same Holy Spirit, now and forever. Amen.

The Dismissal

Then shall the people be sent forth to their life and witness in the world, as follows:

MINISTER: The peace of God, which passes all understanding, keep your hearts and minds in the knowledge and love of God, and of his Son Jesus Christ our Lord:

And the blessing of God Almighty, the Father, the Son, and the Holy Spirit, be among you and remain with you always.

PEOPLE: **Amen.**

MINISTER: Go in peace, to love and serve the Lord.

PEOPLE: **Thanks be to God.**

[When all have received the Communion, the minister shall consume or otherwise reverently dispose of all that remains of the elements which have been blessed, either after the Communion or at the conclusion of the service.

The minister may also reserve such bread and wine as may be needed for the Communion of the sick and of others who are necessarily hindered from being present with the people.]

Alternate Form of the Thanksgiving

MINISTER: The Lord be with you.

PEOPLE: **And also with you.**

MINISTER: Lift up your hearts.

PEOPLE: **We lift them up to the Lord.**

586

MINISTER: Let us give thanks to the Lord our God.

PEOPLE: **It is right to give him thanks and praise.**

MINISTER: It is our duty and delight
at all times and in all places
to give thanks to you,
O Lord, holy Father, through Christ our Lord,
who on this day overcame death and the grave,
and by his glorious resurrection
opened to us the way of everlasting life.
And so, with the church on earth and the hosts of heaven
we praise your name
and join their unending hymn: *

ALL: **Holy, holy, holy Lord, God of power and might,
heaven and earth are full of your glory.
Hosanna in the highest.**

**Blessed is he who comes in the name of the Lord.
Hosanna in the highest.**

MINISTER: Holy God, mighty Lord, gracious Father:
endless is your mercy and eternal your reign.
You have filled all creation with light and life:
everything everywhere is full of your glory.
You made man in your image, the crown of creation.
Through Abraham you promised to bless all mankind.
You rescued Israel, your chosen, the people of your promise;
you sent them prophets with words of judgment and of hope.
And, when the time had come, you sent your Son,
born of Mary by the power of the Holy Spirit.
In words and wonders he proclaimed your kingdom
and was obedient to your will, even to giving his life.

At supper the night he was betrayed,
our Lord Jesus took some bread in his hands;

He takes the bread in his hands.

and then, when he had given thanks to you,
he broke it and he gave it to his friends.
And he said, "Take this, and eat it:
This is my body; it is given for you:
Do this to remember me."
After supper he took a cup of wine

---

*Seasonal prefaces may be substituted.

He takes the cup in his hands.

and after giving thanks, he gave it to them.
And he said, "Drink from this, all of you:
This cup is God's new covenant in my blood
which is poured out for all mankind
for the forgiveness of sins.
Whenever you drink from it from now on,
do this to remember me."

Gracious Father, we therefore celebrate the sacrifice
of our Lord
by means of this holy bread and cup:
rejoicing to receive all that he accomplished for us
in his life and death, his resurrection and ascension;
and awaiting his coming again
to share with us the heavenly feast.

PEOPLE: **Amen. Come, Lord Jesus.**

MINISTER: Send the power of your Holy Spirit upon us

He extends his hands over the bread and wine.

and upon this bread and wine,
that we who receive the body and blood of Christ
may be his body in the world,
living according to his example,
to bring peace and healing to all mankind.
Join our prayers with those of your servants
of every time and every place,
and unite them in the ceaseless petitions
of our great High Priest
until he comes in power and great glory
as victorious Lord of all.

ALL: **Through him, with him, in him,**
in the unity of the Holy Spirit,
all honor and glory is yours,
almighty Father,
now and forever.
Amen.

Our Father in heaven,
holy be your name,
your kingdom come,
your will be done,
on earth as in heaven.

Give us today our daily bread.
Forgive us our sins
    as we forgive those who sin against us.
Do not bring us to the test
    but deliver us from evil.
For the kingdom, the power, and the glory are yours
    now and forever.

As he breaks the bread:

MINISTER: When we eat this bread we share the body of Christ.

As he lifts the cup:

When we drink this cup we share the blood of Christ.

PEOPLE: **Reveal yourself to us, O Lord,
in the breaking of bread,
as you once revealed yourself to the disciples.**

Sit *

Then shall be said, either to the whole congregation or to each individual communicant, by the minister who gives the bread:

The body of Christ, the bread of heaven.

And by the minister who gives the wine:

The blood of Christ, the cup of salvation.

During the Communion time, silence may be kept, or hymns, psalms, and anthems may be sung.

Stand   **An Act of Praise**

A hymn or a psalm of doxology may be sung, or this canticle:

Nunc dimittis

Now, Master, you have kept your word:
    you let your servant go in peace.
With my own eyes I have seen the salvation
    which you have prepared in the sight of every people:
a light to reveal you to the nations
    and the glory of your people Israel.

---

*Or kneel.

589

AN ORDER OF WORSHIP, PROTESTANT

And the minister and people may say this prayer of thanksgiving:

Almighty and everliving God, we give you thanks for receiving our sacrifice of praise and thanksgiving, and for feeding us with the spiritual food of the body and blood of our Savior Jesus Christ. Strengthen us ever with your Holy Spirit, that we may serve you in faith and love, by word and deed, until we come to the joy of your eternal kingdom; through the same Jesus Christ our Lord, who lives and reigns with you and the same Holy Spirit, now and forever. Amen.

Then shall the people be sent forth to their life and witness in the world, as follows:

MINISTER: The peace of God, which passes all understanding, keep your hearts and minds in the knowledge and love of God, and of his Son Jesus Christ our Lord:

And the blessing of God Almighty, the Father, the Son, and the Holy Spirit, be among you and remain with you always.

PEOPLE: **Amen.**

MINISTER: Go in peace, to love and serve the Lord.

PEOPLE: **Thanks be to God.**

A Service of Unity and Peace 615

Hymn. (Contemporary folk hymns are suggested.)

LEADER: In every prayer for peace there is a touch of
blasphemy.
It is as though war were inevitable and only God
could extricate us.

But we are the warriors, the makers and wagers
of destruction.
(Not God. Not even "they.")
Perhaps our prayers for peace should be for
forgiveness.
And perhaps they should be said first to
our brothers.

For "if you are bringing your offering to the altar
and there remember that your brother has
something against you, leave your offering
there before the altar, go and be reconciled
with your brother first . . ."

Brother, forgive us.
Brother, help us to understand.
And when to the Lord:
A prayer for courage. Help in living with the truth.
We are brothers who seek to destroy.
But brothers.
Peace is a truth lived.
A prayer for peace is an outstretched hand.
Unarmed.

Let us pray: O God, you correct injustices and gather together
the dispersed to protect them. Mercifully fill your people with the
spirit of peace and unity, that they may cast aside their differences
and serve you worthily in union with our Lord Jesus Christ.

ALL: **Amen.**

The following, or similar selections, may be read.

591

READER: A beautiful, perilous vision of man in history! Almost as though one were to say, mankind, like a truncated body, can grow new limbs in response to new words.

But it is precisely here that the biological analogy breaks down, and the spiritual reality bursts through. That is to say— . . . man cannot grow new limbs no matter how urgent his needs or how fervent his longings.

And—of course mankind can grow into new forms of community, new international agreements, new alternatives to violence, new expressions of faith and love, new heights of altruism—all in accord with the new demands which his times place on him.

Hope for man! . . . Here are some of the practical things to be done, if hope is to win out . . .

Share your goods. Have compassion. Make peace with your enemies. Grant others breathing space. Stop wasting the earth. Unlearn avarice and selfishness.

Men need hope most when despair seems most reasonable. . . . Despair is seductive and rank and pollutes the atmosphere. We have been hearing so much bad news about ourselves, for so long, we have come almost to believe it—to live by it, to fear it, to arm for its sake, to die of it.

We have grown less and less able to grow limbs for reducing distances, limbs for drawing other lives to our own, limbs for building, and planning and loving and dancing and making music and . . . but where does man stop, if he is man, if he has grown up, if his body is whole?

He never does, of course. He is his own good news. He is discharged from the hospital. He is risen.

Response. (Sing a hymn on brotherhood.)

READER: Hear what God tells us how he would have mankind be. (*Read Philippians 2:2–11, or similar selections.*)

Homily or Brief Sermon.

LEADER: We offer our individual prayers for peace and unity. Following each prayer, please respond **"Hear us, O Lord."**

At the conclusion of the spontaneous prayers, the reader continues:

READER: Lord,
I am confused. There are so many of us here.
What do we do? Where do we begin?
How do we really love each other?
   each show-off
   each loner
   each person who grates us
      uses us
      rejects us?
How do we really know one another
   help one another
   rid one another of superficial human respect
      face-value judgments
      meaningless talk?
Lord,
There are so many of us here
   so many who wander through
      push through
      run through
   so many who are bitter
      sightless
      afraid.
Yes, Lord,
I am grateful for those here who inspire us
   strengthen us
   those with the courage to lead us
      to challenge us
      to be themselves with us.
But, Lord,
What about the rest of us?
If we are strangers to one another now
   will we be brother to your people later on?
If we don't give ourselves now
   will we offer ourselves later on?
Lord,
I am confused. There are so many of us here.
Where do we begin? What do we do?
We do not know now but we are eager to change
   help us to change.
Lord,
   help us to stop talking
      to start listening
      to start believing.

LEADER: Some will say we should not be praying for peace and unity. The real problem in prayer is not that God is effecting no changes in the world; nor that he is distant; nor even that he is silent. The problem is that, being so close and so broadly diffused, men still miss him. That is why the process of prayer is the process of man changing, not God. One travels a route often marked by desperation, and many speak of death and misery and the absence of God. But the reality, known by faith, is quite the contrary.

READER: A prayer for peace is an outstretched hand.

READER: And a truth to be lived as we say, "Brother, forgive us."

A greeting of peace is now exchanged.

Hymn. (A contemporary folk hymn is suggested.)

Hymn.

LEADER: The Christian way is a faith commitment for adults. But its faith is the faith of a community. This faith is initiated and nourished in the believing community, a local assembly which is a community of worship and a community of mission.

One might think it were enough to be born once. But life is not that simple. Our search for meaning cries out to heights and depths beyond human grasp — to God, whose call and favor are a covenant-gift, witnessed by Scripture and made flesh in Christ Jesus. In his cross, in his death and resurrection, is the pattern of our struggle and our new life.

Hymn. (A hymn in contemporary folk idiom is suggested.)

READER: Freedom . . . is inwardness, spontaneity, the capacity of a man to find within himself the reasons and the motives of his own right decisions and action, apart from external coercion. Freedom therefore is authenticity, truthfulness, fidelity to the pursuit of truth and to the truth when found. In further consequence, freedom is experienced as duty, as responsibility — as a response to the claims of justice, to the demands of rightful law, to the governance and guidance of legitimate authority. In its intimately Christian sense, however, freedom has a higher meaning than all of this. Freedom, in the deepest experience of it, is love. To be free is to be-for-the-others. The Christian call to freedom is inherently a call to community, a summons out of isolation, an invitation to be-with-others, an impulse to service of the others.

Response. (A selection from the Psalter is suggested, e.g., Psalm 41 [40], No. 653.)

LEADER: A reading from the letter of Saint Paul to the church of Galatia. *(Galatians 5:13–15, or a similar selection similarly introduced.)*

Homily or Brief Sermon.

LEADER: Let us ask our Lord Jesus Christ to renew our baptismal promises. By the mystery of your death and resurrection, Lord Jesus, may we renew our baptismal life.

ALL: **Lord, hear our prayer.**

LEADER: May we be faithful followers and witnesses of your gospel.

ALL: **Lord, hear our prayer.**

LEADER: Lead us by a holy life to the joy of your kingdom.

ALL: **Lord, hear our prayer.**

LEADER: Keep our families always in your love.

ALL: **Lord, hear our prayer.**

LEADER: Renew the promise of our baptism in each one of us,

ALL: **Lord, hear our prayer.**

LEADER: That, buried in the likeness of Christ's death through baptism, we may also share in the glory of his resurrection:

ALL: **Lord, hear our prayer.**

LEADER: May all of Christ's followers, baptized into one body, always live united in faith and love.

ALL: **Lord, hear our prayer.**

READER I: Do you promise to seek the good life for yourselves and for your brothers and your sisters everywhere, rejecting sin and living in the freedom of God's children?

ALL: **We do.**

READER II: Do you promise to build the kingdom of human brotherhood and love, rejecting the idols of money and property and color and class and position?

ALL: **We do.**

READER I: Do you promise to seek peace and to live in peace, in one human family, rejecting Satan's prejudice and all barriers to unity?

ALL: **We do.**

LEADER: Do you believe in God, the Father Almighty, creator of heaven and earth?

ALL: **We do.**

LEADER: Do you believe in Jesus Christ, his only Son, our Lord, who was born of the Virgin Mary, was crucified, died, and was buried, rose from the dead, and is now seated at the right hand of the Father?

ALL: **We do.**

LEADER: Do you believe in the Holy Spirit, the holy catholic church, the communion of saints, the forgiveness of sins, the resurrection of the body, and life everlasting?

ALL: **We do.**

LEADER: Man was put on this earth, as Scripture tells us, not to leave things the way they were — God created Adam and he put him in the garden to take care of it; man is supposed to transform his world so that it bears a mark of his own intelligence and his own art and his own concern, because only if that is there, can there be a Christian dimension to all this. If the world is going to be Christianized, it automatically means to be humanized.

LEADER: God the Father of our Lord Jesus Christ has freed us from sin, given us new birth by water and the Holy Spirit, and welcomed us into his holy people. He has anointed us with the oil of salvation. As Christ was anointed Priest, Prophet, and King, so may we live always as members of his body, serving one another and sharing everlasting life.

ALL: **Amen.**

Hymn.

617 Reflections on the Suffering, Death, and Resurrection of Jesus

FIRST MEDITATION
Jesus is condemned to death.

LEADER: We adore you, O Christ, and we praise you:

ALL: **Because by your holy cross and resurrection you have redeemed the world.**

Again the high priest questioned him: "Are you the Messiah, the Son of the Blessed God?" "I am," answered Jesus, "and you will all see the Son of Man seated at the right side of the Almighty, and coming with the clouds of heaven!" The high priest tore his robes and said, "We don't need any more witnesses! You heard his wicked words. What is your decision?" They all voted against him: he was guilty and should be put to death. (*Mark 14:61–64.*)

LEADER: Let us pray.
All-powerful and eternal God, for proclaiming the truth, your Son, Jesus Christ, is condemned to death by crucifixion. Stir up your love in our hearts so that we might be ever faithful to all that you have told us and fear nothing more than the loss of your friendship through sin.

ALL: **Amen.**

SECOND MEDITATION
Jesus carries his cross.

LEADER: We adore you, O Christ, and we praise you:

ALL: **Because by your holy cross you have redeemed the world.**

Pilate said to the Jews, "Here is your king!" They shouted back, "Kill him! Kill him! Nail him to the cross!" Pilate asked them, "Do you want me to nail your king to the cross?" The chief priests answered, "The only king we have is the Emperor!" Then Pilate handed Jesus over to them to be nailed to the cross. So they took charge of Jesus. He went out, carrying his own cross. (*John 19:14–17.*)

LEADER: Let us pray.
Father in heaven, your Son, Jesus Christ, still carries his cross in his persecuted brothers throughout the world. Make us feel the needs of all men, so that we might as readily help them as we would help Jesus himself.

ALL: **Amen.**

THIRD MEDITATION
Jesus falls the first time.

LEADER: We adore you, O Christ, and we praise you:

ALL: **Because by your holy cross you have redeemed the world.**

If the world hates you, you must remember that it has hated me first. If you belonged to the world, then the world would love you as its own. But I chose you from this world, and you do not belong to it; this is why the world hates you. Remember what I told you: "No slave is greater than his master." If they persecuted me, they will persecute you too. (*John 15:18–20.*)

LEADER: Let us pray.
O God, to free us from sin and weakness your Son, Jesus Christ, embraced his fearful passion and crucifixion. Strengthen us in our baptismal resolutions by which we renounced sin and Satan, so that through the passion of this life's sufferings we might rise to a new life of joyful service, free of all selfishness.

ALL: **Amen.**

FOURTH MEDITATION
Jesus meets his afflicted mother.

LEADER: We adore you, O Christ, and we praise you:

ALL: **Because by your holy cross you have redeemed the world.**

Standing close to Jesus' cross were his mother, his mother's sister, Mary the wife of Clopas, and Mary Magdalene. Jesus saw his mother and the disciple he loved standing there; so he said to his mother, "Woman, here is your son." Then he said to the disciple, "Here is your mother." And from that time the disciple took her to live in his home. (*John 19:25–27.*)

LEADER: Let us pray.
O blessed Lord, at your passion a sword of sorrow pierced the loving heart of your mother as Simeon had foretold. Grant that

we who look back on her sorrows with compassion might receive
the healing fruits of your sufferings.

ALL: **Amen.**

FIFTH MEDITATION
Simon of Cyrene helps Jesus to carry his cross.

LEADER: We adore you, O Christ, and we praise you:

ALL: **Because by your holy cross you have redeemed the world.**

When they had finished making fun of him, they took off the purple
robe and put his own clothes back on him. Then they led him out
to nail him to the cross. On the way they met a man named Simon,
who was coming into the city from the country, and they forced
him to carry Jesus' cross. (This was Simon from Cyrene, the father
of Alexander and Rufus.) They brought Jesus to a place called
Golgotha, which means "The Place of the Skull." (*Mark 15:20–22.*)

LEADER: Let us pray.
My Lord and my God, help me to see in the sufferings and short-
comings of my life a share in your cross; strengthen and console
us in the belief that we bear all things in union with you, who have
taken upon yourself even our guilt.

ALL: **Amen.**

SIXTH MEDITATION
Veronica wipes the face of Jesus.

LEADER: We adore you, O Christ, and we praise you:

ALL: **Because by your holy cross you have redeemed the world.**

"When, Lord, did we ever see you hungry and feed you, or thirsty
and give you drink? When did we ever see you a stranger and
welcome you in our homes, or naked and clothe you? When did
we ever see you sick or in prison, and visit you?" The King will
answer back, "I tell you, indeed, whenever you did this for one of
the least important of these brothers of mine, you did it for me!"
(*Matthew 25:37–40.*)

LEADER: Let us pray.
Almighty and ever-loving God, we feel your love and understanding in the consolation and support we receive from one another.
Give us, we beg you, the courage and dedication to sacrifice and
suffer with those who are in need, the least of your brethren.

ALL: **Amen.**

600

SEVENTH MEDITATION
Jesus falls the second time.

LEADER: We adore you, O Christ, and we praise you:

ALL: **Because by your holy cross you have redeemed the world.**

It was our weaknesses that he carried, our sufferings that he endured, while we thought of him as stricken, as one struck by God and afflicted. But he was pierced for our offenses, crushed for our sins; upon him was the punishment that makes us whole, by his stripes we were healed. We had all gone astray like sheep, each following his own way; but the Lord laid upon him the guilt of us all. (*Isaiah 53:4–6.*)

LEADER: Let us pray.
My Lord and my God, you shared in our weaknesses and accepted our guilt. Grant me the favor of rejoicing over my human weaknesses, so that in all I do, your strength, dwelling in me, may be shown to all men.

ALL: **Amen.**

EIGHTH MEDITATION
Jesus meets the women of Jerusalem.

LEADER: We adore you, O Christ, and we praise you:

ALL: **Because by your holy cross you have redeemed the world.**

A large crowd of people followed him; among them were some women who were weeping and wailing for him. Jesus turned to them and said, "Women of Jerusalem! Don't cry for me, but for yourselves and your children." (*Luke 23:27–28.*)

LEADER: Let us pray.
My beloved Jesus, with tears of pity these women of Jerusalem responded to you, broken, bruised, and beaten, on the road to Calvary. Deepen my faith, I beg you, so that I might see you in my brother, bruised by my envy, beaten down by injustice, and broken by my greed and my indifference.

ALL: **Amen.**

NINTH MEDITATION
Jesus falls again.

LEADER: We adore you, O Christ, and we praise you:

ALL: **Because by your holy cross you have redeemed the world.**

I am ready to turn to dust. Revive me with your word! I reveal my ways and you sneer. Teach me your laws! Let me understand your decrees, that I may rejoice at your wonders! My life is sleepless with grief. Raise me with your word! (*Psalm 119[118]:25-28.*)

LEADER: Let us pray.
Almighty and eternal God, you permitted your Son to be weakened, crushed, and profaned, so that he might rise from the dead freed from the ravages of sin. Help us to accept our weaknesses and failings as forerunners of our glorious resurrection in union with your Son.

ALL: **Amen.**

TENTH MEDITATION
Jesus is stripped of his clothes.

LEADER: We adore you, O Christ, and we praise you:

ALL: **Because by your holy cross you have redeemed the world.**

They offered him wine to drink, mixed with gall; after tasting it, however, he would not drink it. They nailed him to the cross, and then divided his clothes among them by throwing dice. (*Matthew 27:34-35.*)

LEADER: Let us pray.
My Lord and my God, stripped of everything, you stood exposed to the jeers and contempt of the people whom you loved. Clothe me with genuine love of others, so that nothing I suffer may ever fill my heart with hatred or bitterness.

ALL: **Amen.**

ELEVENTH MEDITATION
Jesus is nailed to the cross.

LEADER: We adore you, O Christ, and we praise you:

ALL: **Because by your holy cross you have redeemed the world.**

When they came to the place called "The Skull," they nailed Jesus to the cross there, and the two criminals, one on his right and one on his left. Jesus said, "Forgive them, Father! They don't know what they are doing." (*Luke 23:33-34.*)

LEADER: Let us pray.
My Lord and Savior, you have told us that we too must accept crucifixion if we are to accept resurrection with you. Help us to

rejoice in the sufferings that come with the fulfillment of our daily duties, seeing in them the royal road of the cross to the resurrection.

ALL: **Amen.**

TWELFTH MEDITATION
Jesus dies on the cross.

LEADER: We adore you, O Christ, and we praise you:

ALL: **Because by your holy cross you have redeemed the world.**

It was about twelve o'clock when the sun stopped shining and darkness covered the whole country until three o'clock; and the curtain hanging in the Temple was torn in two. Jesus cried out in a loud voice, "It is finished! Father! In your hands I place my spirit!" Then he bowed his head and died. (*Luke 23:44–46; John 19:30.*)

ALL: **Our Father, who art in heaven, hallowed be thy name. Thy kingdom come; thy will be done on earth as it is in heaven. Give us this day our daily bread; and forgive us our trespasses as we forgive those who trespass against us. And lead us not into temptation, but deliver us from evil. Amen.**

THIRTEENTH MEDITATION
Jesus is laid in the tomb.

LEADER: We adore you, O Christ, and we praise you:

ALL: **Because by your holy cross you have redeemed the world.**

Joseph of Arimathea took the body of Jesus, wrapped it in a new linen sheet, and placed it in his own grave, which he had just recently dug out of the rock. Then he rolled a large stone across the entrance to the grave and went away. (*Matthew 27:59–60.*)

LEADER: Let us pray.
Almighty and eternal God, on the edge of sadness when all seemed lost, you restored to us the Savior we thought defeated and conquered. Help us, we beg you, so to empty ourselves of self-concern that we might see your hand in every failure and your victory in every defeat. These things we ask in the name of your Son, Jesus Christ, who lives and reigns forever with you in the unity of the Holy Spirit.

ALL: **Amen.**

CLOSING MEDITATION
The resurrection of Jesus.

LEADER: We adore you, O Christ, and we praise you:

ALL: **Because by your holy cross and resurrection you have redeemed the world.**

After the Sabbath day was over, Mary Magdalene, Mary the mother of James, and Salome bought spices to go and anoint the body of Jesus. Very early on Sunday morning, at sunrise, they went to the grave. On the way they said to one another, "Who will roll away the stone from the entrance to the grave for us?" (It was a very large stone.) Then they looked up and saw that the stone had already been rolled back. So they entered the grave, where they saw a young man, sitting at the right, who wore a white robe—and they were filled with alarm. "Don't be alarmed," he said. "You are looking for Jesus of Nazareth, who was nailed to the cross. But he is not here—he has risen! Look, here is the place where they laid him." (*Mark 16:1-6.*)

ALL: **I believe in God, the Father Almighty, creator of heaven and earth; and in Jesus Christ, his only Son, our Lord, who was conceived by the Holy Spirit, born of the Virgin Mary, suffered under Pontius Pilate, was crucified, died, and was buried. He descended into hell; the third day he arose again from the dead. I believe in the Holy Spirit, the holy catholic church, the communion of saints, the forgiveness of sins, the resurrection of the body, and life everlasting. Amen.**

A Community Celebration 618
of Repentance

The readers, leader, and musicians should be in place before the service begins. The leader should ask the persons on the one side of the assembly to read the parts marked I, and those on the other side to read the parts marked II. It is advisable for the musicians to review the music for the service in advance. The chaplains enter during the singing of the opening hymn.

LEADER: Welcome! Our chaplains come among us in the name of Jesus. Let us rise and greet them as we sing Hymn 168.

CHAPLAIN: Let us join in prayer.

GROUP I: **O God, you have indeed been good to us.**
You have prospered our land.
You have opened your heart to us in love.
You have forgiven our sins
and adopted us as your sons.

GROUP II: **We know that you have not turned away from us.**
You touch with joy and peace
the hearts that are open to you.
You stand ready to show your salvation
to all who will trust in you.

CHAPLAIN: As we speak to you in faith,
you respond in loving concern.
You will give us what is good
and will prosper us
with gifts from your hand.

LEADER: Please be seated.

READER: A reading from The Book of Daniel. (*Daniel 9:4–17, or a similar selection from the Old Testament, similarly introduced.*)

CHOIR: (*Meditation song. Stanzas 2 and 3 of Hymn 168, "Where Charity and Love Prevail," or similar stanzas, are suggested.*)

READER: Jesus calls all men to personal union with himself. His call goes forth especially to those who consider themselves unworthy of his sacred presence. Let us listen to the call of Matthew the apostle. (*Matthew 9:9–13, or a similar selection, similarly introduced.*)

CHOIR: (*Meditation song. The same stanzas used before, or others, may be sung.*)

CHAPLAIN: *Homily or Brief Sermon.*

LEADER: Please kneel. We pray for pardon.
If we say we have no sin, we deceive ourselves and the truth is not in us.

ALL: **Hear, O Lord, and grant pardon.**

LEADER: With Peter the apostle we say, Depart from me, Lord, for I am a sinful man.

ALL: **Hear, O Lord, and grant pardon.**

LEADER: Mindful of Mary Magdalene, Peter, and the thief on the cross, we come to you in confidence.

ALL: **Hear, O Lord, and grant pardon.**

LEADER: You, O Christ, remain our advocate to plead our cause before the Father.

ALL: **Hear, O Lord, and grant pardon.**

LEADER: Not those in health, but the sick have need of a physician.

ALL: **Hear, O Lord, and grant pardon.**

LEADER: You, O Lord, the Most Holy, have taken our sins upon yourself; in your body you bore them on the wood of the cross.

ALL: **Hear, O Lord, and grant pardon.**

LEADER: Together we express to God our sorrow for our sins:

ALL: **O my God, I am very sorry for my sins. Give me your help to sin no more. Give me your love to love you. Give me your love to love everyone better. Amen.**

CHAPLAIN: The Lord be with you.

ALL: **And also with you.**

CHAPLAIN: Let us pray in silence.

After a pause, the chaplain reads the following prayer aloud:
O God, you desire the repentance of the sinner and not his

death. Take into consideration our frail human nature. Be merciful to us, for we know that we are dust and to dust we shall return because of our sinfulness. Forgive us and grant us the rewards you have promised to sincere penitents. We ask this in the name of Christ our Lord.

ALL: **Amen.**

LEADER: Our chaplain is here in the name of Jesus. Listen to what he says.

CHAPLAIN: This is what Jesus says to his disciples: Peace be with you. As my Father has sent me, so I am sending you. If anyone comes to you and asks you to forgive his sins, forgive them in my name.

Therefore, brother chaplains, go. Go to those who come to you asking you to forgive their sins, and forgive them in Jesus' name. (*The presiding chaplain gestures and the chaplains go to their assigned stations for confession.*)

LEADER: My brothers in Christ, we are all guilty before the pure and holy God. But in his mercy God has given to his church, to his holy people, the sacrament of reconciliation. For ourselves and our brothers who are about to partake in this holy rite we beg the grace of humility, of sincerity and true sorrow. Let us pray that God may sanctify us and make us one through the bond of his grace.

During the period of confessions, the choir, assembly, and readers shall alternate in the following activities. The choir sings the antiphon, the assembly repeats the antiphon, and the choir sings the stanza or stanzas indicated. The reader assists as indicated. Brief instrumental (organ) interludes provide flexibility for this portion of the service which is intended to end at the conclusion of all confessions.

Hymn: "Yes, I Shall Arise and Return to My Father," Hymn 396, stanza 1.

READER: O God, you are the creator
and the sustainer of your church.
You have protected and prospered
your faithful followers
throughout the stormy and tumultuous past.

Hymn: "My Soul Is Longing for Your Peace," Hymn 131, stanza 1.

READER: Today we are in trouble.
          Listen to our cries of consternation, O God.
          We are confused and confounded.
          We don't know where to turn,
              in what direction to go.

          Instrumental Interlude.

          Hymn: "Yes, I Shall Arise and Return to My Father," stanza 2.

READER: We have prayed, O God.
          We have sung your praises.
          We have proclaimed your love to the world.
          But today our power is slipping away;
              our prestige is wearing thin.
          People seem to have little respect for us anymore.
          Those who have been brought up
              within our structures
              and have embraced our doctrines
              are leaving the fold.
          They say we are no longer meeting their needs
              or the needs of the world.

          Hymn: "My Soul Is Longing for Your Peace," stanza 2.

READER: You were with us in the beginning, Lord.
          You planted us in the midst
              of this world's turmoil.
          You nurtured us and watched over us.
          In spite of your enemies,
              who sought to destroy us,
              we grew until we encircled the earth.
          Great shrines were built in your honor, Lord.
          Magnificent institutions were established
              to carry out your purposes.
          Men dedicated their many skills
              to perpetuate your teachings.
          Multitudes gathered to declare your praises.

          Instrumental Interlude.

          Hymn: "Yes, I Shall Arise and Return to My Father," stanza 3.

READER: Today we are in trouble, Lord.
          The walls are crumbling.
          Our sanctuaries no longer attract the masses.
          Men's skills are dedicated to other purposes.

We no longer are making much of an impression
on this world of ours.

Hymn: "My Soul Is Longing for Your Peace," stanza 3.

READER: Renew your church, O God.
We know you will never turn away
those who come to you,
those who trust in you.

Instrumental Interlude.

Hymn: "Yes, I Shall Arise and Return to My Father," stanza 4.

READER: Fan the dying embers, Lord.
Stir us up, and restore us to the position
of power and effectiveness.
Give us new life and new vision.

Hymn: "My Soul Is Longing for Your Peace," stanza 4.

READER: Give us new life and new vision,
that we may advance your kingdom
in our disjointed world.
Renew your church, O God,
and revive your servants,
so that the whole world may know of your love.

*Repeat the alternation between the two hymns until the period
for confessions is completed. When all have reassembled, the
service continues.*

CHAPLAIN: Now we understand better that God is our merciful Father.
We realize better that our neighbor is our brother. For our
failings, our lack of love, we shall recite Psalm 31 (30) and
perform some freely chosen act of love which will contribute
to the good of the community. Everyone present is invited to
share the penance and to pray for our perseverance and
spiritual improvement in the Lord.

LEADER: Let us kneel and pray the psalm alternately.

ALL: *(Psalm 31 [30], No. 647, group I reading first, group II
reading the parts marked for the congregational response.)*

CHAPLAIN: Let us arise and exchange the greeting of peace as a sign of
our love and forgiveness. *(All may exchange handshakes, saying "The peace of the Lord," or a similar greeting.)*

CHAPLAIN: Our help is in the name of the Lord,

ALL: **Who made heaven and earth.**

CHAPLAIN: Save your servants,

ALL: **Who trust in you, O God.**

CHAPLAIN: Let the enemy have no power over them;

ALL: **And let not the son of evil dare to harm them.**

CHAPLAIN: Be a tower of strength for them, O Lord,

ALL: **Against the attack of the enemy.**

CHAPLAIN: Hear our prayer, O Lord;

ALL: **And let our cry come to you.**

CHAPLAIN: The Lord be with you.

ALL: **And also with you.**

CHAPLAIN: Let us pray. O God, to whom it belongs always to show mercy and to spare, receive our prayer, that these your servants who have admitted their sinfulness before you and the whole court of heaven and before their brothers may be pardoned by your mercy; through Christ our Lord.

ALL: **Amen.**

CHAPLAINS: (*The chaplains together say the words of absolution.*)

CHAPLAIN: Lord, we have come before you;
we have asked forgiveness for our sins.
Give us now your strength to love you better.
Give us your love to make others happy.
Through Jesus Christ, our Lord,
Give us your peace and your joy.

CHAPLAINS: (*Lifting their hands and blessing the assembly*)
May the peace of God
always remain in your hearts
in the name of the Father
and of the Son
and of the Holy Spirit.

ALL: **Amen.**

LEADER: In thanksgiving, let us sing Hymn _____. (*An appropriate hymn of thanksgiving or closing of worship should be selected from the hymnal.*)

Hymn. (A hymn of praise or of the Lord's Supper is suggested.)

LEADER: Father, we gather here in the name of your Son
and at his request.
He calls us friend and brother, and gives us one command:
That our love for each other be real.
May we finally learn what he has come to teach, and set aside
the barriers we have made between us,
of hate and suspicion, which love cannot pierce.
Only then will men say we are his friends;
for if we do not love our brothers, men whom we can see,
we cannot truly love you who are hidden from our eyes.
We ask this in the name of Jesus Christ, your Son,
who is with us still
and who promises peace now and forever.

ALL: **Amen.**

READER: Hear what God says about his covenant with his people. *(Read Exodus 24:3–8, or similar selections.)*

Hymn: (See Topical Index for hymns on "Love.")

LEADER: In early apostolic times the Eucharist was received at the agape, the community love feast. But these dinners at Corinth were marred by factions, with divisions developing between one group and another, between rich and poor, between the well-fed and the hungry. It seems that they—like ourselves—realized only imperfectly the nature of the sacrament that Christ founded at the Last Supper. If we are to think less of the accidentals that separate us, we will have to concentrate in prayer on the great mystery of our supernatural unity—with the body and blood of the Lord making us one with him and with one another.

Lord, we confess in sorrow and shame that often when we assemble as Christians, there are divisions among us. . . . So that when we meet together, it is not really your supper that we eat, for we do not have enough love in our hearts.

The account that Paul received from you, Lord, which he also delivered to us, is that on the night you were betrayed you took bread, and when you had given thanks, you broke it, and said: "This is my body which is for you. Do this in remembrance of me." For as often as we eat this bread and drink the cup, we proclaim your death, O Lord, until you come. Whoever, therefore, eats the bread or drinks your cup in an unworthy manner will be guilty of profaning your body and blood. Help us, then, to examine ourselves, and so eat of the bread and drink of the cup that we may be made worthy to become one with you and one with our neighbor.

ALL: **Amen.**

Homily or Brief Sermon.

LEADER: We express our common bond of brotherhood by praying the words our Lord has taught us.

ALL: *The Lord's Prayer.*

LEADER: Let us pray for peace. (*Various prayers for peace may be selected for use at this time.*)

ALL: **For the kingdom, the power, and the glory are yours, now and forever.**

LEADER: We break bread together for ourselves and for each other,
    that the peace and joy of the risen Christ
    be with us forever.

The leader and the assembly exchange the greeting of peace.

LEADER: (*Raising the bread and the cup*)
Come to the table of the Lord in peace and in brotherhood. It is the Lord who invites us, and the Lord who nourishes us. It is the Lord who gives us his peace.

ALL: **Amen.**

ALL: **Glory be to the Father and to the Son and to the Holy Spirit, as it was in the beginning, is now, and ever shall be, world without end. Amen.**

LEADER: May the body and the blood of our Lord Jesus Christ
    fill us with new life,
    enable us to love one another,
    and be for us a promise of lasting peace.

ALL: **Amen.**

Communion. (During communion a suitable hymn may be sung. After communion, the leader continues:)

LEADER: We beseech you,
send over us your Holy Spirit
and give a new face
to this earth that is dear to us.
May there be peace
wherever people live,
the peace that we cannot make ourselves
and that is more powerful than all violence,
your peace like a bond,
a new covenant between all men,
the power of Jesus Christ
here among us.
Then your name will be made holy,
Lord our God,
through him and with him and in him
everywhere on earth
and in this fellowship of the Holy Spirit
this hour and every day,
world without end.

ALL: **Amen.**

LEADER: *Blessing, Benediction, or Dismissal.*

Hymn. (A hymn of peace in Christ is suggested.)

THE INVOCATION

CHAPLAIN: Blessed is the kingdom of the Father, and of the Son, and of the Holy Spirit, now and ever, and unto ages of ages.

During Eastertide

Christ is risen from the dead, trampling down death by death and upon those in the tomb bestowing life.

PEOPLE: **Amen.**

THE GREAT LITANY

CHAPLAIN: In peace let us pray to the Lord:

PEOPLE: **Lord, have mercy.**

CHAPLAIN: For the peace from above, and for the salvation of our souls, let us pray to the Lord:

PEOPLE: **Lord, have mercy.** *Repeat after each petition.*

CHAPLAIN: For the peace of the whole world; for the welfare of the holy churches of God; and for the union of all men, let us pray to the Lord: **R**

For this holy temple and for those who enter it with faith, reverence, and fear of God, let us pray to the Lord: **R**

For the holy orthodox patriarchs of the east; for the Most Reverend_____; for the honorable priesthood; for the diaconate in Christ; for all the clergy and the people, let us pray to the Lord: **R**

For our nation, our president, our Congress, and all those in authority enabled by the American people; and for our armed forces everywhere, let us pray to the Lord: **R**

For this city [camp, base, ship, etc.], and for those faithful who dwell therein, let us pray to the Lord: **R**

For seasonable weather, for abundance of the fruits of the earth, and for peaceful times, let us pray to the Lord: **R**

For travelers by land, air, and water; for the sick and the suffering; for prisoners and captives and for their salvation, let us pray to the Lord: **R**

That he will deliver us from all tribulation, fear, danger, and want, let us pray to the Lord: **R**

Help us, save us, have mercy on us, and keep us, O God, by thy grace: **R**

CHAPLAIN: Remembering our most holy, most pure, most blessed and glorious lady, the Birth-giver of God and ever-virgin Mary, with all the saints, let us entrust ourselves and each other, and all our life, unto Christ our God:

PEOPLE: **To thee, O Lord!**

CHAPLAIN: For to thee are due all glory, honor, and worship: to the Father, and to the Son, and to the Holy Spirit, now and ever, and unto ages of ages.

PEOPLE: **Amen.**

THE FIRST ANTIPHON

See Nos. 605 to 607 for the Antiphons.

THE FIRST LITTLE LITANY

CHAPLAIN: Again and again in peace let us pray to the Lord:

PEOPLE: **Lord, have mercy.**

CHAPLAIN: Help us, save us, have mercy on us, and keep us, O God, by thy grace:

PEOPLE: **Lord, have mercy.**

CHAPLAIN: Remembering our most holy, most pure, most blessed and glorious lady, the Birth-giver of God and ever-virgin Mary, with all the saints, let us entrust ourselves and each other, and all our life, unto Christ our God:

PEOPLE: **To thee, O Lord!**

CHAPLAIN: For thine is the dominion, thine is the kingdom, the power, and the glory, of the Father, and of the Son, and of the Holy Spirit, now and ever, and unto ages of ages.

PEOPLE: **Amen.**

THE SECOND ANTIPHON

THE SECOND LITTLE LITANY

CHAPLAIN: Again and again in peace let us pray to the Lord:

PEOPLE: **Lord, have mercy.**

CHAPLAIN: Help us, save us, have mercy upon us, and keep us, O God, by thy grace:

PEOPLE: **Lord, have mercy.**

CHAPLAIN: Remembering our most holy, most pure, most blessed and glorious lady, the Birth-giver of God and ever-virgin Mary, with all the saints, let us entrust ourselves and each other, and all our life, unto Christ our God:

PEOPLE: **To thee, O Lord!**

CHAPLAIN: For thou art a loving God and a lover of mankind, and to thee we send up glory, to the Father, and to the Son, and to the Holy Spirit, now and ever, and unto ages of ages.

PEOPLE: **Amen.**

THE THIRD ANTIPHON

The Antiphon ended:

CHAPLAIN: Let us pray to the Lord:

PEOPLE: **Lord, have mercy. Rejoice and be exceedingly glad, for great is your reward in heaven.**

THE LITTLE ENTRANCE

CHAPLAIN: Wisdom! Let us attend!

PEOPLE: **O come, let us worship and bow down before Christ. Save us, O Son of God, who didst rise from the dead,* for now we sing unto thee, Alleluia!**

> **For weekdays:* **who art wonderful in the saints**
> *For Holy Birth-giver feasts:* **through the prayers of thy Birth-giver**

THE TROPARION OF THE DAY

The people sing the Troparion of the Day. See Nos. 326 ff.

616

THE DIVINE LITURGY

THE TRISAGION

PEOPLE: Holy God, holy Mighty, holy Immortal, have mercy on us. (*Three times*)

Glory to the Father, and to the Son, and to the Holy Spirit, now and ever, and unto ages of ages. Amen. Holy Immortal, have mercy on us. Holy God, holy Mighty, holy Immortal, have mercy on us.

THE EPISTLE

CHAPLAIN: Let us attend! Peace be unto you all:

READER: And to thy spirit. The Prokimenon in the _____ tone.

CHAPLAIN: Wisdom!

The people then sing the Prokimenon. See No. 608.

READER: The reading is from_____.

CHAPLAIN: Let us attend!

The reader reads the Epistle. The reading ended:

CHAPLAIN: Peace be unto thee:

READER: And to thy spirit.

CHAPLAIN: Wisdom!

PEOPLE: **Alleluia! Alleluia! Alleluia!**

THE GOSPEL

CHAPLAIN: Wisdom! Let us attend! Let us listen to the Holy Gospel. Peace be to all:

PEOPLE: **And to thy spirit.**

CHAPLAIN: The reading of the Holy Gospel according to St._____.

PEOPLE: **Glory to thee, O Lord, glory to thee.**

CHAPLAIN: Let us attend! *He then reads the Gospel. The reading ended:*

PEOPLE: **Glory to thee, O Lord, glory to thee.**

THE SERMON
THE LITANY OF FERVENT SUPPLICATION

CHAPLAIN: Let us say with all our soul and with all our mind, let us say:

PEOPLE: **Lord, have mercy.**

CHAPLAIN: O Lord Almighty, the God of our fathers, we pray thee, hearken and have mercy:

PEOPLE: **Lord, have mercy.**

CHAPLAIN: Have mercy upon us, O God, according to thy great goodness, we pray thee, hearken and have mercy:

PEOPLE: **Lord, have mercy; Lord, have mercy; Lord, have mercy.** *Repeat after each petition.*

CHAPLAIN: Again we pray for the holy orthodox patriarchs of the east, for the Most Reverend_____, and for all our brothers in Christ: **R**

Again we pray for our nation, our president, our Congress, for all those in authority enabled by the American people, and for our armed forces everywhere: **R**

Again we pray for the blessed and ever memorable holy orthodox patriarchs, for the honorable and right-believing rulers, for the founders of this holy temple, and for all our fathers and brothers, orthodox believers, departed this life before us, who here and in all the world lie asleep in the Lord: **R**

Again we pray for those who bear fruit and do good works in this holy and all-venerable temple; for the workers, the singers; and for the people here present, who look for thy great and rich mercies: **R**

For thou art a merciful God and lover of mankind, and to thee we send up glory, to the Father, and to the Son, and to the Holy Spirit, now and ever, and unto ages of ages.

PEOPLE: **Amen.**

THE LITANY FOR THE DEPARTED

CHAPLAIN: Have mercy on us, O God, according to thy great mercy; we pray thee, hearken and have mercy:

PEOPLE: **Lord, have mercy; Lord, have mercy; Lord, have mercy.** *Repeat after each petition.*

CHAPLAIN: Again we pray for the repose of the souls of the servants of God departed this life, _____, and that thou wilt pardon all their sins voluntary and involuntary: **R**

That the Lord God will establish their souls where the righteous repose: **R**

CHAPLAIN: The mercy of God, the kingdom of heaven, and the remission of sins, let us ask of Christ, our immortal King and our God.

PEOPLE: **Grant this, O Lord.**

CHAPLAIN: Let us pray to the Lord:

PEOPLE: **Lord, have mercy!**

CHAPLAIN: For thou art the resurrection, and the life, and the repose of thy departed servant —————, O Christ God, and unto thee we send up glory together with thy Father, who is from everlasting, and thine all-holy and life-giving Spirit, now and ever, and unto ages of ages.

PEOPLE: **Amen.**

THE LITANY OF THE CATECHUMENS

CHAPLAIN: Catechumens, pray unto the Lord:

PEOPLE: **Lord, have mercy!** *Repeat after each petition.*

CHAPLAIN: Let us, the faithful, pray for the catechumens, that the Lord will have mercy on them: **R**

That he will teach them the word of truth: **R**

That he will reveal to them the gospel of righteousness: **R**

That he will unite them to his holy catholic and apostolic church: **R**

CHAPLAIN: Catechumens, bow your heads unto the Lord.

PEOPLE: **To thee, O Lord!**

CHAPLAIN: That with us they may glorify thine all-honorable and majestic name of the Father and of the Son and of the Holy Spirit, now and ever, and unto ages of ages.

PEOPLE: **Amen.**

THE FIRST LITANY OF THE FAITHFUL

CHAPLAIN: All you who are catechumens, depart. Catechumens, depart. Let all catechumens depart. Let none of the catechumens remain. Let us, the faithful, again and again, in peace pray to the Lord:

PEOPLE: **Lord, have mercy.**

CHAPLAIN: Help us, save us, have mercy on us, and keep us, O God, by thy grace:

PEOPLE: **Lord, have mercy.**

CHAPLAIN: Wisdom! For unto thee are due all glory, honor, and worship, to the Father, and to the Son, and to the Holy Spirit, now and ever, and unto ages of ages.

PEOPLE: **Amen.**

CHAPLAIN: Again and again in peace let us pray to the Lord:

PEOPLE: **Lord, have mercy.**

CHAPLAIN: Help us, save us, have mercy upon us, and keep us by thy grace:

PEOPLE: **Lord, have mercy.**

CHAPLAIN: Wisdom! That guarded always by thy might we may send up glory unto thee, to the Father, and to the Son, and to the Holy Spirit, now and ever, and unto ages of ages.

PEOPLE: **Amen. Amen.**

THE CHERUBIC HYMN

The people sing the Cherubic Hymn, No. 334.

THE OFFERTORY LITANY

CHAPLAIN: Let us complete our prayer unto the Lord.

PEOPLE: **Lord, have mercy.** *Repeat after each petition.*

CHAPLAIN: For the precious gifts that are being offered, let us pray to the Lord: **R**

For this holy temple, and for those who with faith enter it, let us pray to the Lord: **R**

That he will deliver us from all tribulation, fear, danger, and want, let us pray to the Lord: **R**

Help us, save us, have mercy on us, and keep us, O God, by thy grace: **R**

CHAPLAIN: That the whole day may be perfect, holy, peaceful, and sinless, let us ask of the Lord:

PEOPLE: **Grant this, O Lord.** *Repeat after each petition.*

CHAPLAIN: An angel of peace, a faithful guide, a guardian of our souls and bodies, let us ask of the Lord: **R**

The pardon and forgiveness of our sins and transgressions, let us ask of the Lord: **R**

The things that are good and profitable for our souls, and peace for the world, let us ask of the Lord: **R**

That we may finish the remainder of our life in peace and penitence, let us ask of the Lord: **R**

A Christian end to our life, painless, blameless, peaceful; and a good defense before the awesome judgment seat of Christ, let us ask of the Lord: **R**

Remembering our most holy, most pure, most blessed and glorious lady, the Birth-giver of God and ever-virgin Mary, and all the saints, let us entrust ourselves and each other, and all our lives, unto Christ our God:

PEOPLE: **To thee, O Lord!**

CHAPLAIN: Through the mercies of thine only-begotten Son, with whom thou art blessed, with the all-holy and good and life-giving Spirit, now and ever, and unto ages of ages.

PEOPLE: **Amen.**

THE PEACE

CHAPLAIN: Peace be to all:

PEOPLE: **And to thy spirit.**

CHAPLAIN: Let us love one another, that with one mind we may confess:

PEOPLE: **Father, Son, and Holy Spirit, the Trinity, One in essence and undivided.**

CHAPLAIN: Let us stand aright; let us stand in fear; let us attend.

THE CREED

PEOPLE: **I believe in one God, the Father Almighty, maker of heaven and earth, and all things visible and invisible;**

And in one Lord Jesus Christ, the Son of God, the Only-begotten, begotten of the Father before all worlds, Light of Light, very God of very God, begotten, not made; of one essence with the Father; by whom all things were made;
Who for us men and for our salvation came down from heaven, and was incarnate of the Holy Spirit and the Virgin Mary, and was made man;

621

And was crucified also for us under Pontius Pilate, and suffered
and was buried;
And the third day he rose again, according to the Scriptures; and
ascended into heaven, and sitteth at the right hand of the Father;
and he shall come again with glory to judge the quick and the
dead, whose kingdom shall have no end;

And I believe in the Holy Spirit, the Lord and giver of life, who
proceedeth from the Father, who with the Father and the Son
together is worshiped and glorified, who spake by the prophets;
And I believe in one holy, catholic and apostolic church;
I acknowledge one baptism for the remission of sins;
I look for the resurrection of the dead;
And the life of the world to come. Amen.

THE ANAPHORA

CHAPLAIN: Let us stand aright; let us stand with fear; let us attend, that we
may offer the holy oblation in peace.

PEOPLE: **A mercy of peace, a sacrifice of praise!**

CHAPLAIN: The grace of our Lord Jesus Christ, and the love of God the
Father, and the communion of the Holy Spirit, be with you all:

PEOPLE: **And with thy spirit.**

CHAPLAIN: Let us lift up our hearts.

PEOPLE: **We lift them up unto the Lord.**

CHAPLAIN: Let us give thanks unto the Lord.

PEOPLE: **It is meet and right to worship Father, Son, and Holy Spirit, the
Trinity, One in essence and undivided:**

CHAPLAIN: Singing, crying, calling aloud the triumphal hymn, and saying:

PEOPLE: **Holy, holy, holy, Lord God of hosts; heaven and earth are full of
thy glory. Hosanna in the highest. Blessed is he that cometh in the
name of the Lord. Hosanna in the highest.**

CHAPLAIN: (*Quietly*) . . . (*aloud*) Take, eat it; this is my body which is
broken for you, for the remission of sins.

PEOPLE: **Amen.**

CHAPLAIN: (*Quietly*) And likewise, after supper, he took the cup, saying:
(*aloud*) Drink ye all of this; this is my blood of the new testament
which is shed for you and for many, for the remission of sins.

PEOPLE: **Amen. Amen.**

CHAPLAIN: Thine own, of thine own, we offer unto thee, in behalf of all and because of all.

PEOPLE: **We praise thee; we bless thee; we give thanks unto thee, O Lord; and we pray unto thee; we pray unto thee; we pray unto thee, O our God.**

THE HYMN TO THE VIRGIN

CHAPLAIN: Especially for our most holy, most pure, most blessed and glorious lady, the Birth-giver of God and ever-virgin Mary:

PEOPLE: **It is truly meet to bless thee, O Birth-giver of God, ever-blessed and most pure and the mother of our God; more honorable than the cherubim and beyond compare, more glorious than the seraphim, thou who without defilement didst bear God, the Word, true Birth-giver of God, we magnify thee.**

CHAPLAIN: Especially, O Lord, remember the holy orthodox patriarchs _____, the Most Reverend _____, and guard them for thy holy churches, that in peace, safety, honor, and health they may long live to teach aright the word of thy truth:

PEOPLE: **For each and for all!**

CHAPLAIN: And grant us with one mouth and one heart to glorify and praise thine all-honorable and majestic name of the Father and of the Son and of the Holy Spirit, now and ever, and unto ages of ages.

PEOPLE: **Amen.**

CHAPLAIN: And the mercies of our great God and Savior, Jesus Christ, be with you all:

PEOPLE: **And with thy spirit.**

THE LITANY OF PREPARATION

CHAPLAIN: Having remembered all the saints, again and again let us pray to the Lord:

PEOPLE: **Lord, have mercy.** *Repeat after each petition.*

CHAPLAIN: For the precious gifts that have been offered and sanctified, let us pray to the Lord: **R**

That our God, lover of mankind, who has received them at his holy, heavenly, and spiritual altar for a perfume of spiritual fragrance, may send down on us his divine grace and the gift of the Holy Spirit, let us pray to the Lord: **R**

That he will deliver us from all tribulation, fear, danger, and want, let us pray to the Lord: **R**

Help us, save us, have mercy on us, and keep us, O God, by thy grace: **R**

CHAPLAIN: That the whole day may be perfect, holy, peaceful, and sinless, let us ask of the Lord:

PEOPLE: **Grant this, O Lord.** *Repeat after each petition.*

CHAPLAIN: An angel of peace, a faithful guide, a guardian of our souls and bodies, let us ask of the Lord: **R**

Pardon and forgiveness of our sins and transgressions, let us ask of the Lord: **R**

The things that are good and profitable for our souls, and peace for the world, let us ask of the Lord: **R**

That we may finish the remainder of our life in peace and penitence, let us ask of the Lord: **R**

A Christian end to our life, painless, blameless, peaceful, and a good defense before the awesome judgment seat of Christ, let us ask of the Lord: **R**

CHAPLAIN: Having prayed for the unity of the faith and the communion of the Holy Spirit, let us entrust ourselves and each other unto Christ, our God:

PEOPLE: **To thee, O Lord!**

CHAPLAIN: And make us worthy, O Lord, with boldness and without condemnation to dare to call upon thee, the heavenly God, as Father, and to say:

THE LORD'S PRAYER

PEOPLE: **Our Father, who art in heaven: hallowed be thy name; thy kingdom come; thy will be done on earth as it is in heaven; give us this day our daily bread; and forgive us our trespasses, as we forgive those who trespass against us; and lead us not into temptation; but deliver us from evil;**

CHAPLAIN: For thine is the kingdom and the power and the glory, of the Father and of the Son and of the Holy Spirit, now and ever, and unto ages of ages.

624

PEOPLE: **Amen.**

CHAPLAIN: Peace be to all:

PEOPLE: **And to thy spirit.**

CHAPLAIN: Let us bow our heads unto the Lord:

PEOPLE: **To thee, O Lord!**

CHAPLAIN: Through the grace and compassion and love for mankind of thine only-begotten Son, with whom thou art blessed, together with thine all-holy, and good, and life-giving Spirit, now and ever, and unto ages of ages.

PEOPLE: **Amen. Amen.**

THE ELEVATION

CHAPLAIN: Let us attend! The holy things are for the holy.

PEOPLE: **One is holy, One is Lord, Jesus Christ, to the glory of God the Father. Amen. Praise ye the Lord from the heavens. Praise him in the highest. Alleluia. Alleluia. Alleluia.**

THE COMMUNION

CHAPLAIN: With fear of God, faith and love, draw near.

Holy Communion is now distributed to those desiring to commune.

PEOPLE: **Blessed is he who comes in the name of the Lord. The Lord is God and has appeared unto us. Receive the body and blood of Christ; taste the fountain of immortality. Alleluia. Alleluia. Alleluia.**

CHAPLAIN: O God, save thy people and bless thine inheritance.

PEOPLE: **We have seen the true light; we have received the heavenly Spirit; we have found the true faith by worshiping the undivided Trinity. This has saved us.**

CHAPLAIN: (*Quietly*) Blessed is our God . . . (*aloud*) always now and ever, and unto ages of ages.

PEOPLE: **Amen. Let our mouth be filled with thy praise, O Lord, that we may sing of thy glory; for thou hast granted us to partake of thy holy, divine, immortal, and life-giving mysteries. Keep us in thy holiness, that we may meditate on thy justice all the day long. Alleluia. Alleluia. Alleluia.**

THE LITANY OF THANKSGIVING

CHAPLAIN: Having received the divine, holy, pure, immortal, heavenly, life-giving, and awesome mysteries of Christ, let us worthily give thanks unto the Lord:

PEOPLE: **Lord, have mercy.**

CHAPLAIN: Help us, save us, have mercy on us, and keep us, O God, by thy grace:

PEOPLE: **Lord, have mercy.**

CHAPLAIN: Having prayed that the whole day may be perfect, holy, peaceful, and sinless, let us entrust ourselves and each other, and all our life, unto Christ, our God:

PEOPLE: **To thee, O Lord!**

CHAPLAIN: For thou art our sanctification, and to thee we send up glory, to the Father and to the Son and to the Holy Spirit, now and ever, and unto ages of ages.

PEOPLE: **Amen.**

CHAPLAIN: Let us depart in peace:

PEOPLE: **In the name of the Lord.**

CHAPLAIN: Let us pray to the Lord.

PEOPLE: **Lord, have mercy.**

CHAPLAIN: O Lord, who blessest those who bless thee, and sanctifiest those who put their trust in thee: save thy people and bless thine inheritance; preserve the fullness of thy church; sanctify those who love the beauty of thy house; glorify them with thy divine power, and forsake us not who put our hope in thee. Grant peace to thy world, to thy churches, to thy priests, to the President, the Congress, all those in authority enabled by the American people, and to all thy people; for every blessing and every perfect gift is from above and cometh down from thee, the Father of lights, and unto thee we send up glory, thanksgiving, and worship: to the Father and to the Son and to the Holy Spirit, now and ever, and unto ages of ages.

PEOPLE: **Amen. Blessed be the name of the Lord from this time forth and forevermore** (*three times, the third time continuing:*) **and forevermore.**

626

THE DISMISSAL

CHAPLAIN: The blessing and mercy of the Lord be upon you by his divine grace and love for mankind, always, now and ever, and unto ages of ages.

PEOPLE: **Amen.**

CHAPLAIN: Glory to thee, O Christ, our God, and our Hope, glory to thee.

PEOPLE: **Glory to the Father and to the Son and to the Holy Spirit, now and ever, and unto ages of ages. Amen. Lord, have mercy; Lord, have mercy; Lord, have mercy. Father, bless!**

CHAPLAIN: May he who rose from the dead, Christ, our true God — through the prayers of his pure and holy mother; of the holy and glorious apostles; of our father among the saints, John Chrysostom, archbishop of Constantinople; of the holy and righteous ancestors of God, Joachim and Anna; and of all the saints — have mercy upon and save us, as he is good and the lover of mankind.

PEOPLE: **Amen. Amen.**

621   Benediction of the
Blessed Sacrament

Entrance.
The rite begins with the singing of a hymn appropriate to the occasion, or all together may recite a psalm (e.g., Psalm 22 [21], No. 642; or Psalm 33 [32], No. 649.

Scripture Reading.
Suggested readings are Luke 24:13–25; John 6:1–14; 21:1–13; I Corinthians 11:23–32; 12:12–27; I John 4:7–21.

Homily.
The chaplain preaches a brief homily.

Hymn.

CHAPLAIN: You have given them the bread of heaven,

ALL: **Which has all delight within it.**

CHAPLAIN: O God, who in this wonderful sacrament left us a memorial of your passion: grant, we implore you, that we may so venerate the sacred mysteries of your body and blood as always to be conscious of the fruit of your redemption: you who live and reign with God the Father in the unity of the Holy Spirit, God, forever and ever.

ALL: **Amen.**

Blessing.
The chaplain then gives the blessing with the Blessed Sacrament.
Divine Praises.
Then shall all join in reciting the Divine Praises.

ALL: **Blessed be God.**
Blessed be his holy name.
Blessed be Jesus Christ, true God and true man.
Blessed be the name of Jesus.
Blessed be his most sacred heart.
Blessed be his most precious blood.
Blessed be Jesus in the most holy sacrament of the altar.
Blessed be the Holy Spirit, the Paraclete.

Blessed be the great mother of God, Mary most holy.
Blessed be her holy and immaculate conception.
Blessed be her glorious assumption.
Blessed be the name of Mary, virgin and mother.
Blessed be Saint Joseph, her most chaste spouse.
Blessed be God in his angels and in his saints.

Hymn.

The Rosary calls to mind the joyful, sorrowful, and glorious mysteries (events) in the life of Christ and his blessed mother. It is composed of fifteen decades—each decade consisting of one "Our Father," ten "Hail Mary's," and one "Glory be to the Father." Usually only five decades are said at one time, using one of the major divisions given above, i.e., joyful, sorrowful, or glorious mysteries.

The Apostolic Creed is said on the crucifix, the "Our Father" is said on each of the large beads, the "Hail Mary" on each of the small beads, the "Glory be to the Father" after the three "Hail Mary's" at the beginning of the rosary and after each group of small beads.

While the individual prayers are being said, we are asked to meditate or consider the event, or mystery, associated with that particular decade.

JOYFUL MYSTERIES

1. ANNOUNCEMENT TO MARY
The angel said to her: "Don't be afraid, Mary, for God has been gracious to you. You will become pregnant and give birth to a son, and you will name him Jesus. He will be great and will be called the Son of the Most High God. The Lord God will make him a king, as his ancestor David was, and he will be the king of the descendants of Jacob forever; his kingdom will never end!"

Luke 1:30–33

2. VISIT OF MARY
He shows mercy to all who fear him,
From one generation to another.
He stretched out his mighty arm
And scattered the proud people with all their plans.
He brought down mighty kings from their thrones,
And lifted up the lowly.
He filled the hungry with good things,
And sent the rich away with empty hands.

Luke 1:50–53

3. BIRTH OF CHRIST
The angel said to them: "Don't be afraid! For I am here with good news for you, which will bring great joy to all the people. This very night in David's town your Savior was born—Christ the Lord!"

Luke 2:10–11

4. PRESENTATION OF JESUS

Simeon blessed them and said to Mary, his mother: "This child is chosen by God for the destruction and the salvation of many in Israel; he will be a sign from God which many people will speak against."

Luke 2:34

5. FINDING OF JESUS IN THE TEMPLE

So Jesus went back with them to Nazareth, where he was obedient to them. His mother treasured all these things in her heart. And Jesus grew up, both in body and in wisdom, gaining favor with God and men.

Luke 2:51–52

SORROWFUL MYSTERIES

6. AGONY IN THE GARDEN

"The sorrow in my heart is so great that it almost crushes me. Stay here and watch with me." He went a little farther on, threw himself face down to the ground, and prayed, "My Father, if it is possible, take this cup away from me! But not what I want, but what you want."

Matthew 26:38–39

7. SCOURGING AT THE PILLAR

Surely he has borne our griefs
    and carried our sorrows;
yet we esteemed him stricken,
    smitten by God, and afflicted.
But he was wounded for our transgressions,
    he was bruised for our iniquities;
upon him was the chastisement that made us whole,
    and with his stripes we are healed.

Isaiah 53:4–5

8. CROWNING WITH THORNS

The soldiers made a crown of thorny branches and put it on his head; they put a purple robe on him, and came to him and said, "Long live the King of the Jews!" And they went up and slapped him. Pilate went back out once more and said to the crowd, "Look, I will bring him out here to you, to let you see that I cannot find any reason to condemn him." So Jesus went outside, wearing the crown of thorns and the purple robe. Pilate said to them, "Look! Here is the man!"

John 19:2–5

9. CARRYING THE CROSS

Fear not, for you will not be ashamed;
    be not confounded, for you will not be put to shame.
For your Maker is your husband,
    the LORD of hosts is his name;
and the Holy One of Israel is your Redeemer,
    the God of the whole earth he is called.

For the mountains may depart
  and the hills be removed,
but my steadfast love shall not depart from you,
  and my covenant of peace shall not be removed.

Isaiah 54:4,5,10

10. CRUCIFIXION

God has shown that this world's wisdom is foolishness! For God in his wisdom made it impossible for men to know him by any means of their own wisdom. Instead, God decided to save those who believe, by means of the "foolish" message we preach. Jews want miracles for proof, and Greeks look for wisdom. As for us, we proclaim Christ on the cross, a message that is offensive to the Jews and nonsense to the Gentiles; but for those whom God has called, both Jews and Gentiles, this message is Christ, who is the power of God and the wisdom of God.

I Corinthians 1:20-24

GLORIOUS MYSTERIES

11. THE RESURRECTION

God, in his own will and knowledge, had already decided that Jesus would be handed over to you; and you killed him, by letting sinful men nail him to the cross. But God raised him from the dead; he set him free from the pains of death, for it was impossible that death should hold him prisoner. God has raised this very Jesus from the dead, and we are all witnesses to this fact.

Acts 2:23-24,32

12. THE ASCENSION

"Do not hold on to me," Jesus told her, "because I have not yet gone back up to the Father. But go to my brothers and tell them for me, 'I go back up to him who is my Father and your Father, my God and your God.' "

John 20:17

13. THE COMING OF THE HOLY SPIRIT

And it shall come to pass afterward,
  that I will pour out my spirit on all flesh;
your sons and your daughters shall prophesy,
  your old men shall dream dreams,
  and your young men shall see visions.
Even upon the menservants and maidservants
  in those days, I will pour out my spirit.

Joel 2:28-29

14. THE ASSUMPTION OF MARY

With great delight I sat in his shadow,
  and his fruit was sweet to my taste.

He brought me to the banqueting house,
 and his banner over me was love.
Sustain me with raisins,
  refresh me with apples;
  for I am sick with love.
O that his left hand were under my head,
  and that his right hand embraced me!

Song of Solomon 2:3–6

15. THE CORONATION OF MARY
He stretched out his mighty arm
And lifted up the lowly.
He came to the help of his servant Israel,
And remembered to show mercy.

Luke 1:51, 52, 54

623   Sabbath and Festival Prayers

OPENING PRAYER: Psalm 95 (94)

Come, let us sing to the LORD!
Let us shout to our mighty Savior!
Let us approach him with praise
and laud him with music,
for the LORD is a powerful God,
the ruler of all other gods.
He possesses all parts of the earth,
even the tops of the mountains.
The sea is his, for he made it,
and his hands formed the dry land.
Enter! Bow down and worship!
Let us kneel to the LORD, our maker,
for he is our God
and we are his people,
his flock, the sheep of his hand.
If today you can hear his voice
do not be stubborn as you were
in the days of your wilderness wanderings,
when your forefathers tried my patience,
when they tested and saw what I did!
For forty years I despaired.
I said, "They are prone to stray.
They cannot understand my ways."
So, in my anger, I vowed
that they would not enter my haven.

SHO-LOHM AH-LAY-CHEM

(See No. 62 for this hymn.)

L'-CHO DOH-DEE

PEOPLE: **L'-cho doh-dee lik-rahs kah-lo p'-nay shah-bos n'-kah-b'-lo.**

LEADER: Come, my friend, let us welcome the Sabbath as one would go
to greet a bride.

RESPONSIVE READING

Psalm 92 (91), A Song for the Sabbath Day. (See No. 671.)

LEADER: Bless ye the Lord, who is to be blessed.

PEOPLE: **Blessed is the Lord, who is to be blessed forever and ever.**

BO-R'CHOO ES AH-DOH-NOI

LEADER: Bo-r'choo es Ah-doh-noi hah-m'-voh-roch.

PEOPLE: **Bo-rooch Ah-doh-noi hah-m'voh-roch l'oh-lom vo-ed.**

PEOPLE: **Blessed art thou, O Lord our God, King of the universe, who at thy word bringest on the evening twilight, with wisdom openest the gates of the heavens, and with understanding changest times and variest the seasons, and arrangest the stars in their watches in the sky, according to thy will. Thou createst day and night; thou rollest away the light from before the darkness, and the darkness from before the light; thou makest the day to pass and the night to approach, and dividest the day from the night; the Lord of hosts is thy name; a God living and enduring continually, mayest thou reign over us forever and ever. Blessed art thou, O Lord, who bringest on the evening twilight.**

SH'MAH YIS-RO-AYL

ALL: **Sh'mah Yis-ro-ayl Ah-doh-noi e-loh-hay-noo Ah-doh-noi e-chod.**

LEADER: Hear, O Israel: the Lord our God, the Lord is One.

PEOPLE: **And thou shalt love the Lord thy God with all thy heart, and with all thy soul, and with all thy might. And these words which I command thee this day shall be in thy heart. And thou shalt teach them diligently unto thy children, speaking of them when thou sittest in thy house and when thou walkest by the way, when thou liest down and when thou risest up. And thou shalt bind them for a sign upon thy hand, and they shall be as frontlets between thine eyes. And thou shalt write them upon the doorposts of thy house and upon thy gates.**

LEADER: True and unchanging is all this, and binding upon us, that he is the Lord our God with none beside him, and we, Israel, are his people. To thee sang Moses and all the Children of Israel, proclaiming, with great exultation:

ALL: **Mee cho-moh-cho bo-ay-leem Ah-doh-noi; mee ko-moh-cho ne-dor bah-koh-desh, noh-ro s'hil-lohs oh-say fe-le.**

PEOPLE: Who is like unto thee, Lord, among the mighty, who is like unto thee, glorious in holiness, inspiring in praises, working wonders?

MAH-L'CHOO-S'CHO

PEOPLE: Mah-l'choo-s'cho ro-oo vo-ne-cho boh-kay-ah yom lif-nay Moh-she ze ay-lee o-noo v'-om-roo. Ah-doh-noi yim-loch l'-oh-lom vo-ed.

LEADER: Thy children beheld thy sovereignty as thou didst cleave the sea before Moses; they exclaimed, "This is my God," and said, "The Lord shall reign forever and ever."

V' NE-E-MAHR

PEOPLE: V' ne-e-mahr kee fo-do Ah-doh-noi es Yah-ah-kohv oo-g'-o-loh mi-yahd cho-zok mi-me-noo; bo-rooch ah-to Ah-doh-noi go-ahl Yis-ro-ayl.

LEADER: Thus also declared Jeremiah, thy prophet, "The Lord will surely redeem Jacob and rescue him from the hand of one stronger than he." Blessed art thou, Lord, who hast redeemed Israel.

HAHSH-KEE-VAY-NOO (EVENING PRAYER)

PEOPLE: Our Father and King, grant that we may lie down in peace, and raise us up to happy and peaceful life. Spread thy shelter of peace over us and direct us with thy wise guidance. Save us speedily for thy sake. Shield us and ward off from us the stroke of enmity and the sword, pestilence and famine, misery and every form of grievous calamity and destructive disaster. Break the force of evil incitation besetting us on every side and remove it from us. Shelter us in the shadow of thy wings. Guard our going out and our coming in, that our life may be happy and peaceful henceforth forevermore. For thou art God, our guardian and deliverer from every evil and from fear in night's darkness. Blessed art thou, Lord, who ever guardest thy people Israel. Amen.

V'-SHOM-ROO

PEOPLE: V'-shom-roo v'-nay Yis-ro-ayl es hah-shah-bos [es hah-shah-bos] lah-ah-sohs es hah-shah-bos l'doh-roh-som b'rees oh-lom.

Bay-nee oo-vayn b'nay Yis-ro-ayl ohs hee l'-oh-lom [Bay-nee oo-vayn b'nay Yis-ro-ayl ohs hee l'oh-lom].

Kee shay-shes yo-meem o-so Ah-doh-noi es hah-sho-mah-yim v'es ho-o-retz oo-vah-yohm hah-sh'vee-ee sho-vahs vah-yi-no-fahsh.

636

"The Children of Israel shall keep the Sabbath, observing the Sabbath through all their generation as an everlasting covenant. It is a token between me and the Children of Israel for all time (that the Lord made heaven and earth in six days but on the seventh day he ceased from work and rested)."

KADDISH

LEADER: Yis-gah-dahl v'-yis-kah-dahsh sh'-may rah-bo!

PEOPLE: **O-mayn.**

LEADER: B'-o-l'mo dee v'-ro chi-r'oo-say, v'-yahm-leech mah-l'choo-say, b'-chah-yay-chohn oo-v'yoh-may-chohn, oo-v'cha-yay d'-chol bays Yis-ro-ayl,

PEOPLE: **bah-ah-go-lo [bah-ah-go-lo] oo-vi-z'mahn ko-reev,**

LEADER: v'-im-roo,

PEOPLE: **o-mayn. Y'-hay sh'may rah-bo m'-vo-rahch, l'-o-lahm oo-l'o-l'may-yo yis-bo-rahch.**

LEADER: Yis-bo-rahch, v'yish-tah-bahch, v'yis-po-ahr v'yis-roh-mahm, v'yis-nah-say v'yis-hah-dahr, v'yis-ah-leh, v'yis-hah-lahl sh'-may d'-koo-d'sho

PEOPLE: **b'reech hoo;**

LEADER: l'-ay-lo min kol bi-r'cho-so, v'-shee-ro-so,

PEOPLE: **tush-b'-cho-so v'-ne-che-mo-so, dah-ah-mee-ron b'-o-l'-mo,**

LEADER: v'-im-roo,

PEOPLE: **o-mayn.**

VAH-Y'CHOO-LOO

LEADER: Vah-y'choo-loo hah-sho-mah-yeem v'-ho-o-retz v'chol tz'-vo-om. Vah-y'-chahl e-loh-heem bah-yohm hah-sh'-vee-ee m'-lach-toh ah-sher o-so, vah-yish-bohs bah-yohm ha-sh'-vee-ee mi-kol m'-lahch-toh ah-sher o-so. Vah-y'-vo-rech e-loh-heem es yohm hah-sh'-vee-ee vah-y'kah-daysh o-so, kee voh sho-vahs mi-kol m'-lahch-toh a-sher bo-ro e-loh-heem lah-ah-sohs.

LEADER: "Then were finished the heavens and the earth and all their host. And God had finished by the seventh day his work which he had made, and he rested on the seventh day from all his work which he had made. Then God blessed the seventh day and hallowed it, because thereon he rested from all his work which he had created."

*At this point, the **Amidah** is read in silent devotion.*

BIR-CHAHS O-VOHS

PEOPLE: **Bo-rooch ah-to Ah-doh-noi eh-loh-hay-noo vay-loh-hay ah-voh-say-noo, eh-loh-hay Ah-v'roh-hom eh-loh-hay Yitz-chok vay-loh-hay Yah-ah-kohv, ho-ayl ha-go-dohl ha-gi-bohr v'-hah-noh-ro ayl el-yohn, koh-nay sho-mah-yeem vo-o-retz.**

PEOPLE: **Blessed art thou, Lord our God, God of our fathers, God of Abraham, God of Isaac, God of Jacob, God great, powerful and awe-inspiring, God sublime, lavishing tender love. Master of all, thou yet art mindful of the pious love of our fathers, and for thine own sake thou wilt lovingly bring a Redeemer to their children's children.**

   O King, who dost succor, save, and shield, blessed art thou, Lord, shield of Abraham.

LEADER: Lord, who art mighty unto eternity, thou givest life to the dead. Thou art mighty in saving the living, in love sustaining them. Thou upholdest the falling, thou healest the sick, thou loosenest the bound. In thy great love thou givest life to the dead, keeping faith with them who sleep in dust. Who is like unto thee, Lord of power; who resembles thee, King who sendest death and in the flowering of thy saving power givest life?

   Faithful art thou to give life to the dead, Lord; blessed art thou who givest life to the dead.

PEOPLE: **Thou art holy; thy name is holy and the holy ones each day shall praise thee evermore; blessed art thou, Lord, the holy God.**

SABBATH REST AND PEACE

PEOPLE: **Our God and God of our fathers, accept our rest; sanctify us by thy commandments, and grant our portion in thy law; satisfy us with thy goodness, and gladden us with thy salvation; purify our hearts to serve thee in truth; and in thy love and favor, O Lord our God, let us inherit thy holy Sabbath; and may Israel, who hallow thy name, rest thereon. Blessed art thou, O Lord, who hallowest the Sabbath.**

LEADER: Grant us peace, thy most precious gift, O thou eternal source of peace, and enable Israel to be its messenger unto the peoples of the earth. Bless our country, that it may ever be a stronghold of peace, and the advocate of peace in council of nations. May contentment reign within its borders, health and happiness within its homes. Strengthen the bonds of friendship and fellowship among all the inhabitants of our land. Plant virtue in every soul, and may the love of thy name hallow every home and every heart. Praised be thou, Giver of peace.

MAY THE WORDS OF MY MOUTH

ALL: **May the words of my mouth and the meditations of my heart be acceptable in thy sight, O Lord, my Strength and my Redeemer. Amen.**

KIDDUSH

(See No. 611 for the words and music of the Kiddush.)

ADORATION

Arise and read in unison.

PEOPLE: **Let us praise the Lord of all the earth
And acclaim the might of the God of creation.
For he has not made us heathens,
Nor allowed us to be a pagan people.
We bow low before the supreme King of kings,
The Holy One, blessed be he.**

VAH-AH-NAHCH-NOO

PEOPLE: **Vah-ah-nahch-noo koh-r'-eem oo-mish-tah-chah-veem oo-moh-deem li-f'nay me-lech mah-l'chay hah-m'lo-cheem hah-ko-dohsh bo-rooch hoo.**

PEOPLE: **May the time not be distant, O God, when thy name shall be worshiped in all the earth, when unbelief shall disappear and error be no more. We fervently pray that the day may come when all men shall invoke thy name, when corruption and evil shall give way to purity and goodness, when superstition shall no longer enslave the mind, nor idolatry blind the eye, when all inhabitants of the earth shall know that to thee alone every knee must bend and every tongue give homage. O may all, created in thine image, recognize that they are brethren, so that, one in spirit and one in fellowship, they may be forever united before thee. Then shall thy kingdom be established on earth and the word of thine ancient seer be fulfilled: The Lord will reign forever and ever. On that day the Lord shall be One and his name shall be One.**

BAH-YOHM

PEOPLE: Bah-yohm hah-hoo, [bah-yohm hah-hoo] yi-h'ye Ah-doh-noi e-chod oo-sh'-moh, [oo-sh'-moh, oo-sh'-moh] e-chod.

MOURNERS' KADDISH

LEADER: And now ere we part, let us call to mind those who have finished their earthly course and have been gathered to the eternal home. Wait patiently, all ye that mourn, and be ye of good courage, for surely your longing souls shall be satisfied.

Mourners recite **Kaddish** *at this time.*

MOURNERS: Yis-gah-dahl v'yis-kah-dahsh sh'may rah-bo; B'o-l'mo dee-v'ro chi-r'oo-say, v'yahm-leech mah-l'choo-say, b'chah-yay-chohn oo-v'yoh-may-chon, oo-v'cha-yay d'chol bays Yis-ro-ayl, bah-ah-go-lo oo-vi-z'mahn ko-reev, v'i-m'roo o-mayn.

Y'hay sh'may rah-bo m'vo-rahch, l'o-lahm oo-l'o-l'may o-l'may-yo.

Yis-bo-rahch, v'yish-tah-bahch, v'yis-po-ahr v'yis-roh-mahm, v'yis-nah-say v'yis-hah-dahr, v'yis-ah-leh, v'yis-hah-lahl sh'may d'koo-d'sho b'reech hoo; l'ay-lo min kol bi-r'cho-so, v'shee-ro-so, tush-b'cho-so v'ne-che-mo-so, dah-ah-mee-ron b'o-l'mo, v'i-m'roo o-mayn. Y'hay sh'lo-mo rah-bo min sh'mah-yo v'chah-yeem o-lay-noo v'ahl kol Yis-ro-ayl v'i-m'roo o-mayn.

O-se sho-lohm bim-roh-mov hoo yah-ah-se sho-lohm o-lay-noo v'ahl kol Yis-ro-ayl v'i-m'roo o-mayn.

CLOSING HYMNS

(See Nos. 61, 65, 66, 68 for these hymns.)

READING OF SCRIPTURE: Psalm 24 (23)

The LORD owns the earth and its contents,
the world and its creatures.
On the waters primeval he built it;
over the torrents he made it.
Who can climb the LORD's hill?
Who can go up to his sanctuary?
The man with clean hands and an honest mind,
who does not foolishly pledge his life
nor take an oath in deceit.
He carries a blessing away from the LORD,
vindication from the God who saves him.
Seek the Eternal One,
You who search for the Presence of Jacob!
Lift up your heads, O gates!
Be raised, O ancient doors!
The glorious King arrives.
Who is this glorious King?
The LORD, the strong, the hero,
The LORD, the hero of war.
Lift up your heads, O gates!
Be raised, O ancient doors!
The glorious King arrives.
Who is this glorious King?
The LORD of armies,
he is the glorious King.

VAH-Y'-HEE BIN-SOH-AH

Vah-y'-hee bin-soh-ah ho-o-rohn vah-yoh-mer Moh-she: koo-mo Ah-doh-noi
v'-yo-foo-tzoo oh-y'-ve-cho v'-yo-noo-soo m'-sahn-e-cho mi-po-ne-cho.

KEE MI-TZEE-YOHN

Kee mi-tzee-yohn tay-tzay soh-ro, Kee mi-tzee-yohn tay-tzay soh-ro, oo-
d'var Ah-doh-noi mee-roo-sho-lo-yim.

SH'MAH YIS-RO-AYL

Sh'mah Yis-ro-ayl Ah-doh-noi e-loh-hay-noo Ah-doh-noi e-chod. E-chod
e-hoh-hay-noo go-dohl ah-doh-nay-noo ko-dohsh sh'-moh.

GAH-D'LOO

Gah-d'-loo lah-doh-noi i-tee oo-n'-roh-m'-mo sh'-moh yach-dov.

L'CHO AH-DOH-NOI HAH-G'DOO-LO

L'-cho Ah-doh-noi hah-g'-doo-lo v'-hah-g'-voo-ro v'hah-tif-e-res v'-hah-nai-tzach v'hah-hohd. Kee chol bah-sho-mah-yim oo-vo-o-retz, [kee chol bah-sho-mah-yim oo-vo-o-retz] l'-cho Ah-doh-noi ha-mahm-lo-cho v'hah-mis-nah-say l'chol l'-rohsh.

BLESSING BEFORE READING THE TORAH

Bo-r'-choo es Ah-doh-noi hah-m'-voh-roch. Bo-rooch Ah-doh-noi hah-m'voh-roch l'oh-lom vo-ed. Bo-rooch ah-to Ah-doh-noi e-loh-hay-noo me-lech ho-oh-lom ah-sher bo-chahr bo-noo mi-kol ho-ah-meem v'-no-sahn lo-noo es toh-ro-soh. Bo-rooch ah-to Ah-doh-noi noh-sayn hah-toh-ro.

BLESSING AFTER READING THE TORAH

Bo-rooch ah-to Ah-doh-noi e-loh-hay-noo me-lech ho-oh-lom ah-sher no-sahn lo-noo toh-rahs e-mes v'chah-yay oh-lom no-tah b'soh-chay-noo. Bo-rooch ah-to Ah-doh-noi noh-sayn hah-toh-ro.

Y'HAH-L'LOO

Y'hah-l'-loo es shaym Ah-doh-noi kee nis-gov sh'mo l'-vah-doh.

HOH-DOH AHL E-RETZ

Hoh-doh ahl e-retz v'-sho-mo-yim vah-yo-rem ke-ren l'-ah-mo, t'-hi-lo l'-chol chah-see-dov li-v'-nay Yis-ro-ayl ahm k'-roh-voh hah-l'-loo-yo, hah-l'loo-yo.

AYTZ CHAH-YEEM

Aytz chah-yeem hee lah-mah-chah-zee-keem bo v'-soh-m'-che-ho m'-oo-shor. D'-ro-che-ho dah-r'-chay noh-ahm v-chol n'-see-voh-se-ho sho-lohm. Hah-shee-vay-noo Ah-doh-noi ay-le-cho v'-no-shoo-vo cha-daysh, cha-daysh yo-may-noo, cha-daysh yo-may-noo k'-ke-dem. O-mayn.

SABBATH HYMNS

(See Nos. 58 and 60 for these hymns.)

FESTIVAL HYMNS

(See Nos. 59, 63, 64, 67, 69 for these hymns.)

THE TEN COMMANDMENTS

(See No. 705 for this text.)

PRELUDE

OPENING SENTENCE(S)
(One or more of the following may be used: Deuteronomy 33:27a; Psalm 27 [26]:1; Isaiah 35:4.)

HYMN

INVOCATION
(This prayer must be general and ecumenical.*)

RESPONSIVE READING
(See the Psalter, Nos. 632–684, or Other Scripture Selections, Nos. 685–726.)

SPECIAL MUSIC
(This may be instrumental or choral.)

SCRIPTURE LESSON
(This may be from the Scripture Readings for the Year, Nos. 628–629; the Psalter, Nos. 632–684; or Other Scripture Selections, Nos. 685–726.)

ADDRESS

MOMENT OF SILENCE

TAPS

HYMN

BENEDICTION

POSTLUDE

(Consult the Service Manual for possible military honors.)

*If desired, the following litany may be used:
Let us give thanks to God for the land of our birth with all its chartered liberties. For all the wonder of our country's story:

We give you thanks, O God.

For leaders in nation and state, and for those who in days past and in these present times have labored for the commonwealth:

We give you thanks, O God.

For those who in all times and places have been true and brave, and in the world's common ways have lived upright lives and ministered to their fellows:

We give you thanks, O God.

For those who served their country in her hour of need, and especially for those who gave even their lives in that service:

We give you thanks, O God.

O almighty God and most merciful Father, as we remember these your servants, remembering with gratitude their courage and strength, we hold before you those who mourn them. Look upon your bereaved servants with your mercy. As this day brings them memories of those they have lost awhile, may it also bring your consolation and the assurance that their loved ones are alive now and forever in your living presence.

Amen.

PRELUDE

POSTING OF THE COLORS

NATIONAL ANTHEM
   (*No. 201.*)

INVOCATION

RESPONSIVE READING
   (*See Nos. 685–726.*)

INTRODUCTION OF SPECIAL GUESTS
   (*optional*)

SPECIAL MUSIC

SCRIPTURE LESSON(S)
   (*See Suggested Scripture Readings for the Year, Nos. 628–629.*)

ADDRESS

HYMN

RETIRING OF THE COLORS

BENEDICTION

POSTLUDE

   (*Consult the Service Manual for possible military honors.*)

627　Dedication of Religious Facility, Interfaith

PRELUDE

PRESENTATION OF COLORS

NATIONAL ANTHEM (*No. 201*)

INVOCATION

HYMN

PRESENTATION OF FACILITY

ACCEPTANCE OF FACILITY

INTRODUCTION OF GUESTS

SPECIAL MUSIC

ADDRESS

ACT OF DEDICATION
　　Psalm 95 (94), No. 673; 100 (99), No. 677

PRAYER OF DEDICATION

HYMN

BENEDICTION

CHORAL RESPONSE

POSTLUDE

Lectionary

Selections for the Christian Year **628**

This lectionary is a table of lessons and Gospel readings for the Sundays, festivals, and special days of the church year. Suggested readings are listed to cover a three-year period. The general structure of the lectionary, as well as the passages listed for particular days, follows widely accepted ecumenical usage.

In most cases the Gospel reading may be considered primary, the two other lessons being chosen to go with it. No attempt has been made to achieve a rigid thematic structure of readings for each Sunday. The lessons are intended, rather, to be appropriate to the season under which they are listed. If only two of the three readings are used, the Gospel should ordinarily be retained as one of them. The length of passages shown in the tables assumes that all three will be read. They may, of course, be appropriately lengthened or shortened to fit particular circumstances, as desired.

Psalms and responsive readings for each season have been listed in another section of this book. Prayers appropriate to various times of the Christian year are also printed in this book.

For those chapels accustomed to using the symbolism of color in observing the church year, the following summary of popular usage will be helpful:

Advent.. Violet
Christmas Eve and Christmastide............................... White
Epiphany... White
Lent.. Violet
Holy Week
    Monday, Tuesday, Wednesday............................. Violet
    Maundy Thursday.. White
    Good Friday.. Red
Eastertide.. White
Pentecost Sunday (and week following)........................ Red
Trinity Sunday (and week following)............................ White
Other Sundays after Pentecost (and weekdays).............. Green

ADVENT

A period in which the church joyfully remembers the coming of Christ and eagerly looks forward to his coming again. Beginning with the Sunday nearest November 30, the season is observed for the four Sundays prior to Christmas.

Sunday or Festival	Year	First Lesson	Second Lesson	Gospel
1 Advent	A	Isa. 2:1–5	Rom. 13:11–14	Matt. 24:36–44
	B	Isa. 63:16 to 64:4	I Cor. 1:3–9	Mark 13:32–37
	C	Jer. 33:14–16	I Thess. 5:1–6	Luke 21:25–36
2 Advent	A	Isa. 11:1–10	Rom. 15:4–9	Matt. 3:1–12
	B	Isa. 40:1–5, 9–11	II Peter 3:8–14	Mark 1:1–8
	C	Isa. 9:2, 6–7	Phil. 1:3–11	Luke 3:1–6
3 Advent	A	Isa. 35:1–6, 10	James 5:7–10	Matt. 11:2–11
	B	Isa. 61:1–4, 8–11	I Thess. 5:16–24	John 1:6–8, 19–28
	C	Zeph. 3:14–19	Phil. 4:4–9	Luke 3:10–18
4 Advent	A	Isa. 7:10–15	Rom. 1:1–7	Matt. 1:18–25
	B	II Sam. 7:8–16	Rom. 16:25–27	Luke 1:26–38
	C	Micah 5:1–4	Heb. 10:5–10	Luke 1:39–47
Christmas Eve	A	Isa. 62:1–4	Col. 1:15–20	Luke 2:1–14
	B	Isa. 52:7–10	Heb. 1:1–9	John 1:1–14
	C	Zech. 2:10–13	Phil. 4:4–7	Luke 2:15–20

CHRISTMASTIDE

The festival of the birth of Christ, the celebration of the incarnation; a twelve-day period from December 25 to January 5, which may include either one or two Sundays after Christmas.

Sunday or Festival	Year	First Lesson	Second Lesson	Gospel
Christmas Day	A	Isa. 9:2, 6–7	Titus 2:11–15	Luke 2:1–14
	B	Isa. 62:6–12	Col. 1:15–20	Matt. 1:18–25
	C	Isa. 52:6–10	Eph. 1:3–10	John 1:1–14
Christmas I	A	Eccl. 3:1–9, 14–17	Col. 3:12–17	Matt. 2:13–15, 19–23
	B	Jer. 31:10–13	Heb. 2:10–18	Luke 2:25–35
	C	Isa. 45:18–22	Rom. 11:33 to 12:2	Luke 2:41–52
Christmas II	A	Prov. 8:22–31	Eph. 1:15–23	John 1:1–5, 9–14
	B	Isa. 60:1–5	Rev. 21:22 to 22:2	Luke 2:21–24
	C	Job 28:20–28	I Cor. 1:18–25	Luke 2:36–40

EPIPHANY

A season marking the revelation of God's gift of himself to all men. Beginning with the day of Epiphany (January 6), this season continues until Ash Wednesday and can include from four to nine Sundays.

Sunday or Festival	Year	First Lesson	Second Lesson	Gospel
Epiphany	ABC	Isa. 60:1-6	Eph. 3:1-6	Matt. 2:1-12
Epiphany I	A	Isa. 42:1-7	Acts 10:34-43	Matt. 3:13-17
	B	Isa. 61:1-4	Acts 11:4-18	Mark 1:4-11
	C	Gen. 1:1-5	Eph. 2:11-18	Luke 3:15-17, 21-22
			(or readings for day of Epiphany if observed on Sunday)	
Epiphany II	A	Isa. 49:3-6	I Cor. 1:1-9	John 1:29-34
	B	I Sam. 3:1-10	I Cor. 6:12-20	John 1:35-42
	C	Isa. 62:2-5	I Cor. 12:4-11	John 2:1-12
Epiphany III	A	Isa. 9:1-4	I Cor. 1:10-17	Matt. 4:12-23
	B	Jonah 3:1-5, 10	I Cor. 7:29-31	Mark 1:14-22
	C	Neh. 8:1-3, 5-6, 8-10	I Cor. 12:12-30	Luke 4:14-21
Epiphany IV	A	Zeph. 2:3; 3:11-13	I Cor. 1:26-31	Matt. 5:1-12
	B	Deut. 18:15-22	I Cor. 7:32-35	Mark 1:21-28
	C	Jer. 1:4-10	I Cor. 13:1-13	Luke 4:22-30
Epiphany V	A	Isa. 58:7-10	I Cor. 2:1-5	Matt. 5:13-16
	B	Job 7:1-7	I Cor. 9:16-19, 22-23	Mark 1:29-39
	C	Isa. 6:1-8	I Cor. 15:1-11	Luke 5:1-11
Epiphany VI	A	Deut. 30:15-20	I Cor. 2:6-10	Matt. 5:27-37
	B	Lev. 13:1-2, 44-46	I Cor. 10:31 to 11:1	Mark 1:40-45
	C	Jer. 17:5-8	I Cor. 15:12-20	Luke 6:17-26
Epiphany VII	A	Lev. 19:1-2, 17-18	I Cor. 3:16-23	Matt. 5:38-48
	B	Isa. 43:18-25	II Cor. 1:18-22	Mark 2:1-12
	C	I Sam. 26:6-12	I Cor. 15:42-50	Luke 6:27-36
Epiphany VIII	A	Isa. 49:14-18	I Cor. 4:1-5	Matt. 6:24-34
	B	Hos. 2:14-20	II Cor. 3:17 to 4:2	Mark 2:18-22
	C	Job 23:1-7	I Cor. 15:54-58	Luke 6:39-45
Epiphany IX		(Use readings for Pentecost XXVII)		

649

LENT

A period of forty days (not counting Sundays), beginning Ash Wednesday and continuing through Holy Saturday. In joy and sorrow during this season, the church proclaims, remembers, and responds to the death and resurrection of Christ.

Sunday or Day	Year	First Lesson	Second Lesson	Gospel
Ash Wednesday	A	Joel 2:12–18	II Cor. 5:20 to 6:2	Matt. 6:1–6, 16–18
	B	Isa. 58:3–12	James 1:12–18	Mark 2:15–20
	C	Zech. 7:4–10	I Cor. 9:19–27	Luke 5:29–35
1 in Lent	A	Gen. 2:7–9; 3:1–7	Rom. 5:12–19	Matt. 4:1–11
	B	Gen. 9:8–15	I Peter 3:18–22	Mark 1:12–15
	C	Deut. 26:5–11	Rom. 10:8–13	Luke 4:1–13
2 in Lent	A	Gen. 12:1–7	II Tim. 1:8–14	Matt. 17:1–9
	B	Gen. 22:1–2, 9–13	Rom. 8:31–39	Mark 9:1–9
	C	Gen. 15:5–12, 17–18	Phil. 3:17 to 4:1	Luke 9:28–36
3 in Lent	A	Ex. 24:12–18	Rom. 5:1–5	John 4:5–15, 19–26
	B	Ex. 20:1–3, 7–8, 12–17	I Cor. 1:22–25	John 2:13–25
	C	Ex. 3:1–8, 13–15	I Cor. 10:1–12	Luke 13:1–9
4 in Lent	A	II Sam. 5:1–5	Eph. 5:8–14	John 9:1–11
	B	II Chron. 36:14–21	Eph. 2:1–10	John 3:14–21
	C	Josh. 5:9–12	II Cor. 5:16–21	Luke 15:11–32
5 in Lent	A	Ezek. 37:11–14	Rom. 8:6–11	John 11:1–4, 17, 34–44
	B	Jer. 31:31–34	Heb. 5:7–10	John 12:20–33
	C	Isa. 43:16–21	Phil. 3:8–14	Luke 22:14–30
Palm Sunday	A	Isa. 50:4–7	Phil. 2:5–11	Matt. 21:1–11
	B	Zech. 9:9–12	Heb. 12:1–6	Mark 11:1–11
	C	Isa. 59:14–20	I Tim. 1:12–17	Luke 19:28–40

HOLY WEEK

The week prior to Easter, during which the church gratefully celebrates the suffering and death of Jesus Christ.

Day of Holy Week	Year	First Lesson	Second Lesson	Gospel
Monday	ABC	Isa. 50:4–10	Heb. 9:11–15	Luke 19:41–48
Tuesday	ABC	Isa. 42:1–9	I Tim. 6:11–16	John 12:37–50
Wednesday	ABC	Isa. 52:13 to 53:12	Rom. 5:6–11	Luke 22:1–16
Maundy Thursday	A	Ex. 12:1–8, 11–14	I Cor. 11:23–32	John 13:1–15
	B	Deut. 16:1–8	Rev. 1:4–8	Matt. 26:17–30
	C	Num. 9:1–3, 11–12	I Cor. 5:6–8	Mark 14:12–26

HOLY WEEK (Continued)

Day of Holy Week	Year	First Lesson	Second Lesson	Gospel
Good Friday	A	Isa. 52:13 to 53:12	Heb. 4:14–16; 5:7–9	John 19:17–30
	B	Lam. 1:7–12	Heb. 10:4–18	Luke 23:33–46
	C	Hos. 6:1–6	Rev. 5:6–14	Matt. 27:31–50

EASTERTIDE

A fifty-day period of seven Sundays, beginning with Easter, the festival of Christ's resurrection. Ascension Day, forty days after Easter, is celebrated to affirm that Jesus Christ is Lord of all times and places.

Sunday or Festival	Year	First Lesson	Second Lesson	Gospel
Easter Day	A	Acts 10:34–43	Col. 3:1–11	John 20:1–9
	B	Isa. 25:6–9	I Peter 1:3–9	Mark 16:1–8
	C	Ex. 15:1–11	I Cor. 15:20–26	Luke 24:13–35
Easter II	A	Acts 2:42–47	I Peter 1:3–9	John 20:19–31
	B	Acts 4:32–35	I John 5:1–6	Matt. 28:11–20
	C	Acts 5:12–16	Rev. 1:9–13, 17–19	John 21:1–14
Easter III	A	Acts 2:22–28	I Peter 1:17–21	Luke 24:13–35
	B	Acts 3:13–15, 17–19	I John 2:1–6	Luke 24:36–49
	C	Acts 5:27–32	Rev. 5:11–14	John 21:15–19
Easter IV	A	Acts 2:36–41	I Peter 2:19–25	John 10:1–10
	B	Acts 4:8–12	I John 3:1–3	John 10:11–18
	C	Acts 13:44–52	Rev. 7:9–17	John 10:22–30
Easter V	A	Acts 6:1–7	I Peter 2:4–10	John 14:1–12
	B	Acts 9:26–31	I John 3:18–24	John 15:1–8
	C	Acts 14:19–28	Rev. 21:1–5	John 13:31–35
Easter VI	A	Acts 8:4–8, 14–17	I Peter 3:13–18	John 14:15–21
	B	Acts 10:34–48	I John 4:1–7	John 15:9–17
	C	Acts 15:1–2, 22–29	Rev. 21:10–14, 22–23	John 14:23–29
Ascension	ABC	Acts 1:1–11	Eph. 1:16–23	Luke 24:44–53
Easter VII	A	Acts 1:12–14	I Peter 4:12–19	John 17:1–11
	B	Acts 1:15–17, 21–26	I John 4:11–16	John 17:11–19
	C	Acts 7:55–60	Rev. 22:12–14, 16–17, 20	John 17:20–26

(or readings for Ascension if observed on Sunday)

PENTECOST

The festival celebrating the giving of the Holy Spirit to the church, and an extended season to reflect on the life of God's people under the guidance of his Spirit. The season extends from Pentecost, or Whitsunday, to the beginning of Advent.

Sunday	Year	First Lesson	Second Lesson	Gospel
Pentecost	A	I Cor. 12:4–13	Acts 2:1–13	John 14:15–26
	B	Joel 2:28–32	(as in A)	John 16:5–15
	C	Isa. 65:17–25	(as in A)	John 14:25–31
Pentecost I	A	Ezek. 37:1–4	II Cor. 13:5–13	Matt. 28:16–20
(Trinity)	B	Isa. 6:1–8	Rom. 8:12–17	John 3:1–8
	C	Prov. 8:22–31	I Peter 1:1–9	John 20:19–23
Pentecost II	A	Deut. 11:18–21	Rom. 3:21–28	Matt. 7:21–29
	B	Deut. 5:12–15	II Cor. 4:6–11	Mark 2:23 to 3:6
	C	I Kings 8:41–43	Gal. 1:1–10	Luke 7:1–10
Pentecost III	A	Hos. 6:1–6	Rom. 4:13–25	Matt. 9:9–13
	B	Gen. 3:9–15	II Cor. 4:13 to 5:1	Mark 3:20–35
	C	I Kings 17:17–24	Gal. 1:11–19	Luke 7:11–17
Pentecost IV	A	Ex. 19:2–6	Rom. 5:6–11	Matt. 9:36 to 10:8
	B	Ezek. 17:22–24	II Cor. 5:6–10	Mark 4:26–34
	C	II Sam. 12:1–7a	Gal. 2:15–21	Luke 7:36–50
Pentecost V	A	Jer. 20:10–13	Rom. 5:12–15	Matt. 10:26–33
	B	Job 38:1–11	II Cor. 5:16–21	Mark 4:35–41
	C	Zech. 12:7–10	Gal. 3:23–29	Luke 9:18–24
Pentecost VI	A	II Kings 4:8–16	Rom. 6:1–11	Matt. 10:37–42
	B	Gen. 4:3–10	II Cor. 8:7–15	Mark 5:21–43
	C	I Kings 19:15–21	Gal. 5:1, 13–18	Luke 9:51–62
Pentecost VII	A	Zech. 9:9–13	Rom. 8:6–11	Matt. 11:25–30
	B	Ezek. 2:1–5	II Cor. 12:7–10	Mark 6:1–6
	C	Isa. 66:10–14	Gal. 6:11–18	Luke 10:1–9
Pentecost VIII	A	Isa. 55:10–13	Rom. 8:12–17	Matt. 13:1–17
	B	Amos 7:12–17	Eph. 1:3–10	Mark 6:7–13
	C	Deut. 30:9–14	Col. 1:15–20	Luke 10:25–37
Pentecost IX	A	II Sam. 7:18–22	Rom. 8:18–25	Matt. 13:24–35
	B	Jer. 23:1–6	Eph. 2:11–18	Mark 6:30–34
	C	Gen. 18:1–11	Col. 1:24–28	Luke 10:38–42
Pentecost X	A	I Kings 3:5–12	Rom. 8:26–30	Matt. 13:44–52
	B	II Kings 4:42–44	Eph. 4:1–6, 11–16	John 6:1–15
	C	Gen. 18:20–33	Col. 2:8–15	Luke 11:1–13
Pentecost XI	A	Isa. 55:1–3	Rom. 8:31–39	Matt. 14:13–21
	B	Ex. 16:2–4, 12–15	Eph. 4:17–24	John 6:24–35
	C	Eccl. 2:18–23	Col. 3:1–11	Luke 12:13–21

PENTECOST (Continued)

Pentecost XII	A	I Kings 19:9–16	Rom. 9:1–5	Matt. 14:22–33
	B	I Kings 19:4–8	Eph. 4:30 to 5:2	John 6:41–51
	C	II Kings 17:33–40	Heb. 11:1–3, 8–12	Luke 12:35–40
Pentecost XIII	A	Isa. 56:1–7	Rom. 11:13–16, 29–32	Matt. 15:21–28
	B	Prov. 9:1–6	Eph. 5:15–20	John 6:51–59
	C	Jer. 38:1b–13	Heb. 12:1–6	Luke 12:49–53
Pentecost XIV	A	Isa. 22:19–23	Rom. 11:33–36	Matt. 16:13–20
	B	Josh. 24:14–18	Eph. 5:21–33	John 6:60–69
	C	Isa. 66:18–23	Heb. 12:7–13	Luke 13:22–30
Pentecost XV	A	Jer. 20:7–9	Rom. 12:1–7	Matt. 16:21–28
	B	Deut. 4:1–8	James 1:19–25	Mark 7:1–8, 14–15, 21–23
	C	Prov. 22:1–9	Heb. 12:18–24	Luke 14:1, 7–14
Pentecost XVI	A	Ezek. 33:7–9	Rom. 13:8–10	Matt. 18:15–20
	B	Isa. 35:4–7	James 2:1–5	Mark 7:31–37
	C	Prov. 9:8–12	Philemon 8–17	Luke 14:25–33
Pentecost XVII	A	Gen. 4:13–16	Rom. 14:5–9	Matt. 18:21–35
	B	Isa. 50:4–9	James 2:14–18	Mark 8:27–35
	C	Ex. 32:7–14	I Tim. 1:12–17	Luke 15:1–32
Pentecost XVIII	A	Isa. 55:6–11	Phil. 1:21–27	Matt. 20:1–16
	B	Jer. 11:18–20	James 3:13 to 4:3	Mark 9:30–37
	C	Amos 8:4–8	I Tim. 2:1–8	Luke 16:1–13
Pentecost XIX	A	Ezek. 18:25–29	Phil. 2:1–11	Matt. 21:28–32
	B	Num. 11:24–30	James 5:1–6	Mark 9:38–48
	C	Amos 6:1, 4–7	I Tim. 6:11–16	Luke 16:19–31
Pentecost XX	A	Isa. 5:1–7	Phil. 4:4–9	Matt. 21:33–43
	B	Gen. 2:18–24	Heb. 2:9–13	Mark 10:2–16
	C	Hab. 1:1–3; 2:1–4	II Tim. 1:3–12	Luke 17:5–10
Pentecost XXI	A	Isa. 25:6–9	Phil. 4:12–20	Matt. 22:1–14
	B	Prov. 3:13–18	Heb. 4:12–16	Mark 10:17–27
	C	II Kings 5:9–17	II Tim. 2:8–13	Luke 17:11–19
Pentecost XXII	A	Isa. 45:1–6	I Thess. 1:1–5b	Matt. 22:15–22
	B	Isa. 53:10–12	Heb. 5:1–10	Mark 10:35–45
	C	Ex. 17:8–13	II Tim. 3:14 to 4:2	Luke 18:1–8
Pentecost XXIII	A	Ex. 22:21–27	I Thess. 1:2–10	Matt. 22:34–40
	B	Jer. 31:7–9	Heb. 5:1–6	Mark 10:46–52
	C	Deut. 10:16–22	II Tim. 4:6–8, 16–18	Luke 18:9–14
Pentecost XXIV	A	Mal. 2:1–10	I Thess. 2:7–13	Matt. 23:1–12
	B	Deut. 6:1–9	Heb. 7:23–28	Mark 12:28–34
	C	Ex. 34:5–9	II Thess. 1:11 to 2:2	Luke 19:1–10

PENTECOST (Continued)

Sunday	Year	First Lesson	Second Lesson	Gospel
Pentecost XXV	A	S. of Sol. 3:1–5	I Thess. 4:13–18	Matt. 25:1–13
	B	I Kings 17:8–16	Heb. 9:24–28	Mark 12:38–44
	C	I Chron. 29:10–13	II Thess. 2:16 to 3:5	Luke 20:27–38
Pentecost XXVI	A	Prov. 31:10–13, 19–20, 30–31	I Thess. 5:1–6	Matt. 25:14–30
	B	Dan. 12:1–4	Heb. 10:11–18	Mark 13:24–32
	C	Mal. 3:16 to 4:2	II Thess. 3:6–13	Luke 21:5–19
Pentecost XXVII	A	Ezek. 34:11–17	I Cor. 15:20–28	Matt. 25:31–46
	B	Dan. 7:13–14	Rev. 1:4–8	John 18:33–37
	C	II Sam. 5:1–4	Col. 1:11–20	Luke 23:35–43
Pentecost XXVIII			(Use readings for Epiphany VIII)	

SPECIAL DAYS

It is fitting that other days be celebrated which recall the heritage of the church, proclaim its mission, and forward its work; and also days which recognize the civic responsibilities of the people.

Special Day	Year	First Lesson	Second Lesson	Gospel
New Year's Eve or Day	A	Deut. 8:1–10	Rev. 21:1–7	Matt. 25:31–46
	B	Eccl. 3:1–13	Col. 2:1–7	Matt. 9:14–17
	C	Isa. 49:1–10	Eph. 3:1–10	Luke 14:16–24
Christian Unity	A	Isa. 11:1–9	Eph. 4:1–16	John 15:1–8
	B	Isa. 35:3–10	I Cor. 3:1–11	Matt. 28:16–20
	C	Isa. 55:1–5	Rev. 5:11–14	John 17:1–11
World Communion	A	Isa. 49:18–23	Rev. 3:17–22	John 10:11–18
	B	Isa. 25:6–9	Rev. 7:9–17	Luke 24:13–35
	C	I Chron. 16:23–34	Acts 2:42–47	Matt. 8:5–13
Reformation	A	Hab. 2:1–4	Rom. 3:21–28	John 8:31–36
	B	Gen. 12:1–4	II Cor. 5:16–21	Matt. 21:17–22
	C	Ex. 33:12–17	Heb. 11:1–10	Luke 18:9–14
Thanksgiving	A	Isa. 61:10–11	I Tim. 2:1–8	Luke 12:22–31
	B	Deut. 26:1–11	Gal. 6:6–10	Luke 17:11–19
	C	Deut. 8:6–17	II Cor. 9:6–15	John 6:24–35
Day of Civic or National Significance	A	Deut. 28:1–9	Rom. 13:1–8	Luke 1:68–79
	B	Isa. 26:1–8	I Thess. 5:12–23	Mark 12:13–17
	C	Dan. 9:3–10	I Peter 2:11–17	Luke 20:21–26

Church Calendar	Epistle	Gospel
Easter	Acts 1:1–8	John 1:1–17
Easter I	Acts 5:12–20	John 20:19–31
II	Acts 6:1–7	Mark 15:43 to 16:8
III	Acts 9:32–42	John 5:1–15
IV	Acts 11:19–30	John 4:5–42
V	Acts 16:16–34	John 9:1–38
VI	Acts 20:16–18, 28–36	John 17:1–13
VII	Acts 2:1–11	John 7:37–52; 8:12
All Saints I	Heb. 11:33 to 12:2	Matt. 10:32–33, 37–38; 19:27–30
II	Rom. 2:10–16	Matt. 4:18–23
III	Gal. 5:22 to 6:2	Matt. 6:22–33
IV	Rom. 6:18–23	Matt. 8:5–13
V	Rom. 10:1–10	Matt. 8:28 to 9:1
VI	Rom. 12:6–14	Matt. 9:1–8
VII	Rom. 15:1–7	Matt. 9:27–35
VIII	I Cor. 1:10–17	Matt. 14:14–22
IX	I Cor. 3:9–17	Matt. 14:22–34
X	I Cor. 4:9–16	Matt. 17:14–23
XI	I Cor. 9:2–12	Matt. 18:23–35
XII	I Cor. 15:1–11	Matt. 19:16–26
XIII	I Cor. 16:13–24	Matt. 21:33–42
XIV	II Cor. 1:21 to 2:4	Matt. 22:1–14
XV	II Cor. 4:6–15	Matt. 22:35–46
XVI	II Cor. 6:1–10	Matt. 25:14–30
XVII	II Cor. 6:16 to 7:1	Matt. 15:21–28
XVIII	II Cor. 9:6–11	Luke 5:1–11
XIX	II Cor. 11:31 to 12:9	Luke 6:31–36
XX	Gal. 1:11–19	Luke 7:11–16
XXI	Gal. 2:16–20	Luke 8:5–15
XXII	Gal. 6:11–18	Luke 16:19–31
XXIII	Eph. 2:4–10	Luke 8:26–39
XXIV	Eph. 2:14–22	Luke 8:41–56
XXV	Eph. 4:1–6	Luke 10:25–37
XXVI	Eph. 5:9–19	Luke 12:16–21
XXVII	Eph. 6:10–17	Luke 13:10–17
XXVIII	Col. 1:12–18	Luke 14:16–24
XXIX	Col. 3:3–11	Luke 17:12–19
XXX	Col. 3:12–16	Luke 18:18–27
XXXI	I Tim. 1:15–17	Luke 18:35–43
XXXII	I Tim. 4:9–15	Luke 19:1–10
Sun. before Exalt. Cross	Gal. 6:11–18	John 3:13–17
Sun. after Exalt. Cross	Gal. 2:16–20	Mark 8:34–38; 9:1
Sun. before Christmas	Heb. 9:9–10, 17–40	Matt. 1:1–25
Sun. after Christmas	Gal. 1:11–19	Matt. 2:13–23
Sun. before Epiphany	II Tim. 4:5–8	Mark 1:1–8
Sun. after Epiphany	Eph. 4:7–13	Matt. 4:12–17
Publican/Pharisee	II Tim. 3:10–15	Luke 18:10–14
Prodigal Son	I Cor. 6:12–20	Luke 15:11–32
Meat Fast	I Cor. 8:8 to 9:2	Matt. 25:31–46
Cheese Fast	Rom. 13:11 to 14:4	Matt. 6:14–21

Selections for the Christian Year — for Orthodox Use (Continued)

Church Calendar	Epistle	Gospel
Great Fast		
(Lent) I	Heb. 9:24–26, 32; 12:2	John 1:44–52
II	Heb. 1:10 to 2:3	Mark 2:1–12
III	Heb. 4:14 to 5:6	Mark 8:34 to 9:1
IV	Heb. 6:13–20	Mark 9:17–31
V	Heb. 9:11–14	Mark 1:32–45
VI	Phil. 4:4–9	John 12:1–18

630

Selections from the Psalms* Appropriate to the Christian Year

Church Calendar	Psalm
Advent	Psalm 8; 19(18); 24(23); 25(24); 42(41); 122(121); 145(144)
Christmas	Psalm 2; 19(18); 98(97); 148
Epiphany	Psalm 19(18); 46(45); 66(65); 67(66); 84(83); 86(85); 96(95); 97(96); 100(99)
Ash Wednesday	Psalm 32(33); 34(33); 51(50); 130(129)
Lent	Psalm 25(24); 32(31); 34(33); 90(89); 122(121); 130(129)
Holy Week	Psalm 16(15); 22(21); 31(30); 32(31); 40(39); 51(50); 91(90); 130(129)
Easter Day	Psalm 2; 8; 16(15); 98(97)
Eastertide	Psalm 23(22); 33(32); 66(65); 98(97); 100(99); 148
Ascension	Psalm 93(92)
Pentecost	Psalm 19(18); 48(47); 145(144)
Trinity	Psalm 8; 33(32); 96(95); 97(96); 148
After Pentecost	Psalm 8; 15(14); 19(18); 24(23); 25(24); 33(32); 34(33); 37(36); 46(45); 62(61); 63(62); 73(72); 96(95)
Kingdomtide	Psalm 90(89); 91(90); 103(102); 145(144); 148
New Year	Psalm 8; 40(39); 65(64); 103(102); 122(121)

*In references to the Psalms, the Protestant/Jewish numbering is given first, followed by the Catholic/Orthodox numbering in parentheses. A few Psalms have the same numbering in all Bibles. For these, only one number is given.

Selections from the Psalms Appropriate to the Civil Year   631

Special Day	Psalm
Armed Forces Day	Psalm 2; 3; 19(18); 27(26); 46(45); 126(125)
Brotherhood or Race Relations Day	Psalm 24(23); 51(50); 119(118):105–112; 121(120); 126(125); 133(132)
Father's Day	Psalm 1; 8; 24(23); 32(31); 119(118):1–6; 128(127)
Flag Day	Psalm 19(18); 46(45); 150
Independence Day	Psalm 37(36); 46(45); 63(62):1–8; 66(65); 96(95); 121(120)
Memorial Day	Psalm 11(10); 13(12); 23(22); 37(36); 61(60); 77(76); 84(83); 90(89); 137(136)
Mother's Day	Psalm 113(112); 127(126); 128(127)
New Year's Day	Psalm 8; 40(39); 65(64); 90(89); 103(102); 122(121)
Thanksgiving Day	Psalm 65(64); 67(66); 92(91); 95(94); 98(97); 100(99); 103(102); 105(104); 107(106); 111(110); 128(127); 136(135); 145(144); 147(146–147); 148
Veterans' Day	Psalm 27(26); 67(66); 77(76); 85(84); 90(89)

SELECTIONS FROM THE PSALTER

632

Happy is the man who walks not the way of the wicked,
who treads not the highway of sin
nor sits in the seat of the cynic,
because he delights in the LORD's instruction
and studies that teaching both day and night!

He becomes like a tree
planted by rivers of water,
bearing its fruit in due season,
with leaves that are always green.
In all that he does he succeeds.

Not so the wicked,
for he is like the windblown chaff.
Therefore the wicked cannot stand in judgment
nor sinners in the righteous assembly.

The LORD watches over the path of the righteous,
but the way of the wicked leads nowhere.

Psalm 1*

633

Why are the nations assembling,
the peoples mustering troops,
the kings of the earth declaring positions,
the rulers consulting together
against the LORD, against his Anointed?
"Let us tear off their fetters!
Let us cast off their bonds!"

He who dwells in the heavens is laughing;
The Master derides them all.
He speaks to them in his wrath;
in his anger he puts them in fear.
"I have anointed my king
on Zion, my holy hill."

---

*In references to the Psalms, the Protestant/Jewish numbering is given, followed by
the Catholic/Orthodox numbering in parentheses. A few Psalms have the same numbering
in all Bibles. For these, only one number is given.

Let me proclaim the decree of the LORD.
He told me, "You are my son.
Today I bring you to birth."

Happy are all who trust him!   *Psalm 2:1–7, 12b*

634

O LORD, how my foes have increased!
How many are rising against me!
How many who say of my life,
"There is no help from God for him"!

**You, LORD, are my lifelong master,
my honor, my reason for pride.
When I cry aloud to the LORD
he responds from his holy hill.**

As for me, I can lie down and sleep,
then arise, for the LORD sustains me.
I fear not though thousands of men
gather around to oppose me.
Arise, LORD! Save me, my God!
You can slap the face of my foes
and break the teeth of the wicked.

**Salvation, O LORD!
May your blessing rest on your people!**   *Psalm 3*

635

Answer when I call, my Victorious God!
When I am oppressed release me!
Have mercy and hear my prayer!
How long, O men, will you insult my Glory,
worship deceit, and seek what is false?
Understand that the LORD will rescue his saint.
The LORD will hear when I call him.

**Tremble and sin not,
examine your conscience,
lament in your bed,
offer right offerings
and trust in the LORD.**

Many say, "Who can bring good?
Smile upon us, O LORD!"
You have put more joy in my heart
than a bountiful harvest of crops.

I can lie down in peace; I can sleep.
Only you, LORD, permit me to lie down in trust.

Psalm 4

636

O LORD, do not in your anger rebuke me!
Do not in your wrath chastise me!

Be merciful, LORD, for I have grown feeble!
Heal me, O LORD! I tremble in terror.

My life is in terrible danger.
You, O LORD! How long?

Turn, O LORD! Spare my life!
Save me! Your kindness demands it.

The dead can never recall you.
Who can sing praise from the grave?

I am wearied from groaning.
I flood my pillow all night,
soaking my couch with my tears.

My eyes are wasted with grief,
dried up through all my distress.

But now begone, you bringers of pain!
The LORD has heard my weeping;

the LORD has heeded my crying;
the LORD accepts my prayer.

Let all my tormentors be shamed and disgraced!
May they leave in sudden dismay!

Psalm 6

637

LORD, our Master,
how great is your name in the earth!
Your praise is cast through the sky!

660

From the mouths of babes and infants
you have called forth strength despite foes,
silencing enemies and avengers.

> **When I look at your heavens, the work of your fingers,**
> **the moon and the stars which you have created,**
> **why should you notice a human?**
> **Why should you make use of man?**
> **You have made him almost like God**
> **and crowned him with glory and honor.**
> **You gave him command of your works;**
> **you have placed it all at his feet**
> **— the sheep, the oxen, all of them,**
> **yes, even the beasts of the field,**
> **the birds in the sky, the fish in the sea,**
> **swimming the paths of the ocean.**

LORD, our Master,
how great is your name in the earth!   *Psalm 8*

638

I earnestly confess the LORD.

> **I will tell all your wondrous deeds;**
> **I will celebrate you and rejoice;**
> **I will sing to your name, O Highest.**

When my enemies turned away
they staggered and perished before you.
You upheld my cause and my case;
you sat on your throne, judging with justice.

> **May the LORD be the refuge of the poor,**
> **a refuge for times of oppression!**
> **May those who know your name trust you,**
> **for you never forsake those who seek you!**

The nations sink in the pit they have dug;
their own feet are caught in the net they have hid.
It is known that the LORD works justice:
by the deeds of their own hands the wicked are caught.
The wicked return to Deathland
— all nations forgetful of God.

The poor are not always forgotten;
the hope of the lowly does not always perish.
Arise, O LORD! Let man not prevail!
Let the nations be judged in your presence!
Decree, LORD, a terror upon them
that the nations may know they are men.   *Psalm 9:1–4, 9–10, 15–20*

639

LORD, who may dwell in your tent,
reside in your holy hill?

**The trustworthy man,
who does what is right
and thinks with an honest mind,
who has not been a slandering gossip,
who has not been bad to his neighbor,
who has not insulted his friends.**

One vile in his eyes is rejected;
he who fears the LORD is honored.

**When he swears to do evil he does it;
he has loaned no money for interest
nor been bribed to betray the innocent.**

Whoever does these things shall never fail.   *Psalm 15(14)*

640

**Guard me, O God,
for I seek your protection!**

**I say, "O LORD,
you are my greatest good."**

**The holy powers that were in the land
are only your nobles.
I do not like them.**

**They bring only troubles.
In haste they regress.
I will pour no libations of blood!
I will not say their names with my lips!**

You have measured my portion;
it is you who sustain my allotment.

My boundaries fall in fine places;
my inheritance pleases me well.

I will bless the LORD for he guides me
(by night my heart so instructs me).

I put the LORD always before me.
He always will stay at my side.

Therefore my heart is now glad;
my pride is rejoicing.
My body can live in safety,

for you will not leave me to die
nor commit your saint to the grave.

You will show me the pathway of life.
Your favor means the fullness of joy;
your hand offers pleasures forever.

Psalm 16(15)

641

The heavens declare God's glory;
the skies display his handiwork.
Each day pours forth a speech;
each night proclaims some knowledge.
There is no speech, not a word,
but what their voice is heard.
Their sound has gone out in the earth,
their words to the edge of the world.

He set the sun's tent in the sea.
Like a bridegroom it comes from its chamber,
exulting like a warrior,
sprinting on its pathway;
its entrance, the heaven's horizon,
its finish, the farthest extreme.
Nothing is hid from its rays.

The LORD's instructions are perfect,
refreshing the spirit.
The decree of the LORD is trusty,
instructing my brain.

The laws of the LORD are right,
delighting the mind,
The commands of the LORD are clear,
enlightening the eyes.
The fear of the LORD is pure,
enduring forever.
The judgments of the LORD are reliable,
prevailing together.

More precious than gold,
than much fine gold!
Sweeter than honey,
than drippings of the comb!
For by them your servant is taught;
it is very rewarding to keep them.
Who can find fault?
O cleanse me from error!

Ah, keep your servant from scorn!
Let it not overcome me.
Then I shall be healthy and free
of any great sin.

May the words of my mouth be pleasing
and the thoughts of my mind be accepted,
O LORD, my rock, my redeemer!   *Psalm 19(18)*

642

My God, my God, O why have you left me?
The words that I groan bring help no closer.
My God, I call by day without answer,
by night, and I still find no rest.

You are the Holy One,
throned on the praises of Israel.
Our fathers believed in you;
they trusted and you set them free.
They cried unto you and you freed them;
they hoped and were not disappointed.

But I?—a worm, not a man!
—scorned and despised by mankind.
All who see me insult me,
protruding their lips
and wagging their heads.

664

"He trusts the LORD. Will he save him?
Let him help if he loves him!"

> They divide my garments among them;
> they sit and cast lots for my clothes.

> But you, O LORD, stay near!
> O my strength, hasten to help me!

I proclaim your name to my brothers;
in the midst of the gathering I praise you.
Praise him, O worshiper of the LORD!
Honor him, all offspring of Jacob!
Respect him, O seed of Israel!
For he does not despise
nor reject the cry of the needy.
He does not turn away his face;
when he cries unto him he listens.

> I repeat my hymn in the great congregation.
> I pay my vows before those who worship.
> The afflicted shall eat and be full.
> The LORD's disciples shall praise him.
> May their hearts live on!
> May all the ends of the earth
> take note and return to the LORD.
> May all the tribes of the nations
> bow in worship before him!
> For dominion belongs to the LORD;
> he rules the nations.   *Psalm 22(21):1–8, 18–19. 22–28*

643

> My shepherd is the LORD: I lack nothing.
> He lets me stretch out in green meadows;
> he takes me to well-watered places,
>   refreshing my spirit;
> He leads me along the right paths
>   for the honor of his name.
> Even when I walk in great danger
>   I fear no harm,
> because you are with me.
> Your club and your staff,
>   they are my comfort.
> You spread out the table before me
>   in front of my foes.

You anoint my head with oil
  as my cup overflows.
Yes, kindness and goodness pursue me
  all through my life.
I will dwell in the house of the LORD
  as long as I live.   *Psalm 23(22)*

644

The LORD owns the earth and its contents,
the world and its creatures.
On the waters primeval he built it;
over the torrents he made it.

  Who can climb the LORD's hill?
  Who can go up to his sanctuary?

The man with clean hands and an honest mind.
who does not foolishly pledge his life
nor take an oath of deceit.
He carries a blessing away from the LORD,
vindication from the God who saves him.

  Seek the Eternal One,
  you who search for the Presence of Jacob!

Lift up your heads, O gates!
Be raised, O ancient doors!
The glorious King arrives.

  Who is this glorious King?
  The LORD, the strong, the hero,
  the LORD, the hero of war.

Lift up your heads, O gates!
Be raised, O ancient doors!
The glorious King arrives.

  Who is this glorious King?
  The LORD of armies,
  he is the glorious King.   *Psalm 24(23)*

645

I commit myself unto you, O LORD.
I trust you, my God:

let me not be ashamed.
Let no foe exult over me.
Surely, none who look to you are disappointed;
disappointment is for treacherous deceivers.

> **Show me, O LORD, your pathways;**
> **teach me your ways.**
> **Lead me in faithfulness; teach me,**
> **for you are the God who can help me.**
> **I am looking to you all the day.**
> **Remember your mercy and kindness, O LORD,**
> **for they are eternal.**
> **Forget, please, the sins of my youth, my rebellions,**
> **and remember me through your kindness,**
> **on the grounds of your goodness, O LORD!**

The LORD is good and right.
Therefore, he shows sinners the way.
He can lead the afflicted to justice;
he can teach the afflicted his way.
All the LORD's pathways are kind and dependable
to the guardians of his covenant and testimonies.

> **May honesty and uprightness guard me**
> **as I hope in you!**
> **Redeem Israel, O God, from all of her troubles!**

Psalm 25(24):1–10, 21–22

646

The LORD is my light and my savior:
whom shall I fear?
The LORD is the strength of my life:
whom shall I dread?

> **When men of evil approach me**
> **to eat at my flesh,**
> **it is they, my troublers and foes,**
> **who stumble and fall.**

If an army should gather against me
my heart shall not fear;
if war should be waged against me,
even then I can trust.

> **But one thing I ask from the LORD**
> **and for that I plead:**

I would dwell in the house of the LORD
as long as I live,
to behold the mercy of the LORD,
to pray in his temple.

Let him hide me within his tent
in the day of trouble
—conceal me inside his pavilion
and exalt me in danger!

**Even now may he lift up my head
above my gathering foes.
In his tent I will offer an offering of joy.
I will chant and sing praise to the LORD!**   *Psalm 27(26):1–6*

647

I trust you, O LORD:
put an end to my shame!
In your justice release me,
O lend me your ear!
Come quickly to rescue!
O be my defense
—a fortified home for my safety,
for you are my rock and my stronghold!
For your own reputation lead me and guide me.

**Free me from the net they have hidden for me.
You are my defense:
I commit my life to your keeping.
You have purchased my freedom, O LORD, dependable God.**

How great, O LORD, is the goodness
you have treasured for those who fear you,
what you have done for your followers
before all mankind!
In your intimate presence you have hid them
from the turmoils of men,
concealed under cover
from those who accuse.

**Blessed be the LORD!
His kindness did wonders for me
in a time of distress.
When I was frightened I said,**

"I perish before your eyes!"
But you listened to the sound of my plea
when I cried out to you.
Adore the LORD, all his saints,
for the LORD protects the faithful!
Yet he pays in full the ones who act proudly.
Be strong and encourage yourselves,
all you who wait for the LORD!   *Psalm 31(30):1–5, 19–24*

648

Happy is he whose guilt is removed,
whose sin is forgiven!
Happy the man whom the LORD reckons no evil,
whose spirit is free from guile!

> **Then I told you my sin;**
> **I hid not my guilt.**
> **I said, "I confess, O Most High, my transgressions,**
> **O LORD."**
> **As for you, you removed the guilt of my sin.**

Therefore every saint prays unto you.
When an army approaches or flood waters rise,
he is not overtaken.

> **You are my refuge.**
> **You protect me from danger;**
> **you surround me with shouts of triumph.**   *Psalm 32(31):1–7*

649

Rejoice in the LORD, you righteous!
A hymn by the upright is lovely.

> **Give praise to the LORD with a harp;**
> **make music to him with a lyre.**

Sing him a song that is new:
play it well on a brilliant horn!

> **For the word of the LORD does not err**
> **and all he has done stands true.**

He loves what is just and right
and the earth is full of his kindness.

**By his word the heavens were made;
by the breath of his mouth all its stars.**

It is he who scooped up the sea's waters,
who put the great deep into basins.

**Let all the earth worship the LORD!
Let all the world's citizens fear!**

He spoke and things came into being;
he gave the command and they stayed.

**O LORD, send your kindness upon us,
inasmuch as our hope is in you.**

Psalm 33(32):1–9, 22

650

I will bless you, O LORD, at all times;

in my mouth there is always a hymn.

My whole being boasts of the LORD:

let the lowly folk hear and be glad.

Extol the LORD, now, with me!

Let us laud his name together!

I sought the LORD and he answered;

he saved me from all my foes.

Look unto him and be radiant!

Let not your face be downcast!

This poor man called and the LORD heard;

he saved him from all of his troubles.

The angel of the LORD encamps

around those who fear him to save them.

Taste, and discover the LORD's goodness!

Happy is the man who will trust him.

Fear the LORD, O you saints:

There is no want for those who fear him.

Psalm 34(33):1–9

651

Do not fret over those who do evil
nor worry because they do wrong,
for like grass they shall suddenly wither;
like the greenness of grass they shall fade.

**Trust in the LORD and do good;
enjoy the earth in security.
Take delight in the LORD:
he will give what your heart desires.**

Commit your way to the LORD;
trust him, for he is active.
He will make justice come like the dawn
like noon daylight, your justification.

**The LORD has help for the righteous;
in troubled times he is their refuge.
The LORD gives them help;
he delivers them from the wicked.
He saves them, for they trust him.**   *Psalm 37(36):1–6, 39–40*

652

**I patiently waited for the LORD
and he turned and listened to my cry.
He lifted me out of death's pit,
from the mire of the mud.
He planted my feet on a rock,
anchoring my steps.**

**He put a new song in my mouth:
a hymn to our God.
Many shall view it with awe
and trust in the LORD.**

**Happy is the fellow who puts
his trust in the LORD,
who does not turn for help to the proud,
to tangles of lies!**

**As for you, you have done mighty deeds,
O LORD, O my God, great wonders!
And the plans you have for us:
no one can match you!**

671

Let me tell them, proclaim them!
They are far beyond number.

You want no offerings or sacrifice,
so you cause me to listen.
You ask no burnt flesh or atonement.
So I say, "Here I come:
in the scroll it is written for me."

I desire, my God, to do what you want:
your teachings are in me.
I correctly confessed in the great assembly;
lo, I restrained not my lips
and you, O LORD, know it.

I did not keep your triumphs to myself;
I proclaimed you as savior and faithful.
I have not concealed your kindness
nor your truth from the great assembly.

And you, LORD, restrain not yourself
from having mercy on me.
May your kindness and truth
continually guard me!   *Psalm 40(39):1–11*

653

Happy is he who considers the poor:
in a day of distress the LORD saves him.

May the LORD guard and sustain him,
give him joy in the land!
May he not let his foes overcome!
May the LORD give him strength on his sickbed!
To his bed you have sent him in illness.

I say, "O LORD, pity me!
I have sinned against you, so heal me!"
My foes say bad things about me
("When will he die that his name may perish?").
When anyone comes to see me he dreams up a lie.
Gathering gossip for himself,
he goes out in public and tells it.
All those who hate me
whisper together against me.
They spew out a foul message for me:

"When he lies down may he nevermore rise!"
Even my good friend, a man whom I trusted,
has thoroughly betrayed me.

But you, O LORD, have compassion and lift me!
Let me repay them!
By this I will know that you like me:
When my foes no longer insult me.
As for me, you have kept me in safety
and permanently set me before you.

Blessed be the LORD, the God of Israel,
from of old to the future!
Amen! Amen!

Psalm 41(40)

654

As a deer goes panting
for brooks full of water,
even so do I pant
after you, O God.
My spirit has thirsted for God,
for the Living God.
O when can I come and behold
the countenance of God?
My tears have served as my food
by day and by night
as they constantly say unto me,
"Where is your God?"

O why do you bend low, my spirit,
and roar out against me?
Believe in God, for still I confess him
as my vindication, my God!
my own spirit bends low against me:
therefore I recall you.

By day the LORD orders his kindness;
in the night his song is with me
— a prayer to the Living God.
It says,
O God, my Rock,
why do you ignore me?
Why must I grieve
while the enemy does violence

and bruises my bones?
My oppressors degrade me
by saying all day,
"Where is your God?"

O why do you bend low, my spirit,
and roar out against me?
Believe in God, for still I confess him
as my vindication, my God!   *Psalm 42(41):1–3, 5–6, 8–11*

655

God is for us a refuge and strength,
an often-proved help in times of distress.
Therefore we fear not though the earth be shifting,
though mountains move in the heart of the sea.
Its waters may roll and roar;
the mountains may shake with its rising.

There is a river whose channels gladden the city of God.
Holy is the home of the Highest.
God is within her: she stands;
at the first break of day God will help her.

Nations rumble; kingdoms totter.
He speaks with his voice: earth melts away.
The LORD of Armies is with us;
Jacob's God is our fort.

Come, see the deeds of the LORD
— how he brings devastation to earth
by ending wars to the uttermost lands!
He shatters the bow, splinters the spear
and burns the chariots with fire.

Relax and acknowledge that I am God.
I arise among nations;
I arise in the earth.

The LORD of Armies is with us;
Jacob's God is our fort.   *Psalm 46(45)*

656

The LORD is great and mightily praised
in the city of our God, his holy mountain.

Ah, beautiful height,
the joy of the earth,
the hill of Zion, the center of the world,
the great King's city!
The God in her courts
is acknowledged as a fortress.

We have thought, O God, of your kindness
in the midst of your temple.
Your praise, God, befits your name
throughout the earth.
Justice fills your right hand.

Be glad, mount Zion;
let the daughters of Judah rejoice
because of your judgments!

Walk around Zion in procession
and count all her towers.
Consider in your mind her defenses,
explore her chambers,
that you may describe it to later generations,
for this is God's.

Our God, eternal, enduring,
is he who can lead us forever.   *Psalm 48(47):1–3, 9–14*

657

Pity me, God, in your kindness!
With abundant compassion blot out my guilt!
Thoroughly wash out my evil
and cleanse me from sin!
I know my rebellions full well;
my sin is ever before me.
Against you alone have I sinned;
in your sight I have done this bad thing.
Therefore you are right to accuse,
correct in your judgment.

I would teach the rebellious your ways,
that sinners might turn unto you.
Deliver me from idols, O God,
O God, my salvation,
that my tongue may sing of your triumph!
Open my lips, O Master,
that my mouth may proclaim your praise!   *Psalm 51(50):1–4, 13–15*

658

Pity me, God, pity me!
In you my soul has sought refuge.
In the shade of your wings I take refuge
until the dangers pass by.
I cry unto God, the Most High,
to God, the Accomplisher, the Highest.

> **May he reach out from heaven and save me!**
> **May he put my oppressors to shame!**
> **May God reach out with his kindness and truth**
> **and save my life!**

I lie down to sleep among lions,
devourers of men,
whose teeth are spears and arrows,
whose tongues are sharpened swords.

> **God stands higher than the heavens;**
> **his glory is above the whole world.**

Psalm 57(56):1-5

659

Be silent before God, my soul:
he bears my salvation!
Yes, he is my rock and my help
—my fortress: I will not be shaken.

> **Be silent before God, my soul,**
> **for he bears my hope.**
> **He is my rock and my help**
> **—my fortress: I will not be shaken.**

God has gone up!—my Salvation, my Glory,
my Rock and my Strength!
In God I take refuge.
Trust him at all times, O people!
Pour out your hearts before him.
God is the refuge for us.

Trust not unfair gain;
do not desire plunder.
When wealth is abounding, rely not upon it.

God spoke once;
twice I have heard it:
strength is of God.
Kindness is yours, O Master.
It is you who repay
a man for his deeds. *Psalm 62(61):1–2, 5–8, 10–12*

660

O God, my God, I eagerly await you.
My life thirsts for you;
my flesh yearns for you
in a waterless, desolate desert.

My lips shall praise.
While I live I will bless you
and pray in your name.

My life most desperately needs you;
your right arm has hold of me.

May the king rejoice in God's strength!
May all who swear by him boast,
for he shuts the mouth of deceivers! *Psalm 63(62):1, 3b–4, 8, 11*

661

A praise hymn befits you in Zion, O God;
a paid pledge as well,
you, who listen to prayer.
All flesh should come before you.

Happy is he whom you choose and bring near,
who can dwell in your courts,
satisfied by the goodness of your house,
by the holiness of your temple!

You triumph with victorious wonders,
our saving God,
as you tie down the ends of the earth
and the wide, open sea,
as you mightily set up the mountains
all girded with strength,

as you silence the swell of the seas,
the swell of its waves,
and the tumult of peoples.
Those who live far away
stand in awe at your signs.

The cycles of morning and evening sing out.
You have visited the earth with water;
you abundantly enrich it.

The fields of the wilderness are wet
and the hills are clothed with gladness.
The slopes are covered with flocks
and the valleys are groaning with grain.
They shout, yes, they sing.   *Psalm 65(64):1-2, 4-9a, 12-13*

662

Cry out unto God, all the earth!
Sing out the glory of his name!
Chant the glory of his praise!
Say unto God, "How awesome your deeds!"

Come now and see the things God has done!
The awe of his action is over all men.
He dried up the sea
and they passed through the river on foot.
Let us be happy in him!

He rules the world with his might.
His eyes keep watch on the nations.
No rebel dare stand up before him.

Bless our God, O peoples!
Let him hear the sound of his praise!
He sustains our being with life
and prevents our feet from stumbling.

Come, listen as I tell you, all you who fear God,
just what he has done for my life.
I called out to him,
keeping pride under my tongue
and then God listened.
He heard the sound of my prayer.

Blessed be God!
He did not reject my prayer
nor his covenant-love with me!

Psalm 66(65):1–3a, 5–9, 16–17, 19–20

663

May God pity us and bless us!
May his face beam kindly upon us
that his way may be known upon earth,
his saving acts in all nations!

> **May the peoples confess you, O God!**
> **May all of the peoples confess you!**
> **May the masses rejoice and sing out,**
> **for you judge the peoples correctly**
> **and pity the masses on earth!**

May the peoples confess you, O God!
May all of the peoples confess you!
The earth has yielded its produce.

> **May God, our God, bless us!**
> **May God bless us**
> **that all the world may respect him!**

Psalm 67(66)

664

I trust you, O LORD:
let me never be shamed!
In your justice rescue, deliver me!
Bend your ear toward me and save me!

> **Become now my rockbound dwelling,**
> **my fortified house for salvation,**
> **for you are my rock-cliff, my fortress!**

Deliver me, my God, from the wicked,
from the hand of the criminal, the oppressor,
for you are my hope, O Master,
O LORD, my security since childhood!

> **I have leaned upon you since birth;**
> **you took me as soon as I was born.**
> **You are always my boast.**

The fact that you mightily guard me
is a sign unto many.
My mouth is full of your praise,
always giving glory.

**My lips shall ring out
as I sing unto you
for the life which you have redeemed.
My tongue at all times will speak of your triumph,
while those who sought evil
are shamed and dismayed.** *Psalm 71(70):1–8, 23–24*

665

How good is God for Israel,
for the pure of heart!

**As for me, my feet had almost stumbled;
my steps had well-nigh slipped.
I was jealous of the arrogant
and envied the prosperity of the wicked.**

My mind is embittered;
my thoughts, irritating.
I am so stupid, so ignorant!
I am but a dumb brute before you.

**And yet I am always before you:
you keep me in your hand.
With counsel you lead me;
you take me by the hand behind you.**

I have but you in the heavens
and nothing more on earth.
My flesh and my brain may fail
but my Rock, the desire of my mind, is God evermore.

**Those who avoid you will perish;
you exterminate all those who stray.
God's presence is good for me;
I make the LORD my refuge
and I will witness to his deeds.** *Psalm 73(72):1–3, 21–28*

666

How pleasant are your encampments,
O LORD of Armies!
My spirit has longed, yes, yearned
for the courts of the LORD.
My mind and my flesh sing out
to the Living God.

> **Even the bird finds a home,**
> **the swallow a nest,**
> **where she may hatch her young ones:**
> **your altar, O LORD of Armies,**
> **my King, my God.**

Happy are the residents of your house!
They praise you forever.

> **A day in your courts is better**
> **than a thousand in any other;**
> **standing at the door of God's house,**
> **than a lifetime in tents of the wicked.**

Yes, the LORD is a sun and shield,
giving mercy and honor.
The LORD withholds nothing good
from men of integrity.

> **O LORD of Armies,**
> **happy is the man who trusts you!**   *Psalm 84(83):1–4, 10–12*

667

You have favored your land, O LORD:
you removed the captivity of Jacob.
You have lifted the guilt of your people;
you have covered all of their sins.
You have withdrawn all your wrath;
you have turned from the heat of your anger.

> **Restore us, our saving God!**
> **Remove your vexation against us!**
> **Must you ever be angry at us,**
> **unceasingly pour out your wrath?**
> **Can you not restore us again**
> **that your folk may rejoice for your sake?**

Show us, O LORD, your kindness!
Grant us your help!

Let me hear what God, the LORD, has to say,
for he is speaking of peace
—to his people, to those who are faithful.
Let them not turn to folly!
His help is there for his worshipers
that his honor may dwell in our land.
Kindness and faithfulness have met;
justice and peace have kissed.
Faithfulness sprouts from the ground
as justice looks down from the sky.

The LORD can provide what is good;
he can grant to our land its produce.
Righteousness walks on before him
as he plants his steps on the road.   *Psalm 85(84)*

668

Incline your ear, LORD, and answer me,
for I am afflicted and needy!

Guard my life: I am faithful.
Give help to your servant who trusts you.

Have mercy, O Master, my God,
for to you I continually cry!

Give joy to the life of your servant,
for to you, O Master, I dedicate my life!

You, O Master, are good and forgiving,
pouring kindness on those who cry out.

Listen, O LORD, to my prayer!
Give heed to the sound of my plea!
I call you when I am in trouble,
for you answer me.   *Psalm 86(85):1–7*

669

You have been our abode, O Master,
through all generations.

Before the mountains were born,
before the earth was begun,
from beginning to end you are God.

> **You send man back to the dust
> and say, "Return, O mortal!"
> A thousand years in your sight
> seem like a day that is past,
> like a watch in the night.**

Teach us to value our days
that we may learn to act wisely.

> **Turn back soon, O LORD!
> Have mercy upon your servants!**

Treat us to your kindness tomorrow!
Make us joyful and happy forever!

> **Give us as many years of joy
> as the sadness we have already seen!**

Reveal your activity to your servants,
your splendor to your sons!

> **May the mercy of the Master, of our God, be upon us!
> May the works of our hands be established before us!
> Yes, establish the work of our hands!**

Psalm 90(89):1–4, 12–18

670

Whoever sits in the shadow of the Highest,
who sleeps in the shade of the Almighty,
can say to the LORD, "My refuge!
My fortress! The God whom I trust!"

> **He will release you from snares,
> snatch you from dangerous plagues.
> He will cover you with his feathers;
> he will hide you beneath his wings.
> Like a shield he securely surrounds you.**

You will not fear the terror of night,
nor an arrow that flies in the daylight,
a plague that stalks in the darkness
nor destruction that threatens at noon.

A thousand may fall at your side,
a multitude close beside you,
but you shall escape.

> I will save those who hang on to me
> and protect those who know my name.
> When they pray I answer;
> I free and uphold them.
> I give them long life
> and demonstrate my help.　　　　*Psalm 91(90):1-7, 14-16*

671

It is good to confess the LORD's praise,
to sing to the name of the Highest,
to tell of his kindness at morning,
of his faithfulness during the night.

> Your deeds, O LORD, make me happy;
> the works of your hands make me sing.
> How great are your deeds, O LORD!
> How very profound your thoughts!
> The stupid man does not know;
> the fool cannot understand this
> — that the wicked may sprout like grass,
> that evildoers may flourish
> only to be destroyed.

You are exalted forever.
Lo, your enemies, O LORD,
lo, your enemies shall perish.
All evildoers shall be scattered.

> The righteous shall flourish like palm trees;
> they shall grow like cedars of Lebanon.
> Planted in the house of the LORD,
> in the courts of our God, they shall flourish,
> continuing to thrive in old age,
> keeping their vigor and health
> as they speak of the rightness of God,
> my Rock, who never does wrong.　　*Psalm 92(91):1-2, 4-9, 12-15*

672

The LORD becomes King, clothed in splendor.
The LORD is clothed, yes, girded with strength.
You made the world immovable,
your ever-enduring throne.
You exist from of old.

The rivers lift up, O LORD,
the rivers lift up their thunder.
The rivers are raising their waves.

The LORD, in the heights, is more awesome
than the mighty, thundering waters
or the awesome waves of the sea.

Your testimonies are very reliable.
Hence, your house must be holy
forever and ever, O LORD.   *Psalm 93(92)*

673

Come, let us sing to the LORD!
Let us shout to our mighty Savior!

Let us approach him with praise
and laud him with music,

for the LORD is a powerful God,
the ruler of all other gods.

He possesses all parts of the earth,
even the tops of the mountains.

The sea is his, for he made it,
and his hands formed the dry land.

Enter! Bow down and worship!
Let us kneel to the LORD, our maker,
for he is our God
and we are his people,
his flock, the sheep of his hand.   *Psalm 95(94):1–7*

674

Sing to the LORD a new song!
Sing to the LORD, O World!
Sing to the LORD, give him honor!
Preach his salvation each day!

**Tell to the nations his greatness,
to all of the peoples his splendor!
The LORD is great: he is worthy of praise.
He is more awesome than all other gods.**

Ascribe to the LORD, O tribes of the peoples,
ascribe to the LORD both honor and strength!
Ascribe to the LORD the glory of his name!
Bring him a gift and enter his courts!

**Worship the LORD in holy demeanor!
Tremble before him, O Earth!
Say to the nations, "The LORD becomes King.
He causes the world to endure.
He rules his people correctly."** *Psalm 96(95):1–4, 7–10*

675

The LORD rules: let the earth dance!
Let its many islands rejoice!
The heavens proclaim his triumph
while the peoples behold his glory.

**You, O LORD, are the Highest
— much higher than all the earth,
exalted above all gods.**

If we love the LORD we hate evil.

**He guards the lives of his saints;
he frees them from wicked men.**

A sown field awaits the just,
joy for the upright of mind.

**Rejoice in the LORD, you righteous!
Retain his holiness through praise.** *Psalm 97(96):1, 6, 9–12*

676

Sing to the LORD a new song,
for he has done wonders!
His right arm, his holy power,
has gotten him victory.
The LORD has revealed his salvation,
displayed his triumph to the nations.

Shout to the LORD, O Earth!
Break forth with music and singing!
Sing to the LORD with instruments!
With voices and instruments sing!

The sea and its waters are rumbling,
the world and all of its creatures.
The rivers are clapping their hands
and the mountains are singing together,
preceding the LORD as he comes
to rule the earth.

He rules the world and the peoples
correctly and justly. *Psalm 98(97):1–2, 4–5, 7–9*

677

Shout to the LORD, O Earth!
Work for the LORD with gladness
and enter his presence with singing!

Understand that the LORD is God.
We are his, for he made us
—his people, the sheep of his pasture.

Enter his gates with confession,
his courtyards with praise!
Confess him and honor his name!
The LORD is good:
  his kindness endures;
  his faithfulness never ends. *Psalm 100(99)*

678

Bless the LORD, my soul,
every fiber, his holy name!

Bless the LORD, my soul!
Never forget all his goodness.

It is he who forgives all your sins.
It is he who heals every sickness,
who saves your life from the grave,
who crowns you with love and compassion,
who fills you to flowing with goodness,
renewing your strength like the eagle's.

He does not treat us like sinners,
nor has he repaid us for evil.
As the heavens are higher than earth,
so great is his love to his saints.
As far as the east from the west,
so far has he taken our guilt.

As a father's concern for his children
is the LORD's concern for his saints,
for he is aware of our weakness
and remembers that we are but dust.

But the love of the LORD is ancient
and follows his saints to the end.
His righteous deeds are for men,
that they live in his covenant,
remember his laws and do them.

The LORD! He established his throne in the skies.
His dominion extends over all.

Bless the LORD, my soul!

Psalm 103(102):1–5, 10–14, 17–19, 22c

679

I lift my eyes to the hills
from whence my help approaches.

My help is from the LORD,
the Maker of heaven and earth.

May he keep your foot from stumbling!
May your guardian never sleep!

Lo, the guardian of Israel
will not slumber nor sleep.

The LORD is your guardian and shield,
close to your side.

**The sun cannot strike you by day
nor the moon by night.**

May the LORD protect you from evil;
may he guard your life.

**May he guard your coming and going
now and forever.** *Psalm 121(120)*

680

I am happy when someone says,
"Let us go to the House of the LORD!"

**Our feet used to stand
in Jerusalem's gates.**

Jerusalem was built
to be joined to a temple,

**where the tribes could go up,
the tribes of the LORD.**

It is Israel's witness
to confess the LORD's name.

**There sit the thrones of judgment,
the seat of the house of David.**

Ask for the peace of Jerusalem.

**May your friends have rest!
May your workers prosper!
May your courts enjoy peace!**

For the sake of my brother, my friend,
let me say, "Peace for you!"

**For the sake of the LORD-my-God's house
I will seek your good welfare.** *Psalm 122(121)*

681

**I call from the depths, O LORD.
Lord, listen to my voice!**

Let your ears be attuned to hear
the sound of my plea!
If, LORD, you remember guilt,
who, Lord, can stand?
but you are forgiving
and therefore respected.

> I wait, O LORD; my whole being waits.
> I hope in your word.

My whole being hopes for the LORD
more than watchmen wait for the dawn.

> Let Israel hope in the LORD,
> for the LORD deals kindly.
> He continues to redeem.

Psalm 130(129):1–7

682

I exalt you, my God, as king.
I will bless your name forever.

> **Blessed be the LORD!**
> **His name is blessed forever.**

Great is the LORD, greatly praised;
his great deeds, beyond comprehension.

> **Blessed be the LORD!**
> **His name is blessed forever.**

Every generation must laud him
and declare his mighty deeds.

> **Blessed be the LORD!**
> **His name is blessed forever.**

I will think of the story of your wonders
and the splendor of the weight of your glory.

> **Blessed be the LORD!**
> **His name is blessed forever.**

Your kingdom will last forever;
your rule touches all generations.

> **Blessed be the LORD!**
> **His name is blessed forever.**

What God has said is dependable;
all that he does can be trusted.

**Blessed be the LORD!
His name is blessed forever.**

Let my mouth speak the LORD's praise!
Let all flesh bless his holy name.

**Blessed be the LORD!
His name is blessed forever.**   *Psalm 145(144):1, 4–5, 13, 21*

683

Praise the LORD!
Praise the LORD from the heavens!
Praise him in the heights!

**Praise him, all his messengers!
Praise him, all his armies!**

Praise him, sun and moon!
Praise him, all shining stars!

**Praise him, O heavens beyond heavens,
O waters above all the heavens!**

Give praise to the name of the LORD!
At his command you were made.

**He made them immovable forever;
he decreed that they should remain.**

Give praise to the LORD from the earth,
O monsters and all powers of chaos!
— lightning and storm, snow and clouds,
hot desert wind which blows at his word,
mountains and all high hills,
fruit-bearing trees and cedars,
wild creature and very large beast,
reptile and bird on wing,
kings of the earth and all peoples,
princes and all of earth's leaders,
healthy young men and maidens,
old men and children!

Let them all praise the name of the LORD,
his unique, inaccessible name!
His glory covers earth and heaven.

He has lifted strength from his people,
a hymn of praise from his saints,
from Israel, the people who are near him.
Praise the LORD!   *Psalm 148*

684

Praise the LORD!
Praise God in his sanctuary!
Praise him in his mighty sky!
Praise him for his exploits!
Praise him for his transcending greatness!

Praise him with a blast of a trumpet!

Praise him with sound of strings!

Praise him with rhythm and dancing!

Praise him with violins and flutes!

Praise him with ringing of bells!

Praise him with clashing of cymbals!

Let all living things praise the LORD!

Praise the LORD!   *Psalm 150*

OTHER SCRIPTURE SELECTIONS FOR RESPONSIVE OR UNISON READING

685

It shall come to pass in the latter days
that the mountain of the house of the LORD
shall be established as the highest of the mountains,

**and shall be raised above the hills;
and all the nations shall flow to it,**

and many peoples shall come, and say:

**"Come, let us go up to the mountain of the LORD,
to the house of the God of Jacob;
that he may teach us his ways
and that we may walk in his paths."**

For out of Zion shall go forth the law,
and the word of the LORD from Jerusalem.

**He shall judge between the nations,
and shall decide for many peoples;**

and they shall beat their swords into plowshares,
and their spears into pruning hooks;

**nation shall not not lift up sword against nation,
neither shall they learn war any more.**

Isaiah 2:2–4

686

The people who walked in darkness
have seen a great light;

**those who dwelt in a land of deep darkness,
on them has light shined.**

For to us a child is born,
to us a son is given;

and the government will be upon his shoulder,

and his name will be called
"Wonderful Counselor, Mighty God,
Everlasting Father, Prince of Peace."

Of the increase of his government and of peace
there will be no end.

Isaiah 9:2, 6–7

687

Comfort, comfort my people,
says your God.

> **Speak tenderly to Jerusalem,**
> **and cry to her**
> **that her warfare is ended,**
> **that her iniquity is pardoned,**
> **that she has received from the LORD's hand**
> **double for all her sins.**

A voice cries:
"In the wilderness prepare the way of the LORD,
make straight in the desert a highway for our God.

> **"Every valley shall be lifted up,**
> **and every mountain and hill be made low;**
> **the uneven ground shall become level,**
> **and the rough places a plain.**

"And the glory of the LORD shall be revealed,
and all flesh shall see it together,

> **"for the mouth of the LORD has spoken."**

Isaiah 40:1–5

688

Get you up to a high mountain,
O Zion, herald of good tidings;

> **lift up your voice with strength,**
> **O Jerusalem, herald of good tidings,**

lift it up, fear not;
say to the cities of Judah,
"Behold your God!"

> **Behold, the Lord GOD comes with might,**
> **and his arm rules for him;**

behold, his reward is with him,
and his recompense before him.

He will feed his flock like a shepherd,

he will gather the lambs in his arms,
he will carry them in his bosom,

and gently lead those that are with young.

Isaiah 40:9–11

689

My heart praises the Lord,
my soul is glad because of God my Savior.
For he has remembered me, his lowly servant!
And from now on all people will call me blessed,
because of the great things the Mighty God has done for me.

His name is holy;
he shows mercy to all who fear him,
from one generation to another.

He stretched out his mighty arm
and scattered the proud people with all their plans.

He brought down mighty kings from their thrones,
and lifted up the lowly.

He filled the hungry with good things,
and sent the rich away with empty hands.

He kept the promise he made to our ancestors;
he came to the help of his servant Israel,
and remembered to show mercy to Abraham
and to all his descendants forever!

Luke 1:46–55

690

Now there was a man living in Jerusalem whose name was Simeon.
He was a good and God-fearing man,
and was waiting for Israel to be saved.
The Holy Spirit was with him,
and he had been assured by the Holy Spirit
that he would not die before he had seen
the Lord's promised Messiah.

Led by the Spirit, Simeon went into the Temple.
When the parents brought the child Jesus into the Temple
to do for him what the Law required,

Simeon took the child in his arms,
and gave thanks to God:

"Now, Lord, you have kept your promise,
and you may let your servant go in peace.
For with my own eyes I have seen your salvation,
which you have made ready in the presence of all peoples:
a light to reveal your way to the Gentiles,
and to give glory to your people Israel."

Luke 2:25–32

691

This is how God showed his love for us:
he sent his only Son into the world that we might
have life through him.

This is what love is:
it is not that we have loved God,
but that he loved us and sent his Son to be the means
by which our sins are forgiven.

Dear friends, if this is how God loved us,
then we should love one another.

No one has ever seen God;
if we love one another,
God lives in us and his love is made perfect within us.

This is how we are sure that we live in God and
he lives in us: he has given us his Spirit.

And we have seen and tell others that the Father
sent his Son to be the Savior of the world.

Whoever declares that Jesus is the Son of God,
God lives in him, and he lives in God.

I John 4:9–15

692

Then Jesus went to Nazareth, where he had been brought up, and on
the Sabbath day he went as usual to the synagogue. He stood up to
read the Scriptures, and was handed the book of the prophet Isaiah.
He unrolled the scroll and found the place where it is written:

"The Spirit of the Lord is upon me.
He has anointed me to preach the good news to the poor,
He has sent me to proclaim liberty to the captives,
And recovery of sight to the blind,
To set free the oppressed,
To announce the year when the Lord will save his people!"

Jesus rolled up the scroll, gave it back to the attendant, and sat down. All the people in the synagogue had their eyes fixed on him.

He began speaking to them:
"This passage of scripture has come true today,
as you heard it being read."

Luke 4:16–21

693

Then James and John, the sons of Zebedee, came to Jesus. "Teacher," they said, "there is something we want you to do for us."

"What do you want me to do for you?" Jesus asked them.

They answered: "When you sit on your throne in the glorious kingdom, we want you to let us sit with you, one at your right and one at your left."

Jesus said to them: "You don't know what you are asking for. Can you drink the cup that I must drink? Can you be baptized in the way I must be baptized?"

"We can," they answered. Jesus said to them: "You will indeed drink the cup I must drink and be baptized in the way I must be baptized.

"But I do not have the right to choose who will sit at my right and my left. It is God who will give these places to those for whom he has prepared them."

When the other ten disciples heard about this they became angry with James and John.

So Jesus called them all together to him and said: "You know that the men who are considered rulers of the people have power over them, and the leaders rule over them.

"This, however, is not the way it is among you. If one of you wants to be great, he must be the servant of the rest;

"and if one of you wants to be first, he must be the slave of all.

"For even the Son of Man did not come to be served; he came to serve and to give his life to redeem many people." *Mark 10:35–45*

694

Who has believed what we have heard?

And to whom has the arm of the LORD been revealed?

For he grew up before him like a young plant,

and like a root out of dry ground;

he had no form or comeliness that we should look at him,

and no beauty that we should desire him.

He was despised and rejected by men;

a man of sorrows, and acquainted with grief;

and as one from whom men hide their faces

he was despised, and we esteemed him not.

Surely he has borne our griefs
and carried our sorrows;

**yet we esteemed him stricken,
smitten by God, and afflicted.**

But he was wounded for our transgressions,

he was bruised for our iniquities;

upon him was the chastisement that made us whole,

and with his stripes we are healed.

Isaiah 53:1–5

695

**All we like sheep have gone astray;
we have turned every one to his own way;**

and the LORD has laid on him
the iniquity of us all.

**He was oppressed, and he was afflicted,
yet he opened not his mouth;**

like a lamb that is led to the slaughter,

**and like a sheep that before its shearers is dumb,
so he opened not his mouth.**

By oppression and judgment he was taken away;

and as for his generation, who considered
that he was cut off out of the land of the living,
stricken for the transgression of my people?

And they made his grave with the wicked

and with a rich man in his death,

although he had done no violence,

and there was no deceit in his mouth.

Isaiah 53:6–9

696

Do not let anyone deceive you with foolish words: it is because of these very things that God's wrath will come upon those who do not obey him.

So have nothing at all to do with such people.

You yourselves used to be in the darkness, but since you have become the Lord's people you are in the light. So you must live like people who belong to the light.

For it is the light that brings a rich harvest of every kind of goodness, righteousness, and truth.

Try to learn what pleases the Lord.

Have nothing to do with people who do worthless things that belong to the darkness. Instead, bring these out to the light.

And when all things are brought out to the light, then their true nature is clearly revealed;

for anything that is clearly revealed becomes light. That is why it is said,

"Wake up, sleeper,
Rise from the dead!
And Christ will shine upon you."

Ephesians 5:6–11, 13–14

697

But Christ has already come as the High Priest of the good things that are already here. The tent in which he serves is greater and more perfect; it is not made by men, that is, it is not a part of this created world.

When Christ went through the tent and entered once and for all into the Most Holy Place, he did not take the blood of goats and calves to

offer as sacrifice; rather, he took his own blood and obtained eternal salvation for us.

The blood of goats and bulls and the ashes of the burnt calf are sprinkled on the people who are ritually unclean, and make them clean by taking away their ritual impurity.

Since this is true, how much more is accomplished by the blood of Christ! Through the eternal Spirit he offered himself as a perfect sacrifice to God. His blood will make our consciences clean from useless works, so that we may serve the living God.

For Christ did not go into a holy place made by men, a copy of the real one. He went into heaven itself, where he now appears on our behalf in the presence of God.

The Jewish High Priest goes into the Holy Place every year with the blood of an animal. But Christ did not go in to offer himself many times;

for then he would have had to suffer many times ever since the creation of the world. Instead, he has now appeared once and for all, when all ages of time are nearing the end, to remove sin through the sacrifice of himself.

Everyone must die once, and after that be judged by God.

In the same manner, Christ also was offered in sacrifice once to take away the sins of many. He will appear a second time, not to deal with sin, but to save those who are waiting for him.

Hebrews 9:11–14, 24–28

698

The attitude you should have is the one that Christ Jesus had:

He always had the very nature of God,
but he did not think that by force he should try to become equal with God.
Instead, of his own free will he gave it all up,
and took the nature of a servant.
He became like man, he appeared in human likeness;
he was humble and walked the path of obedience to death
— his death on the cross.
For this reason God raised him to the highest place above,
and gave him the name that is greater than any other name,
so that, in honor of the name of Jesus,
all beings in heaven, and on the earth, and in the world below

will fall on their knees,
and all will openly proclaim that Jesus Christ is the Lord,
to the glory of God the Father.

Philippians 2:5–11

699

Let us give thanks to the God and Father of our Lord Jesus Christ! Because of his great mercy, he gave us new life by raising Jesus Christ from the dead. This fills us with a living hope,

and so we look forward to possess the rich blessings that God keeps for his people. He keeps them for you in heaven, where they cannot decay or spoil or fade away.

They are for you, who through faith are kept safe by God's power, as you wait for the salvation which is ready to be revealed at the end of time.

Be glad about this, even though it may now be necessary for you to be sad for a while because of the many kinds of trials you suffer.

Their purpose is to prove that your faith is genuine. Even gold, which can be destroyed, is tested by fire; and so your faith, which is much more precious than gold, must also be tested, that it may endure. Then you will receive praise and glory and honor on the Day when Jesus Christ is revealed.

You love him, although you have not seen him; you believe in him, although you do not now see him; and so you rejoice with a great and glorious joy, which words cannot express.

I Peter 1:3–8

700

One of the elders asked me, "Who are those people dressed in white robes, and where do they come from?"

**"I don't know, sir. You do," I answered.
He said to me: "These are the people who have come safely through the great persecution. They washed their robes and made them white with the blood of the Lamb.**

"That is why they stand before God's throne and serve him day and night in his temple. He who sits on the throne will protect them with his presence.

"Never again will they hunger or thirst; neither sun nor any scorching heat will burn them;

"for the Lamb, who is in the center of the throne, will be their shepherd,
and guide them to springs of living water;

"and God will wipe away every tear from their eyes."

Revelation 7:13–17

701

Next let us praise illustrious men,
our ancestors in their successive generations.

The Lord has created an abundance of glory,
and displayed his greatness from earliest times.

Some wielded authority as kings
and were renowned for their strength;
others were intelligent advisers
and uttered prophetic oracles.
Others directed the people by their advice,
by their understanding of the popular mind,
and by the wise words of their teaching;

some of them left a name behind them,
so that their praises are still sung.

While others have left no memory,
and disappeared as though they had not existed.

But here is a list of generous men
whose good works have not been forgotten.
In their descendants there remains
a rich inheritance born of them.
Their descendants stand by the covenants
and, thanks to them, so do their children's children.
Their offspring will last forever,
their glory will not fade.

Their bodies have been buried in peace,
and their name lives on for all generations.
The peoples will proclaim their wisdom,
the assembly will celebrate their praises.

Ecclesiasticus 44:1–4, 8–9, 10–15

702

So Jesus said to the Jews who believed in him, "If you obey my teaching
you are really my disciples;

702

"you will know the truth, and the truth will make you free."

"We are the descendants of Abraham," they answered, "and we have never been anybody's slaves. What do you mean, then, by saying, 'You will be made free'?"

Jesus said to them: "I tell you the truth: everyone who sins is a slave of sin.

"A slave does not belong to the family always; but a son belongs there forever.

"If the Son makes you free, then you will be really free.

"I know you are Abraham's descendants. Yet you are trying to kill me, because you will not accept my teaching.

"I talk about what my Father has shown me, but you do what your father has told you."

John 8:31–38

703

May you always be joyful in your life in the Lord.
I say it again: rejoice!

Show a gentle attitude toward all.
The Lord is coming soon.
Don't worry about anything,
but in all your prayers ask God for what you need,
always asking him with a thankful heart.

And God's peace, which is far beyond human understanding,
will keep your hearts and minds safe,
in Christ Jesus.

Philippians 4:4–7

704

Happy are those who know they are spiritually poor:
the kingdom of heaven belongs to them!
Happy are those who mourn:
God will comfort them!
Happy are the meek:
they will receive what God has promised!
Happy are those whose greatest desire is to do what God requires:
God will satisfy them fully!
Happy are those who show mercy to others:
God will show mercy to them!

Happy are the pure in heart:
  they will see God!
Happy are those who work for peace among men:
  God will call them his sons!
Happy are those who suffer persecution because they do what God requires:
  the kingdom of heaven belongs to them!
Happy are you when men insult you and mistreat you and tell all kinds of
evil lies against you because you are my followers.
Rejoice and be glad, because a great reward is kept for you in heaven.
This is how men mistreated the prophets who lived before you.

Matthew 5:3–12

705

God spoke all these words, saying,
I am the LORD your God, who brought you out of the land of Egypt, out
of the house of bondage.
You shall have no other gods before me.
You shall not make for yourself a graven image, or any likeness of anything that is in heaven above, or that is in the earth beneath, or that is
in the water under the earth; you shall not bow down to them or serve
them; for I the LORD your God am a jealous God, visiting the iniquity
of the fathers upon the children to the third and the fourth generation of
those who hate me, but showing steadfast love to thousands of those
who love me and keep my commandments.
You shall not take the name of the LORD your God in vain; for the LORD
will not hold him guiltless who takes his name in vain.
Remember the sabbath day, to keep it holy. Six days you shall labor,
and do all your work; but the seventh day is a sabbath to the LORD your
God; in it you shall not do any work, you, or your son, or your daughter,
your manservant, or your maidservant, or your cattle, or the sojourner
who is within your gates; for in six days the LORD made heaven and
earth, the sea, and all that is in them, and rested the seventh day;
therefore the LORD blessed the sabbath day and hallowed it.
Honor your father and your mother, that your days may be long in the
land which the LORD your God gives you.
You shall not kill.
You shall not commit adultery.
You shall not steal.
You shall not bear false witness against your neighbor.
You shall not covet your neighbor's house; you shall not covet your
neighbor's wife, or his manservant, or his maidservant, or his ox, or
his ass, or anything that is your neighbor's.

Exodus 20:1–17

706

And when you fast, do not put on a sad face like the show-offs do. They go around with a hungry look so that everybody will be sure to see that they are fasting. Remember this! They have already been paid in full.

When you go without food, wash your face and comb your hair, so that others cannot know that you are fasting — only your Father, who is unseen, will know. And your Father, who sees what you do in private, will reward you.

Matthew 6:16–18

707

Do not save riches here on earth, where moths and rust destroy, and robbers break in and steal.

Instead, save riches in heaven, where moths and rust cannot destroy, and robbers cannot break in and steal.

For your heart will always be where your riches are.

Matthew 6:19–21

708

Now this is the message that we have heard from his Son
and announce to you:
God is light and there is no darkness at all in him.

If, then, we say that we have fellowship with him,
yet at the same time live in the darkness,
we are lying both in our words and in our actions.

But if we live in the light —
just as he is in the light —
then we have fellowship with one another,
and the blood of Jesus, his Son,
makes us clean from every sin.

If we say that we have no sin, we deceive ourselves
and there is no truth in us.

But if we confess our sins to God,
we can trust him,
for he does what is right —
he will forgive us our sins and make us clean
from all our wrongdoing.

If we say that we have not sinned,
we make a liar out of God,
and his word is not in us.

I John 1:5–10

709

My whole being boasts of the Lord:
let the lowly folk hear and be glad.

**Lord, God Almighty,
how great and wonderful are your deeds!
King of all nations,
how right and true are your ways!**

Who will not fear you, Lord?
Who will refuse to declare your greatness?
For you alone are holy.
All the nations will come
and worship before you,
for your righteous deeds are seen by all.

**O give thanks to the Lord, for he is good;
for his steadfast love endures forever!**

Let the heavens be glad, and let the earth rejoice,
and let them say among the nations, "The Lord reigns!"

**Amen! Praise, and glory, and wisdom, and thanks, and honor,
and power, and might, belong to our God forever and ever! Amen!**
*Psalm 34(33):1; Revelation 15:3–4;
I Chronicles 16:34, 31; Revelation 7:12*

710

In the fear of the LORD one has strong confidence,
and his children will have a refuge.

**Be silent before God, my soul: he bears my salvation!
Yes, he is my rock and help
— my fortress: I will not be shaken.**

Whoever sits in the shadow of the Highest,
who sleeps in the shade of the Almighty,

**the eternal God is your dwelling place,
and underneath are the everlasting arms.**

706

Confess that the LORD is good,

that his kindness endures.

Proverbs 14:26; Psalm 62(61):1-2; 91(90:1);
Deuteronomy 33:27; Psalm 118(117):1

711

Let all the earth worship the Lord!
Let all the world's citizens fear!

Teach me your ways, O Lord:
I would walk in your truth.
Inspire my mind to worship your name.

Holy, holy, holy, is the Lord God Almighty,
who was, who is, and who is to come.

I would praise you, O Master, my God, with all my heart,
and honor your name forever!

Our Lord and God! You are worthy
to receive glory, and honor, and power.
For you created all things,
and by your will they were given existence and life.

How numerous are your deeds, O Lord
— and all of them done with such wisdom!
Your activity fills the earth.
Blessed be the Lord forever.

Psalm 33(32):8; 86(85):11; Revelation 4:8; Psalm 86(85):12;
Revelation 4:11; Psalm 104(103):24; 89(88):52

712

Be strong and of good courage; for you shall cause this people to inherit
the land which I swore to their fathers to give them.
Only be strong and very courageous, being careful to do according to
all the law which Moses my servant commanded you; turn not from it
to the right hand or to the left, that you may have good success wherever
you go.

This book of the law shall not depart out of your mouth, but you shall
meditate on it day and night, that you may be careful to do according
to all that is written in it; for then you shall make your way prosperous,
and then you shall have good success.
Have I not commanded you?

707

Be strong and of good courage;
be not frightened, neither be dismayed;
for the LORD your God is with you wherever you go.

Joshua 1:6–9

713

When the Pharisees heard that Jesus had silenced the Sadducees, they came together, and one of them, a teacher of the Law, tried to trap him with a question.

"Teacher," he asked, "which is the greatest commandment in the Law?"

Jesus answered, " 'You must love the Lord your God with all your heart, and with all your soul, and with all your mind.'

"This is the greatest and the most important commandment.

"The second most important commandment is like it: 'You must love your neighbor as yourself.'

"The whole Law of Moses and the teachings of the prophets depend on these two commandments."

Matthew 22:34–40

714

I may be able to speak the languages of men and even of angels, but if I have not love, my speech is no more than a noisy gong or a clanging bell.

I may have the gift of inspired preaching;
I may have all knowledge and understand all secrets;
I may have all the faith needed to move mountains —
but if I have not love, I am nothing.
I may give away everything I have, and even give up my body to be burned —
but if I have not love, it does me no good.

Love is patient and kind; love is not jealous, or conceited, or proud;

love is not ill-mannered, or selfish, or irritable; love does not keep a record of wrongs;

love is not happy with evil, but is happy with the truth.

Love never gives up: its faith, hope, and patience never fail.

Love is eternal. There are inspired messages, but they are temporary; there are gifts of speaking, but they will cease; there is knowledge, but it will pass.

For our gifts of knowledge and of inspired messages are only partial; but when what is perfect comes, then what is partial will disappear.

When I was a child, my speech, feelings, and thinking were all those of a child; now that I am a man, I have no more use for childish ways.

What we see now is like the dim image in a mirror; then we shall see face to face. What I know now is only partial; then it will be complete, as complete as God's knowledge of me.

Meanwhile these three remain: faith, hope, and love; and the greatest of these is love.

I Corinthians 13:1–13

715

Holy, holy, holy is the LORD of hosts;
the whole earth is full of his glory.

Where can I go to escape?
Where can I hide from your presence?
If I climb to the skies you are there;
if I lie down in Hell, there also.

Could I flee on the wings of the dawn
and camp far beyond the ocean,
even there your presence would follow.
Your strong arm would grasp me.

If I say, "Let the darkness enshroud me!
Let the daylight around me be night!"
I find that the dark cannot daunt you,
that night seems as bright as the day
and darkness like light.

Holy, holy, holy is the LORD of hosts;
the whole earth is full of his glory.

Isaiah 6:3; Psalm 139(138):7–12

716

Surely there is a mine for silver,
and a place for gold which they refine.
But where shall wisdom be found?
And where is the place of understanding?

**Man does not know the way to it,
and it is not found in the land of the living.**

The deep says, "It is not in me,"
and the sea says, "It is not with me."

**It cannot be gotten for gold,
and silver cannot be weighed as its price.**

Whence then comes wisdom?
And where is the place of understanding?

**God understands the way to it,
and he knows its place.
Behold, the fear of the Lord, that is wisdom;
and to depart from evil is understanding.**

Job 28:1, 12–15, 20, 23, 28

717

"Do not be worried and upset," Jesus told them. "Believe in God, and believe also in me.

"There are many rooms in my Father's house, and I am going to prepare a place for you. I would not tell you this if it were not so.

"And after I go and prepare a place for you, I will come back and take you to myself, so that you will be where I am.

"You know how to get to the place where I am going."

Thomas said to him, "Lord, we do not know where you are going, how can we know the way to get there?"

Jesus answered him: "I am the way, I am the truth, I am the life; no one goes to the Father except by me.

"Now that you have known me," he said to them, "you will know my Father also; and from now on you do know him, and you have seen him."

John 14:1–7

718

With God are wisdom and might;
he has counsel and understanding.

**If he tears down, none can rebuild;
if he shuts a man in, none can open.**

If he withholds the waters, they dry up;
if he sends them out, they overwhelm the land.

**With him are strength and wisdom;
the deceived and the deceiver are his.**

He looses the bonds of kings,
and binds a waistcloth on their loins.

**He makes nations great,
and he destroys them:**

he enlarges nations,
and leads them away.

**In his hand is the life of every living thing
and the breath of all mankind.**

Job 12:13–16, 18, 23, 10

719

But the souls of the virtuous are in the hands of God,
no torment shall ever touch them.

**In the eyes of the unwise, they did appear to die,
their going looked like a disaster,
their leaving us, like annihilation;
but they are in peace.**

Yet God did make man imperishable,
he made him in the image of his own nature.

**But the virtuous live forever,
their recompense lies with the Lord.
The Most High takes care of them,**

for he will shelter them with his right hand
and shield them with his arm.

Wisdom 3:1–3; 2:23; 5:15–16, 17

720

So then, my brothers, because of God's many mercies to us, I make this appeal to you: Offer yourselves as a living sacrifice to God, dedicated to his service and pleasing to him. This is the true worship that you should offer.

Do not conform outwardly to the standards of this world, but let God transform you inwardly by a complete change of your mind. Then you will be able to know the will of God – what is good, and is pleasing to him, and is perfect.

Love must be completely sincere. Hate what is evil, hold on to what is good.

Love one another warmly as brothers in Christ, and be eager to show respect for one another.

Work hard, and do not be lazy. Serve the Lord with a heart full of devotion.

Let your hope keep you joyful, be patient in your troubles, and pray at all times.

Share your belongings with your needy brothers, and open your homes to strangers.

Ask God to bless those who persecute you; yes, ask him to bless, not to curse.

Rejoice with those who rejoice, weep with those who weep.

Show the same spirit toward all alike. Do not be proud, but accept humble duties. Do not think of yourselves as wise.

If someone does evil to you, do not pay him back with evil. Try to do what all men consider to be good.

Romans 12:1-2, 9-17

721

If God is for us, who can be against us?

He did not even keep back his own Son, but offered him for us all! He gave us his Son – will he not also freely give us all things?

Who will accuse God's chosen people? God himself declares them not guilty!

Can anyone, then, condemn them? Christ Jesus is the one who died, or rather, who was raised to life and is at the right side of God. He pleads with God for us!

Who, then, can separate us from the love of Christ? Can trouble do it, or hardship, or persecution, or hunger, or poverty, or danger, or death?

As the scripture says,

"For your sake we are in danger of death the whole day long, we are treated like sheep that are going to be slaughtered."

No, in all these things we have complete victory through him who loved us!

For I am certain that nothing can separate us from his love: neither death nor life; neither angels nor other heavenly rulers or powers; neither the present nor the future;

neither the world above nor the world below—there is nothing in all creation that will ever be able to separate us from the love of God which is ours through Christ Jesus our Lord.

Romans 8:31–39

722

I am the real vine, and my Father is the gardener.

He breaks off every branch in me that does not bear fruit, and prunes every branch that does bear fruit, so that it will be clean and bear more fruit.

You have been made clean already by the message I have spoken to you.

Remain in union with me, and I will remain in union with you. Unless you remain in me you cannot bear fruit, just as a branch cannot bear fruit unless it remains in the vine.

I am the vine, you are the branches. Whoever remains in me, and I in him, will bear much fruit; for you can do nothing without me.

Whoever does not remain in me is thrown out, like a branch, and dries up; such branches are gathered up and thrown into the fire, where they are burned.

If you remain in me, and my words remain in you, then you will ask for anything you wish, and you shall have it.

This is how my Father's glory is shown: by your bearing much fruit; and in this way you become my disciples.

I love you just as the Father loves me; remain in my love.

If you obey my commands, you will remain in my love, in the same way that I have obeyed my Father's commands and remain in his love.

I have told you this so that my joy may be in you, and that your joy may be complete.

This is my commandment: love one another, just as I love you.

The greatest love a man can have for his friends is to give his life for them.

John 15:1–13

723

Whoever loves me will obey my message. My Father will love him, and my Father and I will come to him and live with him.

Whoever does not love me does not obey my words. The message you have heard is not mine, but comes from the Father, who sent me.

I have told you this while I am still with you.

The Helper, the Holy Spirit whom the Father will send in my name, will teach you everything, and make you remember all that I have told you.

Peace I leave with you; my own peace I give you. I do not give it to you as the world does. Do not be worried and upset; do not be afraid.

John 14:23–27

724

Holy, holy, holy, is the Lord God Almighty,
who was, who is, and who is to come.

**Lord, God Almighty,
how great and wonderful are your deeds!
King of all nations,
how right and true are your ways!
Who will not fear you, Lord?
Who will refuse to declare your greatness?
For you alone are holy.
All the nations will come
and worship before you,
for your righteous deeds are seen by all.**

Our Lord and God! You are worthy
to receive glory, and honor, and power.
For you created all things,
and by your will they were given existence and life.

**The Lamb who was killed is worthy
to receive power, wealth, wisdom, and strength,
honor, glory, and praise!**

Praise, and glory, and wisdom, and thanks, and honor,
and power, and might, belong to our God forever and ever!

**To him who sits on the throne, and to the Lamb,
be praise and honor, glory and might,
forever and ever!**

Lord God Almighty, the one who is and who was!
We thank you that you have used your great power
and have begun to rule!

> **Praise God! For the Lord, our Almighty God, is King!**
> **Let us rejoice and be glad;**
> **let us praise his greatness!**

> > *Revelation 4:8; 15:3–4; 4:11; 5:12;*
> > *7:12; 5:13; 11:17; 19:6–7*

725

The disciples came to Jesus, asking,
"Who is the greatest in the kingdom of heaven?"

> **Jesus called a child, had him stand in front of them, and said: "Remember this! Unless you change and become like children, you will never enter the kingdom of heaven.**

"The greatest in the kingdom of heaven is the one who humbles himself and becomes like this child.

> **"And the person who welcomes in my name one such child as this, welcomes me."**

Some people brought children to Jesus for him to place his hands upon them and pray, but the disciples scolded those people.

> **Jesus said, "Let the children come to me, and do not stop them, because the kingdom of heaven belongs to such as these." He placed his hands on them.**

> > *Matthew 18:1–5; 19:13–15*

726

Remember your Creator in the days of your youth, before the evil days come,

> **and the years draw nigh, when you will say, "I have no pleasure in them."**

Rejoice, O young man, in your youth, and let your heart cheer you in the days of your youth;

> **walk in the ways of your heart and the sight of your eyes.**

But know that for all these things God will bring you into judgment. Let your heart hold fast my words; keep my commandments, and live.

> **Get wisdom, and whatever you get, get insight.**

And she will keep you; love her, and she will guard you. Prize her highly, and she will exalt you; she will honor you if you embrace her.

She will bestow on you a beautiful crown. Keep your heart with all vigilance; for from it flow the springs of life.

Do not enter the path of the wicked, and do not walk in the way of evil men. Avoid it; do not go on it; turn away from it and pass on. The way of the wicked is like deep darkness.

But the path of the righteous is like the light of dawn, which shines brighter and brighter until full day.

Ecclesiastes 12:1; 11:9;
Proverbs 4:4, 6, 7–9, 23, 14–15, 19, 18

Prayers

727   THE LORD'S PRAYER

Our Father in heaven,
   holy be your name,
   your kingdom come,
   your will be done,
      on earth as in heaven.
Give us today our daily bread.
Forgive us our sins
   as we forgive those who sin against us.
Do not bring us to the test
   but deliver us from evil.

For the kingdom, the power, and the glory are yours
   now and forever.

728   THE APOSTOLIC CREED

I believe in God, the Father almighty,
   creator of heaven and earth.

I believe in Jesus Christ, his only Son, our Lord.
   He was conceived by the power of the Holy Spirit
      and born of the Virgin Mary.
   He suffered under Pontius Pilate,
      was crucified, died, and was buried.
   He descended to the dead.
   On the third day he rose again.
   He ascended into heaven,
      and is seated at the right hand of the Father.
   He will come again to judge the living and the dead.

I believe in the Holy Spirit,
   the holy catholic church,
   the communion of saints,
   the forgiveness of sins,
   the resurrection of the body,
   and the life everlasting.

729 THE NICENE CREED

We believe in one God,
the Father, the Almighty,
maker of heaven and earth,
of all that is seen and unseen.

We believe in one Lord, Jesus Christ,
the only Son of God,
eternally begotten of the Father,
God from God, Light from Light,
true God from true God,
begotten, not made, one in Being with the Father.
Through him all things were made.
For us men and for our salvation
he came down from heaven:
by the power of the Holy Spirit
he was born of the Virgin Mary, and became man.
For our sake he was crucified under Pontius Pilate;
he suffered, died, and was buried.
On the third day he rose again
in fulfillment of the Scriptures;
he ascended into heaven
and is seated at the right hand of the Father.
He will come again in glory to judge the living
and the dead,
and his kingdom will have no end.

We believe in the Holy Spirit, the Lord, the giver of life,
who proceeds from the Father and the Son.
With the Father and the Son he is worshiped and glorified.
He has spoken through the prophets.
We believe in one holy catholic and apostolic church.
We acknowledge one baptism for the forgiveness of sins.
We look for the resurrection of the dead,
and the life of the world to come. Amen.

730 GLORIA IN EXCELSIS

Glory to God in the highest,
and peace to his people on earth.

Lord God, heavenly King,
almighty God and Father,

we worship you, we give you thanks,
we praise you for your glory.

Lord Jesus Christ, only Son of the Father,
Lord God, Lamb of God,
you take away the sin of the world:
    have mercy on us;
you are seated at the right hand of the Father:
    receive our prayer.

For you alone are the Holy One,
you alone are the Lord,
you alone are the Most High,
    Jesus Christ,
    with the Holy Spirit,
    in the glory of God the Father. Amen.

731   SANCTUS AND BENEDICTUS

Holy, holy, holy Lord, God of power and might,
heaven and earth are full of your glory.
    Hosanna in the highest.

Blessed is he who comes in the name of the Lord.
    Hosanna in the highest.

732   GLORIA PATRI

Glory to the Father, and to the Son, and to the Holy Spirit:
    as in the beginning, so now, and forever. Amen.

733   SURSUM CORDA

The Lord be with you.
And also with you.

Lift up your hearts.
We lift them up to the Lord.

Let us give thanks to the Lord our God.
It is right to give him thanks and praise.

734

AGNUS DEI

Jesus, Lamb of God:
  have mercy on us.
Jesus, bearer of our sins:
  have mercy on us.
Jesus, redeemer of the world:
  give us your peace.

735

TE DEUM

You are God: we praise you;
You are the Lord: we acclaim you;
You are the eternal Father:
All creation worships you.
To you all angels, all the powers of heaven,
Cherubim and Seraphim, sing in endless praise:
  Holy, holy, holy Lord, God of power and might,
  heaven and earth are full of your glory.
The glorious company of apostles praise you.
The noble fellowship of prophets praise you.
The white-robed army of martyrs praise you.
Throughout the world the holy Church acclaims you:
  Father, of majesty unbounded,
  your true and only Son, worthy of all worship,
  and the Holy Spirit, advocate and guide.
You, Christ, are the king of glory,
eternal Son of the Father.
When you became man to set us free
you did not disdain the Virgin's womb.
You overcame the sting of death,
and opened the kingdom of heaven to all believers.
You are seated at God's right hand in glory.
We believe that you will come, and be our judge.
  Come then, Lord, sustain your people,
  bought with the price of your own blood,
  and bring us with your saints
  to everlasting glory.

736

CALLS TO WORSHIP

High over all the nations is the Lord God!
His glory is greater than the heavens!
Who is like the Lord our God?
Blessed be the name of God, henceforth and forever!

737

Holy, holy, holy Lord God of hosts,
heaven and earth are filled with your glory.
Hosanna in the highest.
Blessed is he who comes in the name of the Lord.
Hosanna in the highest.

738

You are blessed, O God of our fathers;
blessed, too, is your name forever and ever.
Let the heavens bless you and all things you have made
forevermore.

739

The hour is coming, and now is, when the true worshipers will worship
the Father in spirit and truth, for such the Father seeks to worship him.

740

Make a joyful noise to the Lord, all the lands!
Serve the Lord with gladness!
Come into his presence with singing!
For the Lord is good; his steadfast love endures forever,
and his faithfulness to all generations.

741   INVOCATIONS

Almighty God, unto whom all hearts are open, all desires known, and
from whom no secrets are hid: cleanse the thoughts of our hearts by
the presence of your Holy Spirit, that we may perfectly love you and
glorify your holy name; through Jesus Christ our Lord. **Amen.**

742

O God our Father, you have commanded the light to shine out of
darkness and awakened us again to praise your goodness and to ask
your favor. Accept now the sacrifice of our worship and thanksgiving.
Make us to be children of the light and of the day, heirs of your everlasting inheritance. Remember, O God, your whole church and all our
brothers who stand in need of your favor on land or sea, in air or space.
May our lives ever praise your wonderful and holy name; through Jesus
Christ our Lord. **Amen.**

743

Ever loving and eternal God, Source of the light that never dims and of the love that never fails, Life of our life, Father of our spirits: draw near to us, and by the remembrance of your ancient mercies, by the ministry of your church, teach us and lead us nearer to you. By all our conflicts, by all our aspirations, by all our fears, by all our joys and sorrows, by life and death itself, teach us and lead us nearer to you. **Amen.**

744

O God, who put into our hearts such deep desires that we cannot be at peace until we rest in you: mercifully grant that the longing of our souls may not go unsatisfied because of any unrighteousness of life that may separate us from you. Open our minds to the counsels of eternal wisdom; breathe into our souls the peace which passes understanding. Increase our hunger and thirst for righteousness, and feed us, we beseech you, with the bread of heaven. Give us grace to seek first your kingdom, and help us to grow as you add unto us all things needful. **Amen.**

745

Almighty God, you have given us grace at this time with one accord to make our common supplications unto you, and have promised that you will hear the prayer of faith. Fulfill now, O Lord, the desires and petitions of your servants, granting us in this world knowledge of your truth, and in the world to come life everlasting. **Amen.**

746

We praise you, O God, for all your comings among the sons of men, but we are especially grateful for your coming among us in Jesus Christ our Lord. Help us to live in faithful expectation of his final victory and triumph over all the powers that oppose him. So fill us with hope and enthusiasm that we may celebrate now that glorious day when this world and all its people shall be his and he shall reign forever as Lord of all. **Amen.**

747

O Lord, you have given us the great hope that your kingdom shall come on earth, and your Son has taught us to pray for its coming. Make us ready now to give thanks for the signs of its dawning, and to pray and work for that perfect day when your will shall be done on earth as it is in heaven. We ask this in the name of Christ our Lord. **Amen.**

748

Merciful Father, we are reverently grateful for the coming of your Son, Jesus Christ. We remember his humble birth, his gracious life of love and service, his death for us upon the cross. We acknowledge him as Lord of our life, and as we prepare to celebrate his advent, we dedicate ourselves anew to him. Accept this promise in his name. **Amen.**

749

Almighty God, Father of our Lord Jesus Christ, we give you thanks that in the fullness of time the Light dawned on a dark world and your Son was born in Bethlehem. We praise you that he came and that he shall come again. We confess that the doors of our hearts are too low to receive the King of glory. We are too indifferent to go meet him. Come, we pray you, and by your Holy Spirit banish from us all that resists his entrance into our hearts. Make us, O God, a people who watch and pray for the day of his appearing. Even so, come, Lord Jesus; come quickly! **Amen.**

750

O Lord God, whom no man has seen nor can see, we bless you that you have been pleased to show us yourself in Jesus Christ, your Son. We are grateful that in the fullness of time he came into this world and took upon himself our human nature. In him we see your love for us and are brought into fellowship with you. Accept our thanks, O Father, in the holy name of Jesus for this your inexpressible gift. **Amen.**

751

O God of the guiding star which brought the Gentile kings to worship the Christ-child: strengthen and encourage us who now follow the star, and lead us into all dark places of the earth, letting the light of Christ shine on through us. May that day come when all men shall pay due homage to the King of kings, even Jesus Christ our Lord. **Amen.**

752

Almighty God, you know that of ourselves we have no power to help ourselves. Keep us, we beseech you, both outwardly in our bodies and inwardly in our souls, that we may find defense against all adversities which may afflict the body and all evil which may hurt the soul; through Christ our Lord. **Amen.**

753

O Lord Jesus Christ, as on this day we recall your triumphal entry into Jerusalem, enter our hearts, we pray, and subdue them wholly unto your will. O King of grace and glory, come into our lives with all your strength, gentleness, and goodness. We acknowledge you as Savior and Redeemer, give you our joyous homage, and pledge never-dying loyalty. **Amen.**

754

O God, by the example of your Son, our Savior Jesus Christ, you have taught us the greatness of true humility, and now have called us to watch with him in his suffering. Help us to take the towel and basin and in humbleness of spirit to wash the feet of those who most need our ministry. Give us the graciousness to serve one another in all lowliness and thus fulfill the law of love in the name of your suffering Servant, even Jesus Christ our Lord. **Amen.**

755

Thanks be to you, O God, for Jesus Christ, who for the joy that was set before him endured the cross. Thanks be to you for Jesus Christ, who in the cross triumphed over sin and death, principalities and powers, and over all who desire to thwart your will in the world. Thanks be to you, our Father, for Jesus Christ, who in the cross revealed your love for us by dying for the ungodly; yes, even while we were yet sinners, he died for us. Thanks be to you, O God, for you have called us to take up the cross and follow Christ Jesus. Grant that we may, with courage and joy, remain his disciples, for in Christ's name we pray. **Amen.**

756

Almighty God, you have revealed to us in the life and teaching of your Son the true way to a life that is right and good in your sight. You have also shown us in his suffering and death that the path to the good life may lead to the cross, and the reward of faithfulness and obedience to your will may be a crown of thorns. Give us the grace to learn these hard lessons. May we take up our cross and follow Christ in strength of patience and constancy of faith; may we have such fellowship with him in his sorrow that we may know the secret of his strength and peace, and see, even in our darkest hour, the shining of eternal light. **Amen.**

757

Almighty God, Source of all life, by whose power our Lord Jesus Christ was raised from the dead: we praise you, we give you thanks for this great victory over sin and death. The resurrection of your Son, our Savior, has opened to us the door of abundant and everlasting life. May that same power work in us, raising us from the death of sin to newness of life. Our despair is changed to triumph, our fears to hope. We are grateful. Accept our thanks, O Lord, and may we prove our gratitude by selfless service in behalf of all those who need our love and care. May we show them the risen Christ in all we do. In his living name we pray. **Amen.**

758

O risen and victorious Christ, whose power and love destroyed the darkness of death of sin: ascend, we pray you, the throne of our hearts, and so rule our wills by the might of that immortality wherewith you have set us free, that we may evermore be alive unto God, through the power of your glorious resurrection: world without end. **Amen.**

759

We bless your holy name, O God, for all your servants, who, having finished their course, now rest from their labors. Grant us the courage, we pray you, to follow the example of their steadfastness and faithfulness, to your glory and honor; through Jesus Christ our Lord. **Amen.**

760

O God and Father of us all, we gather in sincere gratitude for all those who, at their country's call, have met the rude shock of battle and have surrendered their lives amid the ruthless brutalities of war. Forbid that their suffering and death should be in vain. We beseech you that, through their devotion to duty and suffering, the horrors of war may pass from earth and that your kingdom of right and honor, of peace and brotherhood, may be established among men. Comfort, O Lord, all who mourn the loss of those near and dear to them, especially the families of our departed brothers. Support them by your love. Give them faith to look beyond the trials of the present and to know that neither life nor death can separate us from the love and care of Christ Jesus, in whose name we pray. **Amen.**

761   FOR PARDON

O God our Father, before whom the lives of all are exposed and the desires of all known, be at work in our lives. Wipe out all our old secret and selfish desires, so that we may perfectly love and truly worship you, in Christ our Lord. **Amen.**

762

Our Father, may all men come to respect and to love you. May you rule in every person and in all of life. Give us, day by day, those things of life we need. Forgive us our sins, just as we forgive those who have done us wrong. Let nothing test us beyond our strength. Save us from our weakness. For yours is the authority and the power, and the credit forever. **Amen.**

763

O God, whom Jesus called Father, we admit that we have done many wrong and wicked things and we have neglected doing many loving things. We are sorry that we have thought, said, and done such foolishness. Now we turn away from our mistakes. We are sick at heart, Father, when we think of them. Forgive us for not knowing what we do. Forgive us; in the name of Jesus, forgive us. Grant that we may so love you and serve you all our days that others will praise you. **Amen.**

764

Gracious Father, accept with favor this our sacrifice of praise which we now present. We offer to you ourselves, giving you thanks for calling us to your service, as your own people, through the perfect offering of your Son Jesus, our Lord; by whom and with whom, in the unity of the Holy Spirit, all honor and glory be to you, Father Almighty, now and forever. **Amen.**

765

Almighty God, in Jesus Christ you called us to be a servant people, but we do not what you command. We are often silent when we should speak, and useless when we could be useful. We are lazy servants, timid and heartless, who turn neighbors away from your love. Have mercy on us, O God, and, though we do not deserve your care, forgive us, and free us from sin; through Jesus Christ our Lord. **Amen.**

766

Almighty God, you love us, but we have not loved you; you call, but we have not listened. We walk away from neighbors in need, wrapped up in our own concerns. We have gone along with evil, with prejudice, warfare, and greed. God our Father, help us to face up to ourselves, so that, as you move toward us in mercy, we may repent, turn to you, and receive forgiveness; through Jesus Christ our Lord. **Amen.**

767

Have mercy upon us, O God, according to your loving-kindness; according to the multitude of your tender mercies blot out our transgressions. Wash us thoroughly from our iniquities, and cleanse us from our sins, for we acknowledge our transgressions, and our sin is ever before us. Create in us clean hearts, O God, and renew a right spirit within us; through Jesus Christ our Lord. **Amen.**

768

Our Father, we know that you would not love us for long except that your love is unchanging. We trust that you will look upon us with a sense of humor, for even when we are trying to confess our sins, we put into words the petty while leaving the gross unspoken. Help us to overcome our clowning and get down to that which is real. Take from us the burden of that which does not matter. Free us from the bewildering array of problems of our own making. Help us to wake up to the fact that in Jesus Christ our sin is forgiven and if we but take up his way of love we are free. **Amen.**

769

We confess to God Almighty, the Father, the Son, and the Holy Spirit, and before the whole company of the faithful, that we have sinned exceedingly in thought, word, and deed, through our own fault; wherefore we pray God to have mercy upon us: Almighty God, have mercy upon us, forgiving us our sins and delivering us from evil, confirming and strengthening us in all goodness and bringing us to everlasting life. **Amen.**

770

Almighty God, who made the light to shine in the darkness, shine now in our hearts. Cleanse us, we pray, from all our sins, and restore us to the light of your glory as we have seen it in the face of Jesus Christ, in whose name we pray. **Amen.**

771

May God the most merciful grant us pardon, forgiveness, and cleansing from all our sins through Jesus Christ our Lord. **Amen.**

772

Grant your faithful people, O gracious and loving Father, pardon and peace, that they may be relieved of the burden of their guilt and serve you with a quiet mind and their fellowmen with humility. **Amen.**

773

Deliver us, O Lord, from the bonds and burdens of our offenses, real or imagined; forgive us for the sins of omission and commission; restore to us the joy of salvation; in the name of him who forgave both his enemies and his friends. **Amen.**

774

Almighty God, our heavenly Father, who of your great mercy have promised forgiveness of sins to all them who with sincere penitence and true faith turn to you: have mercy upon us; pardon and deliver us from all our sins; confirm and strengthen us in all goodness; and bring us into the joyous and abundant life; through Jesus Christ our Lord. **Amen.**

775   WORDS OF ASSURANCE

If we confess our sins to God, we can trust him, for he does what is right — he will forgive us our sins and make us clean from all our wrong-doing. (*I John 1:9.*)

776

Jesus said: I will never turn away anyone who comes to me. (*John 6:37.*)

777

God loved the world so much that he gave his only Son, so that everyone who believes in him may not die but have eternal life. (*John 3:16.*)

778

This is a true saying, to be completely accepted and believed: Christ Jesus came into the world to save sinners. (*I Timothy 1:15.*)

779

There is no condemnation now for those who live in union with Christ Jesus, who live according to the Spirit, not according to human nature. (*Romans 8:1, 4.*)

780

The Lord redeems the life of his servants; those who trust him will not be punished. (*Psalm 34[33]:22.*)

781

As the heavens are higher than earth, so great is his love to his saints. (*Psalm 103[102]:11.*)

782 FOR THE ARMED FORCES

O Lord God of hosts, stretch forth, we pray, your almighty arm to strengthen and protect the soldiers of our country. Support them in the day of battle, and in the time of rest and training keep them safe from all evil. Endue them with courage and loyalty; and grant that in all things they may serve without reproach; through Jesus Christ our Lord. **Amen.**

783

O eternal Lord God, you alone spread out the heavens and rule the raging sea. Take into your most gracious protection our country's navy and all who serve therein. Preserve them from the dangers of the sea and from the violence of the enemy, that they may be a safeguard unto the United States of America, and a security for such as sail upon the seas in peaceful and lawful missions. In serving you, O Lord, may our sailors serve their country; through Jesus Christ our Lord. **Amen.**

784

O Lord God of hosts, you stretch out the heavens like a curtain. Watch over and protect, we pray, the airmen of our country as they fly upon their appointed tasks. Give them courage as they face the foe, and skill in the performance of their duty. Sustain them with your everlasting arms. May your hand lead them, and your right hand hold them up, that they may return to the earth with a grateful sense of your mercy; through Jesus Christ our Lord. **Amen.**

785

O eternal Father, we commend to your protection and care the members of the marine corps. Guide and direct them in the defense of our country and in the maintenance of justice among the nations. Sustain them in the hour of danger. Grant that wherever they serve they may be loyal to their high traditions, and that at all times they may put their trust in you; through Jesus Christ our Lord. **Amen.**

786

O Lord our God, who stilled the raging of the seas by your word of power: watch over, we pray you, the men of the coast guard as they sail upon their missions of vigilant aid. Grant them courage and skill and a safe return. Fill them with a grateful sense of your mercy toward them; through Jesus Christ our Lord. **Amen.**

787

O God of wisdom and order, who filled the universe with the mysteries of your power: guard, we beseech you, those who explore the secrets of space. Sustain them with the knowledge of your mercy and bring them safely back to earth. Let not the achievements of cosmic exploration blind us to the glories of your love for man; through Jesus Christ, your Son, our Lord. **Amen.**

788 FOR CHILDREN

Dear Lord and Father of us all, we give you thanks for the children you have placed in our care. Give us grace and wisdom to train them in your faith and fear and love. May they give you due reverence and all the joyous loyalty of their young hearts, so that as they advance in years they may also grow in the grace and knowledge of the Lord Jesus, who loved all children and blessed them; this we ask in his name. **Amen.**

789

O Lord Jesus Christ, who took the little children into your arms and blessed them with your love: bless, we beseech you, all the little ones who are dear to us. Keep your hand upon them, dear Lord, to protect them from all evil and to uphold and guide them along the pathway of life. May they find joy in both serving and loving you; and may they early learn what this loving service means. To that end give us grace to live before them as your true and faithful servants. **Amen.**

790 FOR YOUTH

O Lord God, source of all strength, fountainhead of all wisdom: look in mercy upon our beloved young people; replenish them with your truth. Teach them to follow the truth. Adorn them with purity of life;

keep them strong in body, keen of mind and sound of soul. Guide them through the shadowy valleys of life. Make them conscious of your presence with them as they gain the heights of glory in the glad sunshine of some victory. Comfort them when they are discouraged. May your peace, which passes all understanding, abide upon them all the days of their life; through Jesus Christ our Lord. **Amen.**

791   CLASSIC PRAYERS

Give me, O Lord, a steadfast heart, which no unworthy thought can drag downward; an unconquered heart, which no tribulation can wear out; an upright heart, which no unworthy purpose may tempt aside. Bestow upon me also, O Lord my God, understanding to know thee, diligence to seek thee, wisdom to find thee, and a faithfulness that may finally embrace thee; through Jesus Christ our Lord. **Amen.**

792

Teach us, good Lord, to serve thee as thou deservest; to give and not to count the cost; to fight and not to heed the wounds; to toil and not to seek for rest; to labor and not to ask for any reward, save that of knowing that we do thy will; through Jesus Christ our Lord. **Amen.**

793

Lord, make us instruments of thy peace. Where there is hatred, let us sow love; where there is injury, pardon; where there is discord, union; where there is doubt, faith; where there is despair, hope; where there is darkness, light; where there is sadness, joy; for thy mercy and for thy truth's sake. **Amen.**

794

Christ be with me, Christ within me,
Christ before me, Christ beside me,
Christ to win me,
Christ to comfort and restore me,
Christ beneath me, Christ above me,
Christ in quiet, Christ in danger,
Christ in hearts of all who love me,
Christ in mouth of friend and stranger. **Amen.**

795

God be in my head, and in my understanding;
God be in mine eyes and in my looking;
God be in my mouth, and in my speaking;
God be in my heart, and in my thinking;
God be at mine end, and at my departing. **Amen.**

796

Grant me:
    The serenity to accept things
      I cannot change,
    The courage to change things
      I can,
    And the wisdom to distinguish
      the one from the other.

797   FOR THE CHURCH IN THE WORLD

(This prayer may be used responsively.)

You have made your dwelling among us, God,
    And you are present wherever men live.
We cling to this grace.
    Make us honor your presence
And make us wise and strong enough
    To build each other up into your city on earth,
The body of Christ,
    A world fit to live in,
Today and forever.
    We ask you for bread and peace
And your answer, God, is Jesus Christ, your Son.
    He is bread for the life of the world,
Our hope and peace.
    We pray that he may be powerful here in our midst
And that we may find gladness in this Man, whom you
have given us
    Here and now and forever. **Amen.**

798

God, it is your happiness and life
  That one Son of Man
Of all the men born into this world
  Should go on living with us,
And that one name, Jesus Christ,
  Should inspire us from generation to generation.
We are gathered here in your presence
  To pray that we may hear and see him
And pass on his name
  To all who wish to receive it.
Let your Spirit move us
  To receive him from each other and from you,
This Man who is our future,
  Who lives with you
For all men
  And for the whole world. **Amen.**

799   FOR PEACE

Lord God, we see the sins of the world in the light of your only Son.
  Since his coming to be your mercy toward us
We have come to suspect how hard and unrelenting we are toward each
other.
  We ask you to renew us according to his example.
Let us grow like him and no longer repay evil with evil,
  But make peace and live in truth
Today and every day of our lives.
  God, you are not happy with us when we make each other unhappy.
You cannot bear it when we kill and destroy each other.
  Break, we pray you, the cycle of evil that holds us captive
And let sin die in us
  As the sin of the world died in Jesus, your Son, and death was killed.
He lives for us today and every day.
  Amen.

800   FOR THE PERSON IN THE WORLD

By your word, Lord God, you set free every man imprisoned within
himself;
  To freedom you have called us and to become men in the image and
  the spirit of Jesus Christ.

734

We beseech you, give us the strength that his life has first provided;
Give us the openness that he has prepared for us.
Make us receptive and free,
So that, with you, we may live for this world.
We thank you, God, our grace, for being alive, tomorrow and today;
For this earth; for bread and light;
For the people around us, today, yesterday, and every day.
We thank you for our lives here and now,
Lives laborious and full of joy.
May neither future nor death separate us from Jesus Christ,
Who is your love for all mankind and all the earth.
Amen.

801 FOR TODAY

O God, you have revealed yourself in the glory of the heavens and in the burning bush, in the still small voice and in the dread power of the hydrogen bomb. Make us aware of your presence as you come in judgment through the events of our time. Grant us to stand in awe and sin not. Help us so to use the fearful powers you have permitted us to know, that we may not work to man's destruction but for his fulfillment. Lift us above the suspicions and fears of our day, that we may bring peace among all men. This we ask, anxious, yet quiet in you; perplexed, yet certain in you; weak, yet strong in you; through him who is the Savior of us all, Jesus Christ our Lord. **Amen.**

802 FOR RESPONSIBILITY

O Lord, we have been called to be in this place at this time. May we be mindful of the responsibility which is ours as military personnel — to maintain order, to establish a rule of law, to protect the peace. Make us obedient always to the laws of God. Grant that in the hour of temptation we may exercise self-control and not be guilty of living an immoral life. Help us to use our skills for the strengthening of the nation. Give us faith in God, and help us to demonstrate our faith through worship and daily life; through Jesus Christ our Lord. **Amen.**

803 IN THE CRISES OF LIFE

O loving Father, help us in the crises of life. Teach us how to meet and conquer temptations, handicaps, frustrations, failures. We know we live in an imperfect world and that life is filled with thorns as well as roses. But sometimes trials come down upon us so suddenly, so swiftly, that we are bewildered; we cannot understand. God of the universe, lift us up at these times. Pour out upon us your mercy and your loving compassion. May we endure crises and testings as good soldiers of Jesus Christ, in whose name we pray. **Amen.**

804

Lord, we need you in our troubles, for they are many. We are burdened with the tragic sorrows of the world, with the needs and griefs of those we love, and with inner perplexities and problems that destroy our peace. We must choose between faith and fear, courage and cynicism, strength of character and collapse of life—and we would choose the better way. Therefore we seek in you vision and power and hope. Grant us grace to accept the materials of life we must accept and to use them worthily. Open our eyes to see opportunity here where we struggle, and to be challenged and not defeated by our troubles, knowing that those who are for us are more than those who are against us. Hear us for the sake of our Lord Jesus Christ. **Amen.**

805

Deepen, we beseech you, our appreciation of the opportunities that face us in this troubled time. Forgive us that so often we ask for comfort and ease. Teach us the high meanings of hardship and adversity. Make us worthy of the fathers and mothers who were before us, and send us out grateful that you have not called us into a finished world, but into an earth unfinished that we might bear a hand with you in its completion; through Christ our Lord. **Amen.**

806

O God, we know that you do not make a good world out of evil men and women. Cleanse our hearts, forgive our sins, amend our ways. Grant that your transforming grace may change our lives. Turn us from the grudges we have borne, the unbrotherliness we have practiced, the uncleanness we have harbored, the selfishness we have clung to. May we go forth a more fit body of your good soldiers to fight for righteousness; through Jesus Christ and in his Spirit we pray. **Amen.**

807

In the light of Jesus' life and teaching, his death and victory, sharpen our consciences, Lord, that we may feel the sin and shame of man's inhumanity to man. Inspire us with insight and courage, that we may combat private greed, social injustice, intolerance and bigotry, the ills of poverty, the misuses of power, and whatever else works enmity between man and man, class and class, race and race, nation and nation. We are sickened by the cries of hatred and the crimes of violence. We see no hope in war piled on war, and bloodshed forever answered by more bloodshed still. O Christ, our Lord, who did bring to your first disciples, frightened and dismayed by your crucifixion, such victorious assurance of your living presence and power, we need you now. Say to us once more, "In the world you have tribulation; but be of good cheer, I have overcome the world." **Amen.**

808

O Lord, beset as we are by misleading counsels and wicked practices, we pray for guidance in a straight way of life. The devices and duplicity of the world are familiar and enticing, the sophistries of the cynical, and the inclinations of our own hearts to self-deceit tempt us to lose the road, and many evil solicitations silence our consciences by their subtle persuasion. Give us, we pray, a firmer hold on your unchangeable laws of righteousness. Search our hearts and drive from them all indirection, equivocation, and pretense. Fortify our decision to live with sincerity, tranquillity, and self-effacement for the sake of Jesus Christ, your Son, our Lord. **Amen.**

809

We would be true servants of your will, Lord, in this troubled time. For this war-torn earth, devastated by violence, we lift our penitent and anxious supplication. Tyranny and hatred rule the world; the light of learning is put out; the liberty of human souls is taken from them; the hopes of the young are destroyed; and the spirit and teaching of Christ, in whom alone is hope for men and nations, are trampled underfoot. Guide our nation in these days of difficult decision. Lord God omnipotent, you are above all nations: use us for your purposes; work in us a moving penitence and amendment of life; save us from the anarchy of unbridled nationalism; teach us alike the necessity and the wisdom of learning to be one family; and through these turbulent days keep our minds and spirits steady. Come close to hearts so troubled over their private griefs that they can hardly feel the grief of the world. See how, discouraged and bereaved, smitten down and wary of life some of your servants are! We pray for a new spirit of triumph and hope. Reveal to us resources of power adequate to make us more than conquerors through Christ Jesus, who conquered all for us. **Amen.**

810   FOR AUTHORITIES

Lord God of hosts, you have made known your authority and delivered your orders for the day in your holy law; you have given persons authority to exercise leadership over us and have bidden us to obey them and to pray for them: we beseech you, fill our officers with zeal for the tasks delegated to them and with understanding and concern for those who, serving under them, must carry out those tasks. May they serve you with pure, exemplary lives and thereby give those whom they lead an ideal to follow. Give them wisdom to judge justly and with compassion in dealings with their subordinates, so that we may be ready to follow their leadership with a willing spirit; through Jesus Christ our Lord. **Amen.**

811

O Father of the just, of your infinite goodness direct the hearts of all who bear authority. Help them with the power of your Holy Spirit to make laws in accordance with your will, and for the advancement of righteousness. Protect them from the snares of the enemy and the deceits of the world; let no pride of power betray them into rejection of your commandments; and grant that both rulers and people may with one mind serve you, our God and King; through Jesus Christ. **Amen.**

812   FOR FAMILY AND HOME

O God, the Father and defender of your people, whom neither space nor time can separate from such as continue in your keeping: be present, we beseech you, with those who are parted from us; prosper them and do them good; guide and direct them in all their undertakings; let nothing hurtful beset them and no evil befall them; and grant that, upheld by your right hand, they may arrive in safety at their journey's end; through Jesus Christ our Lord. **Amen.**

813 FOR ENEMIES

Have mercy, Father, upon those who live to enslave the world rather than let men live in freedom. Bring light to their darkened minds, peace to their warring hearts, and sanity to their warped designs. Hasten the day when international enemies are won to friendship by those who have the power of your love.

Order our lives and our society, O God, that our public enemies decrease and disappear. Through just laws and upright behavior remove the rewards which come from preying on the earnings of others. Convert these enemies to a way of life which will make them friends of the society in which they live.

Especially, O God, let us minister love to the enemies of the cross, whose end is destruction unless they be converted and turn from their evil way. Give them grace to be won as Paul was won, to be your servants with power.

We remember in these moments those who have grieved us personally with their hostility. Save them, O God, and unite us in love rather than being divided in enmity. Where we have sinned in this relationship, forgive, and make us instruments of your peace, after the example and by the power of your Son, our Savior, Jesus Christ. **Amen.**

814 THANKSGIVING

Almighty God, our Father, we turn to you now in thanks and praise, for you are the Giver of our lives and we know ourselves to be your own. For all that we have and are because of your love, we offer you our thanks.

For food and drink,
For clothing and shelter,
For friends and families,
For all who serve us by their professions and their concern,
For pleasant days and the beauties of this earth,
For books and schools and scholars,
For our science and our learning, and the marvels of our
modern age,
For music and laughter and poetry and color,
For help in times of need, and strength for moments of weakness,
For all that we have and are because of your love, we give you
our thanks.
We give you our thanks.

*Yet keep us sensible, O God, of those who do not share our wealth, whose lot is harsh and whose means are few, who struggle with life and often fail.

Look upon the poor of the earth, and the handicapped, and the oppressed, and reach to them with your love.

Help us to help them. Guide us into paths of useful service, and give us the will to serve in every place of need.

*Nor let us forget our responsibility to the whole body of our race. Give us a sense of belonging, one to another, despite our nationalities or our races or our religions.

Uphold those who are set in positions of authority, and give them the grace to be wise and kind, charitable and the seekers of peace.

Let your peace come to our earth, dear Father. Bring an end to war forever. Cause men and nations to live in justice and harmony, with freedom for all.

*And go with us as we go from here, that in all our ways we may be confident of your presence.

When we are discouraged, give us a new heart and a new spirit.

When we are tired, help us to find new strength. When we are afraid, restore our confidence in your power and your purpose for our lives.

So may we serve you, O God, by being your people, in service to all who need us, and in joy for your love.

Through Jesus Christ, your Son, our Lord.

Amen.

815

O God, our Father: we are your own, your children in that we are born of your love, and your people in that we have been gathered to your Son, our Lord Jesus Christ. For all that is your work, we give our thanks.

For life and the abundance of this earth, for the richness of field and orchard, for the materials of our industry and commerce, for all the goods that serve us;

We give you our thanks.

For the opportunity of life, for schools and cultures, for the skills of our science and the imagination of our technology, for the perception of our artists, for the labors of all honest men;

We give you our thanks.

---

*Paragraphs so marked may be read by a single voice other than the leader.

For the compassions of men, for the healers of mind and body, for the brave who seek to right the wrongs of our society, for social workers and lawyers and housewives and managers and truck drivers and teachers and machinists and bankers and merchants and musicians and clerks and secretaries, for all who in their way would give life grace;
>We give you our thanks.

Look upon us in our need. Reach to us with your continuing compassion.
>Uphold us, and improve us.

Frustrate our designs when they are corrupt with our self-conceits. Cause us to stumble under the weight of our self-concerns. Stifle in our throats the sound of our self-pity.
>And enable us to rise to the needs around us.

As there are those within our reach and in our world who are discouraged and lonely, afflicted and diseased, sorrowing and disturbed,
>Move within us to move to them, to love them and to help them, to give them your grace.

As peace and the pursuit of peace are the scorn of the worldly and the object of their wrath, as war and the threat of war are increasingly the blood of our economy, as wise men elect silence and good men bow to fear,
>Move within us to seek the truth and to speak it, to work for peace in our time and justice for all men, to build your kingdom.

As the institutions of men stand threatened by the changes of our day, as our government and our schools, our families and our churches, all struggle for the new stance a new world demands, as the leaders of men are themselves the lost and the perplexed,
>Move within us to bring strength and purpose, to encourage the right and correct the wrong, to find those new means which will best serve us and those who follow us.

Keep us faithful to your love and to your people, that though we meet with reversal and failure, we may yet know the power you give that men might fulfill your will.
>Help us, O God, to serve you by serving others;

Through Jesus Christ, our Lord.
>**Amen.**

816 OFFERTORY

Yours, O Lord, is the greatness and the power and the glory and the preeminence and the majesty, for all in heaven and earth is yours. Yours is the dominion, O Lord, and you are the Supreme Authority. With these gifts we thank you and praise your glorious name. **Amen.**

817

All things come of you, O Lord, and of your own have we given you. **Amen.**

818

O Lord our God, send down upon us your Holy Spirit to cleanse our hearts, to consecrate these gifts, and to perfect the offering of our lives to you. We bring these gifts and we ask this prayer in Jesus' name. **Amen.**

819

We dedicate this offering, O Lord God, to the glory of Jesus Christ; bless the gifts and the givers in his name. **Amen.**

820

O God, you have blessed us with so much: all that we have has come from you and now we return a portion of your blessing; accept it, O Lord, and so guide its use that it may promote peace in the world and justice among men, and advance your kingdom in the hearts of men; through Jesus Christ our Lord. **Amen.**

821

O Lord, our Lord, source of all our joys and all our abundance: receive these gifts of our hands as we dedicate both them and ourselves to your honor and glory in the name of Jesus Christ. **Amen.**

822

Lord Jesus, accept these gifts from our hands; use them for the extension of your kingdom of grace here upon earth. Accept the gift of our hearts; use each one of us as a willing messenger for you, that by our testimony many may learn to know you as Lord and Savior. **Amen.**

823 BENEDICTIONS AND DISMISSALS

The grace of the Lord Jesus Christ, the love of God, and the fellowship of the Holy Spirit be with you all. **Amen.**

824

The grace of our Lord Jesus Christ be with you all. **Amen.**

825

May the peace of God rule in your hearts, and the word of Christ dwell in you richly in all wisdom. **Amen.**

826

The Lord bless you and keep you:
The Lord make his face to shine upon you, and be gracious to you:
The Lord lift up his countenance upon you, and give you peace. **Amen.**

827

God has raised from the dead our Lord Jesus, who is the Great Shepherd of the sheep because of his death, by which the eternal covenant is sealed. May the God of peace provide you with every good thing you need in order to do his will, and may he, through Jesus Christ, do in us what pleases him. And to Christ be the glory forever and ever! **Amen.**

828

Unto God's gracious mercy and protection we commit you; the Lord mercifully look upon you with his favor, and fill you with all spiritual benedictions and grace, that in this life, and in the world to come, you may be partakers of eternal life. **Amen.**

829

Go in peace, remember the poor. Be kind one to another. **Amen.**

830

Go now in love, as those called to do his work. And may God's peace, favor, and mercy bless you always. **Amen.**

831

Go forth in peace, but not in complacency; be strong, but not arrogant; have convictions, but be understanding of the beliefs of others; be eager to love, but not meddlesome; proud enough not to scorn yourselves, but sufficiently humble not to be jealous of your neighbors; through Jesus Christ, our Lord. **Amen.**

832

Our worship is soon ended. Where will you go and what will you do?
We are going out to be God's people in the world.
How will the world know that you belong to Christ?
They will know we are Christians by our love.

FOR THE SICK, WOUNDED, AND DYING

833 Catholic

O my God, I am heartily sorry for having offended you. I detest all my sins because of your just punishments, but most of all because they offend you, my God, who are all good and deserving of all my love. I firmly resolve, with the help of your grace, to sin no more and to avoid the occasions of sin.

834 Protestant

FOR THE SICK AND WOUNDED

O Lord, in your mercy behold, visit, and relieve your servant. Give *him* comfort in the knowledge of your love and sure confidence in your care. Defend *him* from the danger of the enemy and keep *him* in spiritual peace and safety; through our Lord Jesus Christ. **Amen.**

835

Almighty and most merciful God and Savior, extend to your servant the sure comfort of your gracious care. Help *him* to see this sickness as a time for strengthening both *his* spiritual and physical well-being. If it be your will to restore *him* to health, assist *him* by your Holy Spirit to lead the rest of *his* life in godly respect and for your glory. If your fatherly wisdom wills that *his* share in this present life be ended, give *him* grace to accept in faith the salvation won for *him* by Jesus Christ, your Son, and thus to dwell with you in the life everlasting; through the same Jesus Christ, our Lord. **Amen.**

836

FOR SOMEONE AT THE POINT OF DEATH

Father of mercies and God of all comfort, our only help in time of need: we humbly commend to your loving care the soul of our *brother*. We recognize that in this life, through lusts of the flesh and wiles of Satan, *he* defiled *his* soul; yet we entreat you, by the blood of Jesus Christ, to receive *him* as one made pure and without blame before you; through the merits of Jesus Christ, your only Son, our Lord. **Amen.**

837

COMMEMORATION OF THE DEPARTED

Depart, O Christian soul, out of this present world in the name of the almighty Father who created you, in the name of Jesus Christ his Son who redeemed you, in the name of the Holy Spirit who sanctified you. May your rest be in peace and your dwelling place in Paradise with God.

O Lord, support us all the day long until the fever of life is over and our work is done. Then in your mercy grant us a safe lodging and a holy peace at last; through our Lord Jesus Christ. **Amen.**

838 Jewish

O Lord, my God and God of my fathers, my destiny is in your hands. If it be your will, grant me speedy healing of my wounds [illness]. But if not, then grant me complete trust in your wisdom and love, that I may accept whatever may be in store for me. Give me the power to understand that only with you is perfect knowledge and only through you can one find boundless happiness and eternal peace. Most sincerely and humbly I acknowledge my faith and trust in you: Sh'mah Yis-ro-ayl, Ah-doh-noi e-loh-hay-noo Ah-doh-noi e-chod. Hear, O Israel: the Lord our God, the Lord is One!

839

Orthodox

O Master and almighty Lord, the Father of our Lord Jesus Christ, you have told us you desire all men to be saved and to come to the knowledge of the truth, and that you desire not the death of a sinner but that *he* turn again and live. We therefore implore you to absolve your servant from all sins from *his* youth until now. You alone can loose the bonds and restore the contrite. You alone are the hope of the despairing and can remit the sins of everyone who trusts in you. Receive now in peace the soul of your servant and give it rest in that place where all your saints dwell; through the grace of your only-begotten Son, our Lord and Savior Jesus Christ, with whom you are blest, and your all-holy and life-creating Spirit; now and forever and unto ages of ages. **Amen.**

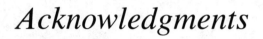

Acknowledgments

Worship Resources Acknowledgment

The Armed Forces Chaplains Board gratefully acknowledges the gracious permission granted it for use of the following copyrighted materials in the Worship Resources section of this hymnal. In all cases, all rights have been reserved by the grantors of permissions for use in this book.

America Press, Inc., New York: No. 616, contains a selection from "Freedom, Authority, and Community," John Courtney Murray in *America*, December 3, 1966, © 1966.

American Bible Society, New York: No. 689 *et al.*, from *Today's English Version of the New Testament*, © 1966.

Church of Scotland: No. 818, adapted from *The Book of Common Order*.

Commission on Worship, The Lutheran Church—Missouri Synod, St. Louis: Nos. 787, 822, written by E. Theo. DeLaney.

Concordia Publishing House, St. Louis: No. 618, contains selections from Leslie F. Brandt, *God Is Here—Let's Celebrate!* © 1969, pp. 44, 48–49.

Consultation on Church Union, Princeton, N.J.: No. 614, *An Order of Worship for the Proclamation of the Word of God and the Celebration of the Lord's Supper*, © 1968; No. 764, *ibid.*, p. 31.

Custodian of the *Book of Common Prayer* (American), New York: Nos. 782, 783.

J. M. Dent & Sons, Ltd., London: No. 756, John Hunter, *Devotional Services for Public Worship* (adapted).

Doubleday & Co., Inc., New York: No. 701 *et al.*, selections from *The Jerusalem Bible*. © 1966 by Darton, Longman & Todd, Ltd., and Doubleday & Company, Inc.

Fortress Press, Philadelphia: Nos. 632–684, selections from *The Psalms in Modern Speech*, tr. and ed. Richard Hanson, © 1968; Nos. 814–815, Carl T. Uehling in *Sing!*

Greek Orthodox Archdiocese of North and South America, New York: No. 620, English translation of The Divine Liturgy; No. 629, lectionary for Orthodox usage.

Harper & Row, Publishers, New York: No. 804, Harry Emerson Fosdick, *A Book of Public Prayers*, © 1959, p. 156 (adapted); Nos. 805, 806, p. 157, *ibid.;* No. 807, pp. 134–135, *ibid.;* No. 808, p. 130, *ibid.;* No. 809, pp. 130–131, *passim, ibid.*

Inter-Lutheran Commission on Worship, Philadelphia: No. 614, alternate form of thanksgiving from *Contemporary Worship—2*, © 1970.

International Committee on English in the Liturgy, Washington, D.C.: No. 612, English translation of the Order of Mass, © 1969.

International Consultation on English Texts, London and Philadelphia: Nos. 727–735, *Prayers We Have in Common*, © 1970 and 1971, translations of liturgical texts which also appear in several of the worship orders.

Jesuit Missions, Inc., New York: No. 615, contains a selection from "Hope for the Handicapped," Daniel Berrigan in *Jesuit Missions*, March, 1966.

John Knox Press, Richmond, Va.: No. 811, George Appleton, *Acts of Devotion*, © 1965, p. 35 (adapted); No. 812, p. 75, *ibid.*

Judson Press, Valley Forge, Pa.: No. 746, John Skoglund, *A Manual of Worship*, p. 359 (adapted); No. 768, p. 164, *ibid.;* No. 769, p. 161, *ibid.*

The Liturgical Conference, Inc., Washington, D.C.: No. 616 contains a selection from chapter two, *Manual of Celebration*, Robert W. Hovda, © 1970.

Lutheran Laymen's League, St. Louis: No. 813, Edward C. May, *Prayers, Intercessions, and Giving of Thanks,* © 1963, p. 53.

National Council of the Churches of Christ in the U.S.A., New York: No. 685 *et al.,* selections from the Revised Standard Version of the Old Testament, © 1952; Nos. 797–800, prayers from William B. Greenspun and Cynthia C. Wedel (eds.), *Second Living Room Dialogues,* © 1967 by Paulist Press and National Council of the Churches of Christ in the U.S.A.

National Jewish Welfare Board, New York: Nos. 623–624.

Oxford University Press, Inc., New York: No. 758, Robert N. Rodenmayer, *The Pastor's Prayerbook,* © 1960; No. 790, adapted from *The Kingdom, the Power and the Glory,* © 1933 Oxford University Press, Inc., and © 1961 Bradford Young.

Paulist/Newman Press, New York: No. 615 contains two items from *Discovery in Prayer,* © 1969, Robert Heyer and Richard Payne, comps., pp. 89 and 54–55; No. 616 contains a paragraph from p. 90, *ibid.;* No. 619 contains a selection from *Eucharistic Liturgies,* John Gallen, ed. © 1969, p. 36, and from *Your Word Is Near,* Huub Oosterhuis, © 1968, p. 117.

Reformed Church in America, New York: No. 749, adapted from *Liturgy and Psalms,* © 1968, p. 373; No. 750, adapted from *Liturgy and Psalms,* © 1940, p. 4.

SCM Press, Ltd., London: No. 747, adapted from *Book of Prayers for Students.*

Seabury Press, New York: Nos. 784, 785, 786 (recast).

Sheed & Ward, Inc., New York: No. 619, contains a selection from Paul Hilsdale, *Prayers from St. Paul,* © 1964.

The Upper Room, Nashville, Tenn.: Nos. 802, 803, L. P. Fitzgerald, *Servicemen at Prayer,* © 1966.

The Westminster Press, Philadelphia: No. 628, slightly adapted from *The Worshipbook,* © 1970; Nos. 765, 766, p. 26, *ibid.*

In a few instances the editors were unable to trace the sources of particular items. If copyright infringements have thereby been incurred, pardon is sincerely requested, since it was not intentionally done.

The following items were adapted from the *Armed Forces Hymnal:* Nos. 743–745, 825, 827–828. Nos. 833–839 were adapted from *Lay Leader's Manual for the U.S. Marine Corps,* Robert F. McComas, David Plank, F. J. Murray, Joseph E. Ryan, Howard Kummer, and A. G. Seniavsky.

Items written or adapted especially for this book: No. 810, by E. Theo. DeLaney; by Larry Paxson, U.S.A.ret., Nos. 748, 751, 753, 755, 759, 760, 762, 763, 771–774, 788, 789, 819–821.

Guitar Chord Fingering

GUITAR FINGERING DIAGRAM LOCATOR

A variety of chord symbols appear with the selections in this hymnal. Instrumentalists are invited to locate the specific name of the chord to be learned in the listings below. Chord groups listed are: A, B♭, B, C, D♭, D, E♭, E, F, G♭, G, and A♭. (Note that *all* A♯ chords are to be found in the B♭ chord group because all A♯ chords are enharmonically equivalent to their sister B♭ chords. The same is true of C♯ chords, which are to be found in the D♭ group. In the same manner, D♯ equals E♭; F♯ equals G♭; and G♯ equals A♭.)

Opposite the name of each chord, guitarists are referred to one or more of the fingering diagrams found on the pages following the listings. Be certain to note upon which frets each specific chord is to be played. Often a particular fingering pattern is common to more than one chord.

By mastering the 88 fingering diagrams in this section the guitarist will have more than 450 chords at his fingertips. All the diagrams assume standard guitar tuning; i.e.: 1st string (highest pitch): E*; 2nd: B; 3rd: G; 4th: D; 5th: A; and 6th (lowest-pitched string): E.

(* This E is two white keys above middle C on a piano.)

Diagram symbols are:

● = black dots indicate where fingers press down on strings
x = do not play strings so marked
o = open string is played (no finger pressing on it)
‿ = a bar grip, wherein one finger presses down two or more strings on the same fret
1 = index finger
2 = middle finger
3 = ring finger
4 = pinky
(The thumb is seldom used in fingering guitar chords)

Chord symbols are:

+	= augmented 5th tone (raised ½ step)
°	= diminished triad (3rd and 5th tones lowered ½ step each)
♭5	= 5th tone lowered ½ step
add 6	= chord includes 6th tone of scale
7	= most frequently refers to dominant 7th chord. Used also with minor 7th and diminished 7th chords
sus	= 4th tone suspended within chord (often 3rd tone is omitted here)
maj7	= 7th tone of major scale (major 7th interval)
9,11	= 9th or 11th tone counting up major scale from "do"
♭9	= 9th tone lowered ½ step
major, maj	= major chord
minor, min, m	= minor chord

When playing hymns on the guitar, the accompanist may wish to substitute easier, more basic chords for the more difficult chords not yet mastered. (The difficult chords are included so that the piano score's harmonization can be matched.) As a general rule, the 7th chord can be substituted for 9th chords; the simple minor chord, for minor 6th and minor 7th chords; the basic major chord, for the 7th and major 6th chords. Simpler chords can also be used in lieu of the ♭5, sus4, and other less-common harmonic structures.

Index for Guitar Fingering Diagrams

A CHORDS

*	**	***
A	1	2,3,4,5
	7	5,6,7
Asus	10	2,3,4,5
A(b5)	12	4,5,6,7
A°7	14	1,2
	14	4,5
A+	15	1,2,3
	16	2,3,4
A+7	18	2,3
A+7b9	19	5,6
A6	21	2
	24	5,6,7
A7	25	2,3
	30	5,6,7,8
A7sus	33	2,3
A7b5	35	1,2,3
A7b9	38	5,6
Amaj7	42	2,3,4
	41	4,5,6,7
Amaj7sus	45	2,3,4
Amaj7b5	47	1,2,3,4
A(b9)	49	5,6,7
A9	52	2,3,4
A9sus	54	2,3
A9b5	56	1,2,3
A9add6	58	2
Amaj9	60	2,3,4
A11	62	2,3,4
Amin	64	1,2
	69	5,6,7
Amsus	71	9,10
Am6	73	1,2
	72	4,5
Am7	76	1,2,3
	77	5
Am7sus	81	7,8
Am7b5	82	1,2,3
Am9	84	5,6,7
Am9add6	87	7,8,9,10

Bb (A#) CHORDS

*	**	***
Bb	2	1,2,3
	7	6,7,8
Bbsus	10	3,4,5,6
Bb(b5)	13	1,2,3
	12	5,6,7,8
Bb°7	14	2,3
	14	5,6
Bb+	15	2,3,4
	16	3,4,5
Bb+7	18	3,4
Bb+7b9	19	6,7
Bb6	21	3
	24	6,7,8
Bb7	25	3,4
	30	6,7,8,9
Bb7sus	33	3,4
Bb7b5	35	2,3,4
Bb7b9	39	1
Bbmaj7	42	3,4,5
	41	5,6,7,8
Bbmaj7sus	45	3,4,5
Bbmaj7b5	47	2,3,4,5
Bb(b9)	49	6,7,8
Bb9	52	3,4,5
Bb9sus	54	3,4
Bb9b5	56	2,3,4
Bb9add6	58	3
Bbmaj9	60	3,4,5
Bb11	62	3,4,5
Bbmin	65	1,2,3
Bbmsus	71	10,11
Bbm6	73	2,3
	72	5,6
Bbm7	76	2,3,4
	77	6
Bbm7sus	80	1,2,3,4
Bbm7b5	82	2,3,4
Bbm9	84	6,7,8
Bbm9add6	87	8,9,10,11

B CHORDS

*	**	***
B	2	2,3,4
	7	7,8,9
Bsus	10	4,5,6,7
B(b5)	13	2,3,4
B°7	14	3,4
	14	6,7
B+	15	3,4,5
	16	4,5,6
B+7	18	4,5
B+7b9	19	7,8
B6	21	4
	24	7,8,9
B7	26	1,2
	25	4,5
B7sus	33	4,5
B7b5	35	3,4,5
B7b9	40	1,2
Bmaj7	42	4,5,6
	41	6,7,8,9
Bmaj7sus	45	4,5,6
Bmaj7b5	47	3,4,5,6
B(b9)	50	1,2
B9	53	1,2
B9sus	54	4,5
B9b5	56	3,4,5
B9add6	59	1,2
Bmaj9	60	4,5,6
B11	62	4,5,6
Bmin	65	2,3,4
Bmsus	71	11,12
Bm6	73	3,4
	72	6,7
Bm7	76	3,4,5
	77	7
Bm7sus	80	2,3,4,5
Bm7b5	82	3,4,5
Bm9	84	7,8,9
Bm9add6	87	9,10,11,12

C CHORDS

*	**	***
C	3	1,2,3
	2	3,4,5
	7	8,9,10
	1	5,6,7,8
Csus	11	1,2,3
C(b5)	13	3,4,5
C°7	14	1,2
	14	4,5
C+	15	4,5,6
	16	1,2,3
C+7	18	5,6
C+7b9	19	8,9
C6	22	1,2,3
	21	5
C7	27	1,2,3
	25	5,6
C7sus	33	5,6
C7b5	36	1,2,3
C7b9	40	2,3
Cmaj7	42	5,6,7
	44	1,2,3
Cmaj7sus	45	5,6,7
Cmaj7b5	47	4,5,6,7
C(b9)	50	2,3
C9	53	2,3
C9sus	54	5,6
C9b5	56	4,5,6
C9add6	59	2,3
Cmaj9	60	5,6,7
C11	63	1,2,3
Cmin	65	3,4,5
Cmsus	70	1
Cm6	74	1,2,3
	73	4,5
Cm7	76	4,5,6
	77	8
Cm7sus	80	3,4,5,6
Cm7b5	82	4,5,6
Cm9	85	1,2,3
Cm9add6	88	1,2,3

Db (C#) CHORDS

*	**	***
Db	4	1,2,3
	5	1,2,3,4
	2	4,5,6
	1	6,7,8,9
Dbsus	9	1,2,3,4
Db(b5)	13	4,5,6
Db°7	14	2,3
	14	5,6
Db+	15	1,2,3
	16	2,3,4
Db+7	18	6,7
Db+7b9	19	9,10
Db6	22	2,3,4
	21	6
Db7	27	2,3,4
	25	6,7
Db7sus	33	6,7
Db7b5	36	2,3,4
Db7b9	40	3,4

*   Chord name
** Use Fingering Diagram number:
*** Play the chord on these frets:

Index for Guitar Fingering Diagrams (*Continued*)

Db (C#) CHORDS

*	**	***
Dbmaj7	42	6,7,8
Dbmaj7sus	45	6,7,8
Dbmaj7b5	47	5,6,7,8
Db(b9)	50	3,4
Db9	53	3,4
Db9sus	54	6,7
Db9b5	56	5,6,7
Db9add6	59	3,4
Dbmaj9	60	6,7,8
Db11	63	2,3,4
Dbmin	65	4,5,6
Dbmsus	71	1,2
Dbm6	74	2,3,4
	73	5,6
Dbm7	78	1,2
	76	5,6,7
Dbm7sus	80	4,5,6,7
Dbm7b5	82	5,6,7
Dbm9	85	2,3,4
Dbm9add6	88	2,3,4

D CHORDS

*	**	***
D	4	2,3,4
	5	2,3,4,5
	2	5,6,7
Dsus	9	2,3,4,5
D(b5)	13	5,6,7
D°7	14	3,4
	14	6,7
D+	15	2,3,4
	16	3,4,5
D+7	18	7,8
D+7b9	20	1,2,3
D6	22	3,4,5
	21	7
D7	28	1,2
	27	3,4,5
D7sus	33	7,8
D7b5	36	3,4,5
D7b9	40	4,5
Dmaj7	42	7,8,9
Dmaj7sus	45	7,8,9
Dmaj7b5	47	6,7,8,9
D(b9)	50	4,5
D9	53	4,5
D9sus	54	7,8
D9b5	56	6,7,8
D9add6	59	4,5
Dmaj9	60	7,8,9
D11	63	3,4,5
Dmin	66	1,2,3
	67	1,2,3
Dmsus	71	2,3
Dm6	74	3,4,5
	73	6,7
Dm7	79	1,2,3
	78	2,3
Dm7sus	80	5,6,7,8
Dm7b5	82	6,7,8
Dm9	85	3,4,5
Dm9add6	88	3,4,5

Eb (Db) CHORDS

*	**	***
Eb	4	3,4,5
	5	3,4,5,6
	2	6,7,8
Ebsus	9	3,4,5,6
Eb(b5)	13	6,7,8
Eb°7	14	1,2
	14	4,5
Eb+	15	3,4,5
	16	4,5,6
Eb+7	18	8,9
Eb+7b9	20	2,3,4
Eb6	22	4,5,6
	21	8
Eb7	27	4,5,6
Eb7sus	33	8,9
Eb7b5	36	4,5,6
Eb7b9	40	5,6
Ebmaj7	43	1,2,3
Ebmaj7sus	45	8,9,10
Ebmaj7b5	48	1,2,3,4
Eb(b9)	50	5,6
Eb9	53	5,6
Eb9sus	55	1,2,3
Eb9b5	57	1,2,3
Eb9add6	59	5,6
Ebmaj9	61	1,2,3
Eb11	63	4,5,6
Ebmin	67	2,3,4
Ebmsus	71	3,4
Ebm6	74	4,5,6
	73	7,8
Ebm7	79	2,3,4
	78	3,4
Ebm7sus	81	1,2
Ebm7b5	83	1,2
Ebm9	86	1,2,3,4
Ebm9add6	87	1,2,3,4

E CHORDS

*	**	***
E	6	1,2
	4	4,5,6
	5	4,5,6,7
	2	7,8,9
Esus	9	4,5,6,7
E(b5)	13	7,8,9
E°7	14	2,3
	14	5,6
E+	15	4,5,6
	16	1,2,3
E+7	17	1,2,3
E+7b9	20	3,4,5
E6	23	1,2
	21	9
E7	29	1,2,3
	27	5,6,7
E7sus	33	9,10
E7b5	37	1,2,3
E7b9	40	6,7

E CHORDS

*	**	***
Emaj7	43	2,3,4
Emaj7sus	45	9,10,11
Emaj7b5	48	2,3,4,5
E(b9)	50	6,7
E9	53	6,7
E9sus	55	2,3,4
E9b5	57	2,3,4
E9add6	59	6,7
Emaj9	61	2,3,4
E11	63	5,6,7
Emin	68	1,2
	67	3,4,5
Emsus	71	4,5
Em6	75	1,2
	74	5,6,7
Em7	79	3,4,5
	78	4,5
Em7sus	81	2,3
Em7b5	83	2,3
Em9	86	2,3,4,5
Em9add6	87	2,3,4,5

F CHORDS

*	**	***
F	7	1,2,3
	4	5,6,7
	5	5,6,7,8
Fsus	9	5,6,7,8
F(b5)	13	8,9,10
F°7	14	3,4
	14	6,7
F+	15	1,2,3
	16	2,3,4
F+7	17	2,3,4
F+7b9	19	1,2
F6	24	1,2,3
F7	30	1,2,3,4
	32	1,2
F7sus	34	1,2,3
F7b5	37	2,3,4
F7b9	38	1,2
Fmaj7	43	3,4,5
Fmaj7sus	45	10,11,12
Fmaj7b5	48	3,4,5,6
F(b9)	49	1,2,3
F9	51	1,2,3
F9sus	55	3,4,5
F9b5	57	3,4,5
F9add6	59	7,8
Fmaj9	61	3,4,5
F11	63	6,7,8
Fmin	69	1,2,3
Fmsus	71	5,6
Fm6	74	6,7,8
Fm7	77	1
	79	4,5,6
Fm7sus	81	3,4
Fm7b5	83	3,4
Fm9	84	1,2,3
Fm9add6	87	3,4,5,6

* Chord name
** Use Fingering Diagram number:
*** Play the chord on these frets:

Gb (F#) CHORDS

*	**	***
Gb	7	2,3,4
	4	6,7,8
	5	6,7,8,9
Gbsus	9	6,7,8,9
Gb(b5)	12	1,2,3,4
Gb°7	14	1,2
	14	4,5
Gb+	15	2,3,4
	16	3,4,5
Gb+7	17	3,4,5
Gb+7b9	19	2,3
Gb6	24	2,3,4
Gb7	30	2,3,4,5
	32	2,3
Gb7sus	34	2,3,4
Gb7b5	37	3,4,5
Gb7b9	38	2,3
Gbmaj7	41	1,2,3,4
	43	4,5,6
Gbmaj7sus	46	1,2,3,4
Gbmaj7b5	48	4,5,6,7
Gb(b9)	49	2,3,4
Gb9	51	2,3,4
Gb9sus	55	4,5,6
Gb9b5	57	4,5,6
Gb9add6	59	8,9
Gbmaj9	61	4,5,6
Gb11	63	7,8,9
Gbmin	69	2,3,4
Gbmsus	71	6,7
Gbm6	72	1,2
Gbm7	77	2
Gbm7sus	81	4,5
Gbm7b5	83	4,5
Gbm9	84	2,3,4
Gbm9add6	87	4,5,6,7

G CHORDS

*	**	***
G	8	1,2,3
	7	3,4,5
	4	7,8,9
Gsus	9	7,8,9,10
G(b5)	12	2,3,4,5
G°7	14	2,3
	14	5,6
G+	15	3,4,5
	16	4,5,6
G+7	17	4,5,6
G+7b9	19	3,4
G6	24	3,4,5
G7	31	1,2,3
	32	3,4
	30	3,4,5,6
G7sus	34	3,4,5
G7b5	37	4,5,6
G7b9	38	3,4
Gmaj7	41	2,3,4,5
	43	5,6,7
Gmaj7sus	46	2,3,4,5
Gmaj7b5	48	5,6,7,8
G(b9)	49	3,4,5
G9	51	3,4,5
G9sus	55	5,6,7
G9b5	57	5,6,7
G9add6	59	9,10
Gmaj9	61	5,6,7
G11	63	8,9,10
Gmin	69	3,4,5
Gmsus	71	7,8
Gm6	72	2,3
Gm7	77	3
Gm7sus	81	5,6
Gm7b5	83	5,6
Gm9	84	3,4,5
Gm9add6	87	5,6,7,8

Ab (G#) CHORDS

*	**	***
Ab	1	1,2,3,4
	7	4,5,6
Absus	10	1,2,3,4
Ab(b5)	12	3,4,5,6
Ab°7	14	3,4
	14	6,7
Ab+	15	4,5,6
	16	1,2,3
Ab+7	18	1,2
Ab+7b9	19	4,5
Ab6	21	1
	24	4,5,6
Ab7	32	4,5
	30	4,5,6,7
Ab7sus	34	4,5,6
	33	1,2
Ab7b5	37	5,6,7
Ab7b9	38	4,5
Abmaj7	42	1,2,3
	41	3,4,5,6
Abmaj7sus	45	1,2,3
Abmaj7b5	48	6,7,8,9
Ab(b9)	49	4,5,6
Ab9	51	4,5,6
	52	1,2,3
Ab9sus	54	1,2
Ab9(b5)	57	6,7,8
Ab9add6	58	1
Abmaj9	60	1,2,3
Ab11	62	1,2,3
Abmin	69	4,5,6
Abmsus	71	8,9
Abm6	72	3,4
Abm7	77	4
Abm7sus	81	6,7
Abm7b5	83	6,7
Abm9	84	4,5,6
Abm9add6	87	6,7,8,9

* Chord name
** Use Fingering Diagram number:
*** Play the chord on these frets:

Special Instructions

For Armed Forces personnel stationed aboard ship or in remote areas:

1. *Before you ship out:* Buy a pitch pipe for tuning your instrument, and extra strings and picks. Purchase the music you will need. Ask your chaplain for a copy of this hymnal. Protect your instrument with a strong case.
2. *In tropical areas and aboard ship:* Watch for buildup of condensation and/or mildew on instruments. Wipe off body of instrument and wax lightly. Cover metal parts (except strings) with a trace of light oil. Keep tuning key gears lightly oiled.
3. *If you find yourself without a pitch pipe,* and if no keyboard instruments are accessible, here are two options for getting tuned up: (*a*) *Find a friend with a harmonica.* Many harmonicas have pitch markings above the tongue holes. Blow (do not draw) breath for correct pitch. (Some harmonicas have numbers rather than pitch markings over the tongue holes. In this case try option b.) (*b*) *See the radioman in your unit.* Ask him to tune to shortwave stations WWV or WWVH at 2.5, 5, 10, 15, 20, or 25 MHz (Megahertz). These stations not only broadcast accurate time checks from the National Bureau of Standards; they also transmit a 440 cycle-per-second audio signal—a perfect "concert A" pitch. (This is the A above middle C on a piano.) With this tone you can tune your instrument accurately anywhere in the world.
4. *Electrified instruments:* Servicemen can enjoy amplified guitars and other instruments on board ship and in many remote areas. The following safety precautions are stressed: (*a*) *Proper grounding:* When standing on steel decks, on damp concrete floors, or on bare earth, be absolutely certain all electrical connections, instruments, and microphones are properly grounded to avoid dangerous shocks. (*b*) *Be sure of your power supply:* Do not run direct current into alternating current units. Find out what *voltage* (110V., 220 V., etc.) your equipment requires and be sure your power source is compatible. Improper voltage can seriously damage amplifiers. (*c*) *Check all power cords* and connectors both for safety and to avoid the embarrassment of equipment failure during a performance.

Guitar Chord Fingering Diagrams

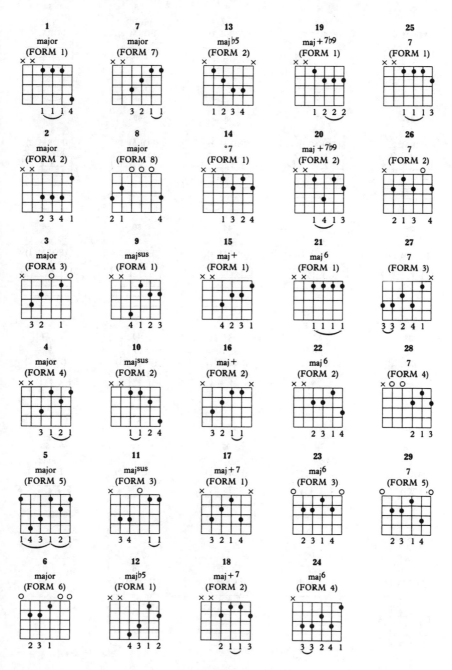

757

Guitar Chord Fingering Diagrams (*Continued*)

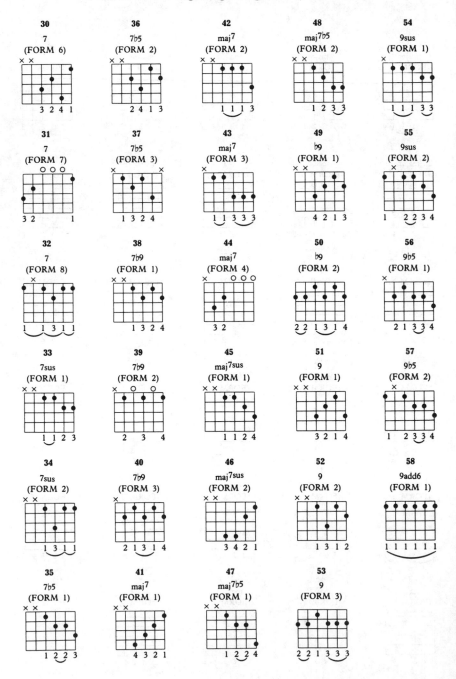

758

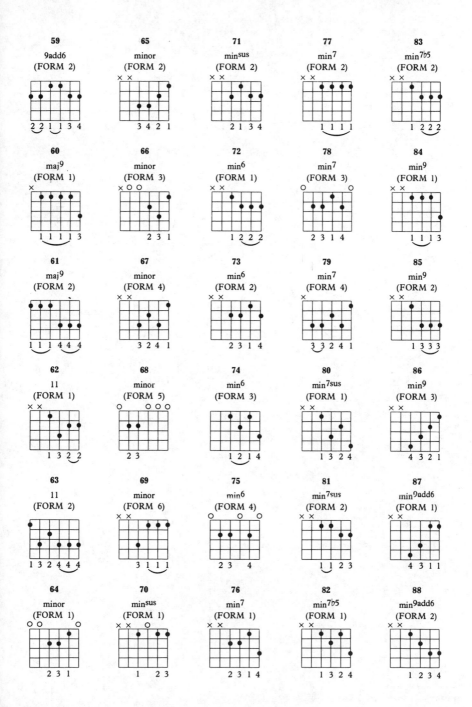

759

Indexes

Contents

Index of Authors, Translators, and Sources

Index of Composers, Arrangers, and Sources

Alphabetical Index of Tunes

Metrical Index of Tunes

10.9.10.9.7.9.
Lonely Voices, 129

10.10.
Lammas, 348
Pax tecum, 109

10.10.9.10.
Slane, 486

10.10.10.4.4.
Sine nomine, 494

10.10.10.6.
Wachusett, 425

10.10.10.9.
with Refrain
Baby Boy, 261

10.10.10.10.
Ellers, 157
Eventide, 153
Hall, 481
Langran, 176
Leoni, 61
Morecambe, 357, 367
National Hymn, 198
O quanta qualia, 13
Penitentia, 413
Sursum corda (*Smith*), 408
Toulon, 199

10.10.10.10.
with Refrain
Living, 452

10.10.10.10.10.
Old 124th, 403, 511

10.10.10.10.10.10.
Finlandia, 382
Unde et memores, 358, 472

10.10.11.11.
Hanover, 7
Lyons, 3

10.10.13.10.
Were You There, 298

11.7.11.7.
with Refrain
Royal Banner, 435
Thompson, 414

11.8.11.9.
with Refrain
It Is Well, 107

11.9.11.9.
with Refrain
Washed in the Blood, 412

11.10.11.9.
Russian Hymn, 172

11.10.11.10.
Charterhouse, 493
Donne secours, 178
Morning Star, 268
Peek, 478
Perfect Love, 522
Russian Hymn, 188
Welwyn, 181
Willingham, 100

11.10.11.10.
with Refrain
Chapman, 274
Faithfulness, 111
Rescue, 411
Tidings, 451

11.10.11.10.10.
Old 124th, 185

11.10.11.10.10.8.
O store Gud, 1

11.10.11.10.D.
Holy Night, 256

11.11.11.5.
Christe sanctorum, 155
Flemming, 121
Herzliebster Jesu, 292

11.11.11.9.
with Refrain
Promises, 138

11.11.11.11.
Foundation, 211
Gordon, 137
Lyons, 380
Mueller, 252
St. Denio, 49

11.11.11.11.
with Refrain
Blessings, 384
To God Be the Glory, 8

11.11.12.12.
Adoro te devote, 347

11.12.12.10.
Nicaea, 2

11.13.11.13.8.14.8.12.
Creation, 183

12.9.12.9.
Wondrous Love, 36

12.10.12.10.11.10.
with Refrain
Joyful Song, 6

12.11.12.11.
Kremser, 44, 52

13.8.
Porter, 524

13.11.11.20.
Salve Regina, 224

13.13.
with Refrain
O Sacrament Most Holy, 340

13.13.13.11.
with Refrain
Ackley, 303

13.13.13.14.
Back to Zion, 439

14.12.12.14.
Conrad, 171

14.14.4.7.8.
Lobe den Herren, 18

15.11.15.11.
with Refrain
The Roll, 513

15.15.15.6.
with Refrain
Battle Hymn of the Republic, 191

Irregular (some with
Refrains or Alleluias)
Adeste fideles, 255
Adon Olam, 65
Al Hanisiym, 63
All My Trials, 143
Angelikai Dynameis, 331
As I Wander, 233
Bring a Torch, 258
Calypso Lord's Prayer, 564
Cherubic Hymn, 334
Christos Aneste, 338
Church Within, 496
Constantly Abiding, 104

Index of Scriptural Allusions

*In references to the Psalms, the Protestant/Jewish numbering is given first, followed by the Catholic/Orthodox numbering in parentheses. A few Psalms have the same numbering in all Bibles. For these, only one number is given.

Isaiah (Continued)	Number	Isaiah (Continued)	Number	Joel	Number
33:20–21	115	63:1	464	2:28	366
35:5	431	66:23	15		
40:8	203				
40:9–11	244	**Jeremiah**		**Amos**	
40:28	49	1:4–10	461	6:1–7	183
40:31	197	1:9	448		
41:10	211	31:3	133, 425		
42:1	17	31:26	160	**Micah**	
42:1–4	127			4:3	175
42:5	122	**Lamentations**		5:2	254, 266, 270
43:1–7	211	3:22–23	111	7:18	407
43:2	116	3:41	164		
48:17	427			**Habakkuk**	
49:1–3	472	**Ezekiel**		2:14	232
49:1–13	183	18:23	451	2:20	23, 541, 542
53:4–5	158,	18:31	403		
288, 292, 294, 296, 340		34:26	140, 402	**Haggai**	
55:7	398	36:26	438	2:7	212, 217
57:15	2	36:27	366		
58:8	154	**Daniel**		**Zechariah**	
58:13–14	14	2:34–35	119	4:6	17
59:20	218	5:23	117	9:17	275
60:1–3	364, 472	7:9–10	26	13:1	397
61:1	391	10:19	473		
61:1–3	413	**Hosea**		**Malachi**	
62:10	483	3:4–5	439	1:11	146
		6:1–3	133	3:6	46, 111

NEW TESTAMENT

Matthew (Continued)	Number		Number		Number
1:18–24	222	6:13	125	13:3–39	74
1:18 to 2:12	261	6:14–15	390	13:14–17	431
1:21	35, 48	6:16–18	385	13:53–58	292
1:23	218	6:25–34	105	14:22–33	378, 416, 425
2:1–12	39, 230, 249,	6:26–30	82	15:30–31	308
256, 259, 262, 264–272		6:33	195, 441	16:18	430, 495, 497
3:12	74	7:9–11	367, 374, 522	16:24–26	133, 285,
3:13–17	335	7:13–14	176	290, 388, 421, 455, 462	
3:16	372	7:21	456	18:1–5	130, 204
4:1–11	385	7:24–27	495	19:3–9	523
4:16	337	8:16	158	19:13–15	130,
4:17	403	8:20	273	204, 208, 276, 280, 516	
4:18–22		8:23–37	116, 196, 384	19:21–29	462
308, 421, 436, 461, 469		9:14–15	385	20:24–28	447, 482
5:5	413	9:20–21	134	21:1–17	277–282
5:14–16	378, 469	9:36	162, 173	21:15–16	125
5:23–24	447	9:37–38	38	21:42	499, 501
5:38–42	488	10:29	102	22:37–39	156
5:43–47	390	11:17	308	23:18–22	447
5:45	57, 76	11:28–30	392, 405, 479	23:37	127
6:9–13	93	12:10–14	308	24:12	301
6:10, 33	185	12:11–12	439		
		12:46–49	467		

785

	Number		Number		Number
Matthew (*Continued*)		**Mark** (*Continued*)		**Luke** (*Continued*)	
24:29-31	19, 139, 513	14:38	383	10:2	38
25:1-13	412, 509	14:50	426	10:23-24	431
25:31-46	165, 182, 184, 376	15:16-26	301	10:27-28	156
25:40	263, 484	15:22-39	284,	11:1	93
26:20-29	337,	286-301, 305, 308, 330,		11:2	185
	340-364, 401	332, 333, 340, 471		11:4	125
26:36-45	283-285, 442	16:1-8	302-319,	11:11-13	522
26:41	383		326-331, 338	11:13	367, 374
26:56	426	16:15-18	174	12:6-7	102
27:24-26	182	16:16	515	12:22-31	105
27:27-56	284, 286-301, 308,			12:24-28	82
330, 332, 333, 340, 471		**Luke**		12:32	428
28:1-10	302-319,	1:26 to 2:7	222, 227	13:23-24	176
	326-331, 338	1:28-33	226	13:34	127
28:16-20	174,	1:39-55	228	14:33	378, 469
424, 439, 449, 451, 503		1:74-79	217	15:18	396
		1:78-79	154, 316	15:24	375
Mark		1:79	119	15:32	434
1:9-11	335	2:1-20	229-262	18:13	406
1:12-13	385	2:7	220	18:16-17	130,
1:15	403	2:7-14	270, 272	208, 276, 280, 516	
1:16-20	421, 436, 461, 469	2:8-16	216	18:22-30	462
1:19-20	308	2:14	9	19:28-38	204, 277, 279-282
1:32-34	158	2:25-38	217	19:41	162, 173
2:18-19	385	2:29	73	20:17	499, 501
3:1-6	308	2:29-32	579	21:25-28	19, 139, 513
3:13	110	2:32	337	22:14-23	
3:31-35	467	2:52	280	339, 340-364, 401, 472	
4:3-20	74	3:17	74	22:24-27	447, 482
4:28-29	74	3:21-22	335	22:29-30	357
4:34-41	116, 196, 384	4:1-13	383, 385-388	22:31-32	387
5:36	418	4:18-19	48, 391	22:40-46	283-285, 442
6:1-6	292	4:40	158	23:24-43	
6:34	162, 173	5:8-15	439	286-301, 330, 332, 333	
6:45-52	378, 416	5:31	185, 195, 441	23:33-46	284
7:31-37	308	5:32	308	23:39-43	339
8:34-38	285,	5:33-34	385	24:1-11	
290, 388, 421, 455, 462		6:5	439	302-319, 326-333, 338	
8:35	133	6:6-11	308	24:27	205, 207, 208, 212
9:33-37	130, 204	6:12	110	24:29	148, 153
9:41	162, 173	6:27-36	390	24:30-35	342,
10:2-12	523	6:29-30	488	344, 349, 351, 353-357,	
10:13-16	130,	6:46	456	359-361, 363, 364	
204, 208, 276, 280, 516		6:47-49	495	24:47	174
10:20-30	462	7:23	292		
10:42-45	447, 482	8:5-15	74	**John**	
11:1-11	277-282	8:19-21	467	1:1-5	308, 330
11:25	390	8:22-25	116, 196, 384	1:4-9	154, 337
12:10	499, 501	8:50	418	1:9-17	248
12:29-31	156	9:23-26	133, 285,	1:14	229-271, 330
13:10	209	290, 388, 421, 455, 462		1:16	405
13:24-27	19, 139, 513	9:46-48	130, 204	1:29, 36, 46	389
14:17-25	339, 340-364, 401	9:49-50	162, 173	1:31-34	335
14:32-42	283-285, 442	9:58	273	2:2	523

Number	*Number*	*Number*

John (*Continued*)		**Acts**		**Romans** (*Continued*)	
3:7	270	1:1-11	31, 90,	14:17	448
3:16	36, 130, 133, 134, 175,		308, 320-323, 325, 361	14:21	434
	245, 395, 416, 463, 515	1:8	209	15:13	178
3:19-21	337	1:14	226		
4:14	405	2:1-4	370	**I Corinthians**	
6:31-35	321, 419	2:2	366	1:18	207
6:34-35	178, 210	2:5-13	472	2:2	293
6:37	389	2:32-33	323	2:9	219
6:44	362	2:37-39	439, 469, 515, 516	3:10-15	177
6:48-58		2:42	94	3:11	211, 457, 501
	339, 340-364, 401, 472	3:1	94	5:7	302, 343
6:68	206	3:8	48	6:19	495
7:37	405	4:12	340, 457	6:19-20	389
8:12	178, 316, 337, 405	4:21	8	8:11-13	434
8:31-32	210	4:24	76	10:4	123
9:5	477	5:31	320	11:23-34	339,
9:24	375	8:26-40	183		340-364, 401, 472
10:1-18	128, 439	9:11	93	11:26	506-509, 513
10:3	414	10	521	12:27-31	184
10:4	98, 113	10:38	166, 181	13	36, 129, 130, 133,
10:11	480	16:14-15	521		134, 137, 175, 284, 416,
10:14	96	16:31	35		460, 463, 488, 492, 523
11:9-10	150	16:31-34	515	15:1-11	314
12:12-15	277	17:24-27	30	15:3-4	306
12:19	279	17:24-28	171	15:20	310
12:26	428	17:26	169, 170	15:25	320
12:34-36	337, 505	20:22	366	15:54-57	153,
13:34	362, 488	20:24	520		302-319, 326-331, 338
14:1-4	349	20:28	501	15:58	380
14:6	404	20:32	73, 141	16:13	417, 420, 433
14:14	106	27	378		
14:15-25	370			**II Corinthians**	
14:18-31	104	**Romans**		1:20	138
14:21	463	2:6-11	511	2:14	436
14:26	213	5:5	15, 372	3:18	463
14:27	87, 109, 157	5:8	288, 294	4:17	462
15:5	424	5:10	390	4:18	195
15:9	110	5:20	395	5:1	12
15:15	106	6:4-8	439	5:7	464
16:13	126, 371, 373, 374	6:4-23	307	5:14-15	389
16:20	291	6:13	294	5:18-19	390
17:4	520	6:19	110, 485	7:1	138
17:18-23	309	8:15-16	17	8:9	273
17:20-23	199, 505	8:22	466	10:5	481
17:21	498	8:26	93	11:21-23	388
19:1-5	296	8:28	18, 122	13:14	17, 365
19:25-27	286-301,	8:31-39	382, 441		
	330, 332, 333, 458	8:34	387	**Galatians**	
20:1	73	8:35-39	105, 114, 133	1:3-4	391
20:1-23	302-315, 317-319,	10:9-10	12	2:20	130, 300, 458
	326-333, 338, 366	10:13	410	3:28	504
20:22	313, 366	10:14-15	451	4:4	30
20:28-29	317, 464	12:1	442, 485	5:1	193
21:9-14	210	12:5	501	5:25	367
21:15	460	13:11-14	132	6:2	504
				6:14	293, 300, 458, 471

	Number		*Number*		*Number*
III John		**Revelation** (*Continued*)		**Revelation** (*Continued*)	
4	125	4:11	78	15:3	16, 409
Jude		5:1–13	26	19:1 ff.	304
3	437	5:8	510	19:6–7	320
		5:9	137, 205	19:9	351
Revelation		5:9, 12	296	19:12, 16	325
1:5–6	48	5:11–13	13	19:16	278
1:8	245	5:12	7	21	177
1:18	320	6:2	455	21:1, 5	92
2:9–10	143, 290, 510	6:11	510	21:1–4	188
3:4–6	132	7:9	444, 494	21:1–11	503
3:12	177	7:9–12	7	21:6	245
3:14, 20	474	7:9–14	510	21:18	512
3:20	273	7:11–12	32	21:22 to 22:5	337
3:21	217	7:12	147	21:23–26	316
4:1–11	321	7:14	412	22:13	245
4:5–11	2	12:11	455	22:16	268, 458
4:6–8	23	14:13	444, 494	22:17	389

Topical Index: Worship Resources

Topical Index: Hymns *and* Other Music for Worship

FAREWELL
God be with you till we meet again, 141
Hush, little baby, don't you cry, 143
FATHER'S DAY. See FAMILY
FEAR. See TRUST
FELLOWSHIP. See also BROTHERHOOD
What a fellowship, what a joy divine, 99
FOLK SONGS
All that I am, all that I do, 487
All the earth proclaim the Lord, 40
Alleluia! Wonderful and great, 77
"Am I my brother's keeper?" 182
By the Babylonian rivers, 377
Christ arose on Easter morn, 309
Christ the Lord is risen From, 315
Come, let's share in the banquet of the Lord, 361
Come, my brothers, priase the Lord, 11
Do you know that the Lord walks on earth? 184
Enter, O people of God, gladly your voices raise, 447
Follow Christ and love the world as he did, 488
Go, tell it on the mountain, 244
Halay! When to God I send a plea, 10
He's got the whole world in his hands, 95
Hush, little baby, don't you cry, 143
I danced in the morning when the world was begun, 308
I wonder as I wander, out under the sky, 233
If we eat of the Lord, 362
In the peace of Christ we sing our thanks to God, 70
It was on a Friday morning, 286
Jesus walked this lonesome valley, 426
Joseph dearest, Joseph mine, 242
Let all creation his glory proclaim, 79
Lonely voices crying all around me, 129
Lord, we pray for golden peace, 186
Many and great, O God, are thy things, 89
My soul is longing for your peace, 131
My soul magnifies the Lord, and my spirit rejoices in God, 228
Praise the Lord in our worship, 54
Sing and rejoice, 9
Still, still, still, He sleeps this night so chill! 243
Take our bread, we ask you, 344
The baby is born, 235
The Mass is ended, all go in peace, 489
The Roman soldier knew not why, 299
The true light that enlightens man, 248
The Virgin Mary had a baby boy, 261

There's a church within us, O Lord, 496
There's a star in the east on Christmas morn, 238
This day God made, 145
What wondrous love is this, 36
When I'm feeling lonely, 142
Yes, I shall arise and return to my Father! 396
You can live while you're dyin', 432
FORGIVENESS. See CONFESSION
FRIENDSHIP. See BROTHERHOOD
FUNERAL. See CHRIST: Easter; DEATH; HEAVEN; HOPE

GIVING. See STEWARDSHIP
GOD

Creator (Creation; Ecology), 75–90
All people that on earth now dwell, 57
All the earth proclaim the Lord, 40
God of earth and planets, 71
"Great is thy faithfulness," O God my Father, 111
I sing the mighty power of God, 16
O mighty God, when I behold the wonder, 1
Praise to the Lord, the Almighty, the King of creation! 18

Eternal
O God, our help in ages past, 5

Grace of
Amazing grace! How sweet the sound, 375
Marvelous grace of our loving Lord, 395

Guide. See also CHRIST: Guide
Be still, my soul: the Lord is on your side, 382
Be thou my Vision, O Lord of my heart, 486
Father, lead me day by day, 125
God of our fathers, whose almighty hand, 198
God of our life, through all the circling years, 117
Great Ruler over time and space, 83
Guide me, O thou great Jehovah, 419
He leadeth me: O blessed thought! 136
If thou but suffer God to guide thee, 118
Lead, kindly Light, amid th'encircling gloom, 119
Lead us, O Father, in the paths of peace, 176
Lord, guard and guide the men who fly, 192
O Lord of hosts, almighty King, 203

Index of First Lines and Familiar Titles: Other Music for Worship

Commonly known titles are listed in italics.

OTHER MUSIC FOR WORSHIP

Index of First Lines and Familiar Titles: Hymns

Commonly known titles are given in italics.

HYMNS

HYMNS

HYMNS

☆ U. S. GOVERNMENT PRINTING OFFICE : 1974 O - 442-791